EVERYMAN,
I WILL GO WITH THEE,
AND BE THY GUIDE,
IN THY MOST NEED
TO GO BY THY SIDE

ANTON CHEKHOV

THE
COMPLETE
SHORT
NOVELS

TRANSLATED FROM THE RUSSIAN BY
RICHARD PEVEAR
AND LARISSA VOLOKHONSKY

WITH AN INTRODUCTION BY
RICHARD PEVEAR

EVERYMAN'S LIBRARY
Alfred A. Knopf New York London Toronto

277

THIS IS A BORZOI BOOK

PUBLISHED BY ALFRED A. KNOPF

English translation Copyright © 2004 by Richard Pevear and
Larissa Volokhonsky
First published in Everyman's Library in 2004
The following stories have previously been published by Everyman's
Library in a different translation: *The Steppe* (1991), *The Duel* (1992),
My Life (1927, 1992).
Bibliography and Chronology Copyright © 2004 by Everyman's Library
Typography by Peter B. Willberg
Fourth printing (US)

US website: www.randomhouse/everymans

ISBN: 1-4000-4049-3 (US)
1-85715-277-8 (UK)

A CIP catalogue reference for this book is available from the
British Library

Book design by Barbara de Wilde and Carol Devine Carson

Printed and bound in Germany by GGP Media GmbH, Pössneck

ANTON CHEKHOV

CONTENTS

INTRODUCTION

God's world is good. One thing is not good: *us.*
                                    – Chekhov to Suvorin, 1891

A good man's indifference is as good as any religion.
                                    – Chekhov's diary, 1897

Chekhov wrote his first and only novel when he was twenty-four. Its title is *Drama na okhote*, or *Drama at the Hunt*, known in English as *A Shooting Party*. It is 170 pages long, was serialized in thirty-two issues of the scandal sheet *Daily News* (which Chekhov renamed *Daily Spews*) from August 1884 to April 1885, and was never reprinted in his lifetime. It is by far his longest work of fiction. As Donald Rayfield wrote in *Chekhov: The Evolution of His Art*, "It reflects almost everything he had ever read, from *The Sorrows of Young Werther* to *The Old Age of Lecoq*. It also contains embryonically everything he was to write." It is part detective story, part psychological study, and very cleverly plotted – a broad parody with a fine sense of the absurd, filled with stock Russian characters and situations, set on a decaying estate that would reappear time and again in Chekhov's subsequent work. One of the characters is a naïve and sympathetic doctor, not unlike Dr. Samoilenko in *The Duel* and some of the other doctors who inhabit Dr. Chekhov's fictional world.

Drama at the Hunt gave fullest expression to Chekhov's early humorous manner, which was otherwise mainly confined to the brief sketches he produced to pay his way through medical school. The five works collected here belong to the period following his entry into serious literature. The first of them, *The Steppe*, published in 1888, the same year in which he won half of the Russian Academy's prestigious Pushkin Prize, was in fact the work which marked that entry. Through the mid-1890s, before the period of the last great plays, the idea of writing a novel continued to entice him. In February 1894 he took a sizeable advance from the Petersburg publisher Adolf

ANTON CHEKHOV

Marx ("I've become a Marxist," he would joke later) for a novel to be serialized in the magazine *Niva* ("The Cornfield"). Meanwhile, he was working on what he described to his brother Mikhail as "a novel about Moscow life." This was *Three Years*, a story set in Moscow merchant circles, which he had been mulling over since 1891. It was published early in 1895 in the liberal journal *Russian Thought*. In the spring of 1896, to fulfill his contract with Marx, he set to work on another "novel," eventually entitled *My Life*, his last extended prose work and, in the opinion of D. S. Mirsky, his masterpiece.

Chekhov's genius defined its formal limits in these works of 90 to 120 pages. It balked at anything longer. Literary genres are notoriously elusive of definition (Chekhov called his last play, *The Cherry Orchard*, a comedy; its first director, Konstantin Stanislavsky, considered it a tragedy), but it seems justifiable to call the five works collected here short novels, and to distinguish them from Chekhov's other works, which are at most half their length. The question is metrical, not mechanical. A hundred-page narrative, whatever generic name we give it, moves to a different measure than a narrative of five, or fifteen, or even fifty pages. It includes the effective time and space of a full-bodied novel, but treats them with the short story's economy of means. The interest in bringing Chekhov's five short novels together in one volume is precisely to focus on that distinction of form.

The Steppe was a pivotal work in Chekhov's artistic development. It opened the door to "serious literature" for him, but it also closed the door on the world of his childhood in southern Russia, in the area around Taganrog on the Sea of Azov, with its unique landscape, wildlife, and culture. He never wrote anything like it again. The prose is lyrical, musically constructed, full of alliterations and internal rhymes, its sentences shaped after what they describe, rendering the movement of the carriage, the mysteriously alive nights and immobile, stifling noondays of the steppe, the flashing and rumbling of what is one of the most famous thunderstorms in Russian literature. While he was working on it, he wrote to a friend that Gogol, "the tsar of the steppe," might be envious. Indeed, Gogol's influence is more marked in *The Steppe* than in anything else Chekhov wrote. Gogol's *Dead Souls* begins with the description of a rather handsome spring britzka driving into the district town of N. *The Steppe* begins with a shabby, springless britzka rolling out of another district town of N. The nod to the master is unmistakable. Like *Dead Souls*, *The Steppe* is virtually plotless, recounting a string of adventures that have no internal connection, a series of encounters with characters who are then left behind. Also like its predecessor, it combines an abundance of natural description with a sense of human flimsiness. Chekhov allows himself the devices of Romantic prose that Gogol reveled in: apostrophes, anthropo-morphisms, addresses to the reader. But the similarities end there, because the hero of *The Steppe* is not that middling, middle-aged apotheosis of banality, Chichikov, but a nine-year-old boy, whose innocent eye takes in the wonders and terrors of his thousand-mile journey with fear and curiosity.

Chekhov never ventured into anything like Gogol's cosmic satire, wild humor, or formal inventiveness. Gogol once boasted of *Dead Souls*: "All Russia will appear in it," but later confessed that he had made it all up. The writer who did know and portray "all Russia" was Nikolai Leskov, a slightly younger contemporary of Dostoevsky, Turgenev, and Tolstoy. Leskov had traveled throughout Russia as an agent for the stewards of a rich Russian landowner, sending back reports that delighted his employers and marked his beginnings as a writer. Chekhov never met Dostoevsky or Turgenev; he was invited to Tolstoy's estate only in 1895, when he was already an established writer; but he ran into Leskov at a decisive moment, in the summer of 1883, when he was twenty-three and Leskov fifty-two. After some low-life carousing in Moscow, he and Leskov ended up in a cab together, where, as Chekhov recounted in a letter to his brother, the following exchange took place: "[Leskov] turns to me half drunk and asks: 'Do you know what I am?' 'I do.' 'No, you don't. I'm a mystic.' 'I know.' He stares at me with his old man's popping eyes and prophesies: 'You will die before your brother.' 'Perhaps.' 'I shall anoint you with oil as Samuel did David ... Write.'"

The consecration was more meaningful than the circum-stances might suggest. Chekhov was indeed Leskov's successor in important ways, not least in his knowledge of Russia. The critic Boris Eichenbaum wrote: "One of the basic principles of Chekhov's artistic work is the endeavor to embrace all of Russian life in its various manifestations, and not to describe selected spheres, as was customary before him." Dostoevsky was an urban intellectual *in excelsis*, Turgenev and Tolstoy belonged to the landed gentry, but Chekhov was the son of a former serf, and not only saw things differently but also saw different things than his aristocratic elders. In its breadth of experience and closeness to life, in its linguistic resources – particularly the use of Church Slavonicisms and the rendering of peasant speech – Chekhov's work continues Leskov's. Chekhov also has a paradoxical, Leskovian vision of the harshness and beauty of the world that goes beyond correct moral or ideological attitudes, and he has something of Leskov's deep comic sense. Leskov was an Orthodox Christian, though of a somewhat unorthodox kind, for whom the evil and sin of the world could suddenly be pierced by holiness, and the "desperate injustice of earthly happening" (the words are Erich Auerbach's, in *Dante, Poet of the Secular World*) was open to "the otherworldly character of justice." Chekhov was an agnostic and a man of science; reason imposed greater restraints on him than on Leskov; but there are moments of transcendence, or near-transcendence, in his stories, understated, hedged round with irony, but nevertheless there, when contradiction becomes so intense and unresolvable that the "veil" is almost torn. Donald Rayfield speaks of this "mystic side of Chekhov – his irrational intuition that there is meaning and beauty in the cosmos," and rightly says that it "aligns him more to Leskov than to Tolstoy in the Russian literary tradition." It is also what distinguishes him from Maupassant and Zola, whom he greatly admired.

One quality of *The Steppe* was to prove a constant of Chekhov's art: his method of composition by means of shifting impressions, the deceptive play of appearances – especially heightened in effect by the naïve incomprehension of the boy Egorushka. The world appears now enticing, now menacing; now good, now evil; now beautiful, now terrible. The picture keeps changing like the weather, and it is the weather that finally predominates: human beings are at its mercy morally as well as physically. Chekhov's predilection for the pathetic fallacy (surprising in a man whose ideal was scientific objectivity) brings about a peculiar interchange in his work: as nature rises towards spirit, human beings sink into matter.

The Steppe contains all the emotion of Chekhov's childhood, but hardly recollected in tranquillity. In 1886 he had begun to publish in the most prominent Petersburg newspaper, the conservative *New Times*, owned and edited by Alexei Suvorin, who was twenty-six years his senior. A close bond developed between the two men, based partly on their similar origins, and, despite stormy disagreements, it lasted for the rest of Chekhov's life. In 1887, Chekhov felt a need for fresh impressions after eight years of medical study and Grub Street hackwork. He took an advance from Suvorin and headed south to revisit his birthplace and travel around the Donets region. He was away for six weeks. Experiencing again the vast freedom and beauty of the steppe was important for him, but the trip also had its painful effects. He was sickened by the provincial narrowness of his native town, as he wrote in his letters: "60,000 inhabitants busy only with eating, drinking and reproducing ... How dirty, empty, idle, illiterate, and boring is Taganrog." (We will hear almost the same lament from the narrator of *My Life* ten years later.) He was also alarmed by the rapid industrialization of the Donets valley. In fact, though he professed a belief in progress, he portrayed only its negative consequences in his work, its natural and human waste, and when he bought the small estate of Melikhovo, near Moscow, he became a dedicated planter of trees, an activity he continued in his last years when he moved to Yalta.

Chekhov produced *The Steppe* only eight months after his return from the south. Its lyricism was born of a sense of irrevocable loss. His youth was finished, as he wrote to his brother, and he looked back enviously at his nine-year-old hero. But a more profound change had also taken place in him. It is clearly marked by the distance that separates *The Steppe* from his next major work, "A Boring Story," written in 1889, which looks ahead to the spiritual problematics of the twentieth century. Here there is no trace of Gogolian Romanticism, nor of the "hypnosis" (Chekhov's word) of Tolstoy's moral influence. The story is quintessential Chekhov, and laid the foundation for all that came after it. "Perhaps in the future it will be revealed to us in the fullest detail who Chekhov's tailor was," wrote the philosopher Lev Shestov, "but we will never know what happened to Chekhov in the time that elapsed between the completion of *The Steppe* and the appearance of 'A Boring Story.'"

In 1884, a year after his anointing by Leskov, Chekhov had suffered a first hemorrhage of the lungs, revealing the illness that would bear out Leskov's prophecy. He never acknowledged that he was consumptive, though as a doctor he could hardly have mistaken the symptoms. They recurred intermittently but more and more alarmingly in the remaining twenty years of his life. His younger brother Nikolai, a gifted artist, was also consumptive. His death in June 1889 deeply shocked Chekhov. Two months later, he began writing "A Boring Story," the first-person account of a famous professor of medicine faced with the knowledge of his imminent death and an absolute solitude, detached from everything and everyone around him. Shestov considers it "the most autobiographical of all his works." But Shestov is right to insist that the change in Chekhov reflected something more profound than the shock of his brother's death and the awareness that the same fate awaited him. We can only learn what it was from the works that followed, among them the four short novels he wrote between 1891 and 1896. In them his impressionism goes from the meteorological to the metaphysical.

By December 1889, Chekhov had decided to make another Russian journey, this time not to the south but across the entire breadth of the continent to Sakhalin Island, off the far eastern coast of Siberia. Given the state of his health, the trip was extremely foolhardy, but he refused to be put off. He was disappointed by the failure of his play *The Wood Demon*, the first version of *Uncle Vanya*, which had opened to boos and catcalls on November 27 and closed immediately; he was generally disgusted with literary life and the role of the fashionable writer; he longed to escape his entanglements with women, editors, theater people, and also to answer his critics, who reproached him with social indifference. He wanted, finally, to do something real. Sakhalin Island was the location of the most notorious penal colony in Russia. He planned to make a detailed survey of conditions on the island and write a report that might help to bring about reforms in the penal system.

After a few months of preparation, reading all he could find about Sakhalin and Siberia, obtaining the necessary permissions, as well as tickets for a return by sea to Odessa, he left on April 21, 1890, traveling by train, riverboat, and covered wagon. Eighty-one days later, on July 11, he set foot on the island, where he spent the next three months gathering information about the prisoners, the guards, their families, the native peoples, the climate, the flora and fauna. He interviewed hundreds of men, women, and children, inspected the mines, the farms, the schools and hospitals (he was especially indignant at the treatment of children and the conditions in the hospitals, and later sent shipments of books and medical supplies to the island). On December 2, 1890, having crossed the China Sea, circumnavigated India, and passed through the Suez Canal and the Bosphorus, he landed back in Odessa, bringing with him a pet mongoose and thousands of indexed notecards.

In January he began what would be his longest published work, *Sakhalin Island*, an intentionally dry sociological dissertation, which was completed and appeared serially in *Russian Thought* only in 1893–94. After his look into the inner abyss in "A Boring Story," he had turned and gone to the worst place on earth, as if to stifle his own metaphysical anguish by plunging into the physical sufferings of others. "Sakhalin," writes Donald Rayfield, "gave Chekhov the first of his experiences of real, irremediable evil ... in Sakhalin he sensed that social evils and individual unhappiness were inextricably involved; his ethics lost their sharp edge of blame and discrimination."

That experience is reflected, though only indirectly, in *The Duel*, which Chekhov worked on alternately with *Sakhalin Island* during the summer of 1891. It is his longest work of fiction. The duel it dramatizes, before it becomes literal, is a conflict of ideas between the two main phases of the Russian intelligentsia in the nineteenth century, the liberal idealism of the 1840s and the rational egoism of the 1860s, in the persons of Laevsky, a self-styled "superfluous man" (a type christened by Ivan Turgenev in 1850), and von Koren, a zoologist and Social Darwinian with an appropriately German name. The one talks like a book (or a small library); the other is so dedicated to science that he decides to participate actively in the process of natural selection. Laevsky and von Koren demolish each other in words behind each other's backs, before they face each other with loaded pistols. But it is rather late in the day for dueling, the clash of ideas has grown weary, the situation has degenerated, and the whole thing is displaced from the capitals to a seedy resort town on the Caucasian coast, where the Russians appear as precarious interlopers among the native peoples.

The Duel verges on satire, even farce, but pulls back; it verges on tragedy but turns comical; it ends by deceiving all our expectations. The closing refrain – "No one knows the real truth" – is first spoken by von Koren, then repeated by Laevsky. Chekhov enters all his characters' minds in turn. No single point of view prevails.

In *The Duel*, Chekhov's art becomes "polyphonic," though not in the Dostoevskian sense. It does not maintain the independence of conflicting "idea-images" or "idea-voices" in "a dialogic communion between consciousnesses," to use Mikhail Bakhtin's terms in *Problems of Dostoevsky's Poetics*. As Bakhtin writes:

The idea [in Dostoevsky] *lives* not in one person's isolated individual consciousness – if it remains there only, it degenerates and dies. The idea begins to live, that is, to take shape, to develop, to find and renew its verbal expression, to give birth to new ideas, only when it enters into genuine dialogic relationships with other ideas, with the ideas of *others*. Human thought becomes genuine thought, that is, an idea, only under conditions of living contact with another and alien thought, a thought embodied in someone else's voice, that is, in someone else's consciousness expressed in discourse. At that point of contact between voice-consciousnesses the idea is born and lives.

In Chekhov it is exactly the opposite: the idea enters into no relationship with the ideas of others; each consciousness is isolated and impenetrable; there is a polyphony of voices but no dialogue; there is compassion but no communion. Chekhov became the master of this protean, quizzical form of narrative, with its radical undercutting of all intellectual positions. *The Duel* begins and ends at sea.

The Story of an Unknown Man is one of the less well-known of Chekhov's works. The title has been mistranslated into English as *An Anonymous Story*. In fact, the first-person narrator, far from being anonymous, has not just one name but two. But though he began with commitment to a revolutionary cause, and ends saying: "One would like to play a prominent, independent, noble role; one would like to make history," he knows he is fated to do nothing, to pass from this world without leaving a trace, to remain "unknown." Chekhov began work on the story in 1888, at the same time as *The Steppe*, but gave it up as too political. In the version he finished four years later, the politics have thinned out to almost nothing. The narrator, based on an actual person, is a former naval officer turned radical, who gets himself hired as a servant in the house of a rich young man named Orlov in order to spy on his father, a well-known elder statesman. At one point he even has a chance to assassinate the old man, but nothing comes of it. The result of all his spying is not action but total inaction. The ideas and ideals that are mentioned never get defined and play no part in the story. There is talk of freedom, of Turgenev's heroes, but it all borders on absurdity, as do Orlov's feasts of irony with his cronies. What interested Chekhov was the ambiguous position of the "servant," who lives as if invisibly with Orlov and his mistress, is there but not there, overhears their most intimate conversations and quarrels, becomes involved in their lives to the point of falling in love with the rejected lady, and all the while is not what he seems.

Central to the story is the passionate and transgressive letter in which the "servant" exposes himself to Orlov, denouncing his own life as well as his unsuspecting master's. He knows that he himself is terminally ill, and this ineluctable fact has altered his radical ideas or simply done away with them. His letter ends as a plea for life:

Why are we worn out? Why do we, who start out so passionate, brave, noble, believing, become totally bankrupt by the age of thirty or thirty-five? Why is it that one is extinguished by consumption, another puts a bullet in his head, a third seeks oblivion in vodka, cards, a fourth, in order to stifle fear and anguish, cynically tramples underfoot the portrait of his pure, beautiful youth? Why is it that, once fallen, we do not try to rise, and, having lost one thing, we do not seek another? Why?

Chekhov's depiction of the dissolution of society goes beyond and even against the political: it is an exploration of human deception and betrayal, of human insubstantiality. The dying man cries out: "I want terribly to live, I want our life to be holy, high, and solemn, like the heavenly vault." But his life turns out to be tawdry, mean, empty. In his final conversation with Orlov, he poses an unanswerable question: "I do believe in the purposefulness and necessity of what happens around us, but what does that necessity have to do with me? Why should my 'I' perish?" At which point the unhearing Orlov shows him to the door.

Though he denied it, Chekhov constantly drew on his own life for his fiction. That is especially true in his portraits of women. They were sometimes quite vindictive and brought pained or angry protests from their real-life counterparts. Others are more complex and compassionate, as in the last two short novels in this collection, which, like so many of his briefer works, are love stories, or stories about the failure to love. The two heroines of *Three Years*, the young beauty Yulia Sergeevna and the edgy, unattractive intellectual "new woman" Rassudina (her name comes from the Russian *rassudok*, "reason"), were drawn in part from two women, Lika Mizinova and Olga Kundasova, who loved Chekhov all their lives. There are other autobiographical elements in the story. The mercantile milieu of the hero's childhood, the strictly religious father, the beatings, the gloom of the warehouse, are Chekhov's experience. Minor characters and incidents also come from Chekhov's circle and his life in Moscow.

INTRODUCTION

The hero, Alexei Laptev, thirty-five years old like his author, a merchant's son declassed by university education but, as certain scenes make clear, not educated enough, is caught between worlds. His story is a variation on the theme of Beauty and the Beast, as Vladimir Kataev has said. It begins with the lovelorn Laptev recalling

> long Moscow conversations in which he himself had taken part still so recently – conversations about how it was possible to live without love, how passionate love was a psychosis, how there was finally no such thing as love, but only physical attraction between the sexes – all in the same vein; he remembered and thought sadly that if he were now asked what love was, he would be at a loss to answer.

Other definitions of nonlove are given as the story unfolds: the brother-in-law Panaurov's ("In every person's skin sit microscopic iron strips which contain currents. If you meet an individual whose currents are parallel to your own, there's love for you"); Yulia Sergeevna's ("You know, I didn't marry Alexei for love. Before, I used to be stupid, I suffered, I kept thinking I'd ruined his life and mine, but now I see there's no need for any love, it's all nonsense"); Yartsev's ("Of course, we're not in love with each other, but I think that ... that makes no difference. I'm glad I can give her shelter and peace and the possibility of not working, in case she gets sick, and it seems to her that if she lives with me, there will be more order in my life, and that under her influence, I'll become a great scholar"). But Laptev finds that he has simply fallen in love, passionately and absurdly, sitting all night in ecstasy under a forgotten parasol.

The decay of the Moscow merchant class, which some critics take to be the real subject of the story, is a secondary theme, sketched in broad strokes; extensive sociological documentary in the manner of Zola was not Chekhov's way. At the center of the story is Yulia Sergeevna. She is a provincial girl, she rarely speaks, she has no fashionable ideas, and she can hardly even explain why she accepted Laptev's proposal without loving him. Chekhov follows this exchange of love and nonlove and its surprising reversals over the three years of the story.

ANTON CHEKHOV

Three Years is filled with striking details, a complex inter-
weaving of impressions, including visionary moments such as
Yartsev's dream of a barbarian invasion and an all-engulfing
fire (Russia's past or her future?), and Laptev's meditations in
the lunar solitude of the garden, when he recalls his far-off,
cheerless boyhood in that same garden, hears lovers whispering and kissing in the next yard, and is strangely stirred:

He went out to the middle of the yard and, unbuttoning his shirt on
his chest, looked at the moon, and he fancied that he would now
order the gate to be opened, go out and never come back there
again; his heart was sweetly wrung by the foretaste of freedom, he
laughed joyfully and imagined what a wonderful, poetic, and maybe
even holy life it could be ...

But the final moment of near-revelation is not an imaginary
one. It is the last image Chekhov grants us of Yulia Sergeevna,
as Laptev watches her walking by herself: "She was thinking
about something, and on her face there was a sad, charming
expression, and tears glistened in her eyes. She was no longer
the slender, fragile, pale-faced girl she once had been, but a
mature, beautiful, strong woman." This image of all that
eludes possession hangs suspended without commentary at the
end of the story.

During 1896, which was to be his last full year at Melikhovo,
Chekhov wrote only two works of fiction: "The House with
the Mezzanine: An Artist's Story" and *My Life: A Provincial's
Story*. The provisional titles he gave them – "My Fiancée" and
"My Marriage" – suggest the closeness of their themes in his
mind. Both are ironic. *My Life* is the most saturated of these
five short novels in the realia of Chekhov's life, from his
childhood in Taganrog and from his four years on the estate.
Taganrog gave him the provincial town, the business of snaring
songbirds, the housepainter Radish, the butcher Prokofy, and
the nickname "Small Profit," which had been pinned on his
brother Alexander. Melikhovo gave him the derelict estate of
Dubechnya, the incursion of the railways, the thousand details
of the building trades, the trials of farming and village life, a
close knowledge of peasants, the construction and consecration
of the schoolhouse. And life gave him the three women, three

variations on failed love, who are central to the narrator's story. It is a *summa* of Chekhov's world.

He described *My Life* as a portrayal of the provincial intelligentsia. The social ideas it embodies had been in the air for two decades in Russia: the Populists' idea of going to the land, and the Tolstoyan ideas of radical simplification, the virtues of honest labor, and the rejection of class distinctions. Misail Poloznev, the narrator, is a young man who rebels against the deadly dullness of provincial life by putting some of those ideas into practice. His story tests them against the complexities of human reality: the uprooting force of modernization embodied in the successful railway constructor Dolzhikov; the collapsing aristocracy represented by Mrs. Cheprakov and her degenerate son; the actualities of the peasants' life and their relations with the "masters," which are far from Populist and Tolstoyan idealization.

Chekhov had been "deeply moved" and "possessed" by Tolstoy's ideas in the 1880s, as he wrote to Suvorin in 1894. But after his trip to Sakhalin, he gradually abandoned them. He told Suvorin:

Maybe it's because I've given up smoking, but Tolstoy's moral philosophy has ceased to move me; down deep I'm hostile to it, which is of course unfair. I have peasant blood flowing in my veins, and I'm not the one to be impressed with peasant virtues ... War is an evil and the court system is an evil, but it doesn't follow that I should wear bast shoes and sleep on a stove alongside the hired hand and his wife ...

My Life has been seen as both an advocacy and a send-up of Tolstoyan "simplification." It is neither. "Chekhov does not debunk Tolstoy," writes Donald Rayfield, "but strips his ideas of sanctimony." Misail, who is the instrument of that process, is an unlikely hero – slow, passive, not very articulate, tolerant except in his revolt against philistine deadness and his search for an alternative way of life. He persists, but in solitude, not in some "rural Eden" of saved humanity. He accepts the consequences of his choice, which Count Tolstoy never had to consider.

The story is symmetrically structured, ending with a final

confrontation between Misail and his father that matches the opening scene. It is preceded by another of those uncanny moments in Chekhov. The housepainter Radish has just told Misail's friend, the young Dr. Blagovo (his name means "goodness"), that he will not find the Kingdom of Heaven. "No help for it," the doctor jokes, "somebody has to be in hell as well." At those words, something suddenly happens to the consciousness of Misail, who has been listening; he has a waking dream, the recapitulation of an earlier episode, but this time verging on the recognition that hell is exactly where they are.

In 1899, Chekhov wrote to his friend Dr. Orlov, a colleague from the district of Melikhovo: "I have no faith in our intelligentsia ... I have faith in individuals, I see salvation in individuals scattered here and there, all over Russia, be they intellectuals or peasants, for they're the ones who really matter, though they are few." Misail's victory is personal and solitary. The ambiguity of his nickname, "Small Profit" – is it ironic or not? – is characteristic of Chekhov's mature vision. In his refusal to force the contradictions of his stories to a resolution, Chekhov seems to come to an impasse. Interestingly, of these five short novels, the last three end with a man left with an orphaned girl on his hands, a being who, beyond all intellectual disputes and human betrayals, simply needs to be cared for. And we may remember the moment in *The Duel* when the deacon, in a comical reverie, imagines himself as a bishop, intoning the bishop's liturgical prayer: "Look down from heaven, O God, and behold and visit this vineyard which Thy right hand hath planted." The quality of Chekhov's attention is akin to prayer. Though he was often accused of being indifferent, and sometimes claimed it himself, that is the last thing he was.

Richard Pevear

SELECT BIBLIOGRAPHY

———

PHILLIP CALLOW, *Chekhov: The Hidden Ground: A Biography*, Ivan R. Dee, Chicago, 1998.

JULIE W. DE SHERBININ, *Chekhov and Russian Religious Culture*, Northwestern University Press, Evanston, IL, 1997. An excellent study of an essential and often ignored aspect of Chekhov's artistic vision.

MICHAEL FINKE, *Metapoesis: The Russian Tradition from Pushkin to Chekhov*, Duke University Press, Durham, NC, 1995.

VERA GOTTLIEB and PAUL ALLEN, eds., *The Cambridge Companion to Chekhov*, Cambridge University Press, Cambridge and New York, 2000. Essays by various hands on Chekhov's fiction and plays.

ROBERT LOUIS JACKSON, ed., *Reading Chekhov's Text*, Northwestern University Press, Evanston, IL, 1993. An interesting collection of recent critical studies.

SIMON KARLINSKY, ed., *Anton Chekhov's Life and Thought: Selected Letters and Commentary*, translated by Michael Henry Heim, commentary by Simon Karlinsky, Northwestern University Press, Evanston, IL, 1997.

VLADIMIR KATAEV, *If Only We Could Know: An Interpretation of Chekhov*, translated by Harvey Pitcher, Ivan R. Dee, Chicago, 2002. An important new work by a leading Russian Chekhov scholar.

AILEEN M. KELLY, *Views from the Other Shore: Essays on Herzen, Chekhov, and Bakhtin*, Yale University Press, New Haven, CT, 1999. Studies by a reputed intellectual historian.

CATHY POPKIN, *The Pragmatics of Insignificance*, Stanford University Press, Stanford, CA, 1993.

V. S. PRITCHETT, *Chekhov: A Spirit Set Free*, Random House, New York, 1988. A critical biography by an English master of the short story and longtime admirer of Chekhov.

DONALD RAYFIELD, *Chekhov: A Life*, Henry Holt, New York, 1997. The most complete and detailed biography of Chekhov in English to date.

———, *Understanding Chekhov*, University of Wisconsin Press, Madison, WI, 1999. An update of Rayfield's *Chekhov: The Evolution of His Art*, Elek Books Ltd., London, 1975.

SAVELY SENDEROVICH and MUNIR SENDICH, eds., *Anton Chekhov Rediscovered*, Russian Language Journal, East Lansing, MI, 1988. A collection including some fine recent studies and a comprehensive bibliography.

LEV SHESTOV, *Chekhov and Other Essays*, translation anonymous, new introduction by Sidney Monas, University of Michigan Press, Ann Arbor, MI, 1966. Essays by a major Russian thinker of the twentieth century, including "Creation from the Void," written on the occasion of Chekhov's death in 1904 and still one of the most penetrating interpretations of his art.

CHRONOLOGY

DATE	AUTHOR'S LIFE	LITERARY CONTEXT
1859		Goncharov: *Oblomov*. Ostrovsky: *The Storm*.
1860	Anton Pavlovich Chekhov born in Taganrog on the Sea of Azov in southern Russia (16 January), the third of seven children of a small shopkeeper, and grandson of a serf who had bought his freedom.	Turgenev: *On the Eve*; "First Love." Dostoevsky: *The House of the Dead* (to 1862). George Eliot: *The Mill on the Floss*.
1861		Herzen publishes *My Past and Thoughts* (to 1866). Dickens: *Great Expectations*.
1862		Turgenev: *Fathers and Children*. Hugo: *Les Misérables*. Flaubert: *Salammbô*.
1863		Tolstoy: *The Cossacks*. Chernyshevsky: *What Is to Be Done?* Nekrasov: *Red-Nosed Frost*.
1864		Dostoevsky: *Notes from Underground*. Fet: "Tormented by life ...".
1865		Leskov: "Lady Macbeth of the Mtensk District." Sleptsov: *Hard Times*. Dickens: *Our Mutual Friend*.
1866		Dostoevsky: *Crime and Punishment*. Daudet: *Lettres de mon moulin*.
1867	Enrolled at parish school attached to Greek Orthodox church. Unable to master modern Greek, he leaves at the end of the school year.	Turgenev: *Smoke*. Dostoevsky: *The Gambler*. Zola: *Thérèse Raquin*. Marx: *Das Kapital*, vol. 1.
1868	Joins preparatory class at the Taganrog *gimnazia*. Following the recent reforms of Dmitry Tolstoy, minister of education,	Lavrov: *Historical Letters*. Nekrasov: "Who Can Be Happy and Free in Russia?"

Alexander II (tsar since 1855) following a reformist policy, in complete opposition to his predecessor, the reactionary Nicholas I. Port of Vladivostok founded to serve Russia's recent annexations (from China). Huge investment in railway building begins.

Emancipation of the serfs (February), the climax of the tsar's program of reform. While his achievement had great moral and symbolic significance, many peasants felt themselves cheated by the terms of the complex emancipation statute. Outbreak of American Civil War. Unification of Italy. Bismarck prime minister of Prussia. 1860s and 1870s: "Nihilism" – rationalist philosophy skeptical of all forms of established authority – becomes widespread among young radical intelligentsia in Russia.
Polish rebellion. Poland incorporated into Russia. Itinerant movement formed by young artists, led by Ivan Kramskoi and later joined by Ivan Shishkin: drawing inspiration from the Russian countryside and peasant life, they are also concerned with taking art to the people.
The first International. Establishment of the Zemstva, organs of self-government and a significant liberal influence in tsarist Russia. Legal reforms do much towards removing class bias from the administration of justice. Trial by jury instituted and a Russian bar established. Russian colonial expansion in Central Asia (to 1868).
Slavery formally abolished in U.S.A.

Young nobleman Dmitry Karakozov tries to assassinate the tsar. Radical journals *The Contemporary* and *The Russian Word* suppressed. Austro-Prussian war.

St. Petersburg section of Moscow Slavonic Benevolent Committee founded (expansion of Pan-Slav movement). Rimsky-Korsakov's symphonic poem *Sadko*.

DATE	AUTHOR'S LIFE	LITERARY CONTEXT
1868 *cont*	Greek and Latin dominate the curriculum and study of "subversive" subjects such as Russian literature is severely restricted.	
1869	Embarks on eight-year course that he completes in ten, being twice kept down. Obliged to work in his father's shop in the evenings and on holidays.	Tolstoy: *War and Peace.* Goncharov: *The Precipice.* Flaubert: *L'Éducation sentimentale.* Gaboriau: *Monsieur Lecoq.* Verne: *Vingt mille lieues sous les mers.*
1870		Turgenev: "King Lear of the Steppes." Death of Herzen and Dickens.
1871	Death of his infant sister, Evgenia.	Dostoevsky: *Demons.* Ostrovsky: *The Forest.* Eliot: *Middlemarch* (to 1872).
1872		Turgenev: "Spring Torrents"; *A Month in the Country* (first performance). Leskov: *Cathedral Folk.* Kushchevsky: *Nikolay Negorev, or The Successful Russian.* Nietzsche: *The Birth of Tragedy.*
1873	Goes to the theater for the first time (Offenbach's *La Belle Hélène*) and is immediately hooked.	Ostrovsky: *The Snow Maiden.*
1874		
1875	Two of his brothers leave for Moscow, Alexander to the university, Nikolai to art college. Anton starts a class magazine, *The Hiccup.*	
1876	Facing bankruptcy, his father flees to Moscow, leaving Anton to negotiate with debtors and creditors (April). His mother and the two youngest children, Maria and Mikhail, follow in July.	Eliot: *Daniel Deronda.* Henry James: *Roderick Hudson.*
1877	When his younger brother Ivan joins the rest of the family, Anton is left alone in Taganrog to complete his education. Finances himself by coaching.	Tolstoy: *Anna Karenina.* Turgenev: *Virgin Soil.* Garshin: "Four Days." Zola: *L'Assommoir.* Flaubert: *Trois contes.*

HISTORICAL EVENTS

Chemist D. I. Mendeleyev wins international fame for his periodic table of chemical elements based on atomic weight.

Lenin born. Franco-Prussian war. End of Second Empire in France and establishment of Third Republic. Repin paints *The Volga Boatmen* (to 1873).

Paris Commune set up and suppressed. Fall of Paris ends war. German Empire established.

Three Emperors' League (Germany, Russia, and Austria-Hungary) formed in Berlin. During the late 1860s and early 1870s, Narodnik (Populist) "going to the people" campaign gathers momentum: young intellectuals incite peasantry to rebel against autocracy.

First performance of Rimsky-Korsakov's first opera, *The Maid of Pskov*.

Mussorgsky's *Pictures at an Exhibition*; first performance of *Boris Godunov*.

Bulgarian Atrocities (Bulgarians massacred by Turks). Founding of Land and Freedom, first Russian political party openly to advocate revolution. Death of anarchist Mikhail Bakunin. Official statute for Women's Higher Courses, whereby women are able to study at the universities of St. Petersburg, Moscow, Kiev, Odessa, and Kazan. By 1881 there are two thousand female students. Queen Victoria proclaimed Empress of India.
Russia declares war on Turkey (conflict inspired by Pan-Slav movement). Tchaikovsky: *Swan Lake*.

ANTON CHEKHOV

DATE	AUTHOR'S LIFE	LITERARY CONTEXT
1878	First attempts to write a play.	Saltykov-Shchedrin: *The Sanctuary of Mon Repos.* Garshin: "An Incident." James: "Daisy Miller."
1879	Matriculates. Leaves Taganrog for Moscow (August), where he joins his parents and younger siblings in lodgings. Enrolls as a medical student at Moscow University.	Dostoevsky: *The Brothers Karamazov* (to 1880). Saltykov-Shchedrin: *The Golovlev Family.*
1880	First stories published in *The Dragonfly* under a pseudonym.	Maupassant: "Boule-de-suif." Death of Flaubert and George Eliot.
1881	Possibly writing his first surviving play, *Platonov.* Contributing regularly to *The Spectator.* Affair with Natalia Golden (who later marries his brother Alexander).	Tolstoy: "What Men Live By." Turgenev: "The Song of Triumphant Love." Leskov: "The Lefthanded Craftsman." Flaubert: *Bouvard et Pécuchet.* Ibsen: *Ghosts.* Death of Dostoevsky.
1882	Writing regularly for *The Alarm Clock.* First contribution to a St. Petersburg paper, *Splinters,* after meeting with the editor, Nikolay Leykin.	Kravchinsky: *Underground Russia* (first chronicle of the revolutionary movement). Uspensky: *The Power of the Soil.*
1883	Spends summer at his brother Ivan's house at Voskresensk, a provincial town forty miles from Moscow. Writes "The Daughter of Albion," his first piece for *Splinters* to win renown. Friendship with Kiseliov family, neighboring landowners. Beginning of long relationship with Olga Kundasova.	Turgenev: "Clara Milich." Garshin: "The Red Flower." Fet: *Evening Lights.* Ostrovsky: *The Handsome Man.* Maupassant: *Une Vie; Clair de Lune.*
1884	Graduates. Summer at Voskresensk, helping at the hospital. Returns to Moscow to practice medicine. First symptoms of TB. Publishes collection of his best stories, *Tales of Melpomene. A Shooting*	Tolstoy: *Confession.* Leskov: "The Toupée Artist." Ostrovsky: *Guilty without Guilt.* Ibsen: *The Wild Duck.* Strindberg: *Getting Married* (to 1885). Maupassant: *Miss Harriet.*

CHRONOLOGY

DATE	AUTHOR'S LIFE	LITERARY CONTEXT
1884 cont	*Party* serialized in *Daily News* (to 1885). First commission for Khudekov's prestigious *Petersburg Gazette*.	
1885	Produces some hundred pieces this year. First of several summers spent in a dacha on the Kiseliovs' estate at Babkino (source of *The Cherry Orchard*). Stories written there include "The Burbot" and "The Huntsman," his first big success in the *Petersburg Gazette*. Visits St. Petersburg for the first time (December) as a guest of Leykin.	Garshin: "Nadezhda Nikolaevna." Leskov: "The Bogey-Man." Zola: *Germinal*. Maupassant: *Bel-Ami*.
1886	Short, secret engagement to Dunia Efros. Begins working for Alexei Suvorin's *New Times*, which becomes his principal outlet; writes under his own name for the first time. Receives letter of praise and encouragement from novelist Dmitry Grigorovich. Publishes the collection *Motley Stories*. Two visits to St. Petersburg (April and December), where his stories are winning him considerable renown. Individual tales this year include "Art," "Easter Eve," "Difficult People," and "On the Road."	Tolstoy: *The Power of Darkness*; *The Death of Ivan Ilyich*. James: *The Bostonians*; *The Princess Casamassima*. Stevenson: *Dr. Jekyll and Mr. Hyde*.
1887	Two visits to St. Petersburg (March and November). Deepening friendship with Suvorin family. Vacation in Taganrog; trip to the Don Steppe (April). Writes "Happiness" (summer). Publishes collection *In the Twilight* (September). First play, *Ivanov*, performed in Moscow (November). "The Kiss" appears in *New Times* (December).	Saltykov-Shchedrin: *Old Days in Poshekhone*. Sluchevsky: *Thirty-three Stories*. Garshin: "The Signal." Leskov: "The Sentry." Fofanov: *Poems*. Strindberg: *The Father*; *The Dwellers of Hemsö*. Maupassant: *Mont-Oriol*; *Le Horla*.

HISTORICAL EVENTS

Students hold a demonstration to commemorate the fiftieth anniversary of the birth of Dobrolyubov. Several of them, disgusted by the brutal way in which the demonstration is suppressed, resolve to assassinate the tsar; the plot is discovered, and among those executed is Lenin's brother Alexander Ulyanov, whose death he swears to avenge.

During the late 1880s Russia begins her industrial revolution.

ANTON CHEKHOV

DATE	AUTHOR'S LIFE	LITERARY CONTEXT
1888	Writes *The Steppe* (January). The Chekhovs rent a summer dacha at Sumy in the Ukraine; friendship with Lintvariov family. Visits Suvorin in the Crimea; goes to Baku with Suvorin's son. Makes first of several abortive attempts to buy a farm in the Ukraine. Awarded half the Russian Academy's 1888 prize for literature. Stays with Suvorin in St. Petersburg (December); meets Tchaikovsky.	Suicide of Vsevolod Garshin. Strindberg: *Miss Julie*. Maupassant: *Pierre et Jean*. James: "The Aspern Papers." Hardy: *Wessex Tales*. Kipling: *Plain Tales from the Hills*.
1889	*Ivanov* a success in St. Petersburg (January). Death of his brother Nikolai, a talented artist, from tuberculosis (June). Spends the summer in Sumy. Short visit to Odessa, where the Moscow Maly Theater company is on tour; writes "A Boring Story" while in the Crimea. *The Wood Demon* produced in Moscow but badly received (November).	Tolstoy: "The Kreutzer Sonata." Kravchinsky: *The Career of a Nihilist*. Ertel: *The Gardenins*. Hauptmann: *Before Sunrise*. Maeterlinck: *La Princesse Maleine*.
1890	In April sets off for Sakhalin, a penal colony off the Pacific coast of Siberia, traveling by road and river. Returns via Hong Kong, Singapore, and Ceylon, arriving in Moscow in December. Writes "Gusev."	Tolstoy: *The Fruits of Enlightenment*. Polonsky: *Evening Bell*. Ibsen: *Hedda Gabler*. Maeterlinck: *Les Aveugles*. Wilde: *The Picture of Dorian Gray*.
1891	To Vienna, Venice, Florence, Rome, Naples, Nice, Monte Carlo, and Paris with Suvorin (March to May). Summer spent at Bogimovo, joined by friends including Lika Mizinova (later to provide the inspiration for the character of Nina in *The Seagull*) and the artist Levitan. Writes *The Duel*. Engaged in fund-raising activities for victims of the famine.	Death of Goncharov. Leskov: "Night Owls." Ertel: *Change*. Conan Doyle: *The Adventures of Sherlock Holmes*.

CHRONOLOGY

HISTORICAL EVENTS

Rimsky-Korsakov: *Scheherazade.*

Introduction of land captains, powerful administrator magnates who increase control of the gentry over the peasants, undermining previous judicial and local government reforms. Shishkin: *Morning in a Pine Forest.*

First performance of Tchaikovsky's opera *The Queen of Spades* and first (posthumous) performance of Borodin's *Prince Igor.* Peasant representation on Zemstva reduced. Bismarck dismissed. During the 1890s growth rate for industrial output averages about 8 percent per annum. Important development of coal mines in southern European Russia. Industrial expansion sustained by growth of banking and joint stock companies, which begin to attract foreign, later native, investment.

Harvest failure in central Russia causes famine and starvation: up to a million peasants die by the end of the winter. Work commences on Trans-Siberian Railway. Twenty thousand Jews brutally evicted from Moscow. Rigorously enforced residence restrictions, quotas limiting entry of Jews into high schools and universities, and other anti-Jewish measures drive more than a million Russian Jews to emigrate, mainly to North America.

DATE	AUTHOR'S LIFE	LITERARY CONTEXT
1892	Purchases country house and estate at Melikhovo, fifty miles south of Moscow, where he moves with his parents, Maria and Mikhail. During cholera epidemic helps man the local clinic; acts as unpaid "cholera superintendent" for twenty-five villages. Writes "The Grasshopper." "Ward No. 6" appears in *Russian Thought*.	Gorky: "Makar Chudra." Fofanov: *Shadows and Secrets*. Hauptmann: *The Weavers*. Maeterlinck: *Pelléas et Mélisande*. Ibsen: *The Master Builder*.
1893	Serial publication of *The Island of Sakhalin* (book version published 1895).	Critic Dmitri Merezhkovsky cites Chekhov, Garshin, Fofanov, and Minsky as heralds of new era in Russian literature. Zola: *Le Docteur Pascal*.
1894	Writes "The Student" (spring). Boat trip down the Volga (August). Travels to Europe with Suvorin (autumn).	Bryusov brings out three collections of *The Russian Symbolists* (to 1895). Balmont: *Under Northern Skies*. Rostand: *Les Romanesques*.
1895	Publishes "Three Years." Visits Tolstoy at Yasnaya Polyana (August). Works on *The Seagull*. Writes "The House with the Mezzanine."	Tolstoy: "Master and Man." Gorky: "The Song of the Falcon"; *Chelkash*. Bryusov: *Chefs d'Oeuvres*. Balmont: *Beyond All Limits*. Fontane: *Effi Briest*. Wilde: *The Importance of Being Earnest*. Rostand: *La Princesse lointaine*.
1896	Writes *My Life*. Builds school at Melikhovo. *The Seagull* staged in St. Petersburg (October). The first night is a disaster, and Chekhov flees to Melikhovo.	Sologub: first collection of Symbolist poetry. Merezhkovsky: *Christ and Antichrist* (to 1905).
1897	Publishes "Peasants" (February). Collapse in health; TB diagnosed (March). Convalesces in Biarritz and Nice. Sides with Zola in the Dreyfus affair; ceases to write for *New Times*, which takes an anti-Semitic line.	Gorky: "Creatures that Once Were Men." Bunin: *To the Edge of the World*. Bryusov: *Me eum esse*. Kuprin: *Miniatures*. Wells: *The Invisible Man*. Rostand: *Cyrano de Bergerac*.

HISTORICAL EVENTS

Tchaikovsky: *The Nutcracker.* Property qualification for franchise raised, reducing number of voters in St. Petersburg from 21,176 to 7,152.

Armenian massacres begin. As part of the russification of the Balkans, the German University of Dorpat is reopened as the University of Yuryev, with a majority of Russian students. Death of Tchaikovsky.

Death of Alexander II; accession of Nicholas II. Growth in popularity of Marxist ideas among university students encouraged by appearance of Struve's *Critical Notes* and Beltov's *Monistic View.*

A. S. Popov, pioneer of wireless telegraphy, gives demonstration and publishes article on his discoveries, coinciding with Marconi's independent discoveries in this field. Establishment of Marxist newspaper *Samarskii Vestnik.* In May, two thousand people crushed to death on Klondynka field when a stand collapses during the coronation ceremony.
Tsar Nicholas II visits President Faure of France: Russo-French alliance. Lenin deported for three years to Siberia. Only systematic census carried out in Imperial Russia reports a population of 128 million, an increase of three and a half times over the century. The industrial labor force of three million (3 percent) is small compared with the West but shows a fifteen-fold increase over the century. Thirteen percent of the population now urban as opposed to only 4 percent a century earlier.

ANTON CHEKHOV

DATE	AUTHOR'S LIFE	LITERARY CONTEXT
1898	Returns from Europe (May). Stories include "Ionych," "Gooseberries," "The Man in the Case," and "About Love." Death of his father (October). Buys a plot of land for a new house in Yalta, where he is spending the winter for his health. First performance in Moscow of *The Seagull* by the newly founded Moscow Arts Theater, run by Stanislavsky and Nemirovich-Danchenko: a triumph (December). Meets the actress Olga Knipper.	Tolstoy: *What Is Art?* Balmont: *Silence.* Zola: *J'Accuse.* Shaw: *Mrs. Warren's Profession.* James: "The Turn of the Screw," "In the Cage." Wells: *The War of the Worlds.*
1899	For 75,000 roubles signs over his copyrights to Adolf Marx, who undertakes to republish his complete works (1899–1902). Friendship with young writers Gorky and Bunin. Falls in love with Olga Knipper. She visits him at Melikhovo and later at Yalta. Chekhov sells estate at Melikhovo. *Uncle Vanya* (reworking of *The Wood Demon*) opens in Moscow (October). Writes "The Lady with the Little Dog" (autumn).	Tolstoy: *Resurrection.* Gorky: *Foma Gordeev; Twenty-six Men and a Girl.* Kropotkin: *Memoirs of a Revolutionist.*
1900	"In the Ravine" published in Gorky's Marxist paper, *Life*. Chekhov, his mother, and his sister installed in new house at Yalta. Elected to the Writers' Section of the Academy. Travels to Caucasus with Gorky. Joins Olga on Moscow Arts Theater tour at Sevastopol. *Three Sisters* completed in October. Attends rehearsals in Moscow.	Freud: *The Interpretation of Dreams.* Solovyov: *Three Conversations on War, Progress, and the End of Human History.* Balmont: *Buildings on Fire.* Bryusov: *Tertia vigilia.* Conrad: *Lord Jim.*
1901	Spends January in Nice. Successful first night of *Three Sisters* (31 January). Marries Olga Knipper in Moscow (25 May). Honeymoon at sanatorium at Aksionovo. Olga returns to	Blok: "Verses on the Beautiful Lady" (to 1902). Mann: *Buddenbrooks.* Kipling: *Kim.*

CHRONOLOGY

HISTORICAL EVENTS

Russian Social Democratic Labor Party founded. Between 1898 and 1901 Caucasian oil production is higher than that of the rest of the world together. Finns begin to lose their rights as a separate nation within the Empire. Sergey Diaghilev and others found the World of Art society, prominent members of which are Benois and Bakst; its most notable production is Diaghilev's Ballet Russe. The magazine, to which "decadent" writers such as Balmont frequently contribute, opposes the "provincial naturalism" of the Itinerant school, and advocates a philosophy of art for art's sake.

Student riots. All universities in Russia temporarily closed. Moscow Law Society also closed. Reactionary Sipyagin becomes minister of the interior. During 1890s the so-called Third Element, consisting of doctors, teachers, statisticians, engineers, and other professionals employed by the Zemstva, becomes a recognized focus of liberal opposition to the tsarist regime. Russian industry enters a period of depression.

Lenin allowed to leave Russia. Founds paper *Iskra* in Germany. Russia ends nineteenth century with a total of 17,000 students spread over nine universities: a hundred years before, the Empire had only one university – Moscow. Nevertheless, the proportion of illiterates in the Empire was recorded at this time as 75 percent of persons aged between nine and forty-nine.

Murder of minister of education Bogolepov by a student marks beginning of wave of political assassinations. For the authorities, the principal menace is the Socialist Revolutionary Party, which looks for support from the peasantry, rather than the Social Democrats, who hope to rouse the urban proletariat. First performance of Rachmaninov's piano concerto No. 2, with the composer as soloist. Death of Queen Victoria.

DATE	AUTHOR'S LIFE	LITERARY CONTEXT
1901 *cont*	the theater for the winter season, but Chekhov, unable to stand the climate, remains in Yalta. Health deteriorates. Writes "The Bishop."	
1902	Olga visits Yalta (February). Back in St. Petersburg, she miscarries and has to undergo an operation; continues to suffer from peritonitis. Chekhov travels to Perm and the Urals (June). Stays, with Olga, at Stanislavsky's country house at Liubimovka (July). Resigns from the Academy when Gorky's election is revoked (September). Visits Olga in Moscow (October to November) and winters in Yalta.	Gorky: *The Lower Depths.* Bely: *Second Symphony.* Andreev: "The Abyss," "In the Fog." Merezhkovsky: *Tolstoy and Dostoevsky.* James: *The Wings of the Dove.* Conrad: *Heart of Darkness.* Gide: *L'Immoraliste.*
1903	Publishes "The Bride." Writing *The Cherry Orchard* (March to October). Attends rehearsals in Moscow (December to January).	Balmont: *Let Us Be Like the Sun.* Bryusov: *Urbi et Orbis.* Shaw: *Man and Superman.* Butler: *The Way of All Flesh.* Mann: *Tonio Kröger.*
1904	First night of *The Cherry Orchard* on 17 January, Chekhov's name day. Public tributes. Goes to Yalta (February), where his health continues to deteriorate. Returns to Moscow (May); leaves with Olga for Black Forest spa of Badenweiler (3 June), where he dies on 2 July. Buried at the Novodevichy Cemetery in Moscow.	Tolstoy completes *Hadji Murad.* Blok: *The City* (to 1908). Bely: *Gold in Azure.* Annensky: *Quiet Songs.* Zinaida Hippius: *Poems.* Shaw: *John Bull's Other Island.* Conrad: *Nostromo.* James: *The Golden Bowl.*
1905		

CHRONOLOGY

Lenin's *What Is to Be Done?* provides blueprint for future Bolshevik party. Sipyagin assassinated by Socialist Revolutionaries.

Conflict between Bolsheviks and Mensheviks at second Congress of Russian Social Democratic Labor Party. Assassination of King Alexander and Queen Draga of Serbia.

Russo-Japanese war (to 1905), both unpopular and unsuccessful from the Russian point of view. Assassination of V. K. Pleve, minister of the interior, and notorious oppressor of minority peoples within the Empire.

First Russian Revolution.

THE STEPPE
The Story of a Journey

I

ON AN EARLY July morning a battered, springless britzka—
one of those antediluvian britzkas now driven in Russia only
by merchants' agents, herdsmen, and poor priests—rolled
out of the district town of N., in Z—— province, and went
thundering down the post road. It rattled and shrieked at the
slightest movement, glumly seconded by the bucket tied to
its rear—and from these sounds alone, and the pitiful leather
tatters hanging from its shabby body, one could tell how
decrepit it was and ready for the scrap heap.

In the britzka sat two residents of N.: the merchant Ivan
Ivanych Kuzmichov, clean-shaven, in spectacles and a straw
hat, looking more like an official than a merchant; and the
other, Father Khristofor Siriysky, rector of the church of St.
Nicholas in N., a small, long-haired old man in a gray canvas
caftan, a broad-brimmed top hat, and a colorfully embroidered belt. The first was thinking intently about something
and kept tossing his head to drive away drowsiness; on his
face a habitual, businesslike dryness struggled with the good
cheer of a man who has just bid farewell to his family and
had a stiff drink; the second gazed at God's world with moist,
astonished little eyes and smiled so broadly that his smile
even seemed to reach his hat brim; his face was red and had
a chilled look. Both of them, Father Khristofor as well as
Kuzmichov, were on their way now to sell wool. Taking
leave of their households, they had just had a filling snack of
doughnuts with sour cream and, despite the early hour, had
drunk a little . . . They were both in excellent spirits.

3

Besides the two men just described and the coachman Deniska, who tirelessly whipped up the pair of frisky bay horses, there was one more passenger in the britzka—a boy of about nine whose face was dark with tan and stained with tears. This was Egorushka, Kuzmichov's nephew. With his uncle's permission and Father Khristofor's blessing, he was going somewhere to enroll in school. His mama, Olga Ivanovna, widow of a collegiate secretary[1] and Kuzmichov's sister, who liked educated people and wellborn society, had entreated her brother, who was going to sell wool, to take Egorushka with him and enroll him in school; and now the boy, not knowing where or why he was going, was sitting on the box beside Deniska, holding on to his elbow so as not to fall off, and bobbing up and down like a kettle on the stove. The quick pace made his red shirt balloon on his back, and his new coachman's hat with a peacock feather kept slipping down on his neck. He felt himself an unhappy person in the highest degree and wanted to cry.

When the britzka drove past the prison, Egorushka looked at the sentries quietly pacing by the high white wall, at the small barred windows, at the cross gleaming on the roof, and remembered how, a week ago, on the day of the Kazan Mother of God,[2] he had gone with his mama to the prison church for the feast; and earlier still, for Easter, he had gone to the prison with the cook Liudmila and Deniska and brought kulichi,[3] eggs, pies, and roasted beef; the prisoners had thanked them and crossed themselves, and one of them had given Egorushka some tin shirt studs of his own making.

The boy peered at the familiar places, and the hateful britzka raced past and left it all behind. After the prison flashed the black, sooty smithies, after them the cozy green cemetery surrounded by a stone wall; the white crosses and tombstones hiding among the green of the cherry trees and showing like white blotches from a distance, peeped merrily from behind the wall. Egorushka remembered that when the cherry trees were in bloom, these white spots blended with the blossoms into a white sea; and when the cherries were ripe, the white tombstones and crosses were strewn with blood-red spots. Behind the wall, under the cherries, Egorushka's father and his grandmother Zinaida Danilovna slept day and night. When the grandmother died, they laid her in a long, narrow coffin and covered her eyes, which refused to close, with two five-kopeck pieces. Before her death she had been alive and had brought soft poppy-seed bagels from the market, but now she sleeps and sleeps...

And beyond the cemetery the brickworks smoked. Thick black smoke came in big puffs from under the long, thatched roofs flattened to the ground, and lazily rose upwards. The sky above the brickworks and cemetery was swarthy, and big shadows from the puffs of smoke crept over the fields and across the road. In the smoke near the roofs moved people and horses covered with red dust...

Beyond the brickworks the town ended and the fields began. Egorushka turned to look at the town for the last time, pressed his face against Deniska's elbow, and wept bitterly...

"So you're not done crying, crybaby!" said Kuzmichov. "Mama's boy, sniveling again! If you don't want to go, stay then. Nobody's forcing you!"

"Never mind, never mind, Egor old boy, never mind..." Father Khristofor murmured quickly. "Never mind, old boy... Call upon God... It's nothing bad you're going to, but something good. Learning is light, as they say, and ignorance is darkness... It's truly so."

"You want to turn back?" asked Kuzmichov.

"Ye... yes..." answered Egorushka with a sob.

"And you should. Anyhow, there's no point in going, it's a long way for nothing."

"Never mind, never mind, old boy..." Father Khristofor

went on. "Call upon God... Lomonosov[4] traveled the same way with fishermen, yet from him came a man for all Europe. Intelligence, received with faith, yields fruit that is pleasing to God. How does the prayer go? 'For the glory of the Creator, for the comfort of our parents, for the benefit of the Church and the fatherland'... That's it."

"Benefits vary..." said Kuzmichov, lighting up a cheap cigar. "There are some that study for twenty years and nothing comes of it."

"It happens."

"Some benefit from learning, but some just have their brains addled. My sister's a woman of no understanding, tries to have it all in a wellborn way, and wants to turn Egorka into a scholar, and she doesn't understand that with my affairs I could make Egorka happy forever. I explain this to you because, if everybody becomes scholars and gentlemen, there'll be nobody to trade or sow grain. We'll all starve to death."

"But if everybody trades and sows grain, then nobody will comprehend learning."

And, thinking that they had both said something convincing and weighty, Kuzmichov and Father Khristofor put on serious faces and coughed simultaneously. Deniska, who was listening to their conversation and understood nothing, tossed his head and, rising a little, whipped up the two bays. Silence ensued.

Meanwhile, before the eyes of the travelers there now spread a wide, endless plain cut across by a chain of hills. Crowding and peeking from behind each other, these hills merge into an elevation that stretches to the right from the road all the way to the horizon and disappears in the purple distance; you go on and on and there is no way to tell where it begins and where it ends... The sun has already peeped out from behind the town and quietly, without fuss, set about its work. At first, far ahead, where the sky meets the earth, near the barrows and a windmill that, from afar, looks like a little man waving his arms, a broad, bright yellow strip crept over the ground; a moment later the same sort of strip lit up somewhat closer, crept to the right, and enveloped the hills; something warm touched Egorushka's back, a strip of light, sneaking up from behind, darted across the britzka and the horses, raced to meet the other strips, and suddenly the whole wide steppe shook off the half-shade of morning, smiled, and sparkled with dew.

Mowed rye, tall weeds, milkwort, wild hemp—all of it brown from the heat, reddish and half dead, now washed by the dew and caressed by the sun—were reviving to flower again. Martins skimmed over the road with merry cries, gophers called to each other in the grass, somewhere far to the left peewits wept. A covey of partridges, frightened by the britzka, fluttered up and, with its soft "trrr," flew off towards the hills. Grasshoppers, crickets, capricorn beetles, mole crickets struck up their monotonous chirring music in the grass.

But a little time passed, the dew evaporated, the air congealed, and the deceived steppe assumed its dismal July look. The grass wilted, life stood still. The sunburnt hills, brown-green, purple in the distance, with their peaceful, shadowy tones, the plain with its distant mistiness, and above them the overturned sky, which, in the steppe, where there are no forests or high mountains, seems terribly deep and transparent, now looked endless, transfixed with anguish...

How stifling and dismal! The britzka runs on, but Egorushka sees one and the same thing—the sky, the plain, the hills...The music in the grass has grown still. The martins have flown away, there are no partridges to be seen. Rooks flit over the faded grass, having nothing else to do; they all look the same and make the steppe still more monotonous.

A kite flies just above the ground, smoothly flapping its

wings, and suddenly stops in the air, as if pondering life's boredom, then shakes its wings and sweeps away across the steppe like an arrow, and there is no telling why it flies and what it wants. And in the distance the windmill beats its wings...

For the sake of diversity, a white skull or a boulder flashes among the weeds; a gray stone idol or a parched willow with a blue roller on its topmost branch rises up for a moment, a gopher scampers across the road, and—again weeds, hills, rooks run past your eyes...

Then, thank God, a cart laden with sheaves comes the opposite way. On the very top lies a peasant girl. Sleepy, exhausted by the heat, she raises her head and looks at the passersby. Deniska gapes at her, the bays stretch their muzzles out to the sheaves, the britzka, shrieking, kisses the cart, and prickly ears of wheat brush like a besom over Father Khristofor's top hat.

"Running people down, eh, pudgy!" shouts Deniska. "See, her mug's all swollen like a bee stung it!"

The girl smiles sleepily, moves her lips, and lies down again...But now a solitary poplar appears on a hill; who planted it and why it is here—God only knows. It is hard to tear your eyes from its slender figure and green garments. Is the handsome fellow happy? Heat in summer, frost and blizzards in winter, terrible autumn nights when you see only darkness and hear nothing but the wayward, furiously howling wind, and above all—you are alone, alone your whole life...Beyond the poplar, fields of wheat stretch in a bright yellow carpet from the top of the hill right down to the road. On the hill the grain has already been cut and gathered into stacks, but below they are still mowing...Six mowers stand in a row and swing their scythes, and the scythes flash merrily and in rhythm, all together making a sound like "vzzhi, vzzhi!" By the movements of the women binding the sheaves, by the faces of the mowers, by the gleaming of the scythes, you can see that the heat is burning and stifling. A black dog, its tongue hanging out, comes running from the mowers to meet the britzka, probably intending to bark, but stops halfway and gazes indifferently at Deniska, who threatens it with his whip: it is too hot to bark! One woman straightens up and, pressing both hands to her weary back, follows Egorushka's red shirt with her eyes. The red color may have pleased her, or she may have been remembering her own children, but she stands for a long time motionless and looks after him...

But now the wheat, too, has flashed by. Again the scorched plain, the sunburnt hills, the torrid sky stretch out, again a kite skims over the ground. The windmill beats its wings in the distance, as before, and still looks like a little man waving his arms. You get sick of looking at it, and it seems you will never reach it, that it is running away from the britzka.

Father Khristofor and Kuzmichov were silent. Deniska kept whipping up the bays and making little cries, and Egorushka no longer wept but gazed indifferently on all sides. The heat and the boredom of the steppe wearied him. It seemed to him that he had already been riding and bobbing about for a long time, that the sun had already been baking his back for a long time. They had not yet gone ten miles, but he was already thinking: "Time for a rest!" The good cheer gradually left his uncle's face, and only the businesslike dryness remained, and to a gaunt, clean-shaven face, especially when it is in spectacles, when its nose and temples are covered with dust, this dryness lends an implacable, inquisitorial expression. Father Khristofor, however, went on gazing in astonishment at God's world and smiled. He was silently thinking of something good and cheerful, and a kindly, good-natured smile congealed on his face. It seemed that the good, cheerful thought also congealed in his brain from the heat...

"What do you say, Deniska, will we catch up with the wagon train today?" asked Kuzmichov.

Deniska glanced at the sky, rose a little, whipped up the horses, and only then replied:

"By nightfall, God willing."

The barking of dogs was heard. Some six huge steppe sheepdogs suddenly rushed at the britzka, as if leaping from ambush, with a fierce, howling barking. Extraordinarily vicious, with shaggy, spiderlike muzzles, their eyes red with malice, they all surrounded the britzka and, shoving each other jealously, set up a hoarse growling. Their hatred was passionate, and they seemed ready to tear to pieces the horses, and the britzka, and the people . . . Deniska, who liked teasing and whipping, was glad of the opportunity and, giving his face an expression of malicious glee, bent over and lashed one of the sheepdogs with his whip. The dogs growled still more, the horses bolted; and Egorushka, barely clinging to the box, looked at the dogs' eyes and teeth and understood that if he were to fall off, he would instantly be torn to pieces, but he felt no fear and looked on with the same malicious glee as Deniska, regretting that he had no whip in his hands.

The britzka overtook a flock of sheep.

"Stop!" cried Kuzmichov. "Hold up! Whoa . . ."

Deniska threw his whole body back and reined in the bays. The britzka stopped.

"Come here!" Kuzmichov shouted to the shepherd. "Calm those dogs down, curse them!"

The old shepherd, ragged and barefoot, in a warm hat, with a dirty bag on his hip and a long staff with a crook— a perfect Old Testament figure—calmed the dogs down and, removing his hat, came up to the britzka. Exactly the same Old Testament figure stood motionless at the other end of the flock and gazed indifferently at the passersby.

"Whose flock is this?" asked Kuzmichov.

"Varlamov's!" the old man replied loudly.

"Varlamov's!" repeated the shepherd standing at the other end of the flock.

"Say, did Varlamov pass by here yesterday or not?"

"No, sir . . . His agent passed by, that's a fact . . ."

"Gee-up!"

The britzka drove on, and the shepherds with their vicious dogs were left behind. Egorushka reluctantly looked ahead into the purple distance, and it was beginning to seem to him that the windmill beating its wings was coming nearer. It was getting bigger and bigger, it really grew, and you could now distinctly make out its two wings. One wing was old, patched up; the other had just recently been made of new wood and gleamed in the sun.

The britzka drove straight on, but the mill for some reason began moving to the left. They drove and drove, but it kept moving to the left and would not disappear from sight.

"A fine windmill Boltva built for his son!" observed Deniska.

"But his farmstead's nowhere to be seen."

"It's over there, beyond that little gully."

Soon Boltva's farmstead appeared as well, but the windmill still would not drop back, would not fall behind, looking at Egorushka with its gleaming wing and beating away. What a sorcerer!

II

AROUND MIDDAY THE britzka turned off the road to the right, drove slowly for a while, and stopped. Egorushka heard a soft, very gentle burbling and felt on his face the cool velvet touch of some different air. Out of a hill that nature had glued together from huge ugly stones, through a little hemlock pipe put in by some unknown benefactor, ran a thin stream of water. It fell to the ground, gay, transparent, sparkling in the sun, and, murmuring quietly, as if imagining itself a strong and swift torrent, quickly flowed off somewhere to the left.

Not far from the hill, the little rivulet broadened into a pool; the hot rays and scorching soil drank it up greedily, diminishing its strength; but a bit further on, it probably merged with another such little rivulet, because some hundred paces from the hill, along its course, dense, lush green sedge was growing, from which, as the britzka approached, three snipe flew up with a cry.

The travelers settled by the brook to rest and feed the horses. Kuzmichov, Father Khristofor, and Egorushka sat down in the thin shade of the britzka and the unharnessed horses, on a spread piece of felt, and began to eat. Once he had drunk his fill of water and eaten a baked egg, the good, cheerful thought congealed by the heat in Father Khristofor's brain asked to be let out. He looked at Egorushka affectionately, munched his lips, and began:

"I myself studied a bit, old boy. From a very early age, God put sense and comprehension into me, so that unlike others, being still as you are now, I comforted my parents and preceptors with my understanding. I was not yet fifteen, and I already spoke and wrote verses in Latin as if it was Russian. I remember when I was a staff-bearer for Bishop Khristofor. Once after the liturgy, I remember it like today, on the name day of the most pious sovereign Alexander Pavlovich the Blessed,[5] while he was taking off his vestments in the sanctuary, he looked at me affectionately and asked: '*Puer bone, quam appellaris?*'* And I answered: '*Christophorus sum.*'† And he: '*Ergo connominati summus,*'§ meaning that we were namesakes... Then he asks in Latin: 'Whose child are you?' I answered, also in Latin, that I was the son of the deacon Siriysky in the village of Lebedinskoe. Seeing such promptness and clarity in my answers, his grace blessed me and said: 'Write to your father that I will not forget him and

---

* "Good boy, what is your name?"
† "I am Christopher."
§ "Then we have the same name."

will keep an eye on you.' The archpriests and priests who were in the sanctuary, listening to the Latin exchange, were also not a little surprised, and each showed his pleasure by praising me. I didn't have whiskers yet, old boy, and was already reading Latin, and Greek, and French, knew philosophy, mathematics, civic history, and all subjects. God gave me an amazing memory. It happened that I would read something twice and learn it by heart. My preceptors and benefactors were amazed and supposed I would become a man of great learning, a Church luminary. And I myself thought of going to Kiev to continue my studies, but my parents would not give me their blessing. 'You'll go on studying for ages,' said my father, 'when will we be done waiting for you?' On hearing these words, I abandoned my studies and took a post. True, no scholar came of me, but I obeyed my parents instead, brought peace to their old age, and buried them honorably. Obedience is greater than fasting and prayer!"

"You must have forgotten all your learning by now!" observed Kuzmichov.

"How could I not? Praise God, I'm in my seventies! I still remember something of philosophy and rhetoric, but languages and mathematics I've quite forgotten."

Father Khristofor closed his eyes, thought, and said in a low voice:

"What is a being? A being is a self-sufficient thing that requires nothing for its completion."

He wagged his head and laughed with sweet emotion.

"Spiritual food!" he said. "Truly, matter nourishes the flesh, and spiritual food for the soul!"

"Learning's learning," sighed Kuzmichov, "but if we don't catch up with Varlamov, that'll learn us all."

"A man's not a needle, we'll find him. He's circling around in these parts now."

The three familiar snipe flew over the sedge, and in their

squawks, anxiety and vexation could be heard at having been driven away from the brook. The horses munched sedately and snorted; Deniska walked around them, trying to show that he was totally indifferent to the cucumbers, pies, and eggs his masters were eating, immersing himself completely in slaughtering the flies and horseflies that covered the horses' bellies and backs. Apathetically, his throat producing some sort of special, sarcastically triumphant sound, he swatted his victims, but in case of failure, he grunted vexedly, his eyes following each of the lucky ones that had escaped death.

"Deniska, where are you? Come and eat!" said Kuzmichov, sighing deeply and thereby letting it be known that he had already had enough.

Deniska timorously approached the felt and chose for himself five big and yellow cucumbers, so-called "yallers" (he was ashamed to choose the smaller and fresher ones), took two baked eggs, blackened and cracked, then irresolutely, as if afraid of being struck on his outstretched hand, touched a little pie with his finger.

"Take it, take it!" Kuzmichov urged him.

Deniska resolutely took the pie and, walking far off to one side, sat down on the ground, his back to the britzka. At once such loud chomping was heard that even the horses turned around and looked at Deniska suspiciously.

Having had a bite to eat, Kuzmichov took a sack with something in it out of the britzka and said to Egorushka:

"I'm going to sleep, and you watch out that nobody pulls this sack from under my head."

Father Khristofor took off his cassock, belt, and caftan, and Egorushka, looking at him, froze in astonishment. He had never supposed that priests wore trousers, but Father Khristofor had on a pair of real canvas trousers tucked into his high boots, and a short buckram jacket. Looking at him, Egorushka found that in this costume so unsuited to his dignity, with his long hair and beard, he looked very much like Robinson Crusoe. After they undressed, Father Khristofor and Kuzmichov lay down face-to-face in the shade under the britzka and closed their eyes. Deniska, having finished chomping, stretched out belly-up in the sun and also closed his eyes.

"Watch out that nobody steals the horses!" he said to Egorushka and fell asleep at once.

Quiet ensued. All that could be heard was the horses snorting and munching and the sleepers snoring; somewhere not close by a peewit wept, and from time to time there came a squawk from the three snipe, who kept coming to check whether the uninvited guests had left; the brook burbled with a soft burr, yet all these sounds did not disturb the quiet or awaken the congealed air, but, on the contrary, drove nature into slumber.

Egorushka, suffocating from the heat, which was especially felt now, after eating, ran to the sedge and from there surveyed the countryside. He saw the same thing he had seen before noon: the plain, the hills, the sky, the purple distance; only the hills stood nearer and there was no windmill, which had been left far behind. Beyond the rocky hill where the brook flowed rose another hill, smoother and wider; to it clung a small hamlet of five or six farmyards. There were no people, or trees, or shadows to be seen by the huts, as if the hamlet had suffocated in the hot air and dried up. Having nothing to do, Egorushka caught a capricorn beetle in the grass, held it to his ear in his fist, and listened to it playing its fiddle for a long time. When he got tired of the music, he chased after a crowd of yellow butterflies that had come to the sedge to drink, and did not notice himself how he wound up by the britzka again. His uncle and Father Khristofor were fast asleep; their sleep was bound to go on for another two or three hours, till the horses were rested . . . How to kill that long time and where to hide from the heat? A tricky problem . . . Mechanically, Egorushka put his mouth to the stream running from the pipe; his mouth felt cold and tasted of hemlock; first he drank eagerly, then forcing himself, until the sharp cold had spread from his mouth to his whole body and the water flowed down his shirt. Then he went over to the britzka and began to look at the sleepers. His uncle's face, as before, showed a businesslike dryness. A fanatic for his business, Kuzmichov always thought about his affairs, even in his sleep, even while praying in church, when they sang the "Cherubic Hymn,"[6] unable to forget them even for a moment, and was now probably dreaming of bales of wool, carts, prices, Varlamov . . . But Father Khristofor was a gentle man, light-minded and given to laughter, who never in all his life had known a single such affair, which could bind his soul like a boa constrictor. In all the numerous affairs he had undertaken in his life, he had never been tempted by the affair itself so much as by the bustle and intercourse with people proper to every undertaking. Thus, in the present journey, he was interested not so much in wool, Varlamov, and prices as in the long route, the conversation on the way, sleeping under the britzka, eating at odd times . . . And now, judging by his face, he must have been dreaming of Bishop Khristofor, the Latin discussion, his wife, doughnuts with sour cream, and all that Kuzmichov never could have dreamed of.

While Egorushka was looking at the sleeping faces, he suddenly heard a soft singing. Somewhere not close by, a woman was singing, but precisely where and in which direction was hard to make out. The song, soft, drawn out, and mournful, like weeping, and barely audible, came now from the right, now from the left, now from above, now from under the ground, as if some invisible spirit was hovering over the steppe and singing. Egorushka looked around and could not tell where this strange song was coming from; then, when he listened better, it began to seem to him that it was the grass singing; in its song, half dead, already perished, wordless, but plaintive and sincere, it was trying to persuade someone that it was not to blame for anything, that the sun was scorching it for nothing; it insisted that it wanted passionately to live, that it was still young and would be beautiful if it were not for the heat and drought; it was not to blame, but even so, it asked forgiveness of someone, swearing that it was suffering unbearably, felt sad and sorry for itself...

Egorushka listened a little, and it began to seem to him that this mournful, drawn-out song made the air still more sultry, hot, and immobile... To stifle the song, he ran to the sedge, humming and trying to stamp his feet. From there he looked in all directions and found the one who was singing. Near the last hut in the hamlet, a peasant woman in a short shift, long-legged and lanky as a heron, stood sifting something. White dust drifted lazily down the knoll from under her sieve. It was now obvious that it was she who was singing. A few feet from her, a little boy stood motionless in nothing but a shirt, and with no hat. As if enchanted by the song, he did not stir and looked down somewhere, probably at Egorushka's red shirt.

The song ceased. Egorushka trudged back to the britzka and again, having nothing to do, occupied himself with the stream of water.

And again he heard the drawn-out song. The same long-legged woman in the hamlet behind the knoll was singing. Egorushka's boredom suddenly came back to him. He abandoned the pipe and raised his eyes. What he saw was so unexpected that he was slightly frightened. Above his head, on one of the big clumsy stones, stood a little boy in nothing but a shirt, pudgy, with a big protruding belly and skinny legs, the same one who had been standing by the woman earlier. With dull astonishment and not without fear, as if seeing otherworldly beings before him, unblinking and openmouthed, he studied Egorushka's red shirt and the britzka. The red color of the shirt lured and caressed him, and the britzka and the people sleeping under it aroused his curiosity; perhaps he himself had not noticed how the pleasing red color and curiosity had drawn him down from the hamlet, and probably he was now astonished at his own boldness. Egorushka studied him for a long time, and he Egorushka. Both were silent and felt a certain awkwardness. After a long silence, Egorushka asked:

"What's your name?"

The stranger's cheeks swelled still more; he pressed his back against the stone, goggled his eyes, moved his lips, and answered in a husky bass:

"Titus."

The boys said not one word more to each other. After a short silence, and not tearing his eyes from Egorushka, the mysterious Titus raised one leg, felt for a foothold behind him with his heel, and climbed up the stone; from there, backing up and staring point-blank at Egorushka, as if afraid he might hit him from behind, he got up onto the next stone and so kept climbing until he vanished altogether over the top of the knoll.

Having followed him with his eyes, Egorushka put his arms around his knees and bowed his head...The hot rays burned his nape, his neck, his back...The mournful song now died down, now drifted again through the stagnant, stifling air, the brook burbled monotonously, the horses munched, and time dragged on endlessly, as if it, too, had congealed and stopped. It seemed that a hundred years had passed since morning...Did God want Egorushka, the britzka, and the horses to stand stock-still in this air and, like the hills, turn to stone and stay forever in one place?

Egorushka raised his head and, with bleary eyes, looked in front of him; the purple distance, which till then had been motionless, swayed and, along with the sky, sped off somewhere still further away...It pulled the brown grass and the sedge with it, and Egorushka, with extraordinary swiftness, sped after the fleeing distance. Some force was noiselessly drawing him somewhere, and in his wake raced the heat and the wearisome song. Egorushka bowed his head and closed his eyes . . .

Deniska was the first to wake up. Something had stung him, because he jumped up, quickly scratched his shoulder, and said:

"Heathenish anathema, the plague's too good for you!"

Then he went to the brook, drank, and washed for a long time. His snorting and splashing brought Egorushka out of oblivion. The boy looked at his wet face, covered with drops and large freckles, which made it look like marble, and asked:

"Will we go soon?"

Deniska looked to see how high the sun was and answered:

"Ought to be soon."

He dried himself with his shirttail and, making a very serious face, began hopping on one leg.

"Hey, let's see who'll reach the sedge first!" he said.

Egorushka was weary with heat and drowsiness, but all the same he went hopping after him. Deniska was already about twenty, he served as a coachman and was going to get married, but he had not yet stopped being a child. He loved flying kites, chasing pigeons, playing knucklebones, playing tag, and always mixed into children's games and quarrels. The masters had only to leave or fall asleep for him to start something like hopping on one leg or throwing stones. It was hard for any adult, seeing the genuine enthusiasm with which he frolicked in the company of the young ones, to keep from saying: "What a dolt!" But children saw nothing strange in the big coachman's invasion of their domain: let him play, so long as he doesn't fight! Just as little dogs see nothing strange when a big, sincere dog mixes into their company and starts playing with them.

Deniska beat Egorushka and apparently remained very pleased with that. He winked and, to show that he could hop on one leg any distance you like, proposed that Egorushka hop down the road with him and from there back to the britzka without resting. Egorushka rejected the proposal, because he was quite breathless and faint.

Suddenly Deniska made a very serious face, such as he never made, even when Kuzmichov reprimanded him or raised his stick to him; listening, he quietly lowered himself on one knee, and an expression of sternness and fear appeared on his face, as happens with people listening to heresy. He aimed his eyes at one point, slowly raised his hand with the palm cupped, and suddenly fell belly-down on the ground, hitting the grass with his hand.

"Got it!" he croaked triumphantly and, getting up, brought to Egorushka's eyes a big grasshopper.

Thinking it was pleasant for the grasshopper, Egorushka and Deniska stroked its broad green back with their fingers and touched its feelers. Then Deniska caught a fat blood-filled fly and offered it to the grasshopper. Very indifferently, as if it had known Deniska for a long time, the latter moved its big visorlike jaws and bit off the fly's stomach. Released, it flashed its pink underwings and, landing in the grass, at once chirped out its song. The fly was also released; it spread its wings and flew off to the horses minus its stomach.

A deep sigh came from under the britzka. This was Kuzmichov waking up. He quickly raised his head, gazed uneasily into the distance, and it was evident from this look, which slipped insensibly past Egorushka and Deniska, that on waking up, he had thought of wool and Varlamov.

"Father Khristofor, get up, it's time!" he began in alarm. "Enough sleeping, we've slept through business as it is! Deniska, harness up!"

Father Khristofor woke up with the same smile he had fallen asleep with. His face was crumpled and wrinkled from sleep and seemed to have become twice smaller. After washing and dressing, he unhurriedly took a small, greasy Psalter from his pocket and, turning his face to the east, began reading in a whisper and crossing himself.

"Father Khristofor!" Kuzmichov said reproachfully. "It's time to go, the horses are ready, and you, by God . . ."

"Right away, right away . . ." Father Khristofor murmured. "I must read the kathismas[7] . . . I haven't read any today."

"The kathismas can wait till later."

"Ivan Ivanych, I have a rule for each day . . . I can't."

"God's not a stickler."

For a whole quarter of an hour Father Khristofor stood motionless, facing the east and moving his lips, while Kuzmichov looked at him almost with hatred and impatiently shrugged his shoulders. He was especially angry when, after each "Glory," Father Khristofor drew his breath, quickly crossed himself, and, deliberately raising his voice so that the others would cross themselves, said three times:

"Alleluia, alleluia, alleluia, glory to Thee, O God!"

At last he smiled, looked up into the sky, and, putting the Psalter into his pocket, said:

"*Finis!*"

A minute later the britzka started on its way. As if it was driving backwards and not forwards, the travelers saw the same things as before noon. The hills were still sinking into the purple distance, and there was no end of them in sight; tall weeds flashed past, boulders, mowed fields rushed by, and the same rooks, and the kite, sedately flapping its wings, flew over the steppe. The air congealed still more from the heat and the stillness, obedient nature grew torpid in the silence. No wind, no brisk, fresh sound, no clouds.

But then, finally, as the sun began to sink in the west, the steppe, the hills, and the air could bear no more oppression, and, worn out, their patience exhausted, they attempted to throw off the yoke. An ash-gray curly cloud unexpectedly appeared from behind the hills. It exchanged glances with the steppe—I'm ready, it seemed to say—and frowned. Suddenly something broke in the stagnant air, a strong gust of wind came and, whistling noisily, went wheeling around the steppe. At once the grass and last year's weeds raised a murmur, the dust of the road whirled into a spiral, ran across the steppe, and, drawing straw, dragonflies, and feathers with it, rose up into the sky in a black, spinning pillar and obscured the sun. Tumbleweed rolled hither and thither, stumbling and leaping, over the steppe, and one bush got into the whirl, spun like a bird, flew up into the sky, and, turning into a black speck there, disappeared from sight. After it swept another, then a third, and Egorushka saw two tumbleweeds collide in the blue height and clutch at each other as if in combat.

A kestrel took flight just by the roadside. Flashing its wings and tail, bathed in sunlight, it looked like an angler's fly or a pond moth whose wings merge with its feelers as it flashes over the water, and it seems to have feelers growing on it in front, and behind, and on the sides . . . Quivering in the air like an insect, sporting its motley colors, the kestrel rose high up in a straight line, then, probably frightened by the cloud of dust, veered off to one side, and its flashing could be seen for a long time . . .

And now, alarmed by the wind and not understanding what it was about, a corncrake flew up from the grass. It flew with the wind, not against it as all birds do; this ruffled its feathers, puffing it up to the size of a hen, and it looked very angry and imposing. Only the rooks, grown old on the steppe and used to its turmoil, calmly raced over the grass or else, paying no attention to anything, indifferently pecked the tough ground with their fat beaks.

From beyond the hills came a dull rumble of thunder; there was a breath of coolness. Deniska whistled merrily and whipped up the horses. Father Khristofor and Kuzmichov, holding on to their hats, turned their eyes to the hills . . . It would be nice if it spat some rain!

A little more, it seemed, the smallest effort, a single push, and the steppe would gain the upper hand. But the invisible oppressive force gradually fettered the wind and the air, settled the dust, and again came stillness, as if nothing had happened. The cloud hid, the sunburnt hills frowned, the air obediently congealed, and only the alarmed peewits wept somewhere and bemoaned their fate . . .

Soon after that, evening came.

III

IN THE EVENING twilight a big, one-story house appeared, with a rusty iron roof and dark windows. This house was called an innyard, though there was no yard around it, and it stood in the midst of the steppe not fenced by anything. Slightly to one side of it, a pathetic little cherry orchard with a wattle fence could be seen, and under its windows, their heavy heads bowed, sunflowers stood sleeping. In the orchard a tiny little windmill rattled away, set there so that the noise would frighten the hares. Besides that, there was nothing to be seen or heard near the house but the steppe.

The britzka had barely stopped by the covered porch when joyful voices were heard inside the house—one male, the other female. The sliding door shrieked on its pulley, and in an instant a tall, skinny figure rose up by the britzka, flapping its arms and coattails. This was the innkeeper Moisei Moiseich, a middle-aged man with a very pale face and a handsome ink-black beard. He was dressed in a worn black frock coat that hung on his narrow shoulders as if on a hanger, and its tails flapped like wings each time Moisei Moiseich clasped his hands in joy or horror. Besides the frock coat, the landlord was wearing wide white untucked trousers and a velvet vest with orange flowers resembling gigantic bedbugs.

Moisei Moiseich, recognizing the visitors, first stopped dead from the flood of emotion, then clasped his hands and groaned. His frock coat flapped its tails, his back bent into a curve, and his pale face twisted into such a smile as if the sight of the britzka was not only pleasant for him but also painfully sweet.

"Ah, my God, my God!" he began in a high singsong voice, breathless and bustling, his movements hindering the passengers from getting out of the britzka. "And what a happy day it is for me! Ah, and what am I to do now! Ivan Ivanych! Father Khristofor! What a pretty little sir is sitting on the box, God punish me! Ah my God, what am I doing standing here and not inviting the guests in? Please, I humbly beg you . . . come in! Give me all your things . . . Ah, my God!"

While rummaging in the britzka and helping the visitors to get out, Moisei Moiseich suddenly turned around and shouted in such a wild, strangled voice, as if he were drowning and calling for help:

"Solomon! Solomon!"

"Solomon, Solomon!" the woman's voice repeated in the house.

The door shrieked on its pulley, and a young Jew appeared on the threshold, of medium height, red-haired, with a big bird's nose and a bald spot in the midst of his stiff, curly hair; he was dressed in a short, very worn jacket with rounded tails and too short sleeves, and tricot trousers, also too short, as a result of which he himself looked short and skimpy, like a plucked bird. This was Solomon, Moisei Moiseich's brother. Silently, not offering any greeting but only smiling somehow strangely, he approached the britzka.

"Ivan Ivanych and Father Khristofor have come!" Moisei Moiseich said to him in such a tone as if he was afraid his brother might not believe him. "Oi, weh, amazing business,

24

such good people up and came! Well, take the things, Solomon. Come in, dear guests!"

A little later Kuzmichov, Father Khristofor, and Egorushka were sitting in a big, gloomy, and empty room at an old oak table. This table was almost solitary, because apart from it, a wide sofa covered with torn oilcloth, and three chairs, there was no other furniture in the room. And not everyone would have ventured to call those chairs chairs. They were some pitiful semblance of furniture, with oilcloth that had outlived its time, and a highly unnatural bend to their backs, which gave them a great likeness to a child's sled. It was hard to see what comfort the unknown cabinetmaker had in mind in bending the backs so mercilessly, and one would rather have thought that it was the fault not of the cabinetmaker but of some itinerant strongman who, wishing to boast of his strength, had bent the chairs' backs, then tried to set them straight and bent them still more. The room looked gloomy. The walls were gray, the ceiling and cornices were covered with soot, the floor was cracked and had holes of unknown origin gaping in it (one might have thought the same strongman had broken through it with his heel), and it seemed that if a dozen lamps were hung up in the room, it would not stop being dark. There was nothing resembling decoration either on the walls or on the windows. However, on one wall, in a gray wooden frame, hung a list of rules of some sort with a double-headed eagle, and on another, in the same sort of frame, some lithograph with the caption: "Men's Indifference." What it was that men were indifferent to was impossible to tell, because the lithograph was badly faded with time and generously flyblown. The room smelled of something musty and sour.

Having led the guests into the room, Moisei Moiseich went on writhing, clasping his hands, squirming, and making joyful exclamations—he considered it necessary to perform all this in order to appear extremely polite and amiable.

"When did our carts pass by here?" Kuzmichov asked him.

"One party passed this morning, and another, Ivan Ivanych, rested here at dinnertime and left before evening."

"Ah... Did Varlamov pass this way or not?"

"No, Ivan Ivanych. Yesterday morning his agent, Grigory Egorych, passed by and said he must now be at the Molokan's[8] farmstead."

"Excellent. That means we'll catch up with the train now, and then go to the Molokan's."

"God help you, Ivan Ivanych!" Moisei Moiseich clasped his hands, horrified. "Where are you going to go with night falling? Have a nice little bite of supper, spend the night, and tomorrow morning, with God's help, you can go and catch up with anybody you want!"

"No time, no time... Sorry, Moisei Moiseich, some other occasion, but now is not the time. We'll stay for a quarter of an hour and then go, and we can spend the night at the Molokan's."

"A quarter of an hour!" shrieked Moisei Moiseich. "You have no fear of God, Ivan Ivanych! You'll force me to hide your hats and lock the door! At least have a bite to eat and some tea!"

"We have no time for any teas and sugars," said Kuzmichov.

Moisei Moiseich inclined his head, bent his knees, and held his palms up in front of him as if defending himself from blows, and with a painfully sweet smile began to implore:

"Ivan Ivanych! Father Khristofor! Be so kind, have some tea with me! Am I such a bad man that you can't even have tea with me? Ivan Ivanych!"

"Why, we might just have a drop of tea," Father Khristofor sighed sympathetically. "It won't keep us long."

"Well, all right!" Kuzmichov agreed.

Moisei Moiseich roused himself, gasped joyfully, and,

squirming as if he had just jumped out of cold water into the warmth, ran to the door and shouted in a wild, strangled voice, the same with which he had called Solomon earlier:

"Rosa! Rosa! Bring the samovar!"

A minute later, the door opened and Solomon came into the room with a big tray in his hands. Setting the tray on the table, he looked mockingly somewhere to the side and smiled strangely, as before. Now, in the light of the lamp, it was possible to examine his smile; it was very complex and expressed many feelings, but one thing was predominant in it—an obvious contempt. It was as if he was thinking of something funny and stupid, could not stand someone and was contemptuous of him, was glad of something and waiting for the appropriate moment to sting someone with his mockery and roll with laughter. His long nose, fat lips, and sly, protruding eyes seemed to be straining with the wish to burst out laughing. Looking at his face, Kuzmichov smiled mockingly and asked:

"Solomon, why didn't you come to the fair this summer in N. to play the Yid for us?"

Two years ago, as Egorushka also remembered perfectly well, in one of the show booths at the fair in N., Solomon had narrated some scenes from Jewish everyday life and had been a great success. The reminder of it did not make any impression on Solomon. He went out without answering and a little later came back with the samovar.

After doing what was to be done at the table, he went to one side and, crossing his arms on his chest, thrusting one foot forward, fixed his mocking eyes on Father Khristofor. There was something defiant, haughty, and contemptuous in his pose, and at the same time something pathetic and comical in the highest degree, because the more imposing it became, the more conspicuous were his short trousers, his skimpy jacket, his caricature of a nose, and his whole plucked-bird-like little figure.

Moisei Moiseich brought a stool from another room and sat down at some distance from the table.

"Good appetite! Tea and sugar!" he began to entertain his guests. "Good health to you. Such rare guests, rare guests, and Father Khristofor I haven't seen for five years already. And does nobody want to tell me whose nice little boy this is?" he asked, looking affectionately at Egorushka.

"He's the son of my sister Olga Ivanovna," answered Kuzmichov.

"And where is he going?"

"To study. We're taking him to school."

Moisei Moiseich, for the sake of politeness, gave his face a look of astonishment and wagged his head meaningfully.

"Oh, this is good!" he said, shaking his finger at the samovar. "This is good! You'll come out of school such a gentleman we'll all take our hats off. You'll be intelligent, rich, ambitious, and your mama will rejoice. Oh, this is good!"

He paused for a while, stroked his knees, and began to speak in a respectfully jocular tone:

"You forgive me now, Father Khristofor, but I'm going to write a letter to the bishop that you're cutting into the merchants' bread. I'll take official paper and write that it means Father Khristofor hasn't got enough money, if he's gone into trade and started selling wool."

"Yes, I've taken a notion in my old age . . ." Father Khristofor said and laughed. "I've gone over from the priests to the merchants, old boy. Instead of staying home and praying to God, I gallop around like pharaoh in his chariot . . . Vanity!"

"But you'll get a lot of moneys!"

"Oh, yes! A fig[9] under my nose, not moneys! The goods aren't mine, they're my son-in-law Mikhailo's!"

"Why didn't he go himself?"

"Because . . . The mother's milk still hasn't dried on his

28

lips. Buy the wool he did, but sell it—no, he's not clever enough, he's still young. He spent all his money, meaning to gain by it and kick up the dust, but he tried here and there, and nobody would even give him what he paid. So the lad knocked about for a year, then came to me and— 'Papa, do me a favor, sell the wool! I don't understand anything about these things!' There you have it. So now I'm papa, but before, he could do without papa. When he bought the wool, he didn't ask, but now he's in a pinch, and so I'm papa. And what about papa? If it weren't for Ivan Ivanych, papa wouldn't be able to do a thing. What a bother they are!"

"Yes, children are a bother, I can tell you!" sighed Moisei Moiseich. "I myself have six of them. One to be taught, another to be doctored, the third to be carried in your arms, and when they grow up, there's still more bother. Not only now, it was so even in Holy Scripture. When Jacob had little children, he wept, and when they grew up, he wept still worse!"[10]

"Mm, yes..." agreed Father Khristofor, gazing pensively at his glass of tea. "Personally, as a matter of fact, I've got no business angering God, I've reached the limit of my life, as God grant everybody... I've married my daughters to good men, I've set my sons up, now I'm free, I've done my duty, and I can go any which way. I live quietly with my wife, eat, drink, and sleep, rejoice in my grandchildren, and pray to God, and I don't need anything else. I'm rolling in clover and I answer to no one. In all my born days, I've never known any grief, and if, say, the tsar now asked me: 'What do you need? What do you want?' Well, there's nothing I'm in need of! I have everything and thank God. There's no happier man than I in the whole town. Only I have many sins, but then they say only God is without sin. Isn't that right?"

"Must be right."

"Well, of course, I've got no teeth, my back aches from old age, this and that... shortness of breath and so forth...

Illnesses, the flesh is weak, but you must agree I've lived enough! I'm in my seventies! You can't go on forever, enough's enough!"

Father Khristofor suddenly recalled something, burst out laughing into his glass, and got into a coughing fit from laughter. Moisei Moiseich, out of politeness, also laughed and coughed.

"So funny!" said Father Khristofor and waved his hand. "My older son Gavrila comes to visit me. He works in the medical line and serves in Chernigov province as a zemstvo[11] doctor . . . Very well, sir . . . I say to him: 'See here,' I say, 'I'm short of breath, this and that . . . You're a doctor, treat your father!' He got me undressed at once, tapped, listened, various other things . . . kneaded my stomach, and then says: 'Papa,' he says, 'you need treatment with compressed air.'"

Father Khristofor laughed convulsively, to tears, and stood up.

"And I say to him: 'God help it, this compressed air!'" he brought out through his laughter and waved both hands. "God help it, this compressed air!"

Moisei Moiseich also stood up and, clutching his stomach, also dissolved in high-pitched laughter, resembling the yelping of a lapdog.

"God help it, this compressed air!" Father Khristofor repeated, laughing loudly.

Moisei Moiseich rose two notes higher and rocked with such convulsive laughter that he barely kept his feet.

"Oh, my God . . ." he moaned amid his laughter. "Let me catch my breath . . . You've made me laugh so much that . . . oh! . . . it's the death of me."

He laughed and talked and meanwhile kept glancing timorously and suspiciously at Solomon. The latter stood in the same pose and smiled. Judging by his eyes and smile, his contempt and hatred were serious, but they were so unsuited to his plucked little figure that it seemed to Egorushka that he assumed this defiant pose and sarcastic, contemptuous expression on purpose in order to play the buffoon and make the dear guests laugh.

Having silently drunk some six glasses, Kuzmichov cleared a space before him on the table, took his sack, the same one that lay under his head while he slept under the britzka, untied the string on it, and shook it. Stacks of banknotes spilled from the sack onto the table.

"Come, Father Khristofor, let's count it while there's time," said Kuzmichov.

Seeing the money, Moisei Moiseich became embarrassed, got up, and, as a tactful man who does not want to know other people's secrets, left the room on tiptoe, balancing himself with his arms. Solomon stayed where he was.

"How many are there in the one-rouble stacks?" Father Khristofor began.

"Fifty in each . . . In the three-rouble stacks, ninety . . . The twenty-fives and hundreds are by the thousands . . . You count out seven thousand eight hundred for Varlamov, and I'll count out for Gusevich. And see that you don't miscount . . ."

Never since the day he was born had Egorushka seen such a pile of money as now lay on the table. It was probably a great deal of money, because the stack of seven thousand eight hundred that Father Khristofor set aside for Varlamov seemed very small compared to the whole pile. Another time such a mass of money might have struck Egorushka and prompted him to reflect on how many bagels, babas, and poppy-seed rolls could be bought with this pile; but now he looked at it impassibly and sensed only the smell of rotten apples and kerosene that the pile gave off. He was worn out from the jolting ride on the britzka, was tired and wanted to sleep. His head was heavy, his eyes kept closing, and his thoughts were tangled like threads. If it had been possible, he would gladly have lowered his head to the table, closed his eyes so as not to see the lamp and the fingers moving over the pile, and let his sluggish, sleepy thoughts tangle still more. When he made an effort not to doze off, the flame of the lamp, the cups, and the fingers went double, the samovar swayed, and the smell of rotten apples seemed still sharper and more repellent.

"Ah, money, money!" sighed Father Khristofor, smiling. "Nothing but woe! Now my Mikhailo is surely sleeping and dreaming of me bringing him such a pile."

"Your Mikhailo Timofeich is a man of no understanding," Kuzmichov said in a low voice, "he took up a business that's not right for him, but you understand and can reason. Why don't you give me your wool, as I said, and go back home, and I—very well—I'll give you fifty kopecks over your asking price, and that only out of respect . . ."

"No, Ivan Ivanovich," sighed Father Khristofor. "Thank you for the offer . . . Of course, if it were up to me, there'd be no discussion, but as you know, the goods aren't mine . . ."

Moisei Moiseich came in on tiptoe. Trying out of delicacy not to look at the pile of money, he crept up to Egorushka and tugged him by the shirt from behind.

"Come along, little lad," he said in a low voice, "I've got a bear cub to show you! Such a terrible, angry one! Ohh!"

Sleepy Egorushka got up and lazily plodded after Moisei Moiseich to look at the bear. He went into a small room where, before he saw anything, his breath was taken away by the smell of something sour and musty, which was much more dense here than in the big room and had probably spread from here all over the house. One half of the room was occupied by a big bed covered with a greasy quilted blanket, and the other by a chest of drawers and heaps of all possible rags, beginning with stiffly starched petticoats and ending with children's trousers and suspenders. A tallow candle was burning on the chest of drawers.

Instead of the promised bear, Egorushka saw a large, very

fat Jewess with loose hair and in a red flannel dress with black specks; she was turning heavily in the narrow passage between the bed and the chest of drawers and letting out long, moaning sighs, as if she had a toothache. Seeing Egorushka, she made a tearful face, heaved a long sigh, and, before he had time to look around, brought to his mouth a chunk of bread smeared with honey.

"Eat, child, eat!" she said. "You're here without your mama, and there's nobody to feed you. Eat."

Egorushka began to eat, though after the fruit drops and poppy-seed rolls he ate every day at home, he found nothing good in honey half mixed with wax and bees' wings. He ate, and Moisei Moiseich and the Jewess watched and sighed.

"Where are you going, child?" asked the Jewess.

"To study," replied Egorushka.

"And how many of you does your mama have?"

"I'm the only one. There's nobody else."

"Och!" sighed the Jewess, and she raised her eyes. "Poor mama, poor mama! How she's going to weep and miss you! In a year we, too, will take our Nahum to study! Och!"

"Ah, Nahum, Nahum!" sighed Moisei Moiseich, and the skin twitched nervously on his pale face. "And he's so sickly."

The greasy blanket stirred, and from under it appeared a child's curly head on a very thin neck; two black eyes flashed and stared at Egorushka with curiosity. Moisei Moiseich and the Jewess, without ceasing to sigh, went over to the chest of drawers and began talking about something in Yiddish. Moisei Moiseich talked softly in a low bass, and generally his Yiddish resembled a ceaseless "gal-gal-gal-gal..." and his wife answered him in a thin hen-turkey's voice, and with her it came out something like "tu-tu-tu-tu..." While they were conferring, another curly head on a thin neck peeked from under the greasy blanket, then a third, then a fourth... If Egorushka had possessed a rich fantasy, he might have thought a hundred-headed hydra was lying under the blanket.

"Gal-gal-gal-gal . . ." said Moisei Moiseich.

"Tu-tu-tu-tu . . ." the Jewess replied.

The conference ended with the Jewess sighing deeply, going to the chest of drawers, unfolding some sort of green rag there, and taking out a big rye gingerbread shaped like a heart.

"Take, child," she said, handing Egorushka the gingerbread. "You've got no mama now, there's nobody to give you a treat."

Egorushka put the gingerbread in his pocket and backed towards the door, no longer able to breathe the musty and sour air in which his hosts lived. Returning to the big room, he snuggled up comfortably on the sofa and let his thoughts run freely.

Kuzmichov had just finished counting the money and was putting it back in the sack. He treated it with no particular respect and shoved it into the dirty sack unceremoniously, with such indifference as if it was not money but wastepaper.

Father Khristofor was conversing with Solomon.

"Well, then, my wise Solomon?" he asked, yawning and crossing his mouth.[12] "How's things?"

"What things are you talking about?" asked Solomon and looked at him with great sarcasm, as if he was hinting at some sort of crime.

"Generally . . . What are you doing?"

"What am I doing?" Solomon repeated and shrugged his shoulders. "The same as everybody . . . You see, I'm a lackey. I'm my brother's lackey, my brother is the travelers' lackey, the travelers are Varlamov's lackeys, and if I had ten million, Varlamov would be my lackey."

"Why would he be your lackey?"

"Why? Because there's no such gentleman or millionaire as wouldn't lick the hands of a scruffy Yid for an extra kopeck. I'm now a scruffy and beggarly Yid, and everybody looks at me like a dog, but if I had money, Varlamov would mince before me like a fool, the way Moisei does before you."

Father Khristofor and Kuzmichov exchanged glances. Neither of them understood Solomon. Kuzmichov looked at him sternly and drily and asked:

"How can a fool like you put yourself on a par with Varlamov?"

"I'm not such a fool as to put myself on a par with Varlamov," Solomon replied, looking his interlocutors over mockingly. "Varlamov may be a Russian, but in his soul he's a scruffy Yid; his whole life is money and gain, but I burned up my money in the stove. I don't need money, or land, or sheep, and I don't need to be feared and have people take their hats off when I drive by. Meaning I'm smarter than your Varlamov and more like a human being!"

A little later, Egorushka, through half-sleep, heard Solomon speaking about the Jews in a voice hollow and hoarse from the hatred that choked him, hurrying and swallowing his R's; at first he spoke correctly, in Russian, then he lapsed into the tone of raconteurs of Jewish life and began speaking with an exaggerated Jewish accent, as he used to in the show booth.

"Wait..." Father Khristofor interrupted him. "If you don't like your faith, change it, but it's a sin to laugh at it; he's the lowest of men who derides his own faith."

"You don't understand anything!" Solomon rudely cut him short. "I'm talking to you about one thing, and you're talking about another..."

"It's obvious at once that you're a stupid man," Father Khristofor sighed. "I admonish you the best I can, and you get angry. I talk to you as an old man, quietly, but you're like a turkey: blah-blah-blah! An odd fellow, really..."

Moisei Moiseich came in. He looked in alarm at Solomon and his guests, and again the skin on his face twitched nervously. Egorushka shook his head and looked around him;

he caught a fleeting glimpse of Solomon's face just at the moment when it was turned three-quarters towards him and the shadow of his long nose crossed his whole left cheek; his contemptuous smile, mingled with this shadow, his glittering, mocking eyes, his haughty expression, and his whole plucked little figure, doubling and flashing in Egorushka's eyes, now made him resemble not a buffoon but something one occasionally dreams of, probably an unclean spirit.

"Some kind of demoniac you've got here, Moisei Moiseich, God help him!" Father Khristofor said with a smile. "You'd better set him up somewhere, get him married or something...He's not like a human being..."

Kuzmichov frowned angrily. Moisei Moiseich again gave his brother and his guests an alarmed and quizzical look.

"Solomon, get out of here!" he said sternly. "Get out."

And he added something else in Yiddish. Solomon laughed abruptly and went out.

"But what is it?" Moisei Moiseich fearfully asked Father Khristofor.

"He forgets himself," replied Kuzmichov. "He's a rude one and thinks a lot of himself."

"I just knew it!" Moisei Moiseich was horrified and clasped his hands. "Ah, my God! My God!" he murmured in a low voice. "Be so kind, forgive and don't be angry. He's such a man, such a man! Ah, my God! My God! He's my own brother, but I've never had anything but grief from him. You know, he's..."

Moisei Moiseich twirled his finger near his forehead and went on:

"Not in his right mind...a lost man. And what I'm to do with him, I don't know! He doesn't love anybody, he doesn't esteem anybody, he's not afraid of anybody...You know, he laughs at everybody, says stupid things, throws it in everybody's face. You won't believe it, but once Varlamov came here, and Solomon said such things to him that the

36

man struck both him and me with his whip . . . But why me? Is it my fault? God took away his reason, that means it's God's will, and is it my fault?"

Some ten minutes passed, and Moisei Moiseich still went on murmuring in a low voice and sighing.

"He doesn't sleep nights and keeps thinking, thinking, thinking, and what he thinks about, God knows. You come to him at night, and he's angry and he laughs. He doesn't love me, either . . . And he doesn't want anything! Father, when he was dying, left us six thousand roubles each. I bought myself an inn, got married, and now have children, but he burned up his money in the stove. Such a pity, such a pity! Why burn it? If you don't need it, give it to me, why burn it?"

Suddenly the door shrieked on its pulley, and the floor trembled from someone's footsteps. A light wind blew at Egorushka, and it seemed to him that a big black bird swept past him and flapped its wings just by his face. He opened his eyes . . . His uncle, the sack in his hands, ready for the road, was standing by the sofa. Father Khristofor, holding his broad-brimmed top hat, was bowing and smiling to someone, not gently and tenderly, as always, but with a strained deference that was very unsuited to his face. And Moisei Moiseich, as if his body had broken into three parts, was balancing and trying all he could not to fall apart. Only Solomon stood in the corner as if nothing had happened, his arms crossed, and smiling as contemptuously as before.

"Your Excellency, forgive us, it's not clean here!" moaned Moisei Moiseich with a painfully sweet smile, no longer noticing Kuzmichov or Father Khristofor, but only balancing his whole body so as not to fall apart. "We're simple people, Your Excellency!"

Egorushka rubbed his eyes. Indeed, in the middle of the room stood an excellency in the guise of a young, very beautiful and shapely woman in a black dress and a straw hat.

Before Egorushka had time to make out her features, he recalled for some reason the solitary slender poplar he had seen that day on a hill.

"Did Varlamov pass here today?" asked a woman's voice.

"No, Your Excellency!" replied Moisei Moiseich.

"If you see him tomorrow, ask him to stop at my place for a minute."

Suddenly, quite unexpectedly, an inch from his eyes, Egorushka saw black velvety eyebrows, big brown eyes, and pampered woman's cheeks with dimples, from which a smile spread all over her face like rays from the sun. There was a scent of something magnificent.

"What a pretty boy!" said the lady. "Whose boy is he? Kazimir Mikhailovich, look, how lovely! My God, he's asleep! My dear little chubsy . . ."

And the lady kissed Egorushka hard on both cheeks, and he smiled and, thinking he was asleep, closed his eyes. The door pulley shrieked, and hurried steps were heard: someone was going in and out.

"Egorushka! Egorushka!" came the thick whisper of two voices. "Get up, we're leaving!"

Someone, probably Deniska, stood Egorushka on his feet and led him by the arm; on the way he half opened his eyes and once more saw the beautiful woman in the black dress who had kissed him. She was standing in the middle of the room and, seeing him leave, smiled and nodded to him amiably. When he reached the door, he saw some handsome and thickset dark-haired man in a bowler hat and leggings. This must have been the lady's escort.

"Whoa!" came from the yard.

By the porch Egorushka saw a new luxurious carriage and a pair of black horses. On the box sat a lackey in livery with a long whip in his hand. Only Solomon came out to see the departing guests off. His face was tense with the desire to burst out laughing; he looked as if he was waiting with great impatience for their departure in order to laugh at them all he wanted.

"Countess Dranitsky," whispered Father Khristofor, getting into the britzka.

"Yes, Countess Dranitsky," Kuzmichov repeated, also in a whisper.

The impression produced by the countess's arrival was probably very strong, because even Deniska spoke in a whisper and only dared to shout and whip up the bays when the britzka had gone about a quarter of a mile and instead of the inn nothing but a dim little light could be seen far behind them.

IV

WHO, FINALLY, WAS this elusive, mysterious Varlamov, of whom there was so much talk, whom Solomon held in contempt, and whom even the beautiful countess needed? Sitting on the box beside Deniska, the half-sleepy Egorushka was thinking precisely about this man. He had never seen him, but he had heard about him very often and had frequently pictured him in his imagination. It was known to him that Varlamov owned several thousand-score acres of land, about a hundred thousand sheep, and a lot of money; of his way of life and activities Egorushka knew only that he was always "circling around in these parts" and was always sought after.

Egorushka had also heard much at home about the countess Dranitsky. She, too, had several thousand-score acres, many sheep, a stud farm, and a lot of money, but she did not "circle around," but lived on her rich estate, about which their acquaintances and Ivan Ivanych, who had visited the countess more than once on business, told many wonders. For instance, they said that in the countess's drawing room, where portraits of all the Polish kings hung, there was a big table clock in the form of a crag, and on the crag stood a rearing golden steed with diamond eyes, and on the steed sat a golden rider who swung his saber right and left each time the clock struck the hour. They also told how twice a year the countess gave a ball to which the nobility and officials of the whole province were invited, and even Varlamov came, the guests all drank tea from silver samovars, ate all sorts of extraordinary things (for instance, raspberries and strawberries were served in winter, for Christmas), and danced to music that played day and night . . .

"And she's so beautiful!" thought Egorushka, remembering her face and smile.

Kuzmichov was probably also thinking about the countess, because when the britzka had gone some two miles, he said:

"This Kazimir Mikhailych robs her good and proper! Two years ago, remember, when I bought wool from her, he made about three thousand on my purchase alone."

"You'd expect nothing else from a Polack," said Father Khristofor.

"And she doesn't care a whit. As they say, young and stupid. Wind blowing around in her head!"

Egorushka, for some reason, wanted to think only about Varlamov and the countess, especially the latter. His sleepy brain totally rejected ordinary thoughts, it was clouded and retained only fantastic fairy-tale images, which have the convenience of emerging in the brain somehow of themselves, without any bother on the thinker's part, and also of themselves—you need only give a good shake of the head—of vanishing without a trace. And besides, nothing around disposed him to ordinary thoughts. To the right were dark hills, which seemed to screen off something unknown and terrible; to the left, the whole sky above the horizon was covered with a crimson glow, and it was hard to tell whether there was a fire somewhere or the moon was about to rise.

The distance was visible, as in the daytime, but now its delicate purple color, shaded by the dusk of evening, disappeared, and the whole steppe was hiding in the dusk, like Moisei Moiseich's children under the blanket.

On July evenings and nights, the quails and corncrakes no longer cry, the nightingales do not sing in the wooded gullies, the flowers give off no scent, but the steppe is still beautiful and filled with life. As soon as the sun sets and the earth is enveloped in dusk, the day's anguish is forgotten, all is forgiven, and the steppe breathes easily with its broad chest. As if because the grass does not see its old age in the darkness, a merry, youthful chirring arises in it, such as does not happen in the daytime; chirping, whistling, scratching, steppe basses, tenors, and trebles—everything blends into a ceaseless, monotonous hum, a good background for remembrance and sorrow. The monotonous chirring lulls you like a cradle song; you ride along and feel you are falling asleep, but then from somewhere comes the abrupt, alarmed cry of a sleepless bird or some indefinite noise resembling someone's voice, like an astonished "Ahh!" and the drowsiness lets go of your eyelids. And then it happens that you drive past a little gully thick with brush, and you hear a bird that the steppe people call a "sleepik," crying "Sleep! Sleep! Sleep!" to someone, and another guffaws or dissolves in hysterical sobbing—that is an owl. Whom they cry to and who listens to them on this plain, God only knows, but there is much sorrow and plaintiveness in their cries... There is a scent of hay, dried grass, and late flowers, but the scent is thick, sweetly cloying, and tender.

Everything is visible in the dusk, but it is hard to make out the colors and outlines of objects. Everything appears to be not what it is. You ride along and suddenly, ahead of you, you see a silhouette like a monk's standing just by the road; he does not move, waits, and is holding something in his hands... Is it a robber? The figure draws near, grows, now it comes even with the britzka, and you see that it is not a man but a solitary bush or a big stone. Such motionless figures, waiting for someone, stand on the hills, hide behind the barrows, peek from amidst the tall weeds, and they all look like people and arouse suspicion.

But when the moon rises, the night becomes pale and dark. It is as if the dusk had never been. The air is transparent, fresh, and warm, everything is clearly visible, and you can even make out the separate stalks of the weeds by the road-side. In the far distance, skulls and stones can be seen. The suspicious monklike figures seem blacker and look more sullen against the bright background of the night. More and more often, amidst the monotonous chirring, someone's astonished "Ah!" is heard, and the cry of a sleepless or deliri-ous bird rings out, troubling the motionless air. Broad shadows drift across the plain like clouds across the sky, and in the incomprehensible distance, if you look at it for a long time, misty, whimsical images loom and heap upon each other . . . It is a little eerie. And once you gaze at the pale green sky spangled with stars, with not a cloud, not a spot on it, you understand why the warm air is motionless, why nature is on the alert and afraid to stir: she feels eerie and sorry to lose even one moment of life. The boundless depth and infinity of the sky can be judged only on the sea or on the steppe at night, when the moon is shining. It is frightening, beautiful, and caressing, it looks at you languorously and beckons, and its caress makes your head spin.

You ride for an hour, two hours . . . On the way you come upon a silent old barrow or a stone idol set up God knows when or by whom, a night bird noiselessly flies over the ground, and steppe legends gradually come to your mind, stories of passing strangers, tales of some old nanny of the steppe, and all that you yourself have managed to see and grasp with your soul. And then, in the chirring of the insects, in the suspicious figures and barrows, in the blue sky, in the moonlight, in the flight of a night bird, in everything you see and hear, you begin to perceive the triumph of beauty, youth, flourishing strength, and a passionate thirst for life; your soul responds to the beautiful, stern motherland, and you want to fly over the steppe with the night bird. And in the triumph of beauty, in the excess of happiness, you feel a tension and anguish, as if the steppe were aware that it is lonely, that its riches and inspiration go for naught in the world, unsung by anyone, unneeded by anyone, and through the joyful hum you hear its anguished, hopeless call: a singer! a singer!

"Who-oa! Greetings, Pantelei! Is all well?"

"Thank God, it is, Ivan Ivanych!"

"Have you boys seen Varlamov?"

"No, haven't seen him."

Egorushka woke up and opened his eyes. The britzka had stopped. Down the road to the right, a wagon train stretched far ahead, with some people scurrying up and down by it. The wagons, because of the big bales of wool piled on them, all seemed very tall and plump, and the horses small and short-legged.

"Well, so that means now we go to the Molokan's!" Kuzmichov was saying loudly. "The Yid said Varlamov would spend the night at the Molokan's. In that case, good-bye, brothers! God be with you!"

"Good-bye, Ivan Ivanych!" several voices anwered.

"Tell you what, boys," Kuzmichov said briskly, "why don't you take my little lad with you! So he doesn't hang about uselessly with us? Put him on a bale, Pantelei, and let him ride slowly, and we'll catch up with you. Go on, Egor! Go, it's all right! . . ."

Egorushka got down from the box. Several hands picked him up, lifted him high, and he found himself on something big, soft, and slightly moist with dew. The sky now seemed close to him and the earth far away.

"Hey, take your coat!" Deniska shouted somewhere far below.

The coat and little bundle, tossed up from below, fell next to Egorushka. Quickly, not wanting to think about anything, he put the bundle under his head, covered himself with his coat, stretched his legs out all the way, squirming from the dew, and laughed with pleasure.

"Sleep, sleep, sleep . . ." he thought.

"Don't rough him up, you devils!" Deniska's voice came from below.

"Good-bye, brothers, God be with you!" shouted Kuzmichov. "I'm counting on you!"

"Don't worry, Ivan Ivanych!"

Deniska hupped the horses, the britzka squealed and started rolling, no longer down the road but somewhere to one side. For two minutes it was silent, as if the wagon train had fallen asleep, and you could hear only the clanking of the bucket tied to the rear of the britzka gradually dying away in the distance. But then at the head of the train someone shouted:

"Gee-up, Kiriukha!"

The wagon at the very front creaked, after it the second, the third . . . Egorushka felt the wagon he was lying on sway and also creak. The train got moving. Egorushka took a tight grip on the rope with which the bundle was tied, laughed again with pleasure, straightened the gingerbread in his pocket, and began to fall asleep the way he used to fall asleep at home in his bed . . .

When he woke up, the sun was already rising; it was screened by a barrow, but in an effort to spray light over the world, it spread its rays tensely in all directions and flooded the horizon with gold. It seemed to Egorushka that it was not where it belonged, because the day before it had risen behind his back, while today it was much more to the left . . . And the whole place was nothing like yesterday. There were no more hills, and wherever you looked, the endless, brown, bleak plain stretched away; here and there small barrows rose up on it, and yesterday's rooks were flying about. Far ahead the belfries and cottages of some village showed white; on account of Sunday, the khokhly[13] stayed home, baking and cooking—that could be seen by the smoke that came from all the chimneys and hung in a transparent dove-gray veil over the village. In the spaces between cottages and behind the church a blue river appeared, and beyond it the misty distance. But there was nothing that so little resembled yesterday as the road. Something extraordinarily broad, sweeping, and mighty stretched across the steppe instead of a road; it was a gray strip, well trodden and covered with dust, like all roads, but it was several dozen yards wide. Its vastness aroused perplexity in Egorushka and suggested folktale thoughts to him. Who drives on it? Who needs such vastness? Incomprehensible and strange. You might really think there were still enormous, long-striding people in Russia, like Ilya Muromets and Nightingale the Robber,[14] and that mighty steeds had not died out yet. Looking at the road, Egorushka imagined some six tall chariots galloping in a row, as he had seen in pictures from sacred history; harnessed to these chariots are six wild, furious horses, and they raise clouds of dust in the sky with their high wheels, and the horses are driven by people such as might appear in dreams or grow in folktale thoughts. And how those figures would suit the steppe and the road, if they existed!

On the right side of the road, for the whole of its length, stood telegraph poles with two wires. Getting smaller and smaller, they disappeared near the village behind the cottages and greenery, and then appeared again in the purple distance, in the guise of very small, thin sticks, like pencils stuck in the ground. On the wires sat hawks, merlins, and crows, looking indifferently at the moving train.

Egorushka lay on the very last wagon and could therefore

see the whole train. There were about twenty wagons in the train, and one wagoner for every three wagons. By the last wagon, where Egorushka was, walked an old man with a gray beard, as skinny and short as Father Khristofor, but with a face dirty brown from sunburn, stern and pensive. It might very well have been that this old man was neither stern nor pensive, but his red eyelids and long, sharp nose gave his face the stern, dry expression that occurs in people who are accustomed to always thinking of serious things, and in solitude. Like Father Khristofor, he was wearing a broad-brimmed top hat, though not a gentleman's, but made of felt and of a dirty brown color, more like a truncated cone than a cylinder. He was barefoot. Probably from a habit acquired during the cold winters, when more than once he must have frozen beside the wagons, he kept slapping his thighs and stamping his feet as he walked. Noticing that Egorushka was awake, he looked at him and said, squirming as if from cold:

"Ah, you're awake, my fine lad! Are you Ivan Ivanovich's son?"

"No, his nephew . . ."

"Ivan Ivanych's? And here I've taken my boots off and go hopping around barefoot. My feet hurt, they got frostbit, and it feels freer without boots . . . Freer, my fine lad . . . Without boots, that is . . . So, you're his nephew? He's a good man, all right . . . God grant him health . . . He's all right . . . Ivan Ivanych, I mean . . . He's gone to the Molokan's . . . Lord have mercy!"

The old man also spoke as if it was very cold, with pauses, and not opening his mouth properly; and he articulated labial consonants poorly, faltering over them as if his lips were frozen. Addressing Egorushka, he never once smiled and appeared stern.

Two wagons ahead walked a man in a long reddish coat, a visored cap, and boots with crumpled tops, holding a whip. This one was not old, about forty. When he turned around,

Egorushka saw a long red face with a thin goatee and a spongy bump under the right eye. Besides this very unattractive bump, he had another special mark that struck the eye sharply: he held the whip in his left hand, and his right hand he waved in such fashion as if he was conducting an invisible choir; occasionally he put the whip under his arm, and then he conducted with both hands and hummed something under his nose.

The next wagoner after this one presented a tall, rectilinear figure with extremely sloping shoulders and a back flat as a board. He held himself erect, as if he was marching or had swallowed a yardstick; his arms did not swing, but hung down like straight sticks, and he strode somehow woodenly, in the manner of toy soldiers, almost without bending his knees, and trying to take the longest stride possible. Where the old man or the owner of the spongy bump took two strides, he managed to take only one, and this made it look as if he was walking more slowly than everyone else and lagging behind. His face was bound in a rag, and something like a monk's skullcap was stuck on his head; he was dressed in a short Ukrainian caftan all sprinkled with patches, and dark blue balloon trousers over his bast shoes.

Those who were further ahead, Egorushka did not examine. He lay belly-down, poked a little hole in the bale, and, having nothing to do, began twisting the wool into threads. The old man striding along below turned out to be not as stern and serious as one might have judged by his face. Once he had started the conversation, he kept it up.

"Where are you going, then?" he asked, stamping his feet.

"To study," answered Egorushka.

"To study? Aha . . . Well, may the Queen of Heaven help you. So. Two heads are better than one. To one man God gives one brain, to another two brains, and to some even three . . . To some even three, that's for sure . . . One brain you're born with, another you get from studies, the third from a good life. So you see, little brother, it's good if some-body has three brains. It's easier for such a man not only to live but even to die. To die, yes . . . And die we all will."

The old man scratched his forehead, glanced up at Ego-rushka with his red eyes, and went on:

"Last year Maxim Nikolaich, a master from near Slavyano-serbsk, also took his lad to study. I don't know how he is regards to learning, but he's an all right lad, a good one . . . God grant them health, they're nice masters. Yes, he also took him to study . . . In Slavyanoserbsk there is no such institution so as to finish your learning . . . None . . . But it's an all right town, a good one . . . There's an ordinary school, for simple folk, but as for greater learning, there's nonesuch . . . None, that's for sure. What's your name?"

"Egorushka."

"Meaning Egory . . . The great and holy martyr Saint Egory the Dragonslayer,[15] whose feast day is the twenty-third of April. And my saint's name is Pantelei . . . Pantelei Zakharovich Kholodov . . . We're Kholodovs . . . I myself was born, you might have heard, in Tim, in Kursk province. My brothers registered themselves as tradesmen and work in town as craftsmen, but I'm a peasant . . . I stayed a peasant. Some seven years ago I went there . . . home, that is. And I was in the village and in the town . . . I was in Tim, I'm saying. Back then, thank God, everybody was alive and well, but I don't know about now . . . Maybe some have died . . . It's time to die now, because everybody's old, there's some are older than me. Death's all right, it's good, only, of course, so long as you don't die unrepentant. There's no greater evil than an impudent death. An impudent death is the devil's joy. And if you want to die repentant, so that the mansions of God aren't barred to you, pray to the great martyr Varvara.[16] She's our intercessor . . . She is, that's for sure . . . Because that's the position God set up for her in heaven, meaning everyone has the full right to pray to her as regards repentance."

Pantelei was muttering and apparently did not care whether Egorushka heard him or not. He spoke listlessly, under his nose, not raising or lowering his voice, but in a short space he managed to tell of many things. Everything he told consisted of fragments that had very little connection with each other and were totally uninteresting to Egorushka. Perhaps he talked only because now, in the morning, after a night spent in silence, he wanted to check his thoughts aloud: were they all at home? Having finished with repentance, he again began speaking about some Maxim Nikolaevich from near Slavyanoserbsk:

"Yes, he took his lad . . . Took him, that's for sure . . ."

One of the wagoners who was walking far ahead tore from his place, ran to the side, and began lashing the ground with his whip. He was a strapping, broad-shouldered man of about thirty, blond, curly-headed, and apparently very strong and healthy. Judging by the movements of his shoulders and whip, by the eagerness his posture expressed, he was beating something live. Another wagoner ran over to him, a short and stocky man with a black spade beard, dressed in a waistcoat and an untucked shirt. This one burst into bass-voiced, coughing laughter and shouted:

"Brothers, Dymov's killed a viper! By God!"

There are people whose intelligence can be judged correctly by their voice and laughter. The black-bearded fellow belonged precisely to such fortunates: in his voice and laughter you could sense an unmitigated stupidity. Having finished whipping, the blond Dymov lifted something resembling a rope from the ground with his whip and flung it towards the wagons with a laugh.

"That's no viper, it's a grass snake," somebody shouted.

The man with the wooden stride and the bound-up face quickly went over to the dead snake, glanced at it, and clasped his sticklike hands.

49

"Jailbird!" he cried in a hollow, tearful voice. "Why'd you kill a grass snake? What did it do to you, curse you! Look, he's killed a grass snake! And what if somebody did the same to you?"

"You shouldn't kill grass snakes, that's for sure . . ." Pantelei muttered placidly. "You shouldn't . . . It's not an asp. It has the looks of a viper, but it's a quiet, innocent beast . . . It loves man . . . Your grass snake . . ."

Dymov and the black-bearded fellow probably felt ashamed, because they laughed loudly and, without answering the protests, trudged lazily to their wagons. When the last wagon came even with the place where the dead snake lay, the man with the bound-up face, standing over the snake, turned to Pantelei and asked in a tearful voice:

"Why'd he kill the grass snake, grandpa?"

His eyes, as Egorushka now made out, were small, lackluster, his face was gray, sickly, and also as if lackluster, and his chin was red and appeared badly swollen.

"Why'd he kill it, grandpa?" he repeated, striding beside Pantelei.

"A stupid man, got an itch in his hands, that's why he killed it," the old man replied. "And you shouldn't kill a grass snake . . . That's for sure . . . We all know Dymov, he's a prankster, he'll kill anything he gets his hands on, and Kiriukha didn't interfere. He ought to have interfered, but it was just ha-ha-ha and ho-ho-ho . . . But don't you get angry, Vasya . . . Why get angry? They killed it, and God help them . . . Dymov's a prankster, and Kiriukha does it from his stupid wits . . . Never mind . . . They're stupid people, with no understanding, and God help them. Emelyan here will never touch what he oughtn't. Never, that's for sure . . . Because he's an educated man, and they're stupid . . . Your Emelyan . . . He won't . . ."

The wagoner in the reddish coat and with the spongy bump, who conducted the invisible choir, stopped on hearing his name, waited until Pantelei and Vasya came even with him, and walked beside them.

"What's the talk about?" he said in a wheezing, stifled voice.

"Vasya here's getting angry," said Pantelei. "I use various words, so he won't get angry, I mean...Eh, my ailing, frostbitten little feet! Ehh! They got itchy for the sake of Sunday, the Lord's feast day!"

"It's from walking," observed Vasya.

"No, lad, no...Not from walking. When I walk, it seems easier, but when I lie down and get warm—it's the death of me. Walking's freer for me."

Emelyan in his reddish coat stood between Pantelei and Vasya and waved his hand as if they were going to sing. After waving it for a while, he lowered his hand and grunted hopelessly.

"I've got no voice!" he said. "Sheer disaster! All night and all morning I've been imagining the triple 'Lord have mercy!' that we sang at Marinovsky's wedding; it's sitting in my head and throat...so it seems I could just up and sing it, but I can't! I've got no voice!"

He fell silent for a moment, thinking about something, then went on:

"For fifteen years I was in the choir, in the whole Lugansk factory, maybe, there was no such voice, but then, deuce take it, I went swimming in the Donets two years ago, and ever since I've been unable to hit a single note clearly. I caught a chill in my throat. And me without a voice is the same as a workman without a hand."

"That's for sure," agreed Pantelei.

"The way I look at myself is, I'm a lost man and nothing more."

At that moment Vasya happened to catch sight of Egorushka. His eyes became unctuous and grew still smaller.

"And there's a young master coming with us!" he said and

covered his nose with his sleeve, as if abashed. "What a grand coachman! Stay with us, you can go around with the wagons carting wool."

The notion of combining a young master and a coachman in one body probably seemed very curious and witty to him, because he tittered loudly and went on developing the thought. Emelyan also glanced up at Egorushka, but fleetingly and coldly. He was occupied with his thoughts, and if it had not been for Vasya, he would not have noticed Egorushka's presence. Before five minutes had passed, he again began waving his hand, then, describing to his companions the beauties of the wedding "Lord have mercy," which had come to his mind during the night, he put the whip under his arm and waved both hands.

A mile from the village, the train stopped by a well with a sweep. Lowering his bucket into the well, the black-bearded Kiriukha leaned his belly on the rail and thrust his shaggy head, shoulders, and part of his chest into the dark hole, so that Egorushka could see only his short legs, which barely touched the ground; seeing the reflection of his head far away at the bottom of the well, he rejoiced and dissolved into stupid bass laughter, and the well's echo answered him the same way; when he stood up, his face and neck were crimson red. Dymov was the first to run over and drink. He drank laughing, often tearing himself away from the bucket and telling Kiriukha about something funny, then he turned and, loudly, for the whole steppe to hear, uttered five bad words. Egorushka did not understand the meaning of these words, but he knew very well that they were bad. He knew the repugnance his family and acquaintances silently nursed for them, shared this feeling, not knowing why himself, and was accustomed to think that only drunk and riotous people had the privilege of uttering these words aloud. He remembered the killing of the grass snake, listened to Dymov's laughter, and felt something like hatred for this man. And, as if on purpose, just then Dymov caught sight of Egorushka, who got off the wagon and was walking towards the well. He laughed loudly and shouted:

"Brothers, the old man gave birth to a boy last night!"

Kiriukha coughed from his bass laughter. Someone else laughed, too, and Egorushka blushed and decided finally that Dymov was a very wicked man.

Blond, curly-headed, hatless, and with the shirt unbuttoned on his chest, Dymov seemed handsome and extraordinarily strong; his every movement revealed the prankster and strongman who knows his own worth. He rolled his shoulders, set his arms akimbo, talked and laughed louder than anybody else, and looked as if he were about to lift something very heavy with one hand and astonish the whole world by it. His mischievous, mocking gaze glided over the road, the wagon train, and the sky, did not pause on anything, and, from having nothing to do, seemed to be looking for some creature to kill or something to make fun of. Evidently he was not afraid of anyone, knew no restraint, and probably had no interest at all in Egorushka's opinion . . . But with all his soul, Egorushka now hated his blond head, clear face, and strength, listened with fear and repugnance to his laughter, and tried to think of some abusive word to say to him in revenge.

Pantelei also went over to the bucket. He took a green icon-lamp glass from his pocket, wiped it with a rag, dipped from the bucket and drank, then dipped again, wrapped the glass in the rag, and put it back in his pocket.

"Grandpa, why do you drink from an icon lamp?" Egorushka was surprised.

"Some drink from a bucket, some from an icon lamp," the old man answered evasively. "To each his own . . . You drink from a bucket, well, so drink in good health . . ."

"My dear little heart, my sweet little beauty," Vasya suddenly started speaking in a tender, tearful voice. "My dear little heart!'

His eyes were aimed off into the distance, they became unctuous, smiled, and his face acquired the same expression as when he had looked at Egorushka earlier.

"Who are you talking to?" asked Kiriukha.

"A sweet little fox . . . it's lying on its back and playing like a puppy . . ."

They all began looking into the distance, seeking the fox with their eyes, but found nothing. Vasya alone saw something with his gray, lackluster little eyes, and admired. As Egorushka later became convinced, he had strikingly keen eyesight. He saw so well that, for him, the dirty brown, empty steppe was always filled with life and content. He had only to peer into the distance to see a fox, a hare, a bustard, or some other animal that keeps away from people. It is not hard to see a fleeing hare or a flying bustard—anyone crossing the steppe has seen that—but it is not given to everyone to see wild animals in their home life, when they are not fleeing, not hiding or looking around in alarm. But Vasya could see foxes frolicking, hares washing themselves with their forepaws, bustards spreading their wings, kestrels beating their wings "in place." Thanks to such keen eyesight, besides the world that everyone could see, Vasya had another world of his own, inaccessible to anyone else, and probably a very nice one, because when he looked and admired, it was hard not to envy him.

As the wagon train moved on, the bells were ringing for the liturgy.

V

THE WAGON TRAIN settled down to the side of the village on the riverbank. The sun burned like the day before, the air was motionless and dismal. Several pussywillows stood on the bank, but their shade fell not on the land but on the water, where it was wasted, and in the shade under the wagons it was stifling and dull. The water, blue from the sky's reflection in it, was passionately alluring.

The wagoner Styopka, to whom Egorushka only now paid attention, an eighteen-year-old Ukrainian boy in a long, belt-less shirt and wide, loose balloon trousers that fluttered like flags as he walked, quickly undressed, ran down the steep bank, and plopped into the water. He dove three times, then turned on his back and closed his eyes with pleasure. His face smiled and wrinkled, as if it felt tickly, painful, and funny to him.

On a hot day, when there is no getting away from the torrid and stifling heat, the splashing of water and the loud breathing of a bather affect the hearing like good music. Dymov and Kiriukha, looking at Styopka, quickly undressed and, with loud laughter and anticipating pleasure, plunged one after the other into the water. And the quiet, modest river resounded with snorting, splashing, and shouting. Kiriukha coughed, laughed, and shouted as if someone was trying to drown him, and Dymov chased after him, trying to grab him by the leg.

"Hey, hey, hey!" he shouted. "Catch him, hold him!"

Kiriukha guffawed and enjoyed himself, but the expression on his face was the same as on dry land: stupid, stunned, as if someone had crept up behind him unseen and whacked him on the head with the butt of an axe. Egorushka also undressed, but he did not go down the bank, but ran up and went flying off the ten-foot height. Describing an arc in the air, he fell into the water, went deep down, but did not reach the bottom; some force, cold and pleasant to the touch, picked him up and carried him back to the surface. He emerged, snorting and blowing bubbles, and opened his eyes; but the sun was reflected in the river just by his face. First blinding sparks, then rainbows and dark spots moved before his eyes; he hastened to dive again, opened his eyes under-water, and saw something muddy green, like the sky on a moonlit night. Again the same force, not letting him touch bottom and stay in the cool, carried him upwards. He emerged and breathed so deeply that he felt vast and refreshed not only in his chest but even in his stomach. Then, to take from the water all that could be taken, he allowed himself every luxury: he lay on his back, basked, splashed, turned somersaults, swam on his stomach, and on his side, and on his back, and upright—however he liked, until he got tired. The opposite bank was thickly overgrown with rushes, shining golden in the sun, and the rush flowers bent their beautiful tufts to the water. In one place the rushes trembled, bent their flowers down, and gave a crunch—this was Styopka and Kiriukha "snatching" crayfish.

"A crayfish! Look, brothers, a crayfish!" Kiriukha shouted triumphantly and indeed held up a crayfish.

Egorushka swam towards the rushes, dove down, and began feeling around near the roots. Digging into the liquid, slimy silt, he felt something sharp and disgusting, maybe really a crayfish, but just then somebody seized him by the leg and pulled him to the surface. Spluttering and coughing, Egorushka opened his eyes and saw before him the wet, laughing face of the prankster Dymov. The prankster was breathing heavily and, judging by his eyes, wanted to go on with his mischief. He held Egorushka tightly by the leg, and was already raising his other hand to seize him by the neck, but Egorushka, with repugnance and fear, as if scornful and afraid that the stalwart fellow would drown him, tore himself free and said:

"Fool! I'll give it to you in the mug!"

Feeling that this was not enough to express his hatred, he thought a moment and added:

"Scoundrel! Son of a bitch!"

But Dymov, as if nothing had happened, no longer paid any attention to Egorushka, but went swimming towards Kiriukha, shouting:

"Hey, hey, hey! Let's do some fishing! Boys, let's go fishing!"

"Why not?" agreed Kiriukha. "There must be lots of fish here..."

"Styopka, run to the village, ask the muzhiks for a net."

"They won't give us one!"

"They will! You just ask! Tell them it's like it's for Christ's sake, because we're the same as wanderers."

"That's for sure!"

Styopka got out of the water, dressed quickly, and, hatless, his wide balloon trousers flapping, ran to the village. After the clash with Dymov, the water lost all its charm for Egorushka. He got out and began to dress. Pantelei and Vasya were sitting on the steep bank, their legs hanging down, and watching the bathers. Emelyan, naked, stood up to his knees in the water just by the bank, holding on to the grass with one hand, so as not to fall, and stroking his body with the other. With his bony shoulder blades, with the bump under his eye, bent over and obviously afraid of the water, he presented a ridiculous figure. His face was serious, stern; he looked at the water crossly, as if about to reprimand it for getting him chilled once in the Donets and taking his voice away.

"And why don't you go for a swim?" Egorushka asked Vasya.

"Just so... I don't like it..." Vasya replied.

"Why's your chin swollen?"

"It hurts... I used to work at a match factory, young master... The doctor told me that's why my jore got swollen. The air there's unhealthy. And besides me, another three boys got bulging jores, and one had it completely rotted away."

Styopka soon came back with a net. Dymov and Kiriukha turned purple and hoarse from staying so long in the water, but they eagerly started fishing. First they walked into a deep place by the rushes; the water there came up to Dymov's neck and over the short Kiriukha's head; the latter spluttered and blew bubbles, while Dymov, stumbling over the prickly roots, kept falling and getting tangled in the net; they both floundered and made noise, and their fishing was nothing but mischief.

"It's too deep," Kiriukha said hoarsely. "You can't catch anything!"

"Don't pull, you devil!" shouted Dymov, trying to set the net in the proper position. "Hold it with your hands!"

"You won't catch anything there!" Pantelei shouted to them from the bank. "You're just frightening the fish, you fools! Head further to the left! It's shallower there!"

Once a bigger fish flashed over the net; everybody gasped, and Dymov brought his fist down on the place where it had disappeared, and his face showed vexation.

"Eh!" Pantelei grunted and stamped his feet. "Missed a perch! Got away!"

Heading to the left, Dymov and Kiriukha gradually came out to the shallows, and here the fishing became real. They wandered some three hundred paces from the wagons; they could be seen barely and silently moving their legs, trying to get to deeper places, closer to the rushes, dragging the net, beating their fists on the water, and rustling the rushes to frighten the fish and drive them into the net. From the rushes they waded to the other bank, dragged the net there, then, with a disappointed air, lifting their knees high, waded back to the rushes. They were talking about something, but what it was, nobody could hear. And the sun burned their backs, flies bit them, and their bodies went from purple to crimson. Styopka waded after them with a bucket in his hand, his shirt tucked up right under his armpits and the hem of it clamped in his teeth. After each successful catch, he held up the fish and, letting it shine in the sun, shouted:

"See what a perch! There are already five like that!"

You could see how Dymov, Kiriukha, and Styopka, each time they pulled out the net, spent a long time digging in the silt, put something into the bucket, threw something out; occasionally they took something caught in the net, handed it to each other, examined it curiously, then also threw it out...

"What'd you have there?" the others shouted from the bank.

Styopka answered something, but it was hard to make out his words. Then he got out of the water and, holding the bucket with both hands, forgetting to let down his shirt, ran to the wagons.

"Already full!" he shouted, breathing heavily. "Give me another!"

Egorushka looked into the bucket; it was full; a young pike stuck its ugly snout from the water, and around it swarmed smaller fish and crayfish. Egorushka thrust his hand to the bottom and stirred up the water; the pike disappeared under the crayfish, and in its place a perch and a tench floated up. Vasya also looked in the bucket. His eyes became unctuous, and his face became tender, as before, when he saw the fox. He took something out of the bucket, put it in his mouth, and began to chew. A crunching was heard.

"Brothers," Styopka was astonished, "Vasya's eating a live gudgeon! Pah!"

"It's not a gudgeon, it's a goby," Vasya replied calmly, continuing to chew.

He took the fish's tail from his mouth, looked at it tenderly, and put it back in his mouth. As he chewed and crunched with his teeth, it seemed to Egorushka that it was not a man he saw before him. Vasya's swollen chin, his lackluster eyes, his extraordinarily keen sight, the fish tail in his mouth, and the tenderness with which he chewed the gudgeon made him look like an animal.

Egorushka got bored being around him. And the fishing

was over. He strolled by the wagons, pondered, and, out of boredom, trudged off to the village.

A little later, he was standing in the church and listening as the choir sang, leaning his head against someone's back, which smelled of hemp. The liturgy was coming to an end. Egorushka understood nothing about church singing and was indifferent to it. He listened for a while, yawned, and began examining napes and backs. In one nape, red-haired and wet from recent bathing, he recognized Emelyan. The hair on his neck was cut square and higher than usual; his temples were also cut higher than they should have been, and Emelyan's red ears stuck out like two burdock leaves and seemed to feel they were not in the right place. Looking at his nape and neck, Egorushka thought for some reason that Emelyan was probably very unhappy. He remembered his conducting, his wheezing voice, his timid look while bathing, and felt an intense pity for him. He wanted to say something affectionate to him.

"I'm here, too!" he said, tugging at his sleeve.

People who sing tenor or bass in a choir, especially those who happen to have conducted at least once in their life, are accustomed to looking sternly and unsociably at little boys. Nor do they drop this habit later, when they stop being singers. Turning to Egorushka, Emelyan looked at him from under his eyebrows and said:

"Don't misbehave in church!"

After that Egorushka made his way to the front, closer to the iconostasis.[17] Here he saw interesting people. In front of everyone else, to the right side on a carpet, stood a gentleman and a lady. Behind each of them stood a chair. The gentleman was dressed in a freshly ironed two-piece tussore suit, stood motionless like a soldier at the salute, and held his blue, clean-shaven chin high. His standing collar, the blueness of his chin, his small bald spot, and his cane expressed a great deal of dignity. His neck was tense with an excess of dignity, and his chin stretched upwards with such force that his head seemed ready at any moment to tear free and fly upwards. But the lady, corpulent and elderly, in a white silk shawl, bent her head sideways and looked as if she had just done someone a favor and wanted to say: "Ah, don't bother thanking me! I don't like it . . ." Around the carpet, Ukrainian men stood in a dense wall.

Egorushka went up to the iconostasis and began to kiss the local icons. He prostrated unhurriedly before each icon, looked back at the people without getting up, then got up and kissed the icon. Touching the cold floor with his forehead gave him great pleasure. When the caretaker came out of the sanctuary with long tongs to extinguish the candles, Egorushka quickly rose from the ground and ran to him.

"Have they already handed out the prosphoras?"[18] he asked.

"All gone, all gone," the sexton muttered sullenly. "You've no business here . . ."

The liturgy was over. Egorushka unhurriedly left the church and started wandering around the square. He had seen not a few villages, squares, and muzhiks in his life, and all that now met his eye was quite uninteresting to him. Having nothing to do, so as to kill time with at least something, he went into a shop that had a strip of scarlet cotton hanging over the door. The shop consisted of two spacious, poorly lit halves: in one groceries and dry goods were sold, and in the other stood barrels of tar, and horse collars hung from the ceiling; from that one came a delicious smell of leather and tar. The floor of the shop had been sprinkled with water; it had probably been sprinkled by a great fantast and freethinker, because it was all covered with patterns and cabbalistic signs. Behind the counter, leaning his belly on a desk, stood a well-nourished shopkeeper with a broad face and a round beard, apparently a Russian. He was sipping tea through a lump of sugar, letting out a deep sigh after each sip. His face showed perfect indifference, but in each sigh you could hear: "Just wait, you're going to get it from me!"

"Give me a kopeck's worth of sunflower seeds!" Egorushka addressed him.

The shopkeeper raised his eyebrows, came from behind the counter, and poured a kopeck's worth of sunflower seeds into Egorushka's pocket, the measure being an empty pomade jar. Egorushka did not want to leave. For a long time he studied the boxes of gingerbreads, pondered and asked, pointing to some small Vyazma gingerbreads that had acquired a rusty film with old age:

"How much are these gingerbreads?"

"Two for a kopeck."

Egorushka took from his pocket the gingerbread that the Jewess had give him the day before, and asked:

"And how much do you sell this kind for?"

The shopkeeper took the gingerbread in his hands, examined it on all sides, and raised one eyebrow:

"This kind?" he asked.

Then he raised the other eyebrow, thought a moment, and replied:

"Two for three kopecks..."

Silence ensued.

"Whose boy are you?" asked the shopkeeper, pouring himself some tea from a red copper kettle.

"I'm Ivan Ivanych's nephew."

"There are all sorts of Ivan Ivanyches," sighed the shopkeeper; he looked over Egorushka's head at the door, paused, and asked: "Would you like a drop of tea?"

"Maybe..." Egorushka accepted with some reluctance, though he had a great longing for his morning tea.

The shopkeeper poured a glass and gave it to him with a nibbled-over piece of sugar. Egorushka sat down on a folding chair and began to drink. He also wanted to ask how much a pound of sugared almonds cost, and had just started the conversation when a customer came in, and the owner, setting his glass aside, got involved in business. He led the customer to the half that smelled of tar and talked for a long time with him about something. The customer, apparently a very stubborn man and with a mind of his own, wagged his head all the time as a sign of disagreement and kept backing towards the door. The shopkeeper convinced him of something and began pouring oats for him into a big sack.

"You call that oats?" the customer said mournfully. "That's not oats, it's chaff, it'd make a chicken grin... No, I'll go to Bondarenko!"

When Egorushka went back to the river, a small fire was smoking on the bank. It was the wagoners cooking their dinner. Styopka stood amidst the smoke and stirred a cauldron with a big nicked spoon. A little to one side, their eyes red from the smoke, Kiriukha and Vasya sat cleaning the fish. Before them lay the silt- and weed-covered net, on which fish glistened and crayfish crawled.

Emelyan, recently come back from church, sat next to Pantelei, waved his hand, and sang barely audibly in a hoarse little voice: "We praise Thee..." Dymov wandered about by the horses.

When they finished cleaning the fish, Kiriukha and Vasya put them and the live crayfish in the bucket, rinsed them, and poured them all from the bucket into the boiling water.

"Shall I put in some lard?" asked Styopka, skimming the froth with his spoon.

"Why? The fish'll give off their own juice," replied Kiriukha.

Before removing the cauldron from the fire, Styopka poured three handfuls of millet and a spoonful of salt into the broth; in conclusion, he tried it, smacked his lips, licked the spoon, and grunted with self-satisfaction—this meant that the kasha[19] was ready.

63

Everybody except Pantelei sat down around the cauldron and went to work with their spoons.

"You! Give the boy a spoon!" Pantelei observed sternly. "I s'pose he must be hungry, too!"

"Ours is peasant fare . . ." sighed Kiriukha.

"And peasant fare may be all to your health, if you've got a liking for it."

They gave Egorushka a spoon. He started to eat, not sitting down, but standing just by the cauldron and looking into it as if into a hole. The kasha smelled of a fishy dampness, and fish scales kept turning up among the millet; the crayfish could not be picked up with a spoon, and the eaters took them straight from the cauldron with their hands; Vasya was especially unconstrained in this respect, wetting not only his hands but his sleeves in the kasha. But all the same the kasha seemed very tasty to Egorushka and reminded him of the crayfish soup his mother cooked at home on fast days. Pantelei sat to one side and chewed bread.

"Why don't you eat, grandpa?" Emelyan asked.

"I don't eat crayfish . . . Dash 'em!" the old man said and turned away squeamishly.

While they ate, a general conversation went on. From this conversation Egorushka understood that all his new acquaintances, despite their differences in age and character, had one thing in common, which made them resemble one another: they were all people with a beautiful past and a very bad present; all of them to a man spoke with rapture about their past, while they greeted the present almost with scorn. The Russian man likes to remember, but does not like to live; Egorushka still did not know that, and, before the kasha was eaten, he was already deeply convinced that the people sitting around the cauldron had been insulted and offended by fate. Pantelei told how, in the old days, when there were no railroads, he went with wagon trains to Moscow and Nizhny and made so much that he didn't know what to do with the money. And what merchants there were in those days, what fish, how cheap everything was! Now the roads had become shorter, the merchants stingier, the people poorer, bread more expensive, everything had become petty and narrow in the extreme. Emelyan told how he used to work in the church choir at the Lugansk factory, had a remarkable voice, and read music very well, but now he had turned into a peasant and ate on the charity of his brother, who sent him out with his horses and took half his earnings for it. Vasya had once worked in a match factory; Kiriukha had served as a coachman for some good people and had been considered the best troika driver in the whole region. Dymov, the son of a well-to-do peasant, had lived for his pleasure, caroused, and known no grief, but as soon as he turned twenty, his strict, stern father, wishing to get him used to work and fearing he would be spoiled at home, began sending him off as a wagoner, like a poor peasant, a hired hand. Styopka alone said nothing, but you could see by his beardless face that before he used to live much better than now.

Remembering his father, Dymov stopped eating and frowned. He looked at his comrades from under his eyebrows and rested his gaze on Egorushka.

"You, heathen, take your hat off!" he said rudely. "You don't eat with your hat on! Some master you are!"

Egorushka took off his hat and did not say a word, but he no longer tasted the kasha and did not hear how Pantelei and Vasya interceded for him. Anger against the prankster stirred heavily in his breast, and he decided at all costs to do him some bad turn.

After dinner they all plodded to the wagons and collapsed in the shade.

"Will we go soon, grandpa?" Egorushka asked Pantelei.

"When God grants, then we'll go...We can't go now, it's hot...Oh, Lord, as Thou wilt, Holy Mother...Lie down, lad!"

Soon, snoring came from under the wagons. Egorushka was about to go to the village again, then thought a little, yawned, and lay down beside the old man.

VI

THE WAGON TRAIN stood by the river all day and set off at sundown.

Again Egorushka lay on a bale, the wagon softly creaked and rocked, Pantelei walked down below, stamped his feet, slapped his thighs, and muttered; in the air the steppe music trilled as the day before.

Egorushka lay on his back, his hands behind his head, and looked up into the sky. He saw how the evening glow lit up, how it then went out; guardian angels, covering the horizon with their golden wings, settled down for the night; the day had passed untroubled, quiet, untroubled night came, and they could peacefully stay at home in the heavens... Egorushka saw how the sky gradually darkened and dusk descended on the earth, how the stars lit up one after another.

When you look for a long time into the deep sky, without taking your eyes away, your thoughts and soul merge for some reason in an awareness of loneliness. You begin to feel yourself irremediably alone, and all that you once considered close and dear becomes infinitely distant and devoid of value. The stars that have gazed down from the sky for thousands of years, the incomprehensible sky itself and the dusk, indifferent to the short life of man, once you remain face-to-face with them and try to perceive their meaning, oppress your soul with their silence; you start thinking about the loneliness that awaits each of us in the grave, and the essence of life seems desperate, terrible...

Egorushka thought of his grandmother, who now slept in the cemetery under the cherry trees; he remembered how she lay in the coffin with copper coins on her eyes, how she was then covered with the lid and lowered into the grave; the dull thud of the lumps of earth against the lid also came back to him . . . He imagined his grandmother in the narrow and dark coffin, abandoned by everyone and helpless. His imagination pictured his grandmother suddenly waking up and unable to understand where she was, knocking on the lid, calling for help, and, in the end, faint with terror, dying again. He imagined his mother, Father Khristofor, Countess Dranitsky, Solomon dead. But however hard he tried to imagine himself in the dark grave, far from home, abandoned, helpless, and dead, he did not succeed, he could not allow the possibility of death for himself personally, and he felt he would never die . . .

And Pantelei, for whom it was already time to die, walked below and took a roll call of his thoughts.

"It's all right . . . nice masters . . ." he muttered. "They took the lad to study, but how he's doing there, nobody hears . . . In Slavyanoserbsk, I say, there's no such institution as gives bigger learning . . . None, that's for sure . . . And he's a good lad, he's all right . . . He'll grow up and help his father. You're small now, Egory, but when you're big, you'll feed your father and mother. That's set up by God . . . Honor your father and mother . . . I had children, too, but they got burned up . . . My wife got burned up and my children . . . That's for sure, on the eve of the Baptism,[20] the cottage caught fire . . . Me, I wasn't home, I'd gone to Orel. To Orel . . . Marya jumped outside, then remembered the children were asleep in the cottage, ran back in, and got burned up with the children . . . Yes . . . The next day they found nothing but bones."

Around midnight the wagoners and Egorushka were again sitting around a small campfire. While the weeds were catching fire, Kiriukha and Vasya went to fetch water somewhere in a little gully; they disappeared into the darkness, but could be heard all the while clanging the buckets and talking; that meant the gully was not far away. The light from the campfire lay in a big, flickering patch on the ground; though the moon was shining, everything outside the red patch seemed impenetrably black. The light struck the wagoners' eyes, and they could see only a part of the high road; in the darkness, the horses and the wagons with their bales were outlined in barely visible mounds of an indefinite shape. Twenty paces from the campfire, on the boundary between the road and the fields, stood a wooden grave cross sunk to one side. When the campfire had not yet been lit and it was possible to see far, Egorushka had noticed exactly the same old sunken cross standing on the other side of the high road.

Coming back with water, Kiriukha and Vasya filled the cauldron and fixed it over the fire. Styopka, with the nicked spoon in his hand, took his place in the smoke by the cauldron and, watching the water pensively, began to wait till froth appeared. Pantelei and Emelyan sat next to each other, kept silent, and thought about something. Dymov lay on his stomach, his head propped on his fists, and looked at the fire; Styopka's shadow leaped across him, so that his handsome face was now covered with darkness, now suddenly blazed up . . . Kiriukha and Vasya wandered a little way off, gathering weeds and birch bark for the fire. Egorushka, his hands in his pockets, stood beside Pantelei and watched how the fire ate the grass.

Everyone rested, thought about something, glanced fleetingly at the cross, over which red patches leaped. There is something sad, dreamy, and in the highest degree poetic in a lonely grave . . . You can hear its silence, and in this silence you sense the presence of the soul of the unknown person who lies under the cross. Is it good for this soul in the steppe? Does it languish on a moonlit night? And the steppe near the grave seems sad, dismal, and pensive, the grass is sorrowful, and the grasshoppers seem to call with more restraint . . .

And there is no passerby who would not give thought to the lonely soul and turn to look back at the grave until it was left far behind and covered in dusk...

"Grandpa, why's that cross standing here?" asked Egorushka.

Pantelei looked at the cross, then at Dymov, and asked:

"Mikolka, mightn't this be the place where the mowers killed the merchants?"

Dymov reluctantly raised himself on his elbow, looked at the road, and replied:

"The very same..."

Silence ensued. Kiriukha made a crackling noise as he crumpled the dry grass into a ball and put it under the cauldron. The fire blazed up more brightly; Styopka was engulfed in black smoke, and the shadow of the cross raced through the darkness over the road by the wagons.

"Yes, killed them..." Dymov said reluctantly. "The merchants, a father and son, were on their way to sell icons. They stopped at an inn nearby, the one that Ignat Fomin keeps now. The old man drank a bit too much and started boasting that he had a lot of money with him. Merchants are known to be boastful folk, God forbid... They can't help showing off at their best before the likes of us. But just then there were some mowers spending the night at the inn. So they heard the merchant boast and made note of it."

"Oh, Lord... Our Lady!" sighed Pantelei.

"The next day, at first light," Dymov went on, "the merchants got ready for the road, and the mowers mixed in with them. 'Let's go together, Your Honor. It's more fun, and less dangerous, because it's a godforsaken place here...' The merchants drove at a slow pace so as not to damage the icons, and that played into the mowers' hands..."

Dymov got up on his knees and stretched himself.

"Yes," he went on, yawning. "Everything went all right, but when the merchants reached this place, the mowers started cleaning them up with their scythes. The son was a fine fellow, he snatched the scythe from one of them and also did some cleaning . . . Well, of course, those fellows overpowered them, because there were about eight of them. They cut the merchants up so there wasn't a live spot left on their bodies; they finished their business and dragged the two of them off the road, the father to one side, the son to the other. Opposite here, on the other side of the road, there's another cross . . . I don't know if it's still there . . . You can't see it from here."

"It's there," said Kiriukha.

"They say afterwards they didn't find much money."

"Not much," Pantelei confirmed. "About a hundred roubles."

"Yes, and three of them died afterwards, because the merchant also cut them badly with the scythe . . . They bled to death. One of them had his arm lopped off, and they say he ran about four miles without his arm, and they found him on a little knoll near Kurikovo. He was crouched there with his head resting on his knees, as if he was deep in thought, but when they took a look, there was no soul in him, he was dead . . ."

"They found him by the trail of blood . . ." said Pantelei.

Everyone looked at the cross, and again silence ensued. From somewhere, probably the little gully, came the mournful cry of a bird: "Sleep! Sleep! Sleep! . . ."

"There's lots of wicked people in the world," said Emelyan.

"Lots, lots!" Pantelei agreed and moved closer to the fire, looking as if he felt eerie. "Lots," he went on in a low voice. "I've seen no end of 'em in my life . . . Wicked people, that is . . . I've seen lots of saintly and righteous people, but the sinful ones there's no counting . . . Queen of Heaven, save us and have mercy . . . I remember once, thirty years ago, maybe more, I was driving a merchant from Morshansk. He was a nice man, fine-looking, and with money...the merchant, that is...a good man, all right...So then we drove on and stopped to spend the night at an inn. And the inns in Russia are not like in these parts. They've got covered yards like cowsheds, or, say, like threshing barns in good farmsteads. Only threshing barns are higher. Well, we stopped, and everything was all right. My merchant was in a little room, I was with the horses, and all was as it should be. So then, brothers, I prayed to God—before sleep, I mean—and went for a stroll in the yard. The night was pitch dark, you couldn't see a thing, no use looking at all. I strolled a little, about as far as from here to the wagons, and I see a light glimmering. What's the story? It seemed the landlords went to bed long ago, and there were no other lodgers besides me and the merchant...Where was the light coming from? Suspicion took hold of me...I went closer...to the light, that is... Lord have mercy and save me, Queen of Heaven! I looked, and right on the ground there was a little window with bars...in the house, that is...I lay on the ground and looked; and the moment I looked, a chill ran through my whole body..."

Kiriukha, trying not to make noise, stuck a bunch of weeds into the fire. The old man waited till the weeds stopped crackling and hissing, and went on:

"I looked inside, and there's a cellar there, a big one, dark and suspicious...A lantern is burning on a barrel. In the middle of the cellar stand some ten men in red shirts, their sleeves rolled up, sharpening long knives...Aha! Well, so we'd fallen in with a band of robbers...What to do? I ran to the merchant, woke him up quietly, and said: 'Don't you get frightened, merchant,' I say, 'but things look bad for us...We've fallen,' I say, 'into a den of robbers.' His face changed, and he asked: 'What do we do now, Pantelei? I have a lot of orphans' money with me...As regards my life,' he says, 'it's as God wills, I'm not afraid to die,' he says, 'but it's

terrible to lose orphans' money . . .' What's to be done? The
gate's locked, there's no getting out by foot or carriage . . . If
there was a fence, you could climb over the fence, but it's
a covered yard! . . . 'Well, merchant,' I say, 'don't you get
frightened, but pray to God. Maybe the Lord won't want to
hurt the orphans. Stay here,' I say, 'and don't give any sign,
and meanwhile maybe I'll think up something . . .' All
right . . . I prayed to God, and God put reason into me . . .
I climbed onto my tarantass and quietly . . . quietly, so that
nobody could hear, I started pulling thatch from the eaves,
made a hole, and got out. Outside, that is . . . Then I jumped
off the roof and ran down the road as fast as I could. I ran
and ran, got dead tired . . . Ran maybe five miles at one go,
maybe more . . . Thank God, I see—there's a village standing
there. I ran up to a cottage and started knocking on the
window. 'Good Orthodox people,' I say, 'thus and so, don't
let a Christian soul perish . . .' I woke them all up . . . The
muzhiks assembled and went with me . . . Some with ropes,
some with sticks, some with pitchforks . . . We broke down
the gates of the inn and went straight to the cellar . . . And
the robbers had finished sharpening their knives and were
about to stick the merchant. The muzhiks took every last
one of them, tied them up, and brought them to the authorities. The merchant was so glad, he donated three hundred
roubles to them, and gave me a fiver, and wrote down my
name to be prayed for. People say afterwards they found no
end of human bones in the cellar. Bones, that is . . . So it
means they robbed folk, and then buried them so there'd
be no traces . . . Well, afterwards they were punished in
Morshansk by the executioners."

Pantelei finished the story and glanced around at his lis-
teners. They were silent and looked at him. The water was
already boiling, and Styopka was skimming the froth.

"Is the lard ready?" Kiriukha asked in a whisper.

"Wait a little . . . Just a minute."

Styopka, not taking his eyes off Pantelei, and as if fearing he would start a story without him, ran to the wagons; he soon came back with a small wooden bowl and started mashing lard in it.

"Another time I also drove with a merchant..." Pantelei went on in a low voice as before, and without blinking his eyes. "His name, I remember as if it were now, was Pyotr Grigoryich. A good man he was...the merchant, that is... We stopped at an inn the same way...He was in a room, and I was with the horses...The landlords, a husband and wife, seemed to be good people, kindly, gentle, the workers also looked all right, and yet, brothers, I couldn't sleep, my heart senses something! Senses it, that's all. The gates were open, and there were many people around, and yet I was afraid, not myself. Everyone had long gone to sleep, it was deep night, soon it would be time to get up, and I alone was lying in my kibitka with my eyes open, like some sort of owl. Only this is what I hear, brothers: tup! tup! tup! Somebody's stealing up to the kibitka. I poke my head out, look—a woman's standing there in nothing but her shift, barefoot... 'What do you want, woman?' I say. And she trembles all over, that one, she looks awful... 'Get up, good man!' she says. 'Trouble...The landlords have decided on an evil thing...They want to do your merchant in. I heard the master and mistress whispering about it,' she says... Well, it was not for nothing my heart ached! 'And who are you?' I ask. 'I'm their cook,' she says...All right...I got out of the kibitka and went to the merchant. I woke him up and said: 'Thus and so,' I say, 'Pyotr Grigoryich, there's dirty business afoot...You can sleep some other time, Your Honor, but now, while there's still time, get dressed,' I say, 'and run for all you're worth out of harm's way...' He'd just started to get dressed when the door opened, and hello!... I look—Mother of God!—the master, the mistress, and three workers come walking into the room on us...Meaning

73

they'd put the workers up to it... The merchant had a lot
of money, so they thought, we'll divide it up... Each of the
five is holding a long knife... a knife, that is... The master
locked the door and said: 'Pray to God, travelers... And if
you start shouting, we won't let you pray before you die...'
As if we could shout! We had our throats stopped up with
fear, we were beyond shouting... The merchant weeps and
says: 'Good Orthodox people!' he says. 'You've decided to
kill me, because my money has seduced you. So be it, I'm
neither the first nor the last; there have been many merchants
killed at inns. But why,' he says, 'Orthodox brothers, why
kill my driver? What's the need of him suffering because of
my money?' And he says it so pitifully! And the master
answers: 'If we let him live,' he says, 'he'll be the first witness
against us. It's all the same,' he says, 'to kill one man or two.
In for a penny, in for a pound... Pray to God, and that's it,
there's no point talking!' The merchant and I knelt beside
each other, wept, and started praying to God. He remembered his little children, but I was young then, I wanted to
live... We look at the icons and pray so pitifully, even now
the tears pour from my eyes... But the mistress, she's a
woman, she looks at us and says: 'Good people,' she says,
'don't remember evil of us in the other world, and don't
heap prayers on our heads, because we do it out of need.'
We prayed and prayed, wept and wept, and God heard us.
Took pity on us, I mean... Just as the master seized the
merchant by the beard to slash his throat with the knife,
somebody suddenly knocked so-o-o hard on the window
from the yard outside! We all just jumped, and the master
lowered his hands... Somebody knocked on the window
and shouted: 'Pyotr Grigoryich, are you here? Get ready,
we're going!' The landlords saw that somebody had come
to fetch the merchant, they got frightened, and off they
ran... And we rushed out to the yard, harnessed up—and
that was the last they saw of us..."

"Who was it knocked on the window?" asked Dymov.

"On the window? Must have been a saint or an angel. Because there was nobody else . . . When we drove out of the yard, there wasn't a single person in the street . . . It was God's doing!"

Pantelei told some other stories, and in all of them "long knives" played the same role, and there was the same made-up feeling. Had he heard these stories from someone else, or had he invented them himself in the distant past and then, when his memory weakened, mixed his experience with fiction and become unable to distinguish one from the other? That all may have been so, but the strange thing was that now and throughout the entire journey, whenever he happened to tell stories, he gave clear preference to the made up and never spoke of what he had experienced. Egorushka took everything at face value now and believed every word, but afterwards it seemed strange to him that a man who had traveled all over Russia in his lifetime, who had seen and known so much, whose wife and children had burned up, devalued his rich life so much that, whenever he sat by the campfire, he either kept silent or spoke of something that had never been.

Over the kasha they were all silent and thought about what they had just heard. Life is fearful and wondrous, and therefore, however fearful a tale you tell in Russia, however you adorn it with robbers' dens, long knives, and miracles, it will always find a real response in the listener's soul, and only a man of well-tried literacy will look askance in mistrust, and even he will say nothing. The cross by the roadside, the dark bales, the vastness, and the destiny of the people gathered around the campfire—all this was so wondrous and fearful in itself that the fantasticality of tall tales and stories paled and merged with life.

They all ate from the cauldron, while Pantelei sat separately to one side and ate from a wooden bowl. His spoon was not like everyone else's, but was made of cypress wood and with a little cross. Egorushka, looking at him, remembered the icon-lamp glass and quietly asked Styopka:

"Why does grandpa sit separately?"

"He's an Old Believer,"[21] Styopka and Vasya answered in a whisper, looking as if they were speaking of a weakness or a secret vice.

They were all silent and thinking. After such fearful tales, no one wanted to speak of ordinary things. Suddenly, in the midst of the silence, Vasya straightened up and, aiming his lackluster eyes at one spot, pricked up his ears.

"What is it?" Dymov asked him.

"There's a man walking," Vasya answered.

"Where do you see him?"

"There he is! A patch of white . . ."

Where Vasya was looking, nothing could be seen except darkness; they all listened, but no footsteps could be heard.

"Is he walking down the road?" asked Dymov.

"No, across the field . . . He's coming here."

A minute passed in silence.

"Maybe it's the merchant buried here, wandering over the steppe," said Dymov.

They all glanced sidelong at the cross and suddenly laughed; they became ashamed of their fear.

"Why would he wander?" said Pantelei. "The only ones that walk about at night are the ones the earth won't receive. But the merchants are all right . . . The merchants received martyrs' crowns."

Now footsteps were heard. Someone was walking hurriedly.

"He's carrying something," said Vasya.

The swish of grass and the crackling of weeds under the walker's feet became audible, but because of the firelight no one could be seen. Finally there was a sound of footsteps close by, someone coughed, the dancing light seemed to part, the scales fell from their eyes, and the wagoners suddenly saw a man before them.

Either because of the way the fire flickered, or because they wanted before all to make out the face of this man, it turned out, oddly enough, that with the first glance at him, everyone saw before all not his face, not his clothes, but his smile. It was an extraordinarily kind, broad, and soft smile, as of an awakened child, one of those infectious smiles that it is hard not to respond to with a smile. The stranger, once they had made him out, proved to be a man of about thirty, not handsome and in no way remarkable. He was a tall Ukrainian, long-nosed, long-armed, and long-legged; in general, everything about him seemed long, and only his neck was short, so much so that it made him look stooped. He was dressed in a clean white shirt with an embroidered collar, white balloon trousers, and new boots, and, compared with the wagoners, looked like a dandy. In his hands he was holding something big, white, and, at first glance, strange, and from behind his shoulder the barrel of a gun appeared, also long.

Emerging from the darkness into the circle of light, he stopped as if rooted to the spot and looked at the wagoners for about half a minute, as if he wanted to say: "See what a smile I've got!" Then he stepped towards the campfire, smiled still more brightly, and said:

"Good health to you all!"

"We bid you welcome!" Pantelei answered for everyone.

The stranger set down what he was holding—it was a dead bustard—and greeted them once more.

They all went over to the bustard and started examining it.

"A grand bird! What did you shoot it with?" asked Dymov.

"Buckshot . . . Birdshot's not enough, it won't reach . . . Buy it, brothers! I'll let you have it for twenty kopecks."

"What do we need it for? It's good roasted, but it's tough boiled—hard to chaw . . ."

"Eh, too bad! I could take it to the head office on the estate, they'd pay fifty kopecks for it, but it's too far—fifteen miles!"

The unknown man sat down, unslung his gun, and placed it beside him. He looked sleepy, languid; he smiled, squinted from the fire, and was apparently thinking about something very pleasant. They gave him a spoon. He began to eat.

"Who might you be?" Dymov asked him.

The stranger did not hear the question; he did not reply and did not even look at Dymov. Most likely this smiling man did not taste the kasha, either, because he chewed somehow mechanically, lazily, bringing to his mouth now a full spoon, now a quite empty one. He was not drunk, but there was something loony wandering in his head.

"I'm asking you: who are you?" Dymov repeated.

"Me?" the unknown man roused himself. "Konstantin Zvonyk, from Rovnoe. About four miles from here."

And, wishing to show first off that he was not a peasant like all the others but a better sort, Konstantin hastened to add:

"We keep bees and raise pigs."

"Do you live with your father or on your own?"

"No, now I live on my own. Separately. Got married this month after Saint Peter's.[22] A married man now!... It's eighteen days I've been under the law."

"That's a good thing!" said Pantelei. "A wife's all right... God's blessing..."

"A young wife asleep at home, and he goes traipsing about the steppe," Kiriukha laughed. "An odd fellow!"

Konstantin, as if pinched on his tenderest spot, roused himself, laughed, turned red...

"But, Lord, she's not at home!" he said, quickly taking the spoon out of his mouth and looking around at them all with joy and surprise. "She's not! She went to her mother for two days! By God, she did, and it's as if I'm not married..."

Konstantin waved his hand and wagged his head; he wanted to go on thinking, but the joy that radiated from his face prevented him. He assumed a different posture, as if he had been sitting uncomfortably, laughed, and again waved his hand. It was embarrassing to give his pleasant thoughts away to strangers, but at the same time he had an irrepressible wish to share his joy.

"She went to her mother in Demidovo!" he said, blushing and putting his gun in a different place. "She'll come back tomorrow... She said she'd be there by dinnertime."

"Do you miss her?" asked Dymov.

"Oh, Lord, as if I don't! It's no time at all since we got married, and she went away... Eh? And she's a spirited one, God punish me! She's so good, so nice, such a laugher and singer—sheer gunpowder! With her my head goes spinning round, and without her it's as if I've lost something, I go about the steppe like a fool. I've been walking since dinnertime, it's either that or start shouting for help."

Konstantin rubbed his eyes, looked at the fire, and laughed.

"You love her, that is..." said Pantelei.

"She's so good, so nice," Konstantin repeated, not listening. "Such a housewife, clever and sensible, you won't find another like her from simple folk in the whole province. She went away... But she misses me, I kno-o-ow it! I know it, the magpie! She said she'd come back tomorrow by dinnertime... But what a story it was!" Konstantin nearly shouted, suddenly taking a higher pitch and changing his position. "Now she loves me and misses me, but she didn't want to marry me!"

"Eat, why don't you!" said Kiriukha.

"She didn't want to marry me," Konstantin went on, not listening. "Three years I struggled with her! I saw her at the fair in Kalachik, fell mortally in love, could have hanged myself... I'm in Rovnoe, she's in Demidovo, twenty-five miles between us, and I just can't take it. I send matchmakers to her, but she says, 'I don't want to!' Ah, you magpie! I try this with her and that with her, earrings, and gingerbreads, and a big pot of honey—'I don't want to!' There you go. Sure, if you reason it out, what kind of match am I for her? She's young, beautiful, gunpowder, and I'm old, I'll soon turn thirty, and so very handsome: a broad beard—like a nail, a clean face—bumps all over. I can't compare with her! The only thing is that we have a rich life, but they, the Vakhramenkos, also live well. They keep three pair of oxen and two hired hands. I fell in love, brothers, and went clean off my head...I don't sleep, don't eat, there's all sorts of thoughts in my head, and such a fuddle, God help me! I want to see her, but she's in Demidovo...And what do you think? God punish me if I'm lying, I went there on foot three times a week just to look at her. I stopped working! Such a darkening came over me, I even wanted to get hired as a farmhand in Demidovo, so as to be closer to her. I wore myself out! My mother called in a wise woman, my father set about beating me some ten times. Well, three years I languished, and then I decided like this: three times anathema on you, I'll go to the city and become a cabby...It means it's not my lot! During Holy Week I went to Demidovo to look at her for the last time..."

Konstantin threw his head back and dissolved into such rapid, merry laughter as if he had just very cleverly hood-winked someone.

"I saw her with the boys by the river," he went on. "I got angry...I called her aside and spent maybe a whole hour saying various words to her...She fell in love with me! For three years she didn't love me, but for my words she fell in love with me!..."

"But what words?" asked Dymov.

"What words? I don't remember...How should I remember? It poured out then like water from a gutter, without stop: rat-a-tat-tat! But now I can't get out a single word...Well, so she married me...She's gone to her mother now, my magpie, and I wander about the steppe without her. I can't sit at home. It's beyond me!"

Konstantin clumsily freed his legs from under him, stretched out on the ground, and propped his head with his fists, then raised himself and sat up again. They all understood perfectly well now that this was a man in love and happy, happy to the point of anguish; his smile, his eyes, and each of his movements expressed a languorous happiness. He could not stay put and did not know what position to assume or what to do so as not to be exhausted by the abundance of pleasant thoughts. Having poured out his soul in front of strangers, he finally sat down quietly, looked at the fire, and fell to pondering.

At the sight of a happy man, they all felt bored and also craved happiness. They all fell to pondering. Dymov stood up, slowly walked about near the fire, and by his gait, by the movement of his shoulder blades, you could see that he felt languid and bored. He stood for a while, looked at Konstantin, and sat down.

But the campfire was dying out. The light no longer danced, and the red patch shrank, grew dim . . . And the more quickly the fire burned out, the more visible the moonlit night became. Now the road could be seen in all its width, the bales, the shafts, the munching horses; on the opposite side the other cross was faintly outlined . . .

Dymov propped his cheek in his hand and began softly singing some plaintive song. Konstantin smiled sleepily and sang along in a thin little voice. They sang for half a minute and fell silent . . . Emelyan roused himself, moved his elbows, and flexed his fingers.

"Brothers!" he said pleadingly. "Let's sing something godly!"

Tears welled up in his eyes.

"Brothers!" he repeated, pressing his hand to his heart. "Let's sing something godly!"

"I can't," said Konstantin.

They all refused; then Emelyan began to sing by himself. He waved both hands, nodded his head, opened his mouth, but nothing except wheezing, soundless breath burst from his throat. He sang with his hands, his head, his eyes, and even his bump, he sang passionately and with pain, and the harder he strained his chest to tear at least one note from it, the more soundless his breath became . . .

Egorushka, like everyone else, was overcome by boredom. He went to his wagon, climbed up on a bale, and lay down. He looked at the sky and thought about the happy Konstantin and his wife. Why do people get married? What are women for in this world? Egorushka asked himself vague questions and thought it is probably nice for a man if a gentle, cheerful, and beautiful woman constantly lives at his side. For some reason he recalled the Countess Dranitsky and thought that it was probably very agreeable to live with such a woman; he might well have married her with great pleasure, if it were not so embarrassing. He remembered her eyebrows, her pupils, her carriage, the clock with the horseman . . . The quiet, warm night was descending on him and whispering something in his ear, and it seemed to him that it was that beautiful woman bending over him, looking at him with a smile, and wanting to kiss him . . .

Only two little red eyes remained from the campfire, and they were growing smaller and smaller. The wagoners and Konstantin sat by them, dark, motionless, and it seemed there were now many more of them than before. Both crosses were equally visible, and far, far away, somewhere on the high road, a red fire glowed—someone else was probably also cooking kasha.

"Our beloved Mother Russia is the head of all the wo-o-orld!" Kiriukha suddenly sang in a wild voice, choked, and fell silent. The steppe echo picked up his voice, carried it, and it seemed stupidity itself was rolling over the steppe on heavy wheels.

"Time to go!" said Pantelei. "Up you get, boys!"

While they were harnessing, Konstantin walked among the wagons and sang his wife's praises.

"Farewell, brothers!" he cried as the wagons started off. "Thanks for your hospitality! And I'll make for that fire. It's beyond me!"

And he quickly vanished into the darkness, and for a long time could be heard striding towards where the little light glowed, in order to tell other strangers of his happiness.

When Egorushka woke up the next day, it was early morning; the sun had not risen yet. The wagon train stood still. Some man in a white peaked cap and a suit of cheap gray cloth, mounted on a Cossack colt, was talking about something with Dymov and Kiriukha by the very first wagon. Two miles or so ahead of the wagon train, long, low barns and little houses with tiled roofs showed white; there were no yards or trees to be seen near the houses.

"What's that village, grandpa?" asked Egorushka.

"Those are Armenian farmsteads, my lad," answered Pantelei. "Armenians live there. They're all right folk... Armenians, that is."

The man in gray finished talking with Dymov and Kiriukha, tightened the reins on his colt, and looked towards the farmsteads.

"Such a business, just think!" sighed Pantelei, also looking towards the farmsteads and shrinking from the morning freshness. "He sent a man to the farmstead for some paper, and the man won't come back... We should send Styopka!"

"But who is that, grandpa?" asked Egorushka.

"Varlamov."

My God! Egorushka quickly jumped up, stood on his knees, and looked at the white cap. The undersized gray little man, shod in big boots, mounted on an ugly horse, and talking with peasants at a time when all decent people were asleep, was hard to identify with the mysterious, elusive Varlamov, sought by everyone, who always "circled around" and had much more money than the Countess Dranitsky.

"He's all right, a good man..." Pantelei said, looking

towards the farmsteads. "God grant him health, he's a nice master...Varlamov, that is, Semyon Alexandrych...The world stands on such people, brother. That's for sure... The cocks haven't crowed yet, and he's already on his feet...Another man would sleep or gibble-gabble with his guests at home, but he's on the steppe the whole day... Circling around...This one won't let any deal slip away... No-o-o! A fine fellow...."

Varlamov would not take his eyes off the farmstead and was saying something; the colt shifted impatiently from one foot to the other.

"Semyon Alexandrych," shouted Pantelei, taking off his hat, "allow us to send Styopka! Emelyan, holler for them to send Styopka!"

But now, at last, a rider detached himself from the farmstead. Leaning strongly to one side and swinging the whip above his head, as if he was a trick horseman and wanted to astonish everybody with his bold riding, he flew towards the wagon train with birdlike swiftness.

"That must be his breaker," said Pantelei. "He's got maybe a hundred of these breakers, if not more."

Coming up to the first wagon, the rider reined in his horse and, taking off his hat, handed Varlamov a book. Varlamov took several papers from the book, read them, and shouted:

"But where's Ivanchuk's note?"

The rider took the book back, looked over the papers, and shrugged; he began to say something, probably justifying himself and asking permission to go to the farmsteads again. The colt suddenly stirred, as if Varlamov had become heavier. Varlamov also stirred.

"Get out!" he shouted angrily and swung his whip at the rider.

Then he turned the horse about and, studying the papers in the book, rode at a slow pace the length of the train. As he approached the last wagon, Egorushka strained his eyes to examine him better. Varlamov was an old man. His face, with its small gray beard, a simple, sunburnt Russian face, was red, wet with dew, and covered with little blue veins; it expressed the same businesslike dryness as Ivan Ivanych's face, the same businesslike fanaticism. But still, what a difference you could feel between him and Ivan Ivanych! Uncle Kuzmichov, along with businesslike dryness, always had care on his face, and fear that he might not find Varlamov, might be late, might miss a good price; nothing of the sort, proper to small and dependent people, could be seen either on the face or in the figure of Varlamov. This man set the prices himself, he did not seek anyone, did not depend on anyone; ordinary as his appearance might be, you could sense in everything, even in his way of holding a whip, an awareness of strength and habitual authority over the steppe.

Riding past Egorushka, he did not glance at him; only the colt deemed Egorushka worthy of his attention and looked at him with his big, stupid eyes, and even that with indifference. Pantelei bowed to Varlamov; the man noticed it and, without taking his eyes from the papers, said, swallowing his R's:

"Ghreetings, ghraybeard!"

Varlamov's conversation with the rider and the swing of the whip evidently made a dispiriting impression on the whole train. They all had serious faces. The rider, discouraged by the strong man's wrath, stood hatless, with slack reins, by the first wagon, silent and as if not believing that the day had begun so badly for him.

"A tough old man . . ." Pantelei muttered. "Awfully tough! But all right, a good man . . . He won't harm you for nothing . . . No fear . . ."

Having examined the papers, Varlamov put the book in his pocket; the colt, as if understanding his thoughts without waiting for orders, gave a start and went racing down the high road.

VII

ON THE FOLLOWING night, the wagoners again made a halt and cooked kasha. This time, from the very beginning, some indefinite anguish was felt in everything. It was stifling; they all drank a great deal and simply could not quench their thirst. The moon rose intensely crimson and morose, as if it was sick; the stars were also morose, the murk was thicker, the distance dimmer. It was as if nature anticipated something and languished.

There was none of yesterday's animation and talk by the campfire. They were all bored and spoke sluggishly and reluctantly. Pantelei only sighed, complained about his feet, and now and then began talking about an impudent death.

Dymov lay on his stomach, said nothing, and chewed on a straw; his expression was squeamish, as if the straw smelled bad, and angry, and weary . . . Vasya complained that his jaw ached and prophesied bad weather; Emelyan did not wave his hands, but sat motionless and sullenly looked at the fire. Egorushka also languished. The slow driving wearied him, and the afternoon heat had given him a headache.

When the kasha was ready, Dymov, out of boredom, began picking on his comrades.

"He sprawls about, the bump, and sticks his spoon in first!" he said, looking spitefully at Emelyan. "Greed! Aims to sit himself down first at the cauldron. He used to sing in the choir, so he thinks he's a master! You find lots of these choir singers begging for alms along the high road!"

"What do you want from me?" Emelyan asked, also looking at him with spite.

"That you don't shove up first to the cauldron. Don't think so much of yourself!"

"A fool, that's all he is," wheezed Emelyan.

Knowing from experience how such conversations usually

end, Pantelei and Vasya intervened and started persuading Dymov not to be abusive for nothing.

"Choir singer . . ." the prankster grinned scornfully, refusing to calm down. "Anybody can sing like that. Go sit on the church porch and sing: 'Alms for the sake of Christ!' Ah, you!"

Emelyan said nothing. His silence had an irritating effect on Dymov. He looked at the former choir singer with still greater hatred and said:

"I don't want to get involved, otherwise I'd teach you to think much of yourself!"

"Why are you bothering me, mazepa?"[23] Emelyan flared up. "Am I touching you?"

"What did you call me?" Dymov asked, straightening up, and his eyes became bloodshot. "What? Me a mazepa? Eh? Take this, then! Go and hunt for it!"

Dymov snatched the spoon from Emelyan's hand and flung it far away. Kiriukha, Vasya, and Styopka jumped up and ran to look for it, while Emelyan stared pleadingly and questioningly at Pantelei. His face suddenly became small, winced, blinked, and the former choir singer cried like a baby.

Egorushka, who had long hated Dymov, felt the air suddenly become unbearably stifling; the flames of the campfire hotly burned his face; he would have liked to run quickly to the wagons in the darkness, but the spiteful, bored eyes of the prankster drew him to them. Passionately wishing to say something offensive in the highest degree, he took a step towards Dymov and said, choking:

"You're the worst of all! I can't stand you!"

After that, he should have run to the wagons, but he could not move from the spot and went on:

"You'll burn in fire in the other world! I'll complain to Ivan Ivanych! Don't you dare offend Emelyan!"

"Well, there's a nice how-do-you-do!" Dymov grinned.

"Some little pig, the milk still not dry on his lips, and he goes giving orders. How about a box on the ear?"

Egorushka felt he had no air left to breathe: he suddenly shook all over—this had never happened to him before—stamped his feet, and shouted piercingly:

"Beat him! Beat him!"

Tears poured from his eyes; he was ashamed and ran staggering to the wagons. What impressions his shout made, he did not see. Lying on a bale and weeping, he thrashed his arms and legs and whispered:

"Mama! Mama!"

These people, and the shadows around the campfire, and the dark bales, and the distant lightning flashing every moment in the distance—all now looked desolate and frightening to him. He was terrified and asked himself in despair how and why he had ended up in an unknown land in the company of frightening muzhiks. Where were his uncle, Father Khristofor, and Deniska now? Why were they so long in coming? Had they forgotten him? The thought that he was forgotten and abandoned to the mercy of fate made him feel cold and so eerie that several times he was about to jump off the bale and run headlong back down the road without looking back, but the memory of the dark, sullen crosses, which he was sure to meet on his way, and lightning flashing in the distance, stopped him . . . And only when he whispered, "Mama! Mama!" did he seem to feel better . . .

The wagoners must also have felt eerie. After Egorushka ran away from the campfire, they were silent for a long time, then began saying in low and muted voices that something was coming and that they had to make ready quickly and get away from it . . . They ate a quick supper, put out the fire, and silently began harnessing up. From their bustling and their curt phrases, one could tell that they foresaw some disaster.

Before they started on their way, Dymov went up to Pantelei and asked quietly:

"What's his name?"

"Egory..." answered Pantelei.

Dymov put one foot on the wheel, took hold of the rope that tied down the bale, and hoisted himself up. Egorushka saw his face and curly head. His face was pale, tired, and serious, but it no longer expressed spite.

"Era!" he said quietly. "Go on, hit me!"

Egorushka looked at him in surprise; just then lightning flashed.

"Never mind, just hit me!" Dymov repeated.

And, without waiting for Egorushka to hit him or talk to him, he jumped down and said:

"I'm bored!"

Then, shifting his weight from one foot to the other, rolling his shoulders, he lazily plodded along the line of wagons and repeated in a half-plaintive, half-vexed voice:

"I'm bored! Oh, Lord! And don't be offended, Emelya," he said as he passed Emelyan. "Our life's cruel, beyond hope!"

Lightning flashed to the right and, as if reflected in a mirror, at once flashed in the distance.

"Egory, take this!" Pantelei shouted, handing up something big and dark from below.

"What is it?" asked Egorushka.

"A bast mat! There'll be rain, you can cover yourself."

Egorushka raised himself and looked around. The distance had become noticeably more black and now blinked more than once a minute with a pale light, as if through eyelids. Its blackness leaned to the right, as though weighted down.

"Will there be a thunderstorm, grandpa?" asked Egorushka.

"Ah, my poor, ailing, frozen feet!" Pantelei said in a sing-song voice, not hearing him and stamping his feet.

To the left, as if someone had struck a match against the sky, a pale phosphorescent strip flashed and went out. There was a sound of someone walking on an iron roof somewhere very far away. He was probably walking barefoot, because the iron made a dull rumble.

"It's all around!" cried Kiriukha.

Between the distance and the horizon to the right, lightning flashed, so bright that it lit up part of the steppe and the place where the clear sky bordered on the blackness. An awful thunderhead was approaching unhurriedly, in a solid mass; from its edge hung big black rags; exactly the same rags, crushing each other, heaped up on the horizon to right and left. This torn, ragged look of the thunderhead gave it a drunken, mischievous expression. Thunder rumbled clearly and not dully. Egorushka crossed himself and quickly began putting on his coat.

"I'm bored!" Dymov's cry came from the front wagons, and one could tell by his voice that he was beginning to get angry again. "Bored!"

Suddenly there was a gust of wind, so strong that it almost tore Egorushka's little bundle and bast mat from his hands; the mat fluttered up, tearing in all directions, and flapped on the bale and on Egorushka's face. The wind raced whistling over the steppe, whirled haphazardly, raising such a din with the grass that because of it neither the thunder nor the creaking of the wheels could be heard. It blew from the black thunderhead, carrying clouds of dust and the smell of rain and wet earth with it. The moonlight grew dim, became as if dirtier, the stars became still more morose, and you could see clouds of dust and their shadows hurrying backwards somewhere along the edge of the road. Now, in all probability, whirlwinds, spinning and drawing dust, dry grass, and feathers up from the ground, were rising all the way into the sky; tumbleweed was probably flying about right by the black thunderhead, and how frightened it must be! But nothing could be seen through the dust that clogged the eyes except flashes of lightning.

Egorushka, thinking the rain would pour down that minute, got to his knees and covered himself with the bast mat.

"Pantel-ei!" someone shouted from the front. "A... a...va!"

"I can't hear you!" Pantelei answered loudly and in a singsong voice.

"A...a...va! Arya...a!"

Thunder crashed angrily, rolling across the sky from right to left, then back, and dying down near the front wagon.

"Holy, holy, holy, Lord Sabaoth," Egorushka whispered, crossing himself, "heaven and earth are full of Thy glory..."[24]

The blackness in the sky opened its mouth and breathed out white fire; at once thunder rolled again; it had barely fallen silent when lightning flashed so broadly that Egorushka suddenly saw, through the openings in the bast mat, the whole of the high road into the far distance, all the wagoners, and even Kiriukha's waistcoat. On the left, the dark rags were already rising upwards, and one of them, crude, clumsy, looking like a paw with fingers, was reaching towards the moon. Egorushka decided to shut his eyes tight, pay no attention, and wait till it was all over.

The rain, for some reason, took a long time to begin. Egorushka, hoping the storm cloud might pass by, peeked out from behind the bast mat. It was awfully dark. Egorushka could not see Pantelei, or the bale, or himself; he glanced sidelong to where the moon had been recently, but there was the same black darkness as on the wagon. And in the dark the lightning seemed more white and dazzling, so that it hurt his eyes.

"Pantelei!" cried Egorushka.

No answer came. But now, finally, the wind tore at the bast mat for a last time and ran off somewhere. A calm, steady noise was heard. A big cold drop fell on Egorushka's knee, another trickled down his arm. He noticed that his knees were not covered and was going to straighten the bast mat, but just then something poured down and beat on the road, then on the shafts, on the bale. It was rain. The rain and the bast mat, as if they understood each other, began talking about something rapidly, merrily, and quite disgustingly, like two magpies.

Egorushka stood on his knees, or, more precisely, sat on his boots. When the rain began to beat on the bast mat, he leaned his body forward to shield his knees, which suddenly became wet; he managed to cover his knees, but in less than a minute he felt a sharp, unpleasant dampness behind, on his lower back and his calves. He reassumed his former position, stuck his knees out into the rain, and began thinking what to do, how to straighten the invisible bast mat in the dark. But his arms were already wet, water ran down his sleeves and behind his collar, his shoulder blades were cold. And he decided to do nothing but sit motionless and wait till it all ended.

"Holy, holy, holy . . ." he whispered.

Suddenly, just above his head, the sky broke up with a frightful, deafening crash; he bent over and held his breath, waiting for the pieces to fall on his neck and back. His eyes opened inadvertently, and he saw a blinding, cutting light flash and blink some five times on his fingers, on his wet sleeves, on the streams running off the bast mat, on the bale, and on the ground below. Another clap resounded, just as strong and terrible. The sky no longer rumbled or crashed, but produced dry, crackling noises, like the creaking of dry wood.

"Trrack! Tak! Tak! Tak!" the thunder rapped out clearly, rolled down the sky, stumbled, and collapsed somewhere by the front wagons or far behind, with an angry, abrupt "Trrah!"

The earlier flashes of lightning had only been scary, but with such thunder, they felt sinister. Their bewitching light penetrated your closed eyelids and spread cold through your whole body. What to do so as not to see them? Egorushka decided to turn and face the other way. Carefully, as if afraid he was being watched, he got up on all fours and, his hands slipping on the wet bale, turned around.

"Trrack! Tak! Tak!" swept over his head, fell under the wagon, and exploded—"Rrrah!"

His eyes again opened inadvertently, and Egorushka saw a new danger; behind the wagon walked three huge giants with long spears. Lightning flashed on the tips of their spears and lit up their figures very clearly. They were people of huge size, with covered faces, drooping heads, and heavy footsteps. They seemed sad and despondent, immersed in thought. Maybe they were not walking after the train in order to do any harm, but still, there was something terrible in their nearness.

Egorushka quickly turned frontwards and, trembling all over, cried out:

"Pantelei! Grandpa!"

"Trrak! Tak! Tak!" the sky answered him.

He opened his eyes to see whether the wagoners were there. Lightning flashed in two places and lit up the road into the far distance, the whole wagon train, and all the wagoners. Streams flowed down the road, and bubbles leaped. Pantelei strode along beside the wagon, his tall hat and shoulders covered by a small bast mat; his figure expressed neither fear nor alarm, as if he had been deafened by the thunder and blinded by the lightning.

"Grandpa, giants!" Egorushka cried to him, weeping.

But the old man did not hear. Emelyan walked further on. He was covered from head to foot with a big bast mat and now had the form of a triangle. Vasya, not covered by anything, strode along as woodenly as ever, lifting his legs high and not bending his knees. In the glare of the lightning, it seemed that the wagon train was not moving and the wagoners were frozen, that Vasya's lifted leg had stopped dead . . .

Egorushka called the old man again. Not getting any answer, he sat without moving, no longer waiting for it all to end. He was certain that a thunderbolt would kill him that very minute, that his eyes would open inadvertently and he would see the frightful giants. And he did not cross himself anymore, did not call out to the old man, did not think of his mother, and only went numb with cold and the certainty that the storm would never end.

But suddenly voices were heard.

"Egory, are you asleep or what?" Pantelei shouted from below. "Climb down! Are you deaf, you little fool?..."

"What a storm!" said some unfamiliar bass, grunting as if he had drunk a good glass of vodka.

Egorushka opened his eyes. Below, by the wagon, stood Pantelei, the triangular Emelyan, and the giants. The latter were now much smaller and, once Egorushka had taken a better look, turned out to be ordinary muzhiks, holding not spears but iron pitchforks on their shoulders. In the space between Pantelei and the triangle shone the lighted window of a low cottage. This meant that the wagon train was standing in a village. Egorushka threw off the bast mat, took his little bundle, and hastened down from the wagon. Now, with people talking nearby and the lighted window, he was no longer afraid, though the thunder crashed as before and lightning slashed across the whole sky.

"A good storm, all right..." muttered Pantelei. "Thank God... My feet got a little soggy from the rain, but that's all right, too... Did you climb down, Egory? Well, go inside the cottage... It's all right..."

"Holy, holy, holy..." wheezed Emelyan. "It must have struck somewhere... Are you from hereabouts?" he asked the giants.

"No, we're from Glinovo... Glinovo folk. We work for the Plater family."

"Threshing or what?"

"All sorts of things. Right now we're harvesting wheat. But what lightning, what lightning! Haven't had such a storm in a long time . . ."

Egorushka went into the cottage. He was met by a skinny, humpbacked old woman with a sharp chin. She was holding a tallow candle, squinting, and letting out long sighs.

"What a storm God sent us!" she said. "And ours spent the night on the steppe, that's hard on 'em, dear hearts! Get undressed, laddie, get undressed . . ."

Trembling with cold and shrinking squeamishly, Egorushka pulled off his drenched coat, then spread his arms and legs wide and did not move for a long time. Each little movement gave him an unpleasant sensation of wetness and cold. The sleeves and back of his shirt were wet, the trousers clung to his legs, his head was dripping . . .

"What are you standing all astraddle for, poppet?" said the old woman. "Go sit down!"

Moving his legs wide apart, Egorushka went over to the table and sat down on a bench by somebody's head. The head stirred, let out a stream of air from its nose, munched its lips, and grew still. From the head, a lump extended along the bench, covered by a sheepskin coat. It was a sleeping peasant woman.

The old woman, sighing, went out and soon came back with a watermelon and a cantaloupe.

"Eat, laddie! There's nothing else to give you . . ." she said, yawning, then rummaged in the table drawer and took out a long, sharp knife, very much like the knives with which robbers kill merchants in roadside inns. "Eat, laddie!"

Egorushka, trembling as in a fever, ate a slice of cantaloupe with some rye bread, then a slice of watermelon, and that made him feel even more chilled.

"Ours spent the night on the steppe . . ." the old woman sighed while he ate. "Suffering Jesus . . . I'd light a candle in front of the icon, but I don't know where Stepanida put them. Eat, laddie, eat..."

The old woman yawned and, thrusting her right hand behind her back, scratched her left shoulder with it.

"Must be two o'clock now," she said. "Soon time to get up. Ours spent the night on the steppe...must be all soaked..."

"Grandma," said Egorushka, "I'm sleepy."

"Lie down, laddie, lie down..." the old woman sighed, yawning. "Lord Jesus Christ! I was asleep, and it seemed I heard somebody knocking. I woke up, looked, and it was this storm God sent us...I should light a candle, but I can't find any."

Talking to herself, she pulled some rags off the bench, probably her own bedding, took two sheepskin coats from a nail by the stove, and started making up a bed for Egorushka.

"The storm won't be still," she muttered. "Hope nothing burns down, worse luck. Ours spent the night on the steppe... Lie down, laddie, sleep...Christ be with you, sonny... I won't put the melon away, maybe you'll get up and eat it."

The old woman's sighs and yawns, the measured breathing of the sleeping woman, the dimness in the cottage, and the sound of the rain outside the window were conducive to sleep. Egorushka was embarrassed to undress in front of the old woman. He took off only his boots, lay down, and covered himself with a sheepskin coat.

"The lad's lying down?" Pantelei's whisper was heard a minute later.

"He is!" the old woman answered in a whisper. "Suffering, suffering Jesus! It rumbles and rumbles, and no end to be heard..."

"It'll soon pass..." Pantelei hissed, sitting down. "It's getting quieter... The boys went to the cottages, but two of them stayed with the horses... The boys, that is...

Otherwise . . . The horses will get stolen . . . I'll sit awhile and go to take my shift . . . Otherwise they'll get stolen . . ."

Pantelei and the old woman sat beside each other at Egorushka's feet and talked in a hissing whisper, interrupting their talk with sighs and yawns. But Egorushka was simply unable to get warm. He was covered with a warm, heavy sheepskin coat, but his whole body was shaking, he had cramps in his arms and legs, his insides trembled . . . He undressed under the sheepskin coat, but that did not help. The chill became stronger and stronger.

Pantelei went to take his shift and then came back again, but Egorushka still could not sleep and was shivering all over. Something weighed on his head and chest, crushing him, and he did not know what it was: the old people's whispering or the heavy smell of the sheepskin? There was an unpleasant metallic taste in his mouth from the cantaloupe and watermelon he had eaten. Besides, the fleas were biting.

"I'm cold, grandpa!" he said and did not recognize his own voice.

"Sleep, sonny, sleep," sighed the old woman.

Titus came up to his bed on skinny legs and began waving his arms, then grew up to the ceiling and turned into a windmill. Father Khristofor, dressed not as in the britzka but in full vestments and with a sprinkler in his hand, walked around the windmill sprinkling it with holy water, and it stopped waving. Egorushka, knowing it was delirium, opened his eyes.

"Grandpa!" he called. "Give me water!"

No one answered. Egorushka felt unbearably suffocated and uncomfortable lying down. He got up, dressed, and left the cottage. It was already morning. The sky was overcast, but there was no rain. Shivering and wrapping himself in his wet coat, Egorushka walked around the dirty yard, listening to the silence; a little shed with a half-open rush door caught his eye. He looked into this shed, went in, and sat in the dark corner on a pile of dry dung.

The thoughts tangled in his heavy head, the metallic taste made his mouth feel dry and disgusting. He examined his hat, straightened the peacock feather on it, and remembered how he had gone with his mother to buy this hat. He put his hand in his pocket and took out a lump of brown, sticky putty. How had this putty ended up in his pocket? He thought, sniffed it: it smelled of honey. Aha, it was the Jewish gingerbread! How soggy it was, poor thing!

Egorushka examined his coat. His coat was gray, with big bone buttons, tailored like a frock coat. As a new and expensive thing, it had hung at home not in the front hall but in the bedroom, next to his mother's dresses; wearing it was permitted only on feast days. Looking it over, Egorushka felt sorry for it, remembered that he and the coat had both been left to the mercy of fate, that they would never return home anymore, and burst into such sobs that he almost fell off the dung pile.

A big white dog, wet with rain, with tufts of fur that looked like curling papers on its muzzle, came into the shed and stared at Egorushka with curiosity. She was apparently wondering whether to bark or not. Deciding there was no need to bark, she warily approached Egorushka, ate the putty, and left.

"They're Varlamov's!" somebody shouted in the street.

Having wept his fill, Egorushka left the shed and, skirting a puddle, trudged out to the street. On the road, just in front of the gate, stood the wagons. The wet wagoners, with dirty feet, sluggish and sleepy as autumnal flies, wandered about or sat on the shafts. Egorushka looked at them and thought: "How boring and uncomfortable it is to be a peasant!" He went up to Pantelei and sat beside him on the shaft.

"I'm cold, grandpa!" he said, shivering and sticking his hands into his sleeves.

"It's all right, we'll soon be there," Pantelei yawned. "You'll get warm all right."

The wagon train started early, because it was not hot. Egorushka lay on the bale and shivered with cold, though the sun soon appeared in the sky and dried his clothes, his bale, and the ground. As soon as he closed his eyes, he again saw Titus and the windmill. Feeling nauseated and heavy all over, he strained his forces to drive these images away, but they no sooner disappeared than the prankster Dymov, with red eyes and upraised fists, threw himself at Egorushka with a roar, or his anguished "I'm bored!" was heard. Varlamov rode by on his Cossack colt; happy Konstantin passed by with his smile and his bustard. And how oppressive, unbearable, and tiresome all these people were!

Once—it was before evening—he raised his head to ask for a drink. The wagon train stood on a big bridge stretched across a wide river. There was dark smoke below, over the river, and through it a steamboat could be seen towing a barge. Ahead, across the river, was a huge motley hill scattered with houses and churches; at the foot of the hill, near the freight cars, a locomotive shuttled back and forth . . .

Egorushka had never seen steamboats before, or locomotives, or wide rivers. Looking at them now, he was neither afraid nor surprised; his face even showed nothing resembling curiosity. He only felt nauseated, and hastened to lean his chest over the edge of the bale. He threw up. Pantelei, who saw it, grunted and shook his head.

"Our little lad's sick!" he said. "Must have caught a chill in his stomach . . . our little lad, that is . . . In foreign parts . . . A bad business!"

VIII

THE WAGON TRAIN stopped not far from the pier at a big trading inn. Climbing down from the wagon, Egorushka heard someone's very familiar voice. Someone helped him down, saying:

"And we already came last evening...Been waiting for you all day today. Wanted to catch up with you yesterday, but it didn't work out, we took another road. Look how you've crumpled your coat! You're going to get it from your uncle!"

Egorushka peered into the speaker's marbled face and remembered that this was Deniska.

"Your uncle and Father Khristofor are in their room now," Deniska went on, "having tea. Come on!"

And he led Egorushka to a big two-story building, dark and gloomy, that looked like the N. almshouse. Going through the entry, up the dark stairs, and down a long narrow corridor, Egorushka and Deniska came to a small room where indeed Ivan Ivanych and Father Khristofor were sitting at the tea table. On seeing the boy, the two old men showed surprise and joy on their faces.

"Ahh, Egor Nikola-a-aich!" Father Khristofor sang out. "Mr. Lomonosov!"

"Ah, Mr. Nobleman!" said Kuzmichov. "Kindly join us."

Egorushka took off his coat, kissed his uncle's and Father Khristofor's hands, and sat down at the table.

"Well, how was the journey, *puer bone*?" Father Khristofor showered him with questions, pouring tea for him and smiling radiantly, as usual. "Sick of it, I suppose? And God keep you from traveling by wagon train or oxcart! You go on and on, Lord forgive me, you look ahead, and the steppe still stretches out as continuously as before: there's no end of it to be seen! That's not traveling, it's sheer punishment. Why aren't you drinking your tea? Drink! And while you were dragging yourself around with the wagon train, we've wrapped up all our business nicely. Thank God! We sold the wool to Cherepakhin, and God grant everybody does as well ... We made a good profit."

With the first glance at his own people, Egorushka felt an irresistible need to complain. He was not listening to Father Khristofor and tried to think how to begin and what in fact to complain about. But Father Khristofor's voice, which seemed sharp and unpleasant, interfered with his concentration and confused his thoughts. After sitting for less than five minutes, he got up from the table, went to the sofa, and lay down.

"Look at this now!" Father Khristofor was surprised. "And what about your tea?"

Trying to think up something to complain about, Egorushka pressed his forehead against the back of the sofa and burst into sobs.

"Look at this now!" Father Khristofor repeated, getting up and going to the sofa. "What's the matter, Georgiy? Why are you crying?"

"I ... I'm sick!" said Egorushka.

"Sick?" Father Khristofor looked perplexed. "That's not good at all, old boy ... How can you be sick on a journey? Ai, ai, what a one you are, old boy ... eh?"

He put his hand to Egorushka's head, touched his cheek, and said:

"Yes, your head's hot ... You must have caught a chill or eaten something ... Call upon God."

"Maybe give him quinine ..." Ivan Ivanych said in perplexity.

"No, give him something hot to eat ... Georgiy, do you want some nice soup? Eh?"

"No ... I don't ..." Egorushka answered.

"Do you have chills, or what?"

"Before I had chills, but now . . . now I'm hot. I ache all over . . ."

Ivan Ivanych went over to the sofa, touched Egorushka's head, grunted perplexedly, and went back to the table.

"See here, you get undressed and go to sleep," said Father Khristofor, "you need a good sleep."

He helped Egorushka to undress, gave him a pillow, covered him with a blanket, and put Ivan Ivanych's coat on top of the blanket, then tiptoed away and sat down at the table. Egorushka closed his eyes, and it seemed to him at once that he was not in a room at an inn but by a campfire on the high road; Emelyan was waving his hand, and red-eyed Dymov was lying on his stomach and looking mockingly at Egorushka.

"Beat him! Beat him!" cried Egorushka.

"He's delirious . . ." Father Khristofor said in a half-whisper.

"Bother!" sighed Ivan Ivanych.

"We'll have to rub him with oil and vinegar. God grant he'll be well by tomorrow."

To get rid of his oppressive reveries, Egorushka opened his eyes and began looking at the fire. Father Khristofor and Ivan Ivanych had finished their tea and were talking about something in a whisper. The former was smiling happily and apparently was quite unable to forget that he had made a good profit on the wool: what made him so glad was not so much the profit itself as the thought that, on coming home, he would gather his whole big family, wink slyly, and burst out laughing; first he would deceive them all and say that he sold the wool for less than it was worth, and then he would give his son-in-law Mikhailo the fat wallet and say: "Here, take it! That's how to do business!" Kuzmichov did not seem pleased. His face, as before, expressed a businesslike dryness and preoccupation.

"Eh, if only I'd known Cherepakhin would give such a price," he said in a low voice, "I wouldn't have sold those five tons to Makarov at home! So vexing! Who could have known the price had gone up here?"

A man in a white shirt put the samovar away and lit the lamp in front of the icon in the corner. Father Khristofor whispered something in his ear; the man made a mysterious face, like a conspirator—meaning "I understand"—went out, and, returning a little later, placed a vessel under the sofa. Ivan Ivanych made up a bed for himself on the floor, yawned several times, prayed lazily, and lay down.

"And tomorrow I think I'll go to the cathedral..." said Father Khristofor. "I know a sacristan there. I should go to see the bishop after the liturgy, but they say he's sick."

He yawned and put out the lamp. Now there was no light except from the icon lamp.

"They say he doesn't receive people," Father Khristofor went on, undressing. "So I'll leave without seeing him."

He took off his caftan, and Egorushka saw Robinson Crusoe before him. Robinson mixed something in a saucer, went over to Egorushka, and whispered:

"Lomonosov, are you asleep? Sit up. I'll rub you with oil and vinegar. It's a good thing, only you must call upon God."

Egorushka quickly raised himself and sat up. Father Khristofor took his shirt off of him and, shrinking and gasping heavily, as though he felt tickled himself, began rubbing Egorushka's chest.

"In the name of the Father, and of the Son, and of the Holy Spirit..." he whispered. "Lie on your stomach!... There. Tomorrow you'll be well, only don't sin anymore... Hot as fire! You must have been on the road during the thunderstorm?"

"We were."

"No wonder you got sick! In the name of the Father, and

of the Son, and of the Holy Spirit...No wonder you got sick!"

After rubbing Egorushka, Father Khristofor put the shirt back on him, covered him up, made a cross over him, and went away. Then Egorushka saw him pray to God. The old man probably knew a great many prayers by heart, because he stood in front of the icon and whispered for a long time. After saying his prayers, he made a cross over the windows, the door, Egorushka, and Ivan Ivanych, lay down on a little couch without a pillow, and covered himself with his caftan. The clock in the corridor struck ten. Egorushka remembered how long it still was till morning, pressed his forehead to the back of the sofa in anguish, and no longer tried to get rid of his foggy, oppressive reveries. But morning came much sooner than he thought.

It seemed to him that he had not lain with his forehead pressed against the back of the sofa for long, but when he opened his eyes, the slanting rays of the sun from both windows in the room were already reaching towards the floor. Father Khristofor and Ivan Ivanych were not there. The little room was tidied up, bright, cozy, and smelled of Father Khristofor, who always gave off a scent of cypress and dried cornflowers (at home he made sprinklers and decorations for icon stands out of dried cornflowers, and had become permeated with their smell). Egorushka looked at the pillow, at the slanting rays, at his boots, which were now polished and stood side by side near the sofa, and laughed. It seemed strange to him that he was not on a bale, that everything around was dry, and that there was no lightning or thunder on the ceiling.

He jumped up from the sofa and began to dress. He felt wonderful; nothing was left of the previous day's illness except a slight weakness in his legs and neck. This meant the oil and vinegar had helped. He remembered the steamboat, the locomotive, and the wide river he had seen vaguely the day before, and he now hastened to dress quickly, so as to run to the pier and look at them. He washed and was putting on his red shirt when the door latch suddenly clicked and Father Khristofor appeared on the threshold in his top hat, holding his staff, and with a brown silk cassock over his canvas caftan. Smiling and radiant (old people who have just come back from church are always radiant), he put a prosphora and a package on the table, repeated a prayer, and said:

"God has been merciful! Well, how do you feel?"

"I'm well now," answered Egorushka, kissing his hand.

"Thank God... And I've been to the liturgy...I went to see a sacristan I know. He invited me to his place for tea, but I didn't go. I don't like to go visiting early in the morning. God be with them!"

He took off his cassock, stroked his chest, and unhurriedly opened the package. Egorushka saw a tin of caviar, a piece of smoked sturgeon, and a loaf of French bread.

"There, I was walking past the fish store and bought them," said Father Khristofor. "There's no reason for this luxury on a weekday, but I thought, we've got a sick boy at home, so it seems pardonable. Good sturgeon caviar..."

A man in a white shirt brought a samovar and a tray of dishes.

"Eat," said Father Khristofor, spreading caviar on a slice of bread and handing it to Egorushka. "Eat and play now, and when the time comes, you can study. See that you study with attention and application, so there's sense in it. What must be learned by heart, learn by heart, and where you should tell the inner meaning in your own words, without touching on the external, use your own words. And try to learn all the subjects. Some know mathematics very well but have never heard of Peter Mogila,[25] and some know about Peter Mogila but can't explain about the moon. No, you should learn in such a way as to understand everything! Learn

Latin, French, German... geography, of course, history, theology, philosophy, mathematics... And once you've learned everything, not hurrying, but with prayer and with zeal, then you can find your work. Once you know everything, it will be easy for you on any path. Only study and acquire grace, and God will show you what you should be. A doctor, or a lawyer, or an engineer..."

Father Khristofor spread a little caviar on a small piece of bread, put it in his mouth, and said:

"The apostle Paul says: 'Be not carried about with divers and strange doctrines.'[26] Of course, if it's black magic, or senseless talk, or calling up spirits from the other world like Saul,[27] or learning subjects that are of no use either to you or to anyone else, then it's better not to study. One should take in only what God has blessed. Just consider... The holy apostles spoke all languages—so you learn languages; Basil the Great taught mathematics and philosophy—so you learn them; Saint Nestor[28] wrote history—so you study and write history. Consider the saints..."

Father Khristofor sipped from his saucer, wiped his mustache, and shook his head.

"Very well!" he said. "I was taught in the old way, I've forgotten a lot, and I also live differently from others. It's even impossible to compare. For instance, somewhere in a big company, at a dinner or a gathering, I say something in Latin, or from history or philosophy, and people are pleased, and I'm pleased myself... Or there's also when the circuit court arrives, and people have to be sworn in; all the other priests are embarrassed, but I hobnob with the judges and prosecutors and lawyers: I have some learned talk, drink tea with them, laugh, ask some questions about things I don't know... And they're pleased. So you see, old boy... Learning is light, and ignorance is darkness. Study! It's hard, of course: these days learning costs a lot... Your mama's a widow, she lives on a pension, well, but then..."

Father Khristofor glanced fearfully at the door and went on in a whisper:

"Ivan Ivanych will help you. He won't abandon you. He has no children of his own, and he'll help you. Don't worry."

He made a serious face and whispered still more softly:

"Only watch out, Georgiy, God keep you from forgetting your mother and Ivan Ivanych. The commandment tells you to honor your mother, and Ivan Ivanych is your benefactor and takes the place of a father. If you become a learned man and, God forbid, begin to feel burdened and scorn people because they're stupider than you are, then woe, woe to you!"

Father Khristofor raised his arm and repeated in a thin little voice:

"Woe! Woe!"

Father Khristofor got warmed up and acquired what is known as a relish for speaking; he would have gone on till dinner, but the door opened and Ivan Ivanych came in. The uncle greeted them hastily, sat down at the table, and began quickly gulping tea.

"Well, I've managed to take care of all my affairs," he said. "We could have gone home today, but there's still Egor to worry about. He's got to be settled. My sister said her friend Nastasya Petrovna lives somewhere around here; maybe she'll give him lodgings."

He rummaged in his wallet, took out a crumpled letter, and read:

"'To Nastasya Petrovna Toskunov, at her own house, Malaya Nizhnyaya Street.' I must go and look her up at once. Bother!"

Soon after tea, Ivan Ivanych and Egorushka left the inn.

"Bother!" the uncle muttered. "You're stuck to me like a burr, deuce take it! For you it's studies and noble ways, but for me you're one big torment . . ."

When they passed through the yard, the wagons and wagoners were no longer there; they had gone to the pier early in the morning. In the far corner of the yard, the familiar britzka could be seen; beside it the two bays stood eating oats.

"Farewell, britzka!" thought Egorushka.

First they had a long climb uphill by the boulevard, then they crossed a big marketplace; here Ivan Ivanych asked a policeman how to get to Malaya Nizhnyaya Street.

"Well, now!" the policeman grinned. "That's pretty far, out there by the common!"

On the way they met several cabs coming towards them, but the uncle allowed himself such a weakness as taking a cab only on exceptional occasions and major feast days. He and Egorushka walked for a long time along paved streets, then along streets where only the sidewalks were paved and not the roadways, and finally ended up on streets that had neither sidewalks nor paved roadways. When their legs and tongues had brought them to Malaya Nizhnyaya Street, they were both red in the face, and, taking off their hats, they wiped away the sweat.

"Tell me, please," Ivan Ivanych addressed an old man who was sitting on a bench by a gateway, "where is Nastasya Petrovna Toskunov's house?"

'There's no Toskunov here," the old man replied, having pondered. "Maybe you mean Timoshenko?"

"No, Toskunov . . ."

"Sorry, there's no Toskunov . . ."

Ivan Ivanych shrugged his shoulders and plodded on.

"Don't go looking!" the old man called out behind him. "If I say no, it means no!"

"Listen, auntie," Ivan Ivanych addressed an old woman who was selling sunflower seeds and pears at a stand on the corner, "where is Nastasya Petrovna Toskunov's house hereabouts?"

The old woman looked at him in astonishment and laughed.

"You mean you think Nastasya Petrovna still lives in her own house?" she asked. "Lord, it's already some eight years since she married off her daughter and made the house over to her son-in-law! Her son-in-law lives in it now!"

And her eyes said: "How is it you fools don't know such a simple thing?"

"And where does she live now?" asked Ivan Ivanych.

"Lord!" the old woman was astonished and clasped her hands. "She's long been living in lodgings! It's already eight years since she made her house over to her son-in-law. What's the matter with you!"

She probably expected that Ivan Ivanych would also be surprised and exclaim: "It can't be!" but he asked very calmly: "Where are her lodgings?"

The marketwoman rolled up her sleeves and, pointing with a bare arm, began to shout in a shrill, piercing voice:

"Keep on straight, straight, straight . . . Once you've passed a little red house, there'll be a lane on your left. Turn down that lane and look for the third gateway on the right . . ."

Ivan Ivanych and Egorushka reached the little red house, turned left into the lane, and made for the third gateway on the right. To both sides of this very old gray gateway stretched a gray wall with wide cracks; the right side of the wall leaned badly forward, threatening to collapse, the left sank backward into the yard, while the gates stood straight and seemed to be choosing whether it would suit them better to fall forward or backward. Ivan Ivanych opened the gate and, along with Egorushka, saw a big yard overgrown with weeds and burdock. A hundred paces from the gate stood a small house with a red roof and green shutters. A stout woman with rolled-up sleeves and a held-out apron stood in the middle of the yard, scattering something on the ground and calling out with the same piercing shrillness as the marketwoman:

"Chick! . . . chick! chick!"

Behind her sat a ginger dog with sharp ears. Seeing the visitors, it ran to the gate and barked in a tenor voice (all ginger dogs bark in a tenor voice).

"Who do you want?" shouted the woman, shielding her eyes from the sun.

"Good morning!" Ivan Ivanych also shouted to her, fending off the ginger dog with his stick. "Tell me, please, does Nastasya Petrovna Toskunov live here?"

"She does! What do you want with her?"

Ivan Ivanych and Egorushka went up to her. She looked them over suspiciously and repeated:

"What do you want with her?"

"Might you be Nastasya Petrovna?"

"So I am!"

"Very pleased . . . You see, your old friend Olga Ivanovna Knyazev sends you her greetings. This is her little son. And I, as you may remember, am her brother, Ivan Ivanych . . . You come from our N. You were born there and married . . ."

Silence ensued. The stout woman stared senselessly at Ivan Ivanych, as if not believing or not understanding, then flushed all over and clasped her hands; oats poured from her apron, tears burst from her eyes.

"Olga Ivanovna!" she shrieked, breathing heavily from excitement. "My own darling! Ah, dear hearts, why am I standing here like a fool? My pretty little angel . . ."

She embraced Egorushka, wetted his face with her tears, and began weeping in earnest.

"Lord!" she said, wringing her hands. "Olechka's little son! What joy! Just like his mother! Exactly! But why are we standing in the yard? Please come in!"

Weeping, breathless, and talking as she went, she hastened to the house; the visitors trudged after her.

"It's not tidied up!" she said, leading the visitors into a small and stuffy parlor all filled with icons and flowerpots. "Ah, Mother of God! Vasilissa, open the blinds, at least! My little angel! My indescribable beauty! I didn't even know Olechka had such a son!"

When she had calmed down and grown used to her visitors, Ivan Ivanych asked to have a private talk with her. Egorushka went to another room; there was a sewing machine there, in the window hung a cage with a starling in it, and there were as many icons and plants as in the parlor. A girl stood motionless by the sewing machine, sunburnt, with cheeks as plump as Titus's, and in a clean cotton dress. She looked at Egorushka without blinking and apparently felt very awkward. Egorushka looked at her for a moment in silence, then asked:

"What's your name?"

The girl moved her lips, made a tearful face, and answered softly:

"Atka..."

This meant "Katka."

"He'll live with you," Ivan Ivanych was whispering in the parlor, "if you'll be so kind, and we'll pay you ten roubles a month. He's a quiet boy, not spoiled..."

"I don't really know what to say to you, Ivan Ivanych!" Nastasya Petrovna sighed tearfully. "Ten roubles is good money, but I'm afraid to take someone else's child! What if he gets sick or something..."

When Egorushka was called back to the parlor, Ivan Ivanych was standing hat in hand and saying good-bye.

"Well? So he can stay with you now," he was saying. "Good-bye! Stay here, Egor!" he said, turning to his nephew. "Behave yourself, listen to Nastasya Petrovna... Good-bye! I'll come again tomorrow."

And he left. Nastasya Petrovna embraced Egorushka once more, called him a little angel, and tearfully began setting the table. In three minutes Egorushka was already sitting beside her, answering her endless questions, and eating rich, hot cabbage soup.

And in the evening he was sitting again at the same table, his head propped on his hand, listening to Nastasya Petrovna. Now laughing, now weeping, she told him about his mother's youth, about her own marriage, about her children... A cricket called out from the stove, and the mantle in the gas lamp hummed barely audibly. The mistress spoke in a low voice and kept dropping her thimble from excitement, and Katya, her granddaughter, went under the table to fetch it, and each time stayed under the table for a long while, probably studying Egorushka's legs. And Egorushka listened drowsily and studied the old woman's face, her wart with hairs on it, the streaks of her tears... And he felt sad, very sad! His bed was made up on a trunk, and he was informed that if he wanted to eat during the night, he should go out to the corridor and take some of the chicken that was there on the windowsill, covered with a plate.

The next morning Ivan Ivanych and Father Khristofor came to say good-bye. Nastasya Petrovna was glad and wanted to prepare the samovar, but Ivan Ivanych, who was in a great hurry, waved his hand and said:

"We have no time for any teas and sugars! We're about to leave."

Before saying good-bye, they all sat down and were silent for a moment. Nastasya Petrovna sighed deeply and looked at the icons with tearful eyes.

"Well," Ivan Ivanych began, getting up, "so you're staying..."

The businesslike dryness suddenly left his face, he turned a little red, smiled sadly, and said:

"See that you study... Don't forget your mother and listen to Nastasya Petrovna... If you study well, Egor, I won't abandon you."

He took a purse from his pocket, turned his back to Egorushka, rummaged for a long time among the small change, and, finding a ten-kopeck piece, gave it to the boy. Father Khristofor sighed and unhurriedly blessed Egorushka.

"In the name of the Father, and of the Son, and of the Holy Spirit...Study," he said. "Work hard, old boy...If I die, remember me. Here's ten kopecks from me, too..."

Egorushka kissed his hand and wept. Something in his soul whispered to him that he would never see the old man again.

"I've already applied to the school, Nastasya Petrovna," Ivan Ivanych said in such a voice as if there was a dead person laid out in the parlor. "On the seventh of August you'll take him to the examination...Well, good-bye! May God be with you. Good-bye, Egor!"

"You should at least have some tea!" Nastasya Petrovna groaned.

Through the tears that clouded his eyes, Egorushka did not see his uncle and Father Khristofor leave. He rushed to the window, but they were no longer in the yard, and the ginger dog, just done barking, trotted back from the gate with a look of duty fulfilled. Egorushka, not knowing why himself, tore from his place and went flying out of the house. When he came running through the gate, Ivan Ivanych and Father Khristofor, the one swinging his curved-handled stick, the other his staff, were just turning the corner. Egorushka felt that with these people, everything he had lived through up to then had vanished forever, like smoke; he sank wearily onto a bench and with bitter tears greeted the new, unknown life that was now beginning for him...

What sort of life would it be?

1888

THE DUEL

IT WAS EIGHT o'clock in the morning—the time when officers, officials, and visitors, after a hot, sultry night, usually took a swim in the sea and then went to the pavilion for coffee or tea. Ivan Andreich Laevsky, a young man about twenty-eight years old, a lean blond, in the peaked cap of the finance ministry[1] and slippers, having come to swim, found many acquaintances on the shore, and among them his friend the army doctor Samoilenko.

With a large, cropped head, neckless, red, big-nosed, with bushy black eyebrows and gray side-whiskers, fat, flabby, and with a hoarse military bass to boot, this Samoilenko made the unpleasant impression of a bully and a blusterer on every newcomer, but two or three days would go by after this first acquaintance, and his face would begin to seem remarkably kind, nice, and even handsome. Despite his clumsiness and slightly rude tone, he was a peaceable man, infinitely kind, good-natured, and responsible. He was on familiar terms with everybody in town, lent money to everybody, treated everybody, made matches, made peace, organized picnics, at which he cooked shashlik and prepared a very tasty mullet soup; he was always soliciting and interceding for someone and always rejoicing over something. According to general opinion, he was sinless and was known to have only two weaknesses: first, he was ashamed of his kindness and tried to mask it with a stern gaze and an assumed rudeness; and second, he liked it when medical assistants and soldiers called him "Your Excellency," though he was only a state councillor.[2]

"Answer me one question, Alexander Davidych," Laevsky began, when the two of them, he and Samoilenko, had gone into the water up to their shoulders. "Let's say you fell in love with a woman and became intimate with her; you lived with her, let's say, for more than two years, and then, as it happens, you fell out of love and began to feel she was a stranger to you. How would you behave in such a case?"

"Very simple. Go, dearie, wherever the wind takes you—and no more talk."

"That's easy to say! But what if she has nowhere to go? She's alone, no family, not a cent, unable to work..."

"What, then? Fork her out five hundred, or twenty-five a month—and that's it. Very simple."

"Suppose you've got both the five hundred and the twenty-five a month, but the woman I'm talking about is intelligent and proud. Can you possibly bring yourself to offer her money? And in what form?"

Samoilenko was about to say something, but just then a big wave covered them both, then broke on the shore and noisily rolled back over the small pebbles. The friends went ashore and began to dress.

"Of course, it's tricky living with a woman if you don't love her," Samoilenko said, shaking sand from his boot. "But Vanya, you've got to reason like a human being. If it happened to me, I wouldn't let it show that I'd fallen out of love, I'd live with her till I died."

He suddenly felt ashamed of his words. He caught himself and said:

"Though, for my part, there's no need for women at all. To the hairy devil with them!"

The friends got dressed and went to the pavilion. Here Samoilenko was his own man, and they even reserved a special place for him. Each morning a cup of coffee, a tall cut glass of ice water, and a shot of brandy were served to him on a tray. First he drank the brandy, then the hot coffee, then the ice water, and all that must have been very tasty, because after he drank it, his eyes became unctuous, he smoothed his side-whiskers with both hands, and said, looking at the sea:

"An astonishingly magnificent view!"

After a long night spent in cheerless, useless thoughts, which kept him from sleeping and seemed to increase the sultriness and gloom of the night, Laevsky felt broken and sluggish. Swimming and coffee did not make him any better.

"Let's continue our conversation, Alexander Davidych," he said. "I won't conceal it, I'll tell you frankly, as a friend: things are bad between Nadezhda Fyodorovna and me, very bad! Excuse me for initiating you into my secrets, but I need to speak it out."

Samoilenko, who anticipated what the talk would be about, lowered his eyes and started tapping his fingers on the table.

"I've lived with her for two years and fallen out of love . . ." Laevsky went on. "That is, more precisely, I've realized that there has never been any love . . . These two years were a delusion."

Laevsky had the habit, during a conversation, of studying his pink palms attentively, biting his nails, or crumpling his cuffs with his fingers. And he was doing the same now.

"I know perfectly well that you can't help me," he said, "but I'm talking to you because, for our kind, luckless fellows and superfluous men,[3] talk is the only salvation. I should generalize my every act, I should find an explanation and a justification of my absurd life in somebody's theories, in literary types, in the fact, for instance, that we noblemen are degenerating, and so on . . . Last night, for instance, I comforted myself by thinking all the time: ah, how right Tolstoy is, how pitilessly right! And that made it easier for me. The fact is, brother, he's a great writer! Whatever they say."

Samoilenko, who had never read Tolstoy and was preparing every day to read him, got embarrassed and said:

"Yes, other writers all write from the imagination, but he writes straight from nature."

"My God," sighed Laevsky, "the degree to which we're crippled by civilization! I fell in love with a married woman, and she with me . . . In the beginning it was all kisses, and quiet evenings, and vows, and Spencer,[4] and ideals, and common interests . . . What a lie! Essentially we were running away from her husband, but we lied to ourselves that we were running away from the emptiness of our intelligentsia life. We pictured our future like this: in the beginning, in the Caucasus, while we acquaint ourselves with the place and the people, I'll put on my uniform and serve, then, once we're free to do so, we'll acquire a piece of land, we'll labor in the sweat of our brow, start a vineyard, fields, and so on. If it were you or that zoologist friend of yours, von Koren, instead of me, you'd live with Nadezhda Fyodorovna for maybe thirty years and leave your heirs a rich vineyard and three thousand acres of corn, while I felt bankrupt from the first day. The town is unbearably hot, boring, peopleless, and if you go out to the fields, you imagine venomous centipedes, scorpions, and snakes under every bush and stone, and beyond the fields there are mountains and wilderness. Alien people, alien nature, a pathetic culture—all that, brother, is not as easy as strolling along Nevsky[5] in a fur coat, arm in arm with Nadezhda Fyodorovna, and dreaming about warm lands. What's needed here is a fight to the death, and what sort of fighter am I? A pathetic neurasthenic, an idler . . . From the very first day, I realized that my thoughts about a life of labor and a vineyard weren't worth a damn. As for love, I must tell you that to live with a woman who has read Spencer and followed you to the ends of the earth is as uninteresting as with any Anfisa or Akulina. The same smell of a hot iron, powder, and medications, the same curling papers every morning, and the same self-delusion . . ."

"You can't do without an iron in the household," said Samoilenko, blushing because Laevsky was talking to him so openly about a lady he knew. "I notice you're out of sorts today, Vanya. Nadezhda Fyodorovna is a wonderful, educated woman, you're a man of the greatest intelligence . . . Of course, you're not married," said Samoilenko, turning to look at the neighboring tables, "but that's not your fault, and besides . . . one must be without prejudices and stand on the level of modern ideas. I myself stand for civil marriage, yes . . . But in my opinion, once you're together, you must go on till death."

"Without love?"

"I'll explain to you presently," said Samoilenko. "Some eight years ago there was an agent here, an old man of the greatest intelligence. And this is what he used to say: the main thing in family life is patience. Do you hear, Vanya? Not love but patience. Love can't last long. You lived in love for two years, but now evidently your family life has entered the period when, to preserve the balance, so to speak, you must put all your patience to use . . ."

"You believe your old agent, but for me his advice is meaningless. Your old man could play the hypocrite, he could exercise patience and at the same time look at the unloved person as an object necessary for his exercise, but I haven't fallen so low yet. If I feel a wish to exercise my patience, I'll buy myself some dumbbells or a restive horse, but the person I'll leave in peace."

Samoilenko ordered white wine with ice. When they had each drunk a glass, Laevsky suddenly asked:

"Tell me, please, what does softening of the brain mean?"

"It's . . . how shall I explain to you? . . . a sort of illness, when the brains become softer . . . thin out, as it were."

"Curable?"

"Yes, if the illness hasn't been neglected. Cold showers, Spanish fly . . . Well, something internal."

"So...So you see what my position is like. Live with her I cannot: it's beyond my strength. While I'm with you, I philosophize and smile, but at home I completely lose heart. It's so creepy for me that if I were told, let's say, that I had to live with her for even one more month, I think I'd put a bullet in my head. And at the same time, it's impossible to break with her. She's alone, unable to work, I have no money, and neither does she...What will she do with herself? Who will she go to? I can't come up with anything...Well, so tell me: what's to be done?"

"Mm-yes..." growled Samoilenko, not knowing how to reply. "Does she love you?"

"Yes, she loves me to the extent that, at her age and with her temperament, she needs a man. It would be as hard for her to part with me as with powder or curling papers. I'm a necessary component of her boudoir."

Samoilenko was embarrassed.

"You're out of sorts today, Vanya," he said. "You must have slept badly."

"Yes, I did...Generally, brother, I feel lousy. My head's empty, my heartbeat's irregular, there's some sort of weakness ... I've got to escape!"

"Where to?"

"There, to the north. To the pines, to the mushrooms, to people, to ideas...I'd give half my life to be somewhere in the province of Moscow or Tula right now, swimming in a little river, getting chilled, you know, then wandering around for a good three hours with the worst of students, chattering away...And the smell of hay! Remember? And in the evenings, when you stroll in the garden, the sounds of a piano come from the house, you hear a train going by..."

Laevsky laughed with pleasure, tears welled up in his eyes, and, to conceal them, he reached to the next table for matches without getting up.

"And it's eighteen years since I've been to Russia," said

Samoilenko. "I've forgotten how it is there. In my opinion, there's no place in the world more magnificent than the Caucasus."

"Vereshchagin[6] has a painting: two men condemned to death languish at the bottom of a deep well. Your magnificent Caucasus looks to me exactly like that well. If I were offered one of two things, to be a chimney sweep in Petersburg or a prince here, I'd take the post of chimney sweep."

Laevsky fell to thinking. Looking at his bent body, at his eyes fixed on one spot, at his pale, sweaty face and sunken temples, his bitten nails, and the slipper run down at the heel, revealing a poorly darned sock, Samoilenko was filled with pity and, probably because Laevsky reminded him of a helpless child, asked:

"Is your mother living?"

"Yes, but she and I have parted ways. She couldn't forgive me this liaison."

Samoilenko liked his friend. He saw in Laevsky a good fellow, a student, an easygoing man with whom one could have a drink and a laugh and a heart-to-heart talk. What he understood in him, he greatly disliked. Laevsky drank a great deal and not at the right time, played cards, despised his job, lived beyond his means, often used indecent expressions in conversation, went about in slippers, and quarreled with Nadezhda Fyodorovna in front of strangers—and that Samoilenko did not like. But the fact that Laevsky had once been a philology student, now subscribed to two thick journals, often spoke so cleverly that only a few people understood him, lived with an intelligent woman—all this Samoilenko did not understand, and he liked that, and he considered Laevsky above him, and respected him.

"One more detail," said Laevsky, tossing his head. "Only this is between you and me. So far I've kept it from Nadezhda Fyodorovna, don't blurt it out in front of her... Two days ago I received a letter saying that her husband has died of a softening of the brain."

"God rest his soul . . ." sighed Samoilenko. "Why are you keeping it from her?"

"To show her this letter would mean: let's kindly go to church and get married. But we have to clarify our relations first. Once she's convinced that we can't go on living together, I'll show her the letter. It will be safe then."

"You know what, Vanya?" said Samoilenko, and his face suddenly assumed a sad and pleading expression, as if he was about to ask for something very sweet and was afraid he would be refused. "Marry her, dear heart!"

"What for?"

"Fulfill your duty before that wonderful woman! Her husband has died, and so Providence itself is showing you what to do!"

"But understand, you odd fellow, that it's impossible. To marry without love is as mean and unworthy of a human being as to serve a liturgy without believing."

"But it's your duty!"

"Why is it my duty?" Laevsky asked with annoyance.

"Because you took her away from her husband and assumed responsibility for her."

"But I'm telling you in plain Russian: I don't love her!"

"Well, so there's no love, then respect her, indulge her . . ."

"Respect her, indulge her . . ." Laevsky parroted. "As if she's a mother superior . . . You're a poor psychologist and physiologist if you think that, living with a woman, you can get by with nothing but deference and respect. A woman needs the bedroom first of all."

"Vanya, Vanya . . ." Samoilenko was embarrassed.

"You're an old little boy, a theoretician, while I'm a young old man and a practician, and we'll never understand each other. Better let's stop this conversation. Mustafa!" Laevsky called out to the waiter. "How much do we owe you?"

"No, no . . ." the doctor was alarmed, seizing Laevsky by the hand. "I'll pay it. I did the ordering. Put it on my account!" he called to Mustafa.

The friends got up and silently walked along the embankment. At the entrance to the boulevard they stopped and shook hands on parting.

"You're much too spoiled, gentlemen!" sighed Samoilenko. "Fate has sent you a young woman, beautiful, educated—and you don't want her, but if God just gave me some lopsided old woman, provided she was gentle and kind, how pleased I'd be! I'd live with her in my little vineyard and . . ."

Samoilenko caught himself and said:

"And the old witch would serve the samovar there."

Having taken leave of Laevsky, he walked down the boulevard. When, corpulent, majestic, a stern expression on his face, in his snow-white tunic and perfectly polished boots, his chest thrust out, adorned by a Vladimir with a bow,[7] he went down the boulevard, for that time he liked himself very much, and it seemed to him that the whole world looked at him with pleasure. Not turning his head, he kept glancing from side to side and found that the boulevard was perfectly well organized, that the young cypresses, eucalyptuses, and scrawny, unattractive palm trees were very beautiful and would, with time, afford ample shade; that the Circassians were an honest and hospitable people. "Strange that Laevsky doesn't like the Caucasus," he thought, "very strange." Five soldiers with rifles passed by and saluted him. On the sidewalk to the right side of the boulevard walked the wife of an official with her schoolboy son.

"Good morning, Marya Konstantinovna!" Samoilenko called out to her, smiling pleasantly. "Have you been for a swim? Ha, ha, ha . . . My respects to Nikodim Alexandrych!"

And he walked on, still smiling pleasantly, but, seeing an army medic coming towards him, he suddenly frowned, stopped him, and asked:

"Is there anyone in the infirmary?"

"No one, Your Excellency."

"Eh?"

"No one, Your Excellency."

"Very well, on your way . . ."

Swaying majestically, he made for a lemonade stand, where an old, full-breasted Jewess who passed herself off as a Georgian sat behind the counter, and said to her as loudly as if he was commanding a regiment:

"Be so kind as to give me a soda water!"

II

LAEVSKY'S DISLIKE OF Nadezhda Fyodorovna expressed itself chiefly in the fact that everything she said or did seemed to him a lie or the semblance of a lie, and that everything he read against women and love seemed to him to go perfectly with himself, Nadezhda Fyodorovna, and her husband. When he came back home, she was sitting by the window, already dressed and with her hair done, drinking coffee with a preoccupied face and leafing through an issue of a thick journal, and he thought that drinking coffee was not such a remarkable event that one should make a preoccupied face at it, and that she need not have spent time on a modish hairdo, because there was no one there to attract and no reason for doing so. In the issue of the journal, he saw a lie as well. He thought she had dressed and done her hair in order to appear beautiful and was reading the journal in order to appear intelligent.

"Is it all right if I go for a swim today?" she asked.

"Why not! I suppose it won't cause an earthquake whether you do or don't go . . ."

"No, I'm asking because the doctor might get angry."

"Well, so ask the doctor. I'm not a doctor."

This time what Laevsky disliked most of all in Nadezhda Fyodorovna was her white, open neck and the little curls of hair on her nape, and he remembered that Anna Karenina, when she stopped loving her husband, disliked his ears first of all, and he thought: "How right that is! How right!" Feeling weak and empty in the head, he went to his study, lay down on the sofa, and covered his face with a handkerchief so as not to be bothered by flies. Sluggish, viscous thoughts, all about the same thing, dragged through his brain like a long wagon train on a rainy autumnal day, and he lapsed into a drowsy, oppressed state. It seemed to him that he was guilty before Nadezhda Fyodorovna and before her husband, and that he was to blame for her husband's death. It seemed to him that he was guilty before his own life, which he had ruined, before the world of lofty ideas, knowledge, and labor, and that this wonderful world appeared possible and existent to him not here on this shore, where hungry Turks and lazy Abkhazians wandered about, but there, in the north, where there were operas, theaters, newspapers, and all forms of intellectual work. One could be honest, intelligent, lofty, and pure only there, not here. He accused himself of having no ideals or guiding idea in his life, though now he vaguely understood what that meant. Two years ago, when he had fallen in love with Nadezhda Fyodorovna, it had seemed to him that he had only to take up with Nadezhda Fyodorovna and leave with her for the Caucasus to be saved from the banality and emptiness of life; so now, too, he was certain that he had only to abandon Nadezhda Fyodorovna and leave for Petersburg to have everything he wanted.

"To escape!" he murmured, sitting up and biting his nails. "To escape!"

His imagination portrayed him getting on a steamer, then having breakfast, drinking cold beer, talking with the ladies on deck, then getting on a train in Sebastopol and going. Hello, freedom! Stations flash by one after another, the air turns ever colder and harsher, here are birches and firs, here is Kursk, Moscow . . . In the buffets, cabbage soup, lamb with kasha, sturgeon, beer, in short, no more Asiaticism, but Russia, real Russia. The passengers on the train talk about trade, new singers, Franco-Russian sympathies; everywhere you feel living, cultured, intelligent, vibrant life . . . Faster, faster! Here, finally, is Nevsky, Bolshaya Morskaya, and here is Kovensky Lane, where he once used to live with the students, here is the dear gray sky, the drizzling rain, the wet cabs . . .

"Ivan Andreich!" someone called from the next room. "Are you at home?"

"I'm here!" Laevsky responded. "What do you want?"

"Papers!"

Laevsky got up lazily, with a spinning head, and, yawning and dragging on his slippers, went to the next room. Outside, at the open window, stood one of his young colleagues laying out official papers on the windowsill.

"One moment, my dear boy," Laevsky said softly and went to look for an inkstand; coming back to the window, he signed the papers without reading them and said: "Hot!"

"Yes, sir. Will you be coming today?"

"Hardly . . . I'm a bit unwell. Tell Sheshkovsky, my dear boy, that I'll stop by to see him after dinner."

The clerk left. Laevsky lay down on the sofa again and began to think:

"So, I must weigh all the circumstances and consider. Before leaving here, I must pay my debts. I owe around two thousand roubles. I have no money . . . That, of course, is not important; I'll pay part of it now somehow and send part of it later from Petersburg. The main thing is Nadezhda Fyodorovna . . . First of all, we must clarify our relations . . . Yes."

A little later, he considered: hadn't he better go to Samoilenko for advice?

I could go, he thought, but what use will it be? Again

I'll speak inappropriately about the boudoir, about women, about what's honest or dishonest. Devil take it, what talk can there be here about honest or dishonest if I have to save my life quickly, if I'm suffocating in this cursed captivity and killing myself?...It must finally be understood that to go on with a life like mine is meanness and cruelty, before which everything else is petty and insignificant. "To escape!" he murmured, sitting up. "To escape!"

The deserted seashore, the relentless heat, and the monotony of the smoky purple mountains, eternally the same and silent, eternally solitary, aroused his anguish and, it seemed, lulled him to sleep and robbed him. Maybe he was very intelligent, talented, remarkably honest; maybe, if he weren't locked in on all sides by the sea and the mountains, he would make an excellent zemstvo activist,[8] a statesman, an orator, a publicist, a zealot. Who knows! If so, wasn't it stupid to discuss whether it was honest or dishonest if a gifted and useful man, a musician or an artist, for example, breaks through the wall and deceives his jailers in order to escape from captivity? In the position of such a man, everything is honest.

At two o'clock Laevsky and Nadezhda Fyodorovna sat down to dinner. When the cook served them rice soup with tomatoes, Laevsky said:

"The same thing every day. Why not make cabbage soup?"

"There's no cabbage."

"Strange. At Samoilenko's they make cabbage soup, and Marya Konstantinovna has cabbage soup, I alone am obliged for some reason to eat this sweetish slop. It's impossible, my dove."

As happens with the immense majority of spouses, formerly not a single dinner went by for Laevsky and Nadezhda Fyodorovna without caprices and scenes, but ever since Laevsky had decided that he no longer loved her, he had tried to yield to Nadezhda Fyodorovna in everything, spoke gently and politely to her, smiled, called her "my dove."

"This soup tastes like licorice," he said, smiling; he forced himself to appear affable, but he could not restrain himself and said: "Nobody looks after the household here . . . If you're so sick or busy reading, then, if you please, I'll take care of our cooking."

Formerly she would have replied: "Go ahead" or: "I see you want to make a cook out of me," but now she only glanced at him timidly and blushed.

"Well, how are you feeling today?" he asked affectionately.

"Not bad today. Just a little weak."

"You must take care of yourself, my dove. I'm terribly afraid for you."

Nadezhda Fyodorovna was sick with something. Samoilenko said she had undulant fever and gave her quinine; the other doctor, Ustimovich, a tall, lean, unsociable man who sat at home during the day and, in the evening, putting his hands behind him and holding his cane up along his spine, quietly strolled on the embankment and coughed, thought she had a feminine ailment and prescribed warm compresses. Formerly, when Laevsky loved her, Nadezhda Fyodorovna's ailment had aroused pity and fear in him, but now he saw a lie in the ailment as well. The yellow, sleepy face, the listless gaze and fits of yawning that Nadezhda Fyodorovna had after the attacks of fever, and the fact that she lay under a plaid during the attack and looked more like a boy than a woman, and that her room was stuffy and smelled bad—all this, in his opinion, destroyed the illusion and was a protest against love and marriage.

For the second course he was served spinach with hard-boiled eggs, while Nadezhda Fyodorovna, being sick, had custard with milk. When, with a preoccupied face, she first prodded the custard with her spoon and then began lazily eating it, sipping milk along with it, and he heard her swallow, such a heavy hatred came over him that his head even began to itch. He was aware that such a feeling would be insulting even to a dog, but he was vexed not with himself but with Nadezhda Fyodorovna for arousing this feeling in him, and he understood why lovers sometimes kill their mistresses. He himself would not kill, of course, but if he had now been on a jury, he would have acquitted the murderer.

"Merci, my dove," he said after dinner and kissed Nadezhda Fyodorovna on the forehead.

Going to his study, he paced up and down for five minutes, looking askance at his boots, then sat down on the sofa and muttered:

"To escape, to escape! To clarify our relations and escape!"

He lay down on the sofa and again remembered that he was perhaps to blame for the death of Nadezhda Fyodorovna's husband.

"To blame a man for falling in love or falling out of love is stupid," he persuaded himself as he lay there and raised his feet in order to put on his boots. "Love and hate are not in our power. As for the husband, perhaps in an indirect way I was one of the causes of his death, but, again, am I to blame that I fell in love with his wife and she with me?"

Then he got up and, finding his peaked cap, took himself to his colleague Sheshkovsky's, where officials gathered each day to play vint and drink cold beer.

"In my indecision I am reminiscent of Hamlet," Laevsky thought on the way. "How rightly Shakespeare observed it! Ah, how rightly!"

III

SO AS NOT to be bored and to condescend to the extreme need of newcomers and the familyless who, for lack of hotels in the town, had nowhere to dine, Dr. Samoilenko kept something like a table d'hôte in his home. At the time of writing, he had only two people at his table: the young zoologist von Koren, who came to the Black Sea in the summers to study the embryology of jellyfish; and the deacon Pobedov, recently graduated from the seminary and sent to our town to take over the functions of the old deacon, who had gone away for a cure. They each paid twelve roubles a month for dinner and supper, and Samoilenko made them give their word of honor that they would appear for dinner at precisely two o'clock.

Von Koren was usually the first to come. He would sit silently in the drawing room and, taking an album from the table, begin studying attentively the faded photographs of some unknown men in wide trousers and top hats and ladies in crinolines and caps. Samoilenko remembered only a few of them by name, and of those he had forgotten he said with a sigh: "An excellent man, of the greatest intelligence!" Having finished with the album, von Koren would take a pistol from the shelf and, squinting his left eye, aim for a long time at the portrait of Prince Vorontsov, or station himself in front of the mirror and study his swarthy face, big forehead, and hair black and curly as a Negro's, and his faded cotton shirt with large flowers, which resembled a Persian carpet, and the wide leather belt he wore instead of a waistcoat. Self-contemplation afforded him hardly less pleasure than looking at the photographs or the pistol in its costly mounting. He was very pleased with his face, and his handsomely trimmed little beard, and his broad shoulders, which served as obvious proof of his good health and sturdy build. He was also pleased with his smart outfit, starting with the tie, picked to match the color of the shirt, and ending with the yellow shoes.

While he was studying the album and standing in front of the mirror, at the same time, in the kitchen and around it, in the hall, Samoilenko, with no frock coat or waistcoat, bare-chested, excited, and drenched in sweat, fussed about the tables, preparing a salad, or some sort of sauce, or meat, cucumbers, and onions for a cold kvass soup, meanwhile angrily rolling his eyes at the orderly who was helping him, and brandishing a knife or a spoon at him.

"Give me the vinegar!" he ordered. "I mean, not the vinegar but the olive oil!" he shouted, stamping his feet. "Where are you going, you brute?"

"For the oil, Your Excellency," the nonplussed orderly said in a cracked tenor.

"Be quick! It's in the cupboard! And tell Darya to add some dill to the jar of pickles! Dill! Cover the sour cream, you gawk, or the flies will get into it!"

The whole house seemed to resound with his voice. When it was ten or fifteen minutes before two, the deacon would come, a young man of about twenty-two, lean, long-haired, beardless, and with a barely noticeable mustache. Coming into the drawing room, he would cross himself in front of the icon, smile, and offer von Koren his hand.

"Greetings," the zoologist would say coldly. "Where have you been?"

"On the pier fishing for bullheads."

"Well, of course...Apparently, Deacon, you're never going to take up any work."

"Why so? Work's not a bear, it won't run off to the woods," the deacon would say, smiling and putting his hands into the deep pockets of his cassock.

"Beating's too good for you!" the zoologist would sigh.

Another fifteen or twenty minutes would go by, but dinner was not announced, and they could still hear the orderly, his boots stomping, running from the hall to the kitchen and back, and Samoilenko shouting:

"Put it on the table! Where are you shoving it? Wash it first!"

Hungry by now, the deacon and von Koren would start

drumming their heels on the floor, expressing their impatience, like spectators in the gallery of a theater. At last the door would open, and the exhausted orderly would announce: "Dinner's ready!" In the dining room they were met by the crimson and irate Samoilenko, stewed in the stifling kitchen. He looked at them spitefully and, with an expression of terror on his face, lifted the lid of the soup tureen and poured them each a plateful, and only when he had made sure that they were eating with appetite and liked the food did he sigh with relief and sit down in his deep armchair. His face became languid, unctuous ... He unhurriedly poured himself a glass of vodka and said:

"To the health of the younger generation!"

After his conversation with Laevsky, all the time from morning till dinner, despite his excellent spirits, Samoilenko felt a slight oppression in the depths of his soul. He felt sorry for Laevsky and wanted to help him. Having drunk a glass of vodka before the soup, he sighed and said:

"I saw Vanya Laevsky today. The fellow's having a hard time of it. The material side of his life is inauspicious, but above all, he's beset by psychology. I feel sorry for the lad."

"There's one person I don't feel sorry for!" said von Koren. "If the dear chap were drowning, I'd help him along with a stick: drown, brother, drown ..."

"Not true. You wouldn't do that."

"Why don't you think so?" the zoologist shrugged his shoulders. "I'm as capable of a good deed as you are."

"Is drowning a man a good deed?" the deacon asked and laughed.

"Laevsky? Yes."

"This kvass soup seems to lack something ..." said Samoilenko, wishing to change the subject.

"Laevsky is unquestionably harmful and as dangerous for society as the cholera microbe," von Koren went on. "Drowning him would be meritorious."

"It's no credit to you that you speak that way of your neighbor. Tell me, what makes you hate him?"

"Don't talk nonsense, Doctor. To hate and despise a microbe is stupid, but to consider anyone who comes along without discrimination as your neighbor—that, I humbly thank you, that means not to reason, to renounce a just attitude towards people, to wash your hands, in short. I consider your Laevsky a scoundrel, I don't conceal it, and I treat him like a scoundrel in good conscience. Well, but you consider him your neighbor—so go and kiss him; you consider him your neighbor, and that means you have the same relation to him as to me and the deacon—that is, none at all. You're equally indifferent to everybody."

"To call a man a scoundrel!" Samoilenko murmured, wincing scornfully. "That's so wrong, I can't even tell you!"

"One judges people by their actions," von Koren went on. "So judge now, Deacon . . . I shall talk to you, Deacon. The activity of Mr. Laevsky is openly unrolled before you like a long Chinese scroll, and you can read it from beginning to end. What has he done in the two years he's been living here? Let's count on our fingers. First, he has taught the town inhabitants to play vint; two years ago the game was unknown here, but now everybody plays vint from morning till night, even women and adolescents; second, he has taught the townspeople to drink beer, which was also unknown here; to him they also owe a knowledge of various kinds of vodka, so that they can now tell Koshelev's from Smirnov's No. 21 blindfolded. Third, before, they lived with other men's wives here secretly, for the same motives that thieves steal secretly and not openly; adultery was considered something that it was shameful to expose to general view; Laevsky appears to be a pioneer in that respect: he lives openly with another man's wife. Fourth . . ."

Von Koren quickly ate his kvass soup and handed the plate to the orderly.

"I understood Laevsky in the very first month of our acquaintance," he went on, addressing the deacon. "We arrived here at the same time. People like him are very fond of friendship, intimacy, solidarity, and the like, because they always need company for vint, drinking, and eating; besides, they're babblers and need an audience. We became friends, that is, he loafed about my place every day, preventing me from working and indulging in confidences about his kept woman. From the very first, he struck me with his extraordinary falseness, which simply made me sick. In the quality of a friend, I chided him, asking why he drank so much, why he lived beyond his means and ran up debts, why he did nothing and read nothing, why he had so little culture and so little knowledge, and in answer to all my questions, he would smile bitterly, sigh, and say: 'I'm a luckless fellow, a superfluous man,' or 'What do you want, old boy, from us remnants of serfdom,' or 'We're degenerating...' Or he would start pouring out some lengthy drivel about Onegin, Pechorin, Byron's Cain, Bazarov,[9] of whom he said: 'They are our fathers in flesh and spirit.' Meaning he is not to blame that official packets lie unopened for weeks and that he drinks and gets others to drink, but the blame goes to Onegin, Pechorin, and Turgenev, who invented the luckless fellow and the superfluous man. The cause of extreme licentiousness and outrageousness, as you see, lies not in him but somewhere outside, in space. And besides—clever trick!—it's not he alone who is dissolute, false, and vile, but we... 'we, the people of the eighties,' 'we, the sluggish and nervous spawn of serfdom,' 'civilization has crippled us...' In short, we should understand that such a great man as Laevsky is also great in his fall; that his dissoluteness, ignorance, and unscrupulousness constitute a natural-historical phenomenon, sanctified by necessity; that the causes here are cosmic, elemental, and Laevsky should have an icon lamp hung before him, because he is a fatal victim of the times, the trends, heredity, and the rest. All the officials and ladies oh'd and ah'd, listening to him, but I couldn't understand for a long time whom I was dealing with: a cynic or a clever huckster. Subjects like him, who look intelligent, are slightly educated, and talk a lot about their own nobility, can pretend to be extraordinarily complex natures."

"Quiet!" Samoilenko flared up. "I won't allow bad things to be said in my presence about a very noble man!"

"Don't interrupt, Alexander Davidych," von Koren said coldly. "I'll finish presently. Laevsky is a rather uncompli-cated organism. Here is his moral structure: in the morning, slippers, bathing, and coffee; then up till dinner, slippers, constitutional, and talk; at two o'clock, slippers, dinner, and drink; at five o'clock, bathing, tea, and drink, then vint and lying; at ten o'clock, supper and drink; and after midnight, sleep and *la femme*. His existence is confined within this tight program like an egg in its shell. Whether he walks, sits, gets angry, writes, rejoices—everything comes down to drink, cards, slippers, and women. Women play a fatal, over-whelming role in his life. He himself tells us that at the age of thirteen, he was already in love; when he was a first-year student, he lived with a lady who had a beneficial influence on him and to whom he owes his musical education. In his second year, he bought out a prostitute from a brothel and raised her to his level—that is, kept her—but she lived with him for about half a year and fled back to her madam, and this flight caused him no little mental suffering. Alas, he suffered so much that he had to leave the university and live at home for two years, doing nothing. But that was for the better. At home he got involved with a widow who advised him to leave the law department and study philology. And so he did. On finishing his studies, he fell passionately in love with his present...what's her name?...the married one, and had to run away with her here to the Caucasus, supposedly in pursuit of ideals...Any day now he'll fall out of love with her and flee back to Petersburg, also in pursuit of ideals."

"How do you know?" Samoilenko growled, looking at the zoologist with spite. "Better just eat."

Poached mullet with Polish sauce was served. Samoilenko placed a whole mullet on each of his boarders' plates and poured the sauce over it with his own hands. A couple of minutes passed in silence.

"Women play an essential role in every man's life," said the deacon. "There's nothing to be done about it."

"Yes, but to what degree? For each of us, woman is a mother, a sister, a wife, a friend, but for Laevsky, she is all that—and at the same time only a mistress. She—that is, cohabiting with her—is the happiness and goal of his life; he is merry, sad, dull, disappointed—on account of a woman; he's sick of his life—it's the woman's fault; the dawn of a new life breaks, ideals are found—look for a woman here as well . . . He's only satisfied by those writings or paintings that have a woman in them. Our age, in his opinion, is bad and worse than the forties and the sixties only because we are unable to give ourselves with self-abandon to amorous ecstasy and passion. These sensualists must have a special growth in their brain, like a sarcoma, that presses on the brain and controls their whole psychology. Try observing Laevsky when he's sitting somewhere in society. You'll notice that when, in his presence, you raise some general question, for instance about cells or instincts, he sits to one side, doesn't speak or listen; he has a languid, disappointed air, nothing interests him, it's all banal and worthless; but as soon as you start talking about males and females, about the fact, for instance, that the female spider eats the male after fertilization, his eyes light up with curiosity, his face brightens, and, in short, the man revives! All his thoughts, however noble, lofty, or disinterested, always have one and the same point of common convergence. You walk down the street with him and meet, say, a donkey... 'Tell me, please,' he asks, 'what would happen if a female donkey was coupled with a camel?' And his dreams! Has he told you his dreams? It's magnificent! Now he dreams he's marrying the moon, then that he's summoned by the police, and there they order him to live with a guitar..."

The deacon burst into ringing laughter; Samoilenko frowned and wrinkled his face angrily, so as not to laugh, but could not help himself and guffawed.

"That's all lies!" he said, wiping his tears. "By God, it's lies!"

IV

THE DEACON WAS much given to laughter and laughed at every trifle till his sides ached, till he dropped. It looked as though he liked being among people only because they had funny qualities and could be given funny nicknames. Samoilenko he called "the tarantula," his orderly "the drake," and he was delighted when von Koren once called Laevsky and Nadezhda Fyodorovna "macaques." He peered greedily into people's faces, listened without blinking, and you could see his eyes fill with laughter and his face strain in anticipation of the moment when he could let himself go and rock with laughter.

"He's a corrupted and perverted subject," the zoologist went on, and the deacon, in anticipation of funny words, fastened his eyes on him. "It's not everywhere you can meet such a nonentity. His body is limp, feeble, and old, and in his intellect he in no way differs from a fat merchant's wife, who only feeds, guzzles, sleeps on a featherbed, and keeps her coachman as a lover."

The deacon guffawed again.

"Don't laugh, Deacon," said von Koren, "it's stupid,

finally. I'd pay no attention to this nonentity," he went on, after waiting for the deacon to stop guffawing, "I'd pass him by, if he weren't so harmful and dangerous. His harmfulness consists first of all in the fact that he has success with women and thus threatens to have progeny, that is, to give the world a dozen Laevskys as feeble and perverted as himself. Second, he's contagious in the highest degree. I've already told you about the vint and the beer. Another year or two and he'll conquer the whole Caucasian coast. You know to what degree the masses, especially their middle stratum, believe in the intelligentsia, in university education, in highborn manners and literary speech. Whatever vileness he may commit, everyone will believe that it's good, that it should be so, since he is an intellectual, a liberal, and a university man. Besides, he's a luckless fellow, a superfluous man, a neurasthenic, a victim of the times, and that means he's allowed to do anything. He's a sweet lad, a good soul, he's so genuinely tolerant of human weaknesses; he's complaisant, yielding, obliging, he's not proud, you can drink with him, and use foul language, and gossip a bit . . . The masses, always inclined to anthropomorphism in religion and morality, like most of all these little idols that have the same weaknesses as themselves. Consider, then, what a wide field for contagion! Besides, he's not a bad actor, he's a clever hypocrite, and he knows perfectly well what o'clock it is. Take his dodges and tricks—his attitude to civilization, for instance. He has no notion of civilization, and yet: 'Ah, how crippled we are by civilization! Ah, how I envy the savages, those children of nature, who know no civilization!' We're to understand, you see, that once upon a time he devoted himself heart and soul to civilization, served it, comprehended it thoroughly, but it exhausted, disappointed, deceived him; you see, he's a Faust, a second Tolstoy . . . He treats Schopenhauer[10] and Spencer like little boys and gives them a fatherly slap on the shoulder: 'Well, how's things, Spencer, old boy?' He hasn't read

Spencer, of course, but how sweet he is when he says of his lady, with a slight, careless irony: 'She's read Spencer!' And people listen to him, and nobody wants to understand that this charlatan has no right not only to speak of Spencer in that tone but merely to kiss Spencer's bootsole! Undermining civilization, authority, other people's altars, slinging mud, winking at them like a buffoon only in order to justify and conceal one's feebleness and moral squalor, is possible only for a vain, mean, and vile brute."

"I don't know what you want from him, Kolya," said Samoilenko, looking at the zoologist now not with anger but guiltily. "He's the same as everybody. Of course, he's not without weaknesses, but he stands on the level of modern ideas, he serves, he's useful to his fatherland. Ten years ago an old man served as an agent here, a man of the greatest intelligence... He used to say..."

"Come, come!" the zoologist interrupted. "You say he serves. But how does he serve? Have the ways here become better and the officials more efficient, more honest and polite, because he appeared? On the contrary, by his authority as an intellectual, university man, he only sanctions their indiscipline. He's usually efficient only on the twentieth, when he receives his salary, and on the other days he only shuffles around the house in slippers and tries to make it look as if he's doing the Russian government a great favor by living in the Caucasus. No, Alexander Davidych, don't defend him. You're insincere from start to finish. If you actually loved him and considered him your neighbor, first of all you wouldn't be indifferent to his weaknesses, you wouldn't indulge them, but would try, for his own good, to render him harmless."

"That is?"

"Render him harmless. Since he's incorrigible, there's only one way he can be rendered harmless..."

Von Koren drew a finger across his neck.

"Or drown him, maybe . . ." he added. "In the interests of mankind and in their own interests, such people should be destroyed. Without fail."

"What are you saying?" Samoilenko murmured, getting up and looking with astonishment at the zoologist's calm, cold face. "Deacon, what is he saying? Are you in your right mind?"

"I don't insist on the death penalty," said von Koren. "If that has been proved harmful, think up something else. It's impossible to destroy Laevsky—well, then isolate him, depersonalize him, send him to common labor . . ."

"What are you saying?" Samoilenko was horrified. "With pepper, with pepper!" he shouted in a desperate voice, noticing that the deacon was eating his stuffed zucchini without pepper. "You, a man of the greatest intelligence, what are you saying?! To send our friend, a proud man, an intellectual, to common labor!!"

"And if he's proud and starts to resist—clap him in irons!"

Samoilenko could no longer utter a single word and only twisted his fingers; the deacon looked at his stunned, truly ridiculous face and burst out laughing.

"Let's stop talking about it," the zoologist said. "Remember only one thing, Alexander Davidych, that primitive mankind was protected from the likes of Laevsky by the struggle for existence and selection; but nowadays our culture has considerably weakened the struggle and the selection, and we ourselves must take care of destroying the feeble and unfit, or else, as the Laevskys multiply, civilization will perish and mankind will become totally degenerate. It will be our fault."

"If it comes to drowning and hanging people," said Samoilenko, "then to hell with your civilization, to hell with mankind! To hell! I'll tell you this: you're a man of the greatest learning and intelligence, and the pride of our fatherland, but you've been spoiled by the Germans. Yes, the Germans! The Germans!"

Since leaving Dorpat,[11] where he had studied medicine, Samoilenko had seldom seen Germans and had not read a single German book, but in his opinion, all the evil in politics and science proceeded from the Germans. Where he had acquired such an opinion, he himself was unable to say, but he held fast to it.

"Yes, the Germans!" he repeated once more. "Let's go and have tea."

The three men got up, put on their hats, went to the front garden, and sat down there under the shade of pale maples, pear trees, and a chestnut. The zoologist and the deacon sat on a bench near a little table, and Samoilenko lowered himself into a wicker chair with a broad, sloping back. The orderly brought tea, preserves, and a bottle of syrup.

It was very hot, about ninety-two in the shade. The torrid air congealed, unmoving, and a long spiderweb, dangling from the chestnut to the ground, hung slackly and did not stir.

The deacon took up the guitar that always lay on the ground by the table, tuned it, and began to sing in a soft, thin little voice: " 'Seminary youths stood nigh the pot-house...' " but at once fell silent from the heat, wiped the sweat from his brow, and looked up at the hot blue sky. Samoilenko dozed off; the torrid heat, the silence, and the sweet after-dinner drowsiness that quickly came over all his members left him weak and drunk; his arms hung down, his eyes grew small, his head lolled on his chest. He looked at von Koren and the deacon with tearful tenderness and murmured:

"The younger generation ... A star of science and a luminary of the Church ... This long-skirted alleluia may someday pop up as a metropolitan,[12] for all I know, I may have to kiss his hand ... So what ... God grant it ..."

Soon snoring was heard. Von Koren and the deacon finished their tea and went out to the street.

"Going back to the pier to fish for bullheads?" asked the zoologist.

"No, it's too hot."

"Let's go to my place. You can wrap a parcel for me and do some copying. Incidentally, we can discuss what you're going to do with yourself. You must work, Deacon. It's impossible like this."

"Your words are just and logical," said the deacon, "but my laziness finds its excuse in the circumstances of my present life. You know yourself that an uncertainty of position contributes significantly to people's apathy. God alone knows whether I've been sent here for a time or forever; I live here in uncertainty, while my wife languishes at her father's and misses me. And, I confess, my brains have melted from the heat."

"That's all nonsense," said the zoologist. "You can get used to the heat, and you can get used to being without a wife. It won't do to pamper yourself. You must keep yourself in hand."

V

NADEZHDA FYODOROVNA WAS going to swim in the morning, followed by her kitchen maid, Olga, who was carrying a jug, a copper basin, towels, and a sponge. Two unfamiliar steamships with dirty white stacks stood at anchor in the roads, evidently foreign freighters. Some men in white, with white shoes, were walking about the pier and shouting loudly in French, and answering calls came from the ships. The bells were ringing briskly in the small town church.

"Today is Sunday!" Nadezhda Fyodorovna recalled with pleasure.

She felt perfectly well and was in a gay, festive mood. Wearing a new loose dress of coarse man's tussore and a big straw hat, its wide brim bent down sharply to her ears, so that her face looked out of it as if out of a box, she fancied herself very sweet. She was thinking that in the whole town there was only one young, beautiful, intelligent woman—herself—and that she alone knew how to dress cheaply, elegantly, and with taste. For example, this dress had cost only twenty-two roubles, and yet how sweet it was! In the whole town, she alone could still attract men, and there were many, and therefore, willy-nilly, they should all envy Laevsky.

She was glad that lately Laevsky had been cold, politely restrained, and at times even impertinent and rude with her; to all his outbursts and all his scornful, cold, or strange, incomprehensible glances, she would formerly have responded with tears, reproaches, and threats to leave him, or to starve herself to death, but now her response was merely to blush, to glance at him guiltily and be glad that he was not nice to her. If he rebuked her or threatened her, it would be still better and more agreeable, because she felt herself roundly guilty before him. It seemed to her that she was guilty, first, because she did not sympathize with his dreams of a life of labor, for the sake of which he had abandoned Petersburg and come here to the Caucasus, and she was certain that he had been cross with her lately precisely for that. As she was going to the Caucasus, it had seemed to her that on the very first day, she would find there a secluded nook on the coast, a cozy garden with shade, birds, brooks, where she could plant flowers and vegetables, raise ducks and chickens, receive neighbors, treat poor muzhiks and distribute books to them; but it turned out that the Caucasus was bare mountains, forests, and enormous valleys, where you had to spend a long time choosing, bustling about, building, and that there weren't any neighbors there, and it was very hot, and they could be robbed. Laevsky was in no rush to acquire a plot; she was glad of that, and it was as if they both agreed mentally never to mention the life of labor. He was silent, she thought, that meant he was angry with her for being silent.

Second, over those two years, unknown to him, she had bought all sorts of trifles in Atchmianov's shop for as much as three hundred roubles. She had bought now a bit of fabric, then some silk, then an umbrella, and the debt had imperceptibly mounted.

"I'll tell him about it today . . ." she decided, but at once realized that, given Laevsky's present mood, it was hardly opportune to talk to him about debts.

Third, she had already twice received Kirilin, the police chief, in Laevsky's absence: once in the morning, when Laevsky had gone to swim, and the other time at midnight, when he was playing cards. Remembering it, Nadezhda Fyodorovna flushed all over and turned to look at the kitchen maid, as if fearing she might eavesdrop on her thoughts. The long, unbearably hot, boring days, the beautiful, languorous evenings, the stifling nights, and this whole life, when one did not know from morning to evening how to spend the useless time, and the importunate thoughts that she was the most beautiful young woman in town and that her youth was going for naught, and Laevsky himself, an honest man with ideas, but monotonous, eternally shuffling in his slippers, biting his nails, and boring her with his caprices—resulted in her being gradually overcome with desires, and, like a madwoman, she thought day and night about one and the same thing. In her breathing, in her glance, in the tone of her voice, and in her gait—all she felt was desire; the sound of the sea told her she had to love, so did the evening darkness, so did the mountains . . . And when Kirilin began to court her, she had no strength, she could not and did not want to resist, and she gave herself to him . . .

Now the foreign steamships and people in white reminded her for some reason of a vast hall; along with the French talk, the sounds of a waltz rang in her ears, and her breast trembled with causeless joy. She wanted to dance and speak French.

She reasoned joyfully that there was nothing terrible in her infidelity; her soul took no part in it; she continues to love Laevsky, and that is obvious from the fact that she is jealous of him, pities him, and misses him when he's not at home. Kirilin turned out to be so-so, a bit crude, though handsome; she's broken everything off with him, and there won't be anything more. What there was is past, it's nobody's business, and if Laevsky finds out, he won't believe it.

There was only one bathing cabin on the shore, for women; the men bathed under the open sky. Going into the bathing cabin, Nadezhda Fyodorovna found an older lady there, Marya Konstantinovna Bitiugov, the wife of an official, and her fifteen-year-old daughter, Katya, a schoolgirl; the two were sitting on a bench undressing. Marya Konstanti-novna was a kind, rapturous, and genteel person who spoke in a drawl and with pathos. Until the age of thirty-two, she had lived as a governess, then she married the official Bitiugov, a small bald person who brushed his hair forward on his temples and was very placid. She was still in love with him, was jealous, blushed at the word "love," and assured everyone that she was very happy.

"My dear!" she said rapturously, seeing Nadezhda Fyodo-rovna and giving her face the expression that all her acquaint-ances called "almond butter." "Darling, how nice that you've come! We'll bathe together—that's charming!"

Olga quickly threw off her dress and chemise and began to undress her mistress.

"The weather's not so hot today as yesterday, isn't that so?" said Nadezhda Fyodorovna, shrinking under the rough touch of the naked kitchen maid. "Yesterday it was so stifling I nearly died."

"Oh, yes, my dear! I nearly suffocated myself. Would you

believe, yesterday I went bathing three times . . . imagine, my dear, three times! Even Nikodim Alexandrych got worried."

"How can they be so unattractive?" thought Nadezhda Fyodorovna, glancing at Olga and the official's wife. She looked at Katya and thought: "The girl's not badly built."

"Your Nikodim Alexandrych is very, very sweet!" she said. "I'm simply in love with him."

"Ha, ha, ha!" Marya Konstantinovna laughed forcedly. "That's charming!"

Having freed herself of her clothes, Nadezhda Fyodorovna felt a wish to fly. And it seemed to her that if she waved her arms, she would certainly take off. Undressed, she noticed that Olga was looking squeamishly at her white body. Olga, married to a young soldier, lived with her lawful husband and therefore considered herself better and higher than her mistress. Nadezhda Fyodorovna also felt that Marya Konstantinovna and Katya did not respect her and were afraid of her. That was unpleasant, and to raise herself in their opinion, she said:

"It's now the height of the dacha season[13] in Petersburg. My husband and I have so many acquaintances! We really must go and visit them."

"It seems your husband's an engineer?" Marya Konstantinovna asked timidly.

"I'm speaking of Laevsky. He has many acquaintances. But unfortunately his mother, a proud aristocrat, rather limited . . ."

Nadezhda Fyodorovna did not finish and threw herself into the water; Marya Konstantinovna and Katya went in after her.

"Our society has many prejudices," Nadezhda Fyodorovna continued, "and life is not as easy as it seems."

Marya Konstantinovna, who had served as a governess in aristocratic families and knew something about society, said:

"Oh, yes! Would you believe, at the Garatynskys' it was

absolutely required that one dress both for lunch and for dinner, so that, like an actress, besides my salary, I also received money for my wardrobe."

She placed herself between Nadezhda Fyodorovna and Katya, as if screening her daughter from the water that lapped at Nadezhda Fyodorovna. Through the open door that gave onto the sea, they could see someone swimming about a hundred paces from the bathing cabin.

"Mama, it's our Kostya!" said Katya.

"Ah, ah!" Marya Konstantinovna clucked in fright. "Ah! Kostya," she cried, "go back! Go back, Kostya!"

Kostya, a boy of about fourteen, to show off his bravery before his mother and sister, dove and swam further out, but got tired and hastened back, and by his grave, strained face, one could see that he did not believe in his strength.

"These boys are trouble, darling!" Marya Konstantinovna said, calming down. "He can break his neck any moment. Ah, darling, it's so pleasant and at the same time so difficult to be a mother! One's afraid of everything."

Nadezhda Fyodorovna put on her straw hat and threw herself out into the sea. She swam some thirty feet away and turned on her back. She could see the sea as far as the horizon, the ships, the people on the shore, the town, and all of it, together with the heat and the transparent, caressing waves, stirred her and whispered to her that she must live, live . . . A sailboat raced swiftly past her, energetically cleaving the waves and the air; the man who sat at the tiller looked at her, and she found it pleasing to be looked at . . .

After bathing, the ladies dressed and went off together.

"I have a fever every other day, and yet I don't get thinner," Nadezhda Fyodorovna said, licking her lips, which were salty from bathing, and responding with smiles to the bows of acquaintances. "I've always been plump, and now it seems I'm plumper still."

"That, darling, is a matter of disposition. If someone is

not disposed to plumpness, like me, for instance, no sort of food will help. But darling, you've got your hat all wet."

"Never mind, it will dry."

Nadezhda Fyodorovna again saw people in white walking on the embankment and talking in French; and for some reason, joy again stirred in her breast, and she vaguely remembered some great hall in which she had once danced, or of which, perhaps, she had once dreamed. And something in the very depths of her soul vaguely and dully whispered to her that she was a petty, trite, trashy, worthless woman . . .

Marya Konstantinovna stopped at her gate and invited her to come in for a moment.

"Come in, my dear!" she said in a pleading voice, at the same time looking at Nadezhda Fyodorovna with anguish and hope: maybe she'll refuse and not come in!

"With pleasure," Nadezhda Fyodorovna accepted. "You know how I love calling on you!"

And she went into the house. Marya Konstantinovna seated her, gave her coffee, offered her some sweet rolls, then showed her photographs of her former charges, the young Garatynsky ladies, who were all married now, and also showed her Katya's and Kostya's grades at the examinations; the grades were very good, but to make them look still better, she sighed and complained about how difficult it was now to study in high school . . . She attended to her visitor, and at the same time pitied her, and suffered from the thought that Nadezhda Fyodorovna, by her presence, might have a bad influence on Katya's and Kostya's morals, and she was glad that her Nikodim Alexandrych was not at home. Since, in her opinion, all men liked "such women," Nadezhda Fyodorovna might have a bad influence on Nikodim Alexandrych as well.

As she talked with her visitor, Marya Konstantinovna remembered all the while that there was to be a picnic that evening and that von Koren had insistently asked that the macaques—that is, Laevsky and Nadezhda Fyodorovna—not be told about it, but she accidentally let it slip, turned all red, and said in confusion:

"I hope you'll be there, too!"

VI

THE ARRANGEMENT WAS to go seven miles out of town on the road to the south, stop by the dukhan[14] at the confluence of the two rivers—the Black and the Yellow—and cook fish soup there. They set out shortly after five. At the head of them all, in a charabanc, rode Samoilenko and Laevsky; after them, in a carriage drawn by a troika, came Marya Konstantinovna, Nadezhda Fyodorovna, Katya, and Kostya; with them came a basket of provisions and dishes. In the next equipage rode the police chief Kirilin and the young Atchmianov, the son of that same merchant Atchmianov to whom Nadezhda Fyodorovna owed three hundred roubles, and on a little stool facing them, his legs tucked under, sat Nikodim Alexandrych, small, neat, with his hair brushed forward. Behind them all rode von Koren and the deacon; at the deacon's feet was a basket of fish.

"Keep r-r-right!" Samoilenko shouted at the top of his lungs whenever they met a native cart or an Abkhazian riding a donkey.

"In two years, when I have the means and the people ready, I'll go on an expedition," von Koren was telling the deacon. "I'll follow the coast from Vladivostok to the Bering Straits and then from the Straits to the mouth of the Yenisei. We'll draw a map, study the flora and fauna, and undertake thorough geological, anthropological, and ethnographic investigations. Whether you come with me or not is up to you."

"It's impossible," said the deacon.

"Why?"

"I'm attached, a family man."

"The deaconess will let you go. We'll provide for her. It would be still better if you persuaded her, for the common good, to be tonsured a nun; that would also enable you to be tonsured and join the expedition as a hieromonk.[15] I could arrange it for you."

The deacon was silent.

"Do you know your theology well?" asked the zoologist.

"Poorly."

"Hm . . . I can't give you any guidance in that regard, because I have little acquaintance with theology. Give me a list of the books you need, and I'll send them to you from Petersburg in the winter. You'll also have to read the notes of clerical travelers: you sometimes find good ethnographers and connoisseurs of Oriental languages among them. When you've familiarized yourself with their manner, it will be easier for you to set to work. Well, and while there are no books, don't waste time, come to me, and we'll study the compass, go through some meteorology. It's all much needed."

"Maybe so . . ." the deacon murmured and laughed. "I've asked for a post in central Russia, and my uncle the archpriest has promised to help me in that. If I go with you, it will turn out that I've bothered him for nothing."

"I don't understand your hesitation. If you go on being an ordinary deacon, who only has to serve on feast days and rests from work all the other days, even after ten years you'll still be the same as you are now; the only addition will be a mustache and a little beard, whereas if you come back from an expedition after the same ten years, you'll be a different man, enriched by the awareness of having accomplished something."

Cries of terror and delight came from the ladies' carriage. The carriages were driving along a road carved into the sheer cliff of the rocky coast, and it seemed to them all that they were riding on a shelf attached to a high wall, and that the carriages were about to fall into the abyss. To the right spread the sea, to the left an uneven brown wall with black spots, red veins, and creeping roots, and above, bending over as if with fear and curiosity, curly evergreens looked down. A minute later, there were shrieks and laughter again: they had to drive under an enormous overhanging rock.

"I don't understand why the devil I'm coming with you," said Laevsky. "How stupid and banal! I need to go north, to escape, to save myself, and for some reason I'm going on this foolish picnic."

"But just look at this panorama!" Samoilenko said to him as the horses turned left, and the valley of the Yellow River came into view, and the river itself glistened—yellow, turbid, mad . . .

"I don't see anything good in it, Sasha," replied Laevsky. "To constantly go into raptures over nature is to show the paucity of your imagination. All these brooks and cliffs are nothing but trash compared to what my imagination can give me."

The carriages were now driving along the riverbank. The high, mountainous banks gradually converged, the valley narrowed, and ahead was what looked like a gorge; the stony mountain they were driving along had been knocked together by nature out of huge stones, which crushed each other with such terrible force that Samoilenko involuntarily grunted each time he looked at them. The somber and beautiful mountain was cut in places by narrow crevices and gorges that breathed dampness and mysteriousness on the travelers; through the gorges, other mountains could be seen, brown, pink, purple, smoky, or flooded with bright light. From time to time, as they drove past the gorges, they could hear water falling from a height somewhere and splashing against the rocks.

"Ah, cursed mountains," sighed Laevsky, "I'm so sick of them!"

At the place where the Black River fell into the Yellow River and its water, black as ink, dirtied the yellow water and struggled with it, the Tartar Kerbalai's dukhan stood by the side of the road, with a Russian flag on the roof and a sign written in chalk: "The Pleasant Dukhan." Next to it was a small garden surrounded by a wattle fence, where tables and benches stood, and a single cypress, beautiful and somber, towered over the pitiful thorny bushes.

Kerbalai, a small, nimble Tartar in a blue shirt and white apron, stood in the road and, holding his stomach, bowed low to the approaching carriages and, smiling, showed his gleaming white teeth.

"Greetings, Kerbalaika!" Samoilenko called out to him. "We'll drive on a little further, and you bring us a samovar and some chairs! Step lively!"

Kerbalai kept nodding his cropped head and muttering something, and only those sitting in the last carriage could hear clearly: "There are trout, Your Excellency!"

"Bring them, bring them!" von Koren said to him.

Having driven some five hundred paces past the dukhan, the carriages stopped. Samoilenko chose a small meadow strewn with stones suitable for sitting on, and where a tree brought down by a storm lay with torn-up, shaggy roots and dry yellow needles. A flimsy log bridge had been thrown across the river at this spot, and on the other bank, just opposite, a shed for drying corn stood on four short pilings, looking like the fairy-tale hut on chicken's legs.[16] A ladder led down from its doorway.

The first impression everyone had was that they would never get out of there. On all sides, wherever one looked, towering mountains loomed up, and the evening shadow was approaching quickly, quickly, from the direction of the dukhan and the somber cypress, and that made the narrow, curved valley of the Black River seem narrower and the mountains higher. One could hear the murmuring of the river and the constant trilling of cicadas.

"Charming!" said Marya Konstantinovna, inhaling deeply with rapture. "Children, see how good it is! What silence!"

"Yes, it is good, in fact," agreed Laevsky, who liked the view and, for some reason, when he looked at the sky and then at the blue smoke coming from the chimney of the dukhan, suddenly grew sad. "Yes, it's good!" he repeated.

"Ivan Andreich, describe this view!" Marya Konstantinovna said tearfully.

"What for?" asked Laevsky. "The impression is better than any description. When writers babble about this wealth of colors and sounds that we all receive from nature by way of impressions, they make it ugly and unrecognizable."

"Do they?" von Koren asked coldly, choosing for himself the biggest stone by the water and trying to climb up and sit on it. "Do they?" he repeated, staring fixedly at Laevsky. "And Romeo and Juliet? And Pushkin's Ukrainian night,[17] for instance? Nature should come and bow down at its feet."

"Perhaps..." agreed Laevsky, too lazy to reason and object. "However," he said a little later, "what are Romeo and Juliet essentially? A beautiful, poetic, sacred love—roses under which they want to hide the rot. Romeo is the same animal as everyone else."

"Whatever one talks with you about, you always bring it all down to..."

Von Koren looked at Katya and did not finish.

"What do I bring it down to?" asked Laevsky.

"Somebody says to you, for instance, 'How beautiful is a bunch of grapes!' and you say, 'Yes, but how ugly when it's chewed and digested in the stomach.' Why say that? It's not new and...generally, it's a strange manner you have."

Laevsky knew that von Koren did not like him, and he was therefore afraid of him and felt in his presence as if they were all crowded together and somebody was standing behind his back. He said nothing in reply, walked away, and regretted that he had come.

"Gentlemen, off you go to fetch brush for the fire!" commanded Samoilenko.

They all wandered off at random, and the only ones who stayed put were Kirilin, Atchmianov, and Nikodim Alexandrych. Kerbalai brought chairs, spread a rug on the ground, and set down several bottles of wine. The police chief, Kirilin, a tall, imposing man who wore an overcoat over his tunic in all weather, with his haughty bearing, pompous stride, and thick, somewhat rasping voice, resembled all provincial police chiefs of the younger generation. His expression was sad and sleepy, as though he had just been awakened against his wishes.

"What is this you've brought, you brute?" he asked Kerbalai, slowly enunciating each word. "I told you to serve Kvareli, and what have you brought, you Tartar mug? Eh? What?"

"We have a lot of wine of our own, Egor Alexeich," Nikodim Alexandrych observed timidly and politely.

"What, sir? But I want my wine to be there, too. I'm taking part in the picnic, and I presume I have every right to contribute my share. I pre-sume! Bring ten bottles of Kvareli!"

"Why so many?" Nikodim Alexandrych, who knew that Kirilin had no money, was surprised.

"Twenty bottles! Thirty!" cried Kirilin.

"Never mind, let him!" Atchmianov whispered to Nikodim Alexandrych. "I'll pay."

Nadezhda Fyodorovna was in a gay, mischievous mood. She wanted to leap, laugh, exclaim, tease, flirt. In her cheap calico dress with blue flecks, red shoes, and the same straw hat, it seemed to her that she was small, simple, light and airy as a butterfly. She ran out on the flimsy bridge and looked into the water for a moment to make herself dizzy, then cried out and, laughing, ran across to the drying shed, and it seemed to her that all the men, even Kerbalai, admired her. When, in the swiftly falling darkness, the trees were merging with the mountains, the horses with the carriages, and a little light shone in the windows of the dukhan, she climbed a path that wound up the mountainside between the stones and thorny bushes and sat on a stone. Below, the fire was already burning. Near the fire, the deacon moved with rolled-up sleeves, and his long black shadow circled radius-like around the flames. He kept putting on more brush and stirring the pot with a spoon tied to a long stick. Samoilenko, with a copper-red face, bustled about the fire as in his own kitchen and shouted fiercely:

"Where's the salt, gentlemen? Did you forget it? Why are you all sitting around like landowners, and I'm the only one bustling about?"

Laevsky and Nikodim Alexandrych sat next to each other on the fallen tree and gazed pensively at the fire. Marya Konstantinovna, Katya, and Kostya were taking the tea service and plates out of the baskets. Von Koren, his arms crossed and one foot placed on a stone, stood on the bank just beside the water and thought about something. Red patches from the fire, together with shadows, moved on the ground near the dark human figures, trembled on the mountainside, on the trees, on the bridge, on the drying shed; on the other side, the steep, eroded bank was all lit up, flickered, and was reflected in the river, and the swift-running, turbulent water tore its reflection to pieces.

The deacon went for the fish, which Kerbalai was cleaning and washing on the bank, but halfway there, he stopped and looked around.

"My God, how good!" he thought. "The people, the stones, the fire, the twilight, the ugly tree—nothing more, but how good!"

On the far bank, by the drying shed, some unknown

people appeared. Because the light flickered and the smoke from the fire was carried to the other side, it was impossible to make out these people all at once, but they caught glimpses now of a shaggy hat and a gray beard, now of a blue shirt, now of rags hanging from shoulders to knees and a dagger across the stomach, now of a swarthy young face with black brows, as thick and bold as if they had been drawn with charcoal. About five of them sat down on the ground in a circle, while the other five went to the drying shed. One stood in the doorway with his back to the fire and, putting his hands behind him, began telling something that must have been very interesting, because, when Samoilenko added more brush and the fire blazed up, spraying sparks and brightly illuminating the drying barn, two physiognomies could be seen looking out the door, calm, expressing deep attention, and the ones sitting in a circle also turned and began listening to the story. A little later, the ones sitting in a circle began softly singing something drawn-out, melodious, like church singing during Lent . . . Listening to them, the deacon imagined how it would be with him in ten years, when he came back from the expedition: a young hiero-monk, a missionary, an author with a name and a splendid past; he is ordained archimandrite, then bishop; he serves the liturgy in a cathedral; in a golden mitre with a panagia, he comes out to the ambo and, blessing the mass of people with the trikíri and dikíri, proclaims: "Look down from heaven, O God, and behold and visit this vineyard which Thy right hand hath planted!" And the children's angelic voices sing in response: "Holy God . . ."[18]

"Where's the fish, Deacon?" Samoilenko's voice rang out.

Returning to the fire, the deacon imagined a procession with the cross going down a dusty road on a hot July day; at the head the muzhiks carry banners, and the women and girls icons; after them come choirboys and a beadle with a bandaged cheek and straw in his hair; then, in due order, himself, the deacon, after him a priest in a skull cap and with a cross, and behind them, raising dust, comes a crowd of muzhiks, women, boys; there, in the crowd, are the priest's wife and the deaconess, with kerchiefs on their heads. The choir sings, babies howl, quails call, a lark pours out its song... Now they stop and sprinkle a herd with holy water ... Go further, and on bended knee pray for rain. Then a bite to eat, conversation ...

"And that, too, is good ..." thought the deacon.

VII

KIRILIN AND ATCHMIANOV were climbing the path up the mountainside. Atchmianov lagged behind and stopped, and Kirilin came up to Nadezhda Fyodorovna.

"Good evening!" he said, saluting her.

"Good evening."

"Yes, ma'am!" Kirilin said, looking up at the sky and thinking.

"Why 'Yes, ma'am'?" asked Nadezhda Fyodorovna after some silence, and noticed that Atchmianov was watching the two of them.

"And so," the officer pronounced slowly, "our love withered away before it had time to flower, so to speak. How am I to understand that? Is it coquetry on your part, or do you regard me as a scapegrace with whom you can act however you please?"

"It was a mistake! Leave me alone!" Nadezhda Fyodorovna said sharply, looking at him with fear on that beautiful, wonderful evening, and asking herself in perplexity if there could indeed have been a moment when she had liked this man and been intimate with him.

"So, ma'am!" said Kirilin. He stood silently for a while, pondering, and said: "What, then? Let's wait till you're in a better mood, and meanwhile, I venture to assure you that I am a respectable man and will not allow anyone to doubt it. I am not to be toyed with! Adieu!"

He saluted her and walked off, making his way through the bushes. A little later, Atchmianov approached hesitantly.

"A fine evening tonight!" he said with a slight Armenian accent.

He was not bad-looking, dressed according to fashion, had the simple manners of a well-bred young man, but Nadezhda Fyodorovna disliked him because she owed his father three hundred roubles; there was also the unpleasantness of a shopkeeper being invited to the picnic, and the unpleasantness of his having approached her precisely that evening, when her soul felt so pure.

"Generally, the picnic's a success," he said after some silence.

"Yes," she agreed, and as if she had just remembered her debt, she said casually: "Ah, yes, tell them in your shop that Ivan Andreich will come one of these days and pay them the three hundred . . . or I don't remember how much."

"I'm ready to give you another three hundred, if only you'll stop mentioning this debt every day. Why such prose?"

Nadezhda Fyodorovna laughed. The amusing thought came to her head that, if she were immoral enough and wished to, she could get rid of this debt in one minute. If, for instance, she were to turn the head of this handsome young fool! How amusing, absurd, wild it would be indeed! And she suddenly wanted to make him fall in love with her, to fleece him, to drop him, and then see what would come of it.

"Allow me to give you one piece of advice," Atchmianov said timidly. "Beware of Kirilin, I beg you. He tells terrible things about you everywhere."

"I'm not interested in knowing what every fool tells about me," Nadezhda Fyodorovna said coldly, and uneasiness came over her, and the amusing thought of toying with the pretty young Atchmianov suddenly lost its charm.

"We must go down," she said. "They're calling."

Down there the fish soup was ready. It was poured into plates and eaten with that religious solemnity which only occurs at picnics. They all found the soup very tasty and said they had never had anything so tasty at home. As happens at all picnics, lost amidst a mass of napkins, packets, needless greasy wrappings scudding about in the wind, no one knew which glass and which piece of bread was whose, they poured wine on the rug and on their knees, spilled salt, and it was dark around them, and the fire burned less brightly, and they were all too lazy to get up and put on more brush. They all drank wine, and Kostya and Katya got half a glass each. Nadezhda Fyodorovna drank a glass, then another, became drunk, and forgot about Kirilin.

"A splendid picnic, a charming evening," said Laevsky, made merry by the wine, "but I'd prefer a nice winter to all this. 'A frosty dust silvers his beaver collar.' "[19]

"Tastes vary," observed von Koren.

Laevsky felt awkward: the heat of the fire struck him in the back, and von Koren's hatred in the front and face; this hatred from a decent, intelligent man, which probably concealed a substantial reason, humiliated him, weakened him, and, unable to confront it, he said in an ingratiating tone:

"I passionately love nature and regret not being a student of natural science. I envy you."

"Well, and I have no regret or envy," said Nadezhda Fyodorovna. "I don't understand how it's possible to be seriously occupied with bugs and gnats when people are suffering."

Laevsky shared her opinion. He was totally unacquainted with natural science and therefore could never reconcile himself to the authoritative tone and learned, profound air of people who studied the feelers of ants and the legs of cockroaches, and it had always vexed him that, on the basis of feelers, legs, and some sort of protoplasm (for some reason, he always imagined it like an oyster), these people should undertake to resolve questions that embraced the origin and life of man. But he heard a ring of falseness in Nadezhda Fyodorovna's words, and he said, only so as to contradict her:

"The point is not in the bugs but in the conclusions!"

VIII

IT WAS LATE, past ten o'clock, when they began getting into the carriages to go home. Everyone settled in, the only ones missing were Nadezhda Fyodorovna and Atchmianov, who were racing each other and laughing on the other side of the river.

"Hurry up, please!" Samoilenko called to them.

"The ladies shouldn't have been given wine," von Koren said in a low voice.

Laevsky, wearied by the picnic, by von Koren's hatred, and by his own thoughts, went to meet Nadezhda Fyodorovna, and when, merry, joyful, feeling light as a feather, breathless and laughing, she seized him by both hands and put her head on his chest, he took a step back and said sternly:

"You behave like a . . . cocotte."

This came out very rudely, so that he even felt sorry for her. On his angry, tired face she read hatred, pity, vexation with her, and she suddenly lost heart. She realized that she had overdone it, that she had behaved too casually, and, saddened, feeling heavy, fat, coarse, and drunk, she sat in the first empty carriage she found, along with Atchmianov. Laevsky sat with Kirilin, the zoologist with Samoilenko, the deacon with the ladies, and the train set off.

"That's how they are, the macaques . . ." von Koren began, wrapping himself in his cloak and closing his eyes. "Did you hear, she doesn't want to study bugs and gnats because people are suffering. That's how all macaques judge the likes of us. A slavish, deceitful tribe, intimidated by the knout and the fist for ten generations; they tremble, they wax tender, they burn incense only before force, but let a macaque into a free area, where there's nobody to take it by the scruff of the neck, and it loses control and shows its real face. Look how brave it is at art exhibitions, in museums, in theaters, or when it passes judgment on science: it struts, it rears up, it denounces, it criticizes . . . And it's sure to criticize—that's a feature of slaves! Just listen: people of the liberal professions are abused more often than swindlers—that's because three-quarters of society consists of slaves, the same macaques as these. It never happens that a slave offers you his hand and thanks you sincerely for the fact that you work."

"I don't know what you want!" Samoilenko said, yawning. "The poor woman, in her simplicity, wanted to chat with you about something intelligent, and you go drawing conclusions. You're angry with him for something, and also with her just for company. But she's a wonderful woman!"

"Oh, come now! An ordinary kept woman, depraved and banal. Listen, Alexander Davidych, when you meet a simple woman who isn't living with her husband and does nothing but hee-hee-hee and ha-ha-ha, you tell her to go and work. Why are you timid and afraid to tell the truth here? Only because Nadezhda Fyodorovna is kept not by a sailor but by an official?"

"What am I to do with her, then?" Samoilenko became angry. "Beat her or something?"

"Don't flatter vice. We curse vice only out of earshot, but that's like a fig in the pocket.[20] I'm a zoologist, or a sociologist, which is the same thing; you are a doctor; society believes us; it's our duty to point out to it the terrible harm with which it and future generations are threatened by the existence of ladies like this Nadezhda Ivanovna."

"Fyodorovna," Samoilenko corrected. "And what should society do?"

"It? That's its business. In my opinion, the most direct and proper way is force. She ought to be sent to her husband *manu militari*,* and if the husband won't have her, then send her to hard labor or some sort of correctional institution."

"Oof!" sighed Samoilenko. He paused and asked softly: "The other day you said people like Laevsky ought to be destroyed . . . Tell me, if somehow . . . suppose the state or society charged you with destroying him, would you . . . do it?"

"With a steady hand."

IX

RETURNING HOME, LAEVSKY and Nadezhda Fyodorovna went into their dark, dull, stuffy rooms. Both were silent. Laevsky lit a candle, and Nadezhda Fyodorovna sat down and, without taking off her cloak and hat, raised her sad, guilty eyes to him.

He realized that she was expecting a talk from him; but to talk would be boring, useless, and wearisome, and he felt downhearted because he had lost control and been rude to her. He chanced to feel in his pocket the letter he had been wanting to read to her every day, and he thought that if he showed her the letter now, it would turn her attention elsewhere.

"It's time to clarify our relations," he thought. "I'll give it to her, come what may."

He took out the letter and handed it to her.

"Read it. It concerns you."

*By military force.

Having said this, he went to his study and lay down on the sofa in the darkness, without a pillow. Nadezhda Fyodorovna read the letter, and it seemed to her that the ceiling had lowered and the walls had closed in on her. It suddenly became cramped, dark, and frightening. She quickly crossed herself three times and said:

"Give rest, O Lord . . . give rest, O Lord . . ."[21]

And she wept.

"Vanya!" she called. "Ivan Andreich!"

There was no answer. Thinking that Laevsky had come in and was standing behind her chair, she sobbed like a child and said:

"Why didn't you tell me earlier that he had died? I wouldn't have gone on the picnic, I wouldn't have laughed so terribly . . . Men were saying vulgar things to me. What sin, what sin! Save me, Vanya, save me . . . I'm going out of my mind . . . I'm lost . . ."

Laevsky heard her sobs. He felt unbearably suffocated, and his heart was pounding hard. In anguish, he got up, stood in the middle of the room for a while, felt in the darkness for the chair by the table, and sat down.

"This is a prison . . ." he thought. "I must get out . . . I can't . . ."

It was too late to go and play cards, there were no restaurants in the town. He lay down again and stopped his ears so as not to hear the sobbing, and suddenly remembered that he could go to Samoilenko's. To avoid walking past Nadezhda Fyodorovna, he climbed out the window to the garden, got over the fence, and went on down the street. It was dark. Some steamer had just arrived—a big passenger ship, judging by its lights . . . An anchor chain clanked. A small red light moved quickly from the coast to the ship: it was the customs boat.

"The passengers are asleep in their cabins . . ." thought Laevsky, and he envied other people's peace.

The windows of Samoilenko's house were open. Laevsky looked through one of them, then another: it was dark and quiet inside.

"Alexander Davidych, are you asleep?" he called. "Alexander Davidych!"

Coughing was heard, and an anxious cry:

"Who's there? What the devil?"

"It's me, Alexander Davidych. Forgive me."

A little later, a door opened; the soft light of an icon lamp gleamed, and the enormous Samoilenko appeared, all in white and wearing a white nightcap.

"What do you want?" he asked, breathing heavily from being awakened and scratching himself. "Wait, I'll open up at once."

"Don't bother, I'll come in the window..."

Laevsky climbed through the window and, going up to Samoilenko, seized him by the hand.

"Alexander Davidych," he said in a trembling voice, "save me! I beseech you, I adjure you, understand me! My situation is tormenting. If it goes on for another day or two, I'll strangle myself like...like a dog!"

"Wait...What exactly are you referring to?"

"Light a candle."

"Ho-hum..." sighed Samoilenko, lighting a candle. "My God, my God...It's already past one o'clock, brother."

"Forgive me, but I can't stay at home," said Laevsky, feeling greatly relieved by the light and Samoilenko's presence. "You, Alexander Davidych, are my best and only friend...All my hope lies in you. Whether you want to or not, for God's sake, help me out. I must leave here at all costs. Lend me some money!"

"Oh, my God, my God!..." Samoilenko sighed, scratching himself. "I'm falling asleep and I hear a whistle—a steamer has come—and then you...How much do you need?"

"At least three hundred roubles. I should leave her a hundred, and I'll need two hundred for my trip . . . I already owe you about four hundred, but I'll send you all of it . . . all of it . . ."

Samoilenko took hold of both his side-whiskers with one hand, stood straddle-legged, and pondered.

"So . . ." he murmured, reflecting. "Three hundred . . . Yes . . . But I haven't got that much. I'll have to borrow it from somebody."

"Borrow it, for God's sake!" said Laevsky, seeing by Samoilenko's face that he wanted to give him the money and was sure to do it. "Borrow it, and I'll be sure to pay it back. I'll send it from Petersburg as soon as I get there. Don't worry about that. Look, Sasha," he said, reviving, "let's have some wine!"

"Wine . . . That's possible."

They both went to the dining room.

"And what about Nadezhda Fyodorovna?" asked Samoilenko, setting three bottles and a plate of peaches on the table. "Can she be staying on?"

"I'll arrange it all, I'll arrange it all . . ." said Laevsky, feeling an unexpected surge of joy. "I'll send her money afterwards, and she'll come to me . . . And then we'll clarify our relations. To your health, friend."

"Wait," said Samoilenko. "Drink this one first . . . It's from my vineyard. This bottle is from Navaridze's vineyard, and this one from Akhatulov's . . . Try all three and tell me frankly . . . Mine seems to be a bit acidic. Eh? Don't you find?"

"Yes. You've really comforted me, Alexander Davidych. Thank you . . . I've revived."

"A bit acidic?"

"Devil knows, I don't know. But you're a splendid, wonderful man!"

Looking at his pale, agitated, kindly face, Samoilenko

ANTON CHEKHOV

remembered von Koren's opinion that such people should be destroyed, and Laevsky seemed to him a weak, defenseless child whom anyone could offend and destroy.

"And when you go, make peace with your mother," he said. "It's not nice."

"Yes, yes, without fail."

They were silent for a while. When they had drunk the first bottle, Samoilenko said:

"Make peace with von Koren as well. You're both most excellent and intelligent people, but you stare at each other like two wolves."

"Yes, he's a most excellent and intelligent man," agreed Laevsky, ready now to praise and forgive everybody. "He's a remarkable man, but it's impossible for me to be friends with him. No! Our natures are too different. I'm sluggish, weak, submissive by nature; I might offer him my hand at a good moment, but he'd turn away from me . . . with scorn."

Laevsky sipped some wine, paced from corner to corner, and, stopping in the middle of the room, went on:

"I understand von Koren very well. He's firm, strong, despotic by nature. You've heard him talking constantly about an expedition, and they're not empty words. He needs the desert, a moonlit night; around him in tents and under the open sky sleep his hungry and sick Cossacks, guides, porters, a doctor, a priest, worn out by the difficult marches, and he alone doesn't sleep and, like Stanley,[22] sits in his folding chair and feels himself the king of the desert and master of these people. He walks, and walks, and walks somewhere, his people groan and die one after the other, but he walks and walks, and in the end dies himself, and still remains the despot and king of the desert, because the cross on his grave can be seen by caravans from thirty or forty miles away, and it reigns over the desert. I'm sorry the man is not in military service. He'd make an excellent, brilliant general. He'd know how to drown his cavalry in the river and make bridges from the corpses, and such boldness is more necessary in war than any fortifications or tactics. Oh, I understand him very well! Tell me, why does he eat himself up here? What does he need here?"

"He's studying marine fauna."

"No. No, brother, no!" sighed Laevsky. "I was told by a scientist traveling on the steamer that the Black Sea is poor in fauna, and that organic life is impossible in the depths of it owing to the abundance of hydrogen sulfate. All serious zoologists work at biological stations in Naples or Ville-franche. But von Koren is independent and stubborn: he works on the Black Sea because nobody works here; he's broken with the university, doesn't want to know any scientists and colleagues, because he's first of all a despot and only then a zoologist. And you'll see, something great will come of him. He's already dreaming now that when he returns from the expedition, he'll smoke out the intrigue and mediocrity in our universities and tie the scientists in knots. Despotism is as strong in science as in war. And he's living for the second summer in this stinking little town, because it's better to be first in a village than second in a city.[23] Here he's a king and an eagle; he's got all the inhabitants under his thumb and oppresses them with his authority. He's taken everybody in hand, he interferes in other people's affairs, he wants to be in on everything, and everybody's afraid of him. I'm slipping out from under his paw, he senses it, and he hates me. Didn't he tell you that I should be destroyed or sent to the public works?"

"Yes," laughed Samoilenko.

Laevsky also laughed and drank some wine.

"His ideals are despotic as well," he said, laughing and taking a bite of peach. "Ordinary mortals, if they work for the general benefit, have their neighbor in mind—me, you, in short, a human being. But for von Koren, people are puppies and nonentities, too small to be the goal of his life.

He works, he'll go on an expedition and break his neck there, not in the name of love for his neighbor but in the name of such abstractions as mankind, future generations, an ideal race of people. He worries about the improvement of the human race, and in that respect we are merely slaves for him, cannon fodder, beasts of burden; he'd destroy some or slap them with hard labor, others he'd bind with discipline, like Arakcheev,[24] make them get up and lie down to the drum, set eunuchs to protect our chastity and morality, order that anyone who steps outside the circle of our narrow, conservative morality be shot at, and all that in the name of improving the human race . . . But what is the human race? An illusion, a mirage . . . Despots have always been given to illusions. I understand him very well, brother. I appreciate him and do not deny his significance; this world stands on men like him, and if the world were placed at the disposal of us alone, with all our kindness and good intentions, we'd do with it just what the flies are doing to that painting. It's true."

Laevsky sat down beside Samoilenko and said with genuine enthusiasm:

"I'm an empty, worthless, fallen man! The air I breathe, this wine, love, in short, life—I've been buying it all up to now at the price of lies, idleness, and pusillanimity. Up to now I've been deceiving people and myself, I've suffered from it, and my sufferings have been cheap and trite. I timidly bend my neck before von Koren's hatred, because at times I, too, hate and despise myself."

Laevsky again paced from corner to corner in agitation and said:

"I'm glad I see my shortcomings clearly and am aware of them. That will help me to resurrect and become a different man. My dear heart, if only you knew how passionately, with what anguish, I thirst for my renewal. And I swear to you, I will be a man! I will! I don't know whether it's the wine speaking in me, or it's so in reality, but it seems to me that it's long since I've lived through such bright, pure moments as now with you."

"Time to sleep, brother..." said Samoilenko.

"Yes, yes... Forgive me. I'll go at once."

Laevsky fussed around the furniture and windows, looking for his cap.

"Thank you..." he murmured, sighing. "Thank you... Gentleness and a kind word are higher than alms. You've revived me."

He found his cap, stopped, and looked guiltily at Samoilenko.

"Alexander Davidych!" he said in a pleading voice.

"What?"

"Allow me, dear heart, to spend the night with you!"

"Please do... why not?"

Laevsky lay down to sleep on the sofa, and for a long time went on talking with the doctor.

X

SOME THREE DAYS after the picnic, Marya Konstantinovna unexpectedly came to Nadezhda Fyodorovna and, without greeting her, without taking off her hat, seized her by both hands, pressed them to her bosom, and said in great agitation:

"My dear, I'm so agitated, so shocked. Our dear, sympathetic doctor told my Nikodim Alexandrych yesterday that your husband has passed away. Tell me, dear... Tell me, is it true?"

"Yes, it's true, he died," Nadezhda Fyodorovna answered.

"My dear, it's terrible, terrible! But there's no bad without some good. Your husband was probably a marvelous, wonderful, holy man, and such people are more needed in heaven than on earth."

All the little lines and points in Marya Konstantinovna's

face trembled, as if tiny needles were leaping under her skin. She smiled an almond-butter smile and said rapturously, breathlessly:

"And so you're free, my dear. Now you can hold your head high and look people boldly in the eye. From now on, God and men will bless your union with Ivan Andreich. It's charming. I'm trembling with joy, I can't find words. My dear, I'll be your sponsor... Nikodim Alexandrych and I have loved you so much, you must allow us to bless your lawful, pure union. When, when are you going to be married?"

"I haven't even thought about it," said Nadezhda Fyodorovna, freeing her hands.

"That's impossible, my dear. You have thought about it, you have!"

"By God, I haven't," laughed Nadezhda Fyodorovna. "Why should we get married? I see no need for it. We'll live as we've lived."

"What are you saying!" Marya Konstantinovna was horrified. "For God's sake, what are you saying!"

"If we get married, it won't be any better. On the contrary, even worse. We'll lose our freedom."

"My dear! My dear, what are you saying!" cried Marya Konstantinovna, stepping back and clasping her hands. "You're being extravagant! Come to your senses! Settle down!"

"What do you mean, settle down? I haven't lived yet, and you tell me to settle down!"

Nadezhda Fyodorovna remembered that indeed she had not lived yet. She had finished the girls' institute and married a man she did not love, then she had taken up with Laevsky and had been living with him the whole time on that dull, deserted coast in expectation of something better. Was that life?

"Yet it would be proper to get married..." she thought but, remembering Kirilin and Atchmianov, blushed and said:

"No, it's impossible. Even if Ivan Andreich were to beg me on his knees, even then I would refuse."

Marya Konstantinovna sat silently on the sofa for a moment, sad, serious, looking at a single point, then got up and said coldly:

"Good-bye, my dear! Excuse me for having troubled you. Though it's not easy for me, I must tell you that from this day on, everything is over between us, and despite my deepest respect for Ivan Andreich, the door of my house is closed to you."

She uttered it with solemnity and was crushed herself by her solemn tone; her face trembled again, took on a soft almond-butter expression; she held out both hands to the frightened and abashed Nadezhda Fyodorovna and said imploringly:

"My dear, allow me at least for one minute to be your mother or an older sister! I'll be open with you, like a mother."

Nadezhda Fyodorovna felt such warmth, joy, and compassion for herself in her breast, as though it really was her mother, risen from the dead, who stood before her. She embraced Marya Konstantinovna impulsively and pressed her face to her shoulder. They both wept. They sat down on the sofa and sobbed for a few minutes, not looking at each other and unable to utter a single word.

"My dear, my child," Marya Konstantinovna began, "I shall tell you some stern truths, without sparing you."

"Do, do, for God's sake!"

"Trust me, my dear. You remember, of all the local ladies, I was the only one to receive you. You horrified me from the very first day, but I was unable to treat you with scorn, like everyone else. I suffered for dear, kind Ivan Andreich as for a son. A young man in a strange land, inexperienced, weak, with no mother, and I was tormented, tormented... My husband was against making his acquaintance, but

I talked him into it...I persuaded him...We began to receive Ivan Andreich, and you with him, of course, otherwise he would have been insulted. I have a daughter, a son... You understand, the tender mind of a child, the pure heart...and whosoever shall offend one of these little ones[25]...I received you and trembled for my children. Oh, when you're a mother, you'll understand my fear. And everyone was surprised that I received you, forgive me, as a respectable woman, people hinted to me...well, of course, there was gossip, speculation...Deep in my soul, I condemned you, but you were unhappy, pathetic, extravagant, and I suffered out of pity."

"But why? Why?" asked Nadezhda Fyodorovna, trembling all over. "What have I done to anyone?"

"You're a terrible sinner. You broke the vow you gave your husband at the altar. You seduced an excellent young man who, if he hadn't met you, might have taken himself a lawful life's companion from a good family of his circle, and he would now be like everybody else. You've ruined his youth. Don't speak, don't speak, my dear! I will not believe that a man can be to blame for our sins. The women are always to blame. In everyday domestic life, men are frivolous, they live by their minds, not their hearts, there's much they don't understand, but a woman understands everything. Everything depends on her. Much is given her, and much will be asked of her. Oh, my dear, if she were stupider or weaker than man in this respect, God wouldn't have entrusted her with the upbringing of little boys and girls. And then, dearest, you entered upon the path of vice, forgetting all shame; another woman in your position would have hidden herself from people, would have sat locked up at home, and people would have seen her only in God's church, pale, dressed all in black, weeping, and each would say with sincere contrition: 'God, this is a sinful angel returning to you again...' But you, my dear, forgot all modesty, you lived openly, extravagantly, as if you were proud of your sin, you frolicked, you laughed, and looking at you, I trembled with horror, fearing lest a thunderbolt from heaven strike our house while you were sitting with us. My dear, don't speak, don't speak!" Marya Konstantinovna cried, noticing that Nadezhda Fyodorovna was about to speak. "Trust me, I won't deceive you, and I won't conceal a single truth from the eyes of your soul. Listen to me, then, dearest . . . God marks great sinners, and you have been marked. Remember, your dresses have always been awful!"

Nadezhda Fyodorovna, who had always had the highest opinion of her dresses, stopped crying and looked at her in astonishment.

"Yes, awful!" Marya Konstantinovna went on. "Anyone could judge your behavior by the refinement and showiness of your clothes. Everyone chuckled and shrugged, looking at you, but I suffered, suffered . . . And forgive me, my dear, but you are slovenly! When I met you in the bathing cabin, you made me tremble. Your dress was still so-so, but the petticoat, the chemise . . . my dear, I blush! Poor Ivan Andreich has no one to tie his necktie properly, and by the poor man's linen and boots, one can see that no one looks after him at home. And you always keep him hungry, my darling, and indeed, if there's no one at home to see to the coffee and the samovar, willy-nilly, one spends half one's salary in the pavilion. And your home is simply terrible, terrible! Nobody in the whole town has flies, but you can't get rid of them, the plates and saucers are black. On the windows and tables, just look—dust, dead flies, glasses . . . What are the glasses doing here? And my dear, your table still hasn't been cleared yet. It's a shame to go into your bedroom: underwear lying about, those various rubber things of yours hanging on the walls, certain vessels standing about . . . My dear! A husband should know nothing, and a wife should be as pure as a little angel before him! I wake up every morning at the first light and wash my face with cold water, so that my Nikodim Alexandrych won't see me looking sleepy."

"That's all trifles," Nadezhda Fyodorovna burst into sobs. "If only I were happy, but I'm so unhappy!"

"Yes, yes, you're very unhappy!" Marya Konstantinovna sighed, barely keeping herself from crying. "And awful grief awaits you in the future! A lonely old age, illnesses, and then your answer before the dread Judgment Seat[26] . . . Terrible, terrible! Now fate itself is offering you a helping hand, and you senselessly push it aside. Get married, get married quickly!"

"Yes, I must, I must," said Nadezhda Fyodorovna, "but it's impossible!"

"Why so?"

"Impossible! Oh, if you only knew!"

Nadezhda Fyodorovna was going to tell her about Kirilin, and about how she had met the young, handsome Atchmianov on the pier the previous evening, and how the crazy, funny thought had come into her head of getting rid of her three-hundred-rouble debt, she had found it very funny, and had returned home late at night, feeling irretrievably fallen and sold. She did not know how it happened herself. And now she was about to swear before Marya Konstantinovna that she would repay the debt without fail, but sobs and shame prevented her from speaking.

"I'll go away," she said. "Ivan Andreich can stay, and I'll go away."

"Where?"

"To Russia."

"But how are you going to live? You have nothing."

"I'll do translations or . . . or open a little library . . ."

"Don't fantasize, my dear. You need money to start a library. Well, I'll leave you now, and you calm down and think, and come to see me tomorrow all cheered up. That will be charming! Well, good-bye, my little angel. Let me kiss you."

Marya Konstantinovna kissed Nadezhda Fyodorovna on the forehead, made a cross over her, and quietly left. It was already growing dark, and Olga lit a light in the kitchen. Still weeping, Nadezhda Fyodorovna went to the bedroom and lay on the bed. She was in a high fever. She undressed lying down, crumpled her clothes towards her feet, and rolled up in a ball under the blanket. She was thirsty, and there was no one to give her a drink.

"I'll pay it back!" she said to herself, and in her delirium it seemed to her that she was sitting by some sick woman and in her recognized herself. "I'll pay it back. It would be stupid to think it was for money that I ... I'll go away and send him money from Petersburg. First a hundred ... then a hundred ... and then another hundred ..."

Laevsky came late at night.

"First a hundred ..." Nadezhda Fyodorovna said to him, "then another hundred ..."

"You should take some quinine," he said and thought: "Tomorrow is Wednesday, the steamer leaves, and I'm not going. That means I'll have to live here till Saturday."

Nadezhda Fyodorovna got up on her knees in bed.

"Did I say anything just now?" she asked, smiling and squinting because of the candle.

"Nothing. We'll have to send for the doctor tomorrow morning. Sleep."

He took a pillow and went to the door. Once he had finally decided to go away and abandon Nadezhda Fyodorovna, she had begun to arouse pity and a feeling of guilt in him; he was slightly ashamed in her presence, as in the presence of an old or ailing horse slated to be killed. He stopped in the doorway and turned to look at her.

"I was annoyed at the picnic and said something rude to you. Forgive me, for God's sake."

Having said this, he went to his study, lay down, and for a long time was unable to fall asleep.

The next morning, when Samoilenko, in full dress uniform with epaulettes and decorations on occasion of the feast day, was coming out of the bedroom after taking Nadezhda Fyodorovna's pulse and examining her tongue, Laevsky, who was standing by the threshold, asked him worriedly:

"Well, so? So?"

His face expressed fear, extreme anxiety, and hope.

"Calm down, it's nothing dangerous," said Samoilenko. "An ordinary fever."

"I'm not asking about that," Laevsky winced impatiently. "Did you get the money?"

"Forgive me, dear heart," Samoilenko whispered, glancing back at the door and getting embarrassed. "For God's sake, forgive me! Nobody has ready cash, and so far I've only collected by fives or tens—a hundred and ten roubles in all. Today I'll talk with someone else. Be patient."

"But Saturday's the last day!" Laevsky whispered, trembling with impatience. "By all that's holy, before Saturday! If I don't leave on Saturday, I'll need nothing... nothing! I don't understand how a doctor can have no money!"

"Thy will be done, O Lord," Samoilenko whispered quickly and tensely, and something even squeaked in his throat, "they've taken everything I've got, I have seven thousand owing to me, and I'm roundly in debt. Is it my fault?"

"So you'll get it by Saturday? Yes?"

"I'll try."

"I beg you, dear heart! So that the money will be in my hands Friday morning."

Samoilenko sat down and wrote a prescription for quinine in a solution of *kalii bromati*, infusion of rhubarb, and *tincturae gentianae aquae foeniculi*—all of it in one mixture, with the addition of rose syrup to remove the bitterness, and left.

XI

"YOU LOOK AS though you're coming to arrest me," said von Koren, seeing Samoilenko coming into his room in full dress uniform.

"I was passing by and thought: why don't I pay a call on zoology?" said Samoilenko, sitting down by the big table the zoologist himself had knocked together out of simple planks. "Greetings, holy father!" he nodded to the deacon, who was sitting by the window copying something. "I'll sit for a minute and then run home to give orders for dinner. It's already time . . . I'm not bothering you?"

"Not at all," replied the zoologist, laying out scraps of paper covered with fine writing on the table. "We're busy copying."

"So . . . Oh, my God, my God . . ." sighed Samoilenko; he cautiously drew from the table a dusty book on which lay a dead, dry phalangid, and said: "However! Imagine some little green bug is going about his business and suddenly meets such an anathema on his way. I can picture how terrifying it is!"

"Yes, I suppose so."

"It's given venom to defend itself from enemies?"

"Yes, to defend itself and to attack."

"So, so, so . . . And everything in nature, my dear hearts, is purposeful and explainable," sighed Samoilenko. "Only here's what I don't understand. You're a man of the greatest intelligence, explain it to me, please. There are these little beasts, you know, no bigger than a rat, pretty to look at but mean and immoral in the highest degree, let me tell you. Suppose such a beast is walking along through the forest; it sees a little bird, catches it, and eats it up. It goes on and sees a nest with eggs in the grass; it doesn't want any more grub, it's not hungry, but even so, it bites into an egg and throws the others out of the nest with its paw. Then it meets a frog and starts playing with it. It tortures the frog to death, goes on, licking its chops, and meets a beetle. Swats the beetle with its paw ... And it ruins and destroys everything in its way ... It crawls into other animals' holes, digs up anthills for nothing, cracks open snail shells ... It meets a rat and gets into a fight with it; it sees a snake or a mouse and has to strangle it. And this goes on all day. So tell me, what is the need for such a beast? Why was it created?"

"I don't know what beast you're talking about," said von Koren, "probably some insectivore. Well, so what? It caught a bird because the bird was careless; it destroyed the nest of eggs because the bird wasn't skillful, it made the nest poorly and didn't camouflage it. The frog probably had some flaw in its coloring, otherwise it wouldn't have seen it, and so on. Your beast destroys only the weak, the unskilled, the careless—in short, those who have flaws that nature does not find it necessary to transmit to posterity. Only the more nimble, careful, strong, and developed remain alive. Thus your little beast, without suspecting it, serves the great purposes of perfection."

"Yes, yes, yes ... By the way, brother," Samoilenko said casually, "how about lending me a hundred roubles?"

"Fine. Among the insectivores, very interesting species occur. For instance, the mole. They say it's useful because it destroys harmful insects. The story goes that a German once sent the emperor Wilhelm I a coat made of moleskins, and that the emperor supposedly reprimanded him for destroying so many of the useful animals. And yet the mole yields nothing to your little beast in cruelty, and is very harmful besides, because it does awful damage to the fields."

Von Koren opened a box and took out a hundred-rouble bill.

"The mole has a strong chest, like the bat," he went on, locking the box, "its bones and muscles are awfully well developed, its jaw is extraordinarily well equipped. If it had the dimensions of an elephant, it would be an all-destructive, invincible animal. It's interesting that when two moles meet underground, they both begin to prepare a flat space, as if by arrangement; they need this space in order to fight more conveniently. Once they've made it, they start a cruel battle and struggle until the weaker one falls. Here, take the hundred roubles," said von Koren, lowering his voice, "but only on condition that you're not taking it for Laevsky."

"And what if it is for Laevsky!" Samoilenko flared up. "Is that any business of yours?"

"I can't give money for Laevsky. I know you like lending. You'd lend to the robber Kerim if he asked you, but, excuse me, in that direction I can't help you."

"Yes, I'm asking for Laevsky!" said Samoilenko, getting up and waving his right arm. "Yes! For Laevsky! And no devil or demon has the right to teach me how I should dispose of my money. You don't want to give it to me? Eh?"

The deacon burst out laughing.

"Don't seethe, but reason," said the zoologist. "To be Mr. Laevsky's benefactor is, in my opinion, as unintelligent as watering weeds or feeding locusts."

"And in my opinion, it's our duty to help our neighbors!" cried Samoilenko.

"In that case, help this hungry Turk who's lying by the hedge! He's a worker and more necessary, more useful than your Laevsky. Give him this hundred roubles! Or donate me a hundred roubles for the expedition!"

"Will you lend it to me or not, I ask you?"

"Tell me frankly: what does he need the money for?"

"It's no secret. He has to go to Petersburg on Saturday."

"So that's it!" von Koren drew out. "Aha . . . We understand. And will she be going with him, or what?"

"She remains here for the time being. He'll settle his affairs in Petersburg and send her money, and then she'll go."

"Clever! . . ." said the zoologist and laughed a brief tenor laugh. "Clever! Smart thinking!"

He quickly went up to Samoilenko and, planting himself face-to-face with him, looking into his eyes, asked:

"Speak frankly to me: he's fallen out of love? Right? Speak: he's fallen out of love? Right?"

"Right," Samoilenko brought out and broke into a sweat.

"How loathsome!" said von Koren, and one could see by his face that he felt loathing. "There are two possibilities, Alexander Davidych: either you're in conspiracy with him or, forgive me, you're a simpleton. Don't you understand that he's taking you in like a little boy, in the most shameful way? It's clear as day that he wants to get rid of her and leave her here. She'll be left on your neck, and it's clear as day that you'll have to send her to Petersburg at your own expense. Has your excellent friend so bedazzled you with his merits that you don't see even the simplest things?"

"Those are nothing but conjectures," said Samoilenko, sitting down.

"Conjectures? And why is he going alone and not with her? And why, ask him, shouldn't she go on ahead and he come later? A sly beast!"

Oppressed by sudden doubts and suspicions concerning his friend, Samoilenko suddenly weakened and lowered his tone.

"But this is impossible!" he said, remembering the night Laevsky had spent at his place. "He suffers so!"

"What of it? Thieves and incendiaries also suffer!"

"Even supposing you're right . . ." Samoilenko said, pondering. "Let's assume . . . But he's a young man, in foreign parts . . . a student, but we've also been students, and except for us, there's nobody to support him."

"To help him in his abomination only because at different points you and he were at the university and both did nothing there! What nonsense!"

"Wait, let's reason with equanimity. It's possible, I suppose, to arrange it like this . . ." Samoilenko reasoned, twisting his fingers. "You see, I'll give him money, but I'll take from him his gentleman's word of honor that he will send Nadezhda Fyodorovna money for the trip in a week."

"And he'll give you his word of honor, and even shed a tear and believe himself, but what is his word worth? He won't keep it, and when, in a year or two, you meet him on Nevsky Prospect arm in arm with a new love, he'll justify himself by saying civilization has crippled him and he's a chip off Rudin's block.[27] Drop him, for God's sake! Walk away from this muck, and don't rummage in it with both hands!"

Samoilenko thought for a minute and said resolutely:

"But even so, I'll give him the money. As you like. I'm unable to refuse a man on the basis of conjectures alone."

"Excellent. Go and kiss him."

"So give me the hundred roubles," Samoilenko asked timidly.

"I won't."

Silence ensued. Samoilenko went completely weak; his face acquired a guilty, ashamed, and fawning expression, and it was somehow strange to see this pitiful, childishly abashed face on a huge man wearing epaulettes and decorations.

"The local bishop goes around his diocese not in a carriage but on horseback," said the deacon, putting down his pen. "The sight of him riding a little horse is extremely touching. His simplicity and modesty are filled with biblical grandeur."

"Is he a good man?" asked von Koren, who was glad to change the subject.

"But of course. If he wasn't good, how could he have been ordained a bishop?"

"There are some very good and gifted people among the bishops," said von Koren. "Only it's a pity that many of them have the weakness of imagining themselves statesmen. One occupies himself with Russification, another criticizes science. That's not their business. They'd do better to stop by at the consistory more often."

"A worldly man cannot judge a bishop."

"Why not, Deacon? A bishop is the same sort of man as I am."

"The same and not the same," the deacon became offended and again took up his pen. "If you were the same, grace would have rested upon you, and you'd have been a bishop yourself, but since you're not a bishop, it means you're not the same."

"Don't drivel, Deacon!" Samoilenko said in anguish. "Listen, here's what I've come up with," he turned to von Koren. "Don't give me that hundred roubles. You're going to be my boarder for another three months before winter, so give me the money for those three months ahead of time."

"I won't."

Samoilenko blinked and turned purple, mechanically drew the book with the phalangid towards him and looked at it, then got up and took his hat. Von Koren felt sorry for him.

"Just try living and having anything to do with such gentlemen!" said the zoologist, and he kicked some paper into the corner in indignation. "Understand that this is not kindness, not love, but pusillanimity, license, poison! What reason achieves, your flabby, worthless hearts destroy! When I was sick with typhoid as a schoolboy, my aunt, in her compassion, overfed me with pickled mushrooms, and I nearly died. Understand, you and my aunt both, that love for man should not be in your heart, not in the pit of your stomach, not in your lower back, but here!"

Von Koren slapped himself on the forehead.

"Take it!" he said and flung the hundred-rouble bill.

"You needn't be angry, Kolya," Samoilenko said meekly, folding the bill. "I understand you very well, but . . . put yourself in my position."

"You're an old woman, that's what!"

The deacon guffawed.

"Listen, Alexander Davidych, one last request!" von Koren said hotly. "When you give that finagler the money, set him a condition: let him leave together with his lady or send her on ahead, otherwise don't give it. There's no point in being ceremonious with him. Just tell him that, and if you don't, on my word of honor, I'll go to his office and chuck him down the stairs, and you I'll have nothing more to do with. Be it known to you!"

"So? If he goes with her or sends her ahead, it's the more convenient for him," said Samoilenko. "He'll even be glad. Well, good-bye."

He affectionately took his leave and went out, but before closing the door behind him, he turned to look at von Koren, made an awful face, and said:

"It's the Germans that spoiled you, brother! Yes! The Germans!"

XII

THE NEXT DAY, Thursday, Marya Konstantinovna celebrated her Kostya's birthday. At noon everyone was invited for cake, and in the evening for hot chocolate. When Laevsky and Nadezhda Fyodorovna came in the evening, the zoologist, already sitting in the drawing room and drinking chocolate, asked Samoilenko:

"Did you speak to him?"

"Not yet."

"Watch out, don't be ceremonious. I don't understand the impudence of these people! They know very well this family's view of their cohabitation, and yet they keep coming here."

"If you pay attention to every prejudice," said Samoilenko, "you won't be able to go anywhere."

"Is the loathing of the masses for licentiousness and love outside marriage a prejudice?"

"Of course. Prejudice and hatefulness. When soldiers see a girl of light behavior, they guffaw and whistle, but ask them what they are themselves."

"It's not for nothing that they whistle. That sluts strangle their illegitimate children and go to hard labor, and that Anna Karenina threw herself under a train, and that they tar people's gates in the villages, and that you and I, for some unknown reason, like Katya's purity, and that everyone vaguely feels the need for pure love, though he knows that such love doesn't exist—is all that a prejudice? That, brother, is all that's left of natural selection, and if it weren't for this obscure force that regulates relations between the sexes, the Messers Laevsky would show us what o'clock it is, and mankind would turn degenerate in two years."

Laevsky came into the drawing room; he greeted everyone and, shaking von Koren's hand, gave him an ingratiating smile. He waited for an opportune moment and said to Samoilenko:

"Excuse me, Alexander Davidych, I must have a couple of words with you."

Samoilenko got up, put his arm around his waist, and the two went to Nikodim Alexandrych's study.

"Tomorrow is Friday . . ." said Laevsky, biting his nails. "Did you get what you promised?"

"I got only two hundred and ten. I'll get the rest today or tomorrow. Don't worry."

"Thank God! . . ." sighed Laevsky, and his hands trembled with joy. "You are saving me, Alexander Davidych, and, I swear to you by God, by my happiness, and by whatever you like, I'll send you this money as soon as I get there. And the old debt as well."

"Look here, Vanya . . ." said Samoilenko, taking him by a button and blushing. "Excuse me for interfering in your

family affairs, but . . . why don't you take Nadezhda Fyodorovna with you?"

"You odd fellow, how could I? One of us certainly has to
stay, otherwise my creditors will start howling. I owe some
seven hundred roubles in various shops, if not more. Wait,
I'll send them the money, stick it in their teeth, and then she
can leave here."

"Well . . . But why don't you send her on ahead?"

"Ah, my God, how can I?" Laevsky was horrified. "She's
a woman, what will she do there alone? What does she
understand? It would just be a loss of time and an unnecessary
waste of money."

"Reasonable . . ." thought Samoilenko, but he remembered his conversation with von Koren, looked down, and
said sullenly:

"I can't agree with you. Either go with her or send her
on ahead, otherwise . . . otherwise I won't give you the
money. That is my final word . . ."

He backed up, collided with the door, and went out into
the drawing room red-faced, in terrible embarrassment.

"Friday . . . Friday," thought Laevsky, returning to the
drawing room. "Friday . . ."

He was handed a cup of chocolate. He burned his lips and
tongue with the hot chocolate and thought:

"Friday . . . Friday . . ."

For some reason, he could not get the word "Friday" out
of his head; he thought of nothing but Friday, and the only
thing clear to him, not in his head but somewhere under his
heart, was that he was not to leave on Saturday. Before him
stood Nikodim Alexandrych, neat, his hair brushed forward
on his temples, and begging him:

"Eat something, I humbly beg you, sir . . ."

Marya Konstantinovna showed her guests Katya's grades,
saying in a drawn-out manner:

"Nowadays it's terribly, terribly difficult to study! So many requirements . . ."

"Mama!" moaned Katya, not knowing where to hide from embarrassment and praise.

Laevsky also looked at her grades and praised her. Bible studies, Russian, conduct, A's and B's began leaping in his eyes, and all of it, together with the importunate Friday, Nikodim Alexandrych's brushed-up temples, and Katya's red cheeks, stood before him as such boundless, invincible boredom that he almost cried out in despair and asked himself: "Can it be, can it be that I won't leave?"

They set two card tables next to each other and sat down to play postman's knock. Laevsky also sat down.

"Friday . . . Friday . . ." he thought, smiling and taking a pencil from his pocket. "Friday . . ."

He wanted to think over his situation and was afraid to think. It frightened him to admit that the doctor had caught him in the deception he had so long and so thoroughly concealed from himself. Each time he thought of his future, he did not give free rein to his thoughts. He would get on the train and go—that solved the problem of his life, and he did not let his thoughts go any further. Like a faint, far-off light in a field, from time to time the thought glimmered in his head that somewhere, in one of Petersburg's lanes, in the distant future, in order to break with Nadezhda Fyodorovna and pay his debts, he would have to resort to a small lie. He would lie only once, and then a complete renewal would come. And that was good: at the cost of a small lie, he would buy a big truth.

Now, though, when the doctor crudely hinted at the deceit by his refusal, it became clear to him that he would need the lie not only in the distant future but today, and tomorrow, and in a month, and maybe even to the end of his life. Indeed, in order to leave, he would have to lie to Nadezhda Fyodorovna, his creditors, and his superiors; then, in order to get money in Petersburg, he would have to lie to his mother and tell her he had already broken with Nadezhda Fyodorovna; and his mother would not give him more than five hundred roubles—meaning that he had already deceived the doctor, because he would not be able to send him the money soon. Then, when Nadezhda Fyodorovna came to Petersburg, he would have to resort to a whole series of small and large deceptions in order to break with her; and again there would be tears, boredom, a hateful life, remorse, and thus no renewal at all. Deception and nothing more. A whole mountain of lies grew in Laevsky's imagination. To leap over it at one jump, and not lie piecemeal, he would have to resolve upon a stiff measure—for instance, without saying a word, to get up from his place, put on his hat, and leave straightaway without money, without a word said, but Laevsky felt that this was impossible for him.

"Friday, Friday . . ." he thought. "Friday . . ."

They wrote notes, folded them in two, and put them in Nikodim Alexandrych's old top hat, and when enough notes had accumulated, Kostya, acting as postman, went around the table handing them out. The deacon, Katya, and Kostya, who received funny notes and tried to write something funny, were delighted.

"We must have a talk," Nadezhda Fyodorovna read in her note. She exchanged glances with Marya Konstantinovna, who gave her almond-butter smile and nodded her head.

"What is there to talk about?" thought Nadezhda Fyodorovna. "If it's impossible to tell everything, there's no point in talking."

Before going to the party, she had tied Laevsky's necktie, and this trifling thing had filled her soul with tenderness and sorrow. The anxiety on his face, his absentminded gazes, his paleness, and the incomprehensible change that had come over him lately, and the fact that she was keeping a terrible, repulsive secret from him, and that her hands had trembled as she tied his necktie—all this, for some reason, told her that they would not be living together for long. She gazed at him as at an icon, with fear and repentance, and thought: "Forgive me, forgive me . . ." Atchmianov sat across the table from her and did not tear his black, amorous eyes from her; desires stirred her, she was ashamed of herself and feared that even anguish and sorrow would not keep her from yielding to the impure passion, if not today, then tomorrow, and that, like a drunkard on a binge, she was no longer able to stop.

So as not to prolong this life, which was disgraceful for her and insulting to Laevsky, she decided to leave. She would tearfully implore him to let her go, and if he objected, she would leave him secretly. She would not tell him what had happened. Let him preserve a pure memory of her.

"Love you, love you, love you," she read. This was from Atchmianov.

She would live somewhere in a remote place, work, and send Laevsky, "from an unknown person," money, embroidered shirts, tobacco, and go back to him only in his old age or in case he became dangerously ill and needed a sick nurse. When, in his old age, he learned the reasons why she had refused to be his wife and had left him, he would appreciate her sacrifice and forgive her.

"You have a long nose." That must be from the deacon or from Kostya.

Nadezhda Fyodorovna imagined how, in saying good-bye to Laevsky, she would hug him tight, kiss his hand, and swear to love him all, all her life, and later, living in a remote place, among strangers, she would think every day that she had a friend somewhere, a beloved man, pure, noble, and lofty, who preserved a pure memory of her.

"If tonight you don't arrange to meet me, I shall take measures, I assure you on my word of honor. One does not treat decent people this way, you must understand that." This was from Kirilin.

XIII

LAEVSKY RECEIVED TWO NOTES; he unfolded one and read: "Don't go away, my dear heart."

"Who could have written that?" he wondered. "Not Samoilenko, of course... And not the deacon, since he doesn't know I want to leave. Von Koren, maybe?"

The zoologist was bent over the table, drawing a pyramid. It seemed to Laevsky that his eyes were smiling.

"Samoilenko probably blabbed..." thought Laevsky.

The other note, written in the same affected handwriting, with long tails and flourishes, read: "Somebody's not leaving on Saturday."

"Stupid jeering," thought Laevsky. "Friday, Friday..."

Something rose in his throat. He touched his collar and coughed, but instead of coughing, laughter burst from his throat.

"Ha, ha, ha!" he guffawed. "Ha, ha, ha!" ("Why am I doing this?" he wondered.) "Ha, ha, ha!"

He tried to control himself, covered his mouth with his hand, but his chest and neck were choking with laughter, and his hand could not cover his mouth.

"How stupid this is, though!" he thought, rocking with laughter. "Have I lost my mind, or what?"

His laughter rose higher and higher and turned into something like a lapdog's yelping. Laevsky wanted to get up from the table, but his legs would not obey him, and his right hand somehow strangely, against his will, leaped across the table, convulsively catching at pieces of paper and clutching them. He saw astonished looks, the serious, frightened face of Samoilenko, and the zoologist's gaze, full of cold mockery and squeamishness, and realized that he was having hysterics.

"How grotesque, how shameful," he thought, feeling the

warmth of tears on his face. "Ah, ah, what shame! This has never happened to me before..."

Then they took him under the arms and, supporting his head from behind, led him somewhere; then a glass gleamed in front of his eyes and knocked against his teeth, and water spilled on his chest; then there was a small room, two beds side by side in the middle, covered with snow-white bedspreads. He collapsed onto one of the beds and broke into sobs.

"Never mind, never mind..." Samoilenko was saying. "It happens... It happens..."

Cold with fear, trembling all over, and anticipating something terrible, Nadezhda Fyodorovna stood by the bed, asking:

"What's wrong with you? What is it? For God's sake, speak..."

"Can Kirilin have written him something?" she wondered.

"Never mind..." said Laevsky, laughing and crying. "Go away... my dove."

His face expressed neither hatred nor revulsion: that meant he knew nothing. Nadezhda Fyodorovna calmed down a little and went to the drawing room.

"Don't worry, dear!" Marya Konstantinovna said, sitting down beside her and taking her hand. "It will pass. Men are as weak as we sinners. The two of you are living through a crisis now... it's so understandable! Well, dear, I'm waiting for an answer. Let's talk."

"No, let's not..." said Nadezhda Fyodorovna, listening to Laevsky's sobbing. "I'm in anguish... Allow me to leave."

"Ah, my dear, my dear!" Marya Konstantinovna was alarmed. "Do you think I'll let you go without supper? We'll have a bite, and then you're free to leave."

"I'm in anguish..." whispered Nadezhda Fyodorovna, and to keep from falling, she gripped the armrest of the chair with both hands.

"He's in convulsions!" von Koren said gaily, coming into the drawing room, but, seeing Nadezhda Fyodorovna, he became embarrassed and left.

When the hysterics were over, Laevsky sat on the strange bed and thought:

"Disgrace, I howled like a little girl! I must be ridiculous and vile. I'll leave by the back stairs . . . Though that would mean I attach serious significance to my hysterics. I ought to downplay them like a joke . . ."

He looked in the mirror, sat for a little while, and went to the drawing room.

"Here I am!" he said, smiling; he was painfully ashamed, and he felt that the others were also ashamed in his presence. "Imagine that," he said, taking a seat. "I was sitting there and suddenly, you know, I felt an awful, stabbing pain in my side . . . unbearable, my nerves couldn't stand it, and . . . and this stupid thing occurred. This nervous age of ours, there's nothing to be done!"

Over supper he drank wine, talked, and from time to time, sighing spasmodically, stroked his side as if to show that the pain could still be felt. And nobody except Nadezhda Fyodorovna believed him, and he saw it.

After nine o'clock they went for a stroll on the boulevard. Nadezhda Fyodorovna, fearing that Kirilin might start talking to her, tried to keep near Marya Konstantinovna and the children all the time. She grew weak from fright and anguish and, anticipating a fever, suffered and could barely move her legs, but she would not go home, because she was sure that either Kirilin or Atchmianov, or both of them, would follow her. Kirilin walked behind her, next to Nikodim Alexandrych, and intoned in a low voice:

"I will not alo-o-ow myself to be to-o-oyed with! I will not alo-o-ow it!"

From the boulevard they turned towards the pavilion, and

for a long time gazed at the phosphorescent sea. Von Koren began to explain what made it phosphoresce.

XIV

"HOWEVER, IT'S TIME for my vint... They're waiting for me," said Laevsky. "Good night, ladies and gentlemen."

"Wait, I'll go with you," said Nadezhda Fyodorovna, and she took his arm. They took leave of the company and walked off. Kirilin also took his leave, said he was going the same way, and walked with them.

"What will be, will be..." thought Nadezhda Fyodorovna. "Let it come..."

It seemed to her that all her bad memories had left her head and were walking in the darkness beside her and breathing heavily, while she herself, like a fly that had fallen into ink, forced herself to crawl down the sidewalk, staining Laevsky's side and arm with black. If Kirilin does something bad, she thought, it will not be his fault, but hers alone. There was a time when no man would have talked to her as Kirilin had done, and she herself had snapped off that time like a thread and destroyed it irretrievably—whose fault was that? Intoxicated by her own desires, she had begun to smile at a totally unknown man, probably only because he was stately and tall, after two meetings she had become bored with him and had dropped him, and didn't that, she now thought, give him the right to act as he pleased with her?

"Here, my dove, I'll say good-bye to you," said Laevsky, stopping. "Ilya Mikhailych will see you home."

He bowed to Kirilin and quickly headed across the boulevard, went down the street to Sheshkovsky's house, where there were lights in the windows, and then they heard the gate slam.

"Allow me to explain myself to you," Kirilin began. "I'm

194

not a boy, not some sort of Atchkasov, or Latchkasov, or Zatchkasov . . . I demand serious attention!"

Nadezhda Fyodorovna's heart was beating fast. She made no reply.

"At first I explained the abrupt change in your behavior towards me by coquetry," Kirilin went on, "but now I see that you simply do not know how to behave with respectable people. You simply wanted to toy with me as with this Armenian boy, but I am a respectable person, and I demand to be treated as a respectable person. And so I am at your service . . ."

"I'm in anguish . . ." said Nadezhda Fyodorovna, and she turned away to hide her tears.

"I am also in anguish, but what follows from that?"

Kirilin was silent for a while and then said distinctly, measuredly:

"I repeat, madam, that if you do not grant me a meeting tonight, then tonight I shall make a scandal."

"Let me go tonight," said Nadezhda Fyodorovna, and she did not recognize her own voice, so pathetic and thin it was.

"I must teach you a lesson . . . Forgive me this rude tone, but it's necessary for me to teach you a lesson. Yes, ma'am, unfortunately I must teach you a lesson. I demand two meetings: tonight and tomorrow. After tomorrow you are completely free and can go wherever you like with whomever you like. Tonight and tomorrow."

Nadezhda Fyodorovna went up to her gate and stopped.

"Let me go!" she whispered, trembling all over and seeing nothing before her in the darkness except a white tunic. "You're right, I'm a terrible woman . . . I'm to blame, but let me go . . . I beg you . . ." she touched his cold hand and shuddered, "I implore you . . ."

"Alas!" sighed Kirilin. "Alas! It is not in my plans to let you go, I merely want to teach you a lesson, to make you understand, and besides, madam, I have very little faith in women."

"I'm in anguish..."

Nadezhda Fyodorovna listened to the steady sound of the sea, looked at the sky strewn with stars, and wished she could end it all quickly and be rid of this cursed sensation of life with its sea, stars, men, fever...

"Only not in my house..." she said coldly. "Take me somewhere."

"Let's go to Miuridov's. That's best."

"Where is it?"

"By the old ramparts."

She walked quickly down the street and then turned into a lane that led to the mountains. It was dark. On the pavement here and there lay pale strips of light from lighted windows, and it seemed to her that she was like a fly that first fell into ink, then crawled out again into the light. Kirilin walked behind her. At one point he stumbled, nearly fell, and laughed.

"He's drunk..." thought Nadezhda Fyodorovna. "It's all the same... all the same... Let it be."

Atchmianov also soon took leave of the company and followed Nadezhda Fyodorovna so as to invite her for a boat ride. He went up to her house and looked across the front garden: the windows were wide open, there was no light.

"Nadezhda Fyodorovna!" he called.

A minute passed. He called again.

"Who's there?" came Olga's voice.

"Is Nadezhda Fyodorovna at home?"

"No. She hasn't come yet."

"Strange... Very strange," thought Atchmianov, beginning to feel greatly worried. "She did go home..."

He strolled along the boulevard, then down the street, and looked in Sheshkovsky's windows. Laevsky, without his frock coat, was sitting at the table and looking intently at his cards.

"Strange, strange..." murmured Atchmianov, and, recollecting the hysterics that had come over Laevsky, he felt ashamed. "If she's not at home, where is she?"

And again he went to Nadezhda Fyodorovna's apartment and looked at the dark windows.

"Deceit, deceit . . ." he thought, remembering that she herself, on meeting him that noon at the Bitiugovs', had promised to go for a boat ride with him in the evening.

The windows of the house where Kirilin lived were dark, and a policeman sat asleep on a bench by the gate. As he looked at the windows and the policeman, everything became clear to Atchmianov. He decided to go home and went, but again wound up by Nadezhda Fyodorovna's. There he sat down on a bench and took off his hat, feeling his head burning with jealousy and offense.

The clock on the town church struck only twice a day, at noon and at midnight. Soon after it struck midnight, he heard hurrying footsteps.

"So, tomorrow evening at Miuridov's again!" Atchmianov heard, and recognized Kirilin's voice. "At eight o'clock. Good-bye, ma'am!"

Nadezhda Fyodorovna appeared by the front garden. Not noticing Atchmianov sitting on the bench, she walked past him like a shadow, opened the gate, and, leaving it open, walked into the house. In her room, she lighted a candle, undressed quickly, yet did not go to bed, but sank onto her knees in front of a chair, put her arms around it, and leaned her forehead against it.

Laevsky came home past two o'clock.

XV

HAVING DECIDED NOT to lie all at once, but piecemeal, Laevsky went to Samoilenko the next day after one o'clock to ask for the money, so as to be sure to leave on Saturday. After yesterday's hysterics, which to the painful state of his mind had added an acute sense of shame, remaining in town was unthinkable. If Samoilenko insists on his conditions, he thought, he could agree to them and take the money, and tomorrow, just at the time of departure, tell him that Nadezhda Fyodorovna had refused to go; he could persuade her in the evening that the whole thing was being done for her benefit. And if Samoilenko, who was obviously under the influence of von Koren, refused entirely or suggested some new conditions, then he, Laevsky, would leave that same day on a freighter or even a sailboat, for Novy Afon or Novorossiisk, send his mother a humiliating telegram from there, and live there until his mother sent him money for the trip.

Coming to Samoilenko's, he found von Koren in the drawing room. The zoologist had just come for dinner and, as usual, had opened the album and was studying the men in top hats and women in caps.

"How inopportune," thought Laevsky, seeing him. "He may hinder everything."

"Good afternoon!"

"Good afternoon," replied von Koren without looking at him.

"Is Alexander Davidych at home?"

"Yes. In the kitchen."

Laevsky went to the kitchen, but, seeing through the doorway that Samoilenko was busy with the salad, he returned to the drawing room and sat down. He always felt awkward in the zoologist's presence, and now he was afraid he would have to talk about his hysterics. More than a minute passed in silence. Von Koren suddenly raised his eyes to Laevsky and asked:

"How do you feel after yesterday?"

"Splendid," Laevsky replied, blushing. "Essentially there was nothing very special . . ."

"Until last night I assumed that only ladies had hysterics, and so I thought at first that what you had was Saint Vitus's dance."

Laevsky smiled ingratiatingly and thought:

"How indelicate on his part. He knows perfectly well that it's painful for me . . ."

"Yes, it was a funny story," he said, still smiling. "I spent this whole morning laughing. The curious thing about a fit of hysterics is that you know it's absurd, and you laugh at it in your heart, and at the same time you're sobbing. In our nervous age, we're slaves to our nerves; they're our masters and do whatever they like with us. In this respect, civilization is a dubious blessing . . ."

Laevsky talked, and found it unpleasant that von Koren listened to him seriously and attentively, and looked at him attentively, without blinking, as if studying him; and he felt vexed with himself for being unable, despite all his dislike of von Koren, to drive the ingratiating smile from his face.

"Though I must confess," he went on, "there were more immediate causes of the fit, and rather substantial ones. My health has been badly shaken lately. Add to that the boredom, the constant lack of money . . . the lack of people and common interests . . . My situation's worse than a governor's."

"Yes, your situation's hopeless," said von Koren.

These calm, cold words, containing either mockery or an uninvited prophecy, offended Laevsky. He remembered the zoologist's gaze yesterday, full of mockery and squeamishness, paused briefly, and asked, no longer smiling:

"And how are you informed of my situation?"

"You've just been talking about it yourself, and your friends take such a warm interest in you that one hears of nothing but you all day long."

"What friends? Samoilenko, is it?"

"Yes, him, too."

"I'd ask Alexander Davidych and my friends generally to be less concerned about me."

"Here comes Samoilenko, ask him to be less concerned about you."

"I don't understand your tone..." Laevsky murmured; he was gripped by such a feeling as though he had only now understood that the zoologist hated him, despised and jeered at him, and that the zoologist was his worst and most implacable enemy. "Save that tone for somebody else," he said softly, unable to speak loudly from the hatred that was already tightening around his chest and neck, as the desire to laugh had done yesterday.

Samoilenko came in without his frock coat, sweaty and crimson from the stuffiness of the kitchen.

"Ah, you're here?" he said. "Greetings, dear heart. Have you had dinner? Don't be ceremonious, tell me: have you had dinner?"

"Alexander Davidych," said Laevsky, getting up, "if I turned to you with an intimate request, it did not mean I was releasing you from the obligation of being modest and respecting other people's secrets."

"What's wrong?" Samoilenko was surprised.

"If you don't have the money," Laevsky went on, raising his voice and shifting from one foot to the other in agitation, "then don't give it to me, refuse, but why announce on every street corner that my situation is hopeless and all that? I cannot bear these benefactions and friendly services when one does a kopeck's worth with a rouble's worth of talk! You may boast of your benefactions as much as you like, but no one gave you the right to reveal my secrets!"

"What secrets?" asked Samoilenko, perplexed and beginning to get angry. "If you came to abuse me, go away. You can come later!"

He remembered the rule that, when angry with your neighbor, you should mentally start counting to a hundred and calm down; and he started counting quickly.

"I beg you not to be concerned about me!" Laevsky went on. "Don't pay attention to me. And who has any business with me and how I live? Yes, I want to go away! Yes, I run up debts, drink, live with another man's wife, I'm hysterical, I'm banal, I'm not as profound as some are, but whose business is that? Respect the person!"

"Excuse me, brother," said Samoilenko, having counted up to thirty-five, "but..."

"Respect the person!" Laevsky interrupted him. "This constant talk on another man's account, the ohs and ahs, the constant sniffing out, the eavesdropping, these friendly commiserations...devil take it! They lend me money and set conditions as if I was a little boy! I'm treated like the devil knows what! I don't want anything!" cried Laevsky, reeling with agitation and fearing he might have hysterics again. "So I won't leave on Saturday," flashed through his mind. "I don't want anything! I only beg you, please, to deliver me from your care! I'm not a little boy and not a madman, and I beg you to relieve me of this supervision!"

The deacon came in and, seeing Laevsky, pale, waving his arms, and addressing his strange speech to the portrait of Prince Vorontsov, stopped by the door as if rooted to the spot.

"This constant peering into my soul," Laevsky went on, "offends my human dignity, and I beg the volunteer detectives to stop their spying! Enough!"

"What...what did you say, sir?" asked Samoilenko, having counted to a hundred, turning purple, and going up to Laevsky.

"Enough!" said Laevsky, gasping and taking his cap.

"I am a Russian doctor, a nobleman, and a state councillor!" Samoilenko said measuredly. "I have never been a spy, and I will not allow anyone to insult me!" he said in a cracked voice, emphasizing the last words. "Silence!"

The deacon, who had never seen the doctor so majestic, puffed up, crimson, and fearsome, covered his mouth, ran out to the front room, and there rocked with laughter. As if through a fog, Laevsky saw von Koren get up and, putting his hands in his trouser pockets, stand in that pose as if waiting for what would happen next. Laevsky found this relaxed pose insolent and offensive in the highest degree.

"Kindly take back your words!" cried Samoilenko.

Laevsky, who no longer remembered what words he had spoken, answered:

"Leave me alone! I don't want anything! All I want is that you and these Germans of Yid extraction leave me alone! Otherwise I'll take measures! I'll fight!"

"Now I see," said von Koren, stepping away from the table. "Mr. Laevsky wants to divert himself with a duel before his departure. I can give him that satisfaction. Mr. Laevsky, I accept your challenge."

"My challenge?" Laevsky said softly, going up to the zoologist and looking with hatred at his swarthy forehead and curly hair. "My challenge? If you please! I hate you! Hate you!"

"Very glad. Tomorrow morning early, by Kerbalai's, with all the details to your taste. And now get out of here."

"I hate you!" Laevsky said softly, breathing heavily. "I've hated you for a long time! A duel! Yes!"

"Take him away, Alexander Davidych, or else I'll leave," said von Koren. "He's going to bite me."

Von Koren's calm tone cooled the doctor down; he somehow suddenly came to himself, recovered his senses, put his arm around Laevsky's waist, and, leading him away from the zoologist, mumured in a gentle voice, trembling with agitation:

"My friends . . . good, kind friends . . . You got excited, but that will do . . . that will do . . . My friends . . ."

Hearing his soft, friendly voice, Laevsky felt that something unprecedented and monstrous had just taken place in his life, as if he had nearly been run over by a train; he almost burst into tears, waved his hand, and rushed from the room.

"To experience another man's hatred of you, to show yourself in the most pathetic, despicable, helpless way before the man who hates you—my God, how painful it is!" he thought shortly afterwards, sitting in the pavilion and feeling something like rust on his body from the just experienced hatred of another man. "How crude it is, my God!"

Cold water with cognac cheered him up. He clearly pictured von Koren's calm, haughty face, his gaze yesterday, his carpetlike shirt, his voice, his white hands, and a heavy hatred, passionate and hungry, stirred in his breast and demanded satisfaction. In his mind, he threw von Koren to the ground and started trampling him with his feet. He recalled everything that had happened in the minutest detail, and wondered how he could smile ingratiatingly at a nonentity and generally value the opinion of petty little people, unknown to anyone, who lived in a worthless town which, it seemed, was not even on the map and which not a single decent person in Petersburg knew about. If this wretched little town were suddenly to fall through the earth or burn down, people in Russia would read the telegram about it with the same boredom as the announcement of a sale of secondhand furniture. To kill von Koren tomorrow or leave him alive was in any case equally useless and uninteresting. To shoot him in the leg or arm, to wound him, then laugh at him, and, as an insect with a torn-off leg gets lost in the grass, so let him with his dull suffering lose himself afterwards in a crowd of the same nonentities as himself.

Laevsky went to Sheshkovsky, told him about it all, and invited him to be his second; then they both went to the head of the post and telegraph office, invited him to be a second as well, and stayed with him for dinner. At dinner they joked and laughed a great deal; Laevsky made fun of the fact that he barely knew how to shoot, and called himself a royal marksman and a Wilhelm Tell.

"This gentleman must be taught a lesson..." he kept saying.

After dinner they sat down to play cards. Laevsky played,

drank wine, and thought how generally stupid and senseless dueling was, because it did not solve the problem but only complicated it, but that sometimes one could not do without it. For instance, in the present case, he could not plead about von Koren before the justice of the peace! And the impending duel was also good in that, after it, he would no longer be able to stay in town. He became slightly drunk, diverted himself with cards, and felt good.

But when the sun set and it grew dark, uneasiness came over him. It was not the fear of death, because all the while he was having dinner and playing cards, the conviction sat in him, for some reason, that the duel would end in nothing; it was a fear of something unknown, which was to take place tomorrow morning for the first time in his life, and a fear of the coming night . . . He knew that the night would be long, sleepless, and that he would have to think not only about von Koren and his hatred but about that mountain of lies he would have to pass through and which he had neither the strength nor the ability to avoid. It looked as though he had unexpectedly fallen ill; he suddenly lost all interest in cards and people, began fussing, and asked to be allowed to go home. He wanted to go to bed quickly, lie still, and prepare his thoughts for the night. Sheshkovsky and the postal official saw him off and went to von Koren to talk about the duel.

Near his apartment, Laevsky met Atchmianov. The young man was breathless and agitated.

"I've been looking for you, Ivan Andreich!" he said. "I beg you, let's go quickly . . ."

"Where?"

"A gentleman you don't know wishes to see you on very important business. He earnestly requests that you come for a moment. He needs to talk to you about something . . . For him it's the same as life and death . . ."

In his excitement, Atchmianov uttered this with a strong Armenian accent, so that it came out not "life" but "lafe."

"Who is he?" asked Laevsky.

"He asked me not to give his name."

"Tell him I'm busy. Tomorrow, if he likes..."

"Impossible!" Atchmianov became frightened. "He wishes to tell you something very important for you... very important! If you don't go, there will be a disaster."

"Strange..." murmured Laevsky, not understanding why Atchmianov was so agitated and what mysteries there could be in this boring, useless little town. "Strange," he repeated, pondering. "However, let's go. It makes no difference."

Atchmianov quickly went ahead, and he followed. They walked down the street, then into a lane.

"How boring this is," said Laevsky.

"One moment, one moment... It's close by."

Near the old ramparts they took a narrow lane between two fenced lots, then entered some big yard and made for a little house.

"That's Miuridov's house, isn't it?" asked Laevsky.

"Yes."

"But why we came through the back alleys, I don't understand. We could have taken the street. It's closer."

"Never mind, never mind..."

Laevsky also found it strange that Atchmianov led him to the back door and waved his hand as if asking him to walk softly and keep silent.

"This way, this way..." said Atchmianov, cautiously opening the door and going into the hallway on tiptoe. "Quiet, quiet, I beg you... They may hear you."

He listened, drew a deep breath, and said in a whisper:

"Open this door and go in... Don't be afraid."

Laevsky, perplexed, opened the door and went into a room with a low ceiling and curtained windows. A candle stood on the table.

"Whom do you want?" someone asked in the next room. "Is that you, Miuridka?"

ANTON CHEKHOV

Laevsky turned to that room and saw Kirilin, and beside him Nadezhda Fyodorovna.

He did not hear what was said to him, backed his way out, and did not notice how he ended up in the street. The hatred of von Koren, and the uneasiness—all of it vanished from his soul. Going home, he awkwardly swung his right arm and looked intently under his feet, trying to walk where it was even. At home, in his study, he paced up and down, rubbing his hands and making angular movements with his shoulders and neck, as though his jacket and shirt were too tight for him, then lighted a candle and sat down at the table . . .

XVI

"THE HUMANE SCIENCES, of which you speak, will only satisfy human thought when, in their movement, they meet the exact sciences and go on alongside them. Whether they will meet under a microscope, or in the soliloquies of a new Hamlet, or in a new religion, I don't know, but I think that the earth will be covered with an icy crust before that happens. The most staunch and vital of all humanitarian doctrines is, of course, the teaching of Christ, but look at how differently people understand even that! Some teach us to love all our neighbors, but at the same time make an exception for soldiers, criminals, and madmen: the first they allow to be killed in war, the second to be isolated or executed, and the third they forbid to marry. Other inter-preters teach the love of all our neighbors without exception, without distinguishing between pluses and minuses. Accord-ing to their teaching, if a consumptive or a murderer or an epileptic comes to you and wants to marry your daughter—give her to him; if cretins declare war on the physically and mentally healthy—offer your heads. This preaching of love

206

for love's sake, like art for art's sake, if it could come to power, in the end would lead mankind to total extinction, and thus the most grandiose villainy of all that have ever been done on earth would be accomplished. There are a great many interpretations, and if there are many, then serious thought cannot be satisfied by any one of them, and to the mass of all interpretations hastens to add its own. Therefore never put the question, as you say, on philosophical or so-called Christian grounds; by doing so, you merely get further away from solving it."

The deacon listened attentively to the zoologist, pondered, and asked:

"Was the moral law, which is proper to each and every person, invented by philosophers, or did God create it along with the body?"

"I don't know. But this law is common to all peoples and epochs to such a degree that it seems to me it ought to be acknowledged as organically connected with man. It hasn't been invented, but is and will be. I won't tell you that it will one day be seen under a microscope, but its organic connection is proved by the evidence: serious afflictions of the brain and all so-called mental illnesses, as far as I know, express themselves first of all in a perversion of the moral law."

"Very well, sir. Meaning that, as the stomach wants to eat, so the moral sense wants us to love our neighbor. Right? But our nature, being selfish, resists the voice of conscience and reason, and therefore many brain-racking questions arise. To whom should we turn for the solution of these questions, if you tell me not to put them on philosophical grounds?"

"Turn to the little precise knowledge we have. Trust the evidence and the logic of facts. True, it's scanty, but then it's not as flimsy and diffuse as philosophy. Let's say the moral law demands that you love people. What, then? Love should consist in renouncing everything that harms people in one way or another and threatens them with danger in the present and the future. Our knowledge and the evidence tell you that mankind is threatened by danger on the part of the morally and physically abnormal. If so, then fight with the abnormal. If you're unable to raise them to the norm, you should have enough strength and skill to render them harmless, that is, destroy them."

"So love consists in the strong overcoming the weak."

"Undoubtedly."

"But it was the strong who crucified our Lord Jesus Christ!" the deacon said hotly.

"The point is precisely that it was not the strong who crucified Him but the weak. Human culture has weakened and strives to nullify the struggle for existence and natural selection; hence the rapid proliferation of the weak and their predominance over the strong. Imagine that you manage to instill humane ideas, in an undeveloped, rudimentary form, into bees. What would come of it? The drones, which must be killed, would remain alive, would eat the honey, would corrupt and stifle the bees—the result being that the weak would prevail over the strong, and the latter would degenerate. The same is now happening with mankind: the weak oppress the strong. Among savages, still untouched by culture, the strongest, the wisest, and the most moral goes to the front; he is the leader and master. While we, the cultured, crucified Christ and go on crucifying Him. It means we lack something... And we must restore that 'something' in ourselves, otherwise there will be no end to these misunderstandings."

"But what is your criterion for distinguishing between the strong and the weak?"

"Knowledge and evidence. The consumptive and the scrofulous are recognized by their ailments, and the immoral and mad by their acts."

"But mistakes are possible!"

"Yes, but there's no use worrying about getting your feet wet when there's the threat of a flood."

"That's philosophy," laughed the deacon.

"Not in the least. You're so spoiled by your seminary philosophy that you want to see nothing but fog in everything. The abstract science your young head is stuffed with is called abstract because it abstracts your mind from the evidence. Look the devil straight in the eye, and if he is the devil, say so, and don't go to Kant or Hegel for explanations."

The zoologist paused and went on:

"Two times two is four, and a stone is a stone. Tomorrow we've got a duel. You and I are going to say it's stupid and absurd, that dueling has outlived its time, that an aristocratic duel is essentially no different from a drunken brawl in a pot-house, and even so, we won't stop, we'll go and fight. There is, therefore, a power that is stronger than our reasonings. We shout that war is banditry, barbarism, horror, fratricide, we cannot look at blood without fainting; but the French or the Germans need only insult us and we at once feel a surge of inspiration, we most sincerely shout 'hurrah' and fall upon the enemy, you will call for God's blessing on our weapons, and our valor will evoke universal, and withal sincere, rapture. So again, there is a power that is if not higher, then stronger, than us and our philosophy. We can no more stop it than we can stop this storm cloud moving in from over the sea. Don't be a hypocrite, then, don't show it a fig in the pocket, and don't say: 'Ah, how stupid! Ah, how outdated! Ah, it doesn't agree with the Scriptures!' but look it straight in the eye, acknowledge its reasonable legitimacy, and when it wants, for instance, to destroy the feeble, scrofulous, depraved tribe, don't hinder it with your pills and quotations from the poorly understood Gospel. In Leskov there's a conscientious Danila,[28] who finds a leper outside of town and feeds him and keeps him warm in the name of love and Christ. If this Danila indeed loved people, he would have dragged the leper further away from the town and thrown him into a ditch, and would have gone himself and served the healthy. Christ, I hope, gave us the commandment of reasonable, sensible, and useful love."

"What a one you are!" laughed the deacon. "You don't believe in Christ, so why do you mention Him so often?"

"No, I do believe. Only in my own way, of course, not in yours. Ah, Deacon, Deacon!" the zoologist laughed; he put his arm around the deacon's waist and said gaily: "Well, what then? Shall we go to the duel tomorrow?"

"My dignity doesn't permit it, otherwise I would."

"And what does that mean—'dignity'?"

"I've been ordained. Grace is upon me."

"Ah, Deacon, Deacon," von Koren repeated, laughing. "I love talking with you."

"You say you have faith," said the deacon. "What kind of faith is it? I have an uncle, a priest, who is such a believer that, if there's a drought and he goes to the fields to ask for rain, he takes an umbrella and a leather coat so that he won't get wet on the way back. That's faith! When he talks about Christ, he gives off a glow, and all the peasants burst into sobs. He could stop this storm cloud and put all your powers to flight. Yes . . . faith moves mountains."

The deacon laughed and patted the zoologist on the shoulder.

"So there . . ." he went on. "You keep teaching, you fathom the depths of the sea, you sort out the weak and the strong, you write books and challenge to duels—and everything stays where it was; but watch out, let some feeble little elder babble one little word by the Holy Spirit, or a new Mohammed with a scimitar come riding out of Arabia on a stallion, and everything of yours will go flying topsy-turvy, and in Europe there will be no stone left upon stone."

"Well, Deacon, that's written in the sky with a pitchfork!"

"Faith without works is dead, but works without faith are worse still,[29] merely a waste of time and nothing more."

The doctor appeared on the embankment. He saw the deacon and the zoologist and went up to them.

"Everything seems to be ready," he said, out of breath. "Govorovsky and Boiko will be the seconds. They'll call at five o'clock in the morning. It's really piling up!" he said, looking at the sky. "Can't see a thing! It'll rain soon."

"You'll come with us, I hope?" asked von Koren.

"No, God forbid, I'm worn out as it is. Ustimovich will come in my place. I've already talked with him."

Far across the sea, lightning flashed, and there was a muffled roll of thunder.

"How stifling it is before a storm!" said von Koren. "I'll bet you've already been to Laevsky's and wept on his bosom."

"Why should I go to him?" the doctor said, embarrassed. "What an idea!"

Before sunset he had walked several times up and down the boulevard and the street, hoping to meet Laevsky. He was ashamed of his outburst and of the sudden kindly impulse that had followed the outburst. He wanted to apologize to Laevsky in jocular tones, to chide him, to placate him, and tell him that dueling was a leftover of medieval barbarism, but that providence itself had pointed them to a duel as a means of reconciliation: tomorrow the two of them, most excellent people, of the greatest intelligence, would exchange shots, appreciate each other's nobility, and become friends. But he never once met Laevsky.

"Why should I go to him?" Samoilenko repeated. "I didn't offend him, he offended me. Tell me, for mercy's sake, why did he fall upon me? Did I do anything bad to him? I come into the drawing room and suddenly, for no reason:

spy! Take that! Tell me, how did it start between you? What did you tell him?"

"I told him that his situation was hopeless. And I was right. Only honest people and crooks can find a way out of any situation, but somebody who wants to be an honest man and a crook at the same time has no way out. However, it's already eleven o'clock, gentlemen, and we have to get up early tomorrow."

There was a sudden gust of wind; it raised the dust on the embankment, whirled it around, roared, and drowned out the sound of the sea.

"A squall!" said the deacon. "We must go, we're getting dust in our eyes."

As they left, Samoilenko sighed and said, holding on to his cap:

"Most likely I won't sleep tonight."

"Don't worry," the zoologist laughed. "You can rest easy, the duel will end in nothing. Laevsky will magnanimously fire into the air, he can't do anything else, and most likely I won't fire at all. Ending up in court on account of Laevsky, losing time—the game's not worth the candle. By the way, what's the legal responsibility for dueling?"

"Arrest, and in case of the adversary's death, imprisonment in the fortress for up to three years."

"The Peter-and-Paul fortress?"[30]

"No, a military one, I think."

"I ought to teach that fellow a lesson, though!"

Behind them, lightning flashed over the sea and momentarily lit up the rooftops and mountains. Near the boulevard, the friends went different ways. As the doctor disappeared into the darkness and his footsteps were already dying away, von Koren shouted to him:

"The weather may hinder us tomorrow!"

"It may well! And God grant it!"

"Good night!"

"What—night? What did you say?"

It was hard to hear because of the noise of the wind and the sea and the rolling thunder.

"Never mind!" shouted the zoologist, and he hurried home.

XVII

> ... in my mind, oppressed by anguish,
> Crowds an excess of heavy thoughts;
> Remembrance speechlessly unrolls
> Its lengthy scroll before me;
> And, reading through my life with loathing,
> I tremble, curse, and bitterly complain,
> And bitter tears pour from my eyes,
> But the sad lines are not washed away.
>   —Pushkin[31]

Whether they killed him tomorrow morning or made a laughingstock of him, that is, left him to this life, in any case he was lost. Whether this disgraced woman killed herself in despair and shame or dragged out her pitiful existence, in any case she was lost...

So thought Laevsky, sitting at the table late at night and still rubbing his hands. The window suddenly opened with a bang, a strong wind burst into the room, and papers flew off the table. Laevsky closed the window and bent down to pick up the papers from the floor. He felt something new in his body, some sort of awkwardness that had not been there before, and he did not recognize his own movements; he walked warily, sticking out his elbows and jerking his shoulders, and when he sat down at the table, he again began rubbing his hands. His body had lost its suppleness.

On the eve of death, one must write to one's family.

Laevsky remembered that. He took up a pen and wrote in a shaky hand:

"Dear Mother!"

He wanted to write to his mother that, in the name of the merciful God in whom she believed, she should give shelter and the warmth of her tenderness to the unfortunate woman he had dishonored, lonely, poor, and weak; that she should forgive and forget everything, everything, everything, and with her sacrifice at least partially redeem her son's terrible sin; but he remembered how his mother, a stout, heavy old woman in a lace cap, went out to the garden in the morning, followed by a companion with a lapdog, how his mother shouted in a commanding voice at the gardener, at the servants, and how proud and arrogant her face was—he remembered it and crossed out the words he had written.

Lightning flashed brightly in all three windows, followed by a deafening, rolling clap of thunder, first muted, then rumbling and cracking, and so strong that the glass in the windows rattled. Laevsky got up, went to the window, and leaned his forehead against the glass. Outside there was a heavy, beautiful thunderstorm. On the horizon, lightning ceaselessly hurled itself in white ribbons from the clouds into the sea and lit up the high black waves far in the distance. Lightning flashed to right and left, and probably directly over the house as well.

"A thunderstorm!" whispered Laevsky; he felt a desire to pray to someone or something, if only to the lightning or the clouds. "Dear thunderstorm!"

He remembered how, in childhood, he had always run out to the garden bareheaded when there was a thunderstorm, and two fair-haired, blue-eyed little girls would chase after him, and the rain would drench them; they would laugh with delight, but when a strong clap of thunder rang out, the girls would press themselves trustfully to the boy, and he would cross himself and hasten to recite: "Holy, holy, holy . . ." Oh, where have you gone, in what sea have you drowned, you germs of a beautiful, pure life? He was no longer afraid of thunderstorms, did not love nature, had no God, all the trustful girls he had ever known had already been ruined by him or his peers, he had never planted a single tree in his own garden, nor grown a single blade of grass, and, living amidst the living, had never saved a single fly, but had only destroyed, ruined, and lied, lied . . .

"What in my past is not vice?" he kept asking himself, trying to clutch at some bright memory, as someone falling into an abyss clutches at a bush.

School? University? But that was a sham. He had been a poor student and had forgotten what he was taught. Serving society? That was also a sham, because he did nothing at work, received a salary gratis, and his service was a vile embezzlement for which one was not taken to court.

He had no need of the truth, and he was not seeking it; his conscience, beguiled by vice and lies, slept or was silent; like a foreigner, or an alien from another planet, he took no part in the common life of people, was indifferent to their sufferings, ideas, religions, knowledge, quests, struggles; he had not a single kind word for people, had never written a single useful, nonbanal line, had never done a groat's worth of anything for people, but only ate their bread, drank their wine, took away their wives, lived by their thoughts, and, to justify his contemptible, parasitic life before them and before himself, had always tried to make himself look higher and better than them . . . Lies, lies, lies . . .

He clearly recalled what he had seen that evening in Miuridov's house, and it gave him an unbearably creepy feeling of loathing and anguish. Kirilin and Atchmianov were disgusting, but they were merely continuing what he had begun; they were his accomplices and disciples. From a weak young woman who trusted him more than a brother, he had taken her husband, her circle of friends, and her native land, and had brought her here to the torrid heat, to fever, and to boredom;

day after day, like a mirror, she had had to reflect in herself his idleness, depravity, and lying—and that, that alone, had filled her weak, sluggish, pitiful life; then he had had enough of her, had begun to hate her, but had not had the courage to abandon her, and he had tried to entangle her in a tight mesh of lies, as in a spiderweb . . . These people had done the rest.

Laevsky now sat at the table, now went again to the window; now he put out the candle, now he lighted it again. He cursed himself aloud, wept, complained, asked forgiveness; several times he rushed to the desk in despair and wrote: "Dear Mother!"

Besides his mother, he had no family or relations; but how could his mother help him? And where was she? He wanted to rush to Nadezhda Fyodorovna, fall at her feet, kiss her hands and feet, beg for forgiveness, but she was his victim, and he was afraid of her, as if she was dead.

"My life is ruined!" he murmured, rubbing his hands. "Why am I still alive, my God! . . ."

He dislodged his own dim star from the sky, it fell, and its traces mingled with the night's darkness; it would never return to the sky, because life is given only once and is not repeated. If it had been possible to bring back the past days and years, he would have replaced the lies in them by truth, the idleness by work, the boredom by joy; he would have given back the purity to those from whom he had taken it, he would have found God and justice, but this was as impossible as putting a fallen star back into the sky. And the fact that it was impossible drove him to despair.

When the thunderstorm had passed, he sat by the open window and calmly thought of what was going to happen to him. Von Koren would probably kill him. The man's clear, cold worldview allowed for the destruction of the feeble and worthless; and if it betrayed him in the decisive moment, he would be helped by the hatred and squeamishness Laevsky inspired in him. But if he missed, or, to mock his hated adversary, only wounded him, or fired into the air, what was he to do then? Where was he to go?

"To Petersburg?" Laevsky asked himself. "But that would mean starting anew the old life I'm cursing. And he who seeks salvation in a change of place, like a migratory bird, will find nothing, because for him the earth is the same everywhere. Seek salvation in people? In whom and how? Samoilenko's kindness and magnanimity are no more saving than the deacon's laughter or von Koren's hatred. One must seek salvation only in oneself, and if one doesn't find it, then why waste time, one must kill oneself, that's all..."

The noise of a carriage was heard. Dawn was already breaking. The carriage drove past, turned, and, its wheels creaking in the wet sand, stopped near the house. Two men were sitting in the carriage.

"Wait, I'll be right there!" Laevsky said out the window. "I'm not asleep. Can it be time already?"

"Yes. Four o'clock. By the time we get there..."

Laevsky put on his coat and a cap, took some cigarettes in his pocket, and stopped to ponder; it seemed to him that something else had to be done. Outside, the seconds talked softly and the horses snorted, and these sounds, on a damp early morning, when everyone was asleep and the sky was barely light, filled Laevsky's soul with a despondency that was like a bad presentiment. He stood pondering for a while and then went to the bedroom.

Nadezhda Fyodorovna lay on her bed, stretched out, wrapped head and all in a plaid; she did not move and was reminiscent, especially by her head, of an Egyptian mummy. Looking at her in silence, Laevsky mentally asked her forgiveness and thought that if heaven was not empty and God was indeed in it, He would protect her, and if there was no God, let her perish, there was no need for her to live.

She suddenly jumped and sat up in her bed. Raising her pale face and looking with terror at Laevsky, she asked:

"Is that you? Is the thunderstorm over?"

"It's over."

She remembered, put both hands to her head, and her whole body shuddered.

"It's so hard for me!" she said. "If you only knew how hard it is for me! I was expecting you to kill me," she went on, narrowing her eyes, "or drive me out of the house into the rain and storm, but you put it off...put it off..."

He embraced her impulsively and tightly, covered her knees and hands with kisses, then, as she murmured something to him and shuddered from her memories, he smoothed her hair and, peering into her face, understood that this unfortunate, depraved woman was the only person who was close, dear, and irreplaceable to him.

When he left the house and was getting into the carriage, he wanted to come back home alive.

XVIII

THE DEACON GOT UP, dressed, took his thick, knobby walking stick, and quietly left the house. It was dark, and for the first moment, as he walked down the street, he did not even see his white stick; there was not a single star in the sky, and it looked as though it was going to rain again. There was a smell of wet sand and sea.

"If only the Chechens don't attack," thought the deacon, listening to his stick tapping the pavement and to the resounding and solitary sound this tapping made in the stillness of the night.

Once he left town, he began to see both the road and his stick; dim spots appeared here and there in the black sky, and soon one star peeped out and timidly winked its one eye. The deacon walked along the high rocky coast and did not see the sea; it was falling asleep below, and its invisible waves broke lazily and heavily against the shore and seemed to sigh: oof! And so slowly! One wave broke, the deacon had time to count eight steps, then another broke, and after six steps, a third. Just as before, nothing could be seen, and in the darkness, the lazy, sleepy noise of the sea could be heard, the infinitely far-off, unimaginable time could be heard when God hovered over chaos.

The deacon felt eerie. He thought God might punish him for keeping company with unbelievers and even going to watch their duel. The duel would be trifling, bloodless, ridiculous, but however it might be, it was a heathen spectacle, and for a clergyman to be present at it was altogether improper. He stopped and thought: shouldn't he go back? But strong, restless curiosity got the upper hand over his doubts, and he went on.

"Though they're unbelievers, they are good people and will be saved," he reassured himself. "They'll surely be saved!" he said aloud, lighting a cigarette.

By what measure must one measure people's qualities, to be able to judge them fairly? The deacon recalled his enemy, the inspector of the seminary, who believed in God, and did not fight duels, and lived in chastity, but used to feed the deacon bread with sand in it and once nearly tore his ear off. If human life was so unwisely formed that everyone in the seminary respected this cruel and dishonest inspector, who stole government flour, and prayed for his health and salvation, was it fair to keep away from such people as von Koren and Laevsky only because they were unbelievers? The deacon started mulling over this question but then recalled what a funny figure Samoilenko had cut that day, and that interrupted the course of his thoughts. How they would laugh tomorrow! The deacon imagined himself sitting behind a bush and spying on them, and when von Koren began boasting tomorrow at dinner, he, the deacon, would laugh and tell him all the details of the duel.

"How do you know all that?" the zoologist would ask.

"It just so happens. I stayed home, but I know."

It would be nice to write a funny description of the duel. His father-in-law would read it and laugh; hearing or reading something funny was better food for him than meat and potatoes.

The valley of the Yellow River opened out. The rain had made the river wider and angrier, and it no longer rumbled as before, but roared. Dawn was breaking. The gray, dull morning, and the clouds racing westward to catch up with the thunderhead, and the mountains girded with mist, and the wet trees—it all seemed ugly and angry to the deacon. He washed in a brook, recited his morning prayers, and wished he could have some tea and the hot puffs with sour cream served every morning at his father-in-law's table. He thought of his deaconess and "The Irretrievable," which she played on the piano. What sort of woman was she? They had introduced the deacon to her, arranged things, and married him to her in a week; he had lived with her for less than a month and had been ordered here, so that he had not yet figured out what kind of person she was. But all the same, he was slightly bored without her.

"I must write her a little letter ..." he thought.

The flag on the dukhan was rain-soaked and drooping, and the dukhan itself, with its wet roof, seemed darker and lower than it had before. A cart stood by the door. Kerbalai, a couple of Abkhazians, and a young Tartar woman in balloon trousers, probably Kerbalai's wife or daughter, were bringing sacks of something out of the dukhan and putting them in the cart on cornhusks. By the cart stood a pair of oxen, their heads lowered. After loading the sacks, the Abkhazians and the Tartar woman began covering them with straw, and Kerbalai hastily began hitching up the donkeys.

"Contraband, probably," thought the deacon.

Here was the fallen tree with its dried needles, here was

the black spot from the fire. He recalled the picnic in all its details, the fire, the singing of the Abkhazians, the sweet dreams of a bishopric and a procession with the cross . . . The Black River had grown blacker and wider from the rain. The deacon cautiously crossed the flimsy bridge, which the muddy waves already reached with their crests, and climbed the ladder into the drying shed.

"A fine head!" he thought, stretching out on the straw and recalling von Koren. "A good head, God grant him health. Only there's cruelty in him . . ."

Why did he hate Laevsky, and Laevsky him? Why were they going to fight a duel? If they had known the same poverty as the deacon had known since childhood, if they had been raised in the midst of ignorant, hard-hearted people, greedy for gain, who reproached you for a crust of bread, coarse and uncouth of behavior, who spat on the floor and belched over dinner and during prayers, if they had not been spoiled since childhood by good surroundings and a select circle of people, how they would cling to each other, how eagerly they would forgive each other's shortcomings and value what each of them did have. For there are so few even outwardly decent people in the world! True, Laevsky was crackbrained, dissolute, strange, but he wouldn't steal, wouldn't spit loudly on the floor, wouldn't reproach his wife: "You stuff yourself, but you don't want to work," wouldn't beat a child with a harness strap or feed his servants putrid salt beef—wasn't that enough for him to be treated with tolerance? Besides, he was the first to suffer from his own shortcomings, like a sick man from his sores. Instead of seeking, out of boredom or some sort of misunderstanding, for degeneracy, extinction, heredity, and other incomprehensible things in each other, wouldn't it be better for them to descend a little lower and direct their hatred and wrath to where whole streets resound with the groans of coarse ignorance, greed, reproach, impurity, curses, female shrieks . . .

There was the sound of an equipage, and it interrupted the deacon's thoughts. He peeked out the door and saw a carriage, and in it three people: Laevsky, Sheshkovsky, and the head of the post and telegraph office.

"Stop!" said Sheshkovsky.

All three got out of the carriage and looked at each other.

"They're not here yet," said Sheshkovsky, shaking mud off himself. "So, then! While the jury's still out, let's go and find a suitable spot. There's hardly room enough to turn around here."

They went further up the river and soon disappeared from sight. The Tartar coachman got into the carriage, lolled his head on his shoulder, and fell asleep. Having waited for about ten minutes, the deacon came out of the drying shed and, taking off his black hat so as not to be noticed, cowering and glancing around, began to make his way along the bank among the bushes and strips of corn; big drops fell on him from the trees and bushes, the grass and corn were wet.

"What a shame!" he muttered, hitching up his wet and dirty skirts. "If I'd known, I wouldn't have come."

Soon he heard voices and saw people. Laevsky, hunched over, his hands tucked into his sleeves, was rapidly pacing up and down a small clearing; his seconds stood just by the bank and rolled cigarettes.

"Strange..." thought the deacon, not recognizing Laevsky's gait. "Looks like an old man."

"How impolite on their part!" said the postal official, looking at his watch. "Maybe for a learned man it's a fine thing to be late, but in my opinion it's swinishness."

Sheshkovsky, a fat man with a black beard, listened and said:

"They're coming."

XIX

"THE FIRST TIME in my life I've seen it! How nice!" said von Koren, emerging into the clearing and holding out both arms to the east. "Look: green rays!"

Two green rays stretched out from behind the mountains in the east, and it was indeed beautiful. The sun was rising.

"Good morning!" the zoologist went on, nodding to Laevsky's seconds. "I'm not late?"

Behind him came his seconds, two very young officers of the same height, Boiko and Govorovsky, in white tunics, and the lean, unsociable Dr. Ustimovich, who was carrying a bundle of something in one hand and put the other behind him; as usual, he was holding his cane up along his spine. Setting the bundle on the ground and not greeting anyone, he sent his other hand behind his back and began pacing out the clearing.

Laevsky felt the weariness and awkwardness of a man who might die soon and therefore attracted general attention. He would have liked to be killed quickly or else taken home. He was now seeing a sunrise for the first time in his life; this early morning, the green rays, the dampness, and the people in wet boots seemed extraneous to his life, unnecessary, and they embarrassed him; all this had no connection with the night he had lived through, with his thoughts, and with the feeling of guilt, and therefore he would gladly have left without waiting for the duel.

Von Koren was noticeably agitated and tried to conceal it, pretending that he was interested most of all in the green rays. The seconds were confused and kept glancing at each other as if asking why they were there and what they were to do.

"I suppose, gentlemen, that there's no need to go further," said Sheshkovsky. "Here is all right."

"Yes, of course," agreed von Koren.

Silence ensued. Ustimovich, as he paced, suddenly turned sharply to Laevsky and said in a low voice, breathing in his face:

"They probably haven't had time to inform you of my conditions. Each side pays me fifteen roubles, and in case of the death of one of the adversaries, the one who is left alive pays the whole thirty."

Laevsky had made this man's acquaintance earlier, but only now did he see distinctly for the first time his dull eyes, stiff mustache, and lean, consumptive neck: a moneylender, not a doctor! His breath had an unpleasant, beefy smell.

"It takes all kinds to make a world," thought Laevsky and replied:

"Very well."

The doctor nodded and again began pacing, and it was clear that he did not need the money at all, but was asking for it simply out of hatred. Everyone felt that it was time to begin, or to end what had been begun, yet they did not begin or end, but walked about, stood, and smoked. The young officers, who were present at a duel for the first time in their lives and now had little faith in this civil and, in their opinion, unnecessary duel, attentively examined their tunics and smoothed their sleeves. Sheshkovsky came up to them and said quietly:

"Gentlemen, we should make every effort to keep the duel from taking place. They must be reconciled."

He blushed and went on:

"Last night Kirilin came to see me and complained that Laevsky had caught him last night with Nadezhda Fyodorovna and all that."

"Yes, we also know about that," said Boiko.

"Well, so you see . . . Laevsky's hands are trembling and all that . . . He won't even be able to hold up a pistol now. It would be as inhuman to fight with him as with a drunk man or someone with typhus. If the reconciliation doesn't take place, then, gentlemen, we must at least postpone the duel or something . . . It's such a devilish thing, I don't even want to look."

"Speak with von Koren."

"I don't know the rules of dueling, devil take them all, and I don't want to know them; maybe he'll think Laevsky turned coward and sent me to him. But anyhow, he can think what he likes, I'll go and speak with him."

Irresolutely, limping slightly, as though his foot had gone to sleep, Sheshkovsky went over to von Koren, and as he walked and grunted, his whole figure breathed indolence.

"There's something I've got to tell you, sir," he began, attentively studying the flowers on the zoologist's shirt. "It's confidential . . . I don't know the rules of dueling, devil take them all, and I don't want to know them, and I'm reasoning not as a second and all that but as a human being, that's all."

"Right. So?"

"When seconds suggest making peace, usually nobody listens to them, looking on it as a formality. Amour propre and nothing more. But I humbly beg you to pay attention to Ivan Andreich. He's not at all in a normal state today, so to speak, not in his right mind, and quite pitiful. A misfortune has befallen him. I can't bear gossip," Sheshkovsky blushed and looked around, "but in view of the duel, I find it necessary to tell you. Last night, in Miuridov's house, he found his lady with . . . a certain gentleman."

"How revolting!" murmured the zoologist; he turned pale, winced, and spat loudly: "Pah!"

His lower lip trembled; he stepped away from Sheshkovsky, not wishing to hear any more, and, as if he had accidentally sampled something bitter, again spat loudly, and for the first time that morning looked at Laevsky with hatred. His agitation and awkwardness passed; he shook his head and said loudly:

"Gentlemen, what are we waiting for, may I ask? Why don't we begin?"

Sheshkovsky exchanged glances with the officers and shrugged his shoulders.

"Gentlemen!" he said loudly, not addressing anyone. "Gentlemen! We suggest that you make peace!"

"Let's get through the formalities quickly," said von Koren. "We've already talked about making peace. What's the next formality now? Let's hurry up, gentlemen, time won't wait."

"But we still insist on making peace," Sheshkovsky said in a guilty voice, like a man forced to interfere in other people's business; he blushed, put his hand to his heart, and went on: "Gentlemen, we see no causal connection between the insult and the duel. An offense that we, in our human weakness, sometimes inflict on each other and a duel have nothing in common. You're university and cultivated people, and, of course, you yourselves see nothing in dueling but an outdated and empty formality and all that. We look at it the same way, otherwise we wouldn't have come, because we can't allow people to shoot at each other in our presence, that's all." Sheshkovsky wiped the sweat from his face and went on: "Let's put an end to your misunderstanding, gentlemen, offer each other your hands, and go home and drink to peace. Word of honor, gentlemen!"

Von Koren was silent. Laevsky, noticing that they were looking at him, said:

"I have nothing against Nikolai Vassilievich. If he finds me to blame, I'm ready to apologize to him."

Von Koren became offended.

"Obviously, gentlemen," he said, "you would like Mr. Laevsky to return home a magnanimous and chivalrous man, but I cannot give you and him that pleasure. And there was no need to get up early and go seven miles out of town only to drink to peace, have a bite to eat, and explain to me that dueling is an outdated formality. A duel is a duel, and it ought not to be made more stupid and false than it is in reality. I want to fight!"

Silence ensued. Officer Boiko took two pistols from a box; one was handed to von Koren, the other to Laevsky, and after that came perplexity, which briefly amused the zoologist and the seconds. It turned out that of all those present, not one had been at a duel even once in his life, and no one knew exactly how they should stand and what the seconds should say and do. But then Boiko remembered and, smiling, began to explain.

"Gentlemen, who remembers how it's described in Lermontov?" von Koren asked, laughing. "In Turgenev, too, Bazarov exchanged shots with somebody or other . . ."

"What is there to remember?" Ustimovich said impatiently, stopping. "Measure out the distance—that's all."

And he made three paces, as if showing them how to measure. Boiko counted off the paces, and his comrade drew his saber and scratched the ground at the extreme points to mark the barrier.

In the general silence, the adversaries took their places.

"Moles," recalled the deacon, who was sitting in the bushes.

Sheshkovsky was saying something, Boiko was explaining something again, but Laevsky did not hear or, more precisely, heard but did not understand. When the time for it came, he cocked and raised the heavy, cold pistol, barrel up. He forgot to unbutton his coat, and it felt very tight in the shoulder and armpit, and his arm was rising as awkwardly as if the sleeve was made of tin. He remembered his hatred yesterday for the swarthy forehead and curly hair, and thought that even yesterday, in a moment of intense hatred and wrath, he could not have shot at a man. Fearing that the bullet might somehow accidentally hit von Koren, he raised the pistol higher and higher, and felt that this much too ostentatious magnanimity was neither delicate nor magnanimous, but he could not and would not do otherwise. Looking at the pale, mockingly smiling face of von Koren, who had evidently been sure from the very beginning that his adversary would fire into the air, Laevsky thought that soon, thank God, it would all be over, and that he had only to squeeze the trigger harder . . .

There was a strong kick in his shoulder, a shot rang out, and in the mountains the echo answered: ka-bang!

Von Koren, too, cocked his pistol and glanced in the direction of Ustimovich, who was pacing as before, his hands thrust behind him, paying no attention to anything.

"Doctor," said the zoologist, "kindly do not walk like a pendulum. You flash in my eyes."

The doctor stopped. Von Koren started aiming at Laevsky.

"It's all over!" thought Laevsky.

The barrel of the pistol pointing straight at his face, the expression of hatred and contempt in the pose and the whole figure of von Koren, and this murder that a decent man was about to commit in broad daylight in the presence of decent people, and this silence, and the unknown force that made Laevsky stand there and not run away—how mysterious, and incomprehensible, and frightening it all was! The time von Koren took to aim seemed longer than a night to Laevsky. He glanced imploringly at the seconds; they did not move and were pale.

"Shoot quickly!" thought Laevsky, and felt that his pale, quivering, pitiful face must arouse still greater hatred in von Koren.

"Now I'll kill him," thought von Koren, aiming at the forehead and already feeling the trigger with his finger. "Yes, of course, I'll kill him . . ."

"He'll kill him!" a desperate cry was suddenly heard somewhere very nearby.

Just then the shot rang out. Seeing that Laevsky was

standing in the same place and did not fall, everyone looked in the direction the cry had come from, and saw the deacon. Pale, his wet hair stuck to his forehead and cheeks, all wet and dirty, he was standing on the other bank in the corn, smiling somehow strangely and waving his wet hat. Sheshkovsky laughed with joy, burst into tears, and walked away . . .

XX

A LITTLE LATER, von Koren and the deacon came together at the little bridge. The deacon was agitated, breathed heavily, and avoided looking him in the eye. He was ashamed both of his fear and of his dirty, wet clothes.

"It seemed to me that you wanted to kill him . . ." he mumbled. "How contrary it is to human nature! Unnatural to such a degree!"

"How did you get here, though?" asked the zoologist.

"Don't ask!" the deacon waved his hand. "The unclean one led me astray: go, yes, go . . . So I went and almost died of fright in the corn. But now, thank God, thank God . . . I'm quite pleased with you," the deacon went on mumbling. "And our grandpa tarantula will be pleased . . . Funny, so funny! Only I beg you insistently not to tell anyone I was here, or else I may get it in the neck from my superiors. They'll say: the deacon acted as a second."

"Gentlemen!" said von Koren. "The deacon asks you not to tell anybody you saw him here. He may get in trouble."

"How contrary it is to human nature!" sighed the deacon. "Forgive me magnanimously, but you had such a look on your face that I thought you were certainly going to kill him."

"I was strongly tempted to finish the scoundrel off," said von Koren, "but you shouted right then, and I missed. However, this whole procedure is revolting to someone unaccustomed to it, and it's made me tired, Deacon. I feel terribly weak. Let's go . . ."

"No, kindly allow me to go on foot. I've got to dry out, I'm all wet and chilly."

"Well, you know best," the weakened zoologist said in a weary voice, getting into the carriage and closing his eyes. "You know best . . ."

While they were walking around the carriages and getting into them, Kerbalai stood by the road and, holding his stomach with both hands, kept bowing low and showing his teeth; he thought the gentlemen had come to enjoy nature and drink tea, and did not understand why they were getting into the carriages. In the general silence, the train started, and the only one left by the dukhan was the deacon.

"Went dukhan, drank tea," he said to Kerbalai. "Mine wants eat."

Kerbalai spoke Russian well, but the deacon thought the Tartar would understand him better if he spoke to him in broken Russian.

"Fried eggs, gave cheese . . ."

"Come in, come in, pope," Kerbalai said, bowing, "I'll give you everything . . . There's cheese, there's wine . . . Eat whatever you like."

"What's God in Tartar?" the deacon asked as he went into the dukhan.

"Your God and my God are all the same," said Kerbalai, not understanding him. "God is one for everybody, only people are different. Some are Russian, some are Turks, or some are English—there are many kinds of people, but God is one."

"Very good, sir. If all people worship one God, why do you Muslims look upon Christians as your eternal enemies?"

"Why get angry?" said Kerbalai, clasping his stomach with both hands. "You're a pope, I'm a Muslim, you say you want to eat, I give . . . Only the rich man sorts out which God is yours, which is mine, but for a poor man, it's all the same. Eat, please."

While a theological discussion was going on in the dukhan, Laevsky drove home and remembered how eerie it had been to drive out at dawn, when the road, the cliffs, and the mountains were wet and dark and the unknown future seemed as frightening as an abyss with no bottom to be seen, while now the raindrops hanging on the grass and rocks sparkled in the sun like diamonds, nature smiled joyfully, and the frightening future was left behind. He kept glancing at the sullen, tear-stained face of Sheshkovsky and ahead at the two carriages in which von Koren, his seconds, and the doctor rode, and it seemed to him as though they were all coming back from a cemetery where they had just buried a difficult, unbearable man who had interfered with all their lives.

"It's all over," he thought about his past, carefully stroking his neck with his fingers.

On the right side of his neck, near the collar, he had a small swelling, as long and thick as a little finger, and he felt pain, as if someone had passed a hot iron over his neck. It was a contusion from a bullet.

Then, when he got home, a long, strange day, sweet and foggy as oblivion, wore on for him. Like a man released from prison or the hospital, he peered at long-familiar objects and was surprised that the tables, the windows, the chairs, the light and the sea aroused a living, childlike joy in him, such as he had not experienced for a long, long time. Nadezhda Fyodorovna, pale and grown very thin, did not understand his meek voice and strange gait; she hurriedly told him everything that had happened to her . . . It seemed to her that he probably listened poorly and did not understand her, and that if he learned everything, he would curse and kill her, yet he listened to her, stroked her face and hair, looked into her eyes, and said:

"I have no one but you . . ."

Then they sat for a long time in the front garden, pressed to each other, and said nothing, or else, dreaming aloud of their happy future life, they uttered short, abrupt phrases, and it seemed to him that he had never spoken so lengthily and beautifully.

XXI

A LITTLE MORE than three months went by.

The day von Koren had appointed for his departure came. Cold rain had been falling in big drops since early morning, a northeast wind was blowing, and the sea churned itself up in big waves. People said that in such weather the steamer could hardly put into the roads. According to the schedule, it should have come after nine, but von Koren, who went out to the embankment at noon and after dinner, saw nothing through his binoculars but gray waves and rain obscuring the horizon.

Towards the end of the day, the rain stopped, and the wind began to drop noticeably. Von Koren was already reconciled with the thought that he was not to leave that day, and he sat down to play chess with Samoilenko; but when it grew dark, the orderly reported that lights had appeared on the sea and a rocket had been seen.

Von Koren began to hurry. He shouldered a bag, kissed Samoilenko and then the deacon, went around all the rooms quite needlessly, said good-bye to the orderly and the cook, and went out feeling as though he had forgotten something at the doctor's or at his own place. He went down the street side by side with Samoilenko, followed by the deacon with a box, and behind them all came the orderly with two suitcases. Only Samoilenko and the orderly could make out the dim lights on the sea; the others looked into the darkness and saw nothing. The steamer had stopped far from shore.

"Quick, quick," von Koren urged. "I'm afraid it will leave!"

Passing by the three-windowed little house Laevsky had moved into soon after the duel, von Koren could not help looking in the window. Laevsky, bent over, was sitting at a desk, his back to the window, and writing.

"I'm astonished," the zoologist said softly. "How he's put the screws to himself!"

"Yes, it's worthy of astonishment," sighed Samoilenko. "He sits like that from morning till evening, sits and works. He wants to pay his debts. And brother, he lives worse than a beggar!"

Half a minute passed in silence. The zoologist, the doctor, and the deacon stood by the window, and they all looked at Laevsky.

"So he never left here, poor fellow," said Samoilenko. "Remember how he fussed about?"

"Yes, he's really put the screws to himself," repeated von Koren. "His marriage, this all-day work for a crust of bread, some new expression in his face, and even his gait—it's all extraordinary to such a degree that I don't even know what to call it." The zoologist took Samoilenko by the sleeve and went on with agitation in his voice: "Tell him and his wife that I was astonished at them as I was leaving, wished them well . . . and ask him, if it's possible, not to think ill of me. He knows me. He knows that if I could have foreseen this change then, I might have become his best friend."

"Go in to him, say good-bye."

"No. It's awkward."

"Why? God knows, maybe you'll never see him again."

The zoologist thought a little and said:

"That's true."

Samoilenko tapped softly on the window with his finger. Laevsky gave a start and turned to look.

"Vanya, Nikolai Vassilyich wishes to say good-bye to you," said Samoilenko. "He's just leaving."

Laevsky got up from the desk and went to the front hall to open the door. Samoilenko, von Koren, and the deacon came in.

"I've come for a moment," the zoologist began, taking off his galoshes in the front hall and already regretting that he had given way to his feelings and come in uninvited. ("As if I'm forcing myself on him," he thought, "and that's stupid.") "Forgive me for bothering you," he said, following Laevsky into his room, "but I'm just leaving, and I felt drawn to you. God knows if we'll ever see each other again."

"I'm very glad . . . I humbly beg you," said Laevsky, and he awkwardly moved chairs for his visitors, as if he wished to bar their way, and stopped in the middle of the room, rubbing his hands.

"I should have left the witnesses outside," thought von Koren, and he said firmly:

"Don't think ill of me, Ivan Andreich. To forget the past is, of course, impossible, it is all too sad, and I haven't come here to apologize or to insist that I'm not to blame. I acted sincerely and have not changed my convictions since . . . True, as I now see, to my great joy, I was mistaken concerning you, but one can stumble even on a smooth road, and such is human fate: if you're not mistaken in the main thing, you'll be mistaken in the details. No one knows the real truth."

"Yes, no one knows the truth . . ." said Laevsky.

"Well, good-bye . . . God grant you all good things."

Von Koren gave Laevsky his hand; he shook it and bowed.

"So don't think ill of me," said von Koren. "Give my greetings to your wife, and tell her I was very sorry I couldn't say good-bye to her."

"She's here."

Laevsky went to the door and said into the other room:

"Nadya, Nikolai Vassilievich wishes to say good-bye to you."

Nadezhda Fyodorovna came in; she stopped by the door and looked timidly at the visitors. Her face was guilty and frightened, and she held her arms like a schoolgirl who is being reprimanded.

"I'm just leaving, Nadezhda Fyodorovna," said von Koren, "and I've come to say good-bye."

She offered him her hand irresolutely, and Laevsky bowed.

"How pitiful they both are, though!" thought von Koren. "They don't come by this life cheaply."

"I'll be in Moscow and Petersburg," he asked, "do you need to have anything sent from there?"

"Need anything?" said Nadezhda Fyodorovna, and she exchanged alarmed glances with her husband. "Nothing, I believe . . ."

"No, nothing . . ." said Laevsky, rubbing his hands. "Say hello for us."

Von Koren did not know what else could or needed to be said, yet earlier, as he was coming in, he thought he would say a great many good, warm, and significant things. He silently shook hands with Laevsky and his wife and went out with a heavy feeling.

"What people!" the deacon was saying in a low voice, walking behind. "My God, what people! Truly, the right hand of God planted this vineyard! Lord, Lord! One defeated thousands and the other tens of thousands.[32] Nikolai Vassilyich," he said ecstatically, "know that today you have defeated the greatest human enemy—pride!"

"Come now, Deacon! What kind of victors are we? Victors look like eagles, but he's pitiful, timid, downtrodden, he keeps bowing like a Chinese doll, and I . . . I feel sad."

There was the sound of footsteps behind them. It was Laevsky catching up to see them off. On the pier stood the orderly with the two suitcases, and a little further off, four oarsmen.

"It's really blowing, though . . . brr!" said Samoilenko. "Must be a whale of a storm out at sea—aie, aie! It's not a good time to be going, Kolya."

"I'm not afraid of seasickness."

"That's not the point . . . These fools may capsize you. You ought to have gone in the agent's skiff. Where's the agent's skiff?" he shouted to the oarsmen.

"Gone, Your Excellency."

"And the customs skiff?"

"Also gone."

"Why wasn't it announced?" Samoilenko got angry. "Dunderheads!"

"Never mind, don't worry . . ." said von Koren. "Well, good-bye. God keep you."

Samoilenko embraced von Koren and crossed him three times.

"Don't forget me, Kolya . . . Write . . . We'll expect you next spring."

"Good-bye, Deacon," said von Koren, shaking the deacon's hand. "Thanks for the company and the good conversation. Think about the expedition."

"Lord, yes, even to the ends of the earth!" laughed the deacon. "Am I against it?"

Von Koren recognized Laevsky in the darkness and silently gave him his hand. The oarsmen were already standing below, holding the boat, which kept knocking against the pilings, though the pier sheltered it from the big swells. Von Koren went down the ladder, jumped into the boat, and sat by the tiller.

"Write!" Samoilenko shouted to him. "Take care of yourself!"

"No one knows the real truth," thought Laevsky, turning up the collar of his coat and tucking his hands into his sleeves.

The boat briskly rounded the pier and headed into the open. It disappeared among the waves, but shot up at once

236

out of the deep hole onto a high hill, so that it was possible to make out the people and even the oars. The boat went ahead about six yards and was thrown back four.

"Write!" shouted Samoilenko. "What the deuce makes you go in such weather!"

"Yes, no one knows the real truth..." thought Laevsky, looking with anguish at the restless, dark sea.

"The boat is thrown back," he thought, "it makes two steps forward and one step back, but the oarsmen are stubborn, they work the oars tirelessly and do not fear the high waves. The boat goes on and on, now it can no longer be seen, and in half an hour the oarsmen will clearly see the steamer's lights, and in an hour they'll already be by the steamer's ladder. So it is in life... In search of the truth, people make two steps forward and one step back. Sufferings, mistakes, and the tedium of life throw them back, but the thirst for truth and a stubborn will drive them on and on. And who knows? Maybe they'll row their way to the real truth..."

"Good-by-y-ye!" shouted Samoilenko.

"No sight or sound of them," said the deacon. "Safe journey!"

It began to drizzle.

1891

THE STORY OF AN
UNKNOWN MAN

I

FOR REASONS OF which now is not the time to speak in detail, I had to go to work as the servant of a certain Petersburg official by the name of Orlov. He was about thirty-five years old and was called Georgiy Ivanych.

I went to work for this Orlov on account of his father, a well-known statesman whom I regarded as a serious enemy of my cause. I reckoned that, from the conversations I would hear and the papers and notes I might find on the desk while living at the son's, I could learn the father's plans and intentions in detail.

Ordinarily, at around eleven o'clock the electric bell rattled in my servants' quarters, letting me know that the master had awakened. When I came to the bedroom with brushed clothing and boots, Georgiy Ivanych would be sitting motionless on the bed, not sleepy, but rather worn out from sleep, and staring at a single spot, showing no pleasure on the occasion of his awakening. I would help him to dress, and he would reluctantly submit to me, silent and not noticing my presence; then, his head wet from washing and smelling of fresh perfume, he would go to the dining room and have coffee. He would sit at the table, drink his coffee, and leaf through the newspapers, while the maid Polya and I stood deferentially by the door and watched him. Two grown-up persons had to watch with the most serious attention as a third drank coffee and nibbled rusks. This is, in all probability, ridiculous and wild, but I did not see anything humiliating to myself in having to stand by the door, though I was as noble and educated a man as Orlov himself.

At that time I had the beginnings of consumption, and along with it something else perhaps more important than consumption. I don't know whether it was under the influence of illness or of a beginning change in worldview, which I hadn't noticed then, but day after day I was over-come by a passionate, nagging thirst for ordinary, humdrum life. I craved inner peace, health, good air, satiety. I was becoming a dreamer and, like a dreamer, did not know what in fact I wanted. One time I wanted to go to a monastery and sit there for whole days at the window, looking out at the trees and fields; then I imagined myself buying some fifteen acres and living like a landowner; then I vowed to take up science and unfailingly become a professor at some provincial university. I'm a retired lieutenant of the navy; I daydreamed of the sea, of our squadron, of the corvette that had taken me around the world. I wanted to experience once again that inexpressible feeling when you're strolling in a tropical forest or watching the sunset on the Bay of Bengal, swooning with rapture and at the same time longing for your motherland. I dreamed of mountains, women, music, and with curiosity, like a boy, peered into faces, listened to voices. And when I stood by the door and watched Orlov drinking coffee, I felt I was not a servant but a man to whom every-thing in the world was interesting, even Orlov.

Orlov had a Petersburg appearance: narrow shoulders, long waist, sunken temples, eyes of an indeterminate color, and a skimpy, drab growth of hair, beard, and mustache. His face was sleek, worn, and unpleasant. It was especially unpleasant when he was deep in thought or asleep. To describe an ordinary appearance is hardly proper; besides, Petersburg is not Spain, a man's appearance is of no great importance here, even in amorous matters, and is needful only for impressive servants and coachmen. I began speaking of Orlov's face and hair only because there was something worth mentioning in his appearance, namely: when Orlov took up a newspaper or book, whatever it might be, or met people, whoever they might be, his eyes began to smile ironically, and his whole face acquired an expression of light, unmalicious mockery. Before reading or listening to something, he prepared his irony each time, like a savage his shield. This was habitual irony of an old cast, and lately it had appeared on his face without any participation of his will, most likely, but as if by reflex. But of that later.

After noon, with an expression of irony, he would take his briefcase stuffed with papers and drive off to work. He would dine out and return home after eight. I would light the lamp and some candles in his study, and he would sit in an armchair, his legs stretched out on a chair, and, sprawled like that, begin to read. Almost every day he brought home new books or had them sent from the shops, and in my servants' quarters in the corners and under my bed lay a host of books in three languages, not counting Russian, already read and discarded. He read with extraordinary speed. They say, tell me what you've read and I'll tell you who you are. That may be true, but it was positively impossible to judge Orlov by the books he read. It was some sort of hodge-podge. Philosophy, French novels, political economy, finance, the new poets, publications of *The Mediator*—and he read it all with equal speed and with the same ironic look in his eyes.

After ten, he would dress carefully, often in a tailcoat, very rarely in his kammerjunker's uniform,[1] and drive off. He would return towards morning.

We lived quietly and peacefully, and there were no misunderstandings between us. Ordinarily he did not notice my presence, and when he spoke to me, there was no ironic expression on his face—evidently he did not regard me as a human being.

Only once did I see him angry. One time—this was a week after I went to work for him—he came back from some dinner at around nine o'clock, his face was capricious, weary. As I followed him into the study to light the candles there, he said to me:

"It stinks of something in our rooms."

"No, the air is clean," I replied.

"And I tell you it stinks," he repeated irritably.

"I air the rooms every day."

"Don't talk back, blockhead!" he shouted.

I was offended and was about to object, and God knows how it would have ended if Polya, who knew her master better than I, had not intervened.

"Indeed, what a bad smell!" she said, raising her eyebrows. "What could it be? Stepan, open the windows in the drawing room and start the fire."

She ah'd and fussed and went around all the rooms, rustling her skirts and hissing with atomizers. But Orlov was still in bad spirits; he obviously kept himself from being angry out loud, sat at the desk, and quickly began writing a letter. After writing several lines, he snorted angrily and tore up the letter, then began writing again.

"Devil take them!" he muttered. "They want to leave me with a monstrous memory!"

Finally the letter got written; he stood up from the desk and said, turning to me:

"Go to Znamenskaya Street and deliver this letter to Zinaida Fyodorovna Krasnovsky, into her own hands. But first ask the porter whether the husband, that is, Mr. Krasnovsky, has returned. If he has, don't deliver the letter, and come back. Wait! . . . In case she asks if there are any people at my place, tell her that some two gentlemen have been sitting with me and writing something since eight in the morning."

I went to Znamenskaya Street. The porter told me that Mr. Krasnovsky had not returned yet, and I went to the third floor. A tall, fat, drab servant with black side-whiskers opened the door for me and sleepily, sluggishly, and rudely, as only a servant can speak to a servant, asked me what I wanted. Before I had time to reply, a lady in a black gown quickly came into the front hall from the drawing room. She narrowed her eyes at me.

"Is Zinaida Fyodorovna at home?" I asked.

"That's me," said the lady.

"A letter from Georgiy Ivanych."

She impatiently unsealed the letter and, holding it in both hands, displaying her diamond rings for me, began to read. I made out a white face with soft features, a prominent chin, long dark eyelashes. By the looks of her, I would have given this lady no more than twenty-five years.

"Greet him and thank him for me," she said when she finished reading. "Is there anyone with Georgiy Ivanych?" she asked softly, joyfully, and as if ashamed of her mistrust.

"Some two gentlemen," I replied. "Writing something."

"Greet him and thank him for me," she repeated, and inclining her head to one side and reading the letter on the way, she noiselessly went out.

I was meeting few women then, and this lady, whom I had seen fleetingly, made an impression on me. Going back home on foot, I recalled her face and the subtle scent of perfume and dreamed. When I returned, Orlov was no longer at home.

II

AND SO MY master and I lived quietly and peacefully, but all the same, the impure and offensive thing I had been so afraid of when I went to work as a servant was there and made itself felt every day. I did not get along with Polya. She was a well-nourished, pampered creature, who adored Orlov because he was a master, and despised me because I was a servant. Probably, from the point of view of a real servant or a cook, she was seductive: ruddy cheeks, upturned nose, narrow eyes, and a fullness of body that verged on plumpness. She used powder, painted her eyebrows and lips, wore tight corsets and a bustle, and a coin bracelet. She walked with small, bouncy steps; as she went, she twitched or, as they say, wagged her shoulders and behind. In the mornings, when she and I tidied the rooms, the rustling of her skirts, the creaking of her corset, and the jingling of her bracelet, and that boorish smell of lipstick, toilet water, and perfume stolen from her master, aroused a feeling in me as though she and I were doing something loathsome together.

Because I didn't steal with her, or didn't show any desire to become her lover, which probably insulted her, or maybe because she sensed a stranger in me, she conceived a hatred for me from the first day on. My ineptitude, my nonservant appearance, and my illness seemed pathetic to her and made her feel squeamish. I coughed badly then and sometimes prevented her from sleeping at night, since her room and mine were separated only by a wooden partition, and every morning she said to me:

"Again you didn't let me sleep. You should be in the hospital, not in a gentleman's house."

She believed so sincerely that I was not a human being but something placed immeasurably beneath her, that, like Roman matrons, who were not embarrassed to bathe in the presence of their slaves, she sometimes went around in front of me in nothing but her shift.

Once over dinner (we had soup and roast brought from a tavern every day), when I was in a splendid dreamy mood, I asked:

"Polya, do you believe in God?"

"As if I didn't!"

"So then you believe," I went on, "that there will be a last judgment and we will answer to God for each of our bad acts?"

She said nothing in reply and only made a scornful grimace, and, looking this time into her cold, sated eyes, I realized that for this wholesome, fully finished nature, there was neither God, nor conscience, nor laws, and that if I had needed to kill, steal, or set a fire, money couldn't have bought me a better accomplice.

In an inhabitual situation, and unaccustomed as I was to being addressed informally and to constant lying (saying "The master is not at home" when he was), my first week of life at Orlov's wasn't easy. In a servant's tailcoat, I felt as if I was wearing armor. But then I got used to it. I served, tidied the rooms, ran and drove about on all sorts of errands like a real servant. When Orlov didn't feel like going to a rendezvous with Zinaida Fyodorovna, or when he forgot that he had promised to call on her, I went to Znamenskaya, delivered a letter there into her own hands, and lied. And the result was not at all what I had expected on becoming a servant; each day of this new life of mine turned out to be a waste both for me and for my cause, since Orlov never spoke of his father, nor did his guests, and of the activity of the well-known statesman all I knew was what I managed, as before, to glean from the newspapers and correspondence with friends. The hundreds of notes and documents I found in the study and read, did not have even a remote connection with what I was looking for. Orlov was totally indifferent to his father's much-touted activity and looked as if he had never heard of it, or as if his father had died long ago.

III

ON THURSDAYS WE received guests.

I would order a roast from a restaurant and telephone Eliseev[2] to have them send us caviar, cheese, oysters, and so forth. I would buy cards. Since morning Polya would be preparing the tea things and laying the supper table. To tell the truth, this slight activity diversified our idle life somewhat, and Thursdays were our most interesting days.

Only three guests used to come. The most solid and perhaps the most interesting was a guest by the name of Pekarsky, a tall lean man of about forty-five, with a long hooked nose, a big black beard, and a bald spot. He had large protruding eyes and a serious, pensive expression on his face, like a Greek philosopher's. He worked in railway administration and in a bank, was a legal adviser in some important government institution, and maintained business relations with a number of private persons as a trustee, committee chairman, and so on. He was of quite low rank and modestly referred to himself as an attorney-at-law, but his influence was enormous. His calling card or a note was enough for you to be received without waiting by a famous doctor, a railway director, or an important official; it was said that through his patronage you even could obtain a fourth-class post or hush up any unpleasant matter you liked. He was considered a very intelligent man, but his was some sort of special, strange intelligence. In an instant he could multiply 213 by 373 or calculate the exchange of sterling for marks without the aid of a pencil or any tables, had an excellent knowledge of the railway business and finance, and nothing that concerned administration held any secrets for him; in civil cases, he was said to be a most skillful lawyer, and it was not easy to go up against him. But this extraordinary intelligence was totally uncomprehending of much that is known even to some stupid men. Thus he decidedly could not comprehend why people get bored, weep, shoot themselves, and even kill others, why they worry over things and events that do not concern them personally, and why they laugh when they read Gogol or Shchedrin[3]... All that is abstract, vanishing into the realm of thought and feeling, was incomprehensible and boring for him, like music for someone with no ear. He looked at people only from a business point of view, and divided them into the capable and the incapable. No other divisions existed for him. Honesty and decency merely constitute a sign of capability. To carouse, play cards, and indulge in depravity is possible but only so long as it doesn't interfere with business. To believe in God is not intelligent, but religion should be protected as a necessary restraining principle for the people, otherwise they won't work. Punishment is needed only to instill fear. There's no reason for going to country houses, since it's quite nice in the city. And so on. He was a widower, had no children, but lived in grand family style and paid three thousand a year in rent.

The second guest, Kukushkin, an actual state councillor[4] of the younger generation, was not very tall and was distinguished by a highly unpleasant expression, which came from the disproportion between his fat, pudgy body and his small, lean face. His lips were shaped like a little heart, and his trimmed little mustache looked as though it had been stuck on with varnish. He was a man with the manner of a lizard. He did not walk but somehow crept in with tiny mincing steps, swaying and tittering, and he bared his teeth when he laughed. He was an official on special assignment to someone, and did nothing, though he earned a big salary, particularly during the summer, when special business trips were invented for him. He was a careerist, not to the marrow of his bones but much deeper, to the last drop of blood and with that, a petty careerist, unsure of himself, who had built his career on nothing but handouts. For some small foreign cross, or for having it published in the newspapers that he had been present at a memorial or a prayer service together with certain high-ranking individuals, he was ready for any humiliation, ready to beg, flatter, promise. He flattered Orlov and Pekarsky out of cowardice, because he considered them powerful, flattered Polya and me because we served an influential person. Each time I relieved him of his fur coat, he tittered and asked me: "Are you married, Stepan?"—and then came scabrous banalities, as a sign of special attention to me. Kukushkin flattered Orlov's weaknesses, his depravity, his satiety; to please him, he pretended to be a godless and wicked scoffer, criticized with him those before whom, in other places, he was a slavish hypocrite. When there was conversation about love and women over supper, he pretended to be a refined and subtle debauchee. In general, it must be noted, Petersburg philanderers enjoy talking about their extraordinary tastes. Your actual state councillor of the younger generation is excellently well satisfied with the caresses of his scullery maid or some wretched girl strolling on Nevsky Prospect,[5] but to listen to him, he is contaminated by all the vices of Orient and Occident, is an honorary member of a whole dozen secret reprehensible societies, and is under police surveillance. Kukushkin lied shamelessly about himself, and it was not that they didn't believe him, but all his fabrications somehow went right past their ears.

The third guest was Gruzin, son of a respectable, learned general, Orlov's peer, long-haired and weak-sighted, blond, with gold spectacles. I recall his long pale fingers, like a pianist's; and in his whole figure there was something of the musician, the virtuoso. Such figures play first violin in orchestras. He coughed and suffered from migraine, and generally seemed sickly and frail. At home they probably helped him to dress and undress like a child. He graduated from law school and served first in the Justice Department, then was transferred to the Senate,[6] left there and received through connections a post in the Ministry of State Property, and soon left again. In my time he was serving in Orlov's department, was a chief clerk, but kept saying that he would soon go back to the Justice Department. He treated his service and his migrations from place to place with a rare light-mindedness, and when people spoke seriously about ranks, decorations, and salaries in his presence, he smiled good-naturedly and repeated an aphorism from Prutkov:[7] "One learns the truth only in government service!" He had a small wife with a shriveled face, a very jealous woman, and five skinny children; he was unfaithful to his wife, loved his children only when he saw them, and in general was quite indifferent to his family and made fun of them. He and his family lived in debt, borrowing wherever and from whomever at every convenient opportunity, not excluding even his superiors and porters. He was of a flimsy nature, lazy to the point of total indifference to himself, and drifted with the current, no one knew where or why. Wherever he was taken, he went. If he was taken to some dive, he went; if wine was put in front of him, he drank; if not, he didn't; if wives were denounced in his presence, he denounced his, maintaining that she had ruined his life; but if they were praised, he also praised his and said sincerely: "I love the poor thing very much." He had no winter coat and always wore a plaid, which smelled of the nursery. When he lapsed into thought over supper, rolling little balls of bread and drinking a good deal of red wine, then, strangely enough, I was almost certain that there was something sitting in him which he probably sensed vaguely himself, but which, because of bustle and banalities, he never managed to understand and appreciate. He played the piano a little. He would sit down at the piano, strike two or three chords, and sing softly:

What does the morrow hold for me?[8]

but then at once, as if frightened, he would get up and move further away from the piano.

The guests usually arrived by ten o'clock. They would play cards in Orlov's study while Polya and I served them tea. Only here could I properly perceive all the sweetness of lackeydom. To stand at the door for a stretch of four or five hours, seeing that no glasses remained empty, changing ashtrays, running to the table to pick up a dropped piece of chalk or a card, but, above all, to stand, to wait, to be attentive, not daring to speak or cough or smile—that, I can assure you, is harder than any hard peasant labor. I once stood a four-hour watch through stormy winter nights, and I find standing watch incomparably easier.

They would play cards till two, sometimes till three, then, stretching, would go to the dining room to have supper, or, as Orlov used to say, a bite to eat. They talked over supper. It usually began with Orlov, his eyes laughing, initiating a conversation about some acquaintance, about a recently read book, about a new appointment or project; the flattering Kukushkin would pick up in the same tone, and there would begin, for the mood I was then in, a most disgusting music. The irony of Orlov and his friends knew no bounds and spared no one and nothing. If they talked about religion—irony; if about philosophy and the meaning and aims of life—irony; if anyone raised the question of the people—irony. In Petersburg there exists a peculiar breed of people who are specially occupied with making fun of every phenomenon of life; they cannot even pass by a starveling or a suicide without uttering some banality. But Orlov and his friends did not joke or make fun, they spoke with irony. They said there is no God and at death a person vanishes completely; immortals exist only in the French Academy.[9] There is no true good and cannot be, because its existence depends on human perfection, and the latter is a logical absurdity. Russia is as dull and squalid a country as Persia. The intelligentsia is hopeless; in Pekarsky's opinion, the vast majority of it consists of incapable and good-for-nothing people. The folk are drunken, lazy, thievish, and degenerate. We have no science, our literature is bumpkinish, trade survives by swindling: "No deceit—no sale." And all of it in the same vein, and all of it funny.

Wine made them merrier towards the end of supper, and they would go on to merry conversations. They would make fun of Gruzin's family life, of Kukushkin's conquests, or of Pekarsky, whose account book supposedly had a page with the heading *For Works of Charity*, and another *For Physiological Needs*. They said there were no faithful wives; there was no wife from whom, given a certain knack, one could not obtain caresses without leaving the drawing room, with the husband sitting right next door in his study. Adolescent girls are depraved and already know everything. Orlov keeps the letter of one fourteen-year-old schoolgirl; on her way home from school, she "hitched up with a little officer on Nevsky" who supposedly took her to his place and let her go only late at night, and she hastened to write to a friend about it in order to share her rapture. They said that there is not and never has been any purity of morals, that it is obviously not needed; mankind has so far done perfectly well without it. The harmfulness of so-called depravity is undoubtedly exaggerated. The perversity specified in our penal code did not keep Diogenes[10] from being a philosopher and a teacher; Caesar and Cicero were debauchees and at the same time great men. Old Cato[11] married a young girl and, even so, went on being considered a strict faster and observer of morals.

At three or four o'clock, the guests would go home or drive out of town together, or to Ofitserskaya Street to visit some Varvara Osipovna, and I would go to my room in the servants' quarters and lie awake for a long time with a headache and a cough.

IV

ABOUT THREE WEEKS after I went to work for Orlov, on a Sunday morning, as I recall, someone rang the bell. It was past ten o'clock, and Orlov was still asleep. I went to open the door. You can imagine my amazement: outside on the landing stood a lady in a veil.

"Is Georgiy Ivanych up?" she asked.

And by her voice I knew it was Zinaida Fyodorovna, to whom I brought letters on Znamenskaya. I don't remember whether I had time or was able to answer her—I was confused by her appearance. But she had no need of my answer. In an instant she darted past me, and, having filled the front hall with the fragrance of her perfume, which to this day I remember perfectly well, she went in, and the sound of her footsteps died away. For at least half an hour after that, nothing was heard. But then someone rang again. This time some spruced-up girl, apparently a maid from a wealthy house, and our porter, both out of breath, brought in two suitcases and a wicker trunk.

"For Zinaida Fyodorovna," said the girl.

And she left without saying another word. All this was mysterious and evoked a sly smile in Polya, who stood in awe of her master's pranks. It was as if she meant to say: "See how we are!"—and she went around all the while on tiptoe. Finally footsteps were heard; Zinaida Fyodorovna quickly came into the front hall and, seeing me in the doorway of my servants' quarters, said:

"Stepan, go and dress Georgiy Ivanych."

When I came into Orlov's room with his clothes and boots, he was sitting on his bed, his feet dangling on the bearskin rug. His whole figure expressed confusion. He didn't notice me, and my servant's opinion didn't interest him: obviously he was confused and abashed before himself, before his own "inner eye." He dressed, washed, and then fussed silently and unhurriedly with his brushes and combs, as if giving himself time to think over and figure out his situation, and even by his back you could see that he was confused and displeased with himself.

They had coffee together. Zinaida Fyodorovna poured for herself and for Orlov, then leaned her elbows on the table and laughed.

"I still can't believe it," she said. "When you travel for a long time and then arrive at a hotel, it's hard to believe there's no need to keep going. It's nice to breathe easy."

With the expression of a little girl who wants very much to do some mischief, she breathed easy and laughed again.

"Excuse me," said Orlov, nodding towards the newspapers. "Reading over coffee is an invincible habit of mine. But I can do the two things at once: read and listen."

"Read, read . . . Your habits and your freedom will remain yours. But why do you have such a lenten look? Are you always this way in the mornings, or just today? You're not glad?"

"On the contrary. But I confess I'm a little stunned."

"Why? You had time to prepare for my invasion. I've been threatening you every day."

"Yes, but I didn't expect you to carry out your threat precisely today."

"I didn't expect it myself, but it's better so. Better, my friend. To pull the aching tooth all at once and—be done."

"Yes, of course."

"Ah, my dear!" she said, closing her eyes. "All's well that ends well, but before it ended well, how much grief there was! Never mind that I laugh; I'm glad, happy, but I feel more like weeping than laughing. Yesterday I went through a whole battle," she continued in French. "God alone knows how hard it was for me. But I'm laughing because I find it hard to believe. It seems to me that I'm sitting and having coffee with you not in reality but in a dream."

Then, continuing to speak in French, she told him how she broke up with her husband the day before, and her eyes now filled with tears, now laughed and looked admiringly at Orlov. She told him that her husband had long suspected her but was avoiding an explanation; they quarreled very often, and usually, at the height of a quarrel, he would suddenly fall silent and go to his study, so as not to voice his suspicions in a sudden outburst, and so that she herself would not begin to explain. Zinaida Fyodorovna felt guilty, worthless, incapable of a bold, serious step, and that made her hate herself and her husband more strongly every day and to suffer as if in hell. But yesterday, during a quarrel, when he cried out in a tearful voice: "My God, when will it all end?"—and went to his study, she chased after him like a cat after a mouse and, keeping him from closing the door behind him, cried out that she hated him with all her soul. Then he let her into the study, and she told him everything and confessed that she loved another man, that this other man was her true, most lawful husband, and she considered it a duty of conscience to move to his place that very day, despite anything, even if she had to go through cannon fire.

"There's the strong pulse of a romantic vein in you," Orlov interrupted her, not taking his eyes from the newspaper.

She laughed and went on with her story, not touching her coffee. Her cheeks were burning, this embarrassed her slightly, and she kept glancing abashedly at me and Polya. From her further account I learned that her husband had answered her with reproaches, threats, and finally with tears, and it would have been more correct to say that it was not she but he who had gone through a battle.

"Yes, my friend, while my nerves were aroused, it all went beautifully," she told him, "but as soon as night came, I lost heart. You don't believe in God, Georges, but I believe a little, and I'm afraid of retribution. God demands patience of us, magnanimity, self-sacrifice, and here I refuse to suffer and want to set up my life in my own way. Is that good? But what if it's suddenly not good from God's point of view? At two o'clock in the morning my husband came into my room and said: 'You won't dare to leave. I'll summons you back with a scandal, through the police.' And a short time later, I see he's in the doorway again, like a shadow. 'Have mercy on me. Your running away may harm my career.' Those words had a rude effect on me, they made me feel covered with rust, I thought the retribution was already beginning, and I began to weep and tremble with fear. It seemed to me that the ceiling was going to collapse on me, that I'd be taken to the police at once, that you would stop loving me—in short, God knows what! I'll go to a convent, I thought, or be a sick-nurse somewhere, and renounce my happiness, but here I remembered that you loved me and that I had no right to dispose of myself without your knowledge, and everything in my head began to get muddled, and I was in despair, I didn't know what to think or do. But the sun rose, and I became cheerful again. I waited till morning and came racing to you. Ah, how worn out I am, my dear! I haven't slept for two nights in a row!"

She was weary and excited. She wanted at the same time to sleep and talk endlessly, and laugh, and cry, and go to a restaurant for lunch, so as to feel herself free.

"Your apartment is cozy, but I'm afraid it will be too small for two," she said after coffee, quickly walking through all the rooms. "Which room will you give me? I like this one, because it's next to your study."

After one, she changed her clothes in the room next to the study, which after that she began to call hers, and drove off with Orlov to have lunch. They also dined in a restaurant and spent the long stretch between lunch and dinner driving from shop to shop. I kept opening the door to shop clerks and messengers till late in the evening, receiving various purchases. Among other things, they brought a magnificent pier glass, a toilet table, a bed, and a splendid tea service, which we didn't need. They brought a whole family of copper pots, which we placed side by side on a shelf in our empty, cold kitchen. As we unwrapped the tea service, Polya's eyes lit up, and she glanced at me two or three times with hatred and fear that maybe not she but I would be the first to steal one of those graceful little cups. They brought a lady's desk, very expensive but uncomfortable. Evidently Zinaida Fyodorovna had the intention of lodging firmly with us as mistress of the house.

She and Orlov came back after nine. Filled with the proud awareness of having accomplished something brave and extraordinary, passionately in love, and, as it seemed to her, loved passionately, languorous, anticipating a sound and happy sleep, Zinaida Fyodorovna reveled in her new life. Overflowing with happiness, she clasped her hands tightly, convinced that everything was beautiful, and vowed that she would love eternally, and these vows, and her naïve, almost childlike confidence that she was also truly loved and would be loved eternally, made her five years younger. She talked sweet nonsense and laughed at herself.

"There's no higher good than freedom!" she said, forcing herself to say something serious and significant. "How preposterous it is, if you stop to think! We give no value to our own opinion, even if it's intelligent, but we tremble before the opinion of various fools. Up to the last minute, I was afraid of other people's opinion, but as soon as I listened to myself and decided to live in my own way, my eyes were opened, I overcame my foolish fear, and now I'm happy and wish everyone such happiness."

But her train of thought immediately broke off, and she began talking about a new apartment, wallpaper, horses, traveling to Switzerland and Italy. Orlov, however, was weary from driving around to restaurants and shops, and continued to feel the same confusion before himself that I had noticed in him that morning. He smiled, but more out of politeness than pleasure, and when she said something serious, he ironically agreed: "Oh, yes!"

"Stepan, you must find a good cook at once," she turned to me.

"No point hurrying with kitchen matters," said Orlov,

giving me a cold look. "We'll have to move to a new apartment first."

He had never kept a cook or horses because, as he put it, he didn't want to "install any mess around him," and he tolerated Polya and me in his apartment only out of necessity. The so-called family hearth with its ordinary joys and squabbles offended his taste, as a banality; to be pregnant or have children and talk about them was bad tone, philistinism. And I now found it extremely curious to picture how these two beings would get along in the same apartment—she, housewifely and practical, with her copper pans and dreams of a good cook and horses, and he, who had often said to his friends that, like a good ship of war, the apartment of a decent, clean man should have nothing superfluous in it— no women, no children, no rags, no kitchenware...

V

NOW I'LL TELL you what happened the next Thursday. On that day Orlov and Zinaida Fyodorovna dined at Contan's or Donon's. Orlov returned home alone, while Zinaida Fyodorovna, as I learned later, went to her old governess on the Petersburg side, to wait out the time while we were having guests. Orlov didn't want to show her to his friends. I realized it in the morning over coffee, when he began assuring her that, for the sake of her peace, it would be necessary to cancel the Thursdays.

The guests, as usual, arrived at almost the same time.

"And is the lady at home?" Kukushkin asked me in a whisper.

"No, sir," I replied.

He went in with sly, unctuous eyes, smiling mysteriously and rubbing his hands from the cold.

"I have the honor of congratulating you," he said to

Orlov, his whole body trembling with obsequious, servile laughter. "I wish you to be fruitful and multiply like the cedars of Lebanon."[12]

The guests went to the bedroom and there exercised their wit at the expense of the woman's slippers, the rug between the two beds, and the gray bed jacket that was hanging on the back of one bed. They found it funny that this stubborn man, who scorned everything ordinary in love, had suddenly been caught in a woman's net in such a simple and ordinary way.

"What thou hast mocked, that hast thou also served," Kukushkin repeated several times, having, incidentally, the unpleasant affectation of flaunting Church Slavonic texts.[13] "Quiet!" he whispered, putting his finger to his lips, as they went from the bedroom to the room next to the study. "Shhh! Here Margarete dreams of her Faust."[14]

And he rocked with laughter, as if he had said something terribly funny. I peered at Gruzin, expecting that his musical soul would be unable to bear that laughter, but I was mistaken. His kind, lean face beamed with pleasure. When they sat down to play cards, he said, swallowing his R's and spluttering with laughter, that to attain full family happiness, it now only remained for Georginka to acquire a cherry-wood chibouk and a guitar. Pekarsky chuckled sedately, but it could be seen from his concentrated expression that he found Orlov's new love story unpleasant. He did not understand what in fact had happened.

"But what about the husband?" he asked in perplexity when they had played three rubbers.

"I don't know," Orlov replied.

Pekarsky combed his big beard with his fingers and fell to thinking and was silent afterwards right up until supper. When they sat down to supper, he said slowly, drawing out each word:

"Generally, excuse me, but I don't understand the two of you. You could be in love with each other and break the

seventh commandment as much as you like—that I understand. Yes, that I understand. But why initiate the husband
into your secrets? Was it really necessary?"

"But does it make any difference?"

"Hm . . ." Pekarsky fell to thinking. "I'll tell you this, my
gentle friend," he went on with evident mental strain, "if
I ever get married a second time, and you decide to make
me a cuckold, do it so that I don't notice. It's much more
honest to deceive a man than to spoil the order of his life
and his reputation. I understand. You both think that by
living openly, you are acting with extraordinary honesty and
liberalism, but with this . . . how is it called? . . . with this
romanticism I cannot agree."

Orlov made no reply. He was out of sorts and did not want
to talk. Pekarsky, continuing to be perplexed, drummed the
table with his fingers, thought, and said:

"I still don't understand the two of you. You're not a
student, and she's not a seamstress. You're both people of
means. I suppose you could arrange a separate apartment
for her."

"No, I couldn't. Go and read Turgenev."[15]

"Why should I read him? I already have."

"Turgenev teaches in his works that every noble-hearted,
honest-minded girl should go to the ends of the earth with
the man she loves and serve his idea," Orlov said, narrowing
his eyes ironically. "The end of the world is *licentia poëtica*:
the whole world, with all its ends, is located in the apartment
of the man she loves. Therefore, not to live in the same
apartment with the woman who loves you—means to reject
her in her lofty purpose and not to share her ideals. Yes, my
dear fellow, Turgenev wrote this porridge, and now I have
to slop it up for him."

"I don't understand what Turgenev has to do with it,"
Gruzin said softly and shrugged his shoulders. "But do you
remember, Georginka, how, in 'Three Meetings,' he's

walking late in the evening somewhere in Italy and suddenly hears: '*Vieni pensando a me segretamente!*'"* Gruzin sang. "That's good!"

"But she didn't force herself on you," said Pekarsky. "You wanted it yourself."

"Well, that's a good one! I not only didn't want it, I didn't even think it would ever happen. When she said she'd move in with me, I thought it was a nice joke."

They all laughed.

"I couldn't want it," Orlov went on in such a tone as if he felt forced to justify himself. "I'm not a Turgenev hero, and if I ever need to liberate Bulgaria,[16] I won't want the company of women. I look at love first of all as a need of my organism, low and hostile to my spirit; it should be satisfied reasonably or renounced entirely, otherwise it will introduce elements as impure as itself into your life. So that it will be an enjoyment and not a torment, I try to make it beautiful and surround it with a host of illusions. I will not go to a woman if I'm not convinced beforehand that she will be beautiful, attractive; nor will I go to her if I'm not at my best myself. And it's only under those conditions that we manage to deceive each other, and it seems to us that we love and are happy. But can I want copper pans and uncombed hair, or that I should be seen when I'm unwashed and out of sorts? Zinaida Fyodorovna, in the simplicity of her heart, wants to make me love something I've been hiding from all my life. She wants my apartment to smell of cooking and dishwashing; she needs to move noisily to a new apartment, drive around with her own horses; she needs to count my linen and look after my health; she needs to interfere in my private life every moment and watch over my every step, and at the same time to assure me sincerely that my habits and freedom will remain my own. She's convinced that we'll

---

*"Come thinking secretly of me!"

take a trip in the nearest future, like newlyweds; that is, she wants to be with me constantly on the train and in hotels, and yet I like to read when I travel and can't bear talking."

"But you can admonish her," said Pekarsky.

"How? Do you think she'd understand me? Mercy, we think so differently! In her opinion, to leave her papa and mama or her husband for the man she loves is the height of civic courage, but in my opinion, it's childishness. To fall in love, to become intimate with a man, means starting a new life for her, but in my opinion, it doesn't mean anything. Love and a man constitute the main essence of her life, and maybe in this respect the philosophy of the unconscious[17] is at work in her. Try convincing her that love is only a simple need, like food and clothing, that the world is by no means perishing because husbands and wives are bad, that one can be a debauchee, a seducer, and at the same time a man of genius and nobility, and, on the other hand, that one can renounce the pleasures of love and at the same time be a stupid, wicked animal. The contemporary cultured man, even if he stands very low—a French worker, for instance— spends ten *sous* a day on dinner, five *sous* on wine to go with dinner, and from five to ten *sous* on a woman, while giving his mind and nerves entirely to his work. Zinaida Fyodorovna gives not *sous* but her whole soul to love. I could perhaps admonish her, but in reply, she'll cry out sincerely that I have ruined her, that she has nothing left in life."

"Don't say anything to her," said Pekarsky, "simply rent a separate apartment for her. That's all."

"It's easy to say..."

A brief silence ensued.

"But she's sweet," said Kukushkin. "She's charming. Such women imagine they're going to love eternally and give themselves with pathos."

"But you've got to have a head on your shoulders," said Orlov, "you've got to reason. All the experiences known to us from everyday life, and set down in the scrolls of countless novels and plays, unanimously confirm that no adulterous relations and cohabitations among decent people, however great their love is in the beginning, last longer than two years, three at the most. She should know that. And so all these moves, pots and pans, and hopes for eternal love and harmony, are nothing more than a wish to deceive herself and me. She's sweet and charming—who's arguing? But she has upset the applecart of my life. What I've considered stuff and nonsense till now, she forces me to raise to the degree of a serious question, I serve an idol I've never considered a god. She's sweet and charming, but for some reason now, when I come home from work, I'm uneasy at heart, as if I expect to encounter some discomfort at home, like stove-makers who have dismantled all the stoves and heaped up mountains of bricks. In short, it's not *sous* that I give for love now, it's part of my peace and my nerves. And that's bad."

"And what if she could hear this villain!" sighed Kukushkin. "My dear sir," he said theatrically, "I shall release you from the onerous duty of loving this charming being! I shall woo Zinaida Fyodorovna away from you!"

"Go ahead . . ." Orlov said carelessly.

For half a minute Kukushkin laughed in a thin little voice and shook all over, then he said:

"Watch out, I'm not joking! Please don't play the Othello afterwards!"

They all began talking about how indefatigable Kukushkin was in amorous affairs, how irresistible he was for women and dangerous for husbands, and how devils would roast him on hot coals in the other world for his dissolute life. He kept silent and narrowed his eyes, and when ladies of his acquaintance were named, he shook his little finger threateningly—meaning, don't give away other people's secrets. Orlov suddenly looked at his watch.

The guests understood and made ready to leave. I remember Gruzin, drunk on wine, this time was painfully long getting dressed. He put on his coat, which resembled the capotes they used to make for children in unwealthy families, raised his collar, and began telling something lengthy; then, seeing that no one was listening to him, he threw his plaid that smelled of the nursery over his shoulder, and asked me, with a guilty, pleading look, to find his hat.

"Georginka, my angel!" he said tenderly. "Listen to me, dearest, let's take a drive out of town!"

"You go, I can't. I have the status of a married man now."

"She's nice, she won't be angry. My kindly superior, let's go! The weather's splendid, a little blizzard, a little frost . . . Word of honor, you need shaking up, you're out of sorts, devil knows . . ."

Orlov stretched, yawned, and looked at Pekarsky.

"Will you go?" he asked, reconsidering.

"Don't know. Perhaps."

"At least get drunk, eh? All right, I'll go," Orlov decided after some hesitation. "Wait, I'll go and get some money."

He went to his study, and Gruzin trudged after him, dragging his plaid behind him. A moment later, they both came back to the front hall. Gruzin, tipsy and very pleased, crumpled a ten-rouble note in his hand.

"We'll settle up tomorrow," he said. "And she's kind, she won't be angry . . . She's my Lizochka's godmother, I love her, poor woman. Ah, my dear man!" he suddenly laughed joyfully and pressed his forehead to Pekarsky's back. "Ah, Pekarsky, my soul! Attornissimus, dry as a dry rusk, but he sure likes women . . ."

"Add: fat ones," said Orlov, putting on his fur coat. "However, let's go, or else we'll meet her in the doorway."

"*Vieni pensando a me segretamente!*" sang Gruzin.

They finally left. Orlov did not spend the night at home and came back only by dinnertime the next day.

ANTON CHEKHOV

VI

ZINAIDA FYODOROVNA'S GOLDEN watch, once given to
her by her father, disappeared. This disappearance astonished
and frightened her. For half a day she walked through all the
rooms, looking in perplexity at the tables and windowsills,
but the watch had vanished into thin air.

Soon after that, about three days later, Zinaida Fyodorovna, having come back from somewhere, forgot her purse
in the front hall. Fortunately for me, it was not I who helped
her out of her things but Polya. When the purse was found
missing, it was no longer in the front hall.

"Strange!" Zinaida Fyodorovna was puzzled. "I remember
perfectly well taking it out of my pocket to pay the
cabby . . . and then putting it here by the mirror. Wonders!"

I hadn't stolen it, but a feeling came over me as if I had
stolen it and had been caught. Tears even came to my eyes.
When they sat down to dinner, Zinaida Fyodorovna said to
Orlov in French:

"We have ghosts here. Today I lost my purse in the front
hall, but I looked just now, and it was lying on my desk. But
it was not an unmercenary trick the ghosts played. They
took a gold piece and twenty roubles for their work."

"First your watch disappeared, and now it's money . . ." said
Orlov. "Why does nothing like that ever happen with me?"

A minute later, Zinaida Fyodorovna no longer remembered the trick the ghosts had played, and was laughingly
telling how she had ordered some stationery a week ago but
had forgotten to leave her new address in the shop, and the
stationery had been sent to her husband at the old apartment,
and her husband had had to pay the bill of twelve roubles.
And she suddenly rested her gaze on Polya and looked at her
intently. With that, she blushed and became confused to such
a degree that she started talking about something else.

When I brought coffee to the study, Orlov was standing by the fireplace with his back to the fire, and she was sitting in an armchair facing him.

"I'm not at all in a bad mood," she was saying in French. "But I've started to figure it out now, and it's all clear to me. I can name you the day and even the hour when she stole my watch. And the purse? There can be no doubts here. Oh!" she laughed, taking the coffee from me. "Now I understand why I lose my handkerchiefs and gloves so often. As you like, but tomorrow I'll let the magpie go and send Stepan for my Sofya. She's not a thief, and she doesn't have such a . . . repugnant look."

"You're out of sorts. Tomorrow you'll be in a different mood, and you'll understand that it's impossible to dismiss a person only because you suspect her of something."

"I don't suspect, I'm certain," said Zinaida Fyodorovna. "All the while I suspected that proletarian with the wretched face, your servant, I never said a word. It's too bad you don't believe me, Georges."

"If you and I think differently about something, it doesn't mean I don't believe you. You may be right," said Orlov, turning to the fire and throwing his cigarette into it, "but even so, you oughtn't to get excited. Generally, I must confess, I didn't expect that my small household would cause you so many serious cares and worries. A gold piece disappeared—well, God be with it, take a hundred of mine, but to change the order, to bring in a new maid from outside, wait till she gets used to it here—it's all long, boring, and not in my character. True, our present maid is fat and maybe has a weakness for gloves and handkerchiefs, but to make up for it, she's quite decent, disciplined, and doesn't squeal when Kukushkin pinches her."

"In short, you can't part with her . . . Just say so."

"Are you jealous?"

"Yes, I'm jealous!" Zinaida Fyodorovna said resolutely.

"Thanks."

"Yes, I'm jealous!" she repeated, and tears glistened in her eyes. "No, it's not jealousy but something worse . . . I have a hard time naming it." She put her hands to her temples and went on impulsively: "You men are sometimes so vile! It's terrible!"

"I see nothing terrible here."

"I haven't seen it, I don't know, but they say still in childhood you men begin with maids and then out of habit don't feel any disgust at it. I don't know, I don't know, but I've even read . . . Georges, you're right, of course," she said, going up to Orlov and changing her tone to a tender and pleading one, "in fact, I am out of sorts today. But understand that I can't be otherwise. I find her repugnant, and I'm afraid of her. It's painful for me to see her."

"Is it really impossible to rise above this pettiness?" said Orlov, shrugging his shoulders in perplexity and stepping away from the fireplace. "Nothing could be simpler: don't pay attention to her, and she won't be repugnant, and there will be no need for you to make a whole drama out of a trifle."

I left the study and do not know what reply Orlov received. Be that as it may, Polya stayed with us. After that, Zinaida Fyodorovna would not address her for anything and obviously tried to do without her services; whenever Polya handed her something, or even merely passed by, jingling her bracelet and rustling her skirts, she shuddered.

I think that if Gruzin or Pekarsky had asked Orlov to dismiss Polya, he would have done it without the slightest hesitation, not troubling himself with any explanations; he was tractable, like all indifferent people. But in his relations with Zinaida Fyodorovna, for some reason, he showed a stubbornness, even in petty things, which at times went as far as tyranny. I just knew that if Zinaida Fyodorovna liked something, he was bound not to like it. When she came back from shopping and hastened to boast to him of her new purchases, he would glance fleetingly at them and say coldly that the more superfluous things there were in the apartment, the less air there was. It would happen that, having already put on his tailcoat to go out somewhere and having already taken leave of Zinaida Fyodorovna, he would suddenly stay home out of stubbornness. It seemed to me then that he was staying home only to feel miserable.

"Why did you stay?" Zinaida Fyodorovna would say with affected vexation and at the same time beaming with pleasure. "Why? You're used to spending your evenings out, and I don't want you to change your habits for my sake. Go, please, if you don't want me to feel guilty."

"Is anyone blaming you?" Orlov would say.

With a victimized look, he would sprawl on the armchair in his study and, shielding his eyes with his hand, pick up a book. But the book would soon drop from his hands, he would turn heavily on the chair and again shield his eyes as if from the sun. Now he was vexed that he had not gone out.

"May I come in?" Zinaida Fyodorovna would say, hesitantly coming into the study. "You're reading? And I got bored and came for one little minute . . . to have a look."

I remember on one of those evenings she came in that way, hesitantly and inopportunely, and lowered herself onto the rug by Orlov's feet, and by her timid, soft movements, it was clear that she did not understand his mood and was afraid.

"And you keep reading . . ." she began ingratiatingly, evidently wishing to flatter him. "Do you know, Georges, what is another secret of your success? You're very educated and intelligent. What book have you got there?"

Orlov told her. Several minutes of silence passed, which seemed very long to me. I stood in the drawing room, observing them both from there and afraid I might start coughing.

"I wanted to say something to you..." Zinaida Fyodorovna said quietly and laughed. "Shall I tell you? Perhaps you'll start laughing and call it self-delusion. You see, I'd like terribly, terribly much to think that you stayed home tonight for my sake...to spend the evening together. Yes? May I think so?"

"Please do," said Orlov, shielding his eyes. "The truly happy man is the one who thinks not only about what is but even about what is not."

"You said something long, and I didn't quite understand it. That is, you want to say that happy people live by imagination? Yes, that's true. I like to sit in your study in the evening and be carried far, far away in my thoughts...It's sometimes nice to dream. Let's dream aloud, Georges!"

"I never went to a girls' institute, I never learned that science."

"Are you out of sorts?" Zinaida Fyodorovna asked, taking Orlov by the hand. "Why, tell me? I'm afraid when you're like this. I can't tell whether you've got a headache or are angry with me..."

Several more long minutes passed in silence.

"Why have you changed?" she said softly. "Why are you no longer cheerful and tender as you were on Znamenskaya? I've lived with you for almost a month, but it seems to me we haven't begun to live yet and have never once talked properly. You answer me each time with little jokes, or else cold and long, like a teacher. And there's something cold in your jokes...Why have you stopped talking seriously with me?"

"I always talk seriously."

"Well, let's talk, then. For God's sake, Georges...let's talk."

"Yes, let's. But about what?"

"Let's talk about our life, about the future..." Zinaida Fyodorovna said dreamily. "I keep making plans for life,

I keep making them—and I feel so good! I'll begin with a question, Georges: when will you leave your service?"

"Why would I do that?" asked Orlov, taking his hand away from his forehead.

"You can't be in the service with your views. You're out of place there."

"My views?" asked Orlov. "My views? By conviction and by nature, I'm an ordinary official, a Shchedrin hero. You take me for someone else, I daresay."

"You're joking again, Georges!"

"Not in the least. The service doesn't satisfy me, maybe, but still it's better for me than anything else. I'm used to it, the people there are the same as I am; I'm not superfluous there, in any case, and feel tolerably well."

"You hate the service, and it sickens you."

"Does it? If I hand in my resignation, start dreaming aloud, and fly off to another world, do you think that world will be less hateful to me than the service?"

"You're even ready to slander yourself in order to contradict me." Zinaida Fyodorovna was hurt and got up. "I'm sorry I started this conversation."

"Why are you angry? I'm not angry that you are not in the service. Each of us lives as he likes."

"But do you really live as you like? Are you really free? Spending your whole life writing papers that are contrary to your convictions," Zinaida Fyodorovna went on, clasping her hands in despair, "obeying, wishing your superiors a happy New Year, then cards, cards, cards, and, above all, serving an order that cannot be sympathetic to you—no, Georges, no! Don't joke so crudely. This is terrible. You're a man of ideas and should serve only your idea."

"Truly, you take me for someone else," Orlov sighed.

"Tell me simply that you don't want to talk with me. I'm repulsive to you, that's all," Zinaida Fyodorovna said through her tears.

"Here's what, my sweet," Orlov said admonishingly, sitting up in his chair. "You yourself kindly observed that I am an intelligent and educated man, and to instruct the instructed only does harm. I'm well acquainted with all the ideas, great and small, that you have in mind when you call me a man of ideas. Which means that if I prefer the service and cards to those ideas, I probably have reasons for doing so. That's one thing. Second, as far as I know, you have never served, and your judgment of government service can only be drawn from anecdotes and bad novels. Therefore it will do us no harm to agree once and for all not to talk about what has long been known to us, or about what does not fall within the circle of our competence."

"Why do you speak to me like that?" Zinaida Fyodorovna said, stepping back as if in horror. "Why? Come to your senses, Georges, for God's sake!"

Her voice trembled and broke off; she apparently wanted to hold back her tears, but suddenly burst into sobs.

"Georges, my dear, I'm perishing!" she said in French, quickly sinking down before Orlov and resting her head on his knees. "I'm tormented, weary, I can't stand it anymore, I can't... In my childhood, a hateful, depraved stepmother, then my husband, and now you... you... You respond to my mad love with irony and coldness... And this dreadful, insolent maid!" she went on, sobbing. "Yes, yes, I see: I'm not a wife to you, not a friend, but a woman you do not respect because she has become your mistress... I'll kill myself!"

I did not expect these words and this weeping to make such a strong impression on Orlov. He blushed, shifted restlessly in his chair, and in place of irony a dull, boyish fear showed on his face.

"My dear, you haven't understood me, I swear to you," he murmured in perplexity, touching her on the hair and shoulders. "Forgive me, I beg you. I was wrong and... I hate myself."

"I offend you with my complaints and whining... You're an honest, magnanimous... rare person, I'm aware of that every moment, but all these days I've suffered anguish..."

Zinaida Fyodorovna impulsively embraced Orlov and kissed his cheek.

"Only don't cry, please," he said.

"No, no... I've cried my fill, and I feel better."

"As for the maid, tomorrow she will not be here," he said, still shifting restlessly in his chair.

"No, she must stay, Georges! Do you hear? I'm no longer afraid of her... One must be above such pettiness and not think stupid things. You're right! You're a rare... an extra-ordinary person!"

She soon stopped crying. With still-undried tears on her lashes, sitting on Orlov's knees, in a low voice she told him something touching, like her memories of childhood and youth, and stroked his face with her hand, kissed and studied attentively his hands with their rings and the seals on his watch chain. She got carried away by her story, and by the nearness of the person she loved, and, probably because her recent tears had purified and refreshed her soul, her voice sounded remarkably pure and sincere. And Orlov played with her chestnut hair and kissed her hands, touching them noiselessly with his lips.

Then they had tea in the study, and Zinaida Fyodorovna read some letters aloud. They went to bed past midnight.

That night I had a bad pain in my side, and right up till morning was unable to get warm and fall asleep. I heard Orlov go from the bedroom to his study. After sitting there for about an hour, he rang. Pain and fatigue made me forget all social rules and decencies, and I went to the study barefoot and in nothing but my underwear. Orlov, in his dressing gown and nightcap, was standing in the doorway waiting for me.

"You should arrive dressed when you're rung for," he said sternly. "Bring more candles."

I was about to apologize but suddenly had a bad fit of coughing and held on to the door frame with one hand so as not to fall.

"Are you ill, sir?" asked Orlov.

I think that, in all the time of our acquaintance, this was the first time he had addressed me like that. God knows why. Probably, in my underwear and with my face distorted by coughing, I played my part badly and hardly resembled a servant.

"If you're sick, why do you work?" he said.

"So as not to starve," I replied.

"How vile this all really is!" he said quietly, going to his desk.

While I, having thrown on my frock coat, set up and lit new candles, he sat by the desk and, with his legs stretched out on the armchair, cut the pages of a book.

I left him immersed in his reading, and the book no longer dropped from his hands, as in the evening.

VII

NOW, AS I WRITE these lines, my hand is restrained by a fear nurtured in me since childhood—of appearing sentimental and ridiculous; when I would like to caress and speak tenderly, I'm unable to be sincere. It is precisely owing to this fear and lack of habit that I am quite unable to express with complete clarity what then happened in my soul.

I was not in love with Zinaida Fyodorovna, but the ordinary human feeling I nursed for her was much younger, fresher, and more joyful than Orlov's love.

In the mornings, working with the shoe brush or the broom, I waited with bated breath till I would at last hear her voice and footsteps. To stand and watch her as she had her coffee and then her breakfast, to help her into her fur coat in the front hall and put galoshes on her little feet while she leaned on my shoulder, then to wait till the porter rang from downstairs, to meet her at the door, rosy, chilled, powdered with snow, to hear her broken exclamations about the cold or the cabby—if you only knew how important it was for me! I would have liked to fall in love, to have my own family, would have liked my future wife to have exactly such a face, such a voice. I dreamed over dinner, and when I was sent out on some errand, and at night when I didn't sleep. Orlov squeamishly thrust aside female rags, children, cooking, copper pans, and I picked it all up and carefully cherished it in my reveries, loved it, asked fate for it, and dreamed of a wife, a nursery, a garden path, a little house . . .

I knew that, if I fell in love with her, I would not dare to count on such a miracle as requital, but this consideration did not trouble me. In my modest, quiet feeling, which resembled ordinary attachment, there was neither jealousy of Orlov nor even envy, since I realized that, for a crippled man like me, personal happiness was possible only in dreams.

When Zinaida Fyodorovna, waiting for her Georges at night, gazed fixedly into a book without turning the pages, or when she gave a start and grew pale because Polya was crossing the room, I suffered with her, and it would occur to me to lance this painful abscess quickly, to make it so that she should quickly learn all that was said here on Thursdays over supper, but—how to do it? More and more often it happened that I saw tears. During the first weeks, she laughed and sang her little song, even when Orlov was not at home, but after another month, there was a dreary silence in our apartment, broken only on Thursdays.

She flattered Orlov, and to obtain an insincere smile or a kiss from him, she went on her knees before him, fawning like a little dog. Going past a mirror, even when her heart was very heavy, she could not help glancing at herself and straightening her hair. It seemed strange to me that she continued to be interested in clothes and went into raptures over her purchases. It somehow didn't go with her genuine sorrow. She observed fashion and had costly dresses made. For what and for whom? I especially remember one new dress that cost four hundred roubles. To pay four hundred roubles for a superfluous, unnecessary dress, while our working women do hard labor at twenty kopecks a day without board, and Venetian and Brussels lace-makers are paid only half a franc a day with the understanding that they will make up the rest by debauchery! And it was strange to me that Zinaida Fyodorovna was not aware of it, it was vexing to me. But she had only to leave the house and I forgave everything, explained everything, and waited for the porter downstairs to ring for me.

She behaved towards me as towards a servant, a lower being. One can pet a dog and at the same time not notice it. I was given orders, asked questions, but my presence was not noticed. The masters considered it indecent to talk with me more than was proper; if, while serving supper, I had mixed into the conversation or laughed, they would probably have considered me mad and dismissed me. But all the same, Zinaida Fyodorovna was benevolent towards me. When she sent me somewhere, or explained how to handle a new lamp or something of that sort, her face was extraordinarily bright, kind, and affable, and her eyes looked directly into my face. Each time it happened, it seemed to me that she remembered gratefully how I had carried letters for her to Znamenskaya. When she rang, Polya, who considered me her favorite and hated me for it, would say with a caustic smile:

"Go, *she's* calling you."

Zinaida Fyodorovna behaved towards me as towards a lower being and did not suspect that, if anyone in the house was humiliated, it was she alone. She didn't know that I, a servant, suffered for her and asked myself twenty times a day what the future held for her and how it would all end. Things were becoming noticeably worse every day. After that evening when they talked about his work, Orlov, who disliked tears, obviously began to fear and avoid conversation; when Zinaida Fyodorovna started arguing or pleading, or was about to weep, he would find some plausible excuse to go to his study or leave the house altogether. He spent the night at home more and more rarely, and dined more rarely still; on Thursdays he himself asked his friends to take him away somewhere. Zinaida Fyodorovna still dreamed of her own kitchen, of a new apartment and a trip abroad, but her dreams remained dreams. Dinner was brought from a restaurant, Orlov asked that the apartment question not be raised till they came back from abroad, and about traveling he said that they could not go before he had grown his hair long, because dragging oneself from hotel to hotel and serving the idea was impossible without long hair.

To crown it all, in Orlov's absence, Kukushkin began to call on us in the evenings. There was nothing special in his behavior, but I was still quite unable to forget that conversation in which he said he would win Zinaida Fyodorovna away from Orlov. He was offered tea and red wine, and he tittered and, wishing to say something pleasant, maintained that civil marriage was higher than church marriage in all respects, and that indeed all decent people should now come to Zinaida Fyodorovna and bow down at her feet.

VIII

CHRISTMASTIME WENT BY boringly, in vague expectation of something bad. On New Year's Eve, over morning coffee, Orlov unexpectedly announced that his superiors were sending him with special powers to a senator who was inspecting some province.

"I don't want to go, but I can't think up an excuse!" he said vexedly. "I'll have to go, there's no help for it."

At this news, Zinaida Fyodorovna's eyes instantly turned red.

"For how long?" she asked.

"Five days or so."

"I'll confess I'm glad you're going," she said after some thought. "You'll be diverted. You'll fall in love with someone on the way and tell me afterwards."

She tried at every opportunity to give Orlov to understand that she was not hampering him in the least and that he could dispose of himself in any way he liked, and this simple, transparent policy deceived no one and only reminded Orlov once again that he was not free.

"I'll leave tonight," he said and began reading the newspapers.

Zinaida Fyodorovna was going to accompany him to the train, but he talked her out of it, saying that he was not going to America, and it was not for five years but only five days or even less.

The leave-taking took place after seven o'clock. He embraced her with one arm and kissed her forehead and lips.

"Be a good girl, and don't mope without me," he said in a tender, heartfelt tone, which moved me, too. "May the Creator protect you."

She peered greedily into his face, so that his dear features would be firmly engraved in her memory, then gracefully put her arms around his neck and laid her head on his chest.

"Forgive me our misunderstandings," she said in French. "A husband and wife can't help quarreling if they love each other, and I love you madly. Don't forget . . . Send me lots of telegrams full of details."

Orlov kissed her once more and, without saying a word, left in confusion. When the lock clicked behind the door, he stopped hesitantly in the middle of the stairs and looked up. It seemed to me that if a single sound had come from upstairs at that moment, he would have gone back. But it was quiet. He straightened his overcoat and began irresolutely to go down.

The cabs had been waiting by the front porch for a long time. Orlov got into one, and I with two suitcases got into the other. It was freezing cold, and bonfires sent up smoke at the intersections. The chill wind from fast driving nipped my face and hands, my breath was taken away, and closing my eyes, I thought: What a magnificent woman she is! How she loves! Nowadays people even collect useless things in courtyards and sell them for charitable purposes, even broken glass is considered good wares, but such a precious, such a rare thing as the love of a graceful, young, intelligent, and decent woman goes completely for naught. One oldtime sociologist looked upon every bad passion as a force which, given the knowhow, could be turned to the good, but with us, even a noble, beautiful passion is born and then dies, powerless, not turned anywhere, misunderstood or trivialized. Why is that?

The cabs stopped unexpectedly. I opened my eyes and saw that we were standing on Sergievskaya Street, by the big house where Pekarsky lived. Orlov got out of the sledge and disappeared through the doorway. About five minutes later, Pekarsky's servant appeared in the doorway without his hat and shouted to me, angry at the cold.

"Are you deaf or what? Dismiss the cabs and go upstairs. You're being called!"

Understanding nothing, I went up to the second floor. I had been at Pekarsky's apartment before; that is, I had stood in the front hall and looked into the drawing room, and each time, after the wet, gloomy street, the gleaming of its picture frames, bronze, and costly furniture had struck me. Now, amidst this gleaming, I saw Gruzin, Kukushkin, and a little later, Orlov.

"It's like this, Stepan," he said, coming up to me. "I'll be living here till Friday or Saturday. If there are any letters or telegrams, bring them here each day. At home, of course, you'll say I left and asked you to convey my greetings. Go with God."

When I returned home, Zinaida Fyodorovna was lying on the sofa in the drawing room and eating a pear. Only one candle was burning, stuck in a candelabra.

"You weren't late for the train?" asked Zinaida Fyodorovna.

"Not at all. The master sends his greetings."

I went to my room in the servants' quarters and also lay down. There was nothing to do, and I didn't want to read. I was not surprised or indignant but simply strained my mind to understand why this deception was necessary. Only adolescents deceive their mistresses that way. Could it be that he, a man who had read and reflected so much, was unable to think up anything more intelligent? I confess, I did not have a bad opinion of his mind. I thought that if he had found it necessary to deceive his minister or some other powerful person, he would have put a lot of energy and art into it, while here, to deceive a woman, he obviously seized upon the first thing that came into his head; if the deception works—good; if not—it was no great disaster, he could lie as simply and quickly a second time without racking his brain.

At midnight, when they began moving chairs and shouting "Hurrah!" on the floor above us, celebrating the New Year, Zinaida Fyodorovna rang for me from the room next to the study. Sluggish from lying down for so long, she sat at the table writing something on a scrap of paper.

"I must send a telegram," she said and smiled. "Drive to the station quickly and ask them to send it after him."

Going outside then, I read on the scrap: "Happy New Year, and best wishes. Wire soon, miss you terribly. A whole eternity has gone by. Pity I can't wire you a thousand kisses and my heart itself. Be cheerful, my joy. Zina."

I sent the telegram and gave her the receipt the next morning.

IX

WORST OF ALL was that Orlov unthinkingly initiated Polya into the secret of his deception as well, telling her to bring his shirts to Sergievskaya. After that she looked at Zinaida Fyodorovna with gloating and with a hatred that I found unfathomable, and never stopped snorting with satisfaction in her room and in the front hall.

"She's overstayed her time here, enough's enough!" she said with delight. "She ought to understand it herself..."

She could already smell that Zinaida Fyodorovna would not be with us much longer, and so as not to miss the moment, she pilfered whatever caught her eye—flacons, tortoiseshell pins, kerchiefs, shoes. On the second day of the new year, Zinaida Fyodorovna summoned me to her room and told me in a low voice that her black dress had disappeared. And afterwards she walked through all the rooms, pale, with a frightened and indignant face, talking to herself:

"How about that? No, how about that? What unheard-of boldness!"

At dinner she wanted to ladle soup for herself, but she couldn't—her hands were trembling. Her lips were trembling, too. She kept glancing helplessly at the soup and the pirozhki, waiting for the trembling to calm down, and suddenly couldn't help herself and looked at Polya.

"You may go, Polya," she said. "Stepan will do by himself."

"No matter, I'll stay, ma'am," Polya replied.

"There's no need for you to stay. Leave here altogether... altogether!" Zinaida Fyodorovna went on, getting up in great agitation. "You may find yourself another place. Leave at once!"

"I can't leave without my master's orders. He hired me. It will be as he orders."

"I'm also ordering you! I'm the mistress here!" said Zinaida Fyodorovna, and she turned all red.

"Maybe you're the mistress, but only the master can dismiss me. He hired me."

"Don't you dare stay here another moment!" cried Zinaida Fyodorovna, and she banged her knife on her plate. "You're a thief! Do you hear?"

Zinaida Fyodorovna flung her napkin on the table and, with a pitiful, suffering face, quickly left the dining room. Polya, sobbing loudly and muttering something, also left. The soup and grouse got cold. And for some reason, all this restaurant luxury on the table now seemed to me paltry, thievish, like Polya. Two pirozhki on a little plate had the most pathetic and criminal look: "Today we'll be taken back to the restaurant," they seemed to be saying, "and tomorrow we'll be served for dinner again to some official or famous diva."

"A grand lady, just think!" came to my ears from Polya's room. "If I wanted, I'd have been just as much of a lady long ago, but I have some shame! We'll see who'll be the first to go! Oh, yes!"

Zinaida Fyodorovna rang the bell. She was sitting in her room, in the corner, with such an expression as if she had been put in the corner as a punishment.

"Have they brought a telegram?" she asked.

"No, ma'am."

"Ask the porter, maybe there's a telegram. And don't leave home," she said after me, "I'm frightened to be left alone."

After that I had to run downstairs to the porter almost every hour to ask whether there was a telegram. It was an eerie time, I must confess! So as not to see Polya, Zinaida Fyodorovna took dinner and tea in her room, slept there on a short couch resembling the letter E, and made her bed herself. For the first few days, it was I who took the telegrams, but, receiving no answer, she stopped trusting me and went to the telegraph office herself. Looking at her, I also waited impatiently for a telegram. I hoped he would invent some lie, for instance, arrange to have a telegram sent to her from some station. If he was too busy playing cards, I thought, or had already managed to become infatuated with another woman, then of course Gruzin and Kukushkin would remind him of us. But we waited in vain. Five times a day I went to Zinaida Fyodorovna's room to tell her the whole truth, but she looked like a goat, her shoulders drooping and her lips moving, and I went away without saying a word. Compassion and pity robbed me of all my courage. Polya, cheerful and content, as though nothing had happened, tidied up the master's study, the bedroom, rummaged in the cupboards and clattered the dishes, and, when going past Zinaida Fyodorovna's door, hummed some tune and coughed. She liked being hidden from. In the evenings she went off somewhere and rang the bell at two or three in the morning, and I had to open the door for her and listen to her remarks about my coughing. There would at once be another ring, I would run to the room next to the study, and Zinaida Fyodorovna, thrusting her head out the door, would ask: "Who rang?" And she would look at my hands to see if there wasn't a telegram in them.

When at last the bell rang downstairs on Saturday and a familiar voice was heard on the stairs, she was so glad that she burst into sobs; she rushed to meet him, embraced him, kissed his chest and sleeves, said something that couldn't be understood. The porter brought in the suitcases, Polya's cheerful voice was heard. As if somebody had come on vacation!

"Why didn't you send me any telegrams?" Zinaida Fyodorovna said, breathing heavily with joy. "Why? I was tormented, I barely survived this time . . . Oh, my God!"

"Very simple! The senator and I went to Moscow that first day, I never received your telegrams," said Orlov. "After dinner, my heart, I'll give you a most detailed report, but now sleep, sleep, sleep . . . I got worn out on the train."

It was obvious that he hadn't slept all night: he probably played cards and drank a lot. Zinaida Fyodorovna put him to bed, and after that, we all went around on tiptoe till evening. Dinner passed quite successfully, but when they went to the study for coffee, a talk began. Zinaida Fyodorovna spoke of something quickly, in a low voice; she spoke in French, and her speech bubbled like a brook, then came a loud sigh from Orlov and the sound of his voice.

"My God!" he said in French. "Don't you have any fresher news than this eternal song about the villainous maid?"

"But my dear, she stole from me and said all sorts of impudent things."

"But why doesn't she steal from me and say impudent things? Why do I never notice maids, or caretakers, or servants? My dear, you're simply capricious and don't want to show character . . . I even suspect you're pregnant. When I offered to dismiss her for you, you demanded that she stay, and now you want me to chase her out. But I'm also stubborn on such occasions: I answer caprice with caprice. You want her to go, well, and now I want her to stay. It's the only way to cure you of your nerves."

"Well, all right, all right!" Zinaida Fyodorovna said fearfully. "Let's stop talking about it . . . Let's put it off till tomorrow. Now tell me about Moscow . . . What's happening in Moscow?"

X

AFTER LUNCH THE next day—it was the seventh of January, the day of John the Baptist—Orlov put on a black tailcoat and a decoration to go to his father and wish him a happy name day. He was to go by two, but when he finished dressing, it was only half past one. How to spend this half hour? He paced about the drawing room and declaimed the congratulatory verses he used to read to his father and mother as a child. Zinaida Fyodorovna, who was about to go to the seamstress or the store, was sitting there and listening to him with a smile. I don't know how the conversation started, but when I brought Orlov his gloves, he was standing in front of Zinaida Fyodorovna, saying to her with a capricious, pleading face:

"For God's sake, for the sake of all that's holy, don't talk about something that's already known to each and every one! What is this unfortunate ability our intelligent, thinking ladies have to speak with passion and an air of profundity about something that has long since set even schoolboys' teeth on edge? Ah, if only you could exclude all these serious questions from our marital program! What a favor it would be!"

"We women should not dare our own judgment to bear."[18]

"I give you full freedom, be liberal and quote any authors you like, but make me one concession, do not discuss these two things in my presence: the perniciousness of high society and the abnormality of marriage. Understand, finally. High society is always denounced, so as to contrast it with the society in which merchants, priests, tradesmen, and muzhiks live—all sorts of Sidors and Nikitas. Both societies are loathsome to me, but if, in all conscience, I were offered the choice between the one and the other, I would choose high society without a second thought, and it would not be a lie or an affectation, because all my tastes are on its side. Our society is trite and trivial, but at least you and I speak decent French, read this and that, and don't start poking each other in the ribs, even when we're having a bad quarrel, while with the Sidors, the Nikitas, and their honors, it's sure thing, right-o, a belt in the gob, and totally unbridled pot-house manners and idolatry."

"The muzhiks and merchants feed you."

"Yes, and what of it? That's a poor recommendation not only for me but for them. They feed me and kowtow to me, meaning they don't have enough intelligence and honesty to act otherwise. I'm not denouncing or praising anybody, I only want to say: high society and low—both are better. In my heart and mind, I'm against them both, but my tastes are on the side of the former. Well, ma'am, and as for the abnormalities of marriage now," Orlov went on, glancing at his watch, "it's time you understood that there are no abnormalities, but as yet there are only indefinite demands on marriage. What do you want of marriage? In lawful and unlawful cohabitation, in all unions and cohabitations, good or bad, there is one and the same essence. You ladies live only for this essence, it's everything for you, without it your existence would have no meaning for you. You need nothing except this essence, and that's what you take, but now that you've read yourselves up on novels, you've become ashamed of taking it, and you rush about hither and thither, recklessly changing men, and to justify this turmoil, you've begun to talk about the abnormalities of marriage. Since you cannot and do not want to eliminate the essence, your chief enemy, your Satan, since you go on serving it slavishly, what serious conversation can there be? Whatever you say to me will be nonsense and affectation. I won't believe you."

I went to find out from the porter whether the cab was there, and when I came back, I found them quarreling. As sailors say, the wind had picked up.

"I see you want to astound me with your cynicism today," Zinaida Fyodorovna was saying, pacing the drawing room in great agitation. "I find it disgusting to listen to you. I am pure before God and men and have nothing to repent of. I left my husband for you, and I'm proud of it. Proud of it, I swear to you on my honor!"

"Well, that's splendid."

"If you're an honorable, decent man, you also should be

proud of my act. It raises me and you above thousands of people who would like to act in the same way as I, but don't dare to out of faintheartedness or petty calculation. But you're not a decent man. You're afraid of freedom and make fun of an honorable impulse for fear that some ignoramus might suspect you of being an honorable man. You're afraid to show me to your acquaintances, there's no higher punishment for you than to drive down the street with me ... What? Isn't it true? Why have you still not introduced me to your father and your cousin? Why? No, I'm tired of it, finally!" cried Zinaida Fyodorovna, and she stamped her foot. "I demand what belongs to me by right. Be so good as to introduce me to your father!"

"If you need him, introduce yourself to him. He receives every morning from ten to ten-thirty."

"How base you are!" said Zinaida Fyodorovna, wringing her hands in despair. "Even if you're not sincere and aren't saying what you think, for this cruelty alone one could come to hate you! Oh, how base you are!"

"We keep circling around and can't talk our way to the real essence. The whole essence is that you were mistaken and don't want to admit it out loud. You imagined I was a hero and had some sort of extraordinary ideas and ideals, but it turned out in reality that I'm a most ordinary official, a cardplayer, and have no interest in any ideas. I'm the worthy offspring of that same rotten society you fled from, outraged at its triviality and triteness. Confess it and be fair: get indignant not with me but with yourself, since it was you who were mistaken, not I."

"Yes, I confess: I was mistaken!"

"That's splendid. We've talked our way to the main thing, thank God. Now listen further, if you like. I can't raise myself up to you, because I'm too corrupt; neither can you lower yourself to me, because you're too high. There remains, then, one thing...."

"What?" Zinaida Fyodorovna asked quickly, with bated breath and suddenly turning white as paper.

"There remains the resort to the aid of logic..."

"Georgiy, why are you tormenting me?" Zinaida Fyodorovna suddenly said in Russian, with a cracked voice. "Why? Understand my suffering..."

Orlov, frightened of tears, quickly went to the study and, I don't know why—wishing to cause her some extra pain, or remembering that this was the practice in such cases— locked the door behind him with a key. She cried out and ran after him, her dress rustling.

"What does this mean?" she asked, knocking on the door. "What...what does this mean?" she repeated in a thin voice breaking with indignation. "Ah, is that how you are? Then know that I hate and despise you! Everything's finished between us! Everything!"

Hysterical weeping and laughter followed. Something small fell off the table in the drawing room and broke. Orlov stole from the study to the front hall by another door and, with a cowardly glance behind him, quickly put on his overcoat and top hat and left.

Half an hour went by, then an hour, and she was still weeping. I remembered that she had no father, no mother, no family, that she was living now between a man who hated her and Polya, who stole from her—and how joyless her life appeared to me! Not knowing why myself, I went to her in the drawing room. Weak, helpless, with beautiful hair, she who seemed to me the image of tenderness and grace suffered like a sick person; she was lying on the sofa, hiding her face, and her whole body shaking.

"Madam, wouldn't you like me to go for the doctor?" I asked quietly.

"No, no need...it's nothing," she said and looked at me with tearful eyes. "I have a slight headache...Thank you."

I went out. But in the evening she wrote letter after letter

288

and sent me now to Pekarsky, now to Kukushkin, now to Gruzin, and finally wherever I liked, so long as I found Orlov quickly and gave him the letter. When I came back each time with the letter, she scolded me, pleaded with me, put money in my hand—as if in a fever. And at night she didn't sleep but sat in the drawing room and talked to herself.

The next day Orlov came back for dinner, and they made peace.

On the first Thursday after that, Orlov complained to his friends about his unbearably hard life; he smoked a lot and said with irritation:

"This isn't life, it's an inquisition. Tears, shouts, wise words, pleas for forgiveness, again tears and shouts, and as a result—I now have no place of my own, I'm worn out and I've worn her out. Can it be I'll have to live like this for another month or two? Can it be? And yet it's possible!"

"Why don't you talk it over with her?" said Pekarsky.

"I've tried, but I can't. You can boldly speak any truth you like to an independent, reasoning man, but here you have to do with a being who has no will, no character, no logic. I can't stand tears, they disarm me. When she cries, I'm ready to vow eternal love and start crying myself."

Pekarsky did not understand, scratched his wide brow, and said:

"Really, you should rent her a separate apartment. It's so simple!"

"She needs me, not an apartment. What's there to talk about?" sighed Orlov. "All I hear is endless talk, but I don't see any way out of my situation. Truly, I'm blamelessly to blame! I didn't sow, but I have to reap. All my life I've shunned the role of hero, I never could stand Turgenev's novels, and suddenly, as if in mockery, I've wound up a veritable hero. I assure her on my word of honor that I'm not a hero at all, I supply irrefutable proofs, but she doesn't

believe me. Why doesn't she believe me? There must indeed
be something heroic in my physiognomy."

"Why don't you go and inspect the provinces?" Kukushkin said with a laugh.

"That's the only thing left."

A week after this conversation, Orlov announced that he
was being sent on business to the senator again, and in the
evening of that same day he drove to Pekarsky's with his
suitcases.

XI

ON THE THRESHOLD stood an old man of about sixty, in a
floor-length fur coat and a beaver hat.

"Is Georgiy Ivanych at home?" he asked.

At first I thought he was a moneylender, one of Gruzin's
creditors, who occasionally came to Orlov for small handouts, but when he came into the front hall and opened his
coat, I saw the thick eyebrows and characteristically compressed lips I had come to know so well from photographs,
and two rows of stars on his uniform tailcoat. I recognized
him: it was Orlov's father, the well-known statesman.

I replied that Georgiy Ivanych was not at home. The
old man pressed his lips tightly together and looked away,
pondering, showing me his dry, toothless profile.

"I'll leave a note," he said. "Show me in."

He left his galoshes in the front hall and, without taking
off his long, heavy fur coat, went to the study. There he sat
down in the armchair at the desk and, before taking up
the pen, thought about something for three minutes or so,
shielding his eyes as if from the sun—exactly as his son did
when he was out of sorts. His face was sad, pensive, with an
expression of that submissiveness which I had seen only in
the faces of old and religious people. I stood behind him,

looking at his bald spot and the depression on his nape, and it was clear as day to me that this weak, ailing old man was now in my hands. For there was not a soul in the whole apartment except me and my enemy. I had only to use a little physical force, then tear off his watch so as to camouflage my purpose, and leave by the back stairs, and I would have gotten immeasurably more than I had counted on when I became a servant. I thought: I'll hardly ever have a luckier chance. But instead of acting, I went on looking with complete indifference now at the bald spot, now at the fur, and calmly reflected on the relations between this man and his only son, and that people spoiled by wealth and power probably don't want to die . . .

"Have you worked for my son long?" he asked, tracing large letters on the paper.

"This is the third month, Your Excellency."

He finished writing and stood up. I still had time. I prodded myself and clenched my teeth, trying to squeeze from my soul at least a drop of my former hatred; I remembered what a passionate, stubborn, and indefatigable enemy I had been still recently . . . But it's hard to strike a match on a crumbling wall. The sad old face and the cold gleam of the stars called up only petty, cheap, and useless thoughts about the frailty of all earthly things, about the proximity of death . . .

"Good-bye, brother!" the old man said, put his hat on, and left.

It was no longer possible to doubt it: a change had taken place in me, I had become different. To test myself, I started to remember, but at once felt eerie, as if I had accidentally glanced into a dark, damp corner. I remembered my friends and acquaintances, and my first thought was of how I would now blush and be at a loss when I met one of them. Who am I now? What am I to think about, and what am I to do? Where am I to go? What am I living for?

I understood nothing and was clearly aware of only one thing: that I must quickly pack my bags and leave. Before the old man's visit, my lackeydom still had meaning, but now it was ridiculous. Teardrops fell into my open suitcase, I was unbearably sad, but how I wanted to live! I was ready to embrace and pack into my short life all that was accessible to man. I wanted to talk, and read, and pound with a hammer somewhere in a big factory, and stand watch, and till the soil. I was drawn to Nevsky Prospect, and to the fields, and to the sea—wherever my imagination could reach. When Zinaida Fyodorovna came back, I rushed to open the door for her, and with special tenderness helped her out of her fur coat. For the last time!

Besides the old man, two others came to us that day. In the evening, when it was already quite dark, Gruzin came unexpectedly to pick up some papers for Orlov. He opened the desk, took out the necessary papers, and, rolling them into a tube, told me to put them in the front hall by his hat while he himself went to Zinaida Fyodorovna. She was lying on the sofa in the drawing room with her hands behind her head. Five or six days had gone by since Orlov left on inspection, and no one knew when he would be back, but she no longer sent telegrams or expected any. Polya still lived with us, but she didn't seem to notice her. "Let it be!"—I read on her dispassionate, very pale face. Like Orlov, she now wanted to be unhappy out of stubbornness; to spite herself and the whole world, she spent whole days lying motionless on the sofa, wishing only the bad for herself and expecting only the bad. She was probably imagining Orlov's return and the inevitable quarrels between them, then his cooling off, his infidelities, then how they would break up, and these tormenting thoughts may have afforded her pleasure. But what would she have said if she had suddenly learned the real truth?

"I love you, my friend," said Gruzin, greeting her and

kissing her hand. "You're so kind! And Georginka's gone away," he lied. "Gone away, the villain!"

He sat down with a sigh and tenderly stroked her hand.

"Allow me, my dove, to sit with you for a little hour," he said. "I don't really want to go home, and it's too early to go to the Birshovs'. Today is their Katya's birthday. A nice girl!"

I served him a glass of tea and a decanter of cognac. He drank the tea slowly, with obvious reluctance, and, as he returned the glass to me, asked timidly:

"My lad, mightn't you have a little something...to eat? I haven't had dinner yet."

We had nothing. I went to the restaurant and brought him an ordinary one-rouble dinner.

"To your health, my dove!" he said to Zinaida Fyodorovna and drank a glass of vodka. "My little one, your goddaughter sends you her greetings. The poor thing has scrofula! Ah, children, children!" he sighed. "Say what you like, my dear, but it's nice to be a father. Georginka doesn't understand that feeling."

He drank again. Skinny, pale, with the napkin on his chest like a bib, he ate greedily and, raising his eyebrows, glanced guiltily now at Zinaida Fyodorovna, now at me, like a little boy. It seemed if I hadn't given him grouse or jelly, he would have wept. Having satisfied his hunger, he cheered up and laughingly began telling something about the Birshovs' family, but, noticing that it was boring and that Zinaida Fyodorovna was not laughing, he fell silent. And somehow it suddenly became boring. After dinner the two of them sat in the drawing room with only one lamp lit and were silent: it was painful for him to lie, and she wanted to ask him about something but could not make up her mind to do it. Half an hour went by that way. Gruzin looked at his watch.

"But perhaps it's time I left."

"No, stay a little...We must talk."

Again they were silent. He sat down at the piano, touched one key, then began to play and sing softly: " 'What does the morrow hold for me?' "—but as usual got up at once and shook his head.

"Play something, my friend," Zinaida Fyodorovna requested.

"But what?" he asked, shrugging his shoulders. "I've forgotten everything. I stopped playing long ago."

Looking at the ceiling as if in recollection, he played two pieces by Tchaikovsky with wonderful expression, so warmly, so intelligently! His face was the same as ever—neither intelligent nor stupid—and to me it seemed simply a wonder that a man whom I was used to seeing in the most mean, impure surroundings was capable of such a high and, for me, inaccessible upsurge of feeling, of such purity. Zinaida Fyodorovna became flushed and began pacing the drawing room in agitation.

"But wait now, my friend, if I can remember it, I'll play a little piece for you," he said. "I heard it played on the cello."

Timidly and tentatively at first, then with assurance, he began playing the "Swan Song" by Saint-Saëns.[19] He played it and repeated it.

"Nice, isn't it?" he said.

Agitated, Zinaida Fyodorovna stopped by him and asked:

"Tell me sincerely, as a friend: what do you think of me?"

"What can I say?" he said, raising his eyebrows. "I love you and think only good things of you. If you want me to speak generally on the question that interests you," he went on, brushing his sleeve at the elbow and frowning, "then, my dear, you know . . . To freely follow the yearnings of one's heart does not always bring good people happiness. To feel yourself free and at the same time happy, it seems to me, you mustn't conceal from yourself the fact that life is cruel, crude, and merciless in its conservatism, and you must respond to it according to its worth; that is, be just as crude and merciless in your yearning for freedom. That's what I think."

"It's beyond me!" Zinaida Fyodorovna smiled sadly. "I'm already weary, my friend. I'm so weary that I won't lift a finger to save myself."

"Go to a convent, my friend."

He said it jokingly, but after his words, Zinaida Fyodorovna and then he himself had tears glistening in their eyes.

"Well, ma'am," he said, "we've sat and sat, now off we go. Good-bye, my dear friend. May God keep you well."

He kissed both her hands and, stroking them tenderly, said he would be sure to visit her one of those days. In the front hall, putting on his coat that resembled a child's capote, he searched in his pockets for a long time, so as to give me a tip, but found nothing.

"Good-bye, my dove!" he said sadly and left.

Never will I forget the mood this man left behind him. Zinaida Fyodorovna still went on pacing the drawing room in agitation. She did not lie down but paced—that was one good thing. I wanted to take advantage of this mood to have a candid talk with her and leave at once, but no sooner had I seen Gruzin off than the bell rang. It was Kukushkin.

"Is Georgiy Ivanych at home?" he asked. "Has he returned? No, you say? What a pity! In that case, I'll go and kiss the mistress's hand and—be off! Zinaida Fyodorovna, may I?" he cried. "I want to kiss your hand. Excuse the late hour."

He did not sit long in the drawing room, no more than ten minutes, but to me, it seemed he had been sitting for a long time and would never go away. I bit my lip with indignation and vexation, and now hated Zinaida Fyodorovna. "Why doesn't she chase him away?" I fulminated, though it was obvious that she was bored with him.

While I held his coat for him, he asked, as a special favor to me, how it was that I could do without a wife.

"But I suppose you're not missing out," he said with a laugh. "You must have all sorts of hanky-panky going on with Polya . . . You rogue!"

Despite my life's experience, I knew very little about people then, and it's very possible that I often exaggerated insignificant things and didn't notice the important at all. I imagined that Kukushkin was tittering and flattering me for a reason: wasn't he hoping that, being a servant, I would blab in servants' quarters and kitchens everywhere about him visiting us in the evenings when Orlov was away and staying with Zinaida Fyodorovna till late at night? And when my gossip reached the ears of his acquaintances, he would drop his eyes abashedly and shake his little finger. And mightn't he—I thought, looking at his honeyed little face—pretend tonight over cards and perhaps let slip that he had already won Zinaida Fyodorovna away from Orlov?

The hatred I had so lacked at noontime, when the old man came, now took possession of me. Kukushkin finally left, and, listening to the shuffling of his leather galoshes, I felt a strong desire to send some rude oath after him in farewell, but I restrained myself. But when the footsteps died away on the stairs, I went back to the front hall and, not knowing what I was doing, seized the bundle of papers Gruzin had forgotten and rushed downstairs. I ran outside without coat or hat. It wasn't cold, but snow was falling in big flakes, and the wind was blowing.

"Your Excellency!" I cried, running after Kukushkin. "Your Excellency!"

He stopped by a streetlamp and looked back in perplexity.

"Your Excellency!" I said breathlessly. "Your Excellency!"

And, unable to think up anything to say, I struck him on the face twice with the bundle of papers. Understanding nothing and not even astonished—so stunned he was—he leaned his back against the streetlamp and covered his face with his hands. At that moment some military doctor walked by and saw me beating a man, but he only looked at us in perplexity and went on.

I felt ashamed and ran back into the house.

XII

BREATHLESS, MY HEAD wet with snow, I ran to the servants' quarters, threw off the tailcoat at once, put on a suit jacket and overcoat, and brought my suitcase out to the front hall. To flee! But before leaving, I quickly sat down and began writing to Orlov:

"I am leaving you my false passport," I began, "asking you to keep it as a souvenir, you false man, Mr. Petersburg Official!

"To sneak into a house under another man's name, to observe your intimate life from behind a servant's mask, to see and hear everything, and then, unbidden, to expose the lie—all that, you will say, resembles theft. Yes, but I cannot worry about nobility now. I lived through dozens of your suppers and dinners, when you said and did whatever you liked, and I had to listen, see, and be silent—I do not want to make you a gift of that. Besides, if there is no living soul around you who would dare to tell you the truth and not flatter, then at least let the servant Stepan wash your splendid physiognomy for you."

I didn't like this beginning, but I had no wish to correct it. And what difference did it make?

The big windows with dark curtains, the bed, the crumpled tailcoat on the floor, and the wet tracks of my feet looked stern and sorrowful. And the silence was somehow peculiar.

Probably because I had run outside without a hat and galoshes, my temperature went up. My face was burning, my legs ached . . . My heavy head bent to the table, and there

ANTON CHEKHOV

was a sort of doubling in my thoughts, when it seems that each thought in your brain is followed by its shadow.

"I am ill, weak, morally depressed," I went on, "I cannot write to you as I would like. In the first moment, I had the wish to insult and humiliate you, but now I do not think I have the right to do so. You and I have both fallen, and neither of us will ever get up, and my letter, even if it were eloquent, strong, and fearsome, would still be like knocking on a coffin lid: knock as you will, there's no waking up! No efforts can warm your cursed cold blood, and you know it better than I do. Why write, then? But my head and heart are on fire, I go on writing, agitated for some reason, as if this letter might still save you and me. Fever keeps the thoughts in my head from cohering, and my pen scratches somehow senselessly on the paper, but the question I want to ask you stands before me as clear as a flame.

"Why I grew weak and fell before my time is not hard to explain. Like the biblical strongman,[20] I lifted the gates of Gaza on my back, so as to carry them to the top of the mountain, but only when I was exhausted, when youth and health were extinguished in me forever, did I notice that those gates were too heavy for me, that I had deceived myself. Besides, I was in constant, cruel pain. I have experienced hunger, cold, illness, the loss of freedom; personal happiness I have not known and do not know, I have no refuge, my memories are a burden, and my conscience is often afraid of them. But you, why have you fallen? What fatal, diabolical reasons kept your life from unfolding into full spring flower? Why, before you had begun to live, did you hasten to shake from yourself the image and likeness of God[21] and turn into a cowardly animal that barks, and frightens others with its barking, because it is afraid? You are afraid of life, afraid, like that Asiatic, the one who sits on a featherbed all day and smokes a hookah. Yes, you read a lot, and wear your European tailcoat dashingly, but still, with what tender, purely Asiatic, khanlike solicitude you protect yourself from hunger, cold, physical strain—from pain and anxiety! How early your soul hid itself in a dressing gown, how you played the coward before real life and nature, with which every healthy and normal person struggles! How soft, cozy, warm, and comfortable it is for you—and how boring! Yes, it is sometimes killingly, irredeemably boring for you, as in solitary confinement, but you try to hide from that enemy as well: you spend eight hours a day playing cards.

"And your irony? Oh, how well I understand it! Living, free, spirited thought is inquisitive and imperious; for a lazy, idle mind, it is unbearable. To keep it from disturbing your peace, you, like thousands of your peers, hastened while still young to set limits to it; you armed yourself with an ironic attitude toward life, or whatever you want to call it, and your restricted, intimidated thought does not dare jump over the little palisade you have set around it, and when you jeer at the ideas that are supposedly *all* known to you, you are like a deserter who shamefully runs away from the field of battle but, to stifle his shame, mocks at war and courage. Cynicism stifles pain. In one of Dostoevsky's stories,[22] an old man tramples underfoot the portrait of his beloved daughter because he is in the wrong before her, and you vilely and tritely make fun of the ideas of good and truth because you are no longer able to go back to them. Any sincere and truthful hint at your fall is frightening to you, and you have deliberately surrounded yourself with people who know only how to flatter your weaknesses. And not for nothing, not for nothing, are you so afraid of tears!

"Incidentally, about your relations with women. We have inherited shamelessness with our flesh and blood, and we are brought up in shamelessness, but it is also for this that we are human beings, so as to overcome the beast in us. With maturity, when *all* ideas became known to you, you could not help seeing the truth; you knew it, but you did not follow it, you were frightened of it, and in order to deceive your conscience, you began loudly assuring yourself that the one to blame was not you but women themselves, that they were as mean as your relations with them. Your cold, scabrous jokes, your horse laugh, all your numberless theories about the essential, the indefinite demands of marriage, the ten *sous* that a French worker pays a woman, your eternal allusions to women's logic, falsity, weakness, and the rest—does it not all look like a desire to force women down into the mud at all costs, so that they and your relations with them stand on the same level? You are a weak, unhappy, unsympathetic man."

In the drawing room, Zinaida Fyodorovna started playing the piano, trying to remember the piece by Saint-Saëns that Gruzin had played. I went and lay on my bed, but, remembering that it was time for me to leave, I forced myself to get up and, with a heavy, hot head, went back to the table.

"But here is the question," I went on. "Why are we worn out? Why do we, who start out so passionate, brave, noble, believing, become totally bankrupt by the age of thirty or thirty-five? Why is it that one is extinguished by consumption, another puts a bullet in his head, a third seeks oblivion in vodka, cards, a fourth, in order to stifle fear and anguish, cynically tramples underfoot the portrait of his pure, beautiful youth? Why is it that, once fallen, we do not try to rise, and, having lost one thing, we do not seek another? Why?

"The thief who hung on the cross[23] managed to recover the joy of life and a bold, realizable hope, though he probably had no more than an hour left to live. You still have long years ahead of you, and most likely I will not die as soon as it seems. What if, by a miracle, the present should turn out to be a dream, a terrible nightmare, and we should wake up renewed, pure, strong, proud of our truth? . . . Sweet dreams burn me, and I can hardly breathe from excitement. I want terribly to live, I want our life to be holy, high, and solemn, like the heavenly vault. Let us live! The sun does not rise twice a day, and life is not given us twice—hold fast to the remains of your life and save them..."

I did not write a word more. I had many thoughts in my head, but they were all scattered and wouldn't fit into the lines. Without finishing the letter, I signed it with my rank, name, and family name, and went into the study. It was dark. I felt for the desk and put the letter on it. I must have bumped into the furniture in the darkness and made a noise.

"Who's there?" an alarmed voice came from the drawing room.

And just then the clock on the desk delicately struck one.

XIII

IN THE DARKNESS I spent at least half a minute scratching the door, feeling it over, then slowly opened it and went into the drawing room. Zinaida Fyodorovna was lying on a couch and, propped on her elbow, met me with her eyes. Not daring to start talking, I slowly walked past her, and she followed me with her gaze. I stood in the reception room for a while and again walked past, and she looked at me attentively and with perplexity, even with fear. Finally I stopped and forced myself to speak:

"He won't come back!"

She quickly stood up and looked at me, not understanding.

"He won't come back!" I repeated, and my heart began pounding terribly. "He won't come back, because he never left Petersburg. He's living at Pekarsky's."

She understood and believed me—that I could see from her sudden pallor and the way she abruptly crossed her hands on her breast with fear and entreaty. In a moment, her recent past flashed through her memory, she put things together and saw the whole truth with implacable clarity. But at the same time, she remembered that I was a servant, an inferior being...A rascal with tousled hair, with a face red from fever, maybe drunk, in some sort of banal coat, had rudely interfered in her private life, and that offended her. She said to me sternly:

"Nobody's asking you. Get out of here."

"Oh, believe me!" I said impulsively, holding my arms out to her. "I'm not a servant, I'm as much a free person as you are!"

I gave my name and quickly, quickly, so that she wouldn't interrupt me or go to her room, explained who I was and why I was living there. This new discovery struck her more strongly than the first one. Earlier, she still had a hope that the servant was lying or mistaken, or had said something stupid, while now, after my confession, she had no doubts left. By the expression of her unhappy eyes and face, which suddenly became unattractive, because it turned old and lost its softness, I saw that it was unbearably painful for her and that nothing good could come of this conversation. Yet I went on impulsively:

"The senator and the inspection were invented to deceive you. In January, just as now, he didn't go anywhere, but lived at Pekarsky's, and I saw him every day and participated in the deception. You were a burden, your presence here was hateful, you were laughed at...If you could have heard how he and his friends here scoffed at you and your love, you wouldn't have stayed here even one minute! Flee this place! Flee!"

"Well, so what?" she said in a trembling voice and passed her hand over her hair. "Well, so what? Let it be."

Her eyes were filled with tears, her lips trembled, and her whole face was strikingly pale and breathed wrath. Orlov's crude, petty lie made her indignant and seemed despicable and ridiculous to her; she was smiling, and I didn't like this smile of hers.

"Well, so what?" she repeated and again passed her hand

over her hair. "Let it be. He imagines I'd die of humiliation, but I find it . . . funny. He needn't be hiding." She stepped away from the piano and said, shrugging her shoulders, "He needn't . . . It would be simpler to have a talk than to hide and knock about in other people's apartments. I have eyes, I saw it long ago . . . and was only waiting for him to come back to have a final talk."

Then she sat in the armchair by the table and, lowering her head onto the armrest of the sofa, wept bitterly. Only one candle was burning in a candelabra in the drawing room, and it was dark around the armchair where she sat, but I saw how her head and shoulders shook and her hair, coming undone, covered her neck, face, hands . . . In her quiet, regular weeping, not hysterical, but ordinary woman's weeping, one could hear insult, humiliated pride, offense, and something irreparable, hopeless, which it was impossible to set right and to which it was impossible to become accustomed. In my agitated, suffering soul, her weeping found an echo; I forgot about my illness and about everything in the world, paced about the drawing room, and muttered perplexedly:

"What sort of life is this? . . . Oh, it's impossible to live this way! Impossible! It's madness, crime, not life!"

"What humiliation!" she said through her tears. "To live together . . . to smile at me, and all the while I'm a burden to him, laughable . . . Oh, what humiliation!"

She raised her head and, looking at me with tearful eyes through her hair, wet with tears, and straightening a strand of hair that kept her from seeing me, asked:

"Did they laugh?"

"These people made fun of you, and of your love, and of Turgenev, whom you have supposedly read too much of. And if we both die of despair right now, they'll also make fun of that. They'll make a funny story out of it and tell it at your panikhida. Why talk about them?" I said with impatience. "We must flee this place. I can't stay here a minute longer."

She started weeping again, and I stepped towards the piano and sat down.

"What are we waiting for?" I asked dejectedly. "It's past two o'clock."

"I'm not waiting for anything," she said. "I'm lost."

"Why say that? Better let's think over together what we're going to do. Neither you nor I can stay here now . . . Where do you intend to go from here?"

Suddenly the bell rang in the front hall. My heart skipped a beat. Might it not be Orlov, to whom Kukushkin had complained about me? How would we meet? I went to open the door. It was Polya. She came in, shook the snow off her cape in the front hall, and, without saying a word to me, went to her room. When I returned to the drawing room, Zinaida Fyodorovna, pale as a corpse, was standing in the middle of the room and looked at me with big eyes as I came in.

"Who came?" she asked softly.

"Polya," I replied.

She ran her hand over her hair and closed her eyes in exhaustion.

"I'll leave here at once," she said. "Be so kind as to take me to the Petersburg side. What time is it now?"

"A quarter to three."

XIV

WHEN WE LEFT the house a little later, the street was dark and deserted. Wet snow was falling, and a damp wind lashed at our faces. I remember it was then the beginning of March, there was a thaw, and for several days the cabs had been driving on wheels. Under the impression of the back stairway, the cold, the darkness of night, and the caretaker in a sheepskin coat, who questioned us before letting us out the gate, Zinaida Fyodorovna became quite faint and dispirited. When we got into the cab and put the top up, she was shivering all over and hastily began telling me how grateful she was to me.

"I don't doubt your good will, but I'm ashamed that you're troubling yourself..." she murmured. "Oh, I understand, I understand... When Gruzin visited today, I felt he was lying and concealing something. Well, so what? Let it be. But even so, I'm ashamed that you're going to such trouble."

She still had some lingering doubts. To disperse them definitively, I told the cabby to drive down Sergievskaya. Stopping by Pekarsky's porch, I got out of the cab and rang the bell. When the porter came out, I asked loudly, so that Zinaida Fyodorovna could hear, whether Georgiy Ivanych was at home.

"He's at home," the porter replied. "He came about half an hour ago. He must be asleep now. What do you want?"

Zinaida Fyodorovna couldn't help herself and stuck her head out of the cab.

"Has Georgiy Ivanovich been living here long?" she asked.

"It's the third week now."

"And he never went away anywhere?"

"No," the porter replied and looked at me in surprise.

"Tell him tomorrow early," I said, "that his sister from Warsaw has come to see him. Good-bye."

Then we drove on. The cab had no front flap, the snow poured on us in big flakes, and the wind, especially on the Neva, pierced us to the bone. It began to seem to me that we had been driving for a long time, suffering for a long time, that I had been listening to Zinaida Fyodorovna's quavering breath for a long time. Fleetingly, in some sort of half-delirium, as if falling asleep, I looked back over my strange, senseless life, and for some reason I remembered the melo-drama *The Beggars of Paris*, which I had seen twice in my childhood. And for some reason, when, in order to shake off this half-delirium, I peeked from under the top and saw the dawn, all the images of the past, all the dim thoughts, suddenly merged in me into one clear, strong thought: Zinaida Fyodorovna and I were now lost irretrievably. This was a certainty, as if the cold blue sky contained a prophecy, but a moment later I was already thinking something else and believing something else.

"What am I now?" Zinaida Fyodorovna was saying in a voice husky from the cold and damp. "Where am I to go? What am I to do? Gruzin said: go to a convent. Oh, I would go! I'd change my clothes, my face, name, thoughts... everything, everything, and hide myself forever. But they won't let me into a convent. I'm pregnant."

"Tomorrow you and I will go abroad," I said.

"That's impossible. My husband won't give me a passport."

"I'll get you there without a passport."

The cab stopped by a two-story wooden house painted a dark color. I rang. Taking from me a light little basket—the only baggage we had brought with us—Zinaida Fyodorovna smiled somehow sourly and said:

"These are my bijoux..."

But she was so weak that she was unable to hold these bijoux. They didn't open the door for a long time. After the third or fourth ring, light flashed in the windows, and footsteps, coughing, and whispering were heard; at last the lock clicked and a fat woman with a red, frightened face appeared in the doorway. Behind her, at some distance, stood a small, thin old lady with short gray hair, in a white chemise, and with a candle in her hand. Zinaida Fyodorovna rushed into the front hall and threw herself on this old lady's neck.

"Nina, I've been deceived!" she sobbed loudly. "I've been crudely, vilely deceived! Nina! Nina!"

I handed the basket to the woman. The door was locked

again, but I could still hear sobbing and the cry: "Nina!" I got into the cab and told the cabby to drive unhurriedly to Nevsky Prospect. I had to think about where to spend the night.

The next day, before evening, I was at Zinaida Fyodorovna's. She was much changed. Her pale face, now grown very thin, showed no trace of tears, and its expression was different. I don't know whether it was because I now saw her in different, far from luxurious surroundings, or because our relations were altered, or maybe strong grief had already left its mark on her, but now she did not appear so graceful and well dressed as always; her figure seemed to have become smaller; in her movements, in her gait, in her face, I noticed an unnecessary nervousness, an impulsiveness, as if she was in a hurry, and there was not even the former softness in her smile. I was now dressed in an expensive two-piece suit, which I had bought in the afternoon. Her eyes first took in this two-piece suit and the hat in my hand, then she rested her impatient, searching gaze on my face, as if studying it.

"Your transformation still seems some sort of miracle to me," she said. "Excuse me for studying you with such curiosity. You really are an extraordinary man."

I told her once again who I was and why I had been living at Orlov's, and I spoke longer and in more detail than the evening before. She listened with great attention and, without letting me finish, said:

"It's all over for me there. You know, I couldn't restrain myself and wrote a letter. Here's the reply."

On the sheet of paper she handed me, there was written in Orlov's hand: "I will not justify myself. But you must agree: it was you who were mistaken, not I. I wish you happiness and ask you to quickly forget your respectful G.O. —P.S. I am sending your belongings."

The trunks and baskets, sent by Orlov, were standing there in the living room, and among them was my pitiful little suitcase as well.

"Which means . . ." said Zinaida Fyodorovna and did not finish.

We were silent for a while. She took the note and for a minute or two held it before her eyes, and at that moment her face took on the same haughty, scornful, and proud, hard expression it had had the day before at the beginning of our talk; tears welled up in her eyes, not timid, not bitter, but proud, angry tears.

"Listen," she said, getting up impulsively and going to the window, so that I couldn't see her face. "I've decided like this: tomorrow I'll go abroad with you."

"That's splendid. I'm even ready to go today."

"Recruit me. Have you read Balzac?" she asked suddenly, turning around. "Have you? His novel *Père Goriot*[24] ends with the hero looking at Paris from the top of a hill and threatening the city: 'Now we'll have it out!' And after that a new life begins. So, too, when I look at Petersburg for the last time from the train, I'll say to it: 'Now we'll have it out!' "

And having said that, she smiled at her joke and, for some reason, shuddered all over.

XV

IN VENICE I began to have pleuritic pains. I had probably caught a cold the evening we went by boat from the train station to the Hotel Bauer. From the first day, I had to take to my bed and stayed in it for about two weeks. Every morning while I was ill, Zinaida Fyodorovna came to me from her room so that we could have coffee together, and then she read aloud to me from French and Russian books, of which we had bought many in Vienna. I had been long familiar with those books or was not interested in them, but beside me was the sound of a dear, kind voice, so that the

contents of them all came down to one thing for me: I was
not lonely. She would go for a walk, come back in her pale
gray dress, in her light straw hat, cheerful, warmed by the
spring sun, and, sitting at my bedside, bending low towards
my face, would tell me something about Venice or read those
books—and I felt good.

At night I was cold, bored, and in pain, but by day I reveled
in life—I can't think of a better expression. The bright, hot
sun beating in through the open windows and the balcony
door, the shouts below, the splashing of oars, the ringing of
bells, the rolling thunder of the cannon at noon, and the
feeling of total, total freedom worked miracles with me; I felt
strong wide wings at my sides, which carried me God knows
where. And what enchantment, how much joy sometimes
at the thought that next to my life now went another life,
that I was the servant, the guardian, the friend, the needed
companion of a beautiful and rich but weak, insulted, lonely
young being! It is even pleasant to be ill when you know
there are people who wait for your recovery as for a feast.
Once I heard her and my doctor whispering outside the
door, and then she came into my room with tearful eyes—a
bad sign—but I was moved and felt extraordinarily light in
my soul.

But now I was allowed to go out on the balcony. The sun
and the light breeze from the sea pamper and caress my ailing
body. I look down on the long-familiar gondolas, which
float with feminine grace, smoothly and majestically, as if
they are alive and feel all the luxury of this original, charming
culture. There is a smell of the sea. Somewhere a stringed
instrument is being played and two voices are singing. How
good! How unlike that Petersburg night when wet snow was
falling and lashing my face so rudely! Now, if you look
directly across the channel, you can see the seashore, and
over the vastness of the horizon, the sun ripples so brightly
on the water that it hurts to look. My soul is drawn there,

to the dear, good sea to which I gave my youth. I want to live! To live—and nothing more!

In two weeks I began going wherever I wanted. I liked to sit in the sun, to listen to a gondolier without understanding, and to spend whole hours looking at the little house where they say Desdemona lived—a naïve, sad little house with a virginal expression, light as lace, so light that it seems you could move it from its spot with one hand. I would stand for a long time by the tomb of Canova,[25] not tearing my eyes from the mournful lion. And in the Doges' Palace, I was always drawn to the corner where the unfortunate Marino Faliero[26] was daubed over with black paint. It's good to be an artist, a poet, a playwright, I thought, but if that's inaccessible to me, I could at least throw myself into mysticism! Ah, if only there was a bit of some sort of faith to add to this untroubled peace and satisfaction that fills my soul.

In the evenings we ate oysters, drank wine, went for boat rides. I remember our black gondola quietly rocking in one spot, the water splashing barely audibly under it. Here and there, reflections of the stars and coastal lights tremble and sway. Not far from us, in a gondola hung with colorful lanterns, which are reflected in the water, some people are sitting and singing. The sounds of guitars, violins, mandolins, male and female voices ring out in the darkness, and Zinaida Fyodorovna, pale, with a serious, almost stern face, sits beside me, tightly clenching her lips and hands. She's thinking about something, and won't even stir an eyebrow, and doesn't hear me. Her face, her posture, her immobile gaze, expressive of nothing, and her memories—unbelievably dismal, eerie, cold as snow—and around us gondolas, lights, music, the song with its energetic, passionate cry: "Jam-mo! . . . Jam-mo! . . ." What contrasts of life! When she sat that way, with her hands clenched, stony, grief-stricken, I imagined both of us participating in some novel in the old-fashioned taste, entitled *An Ill-fated Woman*, *An Abandoned Woman*, or something of the sort. Both of us: she ill-fated, abandoned, and I a true, faithful friend, a dreamer, and, if you like, a superfluous man,[27] a luckless fellow, incapable of anything but coughing and dreaming, and maybe also of sacrificing himself ... but to whom and for what are my sacrifices needed now? And what am I to sacrifice, may I ask?

Each time, after the evening promenade, we drank tea in her room and talked. We weren't afraid of touching old, still-unhealed wounds—on the contrary, for some reason, I even felt pleasure when I told her about my life at Orlov's or openly referred to relations that were known to me and could not have been concealed from me.

"There were moments when I hated you," I said. "When he fussed, condescended, and lied, it struck me how it could be that you didn't see anything, didn't understand, when everything was so clear. You kiss his hands, go on your knees, flatter..."

"When I ... kissed his hands and went on my knees, I loved him..." she said, blushing.

"Could it have been so hard to see through him? A fine sphinx he is! A kammerjunker sphinx! I'm not reproaching you for anything, God forbid!" I went on, feeling that I had been a bit crude, that I lacked worldliness and that delicacy which was so necessary when dealing with another person's soul; before I met her, I had never noticed this shortcoming in myself. "But how could you not have guessed?" I repeated, more softly now and with less assurance.

"You mean to say that you despise my past, and you're right," she said in great agitation. "You belong to a special category of people who can't be measured by the usual yard-stick; your moral demands are distinguished by an exceptional strictness, and, as I understand, you cannot forgive; I understand you, and if I sometimes contradict you, it doesn't mean that I look at things differently than you; I say old rubbish simply because I haven't had time yet to wear

311

out my old dresses and prejudices. I myself hate and despise my past, and Orlov, and my love . . . What kind of love is that? Now it's all even ridiculous," she said, going over to the window and looking down on the canal. "All these loves only darken one's conscience and throw one off. The meaning of life is only in one thing—in struggle. To plant your heel on the vile serpent's head so that it goes 'crack!' The meaning is in that. In that alone, or else there's no meaning at all."

I told her long stories from my past and described for her my indeed amazing adventures. But I never let out a word about the change that had taken place in me. She listened to me with great attention each time and rubbed her hands at the interesting places, as if vexed that she had not yet managed to live through such adventures, fears, and joys, but suddenly she would turn pensive, withdraw into herself, and I could see from her face that she wasn't listening to me.

I'd close the windows looking out on the canal and ask if I shouldn't light the fire.

"No, God help it. I'm not cold," she would say, smiling listlessly, "it's just that I'm all faint. You know, it seems to me that I've become terribly intelligent recently. I have such extraordinary, original thoughts now. When I think about the past, for instance, about my life then . . . well, about people in general, it all merges into one thing in me—the image of my stepmother. Crude, impudent, heartless, false, depraved, and a morphine addict besides. My father, a weak, spineless man, married my mother for money and drove her to consumption, but this second wife, my stepmother, he loved passionately, to distraction . . . The things I suffered! Well, what's there to talk about! So, as I was saying, it all merges into one image . . . And that vexes me: why did my stepmother die? I'd like to meet her now! . . ."

"Why?"

"Just so, I don't know . . ." she answered with a laugh,

shaking her head prettily. "Good night. Get well. As soon as you recover, we'll take care of our affairs ... It's time."

When I had already taken leave and stood holding the door handle, she would say:

"What do you think? Does Polya still live there?"

"Probably."

And I would go to my room. We lived like that for a whole month. One overcast noontime, when we were both standing by the window in my room and silently looking at the clouds coming in from the sea, and at the canal, which had turned dark blue, and expecting the rain to pour down any minute, and when a narrow, dense strip of rain had already covered the coastline like gauze, we both suddenly felt bored. That same day we left for Florence.

XVI

THIS HAPPENED THAT autumn in Nice. One morning when I came to her room, she was sitting in an armchair, her legs crossed, hunched up, shrunken, her face buried in her hands, and weeping bitterly, sobbing, and her long, undone hair fell over her knees. The impression of the marvelous, astonishing sea, which I had only just seen, which I wanted to tell her about, suddenly left me, and my heart was wrung with pain.

"What is it?" I asked. She took one hand away from her face and waved for me to leave. "Well, what is it?" I repeated, and for the first time in our acquaintance, I kissed her hand.

"No, no, it's nothing!" she said quickly. "Oh, nothing, nothing ... Go away ... You can see I'm not dressed."

I left in terrible confusion. My peace and the untroubled mood I had been in for so long were poisoned by compassion. I passionately wanted to fall at her feet, to implore her not to weep alone but to share her sorrow with me, and the even sound of the sea now growled in my ears like a dark prophecy, and I saw new tears ahead, new griefs and losses. What, what was she crying about?—I asked, remembering her face and her suffering eyes. I remembered that she was pregnant. She tried to hide her condition both from people and from her own self. At home she went about in a loose blouse or a chemise with exaggeratedly sumptuous pleats in front, and when she went somewhere, she laced her corset so tightly that she fell into a swoon twice during her walks. She never talked with me about her pregnancy, and once, when I tried to mention that it would do no harm to get a doctor's advice, she turned all red and didn't say a word.

When I came to her room later, she was already dressed, and her hair was done.

"Come, come!" I said, seeing that she was again about to cry. "Better let's go to the sea and have a talk."

"I can't speak. Forgive me, I'm in such a mood now that I'd rather be alone. And please, Vladimir Ivanovich, the next time you want to come into my room, give a preliminary knock on the door."

That "preliminary" had some special, unfeminine ring to it. I left. The cursed Petersburg mood was coming back, and all my dreams curled up and shriveled like leaves in the heat. I felt that I was alone again, that there was no closeness between us. I was the same for her as the spiderweb for this palm tree, which hung on it accidentally and would be torn off and blown away by the wind. I strolled through the square, where music was playing, and went into a casino; there I looked at the dressed-up, much-perfumed women, and each of them looked at me as if she wanted to say: "You're lonely, that's splendid . . ." Then I went out to the terrace and looked at the sea for a long time. Not a single sail on the far horizon; on the shore to the left, hills, gardens, towers, houses in a purple mist; the sun plays on it all, but it's all alien, indifferent, some sort of tangle . . .

XVII

SHE CAME TO me as before to have coffee in the mornings, but we no longer dined together; she, so she said, did not feel like eating, and subsisted on nothing but coffee, tea, and various trifles such as oranges and caramels.

Nor did we have conversations in the evenings. I don't know why that was. After the time I found her in tears, she began to treat me somehow lightly, sometimes carelessly, even with irony, and for some reason called me "my sir." That which earlier had seemed frightening, astonishing, heroic to her, and which had aroused envy and rapture in her, now didn't touch her at all, and usually, having heard me out, she would stretch a little and say:

"Yes, there were big doings at Poltava,[28] my sir, there were indeed."

It even happened that I wouldn't meet her for whole days. I'd knock timidly and guiltily at her door—no answer; I'd knock again—silence . . . I'd stand by the door and listen; but then a maid goes by and announces coldly: "*Madame est partie.*"* Then I'd pace the hotel corridor, pace, pace . . . Englishmen of some sort, full-breasted ladies, garçons in tailcoats . . . And when I've looked for a long time at the long striped carpet that stretches all down the corridor, it occurs to me that I'm playing a strange, probably false role in this woman's life, and that I'm no longer able to change this role; I run to my room, fall on my bed, think and think, and can't think anything up, and it's only clear to me that I want to live, and that the more unattractive, dry, and tough her face becomes, the closer she is to me, and the more strongly and painfully I feel our affinity. Let me be "my sir," let there be this light, disdainful tone, let there be anything, only don't abandon me, my treasure. I'm afraid to be alone now.

*"Madame has left."

315

Then I go out to the corridor again, listen with anxiety . . . I don't have dinner, don't notice how evening comes. Finally, past ten o'clock, I hear familiar footsteps, and Zinaida Fyodorovna appears at the turning by the stairs.

"Taking a stroll?" she asks, passing by. "You'd do better to go out . . . Good night!"

"But won't we see each other today?"

"It's already late, it seems. However, as you wish."

"Tell me, where have you been?" I ask, following her into her room.

"Where? To Monte Carlo." She takes some ten gold pieces from her pocket and says, "Here, my sir. I won. At roulette."

"Well, you're not going to start gambling."

"Why not? And I'll go again tomorrow."

I imagined her with an unpleasant, sickly face, pregnant, tightly laced, standing at the gaming table in a crowd of cocottes, of doddering old women who swarm around gold like flies around honey, remembered that she had left for Monte Carlo in secret from me for some reason . . .

"I don't believe you," I said once. "You won't go there."

"Don't worry. I can't lose much."

"It's not a matter of losing," I said with vexation. "Didn't it occur to you, as you were gambling there, that the gleam of gold, all those women, old and young, the croupier, the whole setting, that it's all a low, vile mockery of a worker's labor, of his sweat and blood?"

"If you don't gamble, what is there to do here?" she asked. "The worker's labor, sweat and blood—set aside that eloquence for another time. But now, since you've started, allow me to continue; allow me to put the question point-blank: what am I to do here, and what will I do?"

"What to do?" I said, shrugging. "It's impossible to answer that question all at once."

"I ask you to answer me in all conscience, Vladimir

316

Ivanych," she said, and her face became angry. "If I've ventured to ask you this question, it is not in order to hear commonplaces. I'm asking you," she went on, rapping the table with her palm as if beating time, "what should I do here? And not only here in Nice, but generally?"

I said nothing and looked out the window at the sea. My heart began to pound terribly.

"Vladimir Ivanych," she said softly, gasping for breath; it was hard for her to speak. "Vladimir Ivanych, if you don't believe in the cause yourself, if you don't intend to return to it, then why . . . why did you drag me away from Petersburg? Why did you promise me, and why did you arouse mad hopes in me? Your convictions have changed, you've become a different person, and no one blames you for that—convictions aren't always in our power, but . . . but Vladimir Ivanych, for God's sake, why are you insincere?" she went on softly, coming up to me. "When I dreamed aloud all these months, raved, admired my plans, reconstructed my life in a new way, why, instead of telling me the truth, did you keep silent or encourage me with stories and behave as if you fully sympathized with me? Why? What did you need that for?"

"It's difficult to confess your bankruptcy," I said, turning around but not looking at her. "No, I don't believe, I'm weary, disheartened . . . It's hard to be sincere, terribly hard, and so I kept silent. God forbid that anyone should go through what I've gone through."

It seemed to me that I was about to burst into tears, and I fell silent.

"Vladimir Ivanych," she said and took me by both hands. "You've experienced and gone through a great deal, you know more than I do; think seriously and tell me: what am I to do? Teach me. If you're no longer able to go yourself and lead others behind you, at least show me where to go. You must agree, I'm a living, feeling, and reasoning person.

To get into a false position . . . to play some absurd role . . . is hard for me. I'm not reproaching, I'm not accusing you, I'm only asking."

Tea was served.

"Well, so?" asked Zinaida Fyodorovna, handing me a glass. "What have you to tell me?"

"There's more than one light in the window," I replied. "There are other people besides me, Zinaida Fyodorovna."

"Point them out for me, then," she said briskly. "That's the only thing I ask of you."

"And I want to say more," I went on. "You can serve the idea in more than just some one field. If you make a mistake and lose faith in one thing, you can find another. The world of ideas is wide and inexhaustible."

"The world of ideas!" she said and looked me mockingly in the face. "Then we'd better stop . . . What's the point . . ."

She blushed.

"The world of ideas!" she repeated and flung the napkin aside, and her face acquired an indignant, squeamish expression. "I see that all your beautiful ideas come down to one inevitable, indispensable step: I must become your mistress. That's what's needed. To fuss with ideas and not be the mistress of the most honest, most idea-conscious man— means not to understand ideas. One must begin with this . . . that is, with the mistress, and the rest will go by itself."

"You're irritated, Zinaida Fyodorovna," I said.

"No, I'm sincere!" she cried, breathing heavily. "I'm sincere."

"Maybe you're sincere, but you're deluded, and it's painful for me to listen to you."

"I'm deluded!" she laughed. "Anyone can say that, but not you, my sir. Let me seem indelicate to you, cruel, but so it goes: you're in love with me, aren't you? Well, aren't you?"

I shrugged my shoulders.

"Yes, shrug your shoulders!" she went on mockingly. "When you were ill, I heard you raving, then there were those constantly adoring eyes, the sighs, the well-intentioned conversations about closeness, spiritual affinity . . . But above all, why have you been insincere up to now? Why did you hide what was there, and talk about what wasn't? You should have told me from the very beginning what, in fact, the ideas were that forced you to drag me away from Petersburg. Then I would have known. I would have poisoned myself, as I wanted to, and there would not have been this tedious comedy now . . . Eh, what's there to talk about!" She waved her hand at me and sat down.

"You speak in such a tone as if you suspect me of dishonorable intentions." I was offended.

"Well, all right now. What's the point. It's not that I suspect your intentions, but that you never had any intentions. If you'd had any, I'd know them. Besides ideas and love, you had nothing. Ideas and love now, and down the road—me as your mistress. Such is the order of things both in life and in novels . . . You denounced him," she said and slapped the table with her palm, "but, willy-nilly, one must agree with him. It's not for nothing he despises all these ideas."

"He doesn't despise ideas, he's afraid of them," I cried. "He's a coward and a liar."

"Well, all right now! He's a coward, a liar, and he deceived me—and you? Forgive my frankness, but who are you? He deceived me and abandoned me to my fate in Petersburg, and you deceived me and abandoned me here. But he at least didn't drag ideas into his deceit, while you . . ."

"For God's sake, why do you say that?" I was horrified and, wringing my hands, quickly went over to her. "No, Zinaida Fyodorovna, no, that's cynicism, you shouldn't be in such despair, hear me out," I went on, seizing upon a thought that had suddenly glimmered vaguely in my head and, it seemed, might still save us both. "Listen to me. I've experienced much in my time, so much that my head is spinning with memories now, and I have now firmly understood with my brain, with my pain-weary soul, that man's purpose is either in nothing or in only one thing—the selfless love of one's neighbor. That's where we should go and what our purpose is! That is my faith!"

I meant to speak further about mercy, about all-forgiveness, but my voice suddenly rang false, and I got embarrassed.

"I want to live!" I said sincerely. "To live, to live! I want peace, quiet, I want warmth, this sea here, your closeness. Oh, how I'd like to inspire this passionate love of life in you as well! You were just talking about love, but for me your closeness alone, your voice, the expression of your face would be enough . . ."

She blushed and said quickly, so as to keep me from talking:

"You love life, but I hate it. Therefore our paths are different."

She poured herself tea but didn't touch it, went to the bedroom, and lay down.

"I suppose it will be better if we stop this conversation," she said to me from there. "For me everything's already over, and I don't need anything . . . Why go on talking about it!"

"No, everything's not over!"

"Well, all right! . . . I know! I'm sick of it . . . Enough."

I stood there for a while, paced from corner to corner, and went out to the corridor. Afterwards, late at night, when I came to her door and listened, I clearly heard weeping.

The next morning the servant, giving me my clothes, told me with a smile that the lady in number thirteen was giving birth. I dressed haphazardly and, sinking with terror, hurried to Zinaida Fyodorovna. In her room were a doctor, a midwife, and an elderly Russian lady from Kharkov by the name of Darya Mikhailovna. There was a smell of ether drops.

I had barely stepped over the threshold when a soft, plaintive moan came from the room where she lay, and it was as if the wind had brought it to me from Russia, I remembered Orlov, his irony, Polya, the Neva, big snowflakes, then the cab with no flap, the prophecy I had read in the cold morning sky, and the desperate cry: "Nina! Nina!"

"Go to her," said the lady.

I went into Zinaida Fyodorovna's room feeling as if I was the father of the child. She lay with her eyes closed, thin, pale, in a white cap trimmed with lace. I remember there were two expressions on her face: one indifferent, cold, listless; the other childlike and helpless, given her by the white cap. She didn't hear me come in, or maybe she did, but paid no attention to me. I stood, looked at her, and waited.

But then her face twisted with pain, she opened her eyes and started looking at the ceiling, as if trying to figure out what was the matter with her... On her face there was a look of disgust.

"Vile," she whispered.

"Zinaida Fyodorovna," I called weakly.

She gave me an indifferent, listless look and closed her eyes. I stood there for a while and then left.

During the night, Darya Mikhailovna told me that the baby was a girl, but the mother was in a dangerous state; then there was running in the corridor, a commotion. Darya Mikhailovna came to me again and, with a desperate look, wringing her hands, said:

"Oh, it's terrible! The doctor suspects she's taken poison! Oh, how badly the Russians behave themselves here!"

And the next day at noon, Zinaida Fyodorovna passed away.

XVIII

TWO YEARS WENT by. My circumstances changed, I went
back to Petersburg and could live there without hiding. I was
no longer afraid to be and to seem sentimental, and gave
myself entirely to the fatherly or, more precisely, the idola-
trous feeling aroused in me by Sonya, Zinaida Fyodorovna's
daughter. I fed her with my own hands, bathed her, put her
to bed, spent whole nights looking at her, and cried out
when I thought the nurse was going to drop her. My thirst
for ordinary, humdrum life grew stronger and more exasper-
ating as time went on, but my vast dreams settled around
Sonya, as if they had finally found in her precisely what
I needed. I loved that little girl madly. I saw in her the
continuation of my life, and it was not that it seemed so to
me, but I felt, and almost believed, that when I had finally
cast off this long, bony, bearded body, I would live in those
light blue eyes, in that blond silky hair and those plump pink
arms that so lovingly stroked my face and embraced my neck.

Sonya's destiny frightened me. Her father was Orlov, on
her birth certificate her name was Krasnovsky, and the only
person who knew of her existence and found it interesting—
that is, I—was already drawing out his last song. I had to
think about her seriously.

The day after my arrival in Petersburg, I went to see Orlov.
A fat old man with red side-whiskers and no mustache,
apparently a German, opened the door. Polya, who was tidy-
ing up in the drawing room, didn't recognize me, but Orlov
did at once.

"Ah, Mr. Seditionist!" he said, looking me over with curiosity and laughing. "What brings you here?"

He hadn't changed at all: the same sleek, unpleasant face,
the same irony. And on the table, as in former times, lay some
new book with an ivory paper knife in place of a bookmark.

He had evidently been reading before I came. He sat me down, offered me a cigar, and, with a delicacy proper only to very well-bred people, hiding the unpleasant feeling provoked in him by my face and my gaunt figure, observed in passing that I hadn't changed at all and was easily recognizable, even though I had grown a beard. We talked of the weather, of Paris. To have done the sooner with the unavoidable painful question that was oppressing both him and me, he asked:

"Did Zinaida Fyodorovna die?"

"Yes, she did," I replied.

"In childbed?"

"Yes, in childbed. The doctor suspected there was some other cause of death, but . . . for you and for me, it's easier to think she died in childbed."

He sighed out of politeness and was silent. An angel passed.

"So, sir. And with me, everything's as before, no particular changes," he said briskly, noticing that I was looking around his study. "Father, as you know, resigned and is now retired, I'm still where I was. Remember Pekarsky? He's the same as ever. Gruzin died last year of diphtheria . . . Well, sir, Kukushkin's alive and often remembers you. Incidentally," Orlov went on, lowering his eyes bashfully, "when Kukush-kin learned who you were, he began telling everywhere that you had supposedly made an assault on him, had wanted to kill him . . . and he had barely escaped with his life."

I said nothing.

"Old servants don't forget their masters . . . It's very nice on your part," Orlov joked. "However, would you like some wine or coffee? I'll order it made."

"No, thank you. I've come to you on very important business, Georgiy Ivanych."

"I'm not a lover of important business, but I'm glad to be of service to you. What is it you want?"

"You see," I began agitatedly, "the daughter of the late Zinaida Fyodorovna is at present here with me . . . Till now

I have occupied myself with her upbringing, but as you see, one of these days I shall turn into an empty sound. I'd like to die with the thought that she has been settled."

Orlov turned slightly red, frowned, and glanced at me sternly, fleetingly. He was unpleasantly affected not so much by the "important business" as by my words about turning into an empty sound, about death.

"Yes, that must be given thought," he said, shielding his eyes as from the sun. "Thank you. You say it's a girl?"

"Yes, a girl. A wonderful girl!"

"So. It's not a pug dog, of course, but a human being... I see it must be given serious thought. I'm ready to take a hand and... and I'm much obliged to you."

He got up, paced about, biting his nails, and stopped before a painting.

"It must be given thought," he said tonelessly, standing with his back to me. "I'll go to Pekarsky today and ask him to call on Krasnovsky. I think Krasnovsky won't make too many difficulties and will agree to take the girl."

"Excuse me, but I don't see what Krasnovsky has to do with it," I said, also getting up and going over to the painting at the other end of the study.

"But she bears his name, I hope!" said Orlov.

"Yes, maybe he's obliged by law to take this girl in, I don't know, but I haven't come to you to talk about laws, Georgiy Ivanych."

"Yes, yes, you're right," he promptly agreed. "It seems I'm talking nonsense. But don't worry. We'll discuss it all to our mutual satisfaction. If not one thing, then another, if not another, then a third, but one way or another, this ticklish question will be resolved. Pekarsky will arrange it all. Kindly leave me your address, and I'll inform you immediately of what decision we come to. Where do you live?"

Orlov wrote down my address, sighed, and said with a smile:

"What a chore, O Creator, to be the father of a little daughter![29] But Pekarsky will arrange it all. He's a 'nintelligent' man. How long did you live in Paris?"

"About two months."

We fell silent. Orlov was obviously afraid I'd bring up the girl again, and to divert my attention in a different direction, he said:

"You've probably forgotten about your letter. But I keep it. I understand your mood at the time, and I confess, I respect that letter. The cursed cold blood, the Asiatic, the horse laugh—it's nice and characteristic," he went on, smiling ironically. "And the main thought is perhaps close to the truth, though one could argue no end. That is," he faltered, "argue not with the thought but with your attitude to the question, with your temperament, so to speak. Yes, my life is abnormal, corrupt, good for nothing, and cowardice keeps me from starting a new life—there you're perfectly right. But that you take it so close to heart, that you worry and despair, is not reasonable—there you're quite wrong."

"A living man can't help worrying and despairing when he sees himself and others around him perishing."

"Who's talking! I'm by no means preaching indifference, I merely want an objective attitude towards life. The more objective, the less risk of falling into error. One must look at the root and seek the cause of all causes in each phenomenon. We've become weak, gone to seed, fallen finally, our generation consists entirely of neurasthenics and whiners, the only thing we know how to do is talk about being tired and overexhausted, but neither you nor I is to blame for it: we're too small for the fate of a whole generation to hang upon our will. Here, one must think, there are large, general causes, which, from a biological point of view, have a sound raison d'être. We are neurasthenics, soured spirits, backsliders, but maybe that's needful and useful for the generations that will live after us. Not a single hair falls from our heads without the will of the Heavenly Father—in other words, nothing in nature and the human environment happens just like that. Everything is well grounded and necessary. But if so, why should we be so especially worried and write desperate letters?"

"That may be so," I said after some reflection. "I believe that for the coming generations, it will be easier and clearer; they will have our experience at their service. But one wants to live independently of the future generations and not merely for them. Life is given only once, and one would like to live it cheerfully, meaningfully, beautifully. One would like to play a prominent, independent, noble role; one would like to make history, so that those same generations would have no right to say of each of us: 'He was a nonentity,' or even worse than that... I do believe in the purposefulness and necessity of what happens around us, but what does that necessity have to do with me? Why should my 'I' perish?"

"Well, what to do!" sighed Orlov, getting up and as if giving me to understand that our conversation was over.

I took my hat.

"We've sat for only half an hour and resolved so many questions, just think!" Orlov said, seeing me off to the front hall. "So I'll take care of that... Today I'll be seeing Pekarsky. Have no doubts."

He stopped to wait while I put on my coat, and obviously felt pleasure at the fact that I would soon be gone.

"Georgiy Ivanych, give me back my letter," I said.

"Yes, sir."

He went to the study and came back a moment later with the letter. I thanked him and left.

The next day I received a note from him. He congratulated me upon the fortunate solution of the problem. A lady of Pekarsky's acquaintance, he wrote, kept a boarding school, something like a kindergarten, where even very small children were accepted. The lady was totally reliable, but, before entering into any agreements with her, it would do no harm to discuss things with Krasnovsky—formality required it. He advised me to go immediately to Pekarsky and, incidentally, to bring the birth certificate with me, if there was such a thing. "Accept the assurance of your humble servant's sincere respect and devotion..."

I was reading this letter, and Sonya was sitting on the table and looking at me attentively, without blinking, as if she knew her fate was being decided.

1892

THREE YEARS

IT WAS NOT dark yet, but here and there lights had been lit in the houses, and beyond the barracks at the end of the street a pale moon was rising. Laptev sat on a bench by the gate and waited for the end of vespers in the Peter-and-Paul church. He reckoned that Yulia Sergeevna, on her way home from vespers, would pass by, and then he would start talking with her and perhaps spend the whole evening with her.

He had been sitting there for about an hour and a half, and his imagination all the while had been picturing his Moscow apartment, his Moscow friends, his footman Pyotr, his desk; he kept glancing in perplexity at the dark, motion-less trees, and it seemed strange to him that he was not now living in his dacha[1] in Sokolniki, but in a provincial town, in a house past which a large herd was driven every morning and evening, accompanied by a frightful cloud of dust and the blowing of a horn. He remembered long Moscow con-versations in which he himself had taken part still so recently—conversations about how it was possible to live without love, how passionate love was a psychosis, how there was finally no such thing as love, but only physical attraction between the sexes—all in the same vein; he remembered and thought sadly that if he were now asked what love was, he would be at a loss to answer.

Vespers were over, people appeared. Laptev peered at the dark figures intently. The bishop had driven past in his car-riage, the bell ringing had stopped, and the red and green lights on the bell tower—this was an illumination on the occasion of the church's feast day[2]—had gone out one by one, yet people still walked unhurriedly, talking, stopping under windows. But then, finally, Laptev heard the familiar voice, his heart began to pound, and because Yulia Sergeevna was not alone but with some two ladies, he was overcome with despair.

"This is terrible, terrible!" he whispered, jealous over her. "This is terrible!"

At the corner, before turning into the lane, she stopped to say good-bye to the ladies and at that moment glanced at Laptev.

"And I'm on my way to your house," he said. "I've come to have a talk with your father. Is he at home?"

"Probably," she replied. "It's too early for him to go to the club."

The lane was all gardens, and lindens grew by the fences, now casting a broad shadow in the moonlight, so that on one side, the fences and gates were completely drowned in darkness; from there came the whisper of women's voices, restrained laughter, and someone very softly played a bala-laika. It smelled of lindens and hay. This smell and the whispering of the invisible ones stirred Laptev. He suddenly wanted passionately to embrace his companion, to cover her face, hands, shoulders with kisses, to burst into sobs, to fall at her feet, to tell her how long he had been waiting for her. She gave off a slight, barely perceptible smell of incense, and it reminded him of the time when he also believed in God and went to vespers and dreamed much of a pure, poetic love. And because this girl did not love him, it seemed to him now that the possibility of the happiness he had dreamed of then was lost to him forever.

She began speaking with concern about the health of his sister, Nina Fyodorovna. Some two months ago, his sister had had a cancer removed, and now everyone expected the illness to return.

"I went to see her this morning," said Yulia Sergeevna, "and it seemed to me that in this last week she has not so much grown thin as faded away."

"Yes, yes," Laptev agreed. "There's no relapse, but with each day, I've noticed, she grows weaker and weaker and wastes away before my eyes. I don't understand what's wrong with her."

"Lord, and how healthy, plump, and red-cheeked she used to be!" said Yulia Sergeevna after a moment's silence. "Here they all used to call her a robin. How she laughed! On feast days she'd dress up like a simple peasant, and it became her very well."

Dr. Sergei Borisych was at home; stout, red-faced, in a long frock coat below his knees, which made him seem short-legged, he paced up and down his study, his hands in his pockets, and hummed in a low voice: "Roo-roo-roo-roo." His gray side-whiskers were disheveled, his hair uncombed, as if he had just gotten out of bed. And his study, with pillows on the sofas, heaps of old papers in the corners, and a sick, dirty poodle under the desk, made the same disheveled and rough impression as the man himself.

"M'sieur Laptev wishes to see you," said the daughter, going into the study.

"Roo-roo-roo-roo," he sang louder and, veering into the drawing room, gave his hand to Laptev and said: "What's the good news?"

It was dark in the drawing room. Laptev, not sitting down, and holding his hat in his hand, began to apologize for the disturbance; he asked what to do so that his sister could sleep at night, and why she was becoming so terribly thin, and he was embarrassed by the thought that he seemed to have asked the doctor these same questions that day during his morning visit.

"Tell me," he asked, "shouldn't we invite some specialist in internal diseases from Moscow? What do you think?"

The doctor sighed, shrugged his shoulders, and made an indefinite gesture with both hands.

It was obvious that he was offended. He was an extremely touchy doctor, very quick to take offense, and always imagined that he was not believed, that he was not recognized and not sufficiently respected, that the public exploited him and his colleagues treated him with ill will. He always laughed at himself, saying such fools as he were created only so that the public could ride on them.

Yulia Sergeevna lighted the lamp. She had gotten tired in church, and that could be noticed by her pale, weary face, by her sluggish gait. She wanted to rest. She sat on the sofa, leaned her arms on her knees, and lapsed into thought. Laptev knew that he was unattractive, and now it seemed to him that he even felt this unattractiveness on his body. He was of small stature, thin, with ruddy cheeks, and his hair was already quite sparse, so that his head got chilled. His expression was totally deprived of that graceful simplicity which makes even coarse, unattractive faces sympathetic; in the company of women, he was awkward, excessively garrulous, affected. And now he almost despised himself for that. To keep Yulia Sergeevna from getting bored in his company, it was necessary to talk. But what about? Again about his sister's illness?

And he began saying what is usually said about medicine, praised hygiene, and mentioned that he had long wished to set up a night shelter in Moscow and that he even had an estimate. According to his plan, a worker coming to the night shelter in the evening would, for five or six kopecks, get a portion of hot cabbage soup with bread, a warm, dry bed with a blanket, and a place to dry his clothes and shoes.

Yulia Sergeevna was usually silent in his presence, and in a strange way, perhaps with the intuition of a man in love, he could guess her thoughts and intentions. And now he realized that if she did not go to her room to change her clothes and have tea after vespers, it meant she was invited somewhere else that evening.

"But I'm in no rush with this night shelter," he went on, now with annoyance and vexation, addressing the doctor, who gazed at him somehow dully and with perplexity, evidently not understanding why on earth he had turned the conversation to medicine and hygiene. "And most likely I won't soon make use of our estimate. I'm afraid our night shelter will fall into the hands of our Moscow hypocrites and philanthropic ladies, who ruin every undertaking."

Yulia Sergeevna got up and gave Laptev her hand.

"Sorry," she said, "it's time for me to go. Please give my greetings to your sister."

"Roo-roo-roo-roo," sang the doctor. "Roo-roo-roo-roo."

Yulia Sergeevna left, and a little later, Laptev took his leave of the doctor and went home. When a man is dissatisfied and feels unhappy, how banal seem to him all these lindens, shadows, clouds, all these self-satisfied and indifferent beauties of nature! The moon was already high, and clouds raced swiftly under it. "But what a naïve, provincial moon, what skimpy, pathetic clouds!" thought Laptev. He was ashamed that he had just spoken of medicine and the night shelter, and he was terrified that tomorrow, too, he would not have character enough, and he would again try to see her and speak with her, and once more be convinced that he was a stranger to her. The day after tomorrow—again the same thing. What for? And when and how would all this end?

At home he went to his sister's room. Nina Fyodorovna still looked sturdy and gave the impression of a well-built, strong woman, but a marked pallor made her look like a dead person, especially when, as now, she lay on her back with her eyes closed. Near her sat her elder daughter, Sasha, ten years old, reading something to her from her school reader.

"Alyosha's come," the sick woman said softly to herself.

Between Sasha and her uncle a silent agreement had long been established: they took turns. Now Sasha closed her reader and, without saying a word, quietly left the room; Laptev took a historical novel from the chest of drawers and, finding the page he needed, sat down and started reading aloud.

Nina Fyodorovna was a native Muscovite. She and her two brothers had spent their childhood and youth on Pyatnitskaya Street, in a family of merchants. It was a long, boring childhood; her father treated her severely and even punished her with a birching three times or so, and her mother was sick with something for a long time and died; the servants were dirty, coarse, hypocritical; priests and monks often came to the house, also coarse and hypocritical; they drank and ate and crudely flattered her father, whom they did not like. The boys had the luck to be sent to school, but Nina remained uneducated, wrote in a scrawl all her life, and read only historical novels. Seventeen years ago, when she was twenty-two, at their dacha in Khimki, she made the acquaintance of her present husband, Panaurov, a landowner, fell in love with him, and married him secretly, against her father's will. Panaurov, handsome, slightly insolent, given to lighting cigarettes from the icon lamp and whistling, seemed utterly worthless to her father, and when, in letters afterward, the son-in-law started demanding a dowry, the old man wrote to his daughter that he would send to her on the estate fur coats, silverware, and various objects left by her mother, and thirty thousand in cash, but without his parental blessing; then he sent another twenty thousand. This money and the dowry were run through, the estate was sold, and Panaurov moved to town with his family and took a job with the provincial government. In town he acquired another family for himself, and that caused much talk every day, since his illegitimate family lived quite openly.

Nina Fyodorovna adored her husband. And now, listening

to the historical novel, she was thinking about how she had lived through so much, had suffered so greatly in all that time, and that if someone were to describe her life, it would come out as very pitiful. Since the tumor was in her breast, she was certain that she had fallen ill from love, from her family life, and that it was jealousy and tears that had brought her to bed.

But here Alexei Fyodorovich closed his book and said:

"The end, and God be praised. Tomorrow we'll start another."

Nina Fyodorovna laughed. She had always laughed readily, but now Laptev had begun to notice that she had moments, on account of illness, when her mind seemed to weaken, and she laughed at the least trifle and even for no reason.

"Yulia came here before dinner, while you were away," she said. "From what I can see, she doesn't have much faith in her father. 'Let my papa treat you,' she says, 'but all the same, write to the holy elder on the quiet and ask him to pray for you.' They've acquired some elder here. Yulechka forgot her parasol here, send it to her tomorrow," she went on after a pause. "No, when it's the end, no doctors or elders will help."

"Nina, why don't you sleep at night?" Laptev asked, to change the subject.

"Just because. I don't sleep, that's all. I lie here and think."

"What do you think about, dear?"

"About the children, about you . . . about my life. I've lived through so much, Alyosha. Once I start remembering, once I start . . . Lord God!" She laughed. "No joke, I've given birth five times, I've buried three children . . . Once I was about to give birth, and my Grigory Nikolaich was with some other woman just then, there was nobody to send for the midwife or a wise woman; I went to the front hall to call for the maid, and there were Jews, shopkeepers, moneylenders—waiting for him to come back. It made my head spin . . . He didn't love me, though he never said so. By

337

now I've calmed down, my heart is more at peace, but before, when I was younger, it hurt me—hurt me, oh, how it hurt me, dear heart! Once—this was still on the estate—I found him in the garden with a lady, and I went away . . . I went wherever my legs would carry me and, I don't know how, I found myself on the church porch, I fell on my knees: 'Queen of Heaven!' I said. And it was night out, a crescent moon was shining . . ."

She was exhausted and began to gasp; then, after resting a little, she took her brother's hand and went on in a weak, soundless voice:

"How kind you are, Alyosha . . . How intelligent you are . . . What a good man you've turned out to be!"

At midnight Laptev said good night to her and, on his way out, took along the parasol forgotten by Yulia Sergeevna. Despite the late hour, the servants, men and women, were having tea in the dining room. What disorder! The children were not asleep and were sitting right there in the dining room. They were talking softly, in low voices, and did not notice that the lamp was growing dim and was about to go out. All these big and small people were upset by a whole series of inauspicious omens, and the mood was oppressive: the mirror in the front hall had broken, the samovar had hummed every day and, as if on purpose, was humming even now; someone said that as Nina Fyodorovna was getting dressed, a mouse had leaped out of her shoe. And the children already knew the awful meaning of these omens; the older girl, Sasha, a thin brunette, sat motionless at the table, and her face was frightened, sorrowful, and the younger, Lida, seven years old, a plump blonde, stood beside her sister and looked at the fire from under her eyebrows.

Laptev went to his rooms on the lower floor, low-ceilinged rooms, where it was stuffy and always smelled of geraniums. In his drawing room sat Panaurov, Nina Fyodorovna's husband, reading a newspaper. Laptev nodded to him and sat down opposite. They both sat and were silent. It sometimes happened that they would spend the whole evening thus silently, and this silence did not embarrass them.

The girls came from upstairs to say good night. Panaurov silently, unhurriedly crossed them both several times and gave them his hand to kiss; they curtseyed, then went over to Laptev, who also had to cross them and give them his hand to kiss. This ceremony with kissing and curtseying was repeated every evening.

When the girls left, Panaurov laid the paper aside and said:

"It's boring in our God-protected town! I confess, my dear," he added with a sigh, "I'm very glad you've finally found yourself some distraction."

"What do you mean?" asked Laptev.

"I saw you earlier coming out of Dr. Belavin's house. I hope you didn't go there for the papa's sake."

"Of course not," said Laptev, reddening.

"Well, of course not. And, incidentally speaking, you won't find another such plug horse as this papa if you search with a lamp in broad daylight. You can't imagine what a slovenly, giftless, and clumsy brute he is! You people there in your capital are still interested in the provinces only from the lyrical side, so to speak, from the *paysage* and Anton the Wretch[3] side, but I swear to you, my friend, there are no lyrics, there's only wildness, meanness, vileness—and nothing more. Take the local high priests of science, the local intelligentsia, so to speak. Can you imagine, there are twenty-eight doctors here in town, they've all made fortunes and live in their own houses, and the populace meanwhile is in the same helpless situation as before. Here Nina had to have an operation, essentially a trifling one, and for that we had to invite a surgeon from Moscow—not a single one here would undertake it. You can't imagine. They know nothing, understand nothing, are interested in nothing. Ask them, for instance, what is cancer? What is it? Where does it come from?"

And Panaurov began to explain what cancer was. He was a specialist in all the sciences and explained scientifically everything that happened to come up in conversation. But he explained it all somehow in his own way. He had his own theory of the circulation of the blood, his own chemistry, his own astronomy. He spoke slowly, quietly, persuasively, and uttered the words "you can't imagine" in a pleading voice, narrowing his eyes, sighing languidly, and smiling benevolently, like a king, and it was obvious that he was very pleased with himself and never thought at all of the fact that he was already fifty years old.

"I'd really like to have something to eat," said Laptev. "It would be pleasant to eat something salty."

"Well, why not? That can be arranged at once."

A little later, Laptev and his brother-in-law were sitting upstairs in the dining room, having supper. Laptev drank a glass of vodka and then began drinking wine, but Panaurov drank nothing. He never drank or played cards and, in spite of that, had all the same run through his own and his wife's fortunes and acquired many debts. To run through so much in such a short time, one had to have not passion but something else, some special talent. Panaurov liked good food, fine place settings, music at the table, speeches, bowing footmen, to whom he casually tossed tips of ten and even twenty-five roubles; he always took part in all the subscriptions and lotteries, sent birthday bouquets to ladies of his acquaintance, bought cups, tea-glass holders, shirt studs, neckties, canes, scent, cigarette holders, pipes, lapdogs, parrots, Japanese objects, antiques; his nightshirts were made of silk, his bed of ebony with mother-of-pearl, his dressing gown was genuine Bokhara, and so on, and all that required a daily outlay of, as he himself said, "no end of money."

Over supper he kept sighing and shaking his head.

"Yes, everything in this world has an end," he said quietly, narrowing his dark eyes. "You'll fall in love, and you'll suffer, fall out of love, be betrayed, because there's no woman who doesn't betray; you'll suffer, become desperate, betray her yourself. But the time will come when it will all turn into a memory, and you'll reason coldly and regard it as completely trifling . . ."

And Laptev, tired, slightly drunk, looked at his handsome head, his black, clipped beard, and it seemed he understood why women so loved this spoiled, self-confident, and physically charming man.

After supper Panaurov did not stay at home but went to his other apartment. Laptev went out to see him off. In the whole town, Panaurov was the only one who wore a top hat, and next to the gray fences, the pitiful three-windowed houses, and the clumps of nettles, his elegant, foppish figure, his top hat and orange gloves, produced each time a strange and sad impression.

After taking leave of him, Laptev returned home unhurriedly. The moon shone brightly, one could see every straw on the ground, and it seemed to Laptev as though the moonlight was caressing his uncovered head, as though someone was stroking his hair with down.

"I'm in love!" he said aloud, and he suddenly wanted to run, overtake Panaurov, embrace him, forgive him, give him a lot of money, and then run off somewhere to the fields, the groves, and keep running without looking back.

At home he saw Yulia Sergeevna's forgotten parasol on a chair, seized it, and greedily kissed it. The parasol was of silk, no longer new, held by an elastic band; the handle was of simple, cheap white bone. Laptev opened it and held it over him, and it seemed to him that there was even a smell of happiness around him.

He settled more comfortably and, without letting go of the parasol, began writing to one of his friends in Moscow:

"My dear Kostya, here is news for you: I am in love again! I say *again*, because some six years ago I was in love with a

Moscow actress with whom I never even managed to get acquainted, and for the last year and a half I have been living with the 'individual' known to you—a woman neither young nor beautiful. Ah, dear heart, how generally unlucky I have been in love! I have never had success with women, and if I say *again*, it is only because it is somehow sad and disappointing to confess to my own self that my youth has passed entirely without love, and that in a real way I am in love for the first time only now, when I am thirty-four. So let it be in love *again*.

"If you only knew what a girl she is! She cannot be called a beauty—her face is broad, and she is very thin—but what a wonderful expression of kindness, what a smile! Her voice, when she speaks, sings and rings. She never gets into conversation with me, I do not know her, but when I am near her, I sense in her a rare, extraordinary being pervaded with intelligence and lofty aspirations. She is religious, and you cannot imagine how that touches me and elevates her in my eyes. On this point I am ready to argue endlessly with you. You are right, let it be your way, but even so, I like it when she prays in church. She is a provincial, but she studied in Moscow, loves our Moscow, dresses in Moscow fashion, and for that I love her, love her, love her . . . I can see you frowning and getting up to give me a long lecture on what love is, and who can and cannot be loved, and so on and so forth. But, dear Kostya, before I fell in love, I myself also knew perfectly well what love was.

"My sister thanks you for your greetings. She often remembers how she once took Kostya Kochevoy to place him in the preparatory class, and to this day she calls you *poor*, because she's kept a memory of you as an orphan boy. And so, poor orphan, I am in love. So far it is a secret, do not say anything *there* to the 'individual' known to you. That, I think, will get settled by itself, or 'shape up,' as the footman says in Tolstoy . . ."[4]

Having finished the letter, Laptev went to bed. His eyes closed of themselves from fatigue, but for some reason, he could not sleep; it seemed that the street noises interfered. The herd was driven past, and the horn was blown, then the bells soon rang for the early liturgy. Now a cart went creaking by, then came the voice of some peasant woman going to market. And the sparrows were chirping all the while.

II

IT WAS A gay, festive morning. At around ten o'clock, Nina Fyodorovna, wearing a brown dress, neatly combed, was brought out to the drawing room, supported under both arms, and there she promenaded a little and stood for a while at the open window, and her smile was broad, naïve, and looking at her reminded one of the local artist, a drunken fellow, who said hers was a face on an icon and wanted to paint her in a Russian Shrovetide scene. And to everybody— the children, the servants, even her brother Alexei Fyodo- rych and herself—it suddenly appeared a certainty that she would unfailingly recover. The girls chased their uncle with shrill laughter, trying to catch him, and the house became noisy.

Strangers came to ask after her health, bringing pros- phoras,[5] saying that prayer services had been held for her that day in almost all the churches. She did charitable work in her town and was loved. She gave charity with extraordinary ease, just like her brother Alexei, who gave money very easily, without considering whether he should give or not. Nina Fyodorovna paid for poor pupils, gave money to old women for tea, sugar, preserves, fitted out needy brides, and if a newspaper happened into her hands, she first looked whether there was any appeal for help or notice of someone in distress.

In her hands now was a bundle of notes by means of which various poor people, her protégés, took goods from the grocery store, and which the merchant had sent her the day before with a request for the payment of eighty-two roubles.

"Just look how much they've taken, shameless folk!" she said, barely making out her bad handwriting on the notes. "No joke! Eighty-two! I'm just not going to pay it!"

"I'll pay it today," said Laptev.

"Why should you? Why?" Nina Fyodorovna became alarmed. "It's enough that I get two hundred and fifty a month from you and our brother. Lord save you," she added quietly, so that the servants would not hear.

"Well, and I run through twenty-five hundred a month," he said. "I repeat to you once more, my dear: you have as much right to spend money as Fyodor and I. Understand that once and for all. Father had the three of us, and of every three kopecks, one is yours."

But Nina Fyodorovna did not understand and had an expression as if she was mentally resolving some very difficult problem. And this obtuseness in money matters always disturbed and confused Laptev. Besides, he suspected that she had personal debts of which she was embarrassed to tell him, and which made her suffer.

Footsteps were heard, and heavy breathing: this was the doctor coming up the stairs, disheveled and uncombed, as usual.

"Roo-roo-roo," he hummed. "Roo-roo."

To avoid meeting him, Laptev went out to the dining room, then downstairs to his own rooms. It was clear to him that to become more intimate with the doctor and visit his house informally was an impossible thing; even to meet this "plug horse," as Panaurov called him, was unpleasant. And that was why he so rarely saw Yulia Sergeevna. He now realized that her father was not at home, that if he brought

Yulia Sergeevna her parasol now, then most likely he would find her at home alone, and his heart was wrung with joy. Quickly, quickly!

He took the parasol and, in great excitement, flew off on the wings of love. It was hot outside. In the doctor's enormous courtyard, overgrown with weeds and nettles, some two dozen boys were playing with a ball. These were all children of the tenants, workers who lived in three old, unsightly wings that the doctor intended to renovate every year and kept putting it off. Healthy, ringing voices resounded. Far to one side, near her porch, stood Yulia Sergeevna, her hands behind her back, watching the game.

"Hello!" called Laptev.

She turned to look. Usually he saw her indifferent, cold, or, as yesterday, tired, but now her expression was lively and frisky, like the boys playing with the ball.

"Look, in Moscow they never play so merrily," she said, coming towards him. "Anyhow, they don't have such big courtyards there, there's no room to run around. And papa has just gone to your house," she added, glancing back at the children.

"I know, but I've come to see you, not him," said Laptev, admiring her youth, which he had not noticed before, and which he seemed to have discovered in her only today; it was as if he was seeing her slender white neck with its golden chain for the first time today. "I've come to see you . . ." he repeated. "My sister sends you your parasol, you forgot it yesterday."

She reached out to take the parasol, but he clutched it to his breast and said passionately, irrepressibly, yielding again to the sweet ecstasy he had experienced the previous night, sitting under the parasol:

"I beg you, give it to me. I'll keep it as a souvenir of you . . . of our acquaintance. It's so wonderful!"

"Take it," she said and blushed. "But there's nothing wonderful about it."

He looked at her in rapture, silently, and not knowing what to say.

"Ah, what am I doing keeping you out in this heat?" she said after some silence and laughed. "Let's go inside."

"But won't I be disturbing you?"

They went into the front hall. Yulia Sergeevna ran up the stairs, her dress rustling, white with little blue flowers.

"It's impossible to disturb me," she said, stopping on the stairs, "I never do anything. Every day is a holiday for me, from morning till evening."

"For me, what you're saying is incomprehensible," he said, going up to her. "I grew up in a milieu where people worked every day, all of them without exception, both the men and the women."

"But if there's nothing to do?" she asked.

"You must set up your life on such conditions that labor will be necessary. Without labor, there can be no pure and joyful life."

He again clutched the parasol to his breast and said softly, unexpectedly for himself, not recognizing his own voice:

"If you would consent to be my wife, I'd give anything. I'd give anything . . . There's no price, no sacrifice I wouldn't go to."

She gave a start and looked at him in surprise and fear.

"What, what are you saying!" she said, turning pale. "It's impossible, I assure you. Forgive me."

Then quickly, with the same rustling of her dress, she went further up and disappeared through the door.

Laptev understood what this meant, and his mood changed at once, abruptly, as if the light had suddenly gone out in his soul. Feeling the shame, the humiliation, of a man who has been scorned, who is disliked, repulsive, maybe vile, whom people flee from, he left the house.

" 'I'd give anything,' " he mocked himself, going home in the heat and remembering the details of his proposal. " 'I'd

346

give anything'—utterly merchantlike. Much need there is for your *anything*!"

Everything he had just said seemed to him stupid to the point of revulsion. Why had he lied about growing up in a milieu where everybody worked without exception? Why had he spoken in an admonitory tone about a pure and joyful life? That was not intelligent, not interesting, false—false Moscow-style. But now a mood of indifference gradually set in, such as criminals lapse into after a harsh sentence, and he thought that, thank God, everything was now past, and there was not that terrible unknowing, there was no need to spend whole days waiting, languishing, thinking about one and the same thing; now everything was clear; he had to abandon any hope of personal happiness, to live without desires, without hopes, not to dream, not to wait, but so that there would not be this boredom he was so sick of nursing, he could be occupied with other people's affairs, other people's happiness, and then old age would set in imperceptibly, life would come to an end—and nothing would be needed anymore. It already made no difference to him, he did not want anything and could reason coldly, but there was some heaviness in his face, especially under his eyes, his forehead was taut as rubber—tears were ready to burst out. Feeling weak all over, he went to bed and in five minutes was fast asleep.

III

THE PROPOSAL LAPTEV had made so unexpectedly brought Yulia Sergeevna to despair.

She knew Laptev only slightly and had become acquainted with him by chance; he was a rich man, a representative of the well-known Moscow firm of Fyodor Laptev and Sons, always very serious, apparently intelligent, preoccupied with his sister's illness; it had seemed to her that he never paid any attention to her, and she herself was totally indifferent to him—and suddenly this declaration on the stairs, this pitiful, admiring face...

The proposal had confused her by its suddenness, and by the fact that the word "*wife*" had been uttered, and by the fact that she had had to answer with a refusal. She no longer remembered what she had said to Laptev, but she went on smarting from the traces of that impulsive, unpleasant feeling with which she had refused him. She did not like him; he had the look of a shopkeeper, was personally uninteresting, she could not have responded otherwise than by refusal, but all the same, she felt awkward, as if she had acted badly.

"My God, without even going in, right on the stairs," she said in despair, addressing the little icon that hung at the head of her bed, "and without courting me beforehand, but somehow strangely, peculiarly..."

In solitude, her anxiety grew stronger with every hour, and it was beyond her strength to deal with this painful feeling alone. She needed someone to hear her out and tell her she had done the right thing. But she had no one to talk to. She had lost her mother long ago, and she considered her father a strange person and could not talk with him seriously. He inhibited her with his caprices, his excessive touchiness and indefinite gestures; and as soon as one got into conversation with him, he would at once begin talking about himself. And during her prayers she was not fully candid, because she did not know for certain what essentially she must ask from God.

The samovar was served. Yulia Sergeevna, very pale, tired, with a helpless look, came out to the dining room, made tea—this was her duty—and poured a glass for her father. Sergei Borisych, in his long frock coat below the knees, red-faced, uncombed, his hands in his pockets, paced the dining room, not up and down, but anyhow, like a caged animal.

He would stop by the table, sip some tea with appetite, and again pace and go on thinking about something.

"Laptev proposed to me today," said Yulia Sergeevna, and she blushed.

The doctor looked at her and seemed not to understand.

"Laptev?" he asked. "Mrs. Panaurov's brother?"

He loved his daughter; it was probable that she would marry sooner or later and leave him, but he tried not to think about it. He was frightened of solitude, and for some reason, it seemed to him that if he was left alone in this big house, he would have an apoplectic stroke, but he did not like to talk about it directly.

"Well, then, I'm very glad," he said and shrugged. "I heartily congratulate you. Now you're presented with a beautiful opportunity for parting with me, to your great satisfaction. I understand you very well. To live with an old father, an ailing half-wit, must be very hard at your age. I understand you perfectly. And if I dropped dead the sooner and got snatched up by devils, everyone would be glad. I heartily congratulate you."

"I refused him."

The doctor felt easier at heart but was no longer able to stop, and went on:

"I'm amazed, I've long been amazed, why they haven't put me in a madhouse yet. Why am I wearing this frock coat and not a straitjacket? I still believe in truth, in the good, I'm a fool of an idealist, and in our time, isn't that madness? And how do they respond to my truth, to my honest attitude? They all but throw stones at me and ride on me. And even my close relations only try to ride on my neck, devil take me, old blockhead that I am . . ."

"It's impossible to have a human conversation with you!" said Yulia.

She got up from the table impulsively and went to her room in great wrath, remembering how often her father had been unfair to her. But a little later, she felt sorry for her father, and when he left for the club, she went downstairs to see him off and locked the door behind him herself. The weather outside was foul, restless; the door trembled from the gusts of wind, and in the front hall, there were drafts from all sides, so that the candle was nearly blown out. Upstairs Yulia went around all the rooms and made crosses at all the windows and doors; the wind howled, and it seemed as though someone was walking on the roof. It had never been so dismal, and she had never felt so alone.

She asked herself: had she acted well in refusing a man only because she did not like his looks? True, this was a man she did not love, and to marry him would mean saying good-bye forever to her dreams, her notions of happiness and married life, but would she ever meet the man she was dreaming of and fall in love with him? She was already twenty-one years old. There were no suitors in town. She pictured to herself all the men she knew—officials, teachers, officers—and some were already married, and their family life struck her as empty and boring, and the others were uninteresting, colorless, unintelligent, immoral. Laptev, whatever else he was, was a Muscovite, he had finished the university, he spoke French; he lived in the capital, where there were many intelligent, noble, remarkable people, where there was noise, splendid theaters, musical evenings, excellent dressmakers, confectioners...It was said in the Holy Scriptures that a wife should love her husband, and in novels love was given enormous significance, but was there not some exaggeration in that? Was family life really impossible without love? Yet they say love soon passes and only habit remains, and that the very goal of family life lies not in love, not in happiness, but in responsibilities, for instance, in bringing up children, taking care of the household, and so on. And the Holy Scriptures may have in mind love for one's husband as for a neighbor, respect for him, tolerance.

That night Yulia Sergeevna attentively read the evening prayers, then knelt and, pressing her hands to her breast, looking at the light of the icon lamp, said with feeling:

"Grant me wisdom, Mother of God! Grant me wisdom, Lord!"

During her life she had happened to meet old maids, poor and insignificant, who bitterly repented and expressed regret that they had once rejected their suitors. Might not the same thing happen to her? Should she not go to a convent or become a sister of mercy?

She undressed and went to bed, crossing herself and crossing the air around her. Suddenly the bell in the corridor rang sharply and plaintively.

"Ah, my God!" she said, feeling a painful irritation all over her body from the ringing. She lay and went on thinking how poor in events this provincial life was, how monotonous and at the same time restless. One kept shuddering, being apprehensive of something, feeling angry or guilty, and in the end one's nerves became upset to such a degree that it was frightening to peek out from under the blanket.

Half an hour later, the bell rang again, as sharply as the first time. It must be that the maid was asleep and did not hear it. Yulia Sergeevna lighted a candle and, trembling, vexed with the maid, began to dress, and when, having dressed, she went out to the corridor, the maid was already locking the door downstairs.

"I thought it was the master, but it was someone sent from a patient," she said.

Yulia Sergeevna went back to her room. She took a pack of cards from the chest of drawers and decided that if she shuffled the cards well and then cut them, and if the card on the bottom was red, it would mean *yes*, that is, she ought to accept Laptev's proposal, but if it was black, it meant *no*. The card was the ten of spades.

That set her at ease, she fell asleep, but in the morning it was again neither *yes* nor *no*, and she thought that if she wished, she could now change her life. The thinking wearied her, she languished and felt ill, but all the same, shortly after eleven o'clock, she got dressed and went to visit Nina Fyodorovna. She wanted to see Laptev: maybe now he would seem better to her; maybe she had been mistaken all the while . . .

It was hard for her to walk against the wind; she inched along, holding her hat with both hands, and could see nothing because of the dust.

IV

GOING INTO HIS sister's room and unexpectedly seeing Yulia Sergeevna, Laptev again experienced the humiliating condition of a man who inspires revulsion. He concluded that if, after what had happened yesterday, she could so easily visit his sister and meet him, it meant she did not notice him, or considered him a total nonentity. But when he greeted her, she, pale, with dust under her eyes, looked at him sadly and guiltily; he realized that she, too, was suffering.

She was unwell. She stayed a very short time, about ten minutes, and began saying good-bye. And, going out, she said to Laptev:

"See me home, Alexei Fyodorych."

They walked down the street in silence, holding their hats, and he, walking behind, tried to shield her from the wind. In the lane, it was quieter, and here they walked side by side.

"If I was unfeeling yesterday, forgive me," she began, and her voice trembled as if she was about to cry. "This is so tormenting! I didn't sleep all night."

"And I slept splendidly all night," Laptev said without looking at her, "but that doesn't mean I'm well. My life is broken, I'm deeply unhappy, and after your refusal yesterday, I walk around as if I've been poisoned. The hardest part was said yesterday, today I feel no constraint with you and can speak directly. I love you more than my sister, more than my late mother...I can and have lived without my sister and my mother, but to live without you—it's senseless for me, I can't..."

And now, as usual, he guessed her intention. It was clear to him that she wanted to continue yesterday's talk and had asked him to accompany her only for that, and now she was leading him to her home. But what more could she add to her refusal? What new thing had she thought up? By everything, by her glances, by her smile, and even by the way she held her head and shoulders as she walked beside him, he could see that she still did not love him, that he was a stranger to her. What more did she want to say?

Dr. Sergei Borisych was at home.

"Welcome, Fyodor Alexeich, very glad to see you," he said, confusing his name and patronymic. "Very, very glad."

Before, he had not been so cordial, and Laptev concluded that the doctor already knew about his proposal; and he did not like that. He was now sitting in the drawing room, and this room made a strange impression, with its poor bourgeois furnishings, its bad paintings, and though there were armchairs in it and an enormous lamp with a lamp shade, it still resembled an uninhabited space, a roomy barn, and it was obvious that only such a man as the doctor could feel at home there; the other room, nearly twice bigger, was called the reception hall, and here there were only straight chairs, as in a dancing school. And Laptev, as he sat in the drawing room and talked with the doctor about his sister, began to be tormented by a certain suspicion. What if Yulia Sergeevna had visited his sister, Nina, and then brought him here in order to announce to him that she accepted his proposal? Oh, how terrible that would be, but most terrible of all was that his soul was accessible to such suspicions. He pictured to himself how yesterday evening and night the father and daughter had discussed it for a long time, maybe argued for a long time, and then come to an agreement that Yulia had acted light-mindedly in refusing a rich man. Even the words parents speak on such occasions rang in his ears:

"True, you don't love him, but then think how much good you can do!"

The doctor was about to go on his sick rounds. Laptev wanted to leave with him, but Yulia Sergeevna said:

"No, please stay."

She was tormented, dispirited, and was now persuading herself that to refuse a decent, kind, loving man only because she did not like him, especially when this marriage would present an opportunity to change her life, her cheerless, monotonous, idle life, when youth was passing by, and there was nothing bright to look forward to in the future—to refuse under such circumstances was madness, it was a caprice and a whim, and God might even punish her for it.

Her father left. When the sound of his footsteps died away, she suddenly stopped in front of Laptev and said resolutely, turning terribly pale:

"I thought for a long time yesterday, Alexei Fyodorych . . . I accept your proposal."

He bent down and kissed her hand, she awkwardly kissed him on the head with cold lips. He felt that in this declaration of love, the main thing—her love—was missing, and there was much that was superfluous, and he wanted to shout, to run away, to leave at once for Moscow, but she was standing close by, she seemed so beautiful to him, and passion suddenly overcame him, he realized that it was now too late to reason, he embraced her passionately, pressed her to his breast, and, murmuring something, calling her *dear*, kissed her on the neck, then on the cheek, on the head . . .

She stepped away to the window, fearing these caresses, and both of them already regretted this declaration and were asking themselves in embarrassment:

"Why has this happened?"

"If you only knew how unhappy I am!" she said, pressing her hands together.

"What's wrong?" he asked, going up to her and also pressing his hands together. "My dear, for God's sake, tell me, what is it? But only the truth, I beg you, only the truth!"

"Don't pay any attention," she said and smiled forcedly. "I promise you, I will be a faithful, devoted wife . . . Come tonight."

Sitting with his sister later and reading a historical novel, he remembered all that, and felt bad that his magnificent, pure, broad feeling had met such a puny response; he was not loved, but his proposal had been accepted, probably only because he was rich; that is, the preference was given to that which he valued least in himself. It might be allowed that Yulia, pure and believing in God, had not thought once about money, but she did not love him, did not love him, and obviously had some calculation, though maybe not fully conscious, vague, but a calculation all the same. The doctor's house was repulsive to him with its bourgeois furnishings, the doctor himself seemed to him like a fat, pathetic niggard, some sort of operetta Gaspard from *The Bells of Corneville*,[6] the very name of Yulia now sounded vulgar. He imagined how he and his Yulia would go to the altar together, essentially complete strangers to each other, without a drop of feeling on her part, as if they had been betrothed by a matchmaker, and there was now only one consolation left him, as banal as this marriage itself, the consolation that he was not the first nor the last, that thousands of people marry that way, and that with time Yulia would get to know him better and might come to love him.

"Romeo and Yulia!" he said, closing the book and laughing. "I'm Romeo, Nina. You can congratulate me, I proposed today to Yulia Belavin."

Nina Fyodorovna thought he was joking, but then believed him and wept. The news did not please her.

"Well, then I congratulate you," she said. "But why is it so sudden?"

"No, it's not sudden. It's been going on since March, only you didn't notice anything...I fell in love back in March, when I made her acquaintance here in your room."

"And I thought you'd marry one of our Moscow girls," Nina Fyodorovna said after a pause. "The girls from our circle would be simpler. But the chief thing, Alyosha, is that you should be happy, that's the chiefest thing. My Grigory Nikolaich didn't love me, and there's no concealing it, you see how we live. Of course, any woman could love you for your kindness and intelligence, but Yulechka is a boarding-school girl and a gentlewoman, for her intelligence and kindness aren't enough. She's young, and you, Alyosha, are no longer young, nor are you handsome."

To soften these last words, she stroked his cheek and said: "You're not handsome, but you're a sweetheart."

She became all excited, so that a slight blush even came to her cheeks, and she spoke with enthusiasm about whether it would be fitting for her to bless Alyosha with an icon; for she was his older sister and took the place of his mother; and she kept trying to persuade her mournful brother that the wedding had to be celebrated in the proper way, festively and merrily, so that people would not condemn them.

After that, he began to visit the Belavins as a fiancé, three or four times a day, and no longer had time to take turns with Sasha reading historical novels. Yulia received him in her own two rooms, far from the drawing room and her father's study, and he liked them very much. Here the walls were dark, and in the corner stood a stand with icons; there was a smell of good perfume and icon-lamp oil. She lived in the farthest rooms, her bed and dressing table were partitioned off by a screen, and the doors of the bookcase were covered from inside with green curtains, and she walked about on rugs, so that her footsteps were not heard at all—

and from that he concluded that she had a secretive character and liked a quiet, peaceful, secluded life. At home she was still in the position of a minor, she had no money of her own, and it happened during walks that she would be embarrassed not to have a kopeck with her. Her father gave her small amounts for clothing and books, no more than a hundred roubles a year. And the doctor himself had hardly any money, even despite a very good practice. He played cards at the club every evening and always lost. Besides that, he bought houses from the mutual credit society with transfer of mortgage and rented them out; the tenants did not pay regularly, but he insisted that these operations with houses were very profitable. He mortgaged his own house, in which he lived with his daughter, and with the money bought a vacant lot and began to build a large two-story house on it, in order to mortgage it.

Laptev now lived in a sort of fog, as though it was not he but his double, and he did many things he would not have ventured to do before. Three times or so he went with the doctor to the club, had supper with him, and offered him money for building; he even visited Panaurov at his other apartment. It happened once that Panaurov invited him for dinner at his place, and Laptev unthinkingly accepted. He was met by a lady of about thirty-five, tall and lean, with slightly graying hair and black eyebrows, apparently not a Russian. There were white blotches of powder on her face; she smiled mawkishly and shook his hand with such zeal that the bracelets jingled on her white arms. It seemed to Laptev that she smiled like that because she wanted to conceal from herself and others that she was unhappy. He also saw two girls, aged five and three, who resembled Sasha. At dinner they were served milk soup, cold veal with carrots, and chocolate—it was sweetish and untasty, but to make up for it, there were gleaming gilt forks on the table, flacons of soy sauce and cayenne pepper, an extraordinarily fanciful cruet stand, a gilt pepper pot.

Only after he finished the milk soup did Laptev realize how inappropriate it actually was for him to have come there for dinner. The lady was embarrassed, smiled all the time, showing her teeth; Panaurov explained scientifically what falling in love was and why it happened.

"We have to do here with one of the phenomena of electricity," he said in French, addressing the lady. "In every person's skin sit microscopic iron strips which contain currents. If you meet an individual whose currents are parallel to your own, there's love for you."

When Laptev returned home and his sister asked where he had been, he felt awkward and did not answer.

All the while before the wedding, he felt himself in a false position. His love grew stronger every day, and Yulia appeared poetic and sublime to him, but all the same there was no mutual love, and the fact of the matter was that he was buying and she was selling herself. Sometimes, as he brooded, he was simply brought to despair and asked himself whether he should not run away. He now spent whole nights without sleeping and kept wondering how, in Moscow after the wedding, he would meet the lady whom he referred to, in his letters to friends, as the "individual," and how his father and brother, difficult people, would regard his marriage and Yulia. He was afraid his father would say something rude to Yulia at their first meeting. As for his brother Fyodor, something strange had been happening to him lately. In his long letters, he wrote about the importance of health, about the influence of illness on one's mental state, about what religion is, but not a word about Moscow and business. These letters annoyed Laptev, and it seemed to him that his brother's character was changing for the worse.

The wedding took place in September. They were married in the Peter-and-Paul church, after the liturgy, and the newlyweds left for Moscow the same day. When Laptev and his wife, in a black dress with a train—no longer a girl, by the look of it, but a real lady—were taking leave of Nina Fyodorovna, the sick woman's whole face went awry, but not a single tear came from her dry eyes. She said:

"If, God forbid, I should die, take my girls to live with you."

"Oh, I promise you!" answered Yulia Sergeevna, and her lips and eyelids also began to twitch nervously.

"I'll come to you in October," said Laptev, deeply moved. "Get well, my dear."

They traveled in a private compartment. Both of them felt sad and awkward. She sat in the corner without taking off her hat and pretended to doze, and he lay on the seat opposite her, troubled by various thoughts: about his father, about the "individual," about whether Yulia was going to like his Moscow apartment. And, glancing at his wife, who did not love him, he thought dejectedly: "Why has this happened?"

V

IN MOSCOW THE Laptevs ran a wholesale trade in haberdashery: fringes, tapes, braid, crocheting cotton, buttons, and so on. The gross receipts reached two million a year; what the net income was no one knew except the old man. The sons and the salesclerks estimated this income at approximately three hundred thousand, and said it would be about a hundred thousand more if the old man did not "extend himself," that is, sell on credit without discernment; in the last ten years they had accumulated almost a million in hopeless promissory notes alone, and the senior salesclerk, when someone mentioned it, would wink slyly and speak words the meaning of which was not clear to everyone:

"The psychological consequences of the age."

The chief trading operations were carried out in the city

market, in premises known as the warehouse. The entrance to the warehouse was from the yard, where it was always dark, there was a smell of bast, and the hooves of dray horses clattered on the asphalt. An iron-bound door, very modest to look at, led from the yard into a room gone brown from dampness, the walls written all over with charcoal, and lighted by a narrow window with iron bars; then, on the left, to another room, slightly larger and cleaner, with a cast-iron stove and two tables, but also with a jailhouse window: this was the office, and from here a narrow stone stairway led to the second story, where the main premises were located. This was a rather large room, but owing to the perpetual darkness, the low ceiling, and the crowding of boxes, bundles, and scurrying people, it made as ill-favored an impression on a fresh person as the two below. Upstairs as well as in the office, goods lay on the shelves in heaps, stacks, and cardboard boxes, no order or beauty could be seen in the way it was organized, and if it had not been for a crimson thread, or a tassel, or a tail of fringe peeking through a hole in the paper wrapping here and there, it would have been impossible to guess at once what they traded in. And, from a glance at these crumpled paper packages and boxes, it was hard to believe that millions were made from such trifles, and that here in the warehouse, fifty people were occupied with business every day, not counting the customers.

When, at noon on the day after his arrival in Moscow, Laptev went to the warehouse, the workers, packing goods, were hammering so loudly on the crates that no one in the front room or the office heard him come in; the familiar postman came down the stairs with a packet of letters in his hand, wincing from the noise, and also did not notice him. The first to meet him upstairs was his brother, Fyodor Fyodorych, who looked so much like him that they were considered twins. This resemblance constantly reminded Laptev of his own appearance, and now, seeing before him a man of small stature, with red cheeks, thinning hair, narrow, underbred hips, looking so uninteresting and unintellectual, he asked himself: "Can I be like that?"

"I'm so glad to see you!" said Fyodor, kissing his brother and firmly shaking his hand. "I've been waiting impatiently for you every day, my dear. As soon as you wrote that you were getting married, I began to be tortured by curiosity, and I missed you as well, brother. Consider for yourself, it's half a year since we've seen each other. Well, so? How are things? Nina's bad? Very?"

"Very bad."

"It's God's will," sighed Fyodor. "Well, and your wife? A beauty, no doubt? I already love her, she's my little sister. We'll pamper her together."

Laptev glimpsed the broad, stooping back of his father, Fyodor Stepanych, a sight long familiar to him. The old man was sitting at the counter on a stool, talking to a customer.

"Papa, God has sent us joy!" cried Fyodor. "Brother has come!"

Fyodor Stepanych was tall and of an extremely sturdy build, so that, despite his eighty years and wrinkles, he still had the look of a hale, strong man. He spoke in a heavy, dense, booming bass, which issued from his broad chest as from a barrel. He shaved his beard, wore a clipped military mustache, and smoked cigars. Since he always felt hot, he wore a roomy canvas jacket at all times of the year, in the warehouse and at home. He had recently had a cataract removed, did not see well, and no longer occupied himself with business but only talked and drank tea with jam.

Laptev bent down and kissed him on the hand, then on the lips.

"We haven't seen each other for a long time, my dear sir," said the old man. "A long time. So, then, congratulations on a lawful marriage are in order? Well, so be it, my congratulations."

And he offered his lips for a kiss. Laptev bent down and kissed him.

"So, then, you've brought your young lady?" asked the old man and, without waiting for an answer, said, turning to a customer: "I hereby inform you, papa, that I am marrying such and such a girl. But as for asking the father's blessing or advice, that's no longer the rule. They keep their own counsel now. When I got married, I was over forty, but I lay at my father's feet and asked for advice. Nowadays it's no longer done."

The old man was glad to see his son but considered it improper to be affectionate with him and in any way show his joy. His voice, his manner of speaking, and the "young lady" cast over Laptev that bad mood he experienced each time in the warehouse. Here every trifle reminded him of the past, when he was whipped and kept on lenten fare; he knew that now, too, boys were whipped and given bloody noses, and that when they grew up, they themselves would do the beating. And it was enough to spend five minutes in the warehouse for him to begin to fancy that he was about to be yelled at or punched in the nose.

Fyodor patted the customer on the shoulder and said to his brother:

"Here, Alyosha, I'd like to introduce you to our Tambov benefactor, Grigory Timofeich. He can serve as an example to contemporary youth: he's past fifty, yet he has nursing babies."

The salesclerks laughed, and the customer, a skinny old man with a pale face, also laughed.

"Nature exceeding its usual activity," observed the senior salesclerk, who was standing behind the counter. "Where it goes in is where it comes out."

The senior salesclerk, a tall man of about fifty, with a dark beard, spectacles, and a pencil behind his ear, usually expressed his thoughts vaguely, in remote hints, and accompanied his words with a sly smile, showing that he had put some especially subtle meaning into them. He liked to obscure his speech with bookish words, which he understood in his own way, and there were many ordinary words that he often employed in a sense other than the one they had. For instance, the word "except." Whenever he expressed some thought categorically and did not want to be contradicted, he would extend his right arm and pronounce:

"Except!"

And most surprising of all was that the other salesclerks and the customers understood him perfectly well. His name was Ivan Vassilyich Pochatkin, and he was from Kashira. Now, congratulating Laptev, he expressed himself thus:

"On your side the merit of courage, for a woman's heart is Shamil."[7]

Another important person in the warehouse was the salesclerk Makeichev, a stout, staid blond man with side-whiskers and a completely bald pate. He came up to Laptev and congratulated him respectfully, in a low voice:

"My respects, sir . . . The Lord has heard the prayers of your parent, sir. Thank God, sir."

Then the other salesclerks began to come up to him and congratulate him on his lawful marriage. They were all fashionably dressed and had the look of quite respectable, well-bred people. They stressed their O's, pronounced their Gh's like the hard Latin G, and because their every third word was sir, their congratulations, pronounced in a quick patter—for instance, the phrase: "I wish you, sir, all the best, sir"—sounded as if someone was lashing the air with a whip: "Whis-s-s-s."

Laptev soon became bored with it all and wanted to go home, but it was awkward to leave. Out of propriety, he had to spend at least two hours in the warehouse. He stepped away from the counter and began asking Makeichev if the summer had gone well and whether there was any news, and the man answered deferentially without looking him in the eye. A boy, crop-headed, in a gray smock, handed Laptev a glass of tea without a saucer; a little later another boy, passing by, stumbled against a crate and almost fell, and the staid Makeichev suddenly made a terrible, wicked face, a fiendish face, and shouted at him:

"Watch your feet!"

The salesclerks were glad that the young master had married and finally come back, they looked at him affably and with curiosity, and each of them, in passing, considered it his duty respectfully to say something pleasant to him. But Laptev was convinced that it was all insincere and that they flattered him because they were afraid. He could never forget how, fifteen years ago, one salesclerk, becoming mentally ill, ran outside barefoot in nothing but his underwear and, shaking his fist at the masters' windows, shouted that they were torturing him; and when the poor man recovered later, they laughed at him for a long time and reminded him of how he had shouted "Plantators!" instead of "Exploiters." In general, the Laptevs' employees had a bad life, and the whole market had long been talking about it. Worst of all was that old Fyodor Stepanych held to some sort of Asiatic policy in regard to them. Thus, no one knew what salary his favorites, Pochatkin and Makeichev, received; they received three thousand a year including bonuses, not more, but he pretended that he paid them seven; bonuses were given annually to all the salesclerks, but in secret, so that, out of vanity, someone who received little would have to say he had received a lot; no boy ever knew when he would be promoted to salesclerk; no employee knew whether the master was pleased with him or not. Nothing was directly forbidden, and therefore, the salesclerks did not know what was allowed and what was not. It was not forbidden to marry, but they did not marry, for fear of displeasing the master and losing their jobs. They were allowed to have acquaintances and pay visits, but the gates were locked at nine o'clock in the evening, and every morning the master looked all the employees over suspiciously and tested whether any of them smelled of vodka: "Go on, breathe!"

On every feast day, the employees were obliged to attend the early liturgy and stand in church so that the master could see them all. Fasts were strictly observed. On festive days, for instance, the name day of the master or one of his family members, the salesclerks had to take up a collection and offer him a cake from Fley's or an album. They lived on the ground floor of the house on Pyatnitskaya or in the wing, three to four men to a room, and at dinner they all ate from the same bowl, though each of them had a plate in front of him. If one of the masters came in during dinner, they all stood up.

Laptev was aware that only those among them who had been corrupted by the old man's tutelage could seriously consider him a benefactor; the rest saw in him an enemy and a "plantator." Now, after six months' absence, he did not see any changes for the better; there was even something new that boded no good. His brother Fyodor, who used to be quiet, pensive, and extremely tactful, now ran about the warehouse with the look of a very occupied and businesslike man, with a pencil behind his ear, patting customers on the shoulder, and shouting "Friends!" to the salesclerks. Apparently he was playing some sort of role, and Alexei did not recognize him in this new role.

The old man's voice boomed incessantly. Being unoccupied, the old man was instructing the customer on how he ought to live and conduct his affairs, and kept setting himself up as an example. This boasting, this authoritative, overbearing tone, Laptev had heard ten and fifteen and twenty years ago. The old man adored himself; to listen to him, he had made the happiness of his late wife and her family, provided for his children, showered his salesclerks and employees with benefactions, and had the whole street and all his acquaintances eternally praying to God for him; whatever he did was all very good, and if things were not going well for people, it was only because they did not want to take his advice; without his advice, nothing could succeed. In church he always stood in front of everyone and even made observations to the priests when, in his opinion, they were not serving correctly, and thought it was pleasing to God, because God loved him.

By two o'clock everybody in the warehouse had gotten down to business, except the old man, who went on booming. Laptev, so as not to stand there doing nothing, took some braid from a maker and dismissed her, then heard out a customer, a merchant from Vologda, and told a salesclerk to take care of him.

"T, V, A!" came from all sides (letters stood for prices and numbers for goods). "R, I, T!"

Going out, Laptev said good-bye only to Fyodor.

"Tomorrow I'll come to Pyatnitskaya with my wife," he said, "but I warn you that if father says just one rude word to her, I won't stay there for a minute."

"And you're still the same," sighed Fyodor. "Married, but unchanged. You must be indulgent to the old man, brother. So, then, tomorrow at around eleven. We'll be waiting impatiently. Come straight from the liturgy."

"I don't go to the liturgy."

"Well, it makes no difference. Above all, no later than eleven, so that we'll have time to pray to God and have lunch together. I send greetings to my little sister and kiss her hand. I have a presentiment that I'll come to love her," Fyodor added quite sincerely. "I'm envious, brother!" he cried when Alexei was already going downstairs.

"And why is it that he keeps cringing somehow bashfully, as if he feels naked?" thought Laptev, walking down Nikolskaya Street and trying to understand the change that had taken place in Fyodor. "And he's got some kind of new language: brother, dear brother, God has sent us mercy, we'll pray to God—just like Shchedrin's Iudushka."[8]

VI

THE NEXT DAY, Sunday, at eleven o'clock, he was driving down Pyatnitskaya in a light one-horse carriage. He feared some sort of escapade on Fyodor Stepanych's part and had an unpleasant feeling beforehand. Yulia Sergeevna, after spending two nights in her husband's home, already considered her marriage a mistake, a misfortune, and if she had had to live with her husband not in Moscow but somewhere in another town, it seemed to her she could not have endured this horror. But Moscow diverted her; she liked the streets, the houses, and the churches very much, and if it had been possible to ride around Moscow in these excellent carriages, with expensive horses, to ride all day long, from morning to evening, and, while going very fast, to breathe the cool autumnal air, perhaps she would not have felt so miserable.

The driver reined in the horse near a white, recently stuccoed two-story house and began turning to the right. Here they were expected. By the gate stood a porter in a new caftan, high boots, and galoshes, and two policemen; the whole space from the middle of the street to the gate, and then through the yard to the porch, had been sprinkled with fresh sand. The porter took off his hat, the policemen saluted. Fyodor met them by the porch with a very serious face.

"I am very glad to make your acquaintance, little sister," he said, kissing Yulia's hand. "You are welcome."

He took her under the arm and led her up the stairs, then down a corridor through a crowd of men and women. The front room was also crowded; there was a smell of incense.

"I'll introduce you to our father now," Fyodor whispered

amidst the solemn, sepulchral silence. "A venerable old man, a paterfamilias."

In a big reception room, near a table prepared for a prayer service, Fyodor Stepanych, a priest in a kamilavka,[9] and a deacon stood in obvious expectation. The old man gave Yulia his hand and did not say a word. Everyone was silent. Yulia became embarrassed.

The priest and the deacon began to put on their vestments. A censer was brought, which showered sparks and gave off a smell of incense and charcoal. The candles were lighted. The salesclerks tiptoed into the room and stood near the wall in two rows. It was quiet; no one even coughed.

"Bless, master," the deacon began.

The prayer service proceeded solemnly, without any omissions, and two akathists[10] were read: to Sweet Jesus and to the Most Holy Mother of God. The choir sang only by the scores and at great length. Laptev noticed how his wife became embarrassed at the beginning; while the akathists were being read, and the choir chanted the triple "Lord have mercy" in various tunes, he waited with inner tension for the old man to turn and make some observation, such as: "You don't know how to cross yourself," and he was vexed: why this crowd, why this whole ceremony with clergy and choir? It was too much in merchant style. But when she, together with the old man, bowed her head to be blessed by the Gospel, and then knelt on several occasions, he realized that she liked it all and calmed down.

At the end of the service, when "Many Years"[11] was sung, the priest held out the cross for Alexei and the old man to kiss, but when Yulia Sergeevna approached, he covered the cross with his hand and indicated that he wanted to speak. They waved for the choir to stop singing.

"The prophet Samuel," began the priest, "came to Bethlehem by order of the Lord, and there the town elders asked him in trembling: 'Comest thou peaceably, O seer?'

And the prophet said: 'Peaceably: I am come to sacrifice unto the Lord, sanctify yourselves and rejoice with me today.'[12] Shall we, too, ask of thee, the servant of God Yulia, whether thou hast come peaceably into this house?..."

Yulia turned all red with agitation. Having finished, the priest gave her the cross to kiss and said in an altogether different tone:

"Now we must get Fyodor Fyodorych married. It's high time."

Again the choir sang, people stirred, it became noisy. The old man, moved, his eyes filled with tears, kissed Yulia three times, made a cross over her face, and said:

"This is your house. I'm an old man, I don't need anything."

The salesclerks congratulated her and said something, but the choir sang so loudly that it was impossible to hear anything. Then they had lunch and drank champagne. She sat next to the old man, and he said to her that it was not good to live separately, that they must live together, in one house, and separations and disagreements lead to ruin.

"I made money, but the children only spend it," he said. "Now you come and live in the same house with me and make money. I'm an old man, it's time for me to rest."

Fyodor was flitting in front of Yulia's eyes all the time, looking very much like her husband, but more fidgety and bashful; he fussed about her and often kissed her hand.

"We're simple people, little sister," he kept saying, and red blotches came to his face. "We live simply, little sister, like Russians, like Christians."

On the way home, Laptev, very pleased that it had all gone well and that, beyond his expectations, nothing particular had happened, said to his wife:

"You're surprised that a big, broad-shouldered father has such undersized, weak-chested children as me and Fyodor. Yes, but it's so understandable! Father married my mother

369

when he was forty-five and she was only seventeen. She went pale and trembled in his presence. Nina was born first, born of a comparatively healthy mother, and therefore came out stronger and better than we did. Fyodor and I were conceived and born when mother was already exhausted by perpetual fear. I remember my father began teaching me, or, to put it simply, beating me, when I was not yet five years old. He whipped me with birches, boxed my ears, hit me on the head, and every morning when I woke up, my first thought was: 'Will I be whipped today?' Fyodor and I were forbidden to play and frolic: we had to go to matins and the early liturgy, kiss the hands of priests and monks, read akathists at home. You are religious and like all that, but I'm afraid of religion, and when I pass a church, I recall my childhood and feel eerie. When I was eight years old, I went to work in the warehouse; I worked as a simple boy, and that was unhealthy, because I was beaten almost every day. Later, when I was sent to school, I studied before dinner and had to sit in that same warehouse from dinner till evening, and so it went till I was twenty-two and at the university made the acquaintance of Yartsev, who persuaded me to leave my father's house. This Yartsev did me a lot of good. You know what," Laptev said and laughed with pleasure, "let's go now and visit Yartsev. He's a most noble man! How touched he'll be!"

VII

ONE SATURDAY IN November, Anton Rubinstein[13] conducted at the symphony. It was very crowded and hot. Laptev stood behind the columns, while his wife and Kostya Kochevoy sat way up front, in the third or fourth row. At the very beginning of the intermission, the "individual," Polina Nikolaevna Rassudina, quite unexpectedly walked past him.

After the wedding he had often thought anxiously about a possible encounter with her. Now, when she looked at him openly and directly, he remembered that so far he had not even managed to have a talk with her or write her at least two or three friendly lines, as if he was hiding from her; he felt ashamed and blushed. She strongly and impetuously shook his hand and asked:

"Have you seen Yartsev?"

And without waiting for a reply, she walked on rapidly, in long strides, as if someone was pushing her from behind.

She was very thin and unattractive, with a long nose, and her face was always exhausted, worn out, and it seemed a great effort for her to keep her eyes open and not fall down. She had beautiful dark eyes and an intelligent, kind, sincere expression, but her movements were angular, abrupt. It was not easy to talk with her, because she was not good at listening or talking calmly. To love her was difficult. It happened, when she was alone with Laptev, that she would laugh for a long time, covering her face with her hands and insisting that love was not the main thing in her life, mincing like a seventeen-year-old girl, and before kissing her, he had to put out all the candles. She was thirty years old. Her husband was a teacher, but she had not lived with him for a long time. She provided for herself by giving music lessons and participating in quartets.

During the Ninth Symphony, she walked past again, as if by chance, but the crowd of men who stood in a thick wall behind the columns blocked her way, and she stopped. Laptev saw on her the same velvet blouse in which she had gone to concerts last year and the year before. Her gloves were new, the fan was also new, but cheap. She loved dressing up but did not know how and was reluctant to spend money on it, and dressed badly and slovenly, so that usually, when she walked down the street in long, hurried strides on her way to a lesson, she could easily be taken for a young novice.

The public applauded and shouted encore.

"You'll spend this evening with me," said Polina Nikola-evna, going up to Laptev and looking at him sternly. "We'll leave here and go to have tea. Do you hear? I demand it. You owe me a lot and have no moral right to deny me this trifle."

"All right, let's go," Laptev agreed.

After the symphony there were endless curtain calls. The public got up from their places and went out extremely slowly, but Laptev could not leave without telling his wife. He had to stand at the door and wait.

"I'm dying for some tea," Rassudina complained. "My soul is on fire."

"We can have it here," said Laptev. "Let's go to the buffet."

"No, I have no money to throw around at buffets. I'm not some little merchant."

He offered her his arm, she refused, uttering a long, tiresome phrase he had heard many times from her, namely that she did not count herself as part of the weak fair sex and had no need of gentlemen's services.

While talking to him, she looked over the public and often greeted acquaintances; these were her classmates from the Guerrier courses[14] and the conservatory, and her pupils, young men and women. She shook their hands strongly and impetuously, almost jerkily. But then she began to hunch her shoulders, as if in a fever, and to tremble, and at last said quietly, looking at Laptev in horror:

"Whom have you married? Where were your eyes, you crazy man? What did you find in that stupid, worthless girl? I loved you for your intelligence, your soul, but this china doll only needs your money!"

"Let's drop that, Polina," he said in a pleading voice. "Everything you can tell me about my marriage, I've already told myself many times . . . Don't cause me any extra pain."

Yulia Sergeevna appeared in a black dress and with a large diamond brooch her father-in-law had sent her after the prayer service; she was followed by her retinue: Kochevoy, two doctors of their acquaintance, an officer, and a stout young man in a student's uniform whose last name was Kish.

"Go with Kostya," Laptev said to his wife. "I'll come later."

Yulia nodded and walked on. Polina Nikolaevna followed her with her eyes, trembling all over and hugging herself nervously, and her look was filled with disgust, hatred, and pain.

Laptev was afraid to go with her, anticipating an unpleasant talk, harsh words, and tears, and he suggested they go and have tea in some restaurant. But she said:

"No, no, let's go to my place. Don't you dare talk to me about restaurants."

She disliked going to restaurants, because restaurant air seemed poisoned to her by tobacco and men's breath. She regarded all unknown men with a strange prejudice, considering them all debauchees capable of throwing themselves at her any moment. Besides that, tavern music irritated her to the point of giving her a headache.

Coming out of the Assembly of Nobility, they hired a cab for Ostozhenka, to Savelovsky Lane, where Rassudina lived. Laptev thought about her all the way. In fact, he did owe her a lot. He had made her acquaintance at his friend Yartsev's, to whom she was teaching the theory of music. She loved him deeply, quite disinterestedly, and, after becoming intimate with him, went on giving lessons and working herself to exhaustion as before. Thanks to her, he began to understand and love music, which previously he had been almost indifferent to.

"My kingdom for a cup of tea!" she said in a hollow voice, covering her mouth with her muff so as not to catch cold. "I gave five lessons today, devil take them! The pupils are such dimwits, such dullards, that I nearly died of spite. And I don't know when this hard labor will end. I'm worn out. As soon as I save three hundred roubles, I'll drop everything and go to the Crimea. I'll lie on the beach and gulp down oxygen. How I love the sea, oh, how I love the sea!"

"You won't go anywhere," said Laptev. "First, you won't save anything, and second, you're stingy. Forgive me, I'll repeat again: is saving these three hundred roubles kopeck by kopeck from idle people, who study music with you because they have nothing to do, really less humiliating than borrowing it from your friends?"

"I have no friends!" she said irritably. "And I beg you not to say foolish things. The working class, to which I belong, has one privilege: the consciousness of its incorruptibility, the right not to owe anything to little merchants and to despise them. No, sir, you won't buy me! I'm not Yulechka!"

Laptev did not try to pay the cabby, knowing it would provoke a whole flood of words he had heard many times before. She paid herself.

She rented a small furnished room, with board, in the apartment of a single lady. Her big Becker grand piano[15] was meanwhile at Yartsev's, on Bolshaya Nikitskaya, and she went there every day to play. There were armchairs in slip-covers in her room, a bed with a white summer coverlet, and the landlady's flowers, some oleographs on the walls, and nothing to remind one that a woman and former student lived there. There was no dressing table, no books, not even a desk. It was evident that she went to bed as soon as she came home and left the house as soon as she got up in the morning.

The cook brought the samovar. Polina Nikolaevna made tea and, still trembling—it was cold in the room—began to denounce the singers who had sung in the Ninth Symphony. Her eyes were closing from fatigue. She drank one glass, then another, then a third.

"And so you got married," she said. "But don't worry, I won't pine away, I'll be able to tear you out of my heart. It's only annoying and bitter that you're the same trash as everybody else, that what you need in a woman is not the mind, the intellect, but the body, beauty, youth . . . Youth!" she pronounced through her nose, as if imitating someone, and laughed. "Youth! You need purity, *Reinheit! Reinheit!*" she laughed loudly, throwing herself back in the armchair. "*Reinheit!*"

When she finished laughing, there were tears in her eyes.

"Are you happy, at least?" she asked.

"No."

"Does she love you?"

"No."

Laptev, agitated, feeling unhappy, got up and began pacing the room.

"No," he repeated. "If you want to know, Polina, I'm very unhappy. What to do? I did a stupid thing, there's no putting it right now. I have to deal with it philosophically. She married without love, stupidly, maybe out of calculation, but without reasoning, and now, obviously, is aware of her mistake and suffers. I can see it. At night we sleep, but in the daytime she's afraid to stay alone with me even for five minutes and seeks diversion, company. She's ashamed and afraid with me."

"And yet she takes money from you?"

"That's stupid, Polina!" cried Laptev. "She takes money from me because it makes decidedly no difference to her whether she has it or not. She's an honest, pure person. She married me simply because she wanted to get away from her father, that's all."

"And you're sure she would have married you if you weren't rich?" asked Rassudina.

"I'm not sure of anything," Laptev said in anguish. "Not of anything. For God's sake, Polina, let's not talk about it."

"You love her?"

"Madly."

Then silence ensued. She was drinking her fourth glass of tea, and he was pacing and thinking that his wife was now most likely having dinner at the Doctors' Club.

"But can one possibly love without knowing why?" Rassudina asked and shrugged her shoulders. "No, it's animal passion speaking in you! You're intoxicated! You're poisoned by that beautiful body, that *Reinheit*! Get away from me, you're dirty! Go to her!"

She waved her hand at him, then took his hat and flung it at him. He silently put on his fur coat and went out, but she ran to the front hall, clutched his arm convulsively near the shoulder, and burst into sobs.

"Stop it, Polina! Enough!" he said, and could not unclench her fingers. "Calm yourself, I beg you!"

She closed her eyes and went pale, and her long nose turned an unpleasant waxen color, like a dead person's, and Laptev still could not unclench her fingers. She was in a swoon. He carefully lifted her up and put her on the bed, and sat beside her for about ten minutes, until she came to. Her hands were cold, her pulse weak and unsteady.

"Go home," she said, opening her eyes. "Go, otherwise I'll howl again. I must get control of myself."

Having left her, he went not to the Doctors' Club, where the company was expecting him, but home. All the way there, he asked himself with reproach: why had he not set up a family for himself with this woman who loved him so much and was already in fact his wife and friend? She was the only human being who was attached to him, and besides, would it not have been a gratifying, worthy task to give happiness, shelter, and peace to this intelligent, proud being who was worn out with work? Did they suit him, he kept asking himself, these pretensions to beauty, youth, to that very happiness which could not be and which, as if in punishment or mockery, had kept him for three months now in a gloomy, depressed state? The honeymoon was long over, and he, funny to say, still did not know what sort of person his wife was. She wrote long five-page letters to her boarding-school friends and her father, and she found what to write about, but with him she talked only about the weather or about it being time for dinner or supper. When she said long prayers to God before sleeping and then kissed her little crosses and icons, he looked at her and thought with hatred: "Here she is praying, but what is she praying for? What?" In his thoughts, he insulted her and himself, saying that when he went to bed with her and took her in his arms, he was taking what he had paid for, but it was terrible to think that; if she had been a robust, bold, sinful woman, but here she was all youth, religiosity, meekness, innocent, pure eyes . . . When she was his fiancée, her religiosity had touched him, but now this conventional definitiveness of views and convictions seemed to him like a screen behind which the real truth could not be seen. Everything had become tormenting in his family life. When his wife, sitting beside him in the theater, sighed or laughed sincerely, he felt bitter that she was enjoying herself alone and did not want to share her delight with him. And remarkably, she made friends with all his friends, and they all knew what kind of person she was, while he knew nothing, and only sulked and was silently jealous.

On coming home, Laptev put on his dressing gown and slippers and sat down in his study to read a novel. His wife was not at home. But before half an hour went by, the bell rang in the front hall, and the muffled steps of Pyotr were heard, running to open the door. It was Yulia. She came into his study in her fur coat, her cheeks red from frost.

"There's a big fire on Presnya," she said breathlessly. "The glow is enormous. I'm going there with Konstantin Ivanych."

"Go with God!"

The look of health, freshness, and childish fear in her eyes

set Laptev at ease. He read for another half hour and went
to bed.

The next day Polina Nikolaevna sent him at the warehouse
two books she had once borrowed from him, all his letters,
and his photographs; with it was a note consisting of only
one word: "*Basta!*"

VIII

BY THE END of October, Nina Fyodorovna's relapse was
clearly marked. She quickly lost weight and changed coun-
tenance. Despite severe pains, she imagined she was getting
better, and dressed each morning as if she was healthy, and
then lay in bed all day dressed. And towards the end she
became very talkative. She would lie on her back telling
something quietly, with effort, breathing heavily. She died
suddenly in the following circumstances.

It was a bright moonlit evening, outside people went
sleigh-riding over the fresh snow, and the noise from outside
came into the room. Nina Fyodorovna lay on her back in
bed, and Sasha, who no longer had anyone to replace her,
sat dozing near her bed.

"I don't remember his patronymic," Nina Fyodorovna was
saying softly, "but he was called Ivan, last name Kochevoy, a
poor clerk. He was an awful drunkard, God rest his soul. He
used to come to us, and we gave him a pound of sugar and
a packet of tea every month. Well, and occasionally money,
of course. Yes . . . Then this is what happened: our Kochevoy
went on a bad binge and died, burnt up on vodka. He left a
little son, a dear little boy of about seven. An orphan . . . We
took him and hid him with the salesclerks, and he lived a
whole year like that, and papa didn't know. But when papa
saw it, he only waved his hand and said nothing. When
Kostya, our orphan, that is, was going on nine—and I was

about to get married then—I took him to all the schools. We went here and there, and they wouldn't accept him. He was weeping... 'Why are you weeping, little fool?' So I took him to Razgulai, to the Second School, and there, God grant them health, they took him... And the little boy went on foot every day from Pyatnitskaya to Razgulai, and from Razgulai to Pyatnitskaya... Alyosha paid for him... Merciful Lord, the boy began to study, grasped things well, and with good results... Now he's a lawyer in Moscow, Alyosha's friend, of the same high learning. We didn't neglect our fellow man, we took him into our house, and no doubt he prays to God for us now... Yes..."

Nina Fyodorovna began speaking more and more softly, with long pauses, then, after some silence, suddenly raised herself and sat up.

"But I'm not so... as if I'm unwell," she said. "Lord have mercy. Ah, I can't breathe!"

Sasha knew her mother was soon to die; now, seeing how her face suddenly became pinched, she guessed that this was the end and was frightened.

"Mama, you mustn't!" she wept. "You mustn't!"

"Run to the kitchen, have them fetch your father. I'm very unwell."

Sasha ran through all the rooms and called, but none of the servants was at home, only Lida was sleeping on a trunk in the dining room, dressed and without a pillow. Just as she was, without galoshes, Sasha ran out to the yard, then to the street. On a bench outside the gate, her nanny sat watching people sleigh-riding. From the river, where the skating rink was, came the sounds of military music.

"Nanny, mama's dying!" Sasha said, weeping. "We must fetch papa!..."

The nanny went upstairs to the bedroom and, after glancing at the sick woman, gave her a lighted wax candle to hold. Terrified, Sasha fussed and begged, herself not knowing whom, to fetch her papa, then she put on her coat and kerchief and ran outside. She knew from the servants that her father had another wife and two daughters with whom he lived on Bazar-naya Square. She ran left from the gate, crying and afraid of strangers, and soon began to sink into the snow and feel cold.

She met an empty cab but did not take it: he might drive her out of town, rob her, and abandon her by the cemetery (the maid had told her over tea that there had been such a case). She walked and walked, breathless from fatigue and sobbing. Coming to Bazarnaya, she asked where Mr. Panau-rov lived. Some unknown woman explained it to her at length and, seeing that she understood nothing, took her by the hand to a one-story house with a porch. The door was not locked. Sasha ran through the front hall, then a corridor, and finally found herself in a bright, warm room where her father was sitting by the samovar, and with him a lady and two little girls. But she could no longer utter a word and only sobbed. Panaurov understood.

"Mama's probably not well?" he asked. "Tell me, girl: is mama unwell?"

He became worried and sent for a cab.

When they reached home, Nina Fyodorovna was sitting, propped on pillows, with a candle in her hand. Her face had darkened, and her eyes were closed. In the bedroom, crowded by the doorway, stood the nanny, the cook, the maid, the muzhik Prokofy, and some other unknown simple people. The nanny was ordering something in a whisper, and they did not understand her. At the far end of the room, by the window, stood Lida, pale, sleepy, sternly gazing at her mother from there.

Panaurov took the candle from Nina Fyodorovna's hands and, wincing squeamishly, flung it onto the chest of drawers.

"This is terrible!" he said, and his shoulders twitched. "Nina, you must lie down," he said tenderly. "Lie down, dear."

She looked and did not recognize him . . . They lay her on her back.

When the priest and Dr. Sergei Borisych came, the servants were already crossing themselves piously and commemorating her.

"There's a story for you!" the doctor said pensively, coming out to the drawing room. "And she was still young, not even forty yet."

The loud sobbing of the girls was heard. Panaurov, pale, with moist eyes, went over to the doctor and said in a weak, languid voice:

"My dear, do me a favor, send a telegram to Moscow. It's decidedly beyond me."

The doctor found the ink and wrote the following telegram to his daughter: "Mrs. Panaurov passed away eight this evening. Tell husband: house on Dvoryanskaya for sale, transfer of mortgage plus nine. Auction twelfth. Advise not let slip."

IX

LAPTEV LIVED IN one of the lanes off Malaya Dmitrovka, not far from Stary Pimen. Besides the big house on the street, he also rented the two-story wing in the yard for his friend Kochevoy, an assistant attorney whom all the Laptevs simply called Kostya, because he had grown up before their eyes. Facing his wing was another, also two-story, in which there lived a French family, consisting of a husband, a wife, and five daughters.

It was ten below zero. The windows were covered with frost. Waking up in the morning, Kostya, with a preoccupied look, took fifteen drops of some medicine, then got two dumbbells from the bookcase and began doing exercises. He was tall, very thin, with a big, reddish mustache; but most conspicuous in his appearance were his remarkably long legs.

Pyotr, a middle-aged muzhik in a jacket and cotton trousers tucked into high boots, brought the samovar and made tea.

"Very nice weather today, Konstantin Ivanych," he said.

"Yes, nice, only the pity is, brother, our life here is nothing to shout about."

Pyotr sighed out of politeness.

"How are the girls?" asked Kochevoy.

"The priest hasn't come, Alexei Fyodorych himself is giving them their lesson."

Kostya found an unfrosted spot on the window and began looking through binoculars at the windows of the French family's house.

"Can't see," he said.

Meanwhile, downstairs Alexei Fyodorych was teaching Sasha and Lida their catechism. They had been living in Moscow for a month and a half, on the ground floor of the wing, with their governess. Three times a week, a teacher from the city school and a priest came. Sasha was studying the New Testament, and Lida had recently started the Old. Lida's homework from the last time was to repeat everything before Abraham.

"And so, Adam and Eve had two sons," said Laptev. "Splendid. But what were their names? Try to remember!"

Lida, stern as ever, said nothing, stared at the table, and only moved her lips; and the older Sasha looked into her face and suffered.

"You know perfectly well, only don't be nervous," said Laptev. "Well, what were the names of Adam's sons?"

"Abel and Cabel," Lida whispered.

"Cain and Abel," Laptev corrected.

A big tear crept down Lida's cheek and fell onto the book. Sasha also lowered her eyes and blushed, ready to weep. Laptev could not speak from pity, a lump rose in his throat; he got up from the table and lit a cigarette. Just then

Kochevoy came downstairs with a newspaper in his hand. The girls stood up and curtseyed without looking at him.

"For God's sake, Kostya, work with them a little," Laptev turned to him. "I'm afraid I'll start crying myself, and I have to get to the warehouse before dinner."

"All right."

Alexei Fyodorych left. Kostya, with a very serious face, frowning, sat down at the table and drew the Catechism towards him.

"Well, missies?" he asked. "How far did you get?"

"She knows about the flood," said Sasha.

"About the flood? All right, let's whiz through the flood. Go ahead." Kostya skimmed through the brief description of the flood in the book and said: "I must point out to you that such a flood as they describe here never actually happened. And there wasn't any Noah. Several thousand years before the birth of Christ, there was an unusual flood on earth, and it's mentioned not only in the Jewish Bible but in the books of other ancient people as well, such as the Greeks, the Chaldeans, the Hindus. But whatever this flood was, it couldn't have covered the whole earth. Well, the plains were flooded, but not the mountains. You can go ahead and read this book, but don't believe it especially."

Lida's tears flowed again; she turned away and suddenly sobbed so loudly that Kostya gave a start and got up from his place in great confusion.

"I want to go home," she said. "To papa and nanny."

Sasha also began to cry. Kostya went upstairs to his rooms and said to Yulia Sergeevna on the telephone:

"Dearest, the girls are crying again. It's simply impossible."

Yulia Sergeevna came running from the big house in nothing but a dress and a knitted shawl, chilled through, and began comforting the girls.

"Believe me, believe me," she said in a pleading voice,

pressing one of the girls to her, then the other, "your papa will come today, he sent a telegram. You're sorry for your mama, and I'm sorry for her, too, it breaks my heart, but what's to be done? We can't go against God!"

When they stopped crying, she wrapped them up and took them for a drive. First they went down Malaya Dmitrovka, then past Strastnoy Boulevard to Tverskaya; they stopped at the Iverskaya Chapel,[16] lit candles, knelt down, and prayed. On the way back, they stopped at Filippov's and bought some lenten rolls with poppyseed.

The Laptevs dined between two and three. Pyotr served the courses. During the day this Pyotr ran to the post office, to the warehouse, to the district court for Kostya, served; in the evenings he rolled cigarettes, during the night he ran to open the door, and by five o'clock in the morning was already stoking the stoves, and nobody knew when he slept. He very much enjoyed uncorking seltzer water, and did it easily, noiselessly, without spilling a drop.

"God bless!" said Kostya, drinking a glass of vodka before dinner.

At first Yulia Sergeevna did not like Kostya; his bass voice, his little phrases like "stood me a bottle," "socked him in the mug," "scum," "portray us the samovar," his habit of clinking and mumbling over the glass seemed trivial to her. But when she got to know him better, she began to feel very easy in his presence. He was frank with her, in the evenings he liked to discuss things with her in a low voice, and he even let her read the novels he wrote, something that so far was a secret even from such friends as Laptev and Yartsev. She read these novels and praised them, so as not to upset him, and he was glad, because he hoped to become a famous writer sooner or later. In his novels he described only the country and landowners' estates, though he had seen the country very rarely, only when visiting his acquaintances in their dachas, and had been on a landowner's estate once in his life, when he went to Volokolamsk on a lawsuit. He avoided the amorous element, as if he was ashamed of it, he frequently described nature, and in his descriptions liked to use such expressions as "the whimsical contours of the mountains," "the fantastic shapes of the clouds," or "the accord of mysterious harmonies" ... His novels were never published, and he explained that by the conditions of censorship.

He liked his activity as a lawyer, but even so, he considered these novels and not the legal profession his chief occupation. It seemed to him that he had a subtle, artistic constitution, and he had always been drawn to the arts. He did not sing or play any instrument himself, and was totally without a musical ear, but he attended all the symphonic and philharmonic gatherings, organized concerts for charitable purposes, met with singers ...

During dinner they talked.

"An amazing thing," said Laptev, "again my Fyodor has nonplussed me! He says we must find out when is the hundredth anniversary of our firm, so as to petition for nobility, and he says it in the most serious way. What's happened to him? Frankly speaking, I'm beginning to worry."

They talked about Fyodor, about the fact that it was now the fashion to affect something or other. Fyodor, for instance, tried to look like a simple merchant, though he was no longer a merchant, and when a teacher from the school where old Laptev was a trustee came to him for his salary, he even changed his voice and gait and behaved like the teacher's superior.

After dinner there was nothing to do, so they went to the study. They talked about the decadents, about *The Maid of Orleans*, and Kostya recited a whole monologue; it seemed to him that he had done a very successful imitation of Ermolova.[17] Then they sat down to play vint. The girls did not go to their wing but, pale and sad, sat both in one armchair, listening to the noise in the street: was it their father coming? In the evening, in the dark and with candles, they felt anguish. The conversation over cards, Pyotr's footsteps, the crackling in the fireplace irritated them, and they did not want to look at the fire; in the evening they no longer even wanted to cry but felt eerie and heavyhearted. And they could not understand how it was possible to talk about something and laugh, when their mama was dead.

"What did you see today through the binoculars?" Yulia Sergeevna asked Kostya.

"Nothing today, but yesterday the old Frenchman himself took a bath."

At seven o'clock Yulia Sergeevna and Kostya went to the Maly Theater. Laptev stayed with the girls.

"It's time your papa came," he kept saying, glancing at the clock. "The train must be late."

The girls sat silently in the armchair, huddled together like little animals in the cold, and he kept pacing the rooms, looking with impatience at his watch. The house was quiet. Then, towards nine o'clock, someone rang the bell. Pyotr went to open the door.

Hearing the familiar voice, the girls cried out, sobbed, and rushed to the front hall. Panaurov was wearing a luxurious fur coat, and his beard and mustache were white with hoarfrost.

"One moment, one moment," he muttered, but Sasha and Lida, sobbing and laughing, kissed his cold hands, his hat, his coat. Handsome, languid, pampered by love, he unhurriedly caressed the girls, then went into the study and said, rubbing his hands:

"But I won't stay with you long, my friends. Tomorrow I'm off to Petersburg. I've been promised a transfer to another town."

He stayed at the Dresden.

X

YARTSEV, IVAN GAVRILYCH, frequently visited the Laptevs. He was a healthy, robust man, black-haired, with an intelligent, pleasant face; he was considered handsome, but lately he had begun to put on weight, and that spoiled his face and figure; another thing that spoiled his looks was his close-cropped, almost shaven head. At the university, owing to his good height and strength, the students used to call him the "bouncer."

He took a degree in philology, along with the Laptev brothers, then studied natural science and now had a master's degree in chemistry. He never counted on having a chair, and did not even work in any laboratory, but taught physics and natural history in a technical high school and in two girls' schools. He was delighted with his students, especially the girls, and said that a wonderful generation was growing up. Besides chemistry, he was also occupied at home with sociology and Russian history, and his brief articles occasionally appeared in newspapers and magazines over the initial Y. When he talked about something from botany or zoology, he resembled a historian; when he discussed some historical question, he resembled a natural scientist.

Another familiar man at the Laptevs' was Kish, nicknamed the eternal student. He had spent three years studying medicine, then had switched to mathematics and had sat through each course there twice. His father, a provincial pharmacist, sent him forty roubles a month, and his mother, in secret from his father, sent another ten, and this money was enough for his expenses and even such luxuries as an overcoat with Polish beaver, gloves, scent, and photography (he often had himself photographed and gave his portraits to acquaintances). Clean, slightly bald on top, with golden side-whiskers at his ears, modest, he had the look of a man ever ready to be of service.

He always bustled about on other people's business: ran around with a subscription list, froze by the theater box office from early in the morning to buy a ticket for a lady of his acquaintance, or went at someone's request to order a wreath or a bouquet. All they said of him was: "Kish will go, Kish will do it, Kish will buy it." For the most part, he performed his errands badly. Reproaches were showered on him, people often forgot to repay him for their purchases, but he never said anything and on embarrassing occasions only sighed. He was never especially glad or sorry, always told long and boring stories, and his witticisms provoked laughter each time only because they were not funny. Thus, one day, intending to make a joke, he said to Pyotr: "Pyotter, you're not an otter," and this provoked general laughter, and he himself laughed a long time, pleased to have made such a successful joke. Whenever some professor was buried, he walked in front with the torchbearers.

Yartsev and Kish usually came in the evening for tea. If the hosts were not going to the theater or a concert, the evening tea stretched till suppertime. On one February evening, the following conversation took place in the dining room:

"A work of art is significant and useful only when its idea includes some serious social problem," Kostya said, looking angrily at Yartsev. "If there is a protest against serfdom in the work, or the author takes up arms against high society with all its banality, such a work is significant and useful. While novels and stories where it's 'Oh' and 'Ah,' and she falls in love with him but he falls out of love with her—these works, I say, are worthless, and to the devil with them."

"I agree with you, Konstantin Ivanych," said Yulia Sergeevna. "One describes a lovers' tryst, another a betrayal, the third a meeting after the separation. Are there really no other subjects? A great many people who are sick, unhappy, worn out by poverty must find it disgusting to read all that."

Laptev was displeased that his wife, a young woman who

was not yet twenty-two years old, should reason about love so seriously and coldly. He could guess why it was so.

"If poetry doesn't resolve the questions that seem important to you," said Yartsev, "turn to works on technology, criminal and financial law, read scholarly articles. Who wants to have *Romeo and Juliet* talk not about love but, let's say, about freedom of instruction or prison sanitation, if you can go to special articles and handbooks for that?"

"That's going to extremes, uncle!" Kostya interrupted. "We're not talking about giants like Shakespeare and Goethe, we're talking about a hundred talented and mediocre writers who would be much more useful if they abandoned love and occupied themselves with bringing knowledge and humane ideas to the masses."

Kish, slightly nasally and rolling his R's, began to recount the content of a short novel he had read recently. He recounted it thoroughly, unhurriedly; three minutes went by, then five, ten, and he still went on, and nobody could understand what it was all about, and his face grew more and more indifferent, and his eyes went dim.

"Tell it more quickly, Kish," Yulia Sergeevna could not stand it, "this is really torture!"

"Stop, Kish!" Kostya yelled at him.

Everybody laughed, including Kish.

Fyodor arrived. Red spots on his face, hurrying, he gave his greetings and led his brother to the study. Lately he had avoided gatherings of many people and preferred the company of a single person.

"Let the young people laugh in there, but here you and I can have a heart-to-heart talk," he said, sitting down in a deep chair away from the lamp. "We haven't seen each other for a long time, brother. When was the last time you came to the warehouse? Must be a week ago."

"Yes. I have nothing to do there. And, I confess, I'm sick of the old man."

"Of course, they can do without us at the warehouse, but one must have some sort of occupation. In the sweat of your brow you shall eat your bread, as they say.[18] God loves labor."

Pyotr brought a glass of tea on a tray. Fyodor drank it without sugar and asked for more. He was a great tea drinker and could drink ten glasses in an evening.

"You know what, brother?" he said, getting up and going over to his brother. "Clever sophistries aside, why don't you get yourself elected representative, and by easy stages we'll make you a member of the board, and then associate head. The further the better; you're an intelligent, educated man, you'll be noticed and invited to Petersburg—zemstvo and city council activists are in fashion there, brother, and lo and behold, you won't be fifty yet, and you'll already be a privy councillor with a ribbon over your shoulder."

Laptev did not reply. He realized that all this—the privy councillor and the ribbon—was what Fyodor himself wanted, and he did not know how to reply.

The brothers sat and said nothing. Fyodor opened his watch and looked into it for a long, long time with strained attention, as if he wanted to observe the movement of the hands, and Laptev found the expression on his face strange.

Supper was served. Laptev went to the dining room, but Fyodor remained in the study. The argument was over, and Yartsev was saying in the tone of a professor reading a lecture:

"Owing to differences of climate, energy, taste, and age, equality among people is physically impossible. But a cultured man can make this inequality harmless, as has already been done with swamps and bears. One scientist did succeed in having a cat, a mouse, a buzzard, and a sparrow eat from the same plate, and education, it must be hoped, will do the same with people. Life keeps going forward, forward, culture makes enormous progress before our eyes, and obviously the time will come when, for instance, the present-day situation of factory workers will seem as absurd as serfdom seems to us, when girls were traded for dogs."

"That won't be soon, it won't be very soon," Kostya said and grinned, "it won't be very soon that Rothschild thinks his cellars of gold are absurd, and until then, the worker can slave away and be swollen with hunger. No, uncle. We mustn't wait, we must fight. If a cat eats from the same plate as a mouse, do you think it's conscious of it? Not at all. It was forced."

"Fyodor and I are rich, our father is a capitalist, a million-aire, it's with us you must fight!" Laptev said and rubbed his forehead with his palm. "Fighting with me—that doesn't fit in with my thinking! I'm rich, but what has money given me so far, what has this power given me? How am I happier than you? My childhood was like hard labor, and money didn't save me from birching. When Nina was sick and dying, my money didn't help her. If someone doesn't love me, I can't force him to love me, though I spend a hundred million."

"But you can do a lot of good," said Kish.

"What sort of good! Yesterday you solicited me for some mathematician who is looking for a post. Believe me, I can do as little for him as you can. I can give him money, but that's not what he wants. Once I solicited a post for a poor violinist from a famous musician, and his answer was: 'You have turned to me precisely because you are not a musician.' And so I will answer you: you've turned to me for help with such assurance, because you've never once been in the position of a rich man."

"Why this comparison with the famous musician, I don't understand!" said Yulia Sergeevna, and she turned red. "What does the famous musician have to do with it!"

Her face trembled with hatred, and she lowered her eyes to conceal this feeling. And not only her husband but everyone sitting at the table understood the expression of her face.

"What does the famous musician have to do with it!" she repeated quietly. "Nothing is easier than helping a poor man."

Silence ensued. Pyotr served grouse, but no one ate it, everyone ate only salad. Laptev no longer remembered what he had said, but it was clear to him that it was not his words that were hateful but merely the fact that he had interfered in the conversation.

After supper he went to his study; tensely, with pounding heart, expecting new humiliations, he listened to what was going on in the drawing room. There again an argument started; then Yartsev sat at the piano and sang a sentimental romance. He was a jack-of-all-trades: he could sing, play, and even do magic tricks.

"As you like, gentlemen, but I don't wish to sit at home," said Yulia. "We must go somewhere."

They decided to drive out of town and sent Kish to the Merchants' Club for a troika. Laptev was not invited, because he usually did not go out of town, and because his brother was now with him, but the way he understood it was that his society bored them, and that in this gay young company, he was quite superfluous. And his vexation, his bitter feeling were so strong that he all but wept; he was even glad that they treated him so unkindly, that they disdained him, that he was a stupid, boring husband, a moneybags, and it seemed to him that he would be even more glad if his wife was unfaithful to him that night with his best friend and then confessed it, looking at him with hatred . . . He was jealous of the students they knew, the actors, the singers, Yartsev, even passersby, and he now passionately wished that she would indeed be unfaithful to him, wanted to find her with someone, then poison himself, to get rid of this nightmare once and for all. Fyodor was drinking tea and swallowing loudly. But then he, too, got ready to go.

"Our old man must be losing his sight," he said, putting on his coat. "He sees quite poorly."

Laptev also put on his coat and left. He saw his brother off to Strastnoy, took a cab, and went to the Yar.

"And this is called family happiness!" he laughed at himself. "This is love!"

His teeth were chattering, and he did not know whether it was jealousy or something else. At the Yar he walked among the tables, listened to a coupleteer in the big hall; he did not have a single phrase prepared in case he met his people, and was certain beforehand that if he met his wife, he would only smile pitifully and stupidly, and everyone would understand what feeling had made him come there. The electric lights, the loud music, the smell of powder, and the fact that the ladies he met stared at him, made him feel sick. He stopped by doorways, trying to see and hear what was going on in the private rooms, and it seemed to him that, along with the coupleteer and those ladies, he was playing some low, contemptible role. Then he went to the Strelna, but did not meet any of his people there, either, and it was only when he drove up to the Yar again on his way back that a troika noisily overtook him; the drunken driver was shouting, and he could hear Yartsev's guffaw: "Ha, ha, ha!"

Laptev came home after three. Yulia Sergeevna was already in bed. Noticing that she was not asleep, he went up to her and said sharply:

"I understand your loathing, your hatred, but you might spare me in front of others, you might conceal your feelings."

She sat up in bed and hung her legs over the side. In the light of the icon lamp, her eyes looked big and dark.

"I ask your forgiveness," she said.

From agitation and the trembling of his whole body, he could no longer utter a single word but stood before her in silence. She was also trembling and sat looking like a criminal, waiting for a talking to.

"How I suffer!" he said at last and clutched his head. "It's like I'm in hell, I've lost my mind!"

"And is it easy for me?" she asked in a quavering voice. "God alone knows what it's like for me."

"You've been my wife for half a year now, but there's not even a spark of love in your soul, no hope, no bright spot! Why did you marry me?" Laptev went on in despair. "Why? What demon pushed you into my arms? What did you hope for? What did you want?"

She looked at him in terror, as if she was afraid he would kill her.

"Was I pleasing to you? Did you love me?" he went on breathlessly. "No! What was it, then? What? Tell me— what?" he shouted. "Oh, cursed money! Cursed money!"

"No, I swear to God!" she cried and crossed herself; she shrank under the insult, and for the first time he heard her weep. "No, I swear to God!" she repeated. "I didn't think of money, I don't need it, I simply thought that if I refused you, it would be a bad thing to do. I was afraid to ruin your life and mine. And now I'm suffering for my mistake, suffering unbearably!"

She sobbed bitterly, and he realized how painful it was for her, and not knowing what to say, he sank down on the rug before her.

"Enough, enough," he murmured. "I insulted you because I love you madly," he suddenly kissed her foot and embraced it passionately. "At least a spark of love!" he murmured. "Well, lie to me! Lie! Don't tell me it was a mistake! . . ."

But she went on weeping, and he felt that she tolerated his caresses only as an inevitable consequence of her mistake. And the foot he had kissed, she drew under her like a bird. He felt sorry for her.

She lay down and pulled the covers over her head; he undressed and also lay down. In the morning they both felt embarrassed and did not know what to talk about, and it even seemed to him that she stepped gingerly on the foot he had kissed.

Before dinner Panaurov came to say good-bye. Yulia felt an irrepressible desire to go home to her birthplace; it would be good, she thought, to rest from family life, from this embarrassment, and from the constant awareness that she had acted badly. Over dinner it was decided that she would leave with Panaurov and visit her father for two or three weeks, until she got bored.

XI

SHE AND PANAUROV traveled in a separate compartment; on his head was a visored lambskin cap of an odd shape.

"No, Petersburg didn't satisfy me," he said measuredly, sighing. "They promise a lot but nothing definite. Yes, my dear. I was a justice of the peace, a permanent member, chairman of the district council, finally an adviser to the provincial board; it would seem I've served my fatherland and have a right to some consideration, but there you have it: I can't get them to transfer me to another town . . ."

Panaurov closed his eyes and shook his head.

"I'm not recognized," he went on, as if falling asleep. "Of course, I'm not an administrative genius, but then I'm a decent, honest man, and in our times even that is a rare thing. I confess, I occasionally deceive women slightly, but in relation to the Russian government, I have always been a gentleman. But enough of that," he said, opening his eyes, "let's talk about you. Why did you suddenly take it into your head to go to your papa?"

"Oh, just a little disagreement with my husband," said Yulia, looking at his cap.

"Yes, he's a bit odd. All the Laptevs are odd. Your husband's all right, more or less, but his brother Fyodor is a complete fool."

Panaurov sighed and asked seriously:

"And do you have a lover yet?"

Yulia looked at him in astonishment and smiled.

"God knows what you're saying."

At a big station, after ten o'clock, they both got out and had supper. When the train rolled on again, Panaurov took off his coat and cap and sat down beside Yulia.

"You're very sweet, I must tell you," he began. "Forgive me the tavern comparison, but you remind me of a freshly pickled cucumber; it still smells of the hotbed, so to speak, but already has a little salt and the scent of dill in it. You're gradually shaping up into a magnificent woman, a wonderful, graceful woman. If this trip had taken place five years ago," he sighed, "I would have felt it my pleasant duty to enter the ranks of your admirers, but now, alas, I'm an invalid."

He smiled sadly and at the same time graciously, and put his arm around her waist.

"You're out of your mind!" she said, flushing, and so frightened that her hands and feet went cold. "Stop it, Grigory Nikolaich!"

"What are you afraid of, my dear?" he asked gently. "What's so terrible? You're simply not used to it."

If a woman protested, for him it only meant that he had made an impression on her and she liked it. Holding Yulia by the waist, he kissed her firmly on the cheek, then on the lips, fully assured that he was affording her the greatest pleasure. Yulia recovered from her fear and embarrassment and began to laugh. He kissed her once more and said, putting on his funny cap:

"That's all the invalid can give you. One Turkish pasha, a kind old man, received as a gift, or maybe as an inheritance, an entire harem. When his beautiful young wives lined up before him, he went to them, kissed each one, and said: 'That's all I'm able to give you now.' I say the same thing."

She found all this silly, extraordinary, and amusing. She

wanted to frolic. Getting up on the seat and humming a tune, she took a box of candies from the shelf and tossed him a piece of chocolate, shouting:

"Catch!"

He caught it. She then threw him another candy with a loud laugh, then a third, and he kept catching them and putting them in his mouth, looking at her with pleading eyes, and it seemed to her that in his face, in its features and expression, there was much that was feminine and childish. And when she sat down breathless on the seat and went on looking at him laughingly, he touched her cheek with two fingers and said as if in vexation:

"Naughty girl!"

"Take it," she said, giving him the box. "I don't like sweets."

He ate the candies to the last one and put the empty box in his suitcase. He liked boxes with pictures on them.

"However, enough frolicking," he said. "It's time for the invalid to go bye-bye."

He took his Bokhara dressing gown and a pillow from his portmanteau, lay down, and covered himself with the gown.

"Good night, my dove!" he said in a soft voice and sighed as if he ached all over.

And soon snoring was heard. Feeling no embarrassment, she also lay down and soon fell asleep.

The next morning, as she drove home from the station in her native town, the streets seemed to her deserted, peopleless, the snow gray, and the houses small, as if someone had flattened them out. She met a procession: a dead man was being carried in an open coffin, with church banners.

"They say it's lucky to meet a funeral," she thought.

The windows of the house where Nina Fyodorovna used to live were now pasted over with white notices.

With a sinking heart, she drove into her courtyard and rang at the door. It was opened by an unfamiliar maid, fat, sleepy, in a warm quilted jacket. Going up the stairs, Yulia recalled how Laptev had made his declaration of love there, but now the stairway was unwashed, covered with stains. Upstairs, in the cold corridor, patients waited in winter coats. And for some reason, her heart pounded strongly, and she could barely walk from agitation.

The doctor, grown fatter still, red as a brick, and with disheveled hair, was having tea. Seeing his daughter, he was very glad and even became tearful; she thought that she was the only joy in this old man's life, and, touched, she hugged him tightly and said she would stay with him for a long time, till Easter. After changing in her own room, she came out to the dining room to have tea with him; he was pacing up and down, his hands thrust in his pockets, and singing "Roo-roo-roo-roo"—meaning that he was displeased with something.

"Your life in Moscow must be very merry," he said. "I'm very glad for you . . . Me, I'm an old man, I don't need anything. I'll croak soon and deliver you all. And it's just a wonder that I've got such a thick hide, that I'm still alive! Amazing!"

He said he was a tough old donkey that everybody rode on. Nina Fyodorovna's treatment had been heaped on him, the care of her children, her funeral; and this coxcomb Panaurov did not want to have anything to do with it and even borrowed a hundred roubles from him and still had not paid it back.

"Take me to Moscow and put me in the madhouse there!" said the doctor. "I'm mad, I'm a naïve child, because I still believe in truth and justice!"

Then he reproached her husband for lack of foresight: he had not bought a house that was up for sale so profitably. And now it seemed to Yulia that she was not the only joy in this old man's life. While he received patients and then went to make calls, she walked around all the rooms, not knowing what to do and what to think about. She was already unaccustomed to her native town and native home; she was now drawn neither outside nor to acquaintances, and she did not feel sad, recalling her former girlfriends and her girl's life, and did not regret the past.

In the evening she dressed smartly and went to the vigil. But there were only simple people in church, and her magnificent fur coat and hat made no impression. And it seemed to her as if some change had taken place in the church and in herself. Before, she had liked it when the canon was read during the vigil and the choir sang the verses, for instance, "I shall open my lips," she had liked moving slowly with the crowd towards the priest standing in the middle of the church, and then feeling the holy oil on her forehead, but now she only waited for the service to be over. And, leaving the church, she was afraid the beggars might ask her for something; it would be boring to stop and search her pockets, and she no longer had copper money but only roubles.

She went to bed early but fell asleep late. Her dreams were all of some sort of portraits and of the funeral procession she had seen in the morning; they carried the open coffin with the dead man into the courtyard, stopped by the door, then for a long time swung the coffin on towels and banged it against the door as hard as they could. Yulia woke up and jumped out of bed in terror. In fact, there was a banging on the door downstairs, and the wire of the bell scraped against the wall, but no ringing was heard.

The doctor coughed. She heard the maid go downstairs, then come back up.

"Madam!" she said, knocking on the door. "Madam!"

"What is it?" asked Yulia.

"A telegram for you!"

Yulia came out to her with a candle. Behind the maid stood the doctor, his coat thrown over his underwear, and also with a candle.

"Our doorbell's broken," he said, yawning sleepily. "It's long been in need of repair."

Yulia unsealed the telegram and read: "We drink your health. Yartsev, Kochevoy."

"Ah, what fools!" she said and laughed; her soul felt light and gay.

Going back to her room, she quietly washed, dressed, then packed for a long time, till dawn, and at noon she left for Moscow.

XII

DURING HOLY WEEK the Laptevs were at the Art School for a picture exhibition. They went there as a household, Moscow fashion, taking along the two girls, the governess, and Kostya.

Laptev knew the names of all the well-known artists and never missed a single exhibition. Sometimes at his dacha in the summer, he himself painted landscapes in oils, and it seemed to him that he had considerable taste, and that if he had studied, he would perhaps have made a good artist. When abroad, he would sometimes visit antique shops, look at old things with the air of a connoisseur and utter his opinion, purchase something or other; the antiquarian would charge him whatever he liked, and afterwards the purchased thing would lie in the carriage house, nailed up in a box, until it disappeared no one knew where. Or else, stopping at a print shop, he would spend a long time attentively examining paintings, bronzes, make various observations, and suddenly buy some homemade frame or a box of trashy paper. The paintings he had at home were all of large size, but bad; the good ones were poorly hung. It happened to him more than once to pay a high price for things that later turned out to be crude fakes. And remarkably, though generally timid in life, he was extremely bold and self-assured at picture exhibitions. Why?

Yulia Sergeevna, like her husband, looked at paintings through her fist or with binoculars, and was surprised that the people in the paintings were as if alive, and the trees as if real; but she had no understanding, and it seemed to her that many of the pictures at the exhibition were alike, and that the whole aim of art lay precisely in this, that the people and objects in the pictures, when looked at through the fist, should stand out as if real.

"This forest is by Shishkin,"[19] her husband explained to her. "He always paints one and the same thing...But pay attention to this: such purple snow has never existed...And this boy's left arm is shorter than his right."

When everyone was tired, and Laptev went looking for Kostya so as to go home, Yulia stopped in front of a small landscape and gazed at it indifferently. In the foreground a rivulet, a wooden bridge across it, a path on the other side disappearing into the dark grass, a field, then to the right a piece of forest, a bonfire nearby: it must have been a night pasture. And in the distance, the last glow of the sunset.

Yulia imagined herelf walking across the little bridge, then down the path further and further, and it is quiet all around, drowsy corncrakes cry, the fire flickers far ahead. And for some reason, it suddenly seemed to her that she had seen those same clouds that stretched across the red part of the sky, and the forest, and the fields long ago and many times; she felt lonely, and she wanted to walk, walk, walk down the path; and where the sunset's glow was, there rested the reflection of something unearthly, eternal.

"How well it's painted!" she said, surprised that she had suddenly understood the painting. "Look, Alyosha! Do you see how quiet it is?"

She tried to explain why she liked this landscape so much, but neither her husband nor Kostya understood her. She kept looking at the landscape with a sad smile, and the fact that the others found nothing special in it troubled her; then she began walking around the rooms again and looking at the pictures, she wanted to understand them, and it no longer seemed to her that many pictures at the exhibition were alike. When, on returning home, she paid attention for the first time to the big painting that hung over the grand piano in the drawing room, she felt animosity towards it and said:

"Who on earth wants to have such pictures!"

And after that the gilded cornices, the Venetian mirrors with flowers, and pictures like the one that hung over the grand piano, as well as the discussions of her husband and Kostya about art, aroused in her a feeling of boredom and vexation and sometimes even hatred.

Life flowed on as usual from day to day, promising nothing special. The theater season was over, the warm time was coming. The weather remained excellent all the while. One morning the Laptevs were going to the district court to hear Kostya, who had been appointed by the court to defend someone. They were delayed at home and arrived at the court when the examination of the witnesses had already begun. A reserve soldier was accused of burglary. Many of the witnesses were washerwomen; they testified that the accused often visited the woman who ran the laundry; on the eve of the Elevation,[20] he came late at night and began asking for money for the hair of the dog, but no one gave him any; then he left, but came back an hour later and brought some beer and mint gingerbreads for the girls. They drank and sang songs almost till daybreak, and when they looked in the morning, the lock on the attic door was broken and laundry was missing: three men's shirts, a skirt, and two sheets. Kostya asked each witness mockingly whether she had drunk the beer brought by the accused on the eve of the Elevation. Evidently what he was driving at was that the washerwomen had stolen from themselves. He delivered his speech without the least excitement, looking angrily at the jury.

He explained what was burglary and what was simple theft. He spoke in great detail, persuasively, displaying an extraordinary capacity for talking at length and in a serious tone about something everybody always knew. And it was hard to understand what he was actually after. From his long speech, the foreman of the jury could only come to the following conclusion: "There was burglary but no theft, because the washerwomen drank up the laundry themselves, or if there was theft, then there was no burglary." But he evidently said precisely what was necessary, because his speech moved the jury and the public, and they liked it very much. When the verdict of acquittal was announced, Yulia nodded to Kostya and later firmly shook his hand.

In May the Laptevs moved to their summer house in Sokolniki. By then Yulia was pregnant.

XIII

MORE THAN A year went by. In Sokolniki, not far from the tracks of the Yaroslavl Railway, Yulia and Yartsev were sitting on the grass; a little to one side, Kochevoy lay with his hands behind his head, looking at the sky. All three had had enough of walking and were waiting for the local six o'clock train to pass before going home to have tea.

"Mothers see something extraordinary in their children— that's the way nature arranged it," Yulia was saying. "A mother stands for hours by a little bed, looking at her baby's little ears, little eyes, little nose, and admiring them. If someone else kisses her child, the poor woman thinks it gives the person great pleasure. And the mother talks about nothing but her child. I know this weakness in mothers and keep an eye on myself, but really, my Olya is extraordinary. How she

ANTON CHEKHOV

gazes while she's nursing! How she laughs! She's only eight
months old, but by God, I haven't seen such intelligent eyes
even in a three-year-old."

"Tell us, by the way," asked Yartsev, "whom do you love
more: your husband or your child?"

Yulia shrugged her shoulders.

"I don't know," she said. "I've never loved my husband
very much, and Olya is essentially my first love. You know,
I didn't marry Alexei for love. Before, I used to be stupid,
I suffered, I kept thinking I'd ruined his life and mine, but
now I see there's no need for any love, it's all nonsense."

"But if it isn't love, what feeling binds you to your
husband? Why do you live with him?"

"I don't know . . . Just so, out of habit, it must be. I respect
him, I miss him when he's away for long, but that—isn't
love. He's an intelligent, honest man, and that's enough for
my happiness. He's very kind, simple . . ."

"Alyosha's intelligent, Alyosha's kind," said Kostya, lazily
raising his head, "but, my dear, to find out that he's intelligent, kind, and interesting, you have to go through hell and
high water with him . . . And what's the use of his kindness
or his intelligence? He'll dish you up as much money as you
like, that he can do, but if there's a need for strength of
character, to resist some brazenheaded boor, he gets embarrassed and loses heart. People like your gentle Alexis are
wonderful people, but they're not fit for struggle. And generally, they're not fit for anything."

At last the train appeared. Perfectly pink steam poured
from the smokestack and rose above the grove, and two
windows in the last car suddenly flashed so brightly in the
sun that it was painful to look.

"Teatime!" said Yulia Sergeevna, getting up.

She had gained weight recently, and her gait was now
ladylike, slightly lazy.

"But all the same, it's not good without love," said Yartsev,

404

walking after her. "We just keep talking and reading about love, but we love little ourselves, and that really isn't good."

"It's all trifles, Ivan Gavrilych," said Yulia. "That's not where happiness lies."

They had tea in a little garden where mignonette, stock, and nicotiana were blooming and the early gladioli were already opening. By Yulia Sergeevna's face, Yartsev and Kochevoy could see that she was living through a happy time of inner peace and balance, and that she needed nothing besides what was already there, and they themselves felt inwardly peaceful and well. Whatever any of them said, it all came out intelligent and to the point. The pines were beautiful, the resin smelled more wonderful than ever, and the cream was very tasty, and Sasha was a nice, intelligent girl . . .

After tea, Yartsev sang romances, accompanying himself on the piano, while Yulia and Kochevoy sat silently and listened, only Yulia got up from time to time and quietly went to look at the baby and at Lida, who for two days now had lain in a fever and eaten nothing.

" 'My friend, my tender friend . . .' " sang Yartsev. "No, ladies and gentlemen, you can put a knife in me," he said and shook his head, "but I don't understand why you're against love! If I weren't busy fifteen hours a day, I'd certainly fall in love."

Supper was served on the terrace; it was warm and still, but Yulia wrapped herself in a shawl and complained of the dampness. When it got dark, she felt out of sorts for some reason, kept shuddering, and asked her guests to stay longer; she offered them wine and had cognac served after supper to keep them from leaving. She did not want to be left alone with the children and the servants.

"We dacha women are organizing a show for the children," she said. "We already have everything—the space and the actors—all we need is a play. About two dozen plays have been sent to us, but not a single one of them will do.

Now, you love theater and you know history well," she turned to Yartsev, "so write us a history play."

"Well, that's possible."

The guests drank all the cognac and got ready to leave. It was past ten o'clock, late by dacha standards.

"How dark, dark as pitch!" Yulia said, seeing them off to the gate. "I don't know how you'll make it, gentlemen. Anyhow, it's cold!"

She wrapped herself more tightly and went back to the porch.

"And my Alexei must be playing cards somewhere!" she called. "Good night!"

After the bright rooms, nothing could be seen. Yartsev and Kostya felt their way like blind men, reached the railroad tracks, and crossed them.

"Can't see a damned thing!" Kostya suddenly said in a bass voice, stopping and looking at the sky. "But the stars, the stars, like new coins! Gavrilych!"

"Eh?" Yartsev responded somewhere.

"I say: can't see a thing. Where are you!"

Yartsev, whistling, came up to him and took his arm.

"Hey, dacha people!" Kostya suddenly shouted at the top of his voice. "We've caught a socialist!"

When tipsy, he was always very restless, shouted, picked on policemen and cabbies, sang, guffawed furiously.

"Nature, devil take it!" he shouted.

"Now, now," Yartsev tried to calm him down. "Mustn't do that. I beg you."

Soon the friends became accustomed to the darkness and began to make out the silhouettes of the tall pines and telephone poles. Rare whistles reached them from the Moscow stations, and the wires hummed plaintively. The grove itself made no sound, and in this silence, something proud, strong, mysterious could be felt, and now, at night, it seemed that the tops of the pines almost touched the sky. The friends found their cutting and went along it. It was quite dark here, and only by the long strip of sky spangled with stars, and the trampled ground under their feet, did they know they were going along a path. They walked side by side in silence, and both fancied there were people coming in the opposite direction. The drunken mood left them. It occurred to Yartsev that the souls of Moscow tsars, boyars, and patriarchs might be flitting about in this grove now, and he was going to say so to Kostya but restrained himself.

When they came to the city gate, there was a slight glimmer in the sky. Still silent, Yartsev and Kochevoy walked along the pavement past cheap dachas, taverns, lumber yards; under the railway arch, the dampness, pleasant, scented with lindens, chilled them, and then a long, wide street opened out, with not a soul on it, not a light... When they reached Krasny Pond, day was already breaking.

"Moscow is a city that still has much suffering ahead of her," Yartsev said, looking at the Alexeevsky Monastery.

"How did that enter your head?"

"It just did. I love Moscow."

Yartsev and Kostya had both been born in Moscow and adored her, and for some reason regarded other cities with hostility; they were convinced that Moscow was a remarkable city and Russia a remarkable country. In the Crimea, in the Caucasus, and abroad, they felt bored, uncomfortable, ill at ease, and they found the gray Moscow weather most pleasant and healthy. Days when cold rain raps at the windows, and dusk falls early, and the walls of houses and churches take on a brown, mournful color, and you do not know what to put on when you go outside—such days pleasantly excited them.

Finally, near a train station, they took a cab.

"In fact, it would be nice to write a history play," said Yartsev, "but you know, without the Liapunovs and the Godunovs, from the times of Yaroslav or Monomakh[21] ... I hate all

Russian history plays, except for Pimen's monologue.[22] When you deal with some historical source, or even when you read a textbook of Russian history, it seems that everything in Russia is remarkably talented, gifted, and interesting, but when I watch a history play in the theater, Russian life begins to seem giftless, unhealthy, and unoriginal to me."

Near Dmitrovka, the friends parted, and Yartsev went further on to his place on Nikitskaya. He dozed, rocking in the cab, and kept thinking about the play. Suddenly he imagined an awful noise, clanging, shouts in some unknown language like Kalmyk; and some village, all caught in flames, and the neighboring forest, covered with hoarfrost and a tender pink from the fire, can be seen far around, and so clearly that each little fir tree is distinct; some wild people, on horseback and on foot, rush about the village, their horses and themselves as crimson as the glow in the sky.

"It's the Polovtsi,"[23] thinks Yartsev.

One of them—old, frightening, with a bloody face, all scorched—is tying a young girl with a white Russian face to his saddle. The old man shouts something furiously, but the girl watches sorrowfully, intelligently... Yartsev shook his head and woke up.

" 'My friend, my tender friend...' " he sang.

Paying the cabby and then going up the stairs to his place, he still could not quite recover, and saw the flames sweep on to the trees, the forest crackle and smoke; an enormous wild boar, mad with terror, rushes through the village... But the girl tied to the saddle keeps watching.

When he entered his apartment, it was already light. On the grand piano, near an open score, two candles were burning down. On the couch lay Rassudina, in a black dress with a sash, a newspaper in her hand, fast asleep. She must have played for a long time, waiting for Yartsev to come back, and fallen asleep before he came.

"Eh, quite worn out!" he thought.

He carefully took the newspaper from her hand, covered her with a plaid, put out the candles, and went to his bedroom. Lying down, he thought about the history play, and the refrain "My friend, my tender friend..." would not leave his head.

Two days later, Laptev stopped by for a moment to tell him that Lida had come down with diphtheria, and that Yulia Sergeevna and the baby had caught it from her, and in another five days came the news that Lida and Yulia were recovering, but the baby had died, and the Laptevs had fled from their Sokolniki dacha to the city.

XIV

IT BECAME UNPLEASANT for Laptev to stay long at home. His wife often went to the wing, telling him she had to do lessons with the girls, but he knew she went there not to give lessons but to weep at Kostya's. The ninth day came, then the twentieth, then the fortieth,[24] and he had to go each time to the Alexeevskoe cemetery and listen to the memorial service, and then torment himself all day thinking only about the unfortunate baby and saying all sorts of banalities to his wife in consolation. He rarely went to the warehouse now and was occupied only with charity, thinking up various cares and chores, and he was glad when he chanced to drive around for a whole day on account of some trifle. Recently he had been preparing to go abroad, in order to acquaint himself there with the setting up of night shelters, and this thought now diverted him.

It was an autumn day. Yulia had just gone to the wing to weep, and Laptev was lying on the couch in his study, trying to think where he would go. Just then Pyotr announced that Rassudina had come. Laptev was very glad, jumped up, and went to meet the unexpected guest, his former friend, whom he had almost begun to forget. Since that evening when he had seen her for the last time, she had not changed in the least and was exactly the same.

"Polina!" he said, reaching both hands out to her. "It's been ages! If you knew how glad I am to see you! Come in!"

Rassudina jerked his hand as she shook it and, without taking off her coat and hat, went into the study and sat down.

"I've come for a minute," she said. "I have no time to talk of trifles. Kindly sit down and listen. Whether you're glad to see me or not is decidedly all one to me, since I don't care a whit about any gracious attention to me from fine gentlemen. If I've come to you, it's because I've already been to five places today and was refused everywhere, and yet it's an urgent matter. Listen," she went on, looking him in the eye, "five students I know, limited and muddleheaded people but unquestionably poor, haven't made their payments and are now being expelled. Your wealth imposes on you the duty of going to the university at once and paying for them."

"With pleasure, Polina."

"Here are their last names," said Rassudina, handing Laptev a little note. "Go this very minute, you'll have time to enjoy family happiness afterwards."

Just then a rustling was heard behind the door to the drawing room: it must have been the dog scratching himself. Rassudina blushed and jumped up.

"Your Dulcinea's[25] eavesdropping on us!" she said. "That is vile!"

Laptev felt offended for Yulia.

"She's not here, she's in the wing," he said. "And do not speak of her like that. Our baby has died, and she is in terrible grief."

"You can reassure her," Rassudina grinned, sitting down again, "there'll be a dozen more. Who hasn't got wits enough to make babies?"[26]

Laptev remembered hearing the same thing or something

like it many times long ago, and the poetry of the past wafted over him, the freedom of solitary, unmarried life, when it seemed to him that he was young and could do whatever he liked, and when there was no love for his wife or memory of their baby.

"Let's go together," he said, stretching.

When they came to the university, Rassudina stopped to wait by the gate, and Laptev went to the office; a little later, he returned and handed Rassudina five receipts.

"Where to now?" he asked.

"Yartsev's."

"I'll come with you."

"But you'll keep him from working."

"No, I assure you!" he said and looked at her imploringly.

She was wearing a black hat trimmed with crape, as if she was in mourning, and a very short, shabby coat with the pockets sticking out. Her nose seemed longer than it used to be, and her face was deathly pale, despite the cold. Laptev found it pleasing to follow her, obey her, and listen to her grumbling. He walked along and thought about her: what inner strength this woman must have if, being so unattractive, angular, restless, unable to dress properly, aways untidily combed, and always somehow ungainly, she still could charm.

They entered Yartsev's apartment by the back door, through the kitchen, where they were met by the cook, a neat little old woman with gray curls; she got very embarrassed, smiled sweetly, which made her face resemble a piece of pastry, and said:

"Please come in."

Yartsev was not at home. Rassudina sat at the piano and took up some dull, difficult exercises, ordering Laptev not to bother her. And he did not distract her with talk but sat to one side and leafed through *The Messenger of Europe*. After playing for two hours—this was her daily helping—she ate something in the kitchen and went to her lessons. Laptev read the sequel to some novel, then sat for a long time, not reading and not feeling bored, and pleased that he was late for dinner at home.

"Ha, ha, ha!" Yartsev's laughter rang out, and he himself came in, hale, cheerful, red-cheeked, in a new tailcoat with bright buttons. "Ha, ha, ha!"

The friends had dinner together. Then Laptev lay down on the sofa, and Yartsev sat by him and lit a cigar. Dusk fell.

"I must be getting old," said Laptev. "Since my sister Nina died, for some reason I've begun thinking frequently of death."

They talked about death, about the immortality of the soul, how it would indeed be nice to resurrect and then fly off somewhere to Mars, to be eternally idle and happy, and above all, to think in some special unearthly way.

"I have no wish to die," Yartsev said softly. "No philosophy can reconcile me with death, and I look upon it simply as a disaster. I want to live."

"You love life, Gavrilych?"

"Yes, I do."

"And I can't understand myself at all in this connection. First I'm in a gloomy mood, then I'm indifferent. I'm timid, unsure of myself, I have a cowardly conscience, I'm quite unable to adjust to life, to master it. Another man talks stupidly, or cheats, and does it so cheerfully, while it happens that I do good consciously and feel nothing but anxiety or total indifference. All this, Gavrilych, I explain by the fact that I'm a slave, the grandson of a bonded serf. Before we smutty-faced ones make it onto the real path, a lot of our kind will have to lay down their bones!"

"That's all to the good, dear heart," Yartsev said and sighed. "It only shows once again how rich and diverse Russian life is. Ah, how rich! You know, I'm more convinced every day that we're living on the eve of the greatest triumph, and I'd like to live long enough to take part in it myself. Believe it or not, but I think a remarkable generation is now growing up. When I teach children, especially girls, it delights me. Wonderful children!"

Yartsev went to the piano and played a chord.

"I'm a chemist, I think chemically, and I'll die a chemist," he went on. "But I'm greedy, I'm afraid I'll die unsated; chemistry alone isn't enough for me, I snatch at Russian history, art history, pedagogy, music . . . Your wife told me once in the summer that I should write a history play, and now I want to write and write; it seems I could just sit for three days and nights, without getting up, and keep writing. Images wear me out, they crowd in my head, and I feel as if my brain is pulsing. I have no wish at all that something special should come from me, that I should create some great thing, I simply want to live, to dream, to hope, to keep up everywhere . . . Life, dear heart, is short, and we must live it the best we can."

After this friendly conversation, which ended only at midnight, Laptev began to visit Yartsev almost every day. He was drawn to him. Usually he came before evening, lay down, and waited patiently for him to come, without feeling the least boredom. Yartsev, having come home from school and eaten, would sit down to work, but Laptev would ask some question, a conversation would begin, work was set aside, and at midnight the friends would part, very pleased with each other.

But this did not last long. Once, coming to Yartsev's, Laptev found Rassudina alone, sitting at the piano and playing her exercises. She looked him over coldly, almost hostilely, and asked, without offering him her hand:

"Tell me, please, when will there be an end to this?"

"To what?" Laptev asked, not understanding.

"You come here every day and hinder Yartsev in his work. Yartsev is not a little merchant, he's a scholar, and every minute of his life is precious. You must understand that and have at least a little delicacy!"

"If you find that I'm hindering him," Laptev said meekly, feeling confused, "I'll discontinue my visits."

"Splendid. Go now, or he may come and find you here."

The tone in which this was said, and Rassudina's indifferent eyes, utterly confused him. She no longer had any feelings for him, except the wish that he leave quickly—and how unlike her former love that was! He left without shaking her hand, and thought she would call after him and tell him to come back, but the sounds of the exercises were heard again, and he understood, as he slowly went down the stairs, that he was now a stranger to her.

After three days or so, Yartsev came to see him and spend the evening together.

"And I've got news," he said and laughed. "Polina Nikolaevna has moved in with me for good." He was slightly embarrassed and went on in a low voice: "What, then? Of course, we're not in love with each other, but I think that... that makes no difference. I'm glad I can give her shelter and peace and the possibility of not working, in case she gets sick, and it seems to her that if she lives with me, there will be more order in my life, and that under her influence, I'll become a great scholar. So she thinks. And let her think it. They have a saying in the south: 'A fool gets rich on fancies.' Ha, ha, ha!"

Laptev was silent. Yartsev strolled about the study, looked at the pictures he had seen many times before, and said with a sigh:

"Yes, my friend, I'm three years older than you, and it's late for me to think about true love, and essentially a woman like Polina Nikolaevna is a find for me, and I could certainly live my life very well with her into old age, but, devil take it, I keep regretting something, keep wanting something, and imagining that I'm lying in the Vale of Dagestan and dreaming of a ball.[27] In short, a man is never content with what he's got."

He went to the drawing room and sang romances as if nothing had happened, but Laptev sat in his study, his eyes closed, trying to understand why Rassudina had gone with Yartsev. And then he became sad that there were no firm, lasting attachments, and felt vexed that Polina Nikolaevna had gone with Yartsev, and vexed with himself that his feeling for his wife was not at all what it had been before.

XV

LAPTEV WAS SITTING in an armchair, reading and rocking; Yulia was there in the study and also reading. There seemed to be nothing to talk about, and both had been silent since morning. Now and then he glanced at her over his book and thought: whether you marry from passionate love or without any love—isn't it all the same? And the time when he was jealous, worried, tormented now seemed far away. He had managed to travel abroad and was now resting from the trip and counting, with the coming of spring, on going to England, which he had liked very much.

And Yulia Sergeevna had grown accustomed to her grief and no longer went to the wing to weep. That winter she did not drive around shopping, did not go to theaters and concerts, but stayed at home. She did not like big rooms and was always either in her husband's study or in her own room, where she kept the encased icons she had received as a dowry, and that landscape she had liked so much at the exhibition hung on the wall. She spent almost no money on herself and lived on as little as she had once lived on in her father's house.

The winter passed cheerlessly. Everywhere in Moscow,

they were playing cards, but if instead of that they invented some other diversion, for instance singing, reading, drawing, it came out still more boring. And because there were few talented people in Moscow, and the same singers and readers participated in all the evenings, the enjoyment of art itself gradually became habitual and, for many, turned into a boring, monotonous duty.

Besides, not a single day passed for the Laptevs without some distress. Old Fyodor Stepanych's eyesight was now very poor, he did not go to the warehouse, and the eye doctors said he would soon be blind; Fyodor also stopped going to the warehouse for some reason and stayed at home all the time writing something. Panaurov obtained a transfer to another town, with a promotion to the rank of actual state councillor,[28] and now lived at the Dresden and came to Laptev almost every day to ask for money. Kish finally left the university and, while waiting for the Laptevs to find some job for him, spent whole days sitting with them, telling long, boring stories. All this was annoying and wearisome and made daily life unpleasant.

Pyotr came into the study and announced that some unknown lady had come. Written on the card he brought was: "Josephina Iosifovna Milan."

Yulia Sergeevna got up lazily and went out, limping slightly because her foot was asleep. A lady appeared in the doorway, thin, very pale, with dark eyebrows, dressed all in black. She clasped her hands to her breast and said pleadingly:

"Monsieur Laptev, save my children!"

The jingling of bracelets and the face with blotches of powder were familiar to Laptev: he recognized her as the same lady in whose house he had happened to dine so inappropriately sometime before his wedding. It was Panaurov's second wife.

"Save my children!" she repeated, and her face quivered and suddenly became old and pathetic, and her eyes reddened. "You alone can save us, and I've come to you in Moscow on my last money! My children will starve!"

She made a movement as if to go on her knees. Laptev became alarmed and grasped her arms above the elbows.

"Sit down, sit down..." he murmured, seating her. "I beg you, sit down."

"We have no money now to buy bread," she said. "Grigory Nikolaich is leaving for his new post, but he does not want to take me and the children with him, and the money that you have been sending us so magnanimously, he spends only on himself. What are we to do? What? Poor, unfortunate children!"

"Calm yourself, I beg you. I'll tell them in the office to send the money in your name."

She burst into sobs, then calmed down, and he noticed that the tears had made tracks on her powdered cheeks, and that she had a mustache sprouting.

"You are endlessly magnanimous, Monsieur Laptev. But be our angel, our good fairy, persuade Grigory Nikolaich not to abandon me but to take me with him. I love him, love him madly, he is my joy."

Laptev gave her a hundred roubles and promised to talk with Panaurov and, seeing her off to the front hall, kept fearing she might burst into sobs or go down on her knees.

After her came Kish. Then came Kostya with his camera. Lately he had become interested in photography, and each day he photographed everyone in the house several times, and this new occupation caused him much distress, and he even lost weight.

Before evening tea, Fyodor came. He sat down in a corner of the study, opened a book, and stared at one page for a long time, apparently without reading it. Then for a long time he drank tea; his face was red. In his presence, Laptev felt inwardly oppressed; he even found his silence disagreeable.

"You may congratulate Russia on the appearance of a new publicist," said Fyodor. "However, joking aside, I've been delivered of a little article, brother, a trial of the pen, so to speak, and I've brought it to show you. Read it, dear heart, and tell me your opinion. Only frankly."

He took a notebook out of his pocket and handed it to his brother. The article was entitled "The Russian Soul." It was written dully, in the colorless style usually employed by untalented, secretly vain people, and its main thought was this: an intelligent man has the right not to believe in the supernatural, but it is his duty to conceal this disbelief, so as not to cause temptation and shake people's faith; without faith, there is no idealism, and idealism is predestined to save Europe and show mankind to the true path.

"But you don't write what Europe must be saved from," said Laptev.

"That's self-evident."

"Nothing is evident," said Laptev, and he paced about in agitation. "It's not evident what you wrote it for. However, that's your affair."

"I want to publish it as a separate brochure."

"That's your affair."

There was a moment's silence. Fyodor sighed and said:

"I'm deeply, infinitely sorry that you and I think differently. Ah, Alyosha, Alyosha, my dear brother! You and I are Russian people, broad Orthodox people; do all these little German and Jewish ideas suit us? We're not some sort of scalawags, we represent a distinguished merchant family."

"What sort of distinguished family?" Laptev said, restraining his irritation. "Distinguished family! Landowners thrashed our grandfather, and every last little official hit him in the mug. Grandfather thrashed our father, father thrashed you and me. What has this distinguished family given us? What nerves and blood have we inherited? For almost three years now you've been reasoning like a beadle, saying all sorts of nonsense, and here you've written it down—it's boorish raving. And me? And me? Look at me . . . No resilience, no courage, no strength of will; I'm afraid at every step, as if I'm going to be whipped, I'm timid before nonentities, idiots, brutes who are incomparably beneath me mentally and morally; I'm afraid of caretakers, porters, policemen, gendarmes, I'm afraid of everybody, because I was born of a cowed mother, I've been beaten down and frightened since childhood! . . . You and I would do well not to have children. Oh, God grant that this distinguished merchant family ends with us!"

Yulia Sergeevna came into the study and sat down by the desk.

"You've been arguing about something?" she said. "Am I interfering?"

"No, little sister," answered Fyodor, "our conversation is on principle. So you say our family is this and that," he turned to his brother, "however, this family has created a million-rouble business. That's something!"

"Big deal—a million-rouble business! A man of no special intelligence or ability happens to become a trader, then a rich man, he trades day in and day out with no system or goal, not even a lust for money, he trades mechanically, and money comes to him, not he to it. All his life he sits in his shop and loves it only because he can dominate his salesclerks and scoff at his customers. He's a church warden because there he can dominate the choir and bend them to his will; he's a school trustee because he likes to think the teacher is his subordinate and he can play the superior before him. The merchant doesn't like to trade, he likes to dominate, and your warehouse is not a trading establishment but a torture chamber! Yes, for such trading as yours, you need depersonalized, deprived salesclerks, and you prepare them that way yourselves, making them bow at your feet from childhood on for a crust of bread, and from childhood on you accustom them to thinking that you're their benefactors. No fear you'd take a university man into your warehouse!"

"University people are no use in our business."

"Not true!" cried Laptev. "That's a lie!"

"Excuse me, but it seems to me you're fouling the well you drink from," Fyodor said and got up. "Our business is hateful to you, and yet you make use of its income."

"Aha, you've finally come out with it!" Laptev said and laughed, looking angrily at his brother. "If I didn't belong to your distinguished family, if I had at least a pennyworth of will and courage, I'd have flung away that income long ago and gone to earn my bread. But you in your warehouse depersonalized me from childhood on! I'm yours!"

Fyodor glanced at his watch and hastily began taking his leave. He kissed Yulia's hand and went out, but instead of going to the front hall, he went to the drawing room, then to the bedroom.

"I've forgotten the layout of the rooms," he said in great perplexity. "A strange house, isn't it? A strange house."

As he was putting on his coat, he looked as if stunned, and his face expressed pain. Laptev no longer felt angry; he was alarmed and, at the same time, sorry for Fyodor, and that warm, good love for his brother, which seemed to have been extinguished in those three years, now awakened in his breast, and he felt a strong desire to express that love.

"Come for dinner tomorrow, Fedya," he said and stroked his shoulder. "Will you?"

"Yes, yes. But give me some water."

Laptev himself ran to the dining room, took the first thing he happened upon in the sideboard—it was a tall beer mug— poured water into it, and brought it to his brother. Fyodor began drinking greedily, then suddenly bit the mug, there was a gnashing sound, then sobbing. Water poured onto his coat and frock coat. And Laptev, who had never seen a man cry before, stood confused and frightened and did not know what to do. He watched like a lost man as Yulia and the maid took Fyodor's coat off and brought him back inside, and he walked after them, feeling himself to blame.

Yulia helped Fyodor to lie down and lowered herself onto her knees before him.

"Never mind," she comforted him. "It's your nerves..."

"Dear heart, it's so hard for me!" he said. "I'm unhappy, unhappy...but I've been concealing it, concealing it all the while!"

He put his arms around her neck and whispered in her ear:

"I see my sister Nina every night. She comes and sits in the armchair by my bed..."

An hour later, as he was again putting his coat on in the front hall, he smiled and felt abashed in front of the maid. Laptev drove with him to Pyatnitskaya.

"Come for dinner with us tomorrow," he said on the way, holding him under the arm, "and for Easter we'll go abroad together. You need airing out, you've grown quite stale as it is."

"Yes, yes. I'll go, I'll go...And we'll take little sister along."

When he returned home, Laptev found his wife in great nervous agitation. The incident with Fyodor had shocked her, and she was unable to calm down. She did not cry, but she was very pale, and thrashed about on her bed, and with her cold fingers tenaciously clutched hold of the blanket, the pillow, her husband's hands. Her eyes were large, frightened.

"Don't go, don't go," she kept saying to her husband. "Tell me, Alyosha, why have I stopped praying to God? Where is my faith? Ah, why did you talk about religion in front of me? You've confused me, you and your friends. I don't pray anymore."

He put compresses on her forehead, warmed her hands, gave her tea, and she clung to him in fear...

Towards morning she grew weary and fell asleep, with

Laptev sitting beside her and holding her hand. He did not have a chance to sleep. The whole next day he felt broken, dull, thought about nothing, and wandered sluggishly through the rooms.

XVI

THE DOCTORS SAID that Fyodor had a mental illness. Laptev did not know what was going on at Pyatnitskaya, and the dark warehouse, in which neither the old man nor Fyodor appeared anymore, gave him the impression of a tomb. When his wife told him that it was necessary for him to go every day both to the warehouse and to Pyatnitskaya, he either said nothing or began talking irritably about his childhood, about his inability to forgive his father for his past, about Pyatnitskaya and the warehouse being hateful to him, and so on.

One Sunday morning Yulia herself drove to Pyatnitskaya. She found old Fyodor Stepanych in the same big room where the prayer service had been held on the occasion of her arrival. In his canvas jacket, without a tie, in slippers, he was sitting motionless in an armchair, blinking his blind eyes.

"It's me, your daughter-in-law," she said, going up to him. "I've come to see how you are."

He started breathing heavily from excitement. Moved by his misfortune, by his solitude, she kissed his hand, and he felt her face and head and, as if he had assured himself that it was her, made the sign of the cross over her.

"Thank you, thank you," he said. "And I've lost my eyes and don't see anything... I can just barely see the window, and also the fire, but not people or objects. Yes, I'm going blind, Fyodor's fallen ill, and it's bad now without a master's supervision. If there's some disorder, nobody's answerable; people will get spoiled. And why is it Fyodor's fallen ill? Was it a cold? I've never taken sick and never been treated. Never known any doctors."

And the old man started boasting as usual. Meanwhile, the servants were hurriedly setting the table in the big room and putting hors d'oeuvres and bottles of wine on it. They put out some ten bottles, and one of them looked like the Eiffel Tower. A dish of hot little pirozhki was served, smelling of boiled rice and fish.

"My dear guest, please have a bite to eat," said the old man.

She took him under the arm, led him to the table, and poured him some vodka.

"I'll come to see you tomorrow, too," she said, "and bring along your two granddaughters, Sasha and Lida. They'll feel sorry and be nice to you."

"No need, don't bring them. They're illegitimate."

"Why illegitimate? Their father and mother were married in church."

"Without my permission. I didn't bless them and don't want to know them. God be with them."

"That's a strange thing for you to say, Fyodor Stepanych," Yulia said with a sigh.

"In the Gospel it says children should respect and fear their parents."

"Nothing of the sort. In the Gospel it says we should even forgive our enemies."

"In our business you can't forgive. If you start forgiving everybody, in three years it'll all fly up the chimney."

"But to forgive, to say an affectionate, friendly word to a man, even if he's to blame—is higher than business, higher than riches!"

Yulia wanted to soften the old man, to fill him with a sense of pity, to awaken repentance in him, but everything she said he listened to only with condescension, as adults listen to children.

"Fyodor Stepanych," Yulia said resolutely, "you're old, and God will soon call you to Him; He will ask you not about your trade, and whether your business went well, but whether you were merciful to people; weren't you severe to those weaker than you, for instance, to servants, to salesclerks?"

"I've always been a benefactor to those who worked for me, and they should eternally pray to God for me," the old man said with conviction; but, touched by Yulia's sincere tone and wishing to give her pleasure, he said: "Very well, bring the granddaughters tomorrow. I'll have presents bought for them."

The old man was untidily dressed and had cigar ashes on his chest and knees; apparently no one cleaned his boots or clothes. The rice in the pirozhki was undercooked, the tablecloth smelled of soap, the servants stamped their feet loudly. Both the old man and this whole house on Pyatnit-skaya had an abandoned air, and Yulia, who felt it, was ashamed of herself and of her husband.

"I'll be sure to come and see you tomorrow," she said.

She walked through the rooms and ordered the old man's bedroom tidied up and the icon lamp lighted. Fyodor was sitting in his room and looking into an open book without reading it; Yulia talked to him and ordered his room tidied up as well, then went downstairs to the salesclerks. In the middle of the room where the salesclerks dined stood an unpainted wooden column that propped up the ceiling, keeping it from collapsing; the ceilings here were low, the walls covered with cheap wallpaper; it smelled of fumes and the kitchen. All the salesclerks were at home for Sunday and sat on their beds waiting for dinner. When Yulia came in, they jumped up from their places and answered her questions timidly, looking at her from under their brows like prisoners.

"Lord, what bad living quarters you have!" she said, clasping her hands. "Aren't you crowded here?"

"Crowded but content," said Makeichev. "We're much pleased with you and offer up our prayers to merciful God."

"The correspondence of life to personal ambition," said Pochatkin.

And, noticing that Yulia had not understood Pochatkin, Makeichev hastened to clarify:

"We're small people and should live according to our rank."

She looked at the boys' living quarters and the kitchen, made the acquaintance of the housekeeper, and remained very displeased.

On returning home, she said to her husband:

"We should move to Pyatnitskaya as soon as possible and live there. And you'll go to the warehouse every day."

Then they both sat side by side in the study and were silent. His heart was heavy, he did not want to go to Pyanitskaya or to the warehouse, but he guessed what his wife was thinking and was unable to contradict her. He stroked her cheek and said:

"I feel as if our life is already over, and what's beginning is some sort of gray half-life. When I learned that my brother Fyodor was hopelessly ill, I wept; we spent our childhood and youth together, I once loved him with all my heart—and here comes catastrophe, and I think that in losing him, I've finally broken with my past. But now, when you said it's necessary for us to move to Pyatnitskaya, into that prison, I began to think that I no longer have any future."

He got up and went to the window.

"Be that as it may, we must bid farewell to thoughts of happiness," he said, looking outside. "There isn't any. I've never known it, and it must be that it simply doesn't exist. However, once in my life I was happy, when I sat all night under your parasol. Remember when you forgot your parasol at my sister Nina's?" he asked, turning to his wife. "I was in love with you then, and I remember sitting all night under that parasol in a state of bliss."

In the study next to the bookcase stood a mahogany chest of drawers trimmed with bronze, in which Laptev kept various useless objects, among them the parasol. He took it out and handed it to his wife.

"Here it is."

Yulia looked at the parasol for a minute, recognized it, and smiled sadly.

"I remember," she said. "When you declared your love to me, you were holding it in your hands," and, noticing that he was about to leave, she said: "If you can, please try to come back early. I'm bored without you."

And then she went to her room and looked for a long time at the parasol.

XVII

THERE WAS NO accountant at the warehouse, despite the complexity of the business and the enormous turnover, and it was impossible to understand anything from the books kept by the clerk at the counter. Every day, customers, Germans and Englishmen, came to the warehouse, and the salesclerks talked politics and religion with them; a nobleman came, a sick, pathetic drunkard who translated foreign correspondence for the office; the salesclerks called him a piddler and put salt in his tea. And in general, the whole trade appeared to Laptev as some great bizarrerie.

He came to the warehouse every day and tried to introduce a new order; he forbade whipping the boys and scoffing at customers; he was beside himself when salesclerks with a merry laugh disposed of musty, worthless wares somewhere in the provinces in the guise of the freshest and most fashionable. He was now the chief person in the warehouse, yet he still did not know how great his fortune was, whether the business was going well, how much salary the senior sales-clerks got, and so on. Pochatkin and Makeichev considered him young and inexperienced, concealed a lot from him, and each evening exchanged mysterious whispers about something with the blind old man.

Once, at the beginning of June, Laptev and Pochatkin went to Bubnov's tavern to have lunch and, incidentally, to discuss business. Pochatkin had worked for the Laptevs a long time, and had entered the firm when he was only eight years old. He was their own man, was trusted completely, and when, on leaving the warehouse, he took all the day's earnings from the cash box and stuffed them in his pockets, it did not arouse any suspicion. He was the chief in the warehouse and at home, and also in church, where he ful-filled the duties of the warden in place of the old man. For his cruel treatment of his subordinates, the salesclerks and boys had nicknamed him Malyuta Skuratov.[29]

When they came to the tavern, he nodded to the waiter and said:

"Well, brother, bring us a half-wonder and twenty-four objectionables."

A little later, the waiter brought a tray with a half-bottle of vodka and several plates of various snacks.

"See here, my man," Pochatkin said to him, "give us a helping of the past master of slander and malignity, with mashed potatoes."

The waiter did not understand and became confused and wanted to say something, but Pochatkin looked at him sternly and said:

"Except!"

The waiter thought with great effort, then went to consult his colleagues, and in the end figured it out and brought a helping of tongue. When they had drunk two glasses each and had some snacks, Laptev said:

"Tell me, Ivan Vassilyich, is it true that our business has begun to fall off in the last few years?"

"By no means."

"Tell me frankly, candidly, how much we've been earning, how much we're earning now, and how great our fortune is. It's simply impossible to walk in the dark. We recently had an accounting done at the warehouse, but, forgive me, I don't believe this accounting; you find it necessary to conceal something from me and tell the truth only to my father. From early on, you've been accustomed to playing politics, and you can no longer do without it. But what use is it? Well, then, I beg you, be frank. What is the state of our business?"

"It all depends on the undulations of credit," Pochatkin said after some reflection.

"What do you mean by the undulations of credit?"

Pochatkin started to explain, but Laptev did not understand anything and sent for Makeichev. The man came at once, said a prayer, had a bite to eat, and, in his sedate, dense baritone, began by saying that salesclerks were obliged to pray to God day and night for their benefactors.

"Splendid, only allow me not to consider myself your benefactor," said Laptev.

"Every man should remember what he is and sense his rank. You, by God's mercy, are our father and benefactor, and we are your slaves."

"I'm sick of all this, finally!" Laptev became angry. "Please be my benefactor now, explain to me the state of our business. Kindly do not consider me a boy, otherwise I'll close the warehouse tomorrow. Father has gone blind, my brother's in the madhouse, my nieces are still young; I hate this business and would gladly walk out, but there's nobody to replace me, you know that yourselves. For God's sake, then, drop the politics!"

They went to the warehouse to do the accounts. Then

they did accounts at home in the evening, and the old man himself helped; initiating his son into his commercial secrets, he spoke in such a tone as if he was occupied not with trade but with sorcery. It turned out that the income increased by approximately a tenth yearly, and that the Laptevs' fortune, counting only money and securities, equaled six million roubles.

When, past midnight, after the accounting, Laptev went out into the fresh air, he felt himself under the charm of those numbers. The night was still, moonlit, stifling; the white walls of the houses across the river, the sight of the heavy, locked gates, the silence, and the black shadows produced the general impression of some sort of fortress, and the only thing lacking was a sentry with a gun. Laptev went to the little garden and sat on a bench by the fence that separated it from the next yard, where there was also a little garden. The bird cherry was in bloom. Laptev remembered that in the time of his childhood, this bird cherry was just as gnarled and just as tall, and had not changed in the least since then. Every little corner of the garden and yard reminded him of the distant past. And in his childhood, just as now, one could see, through the sparse trees, the whole yard flooded with moonlight, the shadows were just as mysterious and severe, the black dog lay in just the same way in the middle of the yard, and the windows of the salesclerks' lodgings were open wide. And these were all cheerless memories.

Light footsteps were heard behind the fence in the neighboring yard.

"My dearest, my darling..." a man's voice whispered just by the fence, so that Laptev could even hear breathing.

Now they kissed... Laptev was sure that the millions and the business, which he had no heart for, would ruin his life and turn him finally into a slave; he imagined how he would gradually become accustomed to his position, would gradually enter into the role of head of a trading firm, would grow dull, old, and finally die, as average people generally die, squalidly, sourly, boring everyone around him. But what prevented him from abandoning both the millions and the business, and leaving this little garden and yard that had been hateful to him ever since childhood?

The whispering and kisses on the other side of the fence stirred him. He went out to the middle of the yard and, unbuttoning his shirt on his chest, looked at the moon, and he fancied that he would now order the gate to be opened, go out and never come back there again; his heart was sweetly wrung by the foretaste of freedom, he laughed joyfully and imagined what a wonderful, poetic, and maybe even holy life it could be . . .

But he went on standing there and asking himself: "What holds me here?" And he was vexed both with himself and with this black dog, which lay on the stones instead of going off to the fields, to the forest, where it would be independent, joyful. Obviously the same thing prevented both him and this dog from leaving the yard: the habit of captivity, of the slavish condition . . .

The next day, at noon, he went to see his wife, and so as not to be bored, he invited Yartsev to come with him. Yulia Sergeevna was living in a dacha in Butovo, and he had not seen her for five days now. Arriving at the station, the friends got into a carriage, and Yartsev kept singing all the way and admiring the splendid weather. The dacha was in a big park not far from the station. About twenty paces from the gate, at the beginning of the main alley, under an old, spreading poplar, sat Yulia Sergeevna, waiting for her guests. She was wearing a light, elegant, lace-trimmed dress of a pale cream color, and in her hands was the same old, familiar parasol. Yartsev greeted her and went to the dacha, from which came the voices of Sasha and Lida, but Laptev sat down beside her to talk about their affairs.

"Why haven't you come for so long?" she asked without

letting go of his hand. "I sit here for whole days and watch to see if you're coming. I'm bored without you!"

She got up and passed her hand over his hair, looking curiously at his face, his shoulders, his hat.

"You know, I love you," she said and blushed. "You're dear to me. Here you've come, I see you, and I'm so happy I can't say. Well, let's talk. Tell me something."

She was declaring her love for him, but he felt as if he had been married to her for ten years already, and he wanted to have lunch. She hugged him around the neck, tickling his cheek with the silk of her dress; he carefully removed her arm, got up, and, without saying a word, went to the dacha. The girls came running to meet him.

"How they've grown!" he thought. "And so many changes in these three years...But maybe I'm to live another thirteen or thirty years...The future still holds something for us! Time will tell."

He embraced Sasha and Lida, who hung on his neck, and said:

"Grandpa sends his greetings...Uncle Fedya will die soon, Uncle Kostya has sent a letter from America and says hello to you. He's bored with the exposition[30] and will come back soon. And Uncle Alyosha's hungry."

Then he sat on the terrace and watched his wife slowly walking down the alley towards the dacha. She was thinking about something, and on her face there was a sad, charming expression, and tears glistened in her eyes. She was no longer the slender, fragile, pale-faced girl she once had been, but a mature, beautiful, strong woman. And Laptev noticed the rapturous look with which Yartsev met her, how her new, beautiful expression was reflected in his face, also sad and admiring. It seemed as if he was seeing her for the first time in his life. And while they were having lunch on the terrace, Yartsev smiled somehow joyfully and bashfully, and kept looking at Yulia, at her beautiful neck. Laptev watched him involuntarily and thought that maybe he was to live another thirteen or thirty years...And what were they to live through in that time? What does the future hold for us?

And he thought:

"Time will tell."

1895

MY LIFE
A Provincial's Story

I

THE MANAGER SAID to me: "I keep you only out of respect for your esteemed father, otherwise I'd have sent you flying long ago." I answered him: "You flatter me too much, Your Excellency, in supposing I can fly." And then I heard him say: "Take the gentleman away, he's bad for my nerves."

Two days later I was dismissed. And so, in all the time I've been considered an adult, to the great chagrin of my father, the town architect, I have changed jobs nine times. I worked in various departments, but all these nine jobs were as alike as drops of water; I had to sit, write, listen to stupid or rude remarks, and wait until they dismissed me.

My father, when I came to him, was sitting in a deep armchair with his eyes closed. His face, lean, dry, with a bluish tinge on the shaved areas (in looks he resembled an old Catholic organist), expressed humility and submissiveness. Without answering my greeting or opening his eyes, he said:

"If my dear wife, your mother, were alive, your life would be a source of constant grief for her. I see divine providence in her premature death. I beg you, unfortunate boy," he went on, opening his eyes, "instruct me: what am I to do with you?"

Formerly, when I was younger, my relations and friends knew what to do with me: some advised me to become a volunteer soldier, others to work in a pharmacy, still others in a telegraph office; but now that I've turned twenty-five, and gray has even appeared at my temples, and I've already been a volunteer soldier and a pharmacist and a telegrapher, everything earthly seems exhausted for me, and people no longer advise me but only sigh or shake their heads.

"What do you think of yourself?" my father went on. "At your age, young people already have a firm social position, but look at you: a proletarian, destitute, living on your father's neck!"

And, as usual, he began his talk about young men nowadays being lost, lost through unbelief, materialism, and superfluous self-confidence, and about how amateur performances ought to be forbidden because they distract young people from religion and their duties.

"Tomorrow we'll go together, and you'll apologize to the manager and promise him to work conscientiously," he concluded. "You shouldn't remain without a social position even for a single day."

"I beg you to hear me out," I said sullenly, expecting nothing good from this conversation. "What you call a social position consists in the privilege of capital and education. Unwealthy and uneducated people earn their crust of bread by physical labor, and I see no reason why I should be an exception."

"When you start talking about physical labor, it comes out stupid and banal," my father said with irritation. "Understand, you dullard, understand, you brainless head, that besides crude physical strength, you also have the spirit of God, the holy fire, which distinguishes you in the highest degree from an ass or a reptile and brings you close to divinity! This fire has been obtained over thousands of years by the best people. Your great-grandfather Poloznev, a general, fought at Borodino,[1] your grandfather was a poet, an orator, and a marshal of the nobility,[2] your uncle is a pedagogue, and lastly, I, your father, am an architect! All the Poloznevs kept the sacred fire just so that you could put it out!"

"One must be fair," I said. "Millions of people bear physical labor."

"And let them bear it! They can't do anything else! Anybody can take up physical labor, even an utter fool or a criminal, such labor is the distinctive quality of the slave and the barbarian, while fire falls to the lot of only a few!"

To prolong this conversation was useless. My father adored himself, and for him, only what he said himself was convincing. Besides, I knew very well that the arrogance with which he referred to common labor had its basis not so much in considerations regarding the sacred fire as in the secret fear that I would become a worker and set the whole town talking about me; and the main thing was that all my peers had long since finished university and were on good paths, and the son of the manager of the State Bank office was already a collegiate assessor,[3] while I, an only son, was nothing! To prolong the conversation was useless and unpleasant, but I went on sitting there and objecting weakly, hoping to be understood at last. For the whole question was simple and clear and only had to do with my means of obtaining a crust of bread, but he didn't see the simplicity and talked to me in sweetly rounded phrases about Borodino, about the sacred fire, about my uncle, a forgotten poet who once wrote bad and false verses, and called me a brainless head and a dullard. And I wanted so much to be understood! Despite all, I love my father and sister, and since childhood the habit has been lodged in me of asking their opinion, lodged so firmly that it's unlikely I'll ever get rid of it; whether I'm right or wrong, I'm constantly afraid of upsetting them, afraid that my father's skinny neck is turning red now with agitation and he may have a stroke.

"To sit in a stuffy room," I said, "to copy papers, to compete with a typewriter, for a man of my age is shameful and insulting. How can there be any talk about sacred fire here!"

"Still, it's intellectual work," said my father. "But enough, let's break off this conversation, and in any case, I'm warning you: if you follow your despicable inclinations and don't go back to work, then I and my daughter will deprive you of our love. I'll deprive you of your inheritance—I swear by the true God!"

With perfect sincerity, to show all the purity of the motives by which I wanted to be guided in my life, I said:

"The question of inheritance seems unimportant to me. I renounce it all beforehand."

For some reason, quite unexpectedly for me, these words greatly offended my father. He turned all purple.

"Don't you dare speak to me like that, stupid boy!" he cried in a high, shrill voice. "Scoundrel!" And quickly and deftly, with an accustomed movement, he struck me on the cheek once and then again. "You begin to forget yourself!"

In childhood, when my father beat me, I had to stand up straight at attention and look him in the face. And now, when he beat me, I was completely at a loss and, as if my childhood was still going on, stood at attention and tried to look him right in the eye. My father was old and very skinny, but his thin muscles must have been strong as straps, because he struck me very painfully.

I backed away into the front hall, and here he seized his umbrella and struck me several times on the head and shoulders; just then my sister opened the door from the drawing room to find out what the noise was, but at once turned away with an expression of horror and pity, not saying a single word in my defense.

The intention not to go back to the office but to start a new working life was unshakable in me. It remained only to choose the kind of trade—and that did not appear especially difficult, because it seemed to me that I was very strong, enduring, capable of the most heavy labor. I had a monotonous working life ahead of me, with hunger, stench, and coarse surroundings, with the constant thought of wages and a crust of bread. And—who knows?—returning from work down Bolshaya Dvoryanskaya Street, maybe more than once I'd envy the engineer Dolzhikov, who lived by intellectual work, but now I enjoyed the thought of all these future adversities of mine. Once I used to dream of mental activity, imagining myself now a teacher, now a doctor, now a writer, but my dreams remained dreams. The inclination to intellectual pleasures, for instance, the theater and reading, was developed in me to the point of passion, but whether I had the capacity for intellectual work, I don't know. In high school I had an invincible aversion to Greek, so that I had to be taken out of the fourth class.[4] For a long time, tutors came and prepared me for the fifth class, then I served in various departments, spending the greater part of the day in total idleness, and was told that it was intellectual work; my activity in the spheres of learning and service called neither for mental effort, nor for talent, nor for personal ability, nor for a creative uplifting of spirit: it was mechanical; and such intellectual work I place lower than physical, and I don't think it can serve even for a moment as justification for an idle, carefree life, since it is nothing but a deception itself, one of the forms of that same idleness. In all likelihood, I have never known real intellectual work.

Evening came. We lived on Bolshaya Dvoryanskaya—it was the main street of the town, and in the evenings our beau monde, for lack of a decent public garden, promenaded on it. This lovely street could partly replace a garden, because on both sides of it grew poplars, which were fragrant, especially after rain, and from behind fences and palisades hung acacias, tall lilac bushes, bird cherries, apple trees. The May twilight, the tender young greenery with its shadows, the smell of the lilacs, the hum of beetles, the silence, the warmth—how new it all is, and how extraordinary, though spring is repeated every year! I stood by the gate and looked at the promenaders. I had grown up and used to play pranks with most of them, but now my proximity might embarrass them, because I was dressed poorly, not fashionably, and on account of my very tight trousers and big, clumsy boots, people called me macaroni on ships. What's more, I had a bad reputation in town because I had no social position and often played billiards in cheap taverns, and maybe also because, without any cause on my part, I was twice taken to the police.

In the big house opposite, at the engineer Dolzhikov's, somebody was playing the piano. It was growing dark, and stars twinkled in the sky. Now my father, in an old top hat with a wide, turned-up brim, arm in arm with my sister, walked by slowly, responding to bows.

"Look!" he was saying to my sister, pointing at the sky with the very umbrella he had struck me with earlier that day. "Look at the sky! The stars, even the smallest of them, are all worlds! How insignificant man is compared to the universe!"

And he said it in such a tone as if he found it extremely flattering and agreeable to be so insignificant. What a giftless man! Unfortunately, he was our only architect, and in the last fifteen or twenty years, as I recall, not a single decent house was built in town. When he was asked for a plan, he usually drew the reception room and drawing room first; as boarding-school girls in the old days could only start dancing on the same foot, so his artistic idea could proceed and develop only from the reception room and drawing room. To them he added a dining room, a nursery, a study, connecting the rooms with doors, so that you inevitably had to pass through one to get to the next, and each had two or even three superfluous doors. His idea must have been unclear, extremely confused, curtailed; each time, as if sensing that something was lacking, he resorted to various sorts of annexes, attaching them one to the other, and I can see even now the narrow little entries, the narrow little corridors, the crooked stairways leading to entresols where you could only stand bent over and where, instead of a floor, there were three huge steps, like shelves in a bathhouse; and the kitchen was unfailingly under the house, with vaulting and a brick floor. The façade had a stubborn, hard expression; the lines were dry, timid, the roof low, flattened; and the fat, muffinlike chimneys unfailingly had wire covers with black, squeaking weathervanes. And for some reason, all these houses my father built, which were so like one another, vaguely reminded me of his top hat, the dry and stubborn nape of his neck. In the course of time, my father's giftlessness became a familiar sight in town, it struck root and became our style.

Father introduced this style into my sister's life as well. Beginning with the fact that he called her Cleopatra (and me Misail).[5] When she was still a little girl, he used to frighten her by telling her about the stars, about the ancient sages, about our ancestors, explaining to her at length what life was, what duty was; and now, when she was twenty-six, he went on the same way, allowing her to walk arm in arm only with him, and imagining for some reason that sooner or later a decent young man must appear who would wish to contract a marriage with her out of respect for his personal qualities. And she adored my father, feared him, and believed in his extraordinary intelligence.

It grew quite dark, and the street gradually became deserted. In the house opposite, the music ceased; the gates were thrust open, and a troika of prancing horses drove down our street with a soft ringing of little bells. It was the engineer and his daughter going for a ride. Time for bed!

I had my own room in the house, but I lived in the yard, in a little shack under the same roof as the brick shed, probably built once for storing harness—there were big spikes driven into the walls—but now no longer needed, and for thirty years my father had been storing his newspapers in it, which for some reason he had bound every six months and

441

allowed no one to touch. Living there, I ran across my father and his visitors less often, and it seemed to me that if I didn't live in my real room and didn't go to the house every day for dinner, my father's words about my living on his neck wouldn't sound so offensive.

My sister was waiting for me. She had brought me supper in secret from my father: a small piece of cold veal and a slice of bread. "Money loves counting," "A kopeck saves a rouble," and the like, were often repeated in our house, and my sister, oppressed by these banalities, did her utmost to reduce expenses, and therefore we ate badly. She set the plate on the table, sat down on my bed, and began to cry.

"Misail," she said, "what are you doing to us?"

She didn't cover her face, the tears dropped on her breast and hands, and her expression was grief-stricken. She fell on the pillow and let her tears flow freely, shaking all over and sobbing.

"Again you've left your job . . ." she said. "Oh, it's so terrible!"

"But understand, sister, understand . . ." I said, and despair came over me because she was crying.

As if on purpose, all the kerosene had burnt up in my lamp, it smoked and was about to go out, and the old spikes in the walls looked stern, and their shadows wavered.

"Spare us!" my sister said, getting up. "Father is awfully grieved, and I'm sick, I'm losing my mind. What will become of you?" she asked, sobbing and reaching her arms out to me. "I beg you, I implore you, in the name of our late mama, I beg you: go back to your job!"

"I can't, Cleopatra!" I said, feeling that a little more and I'd give in. "I can't!"

"Why?" my sister went on. "Why? Well, if you didn't get along with your superior, look for another position. For instance, why don't you go and work for the railway? I was just talking with Anyuta Blagovo, and she assures me you'd be accepted at the railway, and even promised to put in a word for you. For God's sake, Misail, think! Think, I implore you!"

We talked a little more and I gave in. I said the thought of working for the railway that was under construction had never once entered my head, and that maybe I was ready to try.

She smiled joyfully through her tears and pressed my hand, and after that still went on crying because she couldn't stop, and I went to the kitchen to get some kerosene.

II

AMONG THE LOVERS of amateur theater, concerts, and tableaux vivants for charitable purposes, the first place in town went to the Azhogins, who lived in their own house on Bolshaya Dvoryanskaya; they provided the space each time and also took upon themselves all the cares and expenses. This rich landowning family had about ten thousand acres and a magnificent estate in the district, but they didn't like the country and lived in town year-round. It consisted of the mother, a tall, lean, delicate woman who cut her hair short and wore a short jacket and a straight skirt after the English fashion, and three daughters who, when spoken of, were called not by their names but simply the eldest, the middle, and the youngest. They all had unattractively sharp chins, were nearsighted, stoop-shouldered, and dressed the same as their mother, lisped unpleasantly, and despite all that were sure to take part in every performance and were constantly doing something for philanthropic purposes—acting, reciting, singing. They were very serious and never smiled, and even in vaudevilles with songs, acted without the slightest merriment, with a businesslike air, as if they were doing bookkeeping.

I loved our theatricals and especially the rehearsals,

frequent, noisy and often slightly witless, after which we were always given supper. I took no part in choosing the plays and distributing the roles. My part lay backstage. I painted the sets, copied the parts, prompted, did makeup, and was also in charge of arranging various effects such as thunder, nightingales' singing, and so on. Since I had no social position or decent clothes, I kept myself apart at rehearsals, in the shadow of the wings, and was timidly silent.

I painted the sets either in the Azhogins' shed or in the yard. I was helped by a housepainter—or, as he called himself, a housepainting contractor—Andrei Ivanov, a man of about fifty, tall, very thin and pale, with a sunken chest, sunken temples, and blue rings under his eyes, whose appearance was even a little frightening. He was sick with some wasting disease, and every fall and spring they said he was on the way out, but he'd lie down for a while, get up, and then say with surprise: "Again I didn't die!"

In town he was known as Radish, and they said it was his real family name. He loved the theater as much as I did, and as soon as the rumor reached him that a production was being prepared, he'd drop all his work and go to the Azhogins' to paint sets.

The day after my talk with my sister, I worked from morning till night at the Azhogins'. The rehearsal was set for seven o'clock in the evening, and an hour before the start, all the amateurs had gathered in the reception room, and the eldest, the middle, and the youngest walked about the stage reading from their notebooks. Radish, in a long, rusty coat and with a scarf wrapped around his neck, stood leaning his temple against the wall and looking at the stage with a pious expression. The Azhogin mother went up to one guest, then another, and said something pleasant to each of them. She had a manner of looking intently into your face and speaking quietly, as if in secret.

"It must be difficult to paint sets," she said quietly, coming up to me. "And Madame Mufke and I were just talking about prejudice, and I saw you come in. My God, all my life, all my life I've fought against prejudice! To convince the servants of what nonsense all these fears are, I always light three candles in my house and begin all my important business on the thirteenth."

The daughter of the engineer Dolzhikov came in, a beautiful, plump blonde, dressed, as they said here, in everything Parisian. She didn't act, but a chair was placed onstage for her at rehearsals, and the performances would not begin until she appeared in the front row, radiant and amazing everyone with her finery. As a young thing from the capital, she was allowed to make observations during the rehearsals, and she made them with a sweet, condescending smile, and one could see that she looked upon our performances as a childish amusement. It was said of her that she had studied singing at the Petersburg Conservatory and had even sung one whole winter in a private opera. I liked her very much, and usually, at rehearsals and during performances, I never took my eyes off her.

I had already picked up the notebook to start prompting when my sister unexpectedly appeared. Without taking off her coat and hat, she came over to me and said:

"Please come with me."

I went. Backstage, in the doorway, stood Anyuta Blagovo, also wearing a hat with a dark little veil. She was the daughter of the associate court magistrate, who had long served in our town, almost from the very founding of the district court. As she was tall and well built, her participation in tableaux vivants was considered obligatory, and when she represented some sort of fairy or Glory, her face burned with shame; but she didn't take part in the plays and would come to the rehearsals only for a moment, on some errand, and would not go to the reception room. Now, too, it was evident that she had come only for a moment.

"My father has spoken for you," she said drily, not looking at me and blushing. "Dolzhikov has promised you a position on the railway. Go to see him tomorrow, he will be at home."

I bowed and thanked her for taking the trouble.

"And you can drop this," she said, pointing to the notebook.

She and my sister went over to Mrs. Azhogin and exchanged whispers with her for a couple of moments, glancing at me. They were discussing something.

"Indeed," Mrs. Azhogin said quietly, coming up to me and looking intently into my face, "indeed, if this distracts you from serious occupations," she pulled the notebook from my hands, "you may pass it on to someone else. Don't worry, my friend, God be with you."

I took leave of her and went out in embarrassment. As I was going down the stairs, I saw my sister and Anyuta Blagovo leave; they were talking animatedly about something, most likely my starting work at the railway, and were hurrying. My sister had never before come to rehearsals, and now probably had pangs of conscience and was afraid father would find out that she had gone to the Azhogins' without his permission.

I went to see Dolzhikov the next day between twelve and one. The footman took me to a very beautiful room that served the engineer simultaneously as a drawing room and a study. Here everything was soft, elegant, and, for an unaccustomed person like me, even strange. Costly rugs, enormous armchairs, bronze, paintings, gilt and plush frames; in the photographs scattered over the walls, very beautiful women, intelligent, wonderful faces, free poses; the door from the drawing room leads straight to the garden, to the balcony, and one can see lilacs, one can see a table set for lunch, many bottles, a bouquet of roses, it smells of spring and expensive cigars, it smells of happiness—and everything seems to want to say that this is a man who has lived, worked, and achieved that happiness which is possible on earth. The engineer's daughter was sitting at the desk and reading a newspaper.

"You've come to see my father?" she asked. "He's taking a shower, he'll be here presently. Meanwhile, please be seated."

I sat down.

"You live opposite us, I believe?" she said after some silence.

"Yes."

"I watch out the window every day, from boredom, and, you must forgive me," she went on, looking into the newspaper, "I often see you and your sister. She always has such a kind, concentrated expression."

Dolzhikov came in. He was wiping his neck with a towel.

"Papa, Monsieur Poloznev," said his daughter.

"Yes, yes, Blagovo spoke to me," he briskly turned to me without offering me his hand. "But listen, what can I give you? What sort of positions do I have? You're strange people, gentlemen!" he went on loudly, and in such a tone as if he was reprimanding me. "Twenty men come to me every day, they imagine I'm running a department! I'm running a railway, gentlemen, it's hard labor, I need mechanics, metal workers, excavators, carpenters, well diggers, and you all can only sit and write, nothing more! You're all writers!"

And the same happiness breathed on me from him as from his rugs and armchairs. Full-bodied, healthy, with red cheeks, a broad chest, well scrubbed, in a calico shirt and balloon trousers, like a toy china coachman. He had a rounded, curly little beard—and not a single gray hair—a slightly hooked nose, and dark, clear, innocent eyes.

"What are you able to do?" he went on. "You're not able to do anything! I'm an engineer, sir, I'm a well-to-do man, but before I got ahead, I worked hard for a long time, I was an engine driver, I worked for two years in Belgium as a simple oiler. Consider for yourself, my gentle one, what kind of work can I offer you?"

"Of course, that's so . . ." I murmured in great embarrassment, unable to bear his clear, innocent gaze.

"Can you at least manage a telegraph machine?" he asked after a little thought.

"Yes, I worked in a telegraph office."

"Hm . . . Well, we'll see. Go to Dubechnya, meanwhile. I've got a man sitting there already, but he's terrible trash."

"And what will my duties consist of?" I asked.

"We'll see about that. Go, meanwhile, I'll make the arrangements. Only please don't start drinking, and don't bother me with any requests. I'll throw you out."

He walked away from me and didn't even nod his head. I bowed to him and his daughter, who was reading the newspaper, and left. My heart was heavy, so much so that when my sister began asking how the engineer had received me, I couldn't utter a single word.

In order to go to Dubechnya, I got up early in the morning, with the sunrise. There wasn't a soul on our Bolshaya Dvoryanskaya, everybody was still asleep, and my footsteps sounded solitary and muffled. The poplars, covered with dew, filled the air with a delicate fragrance. I felt sad and did not want to leave town. I loved my native town. It seemed to me so beautiful and warm! I loved this greenery, the quiet, sunny mornings, the ringing of our bells; but the people I lived with in this town bored me, were alien and sometimes even repulsive to me. I didn't love them and didn't understand them.

I didn't understand why and from what all these sixty-five thousand people lived. I knew that Kimry subsisted on boots, that Tula made samovars and guns, that Odessa was a seaport, but what our town was and what it did, I didn't know. Bolshaya Dvoryanskaya and the two other proper streets lived on ready capital and on the salaries the officials received from the treasury; but how the remaining eight streets lived, which stretched parallel to each other for some two miles and disappeared beyond the horizon—that for me had always been an unfathomable enigma. And the way those people lived was shameful to tell about! No park, no theater, no decent orchestra; the town and club libraries were visited only by Jewish adolescents, so that magazines and new books lay uncut for months; rich and educated people slept in stuffy little bedrooms, on wooden beds with bedbugs, the children were kept in disgustingly dirty rooms known as nurseries, and the servants, even old and respected ones, slept on the kitchen floor and covered themselves with rags. On ordinary days, the houses smelled of borscht, and on fast days, of sturgeon fried in sunflower oil. The food was not tasty, the water was not good to drink. In the duma,[6] at the governor's, at the bishop's, in houses everywhere, there had been talk for many years about the fact that our town had no good and cheap water, and that it was necessary to borrow two hundred thousand from the treasury for a water system; very rich people, who numbered up to three dozen in our town, and who chanced to lose entire estates at cards, also drank the bad water and all their lives talked passionately about the loan—and I didn't understand that; it seemed simpler to me to take the two hundred thousand from their own pockets.

I didn't know a single honest man in the whole town. My father took bribes and imagined they were given him out of respect for his inner qualities; high school students, in order to pass from grade to grade, boarded with their teachers and paid them big money for it; the wife of the army administrator took bribes from the recruits at call-up time and even let them offer her treats, and once in church was unable to get up from her knees because she was so drunk; the doctors also took bribes during recruitment, and the town physician and the veterinarian levied a tax on the butcher shops and taverns; the district school traded in certificates that provided the benefits of the third category; the dean of the cathedral took bribes from the clergy and church wardens; on the municipal, the tradesmen's, the medical, and all other boards, they shouted at each petitioner's back: "You should say thank you!" and the petitioner would come back and give thirty or forty kopecks. And those who didn't take bribes—for instance, the court administration—were haughty, offered you two fingers to shake, were distinguished by the coldness and narrowness of their judgments, played cards a lot, drank a lot, married rich women, and undoubtedly had a harmful, corrupting influence on their milieu. Only from the young girls came a whiff of moral purity; most of them had lofty yearnings, honest and pure souls; but they didn't understand life and believed that bribes were given out of respect for inner qualities, and, after marrying, aged quickly, went to seed, and drowned hopelessly in the mire of banal, philistine existence.

III

A RAILWAY WAS being constructed in our parts. On the eves of feast days, the town was filled with crowds of rag-amuffins who were known as "railboys" and were feared. Not seldom did I happen to see a ragamuffin, hatless, with a bloodied physiognomy, being taken to the police station; and carried behind him, as material evidence, a samovar or some recently washed, still-wet laundry. The "railboys" usually crowded around the pot-houses and markets; they drank, ate, used bad language, and sent a shrill whistle after every woman of light behavior who passed by. Our shopkeepers, to amuse this hungry riffraff, got dogs and cats to drink vodka, or would tie an empty kerosene can to a dog's tail, give a whistle, and the dog would race down the street squealing with terror, the tin can clanking behind it;

believing some monster was chasing at its heels, it would run far out of town, into the fields, till it was exhausted; and we had several dogs in town who trembled constantly, tails between their legs, of whom it was said that they were unable to endure such amusements and lost their minds.

The station was being built three miles from town. It was said that the engineers had asked for a bribe of fifty thousand to have the railway come right to town, but the town administration had agreed to give only forty, a difference of ten thousand, and now the townspeople regretted it, because they had to build a road to the station, for which the estimate was higher. The ties and rails were already laid the whole length of the line, and service trains were running, bringing building materials and workers, and the only holdup was the bridges, which Dolzhikov was building, and here and there a station wasn't ready yet.

Dubechnya—so our first station was called—was some ten miles from town. I went on foot. The winter and spring crops were bright green, caught by the morning sunlight. The area was level, cheerful, and the station, the barrows, and some remote estates were clearly outlined in the distance... How good it was here at liberty! And how I wanted to be filled with the awareness of freedom, at least for this one morning, and not think of what was going on in town, not think of my needs, not want to eat! Nothing so prevented me from living as the acute sense of hunger, when my best thoughts were strangely mingled with thoughts of buckwheat kasha, meat cakes, fried fish. Here I am standing alone in the field and looking up at a lark, which is hanging in one place in the air and pouring itself out as if in hysterics, and I'm thinking: "It would be good now to have some bread and butter!" Or here I am sitting down by the roadside and closing my eyes to rest, to listen to this wonderful Maytime clamor, and I recall the smell of hot potatoes. Though I was tall and strongly built, I generally had little to eat, and therefore my main feeling in the course of a day was hunger, and that may have been why I understood perfectly well why so many people worked only for a crust of bread and could talk only about grub.

In Dubechnya they were plastering the inside of the station and building a wooden upper story to the pump house. It was hot, there was a smell of lime, and workers wandered sluggishly over heaps of shavings and rubbish; the switchman was asleep by his booth, and the sun burned down directly on his face. Not a single tree. The telegraph wires hummed faintly, and hawks rested on them here and there. Wandering over the same heaps, not knowing what to do, I remembered how the engineer, to my question of what my duties would be, had answered: "We'll see." But what could one see in this desert? The plasterers were talking about the foreman and about some Fedot Vassiliev, I didn't understand, and anguish gradually came over me—physical anguish, when you feel your arms and legs and your whole big body and don't know what to do with them or where to take yourself.

After wandering around for at least two hours, I noticed that there were telegraph poles going from the station somewhere to the right of the line, which ended after a mile or a mile and a half at a white stone wall; the workers said the office was there, and I finally realized that that was precisely where I had to go.

It was an old, long-neglected estate. The wall of porous white stone was weathered and had fallen down in places, and the roof on the wing, whose blank wall looked into the fields, was rusty, and tin patches shone on it here and there. Through the gate, you could see a spacious yard overgrown with tall weeds, and an old master's house with jalousies on the windows and a high roof red-brown with rust. At the sides of the house, to right and left, stood two identical wings; one had its windows boarded up; near the other, whose windows were open, laundry hung on a line, and calves were walking around. The last telegraph pole stood in the yard, and its wire went to the window of the wing whose blank wall looked onto the fields. The door was open, and I went in. At a table by a telegraph machine sat some gentleman with dark curly hair, in a canvas jacket; he looked at me sternly from under his brows but smiled at once and said:

"Greetings, Small Profit!"

This was Ivan Cheprakov, my schoolmate, who had been expelled from the second class for smoking tobacco. In the autumn he and I used to catch siskins, finches, and grosbeaks and sell them at the market early in the morning, while our parents were still asleep. We lay in wait for flocks of migratory starlings and shot them with birdshot, then gathered up the wounded, and some of them died on us in awful torment (I still remember them moaning at night in the cage I had), but others recovered and we sold them, brazenly swearing to God that they were all males. Once, at the market, I had only one starling left, which I kept offering to buyers and finally let go for a kopeck. "Still, it's a small profit!" I said to console myself, pocketing the kopeck, and after that the street urchins and schoolboys nicknamed me "Small Profit"; and even now the street urchins and shopkeepers tease me with it, though no one but me remembers any longer where the nickname came from.

Cheprakov was not strongly built: narrow-chested, stoop-shouldered, long-legged. A string tie, no waistcoat at all, and boots worse than mine—with crooked heels. He rarely blinked and had a look of urgency, as if he was about to grab something, and was always in a flurry.

"But wait," he said in a flurry. "No, listen here! . . . What was it I was just saying?"

We got to talking. I found out that the estate we were then on had belonged still recently to the Cheprakovs and had passed only last autumn to the engineer Dolzhikov, who thought it more profitable to keep his money in land than in securities, and had already bought three considerable estates in our region, with a transfer of mortgages; at the time of the sale, Cheprakov's mother had negotiated for herself the right to live in one of the wings for another two years and had managed to obtain for her son a position in the office.

"How can he not go buying up?" Cheprakov said of the engineer. "He fleeces the contractors alone for that much! He fleeces everybody!"

Then he took me to dinner, having decided in a flurry that I would live in the wing with him and board with his mother.

"She's a niggard," he said, "but she won't take much from you."

In the small rooms where his mother lived, it was very crowded; all of them, even the entry and the front room, were cluttered with furniture, which, after the sale of the estate, had been brought there from the big house; and it was all old mahogany furniture. Mrs. Cheprakov, a very stout, elderly lady with slanted Chinese eyes, was sitting in a big armchair by the window and knitting a stocking. She received me ceremoniously.

"This is Poloznev, mama," Cheprakov introduced me. "He'll be working here."

"Are you a nobleman?" she asked in a strange, unpleasant voice; it seemed to me as if fat was gurgling in her throat.

"Yes," I said.

"Be seated."

The dinner was bad. All that was served was a pie with rancid cottage cheese and milk soup. Elena Nikiforovna, the hostess, blinked somehow strangely, now with one eye, now with the other. She talked, ate, but there was something already dead in her whole figure, and it was as if you could even sense the smell of a corpse. There was barely a glimmer of life in her, along with a glimmer of awareness that she was a landowner who had once had her own serfs, that she was a general's widow whom the servants were obliged to call "Your Excellency"; and when these pathetic remnants of life lit up in her for a moment, she would say to her son:

"Jean, you're holding your knife the wrong way!"

Or else she would tell me, breathing heavily, with the mincing manner of a hostess wishing to entertain a guest:

"And we, you know, have sold our estate. Of course, it's a pity, we're used to it here, but Dolzhikov has promised to make Jean the stationmaster of Dubechnya, so we won't be leaving the place, we'll live here at the station, and it's the same as on the estate. The engineer is so kind! Don't you find him very handsome?"

Still recently the Cherpakovs lived a wealthy life, but after the general's death, everything changed. Elena Nikiforovna started quarreling with the neighbors, went to court, paid less than she owed to her stewards and hired hands, kept fearing she would be robbed—and in some ten years, Dubechnya became unrecognizable.

Behind the big house was an old garden, grown wild, stifled with tall weeds and bushes. I strolled about the terrace, still strong and beautiful; through the glass door, a room with a parquet floor could be seen, probably the drawing room; an old piano, and on the walls, etchings in wide mahogany frames—and nothing more. All that was left of the former flowerbeds were peonies and poppies that lifted their white and scarlet heads from the grass; on the pathways, stretching themselves out, hindering each other, grew young maples and elms, already plucked by the cows. The growth was thick, and the garden looked impenetrable, but that was only near the house, where poplars, pines, and old lindens, all of an age, survivors from the former alleys, still stood, but further behind them the garden had been cleared for hayfields, and here it was no longer so close, the cobwebs did not get into your eyes and mouth, a breeze blew; the further on, the more spacious it became, and here cherries, plums, and spreading apple trees grew in abandon, disfigured by props and canker, and pear trees so tall it was even hard to believe they were pear trees. This part of the garden was rented by our town marketwomen and was guarded from thieves and starlings by a peasant simpleton who lived in a brush hut.

The garden, growing ever sparser, turned into a real meadow, descending to the river, where green bulrushes and willows grew; by the dam there was a pool, deep and full of fish, a small mill with a thatched roof made an angry clamor, frogs croaked furiously. From time to time, the water, smooth as a mirror, would be covered with rings, and the water lilies would shake, disturbed by playful fish. On the other side of the river was the small village of Dubechnya. The quiet blue pool enticed you, promising coolness and peace. And now all of it—the pool, and the mill, and the cozy-looking banks—belonged to the engineer!

And so my new work began. I received telegrams and sent them further on, kept various records, and made clean copies of the requests, claims, and reports sent to our office by illiterate foremen and workmen. But the greater part of the day I did nothing but walk around the room waiting for telegrams, or I'd get a boy to sit there and go to the garden myself, and stroll until the boy came running to tell me the telegraph was tapping. I ate dinners with Mrs. Cheprakov. Meat was served very rarely, the dishes were all from dairy products, but on Wednesdays and Fridays they were lenten, and on those days pink plates, which were known as lenten plates, were set out on the table. Mrs. Cheprakov blinked constantly—such was her habit—and I felt ill at ease each time I was in her presence.

Since there was not enough work in the wing even for one person, Cheprakov did nothing but sleep or go to the pool with a gun to shoot ducks. In the evenings he would get drunk in the village or at the station and, before going to bed, would look in the mirror and shout:

"Greetings, Ivan Cheprakov!"

When drunk, he was very pale and kept rubbing his hands and laughing with a sort of whinny: "Hee, hee, hee!" Out of mischief, he would strip and run naked through the fields. He ate flies and said they tasted sour.

IV

ONCE AFTER DINNER he came running to the wing, out of breath, and said:

"Go, your sister's here."

I went out. Indeed, a hired town droshky was standing by the porch of the big house. My sister had come, and Anyuta Blagovo with her, and some gentleman in a military tunic. Going closer, I recognized the military man: it was Anyuta's brother, a doctor.

"We've come for a picnic," he said. "It that all right?"

My sister and Anyuta would have liked to ask how my life was there, but they both said nothing and only looked at me. I also said nothing. They understood that I didn't like it there, and tears welled up in my sister's eyes, and Anyuta Blagovo turned red. We went to the garden. The doctor went ahead of us, saying rapturously:

"What air! Holy Mother, what air!"

In appearance, he was still quite the student. He spoke and walked like a student, and the gaze of his gray eyes was as lively, simple, and open as in a good student. Next to his tall and beautiful sister, he seemed weak and thin; and his little beard was thin, and his voice also—a thin little tenor, though pleasant enough. He served in a regiment somewhere, and had now come home on leave, and said that in the fall he would go to Petersburg to pass the examination for doctor of medicine. He already had a family of his own—a wife and three children; he had married early, while still in the second year of his studies, and now they said of him in town that he was unhappy in his family life and no longer lived with his wife.

"What time is it now?" My sister was worried. "We should get back early, papa allowed me to visit my brother only till six o'clock."

"Ah, your papa again!" sighed the doctor.

I prepared a samovar. We had tea on a rug in front of the terrace of the big house, and the doctor, on his knees, drank from the saucer and said that he was experiencing bliss. Then Cheprakov fetched the key and opened the glass door, and we all went into the house. Here it was dim, mysterious, it smelled of mushrooms, and our footsteps made a hollow sound, as if there was a basement under the floor. The doctor, standing, touched the keys of the piano, and it responded to him weakly, in quavering, husky, but still harmonious chords; he tested his voice and began to sing some love song, wincing and tapping his foot impatiently when one of the keys turned out to be mute. My sister no longer wanted to go home but went about the room excitedly, saying:

"I feel merry! I feel very, very merry!"

There was surprise in her voice, as if it seemed incredible to her that she also could be in good spirits. It was the first time in her life I had seen her so merry. She even became prettier. In profile she was unattractive, her nose and mouth were somehow thrust forward and made it look as if she was blowing, but she had beautiful dark eyes, a pale, very delicate complexion, and a touching expression of kindness and sorrow, and when she spoke, she looked comely and even beautiful. Both she and I took after our mother—broad-shouldered, strong, enduring—but her paleness was sickly, she coughed frequently, and in her eyes I sometimes caught the expression people have who are seriously ill but for some reason conceal it. In her present merriment, there was something childlike, naïve, as if the joy which, during our childhood, had been suppressed and stifled by a stern upbringing, had now suddenly awakened in her soul and burst out into freedom.

But when evening came and the horses were brought, my sister became quiet, shrank, and got into the droshky looking as if it was the prisoner's bench.

Then they were all gone, the noise died away . . . I remembered that in all that time, Anyuta Blagovo had not said a single word to me.

"An astonishing girl!" I thought. "An astonishing girl!"

Saint Peter's fast[7] came, and we were now given lenten food every day. In my idleness and the uncertainty of my position, I was oppressed by physical anguish, and, displeased with myself, sluggish, hungry, I loitered about the estate and only waited for the appropriate mood in order to leave.

Before evening once, when Radish was sitting in our wing, Dolzhikov came in unexpectedly, very sunburnt and gray with dust. He had spent three days at his work site and had now arrived in Dubechnya by locomotive and come from the station on foot. While waiting for the carriage that was to come from town, he went around the estate with his steward giving orders in a loud voice, then sat for a whole hour in our wing writing some letters; telegrams addressed to him came in his presence, and he tapped out the replies himself. The three of us stood silently at attention.

"Such disorder!" he said, looking scornfully into a report. "In two weeks I'll transfer the office to the station, and I don't know what I'll do with you, gentlemen."

"I try hard, Your Honor," said Cheprakov.

"I see how hard you try. All you know how to do is collect your salary," the engineer went on, looking at me. "You rely on connections, so as to *faire la carrière** quickly and

*Make a career.

easily. Well, I don't look at connections. Nobody put in a word for me, sir. Before I got ahead, I was an engine driver, I worked in Belgium as a simple oiler, sir. And you, Pantelei, what are you doing here?" he asked, turning to Radish. "Drinking with them?"

For some reason, he called all simple people Pantelei, but those like me and Cheprakov he despised and called drunkards, brutes, and scum behind their backs. In general, he was cruel to underlings, fined them, and threw them out of their jobs coldly, without explanations.

At last the horses came for him. As a farewell he promised to dismiss us all in two weeks, called his steward a blockhead, and then, sprawling in the carriage, drove off to town.

"Andrei Ivanych," I said to Radish, "take me on as a hired hand."

"Well, why not!"

And we set off for town together. When the estate and the station were left far behind us, I asked:

"Andrei Ivanych, why did you come to Dubechnya today?"

"First, my boys are working on the line, and second— I came to pay interest to the general's widow. Last summer I borrowed fifty roubles from her, and now I pay her a rouble a month."

The painter stopped and took hold of my button.

"Misail Alexeich, angel mine," he went on, "it's my understanding that if a simple man or a gentleman takes even the smallest interest, he's already a villain. Truth cannot exist in such a man."

Skinny, pale, frightening Radish closed his eyes, shook his head, and pronounced in the tones of a philosopher:

"Worm eats grass, rust eats iron, and lying eats the soul. Lord, save us sinners!"

V

RADISH WAS IMPRACTICAL and a poor planner; he took more work than he could do, became worried and confused when calculating, and therefore almost always wound up in the red. He was a painter, a glazier, a paperhanger, and even did roofing, and I remember him running around for three days looking for roofers for the sake of a worthless job. He was an excellent craftsman, and it happened that he sometimes earned up to ten roubles a day, and if it hadn't been for this wish to be the head at all costs and be called a contractor, he probably would have made good money.

He himself was paid by the job, but me and the other boys he paid by the day, from seventy kopecks to a rouble a day. While the weather stayed hot and dry, we did various outdoor jobs, mainly roof painting. My feet weren't used to it and got as hot as if I was walking on a burning stove, but when I put on felt boots, they sweltered. But that was only at first; later I got used to it, and everything went swimmingly. I now lived among people for whom work was obligatory and inevitable, and who worked like dray horses, often unaware of the moral significance of labor and never even using the word "labor" in conversation; alongside them, I, too, felt like a dray horse, ever more pervaded by the obligatoriness and inevitability of all I did, and that made my life easier, delivering me from all doubts.

At first everything interested me, everything was new, as if I had been newly born. I could sleep on the ground, I could go barefoot—and that was a great pleasure; I could stand in a crowd of simple people without embarrassing anyone, and when a cab horse fell in the street, I ran and helped to lift it up with no fear of dirtying my clothes. And above all, I lived at my own expense and was not a burden to anyone!

Painting roofs, especially with our own oil and paint, was considered very profitable, and therefore even such good craftsmen as Radish did not scorn this crude, boring work. In his short trousers, with his skinny, purple legs, he walked over a roof looking like a stork, and as he worked with his brush, I heard him sigh heavily and say:

"Woe, woe to us sinners!"

He walked on a roof as freely as on the floor. Though ill and pale as a corpse, he was remarkably nimble; just like the young men, he painted the cupolas and domes of churches without scaffolding, only with the aid of ladders and ropes, and it was a bit scary when, standing up there, far from the ground, he would straighten up to his full height and pronounce for who knows whom:

"Worm eats grass, rust eats iron, and lying eats the soul!"

Or else, thinking about something, he would answer his own thoughts aloud:

"Everything's possible! Everything's possible!"

When I came home from work, all those who were sitting on benches by the gateways, all the shop clerks, errand boys, and their masters, sent various mocking and spiteful observations after me, and at first that upset me and seemed simply monstrous.

"Small Profit!" came from all sides. "Housepainter! Ocher!"

And nobody treated me as mercilessly as precisely those who still recently had been simple people themselves and had earned their crust of bread by common labor. In the market, when I passed a hardware store, they poured water on me as if accidentally and once even threw a stick at me. And one fishmonger, a gray-haired old man, stood in my way and said, looking at me with spite:

"It's not you who's to be pitied, you fool! It's your father!"

And my acquaintances, on meeting me, were for some reason embarrassed. Some looked upon me as an eccentric and buffoon, others felt sorry for me, still others did not know how to treat me, and it was hard to understand them. One afternoon, in one of the lanes near our Bolshaya Dvoryanskaya, I met Anyuta Blagovo. I was on my way to work and was carrying two long brushes and a bucket of paint. Recognizing me, Anyuta blushed.

"I beg you not to greet me in the street," she said nervously, sternly, in a trembling voice, without offering me her hand, and tears suddenly glistened in her eyes. "If, in your opinion, all this is necessary, then so be it . . . so be it, but I beg you not to approach me!"

I now lived not on Bolshaya Dvoryanskaya but in the suburb of Makarikha, with my nanny Karpovna, a kind but gloomy old woman who always anticipated something bad, was afraid of all dreams in general, and saw bad omens even in the bees and wasps that flew into her room. And the fact that I had become a worker, in her opinion, did not presage anything good.

"It'll be your head!" she repeated mournfully, shaking her head. "So it will!"

With her in her little house lived her adopted son Prokofy, a butcher, a huge, clumsy fellow of about thirty, red-haired, with a stiff mustache. Meeting me in the front hall, he would silently and deferentially make way for me, and if he was drunk, he would give me a five-finger salute. He took his dinner in the evenings, and I could hear him through the wooden partition grunting and sighing as he drank glass after glass.

"Mama!" he would call in a low voice.

"Well?" Karpovna would answer (she loved her adopted son to distraction). "What is it, sonny?"

"I can do you this indulgence, mama. For all my earthly life, I'll feed you in your old age in this vale, and when you die, I'll bury you at my own expense. I've said it, and it's so."

I got up every day before sunrise and went to bed early.

We housepainters ate a lot and slept soundly, only for some reason my heart beat hard during the night. I never quarreled with my comrades. Abuse, desperate curses, and such wishes as that your eyes should burst, or you should drop dead from cholera, never ceased all day, but nonetheless we still lived together amicably. The boys suspected I was a religious sectarian and made fun of me good-naturedly, saying that even my own father had renounced me, telling me straight off that they seldom saw the inside of God's church themselves, and that many of them hadn't gone to confession for ten years, and justifying such dissipation by saying that a housepainter is among people what a jackdaw is among birds.

The boys respected me and treated me with deference; they apparently liked it that I didn't drink, didn't smoke, and led a quiet, sedate life. They were only unpleasantly shocked that I didn't take part in stealing drying oil and didn't go to the clients with them to ask for a tip. Stealing the owner's oil and paint was habitual among housepainters and was not considered theft, and remarkably, even such an upright man as Radish, each time he left a job, took along a little whiting and oil. And even venerable old men, who owned their own houses in Makarikha, weren't ashamed to ask for a tip, and I found it vexing and shameful when the boys would go in a bunch to congratulate some nonentity for the start or the finish and, getting ten kopecks from him, thank him humbly.

With clients, they behaved like wily courtiers, and I recalled Shakespeare's Polonius almost every day.

"But surely it's going to rain," the client would say, looking at the sky.

"It is, it certainly is!" the painters would agree.

"Though the clouds aren't the rainy sort. Perhaps it won't rain."

"It won't, Your Honor! It sure won't."

Behind their backs, their attitude to the clients was generally ironic, and when, for instance, they saw a gentleman
sitting on a balcony with a newspaper, they would observe:

"Reads the newspaper, but I bet he's got nothing to eat."

I never went home to my family. On returning from work,
I often found notes, short and anxious, in which my sister
wrote to me about father: now he was somehow especially
preoccupied and ate nothing at dinner, now he lost his
balance, now he locked himself in his study and didn't come
out for a long time. Such news disturbed me, I couldn't sleep,
and sometimes even went past our house on Bolshaya Dvoryanskaya at night, looking into the dark windows and trying
to make out whether everything was all right at home. On
Sundays my sister came to see me, but on the sly, as if not to me
but to our nanny. And if she came into my room, she would be
very pale, with tearful eyes, and would begin to cry at once.

"Our father won't survive it!" she would say. "If, God
forbid, something should happen to him, your conscience
will torment you all your life. It's terrible, Misail! I implore
you in our mother's name: mend your ways!"

"Sister, dear," I would say, "how can I mend my ways if
I'm convinced that I'm acting according to conscience? Try
to understand!"

"I know it's according to conscience, but maybe it could
be done somehow differently, so as not to upset anyone."

"Oh, dear me!" the old woman would sigh behind the
door. "It'll be your head! There'll be trouble, my dearies,
there'll be trouble!"

VI

ONE SUNDAY, DR. BLAGOVO unexpectedly appeared at my
place. He was wearing a tunic over a silk shirt, and high
patent-leather boots.

"I've come to see you!" he began, shaking my hand firmly, student-fashion. "I hear about you every day and keep intending to come and have, as they say, a heart-to-heart talk. It's terribly boring in town, not a single live soul, nobody to talk to. Heavenly Mother, it's hot!" he went on, taking off his tunic and remaining in nothing but the silk shirt. "Dear heart, allow me to talk with you!"

I was bored myself and had long wanted to be in the society of other than housepainters. I was sincerely glad to see him.

"I'll begin by saying," he said, sitting down on my bed, "that I sympathize with you wholeheartedly and deeply respect this life of yours. Here in town you're not understood, and there's nobody to understand you, because, you know yourself, here, with very few exceptions, it's all Gogol's pig snouts.[8] But I figured you out at once, that time at the picnic. You're a noble soul, an honest, lofty man! I respect you and regard it as a great honor to shake your hand!" he went on rapturously. "To change your life as sharply and summarily as you did, one must have lived through a complex inner process, and to continue that life now and be constantly at the height of your convictions, you must work intensely in your mind and heart day after day. Now, to begin our conversation, tell me, don't you find that if you expended this willpower, this intensity, this whole potential on something else, for instance, so as to become in time a great scholar or artist, your life would then expand more widely and deeply, and would be more productive in all respects?"

We fell to talking, and when we began to discuss physical labor, I expressed the following thought: it is necessary that the strong not enslave the weak, that the minority not be parasites on the majority or a pump constantly pumping its best juices out of it; that is, it is necessary that everyone without exception—the strong and the weak, the rich and the poor—participate equally in the struggle for existence, each for himself, and there is no better means of leveling in this respect than physical labor in the quality of a common service obligatory for everyone.

"So, in your opinion, everyone without exception should be occupied with physical labor?" asked the doctor.

"Yes."

"But don't you find that if everyone, including the best people, the thinkers and great scholars, as they participate in the struggle for existence, each for himself, begins to spend time crushing stone and painting roofs, it may pose a serious threat to progress?"

"What's the danger?" I asked. "Progress lies in works of love, in the fulfillment of the moral law. If you don't enslave anyone, are not a burden to anyone, what more progress do you want?"

"But excuse me!" Blagovo suddenly flared up, getting to his feet. "But excuse me! If the snail in its shell is occupied with personal self-perfection and dabbles in the moral law, do you call that progress?"

"Why dabbles?" I was offended. "If you don't make your neighbors feed you, clothe you, drive you around, protect you from enemies, then isn't that progress in a life that's all built on slavery? In my opinion, that is the most genuine progress, and perhaps the only kind possible and necessary for man."

"The limits of universally human world progress lie in infinity, and to speak of some 'possible' progress, limited by our needs or temporary views—that, forgive me, is even strange."

"If the limits of progress lie in infinity, as you say, that means its goals are undefined," I said. "To live and not know definitely what you're living for!"

"So be it! But this 'not knowing' is not as boring as your 'knowing.' I'm climbing the ladder known as progress,

civilization, culture, I go on and on without knowing definitely where I'm going, but really, for the sake of this wonderful ladder alone, life is worth living; while you know what
you're living for—so that some people will not enslave
others, so that an artist and the man who grinds pigments for
him will have the same dinner. But that is the gray, philistine,
kitchen side of life, and to live for that alone—isn't that disgusting? If some insects enslave others, devil take them, let
them eat each other! We shouldn't think about them—they'll
die and rot anyway, no matter how you save them from
slavery—we must think about that great X that awaits all
mankind in the distant future."

Blagovo argued hotly with me, but at the same time, he
was noticeably troubled by some extraneous thought.

"Your sister probably won't come," he said, looking at his
watch. "Yesterday she visited my family and said she'd be
here. You keep saying slavery, slavery . . ." he went on. "But
that is a specific problem, and all such problems get solved
by mankind gradually, of themselves."

We began to talk about gradualness. I said that each of us
resolves the question of whether to do good or evil for
himself, without waiting until mankind approaches the resolution of the question by way of gradual development.
Besides, gradualness was a stick with two ends. Alongside
the process of the gradual development of humane ideas,
there could be observed the gradual growth of ideas of a
different sort. There is no serfdom, but capitalism is growing
instead. And at the very height of liberating ideas, the majority, just as in the times of Batu Khan,[9] feeds, clothes, and
protects the minority while going hungry, naked, and un-
protected itself. This order gets along splendidly with all
trends and currents, because the art of enslavement is also
gradually cultivated. We no longer thrash our lackeys in the
stable, but we endow slavery with refined forms, or at least
we know how to find a justification for it in each particular

case. With us, ideas are ideas, but if now, at the end of the nineteenth century, it were possible to heap our most unpleasant physiological functions on workers, we would do it and then, of course, say in order to justify ourselves that if the best people, the thinkers and great scholars, started wasting their precious time on these functions, it might seriously threaten progress.

But then my sister came. Seeing the doctor, she began bustling, worrying, and right away began saying it was time for her to go home to father.

"Cleopatra Alexeevna," Blagovo said persuasively, pressing both hands to his heart, "what will happen to your dear papa if you spend a mere half hour with me and your brother?"

He was simple-hearted and knew how to communicate his animation to others. My sister, having thought for a moment, laughed and became all merry suddenly, unexpectedly, like the other time at the picnic. We went into the fields and, settling in the grass, continued our conversation and looked at the town, where all the windows to the west seemed bright gold because of the setting sun.

After that, each time my sister came to see me, Blagovo appeared as well, and the two greeted each other as if their meeting at my place was accidental. My sister listened to me and the doctor arguing, and her expression then was joyfully rapturous, tender, and curious, and it seemed to me that a different world was gradually opening before her eyes, which she had never seen before even in dreams, and which she now tried to puzzle out. Without the doctor, she was quiet and sad, and if she wept occasionally, sitting on my bed, it was now for reasons she did not speak about.

In August, Radish told us to get ready to go to the railway line. A couple of days before we were "herded" out of town, my father came to see me. He sat down and wiped his red face unhurriedly, without looking at me, then took our town

Messenger from his pocket and slowly, emphasizing each word, read that my peer, the son of the office manager of the State Bank, had been appointed head of a section in the treasury department.

"And now look at yourself," he said, folding the newspaper, "a beggar, a ragamuffin, a scoundrel! Even tradesmen and peasants get educated in order to become human beings, while you, a Poloznev, with noble, wellborn forebears, are striving towards the mud! But I haven't come here to talk to you; I've already waved you aside," he went on in a stifled voice, getting up. "I've come to find out where your sister is, you scoundrel! She left home after dinner, and it's now past seven o'clock, and she's not back. She's started going out frequently without telling me, she's less respectful—and I see in it your wicked, mean influence. Where is she?"

In his hands was the umbrella I knew so well, and I already felt at a loss and stood at attention like a schoolboy, expecting my father to start beating me, but he noticed the glance I cast at the umbrella, and that probably held him back.

"Live as you like!" he said. "I deprive you of my blessing!"

"Saints alive!" my nanny muttered behind the door. "Your poor, miserable head! Oh, there's a foreboding in my heart, a foreboding!"

I worked on the line. It rained ceaselessly all August, it was damp and cold; the grain wasn't taken in from the fields, and on large estates, where they harvested with machines, the wheat lay not in sheaves but in heaps, and I remember how those sad heaps grew darker every day, and the grain sprouted in them. It was hard to work; the downpour ruined everything we managed to get done. We weren't allowed to live and sleep in the station buildings, and took shelter in dirty, damp dugouts where the "railboys" lived in summer, and I couldn't sleep at night from the cold and from the woodlice that crawled over my face and hands. And when we worked near the bridges, bands of "railboys" came in the

evenings just to beat us painters—for them it was a kind of
sport. They beat us, stole our brushes, and to taunt us and
provoke us to fight, they ruined our work, for instance, by
smearing green paint all over the booths. To crown all our
troubles, Radish began to pay very irregularly. All the painting work at the site had been given to a contractor, who had
subcontracted it to someone else, who in turn had subcontracted it to Radish, having negotiated twenty percent for
himself. The work itself was unprofitable, and there was rain
besides; time was lost for nothing, we didn't work, but Radish was obliged to pay the boys by the day. The hungry
painters almost beat him up, called him a crook, a blood-
sucker, a Christ-selling Judas, and he, poor man, sighed,
raised his hands to heaven in despair, and kept going to Mrs.
Cheprakov for money.

VII

A RAINY, DIRTY, dark autumn came. Joblessness came, and
I would sit at home for three days in a row with nothing to
do, or perform various nonpainting jobs, for instance, carting
earth for subflooring, getting twenty kopecks a day for it.
Dr. Blagovo left for Petersburg. My sister stopped coming to
see me. Radish lay at home sick, expecting to die any day.

My mood, too, was autumnal. Maybe because, having
become a worker, I now saw our town life only from its
underside, making discoveries almost every day that simply
drove me to despair. Those of my fellow townsmen of whom
I had previously had no opinion, or who from the outside
had seemed quite decent, now turned out to be low people,
cruel, capable of every nastiness. We simple people were
deceived, cheated, made to wait whole hours in cold entries
or kitchens; we were insulted and treated extremely rudely.
In the autumn I hung wallpaper in the reading room and

two other rooms of our club; I was paid seven kopecks a roll but was told to sign for twelve, and when I refused to do so, a decent-looking gentleman in gold-rimmed spectacles, who must have been one of the club elders, said to me:

"If you say any more about it, you blackguard, I'll push your face in."

And when the footman whispered to him that I was the son of the architect Poloznev, he became embarrassed, turned red, but recovered at once and said:

"Ah, devil take him!"

In the shops, we workers were fobbed off with rotten meat, lumpy flour, and once-brewed tea; the police shoved us in church, the orderlies and nurses robbed us in hospitals, and if we, poor as we were, did not give them bribes, they fed us from dirty dishes in revenge; at the post office, the least clerk considered it his right to treat us like animals and shout rudely and insolently: "Wait! No shoving ahead!" The yard dogs—even they were unfriendly to us and attacked us with some special viciousness. But the main thing that struck me in my new condition was the total lack of fairness, precisely what is defined among the people by the words: "They have forgotten God." Rarely did a day pass without cheating. The shopkeepers who sold us oil cheated; so did the contractors, and the workmen, and the clients themselves. It goes without saying that there could be no talk of any rights for us, and each time, we had to beg for the money we had earned as if it was alms, standing at the back door with our hats off.

I was hanging wallpaper in the club, in one of the rooms adjacent to the reading room; in the evening, as I was about to leave, the daughter of the engineer Dolzhikov came into the room with a stack of books in her hands.

I bowed to her.

"Ah, hello!" she said, recognizing me at once and offering her hand. "I'm very glad to see you."

She was smiling and, with curiosity and perplexity, examined my smock, the bucket of paste, the wallpaper spread out on the floor. I was embarrassed, and she also felt awkward.

"Excuse me for looking at you like this," she said. "They've told me a lot about you. Especially Dr. Blagovo— he's simply in love with you. And I've become acquainted with your sister; a dear, sympathetic girl, but I haven't been able to convince her that there's nothing terrible in your simplification. On the contrary, you're now the most interesting person in town."

She glanced again at the bucket of paste, at the wallpaper, and went on:

"I asked Dr. Blagovo to make me better acquainted with you, but he obviously forgot or had no time. Be that as it may, we're acquainted anyway, and if you were so good as simply to call on me one day, I'd be very much obliged to you. I do so want to talk! I'm a simple person," she said, giving me her hand, "and I hope you won't feel any constraint with me. Father's not there, he's in Petersburg."

She went to the reading room, rustling her skirts, and I, when I got home, was unable to fall asleep for a long time.

During this cheerless autumn, some kindly soul, evidently wishing to alleviate my existence a little, occasionally sent me now some tea and lemons, now some pastry, now a roast hazel grouse. Karpovna said it was brought each time by a soldier, but from whom she didn't know; and the soldier asked whether I was in good health, whether I had dinner every day, and whether I had warm clothes. When the frosts struck, I received in the same way—in my absence, through a soldier—a soft knitted scarf that gave off a delicate, barely perceptible odor of perfume, and I guessed who my good fairy was. The scarf smelled of lily of the valley, Anyuta Blagovo's favorite scent.

Towards winter we got more work, and things became more cheerful. Radish revived again, and we worked together in the cemetery church, where we primed the iconostasis[10] for gilding. This was clean, peaceful work and, as our boys used to say, gainful. We could do a lot in one day, and the time passed quickly, imperceptibly. There was no cursing, or laughter, or loud talk. The place itself imposed silence and good order and was conducive to quiet, serious thoughts. Immersed in our work, we stood or sat motionless, like statues; there was a dead silence, as befitted a cemetery, so that if a tool was dropped or the flame sizzled in an icon lamp, these noises resounded sharply and hollowly—and we turned to look. After long silence, a humming would be heard, like the buzz of bees: this was a funeral service for an infant, being sung unhurriedly, softly, in a side chapel; or the artist painting a dove on the cupola with stars around it would start whistling quietly, then catch himself and fall silent at once; or Radish, answering his own thoughts, would say with a sigh: "Everything's possible! Everything's possible!"; or a slow, mournful ringing would resound over our heads, and the painters would remark that it must be some rich man's burial . . .

I spent my days in this silence, in this churchly dimness, and during the long evenings played billiards or went to the gallery of the theater in my new tricot suit, which I had bought with the money I earned. At the Azhogins', theatricals and concerts had already begun; the sets were now painted by Radish alone. He told me the contents of the plays and tableaux vivants he saw at the Azhogins', and I listened to him with envy. I had a strong yearning to attend the rehearsals, but I couldn't bring myself to go to the Azhogins'.

A week before Christmas, Dr. Blagovo arrived. Again we argued and in the evenings played billiards. When he played, he took off his frock coat and unbuttoned his shirt on his chest, and generally tried to make himself look like a desperate carouser. He drank little but noisily and, in such a poor, cheap tavern as the Volga, managed to leave twenty roubles an evening.

474

Again my sister began to frequent me; the two of them, seeing each other, were surprised each time, but from her joyful, guilty face it was evident that these meetings were not accidental. One evening while we were playing billiards, the doctor said to me:

"Listen, why don't you ever call on Miss Dolzhikov? You don't know Marya Viktorovna, she's intelligent, lovely, a simple, kind soul."

I told him how the engineer had received me in the spring.

"Trifles!" the doctor laughed. "The engineer's one thing, and she's another. Really, dear heart, don't offend her, go and see her one day. For instance, we could go and see her tomorrow evening. Do you want to?"

He persuaded me. The next evening, donning my new tricot suit and feeling worried, I went to see Miss Dolzhikov. The footman no longer seemed so arrogant and fearsome, nor the furniture so luxurious, as on that morning when I went there as a petitioner. Marya Viktorovna was expecting me and greeted me like an old acquaintance, and gave my hand a firm, friendly shake. She was wearing a gray flannel dress with full sleeves, and a hairstyle which, when it became fashionable in our town a year later, was known as "dog's ears." The hair was combed down from the temples and over the ears, and it made Marya Viktorovna's face seem broader, and this time she looked to me very much like her father, whose face was broad, ruddy, and had something of the coachman in its expression. She was beautiful and graceful but not young, around thirty by the look of it, though in reality she was no more than twenty-five.

"The dear doctor, how grateful I am to him!" she said as she was seating me. "If it weren't for him, you wouldn't have come to see me. I'm bored to death! Father went away and left me alone, and I don't know what to do in this town."

Then she began asking me where I was working now, how much I earned, where I lived.

"You spend on yourself only what you earn?" she asked.

"Yes."

"Lucky man!" she sighed. "All the evil in life, it seems to me, comes from idleness, from boredom, from inner emptiness, and that is all inevitable when one is used to living at the expense of others. Don't think I'm showing off, I tell you sincerely: it's uninteresting and unpleasant to be rich. Make to yourselves friends of the mammon of unrighteousness[11]—so it says, because generally there is not and cannot be a mammon of righteousness."

She looked the furniture over with a serious, cold expression, as if she was taking an inventory, and went on:

"Comfort and conveniences possess a magic power; they gradually suck in even strong-willed people. My father and I once lived moderately and simply, but now you see how. Who ever heard of it," she said, shrugging her shoulders, "we go through twenty thousand a year! In the provinces!"

"Comfort and conveniences are to be regarded as the inevitable privilege of capital and education," I said, "and it seems to me that life's conveniences can be combined with any sort of labor, even the heaviest and dirtiest. Your father is rich, yet, as he says, he had to work as an engine driver and a simple oiler."

She smiled and shook her head doubtfully.

"Papa sometimes eats bread soaked in kvass," she said. "It's a whim, for fun!"

Just then the bell rang, and she got up.

"The educated and the rich should work like everyone else," she went on, "and if there's comfort, it should be the same for everyone. There should be no privileges. Well, God help philosophy! Tell me something merry. Tell me about housepainters. What are they like? Funny?"

The doctor came in. I began telling about housepainters but was abashed, being unaccustomed, and spoke like an ethnographer, gravely and ploddingly. The doctor also told

476

a few anecdotes from the workmanly life. He staggered, wept, fell on his knees, and, in portraying a drunkard, even lay on the floor. It was a real actor's performance, and Marya Viktorovna, as she watched him, laughed to the point of tears. Then he played the piano and sang in his pleasant, thin tenor, and Marya Viktorovna stood beside him, choosing what he should sing and correcting him when he made mistakes.

"I hear that you also sing?" I asked.

"Also!" The doctor was horrified. "She's a wonderful singer, an artist, and you say 'also'! That's a bit much!"

"I once studied seriously," she said in answer to my question, "but now I've dropped it."

Sitting on a low stool, she told us about her life in Petersburg and impersonated well-known singers, mimicking their voices and manners of singing; she drew the doctor in her album, then me; she drew badly, but we both came out looking like ourselves. She laughed, was mischievous, grimaced sweetly, and this suited her more than talking about the mammon of unrighteousness, and it seemed to me that what she had said to me earlier about riches and comfort wasn't serious but was an imitation of someone. She was a superb comic actress. I mentally placed her beside our young ladies, and even the beautiful, grave Anyuta Blagovo could not bear comparison with her; the difference was enormous, as between a fine cultivated rose and a wild brier.

The three of us had dinner. The doctor and Marya Viktorovna drank red wine, champagne, and coffee with cognac; they clinked glasses and toasted friendship, reason, progress, freedom, and they didn't get drunk, but only turned red and often laughed loudly for no reason, to the point of tears. So as not to seem dull, I also drank red wine.

"Talented, richly endowed natures," said Miss Dolzhikov, "know how to live and follow their own path; but average people, like me, for instance, don't know anything and can't do anything themselves; nothing remains for them but to pick out some deep social current and float off where it takes them."

"Is it possible to pick out what's not there?" asked the doctor.

"Not there, because we don't see it."

"Is that so? Social currents are an invention of the new literature. We don't have any."

An argument began.

"We don't have and never have had any deep social currents," the doctor said loudly. "What has the new literature not invented! It has also invented some sort of intellectual laborers in the villages, but go around all our villages and you'll find only some Disrespect-Trough[12] in a jacket or a black frock coat who makes four spelling errors in the word 'although.' Our cultural life hasn't begun yet. The same savagery, the same overall boorishness, the same worthlessness as five hundred years ago. Currents, trends, but all this is petty, miserable, hitched to a banal groatsworth of little interests—how can we see anything serious in it? If you imagine you've picked out some deep social current and, following it, devote your life to such tasks in the contemporary taste as liberating insects from slavery or abstaining from beef cutlets, then—I congratulate you, madam. Study is what we must do, study and study, and let's wait a little with social currents: we haven't grown up to them yet and, in all conscience, understand nothing about them."

"You don't understand, but I do," said Marya Viktorovna. "You're God knows how boring today!"

"Our business is to study and study, to try to accumulate as much knowledge as possible, because serious social currents are there where knowledge is, and the happiness of future mankind lies only in knowledge. I drink to learning!"

"One thing is unquestionable: one should set up one's life somehow differently," said Marya Viktorovna, after some silence and reflection, "and life as it has been so far is worth nothing. We won't talk about it."

As we left her house, it was already striking two at the cathedral.

"Did you like her?" asked the doctor. "Nice, isn't she?"

On Christmas day we dined with Marya Viktorovna and then, in the course of all the holidays, went to see her almost every day. No one visited her except us, and she was right when she said that, except for me and the doctor, she had no acquaintances in town. We spent most of the time talking: occasionally the doctor brought along some book or magazine and read aloud to us. Essentially, he was the first educated man I had met in my life. I can't judge how much he knew, but he constantly showed his knowledge, because he wanted others to know as well. When he talked about something related to medicine, he bore no resemblance to any of our town doctors but produced a new, special impression, and it seemed to me that if he had wanted to, he could have become a real scientist. And this was perhaps the only man who had a serious influence on me at that time. Seeing him and reading the books he gave me, I gradually began to feel a need for knowledge that would inspire my cheerless labor. It now seemed strange to me that I hadn't known before, for example, that the entire world consists of sixty elements, hadn't known what linseed oil was, what paints were, and somehow could have done without this knowledge. Acquaintance with the doctor raised me morally as well. I often argued with him, and though I usually stuck to my own opinion, still, owing to him, I gradually began to notice that not everything was clear to me, and I then tried to work out for myself some possibly definite convictions, so that the dictates of my conscience would be definite and have nothing vague about them. Nevertheless, this best and most educated man in town was still far from perfection. In his manners, in his habit of reducing every conversation to an argument, in his pleasant tenor voice, and even in his gentleness, there was something slightly coarse, something of the seminarian,[13] and when he took off his frock coat and remained in nothing but his silk shirt, or when he tossed a tip to a waiter in a tavern, it seemed to me each time that culture is culture, but there was still a Tartar fermenting in him.

At the Baptism,[14] he left for Petersburg again. He left in the morning, and after dinner my sister came to see me. Without taking off her coat and hat, she sat silently, very pale, and stared at one spot. She was shivering but clearly trying to carry on.

"You must have caught a cold," I said.

Her eyes filled with tears, she got up and went to Karpovna without saying a word to me, as if I had offended her. A little later, I heard her speaking in a tone of bitter reproach:

"Nanny, what have I been living for till now? Why? Tell me: haven't I ruined my youth? To spend the best years of your life doing nothing but writing down expenses, pouring tea, counting kopecks, entertaining guests, and thinking that there was nothing higher than that in the world! Nanny, understand, I, too, have human needs, and I want to live, but I've been made into some sort of housekeeper. It's terrible, terrible!"

She flung the keys through the doorway, and they landed in my room with a jingle. These were the keys to the sideboard, the pantry, the cellar, and the tea chest—the same keys my mother once carried.

"Ah, oh, dear hearts!" the old woman was horrified. "Saints in heaven!"

Before going home, my sister came to my room to pick up the keys and said:

"Excuse me. Something strange has been happening to me lately."

VIII

ONCE, COMING HOME from Marya Viktorovna's late in the evening, I found in my room a young police officer in a new uniform; he was sitting at my table and leafing through a book.

"At last!" he said, getting up and stretching. "This is the third time I've come to you. The governor orders you to come to him tomorrow at exactly nine o'clock in the morning. Without fail."

He had me sign a statement that I would carry out His Excellency's order punctually, and left. This late visit from a police officer and the unexpected invitation to the governor's affected me in a most oppressive manner. From early childhood, a fear of gendarmes, policemen, magistrates had remained in me, and I was now tormented by anguish, as if I was indeed guilty of something. And I was quite unable to fall asleep. Nanny and Prokofy were also agitated and couldn't sleep. Besides that, nanny had an earache; she moaned and began to cry several times from the pain. Hearing that I was not asleep, Prokofy cautiously came into my room with a lamp and sat at the table.

"You ought to drink some pepper vodka..." he said, pondering. "In this vale, once you've had a drink, it feels all right. And if mama took a drop of pepper vodka in her ear, it would be a great benefit."

Between two and three o'clock, he got ready to go to the slaughterhouse for meat. I knew I wouldn't sleep before morning, and to while away the time till nine o'clock, I went with him. We walked with a lantern, and his boy, Nikolka, about thirteen years old, with blue spots on his face from the cold and the look of a perfect robber, drove after us with the sledge, urging the horse on in a husky voice.

"Must be they're going to punish you at the governor's,"

Prokofy said to me on the way. "There's governor's learning, there's archimandrite's learning, there's officer's learning, there's doctor's learning, for every title there's its learning. But you don't keep to your learning, and you shouldn't be allowed."

The slaughterhouse was beyond the cemetery, and I had previously seen it only from a distance. It was three dismal sheds surrounded by a gray fence, and on hot summer days, when the wind blew from that direction, it gave off a choking stench. Now, going into the yard, I couldn't see the sheds in the darkness, I kept running into horses and sledges, empty or already loaded with meat; people with lanterns walked about cursing repulsively. Prokofy and Nikolka cursed as vilely, and a constant noise of cursing, coughing, and the whinnying of horses hung in the air.

It smelled of corpses and dung. The melting snow was mixed with mud, and it seemed to me in the darkness that I was walking on pools of blood.

Having filled the sledges with meat, we went to the butcher shop at the market. Dawn was breaking. Cooks with baskets and elderly ladies in overcoats walked by one after the other. Prokofy, with a meat axe in his hand, in a blood-spattered white apron, swore terribly, crossed himself towards the church, shouted loudly enough for the whole marketplace to hear, claiming that he was giving the meat away at cost and was even losing on it. He short-weighed, short-changed, the cooks saw it, but, deafened by his shouting, did not protest but only called him a hangman. As he raised and lowered his terrible meat axe, he assumed picturesque poses and, with a ferocious look, emitted a loud "Hack!" each time, and I was afraid he would indeed cut off somebody's head or arm.

I stayed in the butcher shop all morning, and when I finally went to the governor's, my coat smelled of meat and blood. I was in such a mental state as if, on somebody's orders, I was going for bear with a spear. I remember a high stairway with a striped runner, and a young official in a tailcoat with bright buttons, who silently pointed me to the door with both hands and ran to announce me. I entered a reception hall in which the furnishings were luxurious but cold and tasteless, and the tall, narrow mirrors between the windows and the bright yellow curtains struck the eye especially unpleasantly; one could see that the governors changed but the furnishings remained the same. The young official again pointed me to the door with both hands, and I went to a big green desk behind which stood an army general with a Vladimir on his neck.[15]

"Mr. Poloznev, I have asked you to appear," he began, holding some letter in his hand and opening his mouth round and wide like an O, "I have asked you to appear in order to announce to you the following. Your esteemed father has addressed the provincial marshal of the nobility in writing and verbally, asking him to summon you and bring to your attention all the incompatibility of your behavior with the rank of a nobleman, which you have the honor of bearing. His Excellency Alexander Pavlovich, correctly supposing that your behavior may be a temptation, and finding that on his part, persuasion alone would be insufficient here, and that serious administrative intervention was necessary, has presented me in this letter with his considerations concerning you, which I share."

He said this quietly, respectfully, standing at attention as if I was his superior, and looking at me without any severity. His face was flabby, worn, all wrinkled, there were bags hanging under his eyes, his hair was dyed, and generally it was impossible to tell by his appearance how old he was—forty or sixty.

"I hope," he went on, "that you will appreciate the delicacy of the esteemed Alexander Pavlovich, who has addressed me not officially but in a private manner. I have also summoned you unofficially, and I am speaking to you not as a governor but as a sincere admirer of your parent. And so I ask you either to change your behavior and return to the duties proper to your rank, or, to avoid temptation, to relocate in another place, where people do not know you and where you can occupy yourself with whatever you like. Otherwise I shall have to take extreme measures."

He stood silently for about half a minute, with his mouth open, looking at me.

"Are you a vegetarian?" he asked.

"No, Your Excellency, I eat meat."

He sat down and drew some paper towards him; I bowed and left.

It wasn't worth going to work before dinner. I went home to sleep, but could not fall asleep because of the unpleasant, morbid feeling brought upon me by the slaughterhouse and the talk with the governor, and, waiting till evening, upset, gloomy, I went to see Marya Viktorovna. I told her about my visit to the governor, and she looked at me in perplexity, as if she didn't believe me, and suddenly laughed merrily, loudly, impetuously, as only good-natured, easily amused people know how to laugh.

"If I were to tell that in Petersburg!" she said, nearly dropping with laughter and leaning on her desk. "If I were to tell that in Petersburg!"

IX

WE NOW SAW each other often, about twice a day. Almost every day after dinner she came to the cemetery and, while waiting for me, read the inscriptions on the crosses and tombstones; sometimes she went into the church and, standing beside me, watched me work. The silence, the naïve work of the artists and gilders, Radish's reasonings, and the fact that externally I was no different from the other craftsmen and worked, like them, only in a vest and old shoes, and that they addressed me familiarly—all this was new to her and moved her. Once, in her presence, the artist who was painting the dove up top shouted to me:

"Misail, bring me some whiting!"

I fetched him some whiting, and as I came down the flimsy scaffolding afterwards, she watched me, moved to tears and smiling.

"How nice you are!" she said.

The memory had stayed with me since childhood of how a green parrot belonging to one of our wealthy people escaped its cage, and how after that the beautiful bird wandered about town for a whole month, lazily flying from one garden to another, lonely, shelterless. And Marya Viktorovna reminded me of that bird.

"I now have positively nowhere to go except the cemetery," she said to me, laughing. "This town bores me to the point of loathing. At the Azhogins' they read, sing, lisp, I can't bear them lately; your sister is unsociable, Mlle. Blagovo hates me for some reason, I don't like the theater. What do you suggest I do?"

When I called on her, I smelled of paint and turpentine, my hands were dark—and she liked that; she also wanted me to come to her not otherwise than in my ordinary working clothes; but those clothes hampered me in the drawing room, I was embarrassed, as if I was wearing a uniform, and therefore, when I went to her, I always put on my new tricot suit. And she didn't like it.

"But confess, you don't quite feel comfortable in your new role," she said to me once. "Your working costume hampers you, you feel awkward in it. Tell me, isn't that because you have no assurance and are not satisfied? The very kind of work you've chosen, this painting spell of yours, can it be that it satisfies you?" she asked, laughing. "I know painting makes things prettier and more durable, but these things belong to the townspeople, the rich, and in the end constitute a luxury. Besides, you yourself have said more than once that each man should procure his bread with his own hands, while you procure money, not bread. Why don't you stick to the literal meaning of your words? You should procure precisely bread, that is, you should plow, sow, mow, thresh, or do something that has a direct relation to farming, for instance, tend cattle, till the earth, build cottages . . ."

She opened a pretty bookcase that stood by her desk and said:

"I'm saying all this because I want to initiate you into my secret. Voilà! This is my farming library. Here are fields, and kitchen garden, and orchard, and cattle yard, and apiary. I read them avidly and in terms of theory have already studied everything to the last jot. My dream, my sweet dream, is to go to our Dubechnya as soon as March comes. It's wonderful there, marvelous! Isn't that so? For the first year I'll observe things and get accustomed to them, and the next year I'll work myself in a real way, give it my all, as they say. Father has promised me Dubechnya, and I can do whatever I like with it."

All flushed, excited to the point of tears, and laughing, she dreamed aloud of how she would live in Dubechnya and what an interesting life it would be. And I envied her. March was already near, the days were getting longer and longer, and on bright sunny afternoons the roofs dripped and it smelled of spring. I would have liked to go to the country myself.

And when she said she would move to live in Dubechnya, I vividly pictured how I would remain alone in town, and I felt jealous of her bookcase and of farming. I didn't know and didn't like farming, and was about to tell her that farming was a slavish occupation, but remembered that my father had said something like that more than once, and kept silent.

Lent came. The engineer Viktor Ivanych, whose existence

I was beginning to forget, arrived from Petersburg. He arrived unexpectedly, without even a warning telegram. When I came in the evening as usual, he, scrubbed, hair trimmed, looking ten years younger, was pacing the drawing room and telling about something; his daughter was on her knees, taking boxes, flacons, and books from the suitcases and handing it all to the footman Pavel. Seeing the engineer, I involuntarily stepped back, but he held out both arms to me and said, smiling, showing his white, strong coachman's teeth:

"Here he is, here he is! Very glad to see you, Mr. Housepainter! Masha has told me everything, she's sung a whole panegyric to you here. I fully understand and approve of you!" he went on, taking me under the arm. "To be a decent worker is much more intelligent and honest than to waste official stationery and wear a cockade on your forehead. I myself worked in Belgium, with these hands, then spent two years as an engine driver . . ."

He was wearing a short jacket and slippers for around the house, and walked like a man with gout, waddling slightly and rubbing his hands. Humming something, he murmured softly and kept hugging himself with satisfaction that he had finally come back home and taken his beloved shower.

"Indisputably," he said to me over supper, "indisputably, you're all nice, sympathetic people, but for some reason, gentlemen, as soon as you undertake some physical labor or start saving muzhiks, it all comes down in the end to sectarianism. Aren't you a sectarian? Look, you don't drink vodka. What's that if not sectarianism?"

To give him pleasure, I drank some vodka. I also drank some wine. We sampled cheeses, sausages, pâtés, pickles, and various delicacies the engineer had brought along, and the wines received from abroad during his absence. The wines were excellent. For some reason, the engineer received wines and cigars from abroad tax-free; someone sent him caviar and smoked fish gratis, he paid no rent for his apartment because the owner of the house supplied the railway line with kerosene; and in general, he and his daughter gave me the impression that everything best in the world was at their disposal, and they received it completely gratis.

I continued to frequent them, but no longer as willingly. The engineer hampered me, and I felt constrained in his presence. I couldn't stand his clear, innocent eyes, his reasonings oppressed me, disgusted me; oppressive, too, was the memory of my being so recently a subordinate of this well-nourished, ruddy man, and of his being mercilessly rude to me. True, he put his arm around my waist, patted me benignly on the shoulder, approved of my life, but I felt that he scorned my nonentity as much as before and put up with me only to please his daughter; I could no longer laugh and say what I liked, I behaved unsociably and kept waiting every moment for him to call me Pantelei, as he did his footman Pavel. How exasperated my provincial, philistine pride was! I, a proletarian, a housepainter, go every day to see rich people, strangers to me, whom the whole town looks upon as foreigners, and every day drink expensive wines with them and eat exotic things—my conscience refused to be reconciled with it! On the way to them, I sullenly avoided passersby and looked from under my brows, as if I was indeed a sectarian, and when I went home from the engineer's, I was ashamed of my satiety.

And above all, I was afraid of becoming infatuated. Whether I was walking down the street, or working, or talking with the boys, all I thought about the whole time was how in the evening I would go to Marya Viktorovna's, and I imagined her voice, her laughter, her gait. Before going to her each time, I stood for a long while in front of my nanny's crooked mirror, tying my necktie; I found my tricot suit repulsive, and I suffered and at the same time despised myself for being so petty. When she called to me from the other room to say she was undressed and asked me to wait,

I listened to her getting dressed; this excited me, I felt as if the floor was giving way under me. And when I saw a female figure in the street, even from afar, I invariably made the comparison; it seemed to me then that all our women and girls were vulgarly, absurdly dressed and did not know how to behave; and these comparisons aroused a feeling of pride in me: Marya Viktorovna was the best of all! And at night I saw the two of us in my dreams.

Once, at supper, the engineer and I ate a whole lobster together. Going home then, I remembered that at supper the engineer had twice addressed me as "my most gentle," and I reasoned that I was being petted in this house like a big, unhappy dog that has lost its master, that I was an amusement, and when they tired of me, they would chase me away like a dog. I felt ashamed and pained, pained to the point of tears, as if I had been insulted, and, looking at the heavens, I vowed to put an end to all this.

The next day I did not go to the Dolzhikovs'. Late in the evening, when it was quite dark and pouring rain, I walked down Bolshaya Dvoryanskaya, looking at the windows. The Azhogins were already asleep, and only in one of the end windows was there a light; it was the old Azhogin woman in her bedroom, doing embroidery to the light of three candles, imagining she was fighting prejudice. Our house was dark, and in the house across the street, at the Dolzhikovs', there was light in the windows, but nothing could be seen through the flowers and curtains. I kept walking up and down the street; the cold March rain poured down on me. I heard my father come back from the club; he knocked at the gate, a minute later there was light in the window, and I saw my sister walking hurriedly with a lamp, straightening her thick hair with one hand as she went. Then father paced up and down the drawing room and talked about something, rubbing his hands, and my sister sat motionless in an armchair, thinking about something, not listening to him.

But then they left, the light went out ... I turned to look at the engineer's house—there, too, it was dark now. In the darkness, under the rain, I felt myself hopelessly lonely, abandoned to my fate, felt that, compared with this solitude of mine, compared with my suffering, the present and that which still lay ahead of me in life, all my deeds, desires, and all that I had thought and said till now, were terribly petty. Alas, the deeds and thoughts of living beings are far less significant than their sorrows! And without giving myself a clear account of what I was doing, I pulled with all my might on the doorbell at the Dolzhikovs' gate, tore it off, and ran down the street like a little boy, feeling afraid and thinking that now they were sure to come out and recognize me. When I stopped at the end of the street to catch my breath, the only thing to be heard was the sound of the rain and a night watchman rapping on an iron bar somewhere far away.

For a whole week, I didn't go to the Dolzhikovs'. The tricot suit got sold. There was no painting work, and again I starved, earning ten or twenty kopecks a day, wherever I could, by heavy, unpleasant work. Floundering knee-deep in cold mud, straining my chest, I wanted to stifle my memories, as if taking revenge on myself for all those cheeses and potted meats I had been treated to at the engineer's; but all the same, as soon as I went to bed, hungry and wet, my sinful imagination began at once to paint wonderful, seductive pictures, and I confessed to myself in amazement that I was in love, passionately in love, and I would fall asleep soundly and healthily, feeling that this life of hard labor only made my body stronger and younger.

On one of those evenings, it snowed unseasonably, and the wind blew from the north as if winter was coming again. On returning from work that evening, I found Marya Viktorovna in my room. She was sitting in her fur coat, holding both hands in her muff.

"Why don't you come to see me?" she asked, raising her

intelligent, clear eyes, while I was greatly embarrassed from joy and stood at attention before her, as before my father when he was about to beat me; she looked into my face, and I could see from her eyes that she understood why I was embarrassed.

"Why don't you come to see me?" she repeated. "If you don't want to come, here, I've come myself."

She stood up and came close to me.

"Don't abandon me," she said, and her eyes filled with tears. "I'm alone, completely alone!"

She began to cry and said, covering her face with her muff:

"Alone! It's hard for me to live, very hard, and I have no one in the whole world except you. Don't abandon me!"

Looking for a handkerchief to wipe her tears, she smiled; we were silent for a while, then I embraced and kissed her, getting a bloody scratch on my cheek as I did so from the pin that held her hat.

And we began talking as if we had been close to each other for a long, long time ...

X

SOME TWO DAYS later, she sent me to Dubechnya, and I was unspeakably glad of it. On my way to the station, and then sitting on the train, I laughed for no reason, and people looked at me as if I was drunk. It was snowing, and there were morning frosts, but the roads had already darkened, and rooks, crowing, flitted over them.

At first I planned to set up quarters for the two of us, Masha and me, in the side wing opposite Mrs. Cheprakov's wing, but it turned out that it had long been inhabited by pigeons and ducks, and it would be impossible to clean it out without destroying a multitude of nests. I had, willy-nilly, to go to the inhospitable rooms of the big house with jalousies. The muzhiks called this house a mansion; it had more than twenty rooms and no furniture except the piano and a child's chair that lay in the attic, and if Masha had brought all her furniture from town, even then we would not have managed to get rid of this impression of gloomy emptiness and coldness. I chose three smaller rooms with windows on the garden, and cleaned them from early morning till night, putting in new window glass, hanging wallpaper, filling the cracks and holes in the floor. It was easy, pleasant work. Time and again I ran to the river to see if the ice was breaking up; I kept imagining that the starlings had flown back. And at night, thinking about Masha, I listened, with an inexpressibly sweet feeling, with a thrilling joy, to the sound of the rats and the wind howling and knocking above the ceiling; it seemed as though some old household spirit was coughing in the attic.

The snow was deep; at the end of March, a lot more poured down, but it melted quickly, as if by magic, the spring waters flowed stormily, and by the beginning of April the starlings were already making their racket, and yellow butterflies flew about the garden. The weather was wonderful. Every day towards evening, I headed for town to meet Masha, and what a pleasure it was to go barefoot on the drying, still-soft road! Halfway there, I would sit down and look at the town, not venturing to go nearer. The sight of it perplexed me. I kept thinking: how would my acquaintances treat me when they learned of my love? What would my father say? Especially perplexing was the thought that my life had become more complicated, and I had totally lost the ability to control it, and, like a big balloon, it was carrying me God knows where. I no longer thought of how to provide nourishment for myself, how to live, but thought—I truly can't remember of what.

Masha would come in a carriage; I would get in with her,

and we would go to Dubechnya together, merry, free. Or, after waiting till sunset, I would return home displeased, downcast, puzzling over why Masha hadn't come, and by the gates of the estate or in the garden, a sweet phantom—she!—would meet me unexpectedly! It turned out that she had come by train and walked from the station. How festive it was! In a simple woolen dress, in a kerchief, with a modest parasol, but tightly laced, trim, in expensive imported shoes—this was a talented actress playing the little tradeswoman. We looked over our domain, deciding which room was whose, where we would have alleys, the kitchen garden, the apiary. We already had chickens, ducks, and geese, which we loved because they were ours. We already had oats, clover, timothy, buckwheat, and vegetable seeds ready for sowing, and we examined it all each time and had long discussions of what the harvest might be, and everything Masha said seemed to me remarkably intelligent and beautiful. This was the happiest time of my life.

Soon after Saint Thomas's Sunday,[16] we were married in our parish church, in the village of Kurilovka, two miles from Dubechnya. Masha wanted everything to be done modestly; at her wish, we had peasant lads as best men, the beadle did all the singing, and we came home from church in a small, jolty tarantass, and she herself did the driving. Our only guest from town was my sister Cleopatra, to whom Masha sent a note three days before the wedding. My sister wore a white dress and gloves. During the ceremony, she cried quietly from tenderness and joy, the expression of her face was motherly, infinitely kind. She was drunk with our happiness and smiled as though she was inhaling sweet fumes, and, looking at her during our wedding, I understood that for her there was nothing higher in the world than love, earthly love, and that she dreamed of it secretly, timorously, but constantly and passionately. She embraced and kissed Masha and, not knowing how to express her rapture, kept saying to her about me:

493

"He's kind! He's very kind!"

Before leaving us, she changed into her ordinary dress and led me to the garden to talk with me one to one.

"Father is very upset that you didn't write anything to him," she said. "You should have asked his blessing. But essentially he's very pleased. He says that this marriage will raise you in the eyes of all society, and that under the influence of Marya Viktorovna, you'll take a more serious attitude towards life. In the evenings we talk only about you, and yesterday he even used the phrase 'our Misail.' That made me glad. Evidently he has something in mind, and it seems he wants to show you an example of magnanimity and be the first to start talking about a reconciliation. It's very possible that he'll come to see you one of these days."

She hastily crossed me several times and said:

"Well, God be with you, I wish you happiness. Anyuta Blagovo is a very intelligent girl, she says of your marriage that God is sending you a new test. What, then? In family life there are not only joys but also sufferings. It's impossible without that."

Seeing her off, Masha and I went on foot about two miles; then, on the way back, we walked slowly and silently, as if resting. Masha held my hand, our hearts were light, and we no longer wanted to speak of love; after our marriage, we became still closer and dearer to each other, and it seemed to us that nothing could separate us now.

"Your sister is a sympathetic being," said Masha, "but it looks as though she's been tormented for a long time. Your father must be a terrible man."

I began to tell her how my sister and I had been brought up and indeed how tormenting and senseless our childhood had been. Learning that my father had beaten me still so recently, she shuddered and pressed herself to me.

"Don't tell me any more," she said. "It's frightening."

Now she never parted from me. We lived in the big house,

in three rooms, and in the evening tightly bolted the door leading to the empty part of the house, as if someone lived there whom we did not know and were afraid of. I got up early, at dawn, and straightaway started some work. I repaired the carts, laid out the paths in the garden, dug the flower beds, painted the roof of the house. When the time came for sowing oats, I tried my hand at cross-plowing, harrowing, sowing, and I did it all conscientiously, without lagging behind the hired man; I'd get tired from the rain, and the sharp, cold wind made my face and legs burn for a long time, and at night I dreamed of plowed earth. But working in the fields did not attract me. I didn't know farming and didn't like it; the reason for that might have been that my ancestors were not tillers of the soil, and pure city blood flowed in my veins. Nature I loved tenderly, I loved the fields and meadows, and the kitchen garden, but the muzhik turning over the soil with a wooden plow, bedraggled, wet, his neck stretched out, urging on his pitiful horse, was for me the expression of a crude, wild, ugly force, and each time I looked at his clumsy movements, I involuntarily began to think of that long-gone, legendary life before people knew the use of fire. The stern bull going about with the peasant's herd, and the horses, when they raced through the village, their hooves pounding, inspired fear in me, and everything at all big, strong, and angry, whether it was a ram with horns, a gander, or a watchdog, was to me an expression of the same crude, wild force. This prejudice spoke in me especially strongly during bad weather, when heavy clouds hung over the black plowed fields. But above all, when I plowed or sowed, and two or three people stood and watched me do it, I had no consciousness that this labor was inevitable and obligatory, and it seemed to me that I was amusing myself. And I preferred to do something in the yard and liked nothing so much as painting the roof.

I used to go through the garden and through the meadow

to our mill. It was leased to Stepan, a muzhik from Kurilovka, handsome, swarthy, with a thick black beard, a very strong man by the look of him. He didn't like the work at the mill, and considered it boring and unprofitable, and he lived at the mill only so as not to live at home. He was a harness-maker, and there was always a pleasant smell of tar and leather about him. He didn't like talking, was sluggish, inert, and kept crooning "Oo-loo-loo-loo" to himself as he sat on the riverbank or in the doorway. Occasionally his wife and mother-in-law would come to him from Kurilovka, both of them fair-skinned, languid, meek; they bowed low to him and addressed him formally as "Stepan Petrovich." But he, not responding to their bows either by a gesture or by a word, sat apart on the riverbank and crooned softly "Oo-loo-loo-loo." An hour or two would pass in silence. Mother-in-law and wife would exchange whispers, get up, look at him for some time, waiting for him to turn and look at them, then bow low and say in sweet, singsong voices:

"Good-bye, Stepan Petrovich!"

And go away. After that, picking up a bundle of bread rolls or a shirt, Stepan would sigh and say, winking in their direction:

"The female sex!"

The mill, with its two sets of millstones, worked day and night. I helped Stepan, it was to my liking, and when he went off somewhere, I willingly stayed in his place.

XI

AFTER THE WARM, clear weather came mud time; it rained all through May, and it was cold. The noise of the mill wheels and the rain disposed one to laziness and sleepiness. The floor trembled, there was a smell of flour, and that also made one drowsy. My wife, in a short fur coat and high, man's rubber boots, put in an appearance twice a day and always said one and the same thing:

"And they call this summer! It's worse than October!"

Together we drank tea, cooked kasha, or sat silently for long hours waiting for the rain to stop. Once, when Stepan went off to a country fair somewhere, Masha spent the whole night at the mill. When we got up, it was impossible to tell what time it was, because the rain clouds covered the sky; only sleepy roosters crowed in Dubechnya, and corncrakes called in the meadow; it was still very, very early . . . My wife and I went down to the pool and pulled out the creel Stepan had set in our presence the day before. One big perch was struggling in it, and a bristling crayfish, his claw thrust up.

"Let them out," said Masha. "Let them be happy, too."

Because we got up very early and then did nothing, this day seemed very long, the longest in my life. Before evening Stepan came back, and I went home to the farmhouse.

"Your father came today," Masha told me.

"Where is he?" I asked.

"He left. I didn't receive him."

Seeing that I stood there and said nothing, that I felt sorry for my father, she said:

"One must be consistent. I didn't receive him and sent word to him that he needn't trouble himself anymore by coming to see us."

A minute later, I was out the gate and on my way to town to talk things over with my father. It was muddy, slippery, cold. For the first time since the wedding, I felt sad, and in my brain, weary from this long, gray day, the thought flashed that maybe I wasn't living as I should. I was worn out, I gradually succumbed to faintheartedness, laziness, I didn't want to move, to think, and, having gone a little way, I waved my hand and turned back.

In the middle of the yard stood the engineer in a leather coat with a hood, speaking loudly:

"Where's the furniture? There was fine furniture in the Empire style, there were paintings, there were vases, and now you could play skittles in it! I bought the estate with the furniture, devil take it!"

Beside him, crumpling his hat in his hands, stood the widow Cheprakov's hired man Moisei, a fellow of about twenty-five, skinny, slightly pockmarked, with insolent little eyes; one of his cheeks was slightly bigger than the other, as if he had slept on it.

"You bought it without the furniture, if you please, Your Honor," he said hesitantly. "I remember it, sir."

"Silence!" the engineer shouted, turned purple, shook, and the echo in the garden loudly repeated his shout.

XII

WHENEVER I WAS doing something in the garden or the yard, Moisei stood nearby and, with his hands behind his back, watched me lazily and insolently with his little eyes. And this annoyed me so much that I would abandon my work and leave.

We learned from Stepan that this Moisei was the widow's lover. I noticed that when people came to her for money, they first addressed themselves to Moisei, and once I saw a muzhik, all black, probably a coal shoveler, bow down at his feet; sometimes, after some whispering, he handed the money over himself, without telling the lady, from which I concluded that on occasion he operated independently, on his own account.

He went shooting in the garden under our windows, pilfered food from our cellar, took the horses without asking, and we became indignant, ceasing to believe that Dubechnya was ours, and Masha would say, turning pale:

"Do we really have to live with these vermin for another year and a half?"

The widow's son, Ivan Cheprakov, served as a conductor on our railway. Over the winter he had grown very thin and weak, so that one glass made him drunk, and he felt cold in the shade. He wore conductor's dress with disgust and was ashamed of it, but he considered his post profitable because he could steal candles and sell them. My new position aroused in him mixed feelings of astonishment, envy, and the vague hope that something similar might happen to him. He followed Masha with admiring eyes, asked what I now ate for dinner, and a sad and sweet expression appeared on his emaciated, homely face, and he moved his fingers as if touching my happiness.

"Listen, Small Profit," he said fussily, relighting his cigarette every moment; the place where he stood was always littered, because he used dozens of matches to light one cigarette. "Listen, my life now is the meanest sort. The main thing is that every little officer can shout: 'Hey, you, conductor!' I've heard a lot on the train, brother, all sorts of things, and you know, I realized: what a rotten life! My mother ruined me! A doctor on the train told me: if the parents are depraved, the children come out drunkards or criminals. That's how it is!"

Once he came into the yard reeling. His eyes wandered senselessly, he was breathing heavily; he laughed, cried, said something as if in feverish delirium, and all I could make out in his confused talk were the words: "My mother! Where's my mother?" which he pronounced tearfully, like a child that has lost its mother in a crowd. I took him to our orchard and lay him down under a tree, and then all day and all night Masha and I took turns sitting by him. He was in poor shape, and Masha looked at his pale wet face with loathing, saying:

"Will these vermin really be living in our yard for another year and a half? It's terrible! Terrible!"

And how much grief the peasants caused us! How many

painful disappointments at the very first, in the spring months, when we so wanted to be happy! My wife was building a school. I drew the plan of a school for sixty boys, and the zemstvo[17] council approved of it but advised building the school in Kurilovka, a big village that was only two miles from us; incidentally, the Kurilovka school, in which the children of four villages studied, including those from our Dubechnya, was old and small, and one had to walk warily on its rotted floor. At the end of March, Masha, at her own wish, was appointed trustee of the Kurilovka school, and at the beginning of April, we called meetings three times and tried to persuade the peasants that their school was small and old and that it was necessary to build a new one. A member of the zemstvo council came, and an inspector from the state school system, and also tried to persuade them. After each meeting, they surrounded us and asked for a bucket of vodka; it was hot in the crowd, we soon grew weary and returned home displeased and somewhat abashed. In the end, the peasants allotted a piece of land for the school and took it upon themselves to deliver all the building materials from town with their horses. And as soon as they were finished with the spring crops, on the very first Sunday, carts went from Kurilovka and Dubechnya to bring bricks for the foundation. They left at first light and came back late in the evening; the muzhiks were drunk and said they were exhausted.

As if on purpose, the rain and cold continued all through May. The road was ruined, turned to mud. The carts usually stopped by our yard on their way from town—and what a horror that was! Now a horse appears in the gateway, big-bellied, its forelegs splayed; it curtsies before coming into the yard; a thirty-foot beam comes crawling in on a dray, wet, slimy-looking; beside it, wrapped up against the rain, not looking under his feet, not avoiding the puddles, strides a muzhik, his coat skirts tucked up under his belt. Another cart appears with planks, then a third with a beam, a fourth...and the space in front of the house gradually becomes crammed with horses, beams, boards. Muzhiks and women with wrapped heads and tucked-up skirts look angrily at our windows, noisily demand that the lady come out to them; coarse abuse can be heard. And Moisei stands to one side, and it seems to us that he delights in our disgrace.

"We won't do any more carting!" shout the muzhiks. "We're exhausted! Go and do your own carting!"

Masha, pale, distraught, thinking they were about to break into our house, gives them money for a half-bucket of vodka, after which the noise subsides, and the long beams crawl out of the yard one after another.

When I got ready to go to the construction site, my wife became worried and said:

"The peasants are angry. They might do something to you. No, wait, I'll go with you."

We drove off to Kurilovka together, and there the carpenters asked us for a tip. The frame was ready, it was time to lay the foundation, but the masons did not come; there was a delay, and the carpenters murmured. But when the masons finally came, it turned out that there was no sand: the need for it had somehow been overlooked. Taking advantage of our helpless position, the peasants asked thirty kopecks per cartload, though it was less than a quarter of a mile from the construction site to the river, where they took the sand, and all told, we needed five hundred cartloads. There was no end of misunderstanding, abuse, and extortion, my wife was indignant, and Titus Petrov, the masonry contractor, a seventy-year-old man, took her by the hand and said:

"Look here! Look here! Just get me the sand, and I'll round you up ten men at once, and in two days it'll be ready. Look here!"

But the sand was delivered, two days, four days, a week went by, and a pit still yawned in the place of the future foundation.

"It could drive you crazy!" My wife was agitated. "What people! What people!"

During these disorders, the engineer Viktor Ivanych used to visit us. He would bring bags of wine and delicacies, spend a long time eating, and then fall asleep on the terrace and snore so loudly that the workers shook their heads and said:

"Well, now!"

Masha was usually not glad of his coming, did not trust him, and at the same time asked for his advice; when, having slept after dinner, he woke up out of sorts and said bad things about our farming, or expressed regret that he had bought Dubechnya, which had already caused him so many losses, a look of anguish would come to poor Masha's face; she complained to him, and he yawned and said that peasants should be whipped.

He called our marriage and our life a comedy, said it was a whim and an indulgence.

"Something like this already happened with her," he told me about Masha. "She once fancied herself an opera singer and left me; I searched for her for two months and spent, my gentle one, a thousand roubles on telegrams alone."

He no longer called me a sectarian or Mr. Housepainter, or approved of my working life as before, but said:

"You're a strange man! You're an abnormal man! I wouldn't venture to prophesy, but you'll end badly, sir!"

And Masha slept poorly at night and kept thinking about something, sitting by the window in our bedroom. There was no more laughter over dinner, no making sweet grimaces. I suffered, and when it rained, every drop of rain pierced my heart like birdshot, and I was ready to kneel before Masha and apologize for the weather. When the muzhiks made noise in the yard, I also felt myself guilty. I spent whole hours sitting in one spot, thinking only of what a wonderful, what a magnificent person Masha was. I loved her passionately and admired everything she did, everything she said. She had a penchant for quiet, studious occupations; she liked to spend a long time reading, studying something; she, who knew farming only from books, astonished us all with her knowledge, and the advice she used to give was all useful, and none of it went for naught. And with all that, so much nobility, taste, and good humor, that good humor which occurs only in exceptionally well-brought-up people!

For this woman, with her healthy, positive mind, the disorderly situation we now lived in, with its petty cares and squabbles, was tormenting; I saw it and could not sleep nights myself, my head worked, tears choked me. I thrashed about, not knowing what to do.

I galloped to town and brought Masha books, newspapers, sweets, flowers; I went fishing with Stepan and waded for hours up to my neck in cold water, under the rain, to catch a burbot in order to diversify our meals; I stooped to asking the muzhiks not to make noise, gave them vodka, bribed them, made them various promises. And did so many other foolish things!

The rain finally stopped, the earth dried. You get up early, at four o'clock—dew glistening on the flowers, birds and insects noising about, not a single cloud in the sky; the orchard, the meadow, and the river so beautiful, but then memories of the muzhiks, the carts, the engineer! Masha and I drove out to the fields in a racing droshky to look at the oats. She was the driver, I sat behind; her shoulders were raised, and the wind played with her hair.

"Keep right!" she shouted to oncoming drivers.

"You're just like a coachman!" I said to her once.

"Maybe so! My grandfather, the engineer's father, was a coachman. Didn't you know that?" she asked, turning to me, and at once imitated the way coachmen shout and sing.

"Thank God!" I thought, listening to her. "Thank God!"

And again memories of the muzhiks, the carts, the engineer...

XIII

DR. BLAGOVO CAME out on a bicycle. My sister began to visit often. Again there were conversations about physical labor, about progress, about the mysterious X that awaits mankind in the distant future. The doctor didn't like our farming because it interfered with our arguing, and said that to plow, mow, and tend calves was unworthy of a free man, and that in time people would charge animals and machines with these crude forms of the struggle for existence, and would themselves be occupied solely with scientific studies. And my sister kept asking to be allowed to go home earlier, and if she stayed till late evening or overnight, there was no end to her worrying.

"My God, what a child you still are!" Masha would say in reproach. "It's even ridiculous, finally."

"Yes, ridiculous," my sister would agree, "I'm aware that it's ridiculous; but what am I to do if I'm unable to overcome myself? It always seems to me that I act badly."

During the haymaking, my whole body ached from lack of habit; sitting on the terrace with everybody in the evening and talking, I would suddenly fall asleep, and they laughed loudly at me. They would wake me up and sit me at the table for supper, drowsiness would come over me, and, as in oblivion, I would see lights, faces, plates, hear voices without understanding them. And getting up early in the morning, I would at once take the scythe or go off to the construction site and work all day.

Staying home on holidays, I noticed that my wife and sister were concealing something from me and even seemed to be avoiding me. My wife was tender with me as before, but she had some thoughts of her own that she did not impart to me. There was no doubt that her irritation with the peasants was growing, life was becoming ever more difficult for her, and yet she no longer complained to me. She now talked with the doctor more willingly than with me, and I didn't understand why that was so.

There was a custom in our province: at haymaking and harvest time, workers came in the evenings to the master's yard to be treated to vodka, even young girls drank a glass. We did not observe it; the mowers and women stood in our yard till late in the evening, waiting for vodka, and then went away cursing. Masha frowned sternly during this time and was silent, or said irritably to the doctor in a low voice:

"Savages! Pechenegs!"[18]

In the country, newcomers are given an unfriendly, almost hostile welcome, as at school. We, too, were welcomed in that way. At first we were looked upon as stupid and simple people who had bought an estate only because there was nothing else to do with the money. We were laughed at. The muzhiks let their cattle graze in our woods and even in the orchard, they drove our cows and horses to their village and then came to demand money for damages. They came into our yard in whole companies and noisily complained that, while mowing, we had supposedly encroached on the border of some Bysheevka or Semyonikha that did not belong to us; and since we did not yet know the precise boundaries of our land, we took their word for it and paid the fine; later, it would turn out that we had mowed correctly. They stripped bast[19] in our woods. One Dubechnya muzhik, a kulak[20] who dealt in vodka without a license, bribed our workers and, together with them, deceived us in a most treacherous way: replaced the new wheels on our carts with old ones, took our horse collars and then sold them back to us, and so on. But most offensive of all was what was happening at the Kurilovka construction site; at night the women stole planks, bricks, tiles, sheet iron; the elder searched their houses in the presence of witnesses, the assembly fined each of them two roubles, and then they all drank up the money together.

When Masha learned of it, she would say indignantly to the doctor or my sister:

"What animals! It's awful! Awful!"

And more than once I heard her express regret at undertaking the building of the school.

"Understand," the doctor persuaded her, "understand that if you build this school and generally do good, it's not for the muzhiks but in the name of culture, in the name of the future. And the worse these muzhiks are, the more reason to build the school. Understand that!"

In his voice, however, one could hear a lack of assurance, and it seemed to me that he and Masha both hated the muzhiks.

Masha often went to the mill and took my sister with her, and the two of them laughingly said they were going to look at Stepan, how handsome he was. Stepan, it turned out, was slow and taciturn only with men, but in the company of women behaved quite casually and talked incessantly. Once, going to the river to swim, I involuntarily overheard a conversation. Masha and Cleopatra, both in white dresses, were sitting on the bank under a willow, in a broad patch of shade, and Stepan was standing nearby, his hands behind his back, saying:

"Are peasants people? They aren't people but, excuse me, beastly folk, charlatans. What kind of life does a peasant have? Only eating, drinking, getting cheaper grub, straining his gullet witlessly in the pot-house; and no nice conversation for you, no manners, no form—just boorishness! Sits in dirt himself, and his wife sits in dirt, and his children sit in dirt, he sleeps in whatever he's got on him, he picks potatoes from the cabbage soup straight out with his fingers, he drinks his kvass with cockroaches—might at least blow it aside!"

"But that's poverty!" my sister put in.

"What poverty! Want, true, but then there's want and want, madam. If a man sits in jail or, say, is blind or crippled, that God should better spare us all, but if he's free, can use his intelligence, has eyes and hands, has strength, has God, then what more does he need? It's indulgence, madam, ignorance, and not poverty. If you, let's suppose, as good masters, being educated, want to offer him charitable assistance, he's so vile that he'll drink up your money, or worse still, open a drinking establishment himself and use your money to rob people. Poverty, you're pleased to say. But does the wealthy peasant live better? Excuse me, but he also lives like a pig. A boor, a loudmouth, a blockhead, wider than he is tall, a fat red mug—the scoundrel's just begging you to haul off and whack him. This Larion from Dubechnya is also rich, but don't worry, he strips bast in your forest no worse than a poor man; he's foulmouthed, and his children are foulmouthed, and when he's had a drop too much, he plunks his nose down in a puddle and sleeps. They're all worthless, madam. Living in the village with them is like living in hell. It sticks in my craw, this village, and I thank the Lord, the Heavenly King, that I'm fed and clothed, and have served my term as a dragoon, and spent three years as elder, and am now a free Cossack: I live where I like. I have no wish to live in the village, and nobody has the right to make me. Your wife, they say. You, they say, are obliged to live in the cottage with your wife. Why is that? I'm not hired out to her."

"Tell me, Stepan, did you marry for love?" asked Masha.

"What kind of love do we have in the village?" Stepan asked and grinned. "As a matter of fact, madam, if you wish to know, I'm married for the second time. I'm not from Kurilovka myself, I'm from Zalegoshche, but I was taken to Kurilovka later as a son-in-law. Meaning my parent had no wish to divide his land among us—we're five brothers— so I bowed out and took off, went to another village as a son-in-law. But my first wife died young."

"What from?"

"Foolishness. Used to cry, she did, kept crying and crying for no reason, and just withered away. Kept drinking some kind of herbs to get prettier and must have damaged her insides. And my second wife, from Kurilovka—what about her? A village wench, a peasant, nothing more! When they matched me with her, I took a fancy: I thought, she's young, fair-skinned, they live clean. Her mother was something like a flagellant[21] and drank coffee, but the main thing was, they lived clean! So I married the girl, and the next day we sat down to dinner, I told my mother-in-law to give me a spoon, she gave me a spoon, and I see she wipes it with her finger. There you have it, I thought, that's clean for you! I lived with them a year and left. Maybe I should have married a city girl," he went on after a pause. "They say a wife is her husband's helpmeet. I don't need a helpmeet, I'm my own helpmeet, but you'd better talk to me, and not all that blah, blah, blah, but thoroughly, feelingly. Without good talk—what kind of life is it!"

Stepan suddenly fell silent, and at once came his dull, monotonous "Oo-loo-loo-loo." That meant he had seen me.

Masha often went to the mill and evidently found pleasure in conversing with Stepan; Stepan abused the muzhiks so sincerely and with such conviction—and she was attracted to him. Each time she came back from the mill, the peasant simpleton who watched over the orchard shouted at her:

"Wench Palashka! Hi there, wench Palashka!" and barked at her like a dog: "Bow-wow!"

And she would stop and look at him attentively, as if in that simpleton's barking she found an answer to her thoughts, and he probably attracted her as did Stepan's abuse. And at home some news would be waiting for her, such as, for example, that the village geese had trampled our cabbage patch, or that Larion had stolen the reins, and, shrugging her shoulders, she would say with a smile:

"What do you want from these people!"

She was indignant, she was all seething in her soul, and meanwhile I was getting used to the muzhiks and felt more drawn to them. They were mostly nervous, irritated, insulted people; they were people of suppressed imagination, ignorant, with a poor, dull outlook, with ever the same thoughts about the gray earth, gray days, black bread, people who were sly but, like birds, only hid their heads behind a tree—who didn't know how to count. They wouldn't go to your haymaking for twenty roubles, but they would go for a half-bucket of vodka, though for twenty roubles they could buy four buckets. In fact, there was filth, and drunkenness, and stupidity, and deceit, but with all that you could feel, nevertheless, that the muzhiks' life was generally upheld by some strong, healthy core. However much the muzhik looks like a clumsy beast as he follows his plow, and however much he befuddles himself with vodka, still, on looking closer, you feel that there is in him something necessary and very important that is lacking, for instance, in Masha and the doctor—namely, he believes that the chief thing on earth is truth, and that his salvation and that of all people lies in truth alone, and therefore he loves justice more than anything else in the world. I would tell my wife that she saw the spots on the windowpane, but not the windowpane itself; she would say nothing in reply, or start crooning "Oo-loo-loo-loo" like Stepan . . . When this kind, intelligent woman grew pale with indignation and, in a trembling voice, talked with the doctor about drunkenness and deceit, I was puzzled and struck by her forgetfulness. How could she forget that her father, the engineer, also drank, drank a lot, and that the money that had gone to purchase Dubechnya had been acquired by a whole series of brazen, shameless deceptions? How could she forget?

XIV

AND MY SISTER also lived her own life, which she carefully concealed from me. She often whispered with Masha. When I approached her, she shrank back, and her look became guilty, entreating; obviously something was happening in her soul that she was afraid or ashamed of. So as not to meet me somehow in the garden or be left alone with me, she stayed close to Masha all the time, and I rarely had a chance to talk with her, only over dinner.

One evening I was walking slowly through the garden, coming back from the construction site. It was beginning to get dark. Not noticing me, not hearing my footsteps, my sister was walking near an old, spreading apple tree, quite noiselessly, like a phantom. She was dressed in black and walked quickly, along the same line, back and forth, looking at the ground. An apple fell from the tree; she gave a start at the noise, stopped, and pressed her hands to her temples. Just then I came up to her.

In an impulse of tender love that suddenly flooded my heart, in tears, for some reason remembering our mother, our childhood, I put my arms around her shoulders and kissed her.

"What's the matter with you?" I asked. "You're suffering, I've seen it for a long time. Tell me, what's the matter?"

"I'm frightened..." she said, trembling.

"But what's the matter?" I insisted. "For God's sake, be open with me!"

"I will, I will be open with you, I'll tell you the whole truth. Concealing it from you is so hard, so painful! Misail, I'm in love..." she went on in a whisper. "I'm in love, I'm in love... I'm happy, but why am I so frightened?"

There was the sound of footsteps, Dr. Blagovo appeared among the trees in his silk shirt and high boots. Evidently they had arranged a meeting here by the apple tree. Seeing him, she rushed to him impulsively, with a pained cry, as if he was being taken from her:

"Vladimir! Vladimir!"

She pressed herself to him and looked greedily into his face, and only now did I notice how thin and pale she had become recently. It was especially noticeable by her lace collar, which I had long known and which now lay more loosely than ever around her long and slender neck. The doctor became embarrassed but recovered at once and said, smoothing her hair:

"Well, come, come...Why so nervous? You see, I'm here."

We were silent, glancing shyly at each other. Then the three of us walked on, and I heard the doctor say to me:

"Cultured life has not yet begun with us. The old men comfort themselves that if there's nothing now, there was something in the forties or the sixties;[22] that's the old men, but you and I are young, our brains have not yet been touched by *marasmus senilis*, and we cannot comfort ourselves with such illusions. Russia began in the year 862,[23] but cultured Russia, in my understanding, has never yet begun."

But I didn't enter into these reflections. Strange as it was, I didn't want to believe that my sister was in love, that she was now walking and holding this stranger's hand, looking tenderly at him. My sister, this nervous, intimidated, downtrodden, unfree being, loves a man who is already married and has children! I felt sorry about something, precisely what I didn't know; the doctor's presence was now unpleasant for some reason, and I simply couldn't understand what could come of this love of theirs.

XV

MASHA AND I were driving to Kurilovka for the blessing of the school.[24]

"Autumn, autumn, autumn . . ." Masha was saying softly, looking around. "Summer's over. There are no birds, and only the pussywillows are still green."

Yes, summer was over. The days are clear, warm, but the mornings are chilly, the shepherds now go out in sheepskin coats, and in our garden the dew on the asters doesn't dry the whole day. You hear plaintive noises, and there's no telling whether it's a shutter whining on its rusty hinges or the cranes flying—and you feel so good and want so much to live!

"Summer's over . . ." Masha was saying. "Now you and I can sum things up. We've worked a lot, thought a lot, we're the better for it—honor and glory to us—we've succeeded at personal improvement; but did these successes of ours have any noticeable influence on the life around us, were they of any use to anyone? No. The ignorance, the physical filth, the drunkenness, the shockingly high infant mortality—it all remains as it was, and the fact that you plowed and sowed, and I spent money and read books, hasn't made things better for anyone. Obviously we worked only for ourselves and had broad minds only for ourselves."

Such reasoning disconcerted me, and I didn't know what to think.

"We were sincere from beginning to end," I said, "and whoever is sincere is right."

"Who disputes that? We were right, but we did not rightly accomplish what we were right about. First of all, our external methods themselves—aren't they mistaken? You want to be useful to people, but the very fact of your buying an estate precludes from the start all possibility of doing anything useful for them. Then, if you work, dress, and eat like a muzhik, by your own authority you legitimize, as it were, these heavy, clumsy clothes of theirs, their terrible cottages, their stupid beards . . . On the other hand, suppose you work a long time, very long, all your life, and in the end you get some practical results, but what are they, these results of yours, what can they do against such elemental forces as wholesale ignorance, hunger, cold, degeneracy? A drop in the ocean! Other methods of fighting are needed here, strong, bold, quick! If you really want to be useful, leave the narrow circle of ordinary activity and try to act upon the masses as a whole! What's needed first of all is loud, energetic preaching. Why is art—music, for instance—so vital, so popular, and in fact so strong? Because a musician or a singer acts upon thousands at once. Dear, dear art!" she went on, looking dreamily at the sky. "Art gives wings and carries you far, far away! Whoever is sick of filth, of petty pennyworth interests, whoever is outraged, insulted, and indignant, can find peace and satisfaction only in the beautiful."

As we drove up to Kurilovka, the weather was clear, joyful. In some yards the threshing was under way, there was a smell of rye straw. Bright red rowanberries showed behind the wattle fences, and the trees all around, wherever you looked, were all gold or red. Bells were ringing in the bell towers, icons were being carried to the school, and they were singing "The Fervent Intercessor." And how transparent the air, how high the pigeons flew!

A prayer service was held in the schoolroom. Then the Kurilovka peasants presented Masha with an icon, and the Dubechnya peasants with a big plaited bread and a gilded salt cellar. And Masha broke into sobs.

"And if anything unnecessary was said, or there was any displeasure, forgive us," said one old man, and he bowed to her and to me.

As we drove home, Masha kept turning to look back at the

school; the green roof, which I had painted, now glistened in the sun, and we could see it for a long time. And I felt that the glances Masha cast at it now were farewell glances.

XVI

IN THE EVENING she got ready for town.

Lately she had often gone to town and spent the night there. In her absence, I was unable to work, my hands would drop and go weak; our big yard seemed a dull, disgusting wasteland, the orchard rustled angrily, and without her, the house, the trees, the horses were, for me, no longer "ours."

I didn't go anywhere out of the house but kept sitting at her desk, by her bookcase with the books on farming, those former favorites, now no longer needed, looking at me so abashedly. For hours at a time, while it struck seven, eight, nine, while the autumn night, black as soot, was falling outside the windows, I would examine her old glove, or the pen she always wrote with, or her little scissors; I did nothing and was clearly aware that if I had done something before, if I had plowed, mowed, chopped wood, it was only because she wanted it. And if she had sent me to clean a deep well, where I'd have to stand up to my waist in water, I'd have gone into the well, regardless of whether it was necessary or not. But now, when she was not around, Dubechnya, with its decay, unkemptness, banging shutters, thieves by night and by day, seemed to me a chaos in which any work would be useless. And why should I work here, why worry and think about the future, if I felt that the ground was disappearing from under me, that my role here in Dubechnya had been played, in short, that the same lot awaited me as had befallen the books on farming? Oh, what anguish it was at night, in the hours of solitude, when I listened every moment with anxiety, as if waiting for someone to cry out to me that it was time to go. I wasn't sorry for Dubechnya, I was sorry for my love, whose autumn had obviously also come. What enormous happiness it is to love and be loved, and how terrible to feel that you're beginning to fall from that high tower!

Masha came back from town the next day towards evening. She was displeased with something but concealed it, and only asked why all the storm windows had been put in— you could suffocate that way. I removed two of the storm windows. We had no wish to eat, but we sat down and had supper.

"Go and wash your hands," said my wife. "You smell of putty."

She brought new illustrated magazines from town, and we looked at them together after supper. Some had supplements with fashion pictures and patterns. Masha gave them a cursory glance and set them aside in order to give them a separate and proper examination later; but one dress with a wide, smooth, bell-shaped skirt and big sleeves caught her interest, and she looked at it seriously and attentively for a moment.

"That's not bad," she said.

"Yes, that dress would go very well on you," I said. "Very well!"

And, looking at the dress with loving emotion, admiring that gray spot only because she liked it, I went on tenderly:

"A wonderful, charming dress! Beautiful, splendid Masha! My dear Masha!"

And tears dropped on the picture.

"Splendid Masha..." I murmured. "Dear, sweet Masha..."

She went and lay down, and I sat for another hour looking at the illustrations.

"You shouldn't have removed the storm windows," she said from the bedroom. "I'm afraid it will be cold. Look how it's blowing!"

I read here and there in the "miscellany"—about how to make cheap ink, and about the world's biggest diamond. I again came upon the fashion picture of the dress she liked, and I imagined her at a ball, with a fan, bare shoulders, brilliant, magnificent, well versed in music and painting and literature, and how small, how brief, my role seemed to me!

Our meeting, this marriage of ours, was only an episode of which this alive, richly endowed woman would have many in her life. All that was best in the world, as I've already said, was at her disposal and came to her perfectly gratis, and even ideas and fashionable intellectual trends served for her pleasure, diversifying her life, and I was merely a coachman who drove her from one enthusiasm to another. Now she no longer needed me, she would flutter off, and I would be left alone.

And as if in answer to my thoughts, a desperate cry came from the yard:

"He-e-elp!"

It was a shrill woman's voice, and as if wishing to imitate it, the wind in the chimney also howled in a shrill voice. About half a minute went by, and again I heard through the noise of the wind, but as if from the other end of the yard:

"He-e-elp!"

"Misail, do you hear?" my wife asked softly. "Do you hear?"

She came out to me from the bedroom in just her nightgown, her hair undone, and listened, looking at the dark window.

"Somebody's being strangled!" she said. "Just what we needed."

I took a gun and went out. It was very dark in the yard, a strong wind was blowing, so that it was hard to stand. I walked to the gate, listened: the trees rustled, the wind whistled, and in the orchard a dog howled lazily, probably the peasant simpleton's. Beyond the gate it was pitch dark, not a single light on the tracks. And near the wing where the office was last year, there suddenly came a stifled cry:

"He-e-elp!"

"Who's there?" I called.

Two men were fighting. One was pushing the other out, but the other was resisting, and both were breathing heavily.

"Let go!" said one, and I recognized Ivan Cheprakov; it was he who had cried in a shrill woman's voice. "Let go, curse you, or I'll bite your hands all over!"

I recognized the other as Moisei. I pulled them apart and, with that, couldn't help myself and hit Moisei twice in the face. He fell down, then got up, and I hit him once more.

"He wanted to kill me," he muttered. "He was getting at mother's chest... I wish to lock him up in the wing for safety's sake, sir..."

Cheprakov was drunk, didn't recognize me, and kept taking deep breaths, as if gathering air in order to cry "help" again.

I left them and went back to the house; my wife was lying in bed, already dressed. I told her what had happened in the yard and did not even conceal that I had struck Moisei.

"It's frightening to live in the country," she said. "And God in heaven, what a long night!"

"He-e-elp!" the cry came again a little later.

"I'll go and calm them down," I said.

"No, let them bite each other's throats there," she said with a squeamish air.

She was staring at the ceiling and listening, and I was sitting nearby, not daring to start talking with her, feeling as if it was my fault that they were shouting "help" in the yard and that the night was so long.

We were silent, and I waited impatiently for a glow of light in the windows. But Masha looked all the while as if she had just recovered consciousness and was surprised at how it was that she, so intelligent, educated, so neat, could have wound up in this pitiful provincial wasteland, in a gang of petty, worthless people, and how she could have forgotten herself so far that she had even been captivated by one of those people and, for over six months, had been his wife. It seemed to me that it now made no difference to her whether it was me, or Moisei, or Cheprakov; everything had merged for her into this wild, drunken "help"—me, and our marriage, and our farming, and the bad autumn roads; and whenever she sighed or stirred in order to lie more comfortably, I read in her face: "Oh, if only morning would come sooner!"

In the morning she left.

I stayed in Dubechnya for three more days, waiting for her, then put all our things in one room, locked it, and went to town. When I rang at the engineer's, it was already evening, and the streetlamps were lit along our Bolshaya Dvoryanskaya. Pavel told me there was nobody home: Viktor Ivanych had left for Petersburg, and Marya Viktorovna was most likely rehearsing at the Azhogins'. I remember with what agitation I went to the Azhogins', how my heart pounded and sank as I went up the stairs and stood for a long time on the upper landing, not daring to enter that temple of the muses! In the reception room, candles were burning on the little table, the grand piano, and the stage, three of them everywhere, and the first performance had been set for the thirteenth, and now the first rehearsal was on a Monday—a black day. The struggle against superstition! All the amateurs of the scenic art were gathered; the eldest, the middle, and the youngest walked about onstage, reading their roles from notebooks. Apart from them all, Radish stood motionless, his temple leaning against the wall, and gazed at the stage with adoration, waiting for the rehearsal to begin. Everything as it used to be!

I made for the hostess—I had to greet her, but suddenly everyone hissed and waved at me not to stamp my feet. Silence fell. The lid of the grand piano was opened, some lady sat down, narrowing her nearsighted eyes at the score, and my Masha went to the piano, decked out, beautiful, but beautiful in some special new way, not at all like the Masha who used to come to me at the mill in the spring. She began to sing:

"Why do I love thee, radiant night?"[25]

In all the period of our acquaintance, this was the first time I had heard her sing. She had a good, strong, juicy voice, and it seemed to me while she sang that I was eating a ripe, sweet, fragrant melon. Then she finished, there was applause, and she smiled, very pleased, flashing her eyes, leafing through the scores, straightening her dress like a bird that has escaped its cage at last and preens its feathers in freedom. Her hair was brushed over her ears, and her face had an unpleasant, defiant expression, as if she wanted to challenge us all, or yell at us as at horses: "Hey, you, my pretty ones!"

And just then she must have resembled her grandfather the coachman.

"You here, too?" she asked, giving me her hand. "Did you hear me sing? Well, how did you find it?" And, not waiting for my reply, she went on: "It's very opportune that you're here. Tonight I'm going to Petersburg for a short time. Will you let me go?"

At midnight I saw her to the station. She embraced me tenderly, probably grateful that I hadn't asked her any unnecessary questions, and promised to write to me, and I pressed her hands for a long time and kissed them, barely holding back the tears, not saying a word to her.

And when she was gone, I stood watching the receding lights, caressing her in my imagination, and saying softly:

"My dear Masha, splendid Masha . . ."

I spent the night in Makarikha at Karpovna's, and the next morning was already back with Radish, upholstering furniture for some wealthy merchant who was marrying his daughter to a doctor.

XVII

ON SUNDAY AFTER dinner my sister came to see me and we had tea.

"I read a lot now," she said, showing me a book she had taken from the town library on the way to see me. "Thanks to your wife and Vladimir for awakening my self-awareness. They saved me, they made it so that I now feel myself a human being. Before, I used not to sleep at night from various worries: 'Ah, we've used too much sugar this week! Ah, if only I don't oversalt the pickles!' And now I also don't sleep, but I have different thoughts. I suffer that half of my life has been spent so stupidly, so faintheartedly. I despise my past, I'm ashamed of it, and I look at father now as my enemy. Oh, how grateful I am to your wife! And Vladimir? He's such a wonderful man! They've opened my eyes."

"It's not good that you don't sleep at night," I said.

"You think I'm sick? Not a bit. Vladimir auscultated me and said I'm perfectly healthy. But health is not the point, it's not so important . . . Tell me: am I right?"

She was in need of moral support—that was obvious. Masha was gone, Dr. Blagovo was in Petersburg, and besides me there was no one left in town who could tell her she was right. She peered intently into my face, trying to read my secret thoughts, and if I became pensive in her presence and was silent, she took it to her account and grew sad. I had to be on my guard all the time, and when she asked me if she was right, I hastened to reply that she was right and that I deeply respected her.

"You know? They've given me a role at the Azhogins'," she went on. "I want to act on the stage. I want to live; in short, I want to drink from the full cup. I have no talent at all, and the role's only ten lines long, but that's still immeasurably more lofty and noble than pouring tea five times a day and keeping an eye on the cook lest she eat an extra bite. And above all, let father see, finally, that I, too, am capable of protest."

After tea she lay down on my bed and went on lying there for some time with her eyes closed, very pale.

"Such weakness!" she said, getting up. "Vladimir said that all town women and girls are anemic from idleness. What an intelligent man Vladimir is! He's right, infinitely right. One must work!"

Two days later she came to the rehearsal at the Azhogins' with a notebook. She was wearing a black dress with a string of corals around her neck, a brooch that, from a distance, looked like a puff pastry, and big earrings in her ears, with a diamond sparkling in each of them. When I looked at her, I felt awkward: the tastelessness struck me. Others, too, noticed that she was wearing earrings and diamonds inappropriately and was strangely dressed; I saw smiling faces and heard someone say laughingly:

"Cleopatra of Egypt."

She tried to be worldly, unconstrained, at ease, and that made her look affected and strange. Her simplicity and comeliness abandoned her.

"I just announced to father that I was going to a rehearsal," she began, coming up to me, "and he shouted that he was depriving me of his blessing and even all but struck me. Imagine, I don't know my role," she said, looking into her notebook. "I'm sure to get confused. And so the die is cast," she went on in strong agitation. "The die is cast . . ."

It seemed to her that everyone was looking at her and was amazed at the important step she had ventured upon, that everyone expected something special from her, and it was impossible to convince her that nobody paid attention to such small and uninteresting people as she and I.

She had nothing to do till the third act, and her role as a visiting provincial gossip consisted merely in standing by the door as if eavesdropping and then saying a short monologue. Until her appearance, for at least an hour and a half, while there was walking, reading, tea drinking, arguing onstage, she never left my side and kept murmuring her role and clutching her notebook nervously; and, imagining that everyone was looking at her and waiting for her appearance, she kept straightening her hair with a trembling hand and repeating:

"I'm sure to get confused . . . How heavy my heart is, if you only knew! I'm as frightened as if I was about to be led out to execution."

At last her turn came.

"Cleopatra Alexeevna—you're on!" said the director.

She stepped to the middle of the stage with an expression of terror on her face, unattractive, angular, and for half a minute stood there like a post, completely motionless, and only the big earrings swung under her ears.

"You can use the notebook the first time," somebody said.

It was clear to me that she was trembling and, from trembling, could not speak or open her notebook, and that she was past thinking about her role, and I was just about to go to her and say something when she suddenly sank to her knees in the middle of the stage and burst into loud sobs.

There was movement, there was noise all around, I alone stood leaning against the backdrop, struck by what had happened, not understanding, not knowing what I was to do. I saw her being picked up and led away. I saw Anyuta Blagovo come over to me; earlier I hadn't seen her in the room, and now it was as if she had sprung from the ground. She was wearing a hat with a veil and, as always, had the air of having stopped by only for a minute.

"I told her not to act," she said crossly, pronouncing each word abruptly and blushing. "This is madness! You should have stopped her!"

The Azhogin mother, thin and flat, quickly came over to

me, in a short jacket with short sleeves, and with cigarette ashes on her chest.

"My friend, it's terrible," she said, wringing her hands and, as usual, peering intently into my face. "It's terrible! Your sister's condition...she's pregnant! Take her away, I implore you..."

She was breathing heavily from agitation. And to one side stood her three daughters, as thin and flat as she, and huddled timorously together. They were alarmed, astounded, as if a convict had just been caught in their house. What a disgrace, how frightful! And yet this respectable family spent all their lives fighting prejudice; obviously they assumed that all of mankind's prejudices and errors consisted only in three candles, the number thirteen, and the black day—Monday!

"I implore you...implore you..." Mrs. Azhogin repeated, protruding her lips and drawing out the letter O. "I implo-o-ore you, take her home."

XVIII

A LITTLE LATER, my sister and I went down the stairs. I shielded her with the skirt of my coat; we hurried, choosing back lanes where there were no streetlamps, hiding from passersby, and it was like fleeing. She no longer wept but looked at me with dry eyes. To Makarikha, where I was taking her, it was only a twenty-minute walk, and strangely, in so short a time we managed to recall our whole life, we discussed everything, thought over our situation, considered...

We decided it was no longer possible for us to stay in this town, and that when I earned a little money, we would move somewhere else. In some houses people were already asleep, in others they were playing cards; we hated these houses, feared them, and spoke of the fanaticism, the coarseness of heart, the nonentity of these respectable families, these amateurs of dramatic art whom we frightened so much, and I asked how these stupid, cruel, lazy, dishonest people were better than the drunken and superstitious Kurilovka muzhiks, or how they were better than animals, which are also thrown into consternation when some incident disrupts the monotony of their instinct-bound lives. What would become of my sister now, if she went on living at home? What moral suffering would she experience, talking with father, meeting acquaintances every day? I pictured it to myself, and at once people came to my memory, all people of my acquaintance, who were slowly being pushed out of this world by their families and relations, I recalled tortured dogs driven insane, living sparrows plucked bare by little boys and thrown into the water—and the long, long series of obscure, protracted sufferings I had been observing in this town uninterruptedly since childhood; and it was incomprehensible to me what these sixty thousand inhabitants lived by, why they read the Gospel, why they prayed, why they read books and magazines. What benefit did they derive from all that had been written and said so far, if there was in them the same inner darkness and the same aversion to freedom as a hundred or three hundred years ago? A building contractor builds houses in town all his life, and yet till his dying day he says "galdary" instead of "gallery," and so, too, these sixty thousand inhabitants for generations have been reading and hearing about truth, mercy, and freedom, and yet till their dying day they lie from morning to evening, torment each other, and as for freedom, they fear it and hate it like an enemy.

"And so my fate is decided," said my sister when we came home. "After what has happened, I can't go back *there*. Lord, how good that is! I feel easy in my heart."

She went to bed at once. Tears glistened on her lashes, but her expression was happy, her sleep was sound and sweet, and you could see that she really did feel easy in her heart and that she was resting. She hadn't slept like that for a long, long time!

And so we began to live together. She kept singing and saying that she felt very well, and the books we took from the library were returned unread because she could no longer read; all she wanted was to dream and talk about the future. Mending my linen or helping Karpovna at the stove, she either hummed to herself or talked about her Vladimir, about his intelligence, his beautiful manners, his kindness, about his extraordinary learning, and I agreed with her, though I no longer liked her doctor. She wanted to work, to live independently, to support herself, and said she would become a schoolteacher or a doctor's assistant as soon as her health permitted, and would wash the floors and do the laundry herself. She already passionately loved her little boy; he wasn't born yet, but she already knew what sort of eyes he would have, what sort of hands, and how he would laugh. She liked to talk about his upbringing, and since Vladimir was the best man in the world, all her reasoning about upbringing came down to the boy turning out as charming as his father. There was no end to this talk, and everything she said aroused a lively joy in her. Sometimes I, too, rejoiced, not knowing why myself.

She must have infected me with her dreaming. I also read nothing and only dreamed; in the evenings, despite my fatigue, I paced up and down the room, my hands thrust into my pockets, and talked about Masha.

"When do you think she'll come back?" I asked my sister. "I think she'll come back by Christmas, not later. What does she have to do there?"

"Since she doesn't write, she'll obviously come back very soon."

"That's true," I agreed, though I knew perfectly well that there was no need for Masha to come back to our town.

I missed her terribly, and couldn't help deceiving myself,

ANTON CHEKHOV

and tried to get others to deceive me. My sister waited for
her doctor, I for Masha, and the two of us ceaselessly talked,
laughed, and didn't notice that we disturbed the sleep of
Karpovna, who lay on her stove[26] and kept muttering:

"The samovar hummed in the morning, hum-m-m! Ah,
it's a bad sign, dear hearts, a bad sign."

Nobody called on us except the postman, who brought
my sister letters from the doctor, and Prokofy, who would
occasionally come to our room in the evening, look silently
at my sister, leave, and, when already in the kitchen, say:

"Every title should remember its learning, and whoever
doesn't wish to understand that in his pride, it's the vale
for him."

He liked the word "vale." Once—this was already at
Christmastime—as I was going through the market, he
invited me to his butcher shop and, without shaking hands
with me, announced that he had to talk with me about a
very important matter. He was red from the cold and from
vodka; behind the counter next to him stood Nikolka with
his robber's face, holding a bloody knife in his hand.

"I want to express my words to you," Prokofy began.
"This event cannot exist, because you understand yourself
that for such a 'vale' people won't praise either us or you.
Mama, of course, out of pity cannot say an unpleasantness
to you, that your sister should move to other quarters on
account of her condition, but I don't wish it anymore,
because I cannot approve of her behavior."

I understood him and left the shop. The same day my
sister and I moved to Radish's. We had no money for a cab
and went on foot; I carried a bundle of our belongings on
my back, my sister had nothing to carry, but she choked,
coughed, and kept asking how soon we'd get there.

XIX

AT LAST, A LETTER came from Masha.

"My dear, good M.A.," she wrote, "kind, meek 'angel ours,' as the old housepainter calls you, farewell, I'm going to the exposition in America[27] with my father. In a few days I'll be seeing the ocean—so far from Dubechnya, it's frightening to think of it! It's as far and boundless as the sky, and I long to be there, to be free, I'm triumphant, I'm mad, and you see how incoherent my letter is. My dear, my kind one, set me free, quickly break the thread that still holds us, binding me and you. That I met and knew you was a ray from heaven, lighting up my existence; but that I became your wife was a mistake, you understand that, and now the awareness of the mistake weighs on me, and I beg you on my knees, my magnanimous friend, quickly, quickly, before I go off to the ocean, to telegraph that you agree to correct our mutual mistake, to remove this one stone from my wings, and my father, who will take all the bother on himself, promises not to burden you too much with formalities. And so, freedom on all four sides? Yes?

"Be happy, God bless you, forgive me, a sinner.

"I'm alive, I'm well. I squander money, commit many follies, and thank God every moment that such a bad woman as I has no children. I sing and have success, but this isn't a passion, it is my haven, my cell, where I now withdraw to have peace. King David had a ring with the inscription: 'Everything passes.' When one feels sad, these words make one merry, and when one is merry, they make one sad. And I've acquired such a ring for myself, with Hebrew lettering, and this charm will keep me from passions. Everything passes, life, too, will pass, therefore there's no need for anything. Or there is need only for the awareness of freedom, because when a person is free, he needs nothing, nothing,

nothing. So break the thread. I warmly embrace you and your sister. Forgive and forget your M."

My sister lay in one room, Radish, who had been sick again and was now recovering, in the other. Just as I received this letter, my sister quietly went to the painter's room, sat down beside him, and began to read. She read Ostrovsky[28] or Gogol to him every day, and he listened, staring at the same spot, not laughing, shaking his head and muttering to himself from time to time:

"Everything's possible! Everything's possible!"

If something unseemly or ugly happened in the play, he would say, as if gloatingly, jabbing his finger at the book:

"There it is, the lie! That's what it does, the lie!"

Plays attracted him by their content, by their moral, and by their complex, artful construction, and he was amazed at *him*, never calling *him* by name:

"How deftly *he* put it all together!"

Now my sister quietly read only one page and couldn't go on: she didn't have voice enough. Radish took her by the hand and, moving his dry lips, said barely audibly, in a husky voice:

"The soul of the righteous man is white and smooth as chalk, but the sinner's is like pumice. The soul of the righteous man is clear oil, but the sinner's is coal tar. We must labor, we must grieve, we must feel pain," he went on, "and whichever man does not labor or grieve, his will not be the Kingdom of Heaven. Woe, woe to the sated, woe to the strong, woe to the rich, woe to the moneylenders! They will not see the Kingdom of Heaven. Worm eats grass, rust eats iron . . ."

"And lying eats the soul," my sister finished and laughed.

I read over the letter once more. At that moment the soldier came into the kitchen who, twice a week, on the part of some unknown person, brought us tea, French bread, and hazel grouse that smelled of perfume. I was out of work, had to spend whole days at home, and the person who sent us these loaves probably knew we were in need.

I heard my sister talking with the soldier and laughing merrily. Then, lying down, she ate some bread and said to me:

"When you refused to get a job and became a housepainter, Anyuta Blagovo and I knew from the very beginning that you were right, but we were afraid to say it aloud. Tell me, what power keeps us from confessing what we think? Take Anyuta Blagovo. She loves you, she adores you, she knows you're right; she loves me, too, like a sister, and she knows I'm right, and most likely envies me in her soul, yet some power keeps her from coming to us, she avoids us, fears us."

My sister folded her hands on her breast and said with passion:

"How she loves you, if you only knew! She has confessed this love to me alone, and that secretly, in the dark. She used to lead me to a dark alley in the park and start whispering to me how dear you were to her. You'll see, she'll never marry, because she loves you. Are you sorry for her?"

"Yes."

"It's she who sent the bread. Funny girl, really, why hide herself? I was also funny and stupid, but now I've left that behind, and now I'm not afraid of anybody, I think and say aloud whatever I like—and I've become happy. While I lived at home, I had no notion of happiness, but now I wouldn't change places with a queen."

Dr. Blagovo came. He had received his doctor's degree and was now living in our town with his father, resting and saying he would soon leave for Petersburg again. He wanted to work on vaccines against typhus and, I think, cholera; he wanted to go abroad in order to advance himself, and then take a university chair. He had abandoned military service and wore loose Cheviot jackets, very wide trousers, and excellent neckties. My sister was in raptures over his pins, shirt studs, and the red silk handkerchief he wore in the breast pocket of his jacket, probably out of foppishness. Once, having nothing else to do, she and I started counting up all his outfits we could remember, and decided he must have at least ten. It was clear that he still loved my sister, but he never once said, even jokingly, that he would take her with him to Petersburg or abroad, and I could not picture clearly to myself what would become of her if she remained alive, or what would become of her child. But she only dreamed endlessly, without thinking seriously of the future; let him go wherever he liked, she said, let him even abandon her, so long as he himself was happy, and she would be content with what had been.

Usually, when he came to see us, he auscultated her very attentively and demanded that she drink milk with drops in his presence. And this time it was the same. He auscultated her and made her drink a glass of milk, and after that our rooms smelled of creosote.

"There's a good girl," he said, taking the glass from her. "You mustn't talk too much, yet lately you've been chattering away like a magpie. Please keep quiet."

She laughed. Then he came to Radish's room, where I was sitting, and patted me gently on the shoulder.

"Well, how's things, old man?" he asked, bending over the sick man.

"Your Honor . . ." Radish pronounced, slowly moving his lips, "Your Honor, I venture to declare. . . we all walk under God, we'll all have to die . . . Allow me to tell you the truth . . . Your Honor, there'll be no Kingdom of Heaven for you!"

"No help for it," the doctor joked, "somebody has to be in hell as well."

And suddenly something happened to my consciousness; as if I was dreaming, it was winter, night, I was standing in the yard of the slaughterhouse, and beside me was Prokofy, who smelled of pepper vodka; I tried to pull myself together and rubbed my eyes, and it immediately seemed to me that I was going to the governor's for a talk. Nothing like it has ever happened to me either before or since, and I explained this strange, dreamlike remembrance by overexhausted nerves. I experienced the slaughterhouse and the talk with the governor, and at the same time was vaguely aware that it was not real.

When I came to my senses, I saw that I was no longer at home but in the street, and standing with the doctor near a streetlamp.

"It's sad, sad," he was saying, and tears flowed down his cheeks. "She's gay, she's forever laughing, hoping, but her condition is hopeless, dear heart. Your Radish hates me and wants to bring it home to me that I acted badly with her. He's right, in his own way, but I also have my point of view, and I don't regret in the least what has happened. We must love, we all should love—isn't that so?—without love there would be no life; anyone who fears and avoids love is not free."

He gradually passed on to other themes, talked about science, about his thesis, which was liked in Petersburg; he spoke with enthusiasm and no longer remembered my sister, or his grief, or me. He was carried away by life. That one has America and a ring with an inscription, I thought, and this one has his doctoral degree and a scholarly career, and only my sister and I are left with the old things.

After taking leave of him, I went over to the streetlamp and read the letter once more. And I remembered, vividly remembered, how in spring, in the morning, she came to me at the mill, lay down, and covered herself with a sheepskin jacket—she wanted to be like a simple peasant woman. And when, another time—this was also in the morning—we pulled the creel out of the water, and big drops of rain poured down on us from the willows on the bank, and we laughed . . .

It was dark in our house on Bolshaya Dvoryanskaya. I climbed over the fence and, as I used to do in former times, went through the back entrance to the kitchen, to take a lamp there. There was no one in the kitchen; the samovar was hissing by the stove, waiting for my father. "Who pours tea for father now?" I wondered. Taking a lamp, I went to the shed, improvised a bed for myself there out of old newspapers, and lay down. The spikes in the walls looked stern, as before, and their shadows wavered. It was cold. I fancied that my sister was to come now and bring me supper, but I remembered at once that she was ill and lying in Radish's house, and I thought it strange that I had climbed over the fence and was lying in the unheated shed. My mind was confused, and I fancied all sorts of rubbish.

Ringing. Sounds familiar from childhood: first the scraping of the wire against the wall, then a short, pathetic ringing in the kitchen. It was my father coming back from the club. I got up and went to the kitchen. The cook Aksinya, seeing me, clasped her hands and for some reason burst into tears.

"My child!" she said softly. "Dear! Oh Lord!"

And she began crumpling her apron in her hands from agitation. On the windowsill stood quart bottles with berries and vodka. I poured myself a teacupful and greedily drank it off, because I was very thirsty. Aksinya had only recently washed the tables and benches, and there was the smell of a bright, cozy kitchen kept by a neat cook. And once, in our childhood, this smell and the chirping of a cricket used to entice us children here to the kitchen and disposed us to fairy tales, to playing kings . . .

"And where is Cleopatra?" Aksinya asked softly, hurriedly, with bated breath. "And where's your hat, dearie? And they say your wife has gone to Petersburg?"

She had served us back in my mother's time, and used to bathe me and Cleopatra in a tub, and for her now we were still children who needed admonishing. In a quarter of an hour or so, she laid out for me all her considerations, which she, with the reasonableness of an old servant, had accumulated in the quiet of this kitchen all the while we hadn't seen each other. She said that the doctor could be made to marry Cleopatra—all we needed was to give him a scare, and if the petition was written properly, the bishop would annul his first marriage; that it would be good to sell Dubechnya in secret from my wife and put the money in the bank under my own name; and if my sister and I bowed down at my father's feet and begged him properly, he might forgive us; that a prayer service should be offered to the Queen of Heaven...

"Well, go, dearie, talk to him," she said, hearing my father cough. "Go and talk to him, bow to him, your head won't fall off."

I went. Father was sitting at the table drawing up the plan for a summer house with Gothic windows and a fat turret that resembled a fire tower—something extraordinarily obstinate and giftless. Going into his study, I stopped in such a way that I was able to see this drawing. I didn't know why I had come to my father, but I remember that, when I saw his fleshless face, his red neck, his shadow on the wall, I wanted to throw myself on his neck and, as Aksinya had instructed me, bow down at his feet; but the sight of the summer house with its Gothic windows and fat turret held me back.

"Good evening," I said.

He glanced at me and at once lowered his eyes to his drawing.

"What do you want?" he asked after a pause.

"I've come to tell you—my sister is very ill. She will die soon," I added in a muted voice.

"Well, then?" my father sighed, taking off his spectacles and putting them on the table. "As you sow, so shall you reap. As you sow," he repeated, getting up from the table, "so shall you reap. I ask you to remember how you came to me two years ago, and in this very same place I begged you, I implored you to abandon your errors, reminding you of duty, honor, and your responsibility to your ancestors, whose traditions we should sacredly preserve. Did you obey me? You scorned my advice and stubbornly went on holding to your wrong views; what's more, you dragged your sister into your errors as well and caused her to lose her morality and shame. Now you've both gotten into a bad way. Well, then? As you sow, so shall you reap!"

He was saying this and pacing the study. He probably thought I had come to him to acknowledge my guilt, and he probably expected me to start interceding for myself and my sister. I was cold, I was trembling as in a fever, and I spoke with difficulty, in a hoarse voice.

"And I, too, ask you to remember," I said, "how in this same place I implored you to understand me, to think, to decide together how we should live and for what, and in response you began talking about our ancestors, about our grandfather who wrote poetry. You have now been told that your only daughter is hopelessly ill, and again you talk about ancestors, traditions... And such light-mindedness in old age, when death is not far off, when you have some five or ten years left to live!"

"What have you come here for?" my father asked sternly, obviously offended that I had reproached him for light-mindedness.

"I don't know. I love you, I'm inexpressibly sorry that we are so distant from each other—and so I've come. I still love you, but my sister has broken with you definitively. She doesn't forgive and will never forgive. Your name alone arouses loathing in her for the past, for this life."

"And who is to blame?" my father cried. "You yourself are to blame, you scoundrel!"

"Yes, let me be to blame," I said. "I confess, I'm to blame in many ways, but why is this life of yours, which you also consider obligatory for us—why is it so dull, so giftless, why is it that there are no people in any one of these houses you've been building for thirty years now from whom I could learn how to live so as not to be to blame? Not a single honest man in the whole town! These houses of yours are cursed nests in which mothers and daughters are pushed out of this world, children are tortured... My poor mother!" I went on desperately. "My poor sister! You have to stupefy yourself with vodka, cards, gossip, you have to fawn, play the hypocrite, or spend decade after decade drawing plans, to ignore all the horror hidden in these houses. Our town has existed for hundreds of years, and in all that time it hasn't given our motherland a single useful man—not one! You've stifled in the womb everything that had the least bit of life or brightness! A town of shopkeepers, tavern keepers, clerks, hypocrites, a needless, useless town, for which not a single soul would be sorry if it suddenly sank into the earth."

"I do not wish to listen to you, you scoundrel!" said my father and picked up the ruler from the table. "You're drunk! You dare not appear this way before your father! I tell you for the last time, and you tell it to your immoral sister, that you will get nothing from me. I have torn my disobedient children out of my heart, and if they suffer from their disobedience and stubbornness, I am not sorry for them. You can go back where you came from! God has been pleased to punish me with you, but I endure this test with humility and, like Job, find consolation in suffering and continual toil. You must not cross my threshold until you mend your ways. I am a just man, everything I say is useful, and if you want good for yourself, then you should remember all your life what I have said and am saying to you."

I waved my hand and left. After that, I don't remember what happened during the night and the next day.

They say I walked the streets hatless, staggering, and singing loudly, and that crowds of boys followed me and shouted: "Small Profit! Small Profit!"

XX

IF I HAD THE desire to order myself a ring, I would choose this inscription: "Nothing passes." I believe that nothing passes without a trace and that each of our smallest steps has significance for the present and the future.

What I have lived through has not gone in vain. My great misfortunes, my patience, have touched the hearts of the townspeople, and they no longer call me "Small Profit," they don't laugh at me, and when I go through the market, they no longer pour water on me. They've grown used to my being a workman, and see nothing odd in the fact that I, a nobleman, carry buckets of paint and put in windowpanes; on the contrary, they willingly give me orders, and I'm now considered a good craftsman and the best contractor after Radish, who, though he has recovered from his illness and, as always, paints the cupolas of bell towers without scaffolding, is no longer able to manage his boys; in place of him, I run around town and look for orders, I hire and pay the boys, I borrow money at high interest. And now, having become a contractor, I understand how it's possible, for the sake of a pennyworth job, to run around town for three days hunting up roofers. People are polite to me, they address me formally, and I'm treated to tea in the houses I work in, and they send to ask if I'd like to have dinner. Children and young girls often come and look at me with curiosity and sadness.

Once I was working in the governor's garden, painting

the gazebo in false marble. The governor, strolling, came into the gazebo and, having nothing to do, began talking to me, and I reminded him of how he had once invited me for a talk. He peered into my face for a moment, then formed his lips into an O, spread his arms, and said:

"I don't remember!"

I've aged, become silent, stern, severe, I rarely laugh, and they say I've come to resemble Radish and, like him, bore the boys with my useless admonitions.

Marya Viktorovna, my former wife, now lives abroad, and her father the engineer is building a railway somewhere in the eastern provinces and buying up estates there. Dr. Blagovo is also abroad. Dubechnya has gone back to Mrs. Cheprakov, who bought it after negotiating with the engineer for a twenty percent discount. Moisei now goes about in a bowler hat; he often comes to town in a racing droshky on business of some sort and stops near the bank. They say he has already bought himself an estate with a transfer of mortgage, and constantly inquires at the bank about Dubechnya, which he also intends to buy. Poor Ivan Cheprakov loitered around town for a long time, doing nothing and drinking. I attempted to introduce him to our work, and for a time he painted roofs with us, put in windowpanes, and even developed a taste for it and, like a real housepainter, stole drying oil, asked for tips, and drank. But he soon got sick of the work and went back to Dubechnya, and later the boys confessed to me that he had incited them to go with him one night to kill Moisei and rob the general's widow.

My father has aged greatly, become bent, and at night strolls about near his house. I never visit him.

During a cholera epidemic, Prokofy treated the shopkeepers with pepper vodka and tar, and took money for it, and, as I learned from our newspaper, was punished with a flogging because he sat in his butcher shop and spoke badly of doctors. His assistant, Nikolka, died of cholera. Karpovna is still alive and still loves and fears her Prokofy. Seeing me, she shakes her head woefully each time and says with a sigh:

"It'll be your head!"

On weekdays I'm usually busy from early morning till evening. But on feast days, if the weather is good, I take my little niece in my arms (my sister had hoped for a boy but gave birth to a girl) and walk unhurriedly to the cemetery. There I stand or sit, and look for a long time at the dear grave, and tell the girl that her mama lies there.

Sometimes I find Anyuta Blagovo by the grave. We greet each other and stand silently, or talk about Cleopatra, about her girl, and about how sad it is to live in this world. Then, leaving the cemetery, we walk silently, and she slows her steps—on purpose, in order to spend a longer time walking with me. The girl, joyful, happy, squinting from the bright daylight, laughs and reaches her little arms out to her, and we stop and together caress the dear girl.

But when we come to town, Anyuta Blagovo, worrying and blushing, takes leave of me and continues walking alone, staid, stern. And none of those we meet, looking at her, would think that she had just been walking beside me and had even caressed the child.

1896

NOTES

THE STEPPE

1. Collegiate secretary was tenth in the table of fourteen civil administrative ranks, numbered from highest to lowest, established in 1722 by the emperor Peter the Great (1672–1725), equivalent to the military rank of lieutenant.

2. That is, July 8, feast day of the wonder-working icon of the Mother of God, which, according to tradition, appeared or was discovered in the city of Kazan in 1579.

3. A kulich (pl. kulichi) is a special bread traditionally baked in Russia for Easter.

4. Mikhail Vassilievich Lomonosov (1711–65), the son of a fisherman, born in Deniskovo (now Lomonosov) on the White Sea, went to Petersburg on foot at an early age to enroll in the Imperial Academy of Sciences, founded by Peter the Great. He became a poet, chemist, astronomer, and founder of Moscow State University, now named after him.

5. That is, the emperor Alexander I (1777–1825), defeater of Napoleon and savior of Russia, known popularly as "the Blessed." His name day is August 30.

6. The "Cherubic Hymn" is sung during the Orthodox liturgy while the elements of the eucharist are being prepared to be carried to the altar.

7. Kathismas are daily readings from the Psalms, read while seated (from the Greek *kathizo*, to sit).

8. The Molokans are a Bible-centered sect that arose in Russia during the seventeenth century in protest against the official Orthodox Church and still persists in Russia and America. The name comes from the Russian word for milk *(moloko)*, because the sectarians refused to abstain from milk during fast periods.

9. The fig is a contemptuous gesture (*figue* in French, *fica* in Italian) made by inserting the thumb between the first and second fingers of the fist; in Russia it has been developed in various specific forms: the fig under the nose, the fig with butter, the fig in the pocket.

10. The biblical patriarch Jacob (Genesis 25:26–47:28) was the father of twelve sons and one daughter; his favorite son was Joseph, at whose supposed death he "rent his clothes, and put sackcloth upon his loins, and mourned for . . . many days" (Genesis 37:34).

11. The zemstvo was a local assembly for provincial self-government instituted by the legal reforms of the emperor Alexander II in 1864 and abolished by the 1917 revolution.

12. A popular Russian custom to protect against the inhalation of demons.

13. "Khokhly" (singular "khokhól") is a local Russian name for Ukrainians, from the word for the topknot characteristic of Ukrainian men.

14. Ilya Muromets and Nightingale the Robber are epic heroes from the anonymous medieval Russian poems known as byliny.

15. A popular distortion of the name of Saint George.

16. That is, Saint Barbara, a martyr of the third century and patron saint of artillerymen.

17. In an Orthodox church, the iconostasis, a partition with three doors and decorated with icons, separates the sanctuary from the main body of the church.

18. A prosphora is a small round loaf of leavened bread, offered by the faithful and blessed by the priest, a portion of which is incorporated into the sacrament of the eucharist.

19. Kasha, a preparation of boiled grain, is one of the staples of the Russian diet.

20. The feast of Theophany, known in the West as Epiphany, commemorates Christ's baptism in the Jordan. It falls on January 6.

21. There was a schism in the Russian Orthodox Church following the reforms instituted by the patriarch Nikon in the seventeenth century. Those who rejected the reforms came to be known as Old Believers; they were (and are) generally conservative and of strict behavior, and avoid contacts with the Orthodox.

22. The feast of Saints Peter and Paul falls on June 29.

23. In Ukrainian the common noun *mazepa* means "boor." It was also the proper name or nickname of a hetman of the Ukrainian Cossacks (1644–1709), who first served Peter the Great, then turned against him and joined Charles XII of Sweden. When Charles was defeated at the battle of Poltava, Mazepa (or Mazeppa) fled to Turkey.

24. Egorushka whispers the first words of the hymn from the Anaphora (the "offering up") in the Orthodox liturgy.

25. Peter Mogila (1596–1646), a Moldavian nobleman who, after studying in Paris, returned home to become an Orthodox monk and eventually the metropolitan of Kiev, reformed theological scholarship and wrote a highly influential *Orthodox Catechism*.

26. The quotation is from Saint Paul's epistle to the Hebrews (13:9).

27. Frightened by the host of the Philistines, King Saul sought help from the witch of Endor, who called up the spirit of the dead prophet Samuel (I Samuel 28: 7–25).

28. Saint Basil the Great (329–79), bishop of Caesarea and one of the most important fathers of the Orthodox Church, studied in the platonic Academy of Athens. Saint Nestor the Chronicler (1056–1114), of the Monastery of the Caves in Kiev, probably one of the first Russian chroniclers, also wrote the lives of Saints Boris and Gleb and of Saint Theodosius, one of the founders of the monastery and therefore of Russian monasticism.

THE DUEL

1. Russian civil servants had official uniforms similar to the military.

2. State councillor was the fifth in the table of ranks (see note 1 to *The Steppe*). Only those of the fourth rank and higher, which conferred hereditary nobility, were entitled to be called "Your Excellency."

3. Ivan Turgenev (1818–83) introduced this term in his *Diary of a Superfluous Man* (1850); it came to typify intellectuals from the 1840s to the '60s,

but by Laevsky's time was rather out-dated. The eponymous hero of *Evgeny Onegin* (1823–30), a novel in verse by Alexander Pushkin (1799–1837); Chatsky, the protagonist of the comedy *Woe from Wit*, by Alexander Griboedov (1795–1829); and Pechorin, the protagonist of the novel *A Hero of Our Time* (1840), by Mikhail Lermontov (1814–41), were precursors of Turgenev's character, as were some of Byron's heroes.

4. Herbert Spencer (1820–1903) was an influential British philosopher who applied the theory of evolution to social life in a doctrine sometimes known as Social Darwinism.

5. Nevsky Prospect is the central thoroughfare of Petersburg, very popular for strolling and being seen, and the subject of much literature, most notably the story "Nevsky Prospect," by Nikolai Gogol (1809–52).

6. Vasily V. Vereshchagin (1842–1904), a soldier and traveler as well as an eminent painter, was best known for his military canvases, which portrayed the brutality rather than the glory of war. He was killed in the Russo-Japanese war.

7. The Order of Saint Vladimir was established by the empress Catherine the Great (1729–96) in 1792, in honor of Grand Prince Vladimir (960–1015), who converted Russia to Christianity in 988. It was both a civil and a military order; the military form of the decoration had a cross with crossed swords and a black and red bow.

8. See note 11 to *The Steppe*.

9. See note 3 above. Bazarov is the hero of Turgenev's novel *Fathers and Children* (1862) and the first "nihilist" in Russian literature.

10. The German philosopher Arthur Schopenhauer (1788–1860) was one of the greatest and most influential thinkers of the nineteenth century. His major work is *The World As Will and Representation* (1818).

11. The distinguished University of Dorpat, now Tartu, the second largest city of Estonia, was founded in 1632 by Gustavus II of Sweden. After many vicissitudes, it was reopened in 1802 under a charter from the Russian emperor Alexander I (the territory then being annexed to Russia), with German as its language of instruction.

12. In the Orthodox Church, a metro-politan is a bishop who oversees a large ecclesiastical territory known as a metropolis. He ranks above an archbishop and below a patriarch.

13. In Russia, a dacha can be anything from a large summer house to a rented room in the country or at the seashore, but the "dacha season," from June to August, with its long nights, also implies a special form of social life, with visits, evening parties, theatricals, and so on.

14. A dukhan is a tavern run by local Caucasian people who were traditionally Muslim but catered to the tastes of their Russian rulers.

15. A hieromonk is an Orthodox monk who is also a priest.

16. Baba Yaga, the fearsome witch of Russian fairy tales, lives in a hut on chicken's legs that spins round and round when someone approaches it.

17. A famous passage from Canto 3 of Pushkin's long poem *Poltava* (1829), beginning: "Quiet is the Ukrainian night . . ."

18. An archimandrite is the superior of an Orthodox monastery. A bishop traditionally wears a mitre and a panagia ("all-holy" in Greek, an icon of the Mother of God with the child Christ on a chain around the neck) and blesses the

faithful with a double candlestick (dikíri) in one hand, signifying the two natures of Christ, and a triple candlestick (trikíri) in the other, signifying the three persons of the Trinity. During the liturgy, he speaks the line Chekhov quotes here, after which the choir sings the trisagion (the "thrice holy" supplication: "Holy God, Holy Mighty, Holy Immortal, have mercy on us!").

19. A line from Pushkin's *Evgeny Onegin*, Chapter 1, Stanza XVI.

20. See note 9 to *The Steppe*.

21. Words from the Orthodox funeral or memorial service ("Give rest, O Lord, to the soul of thy servant who has fallen asleep").

22. The Welsh-born journalist Henry Morton Stanley (1841–1904), who was sent as a *New York Times* reporter to find the famous Scottish explorer of Africa, David Livingstone (1813–73), who had not been heard from for five years and was presumed dead. Stanley set out with his expedition in 1869 and in 1871 found Dr. Livingstone, frail but alive.

23. A phrase ultimately derived from an episode in Plutarch's life of Caesar. As the young Caesar was crossing the Alps on his way to Spain, he passed through a wretched village inhabited by a few half-starved people. When his companions began to make fun of them, Caesar replied: "For my part, I had rather be the first man among these fellows than the second man in Rome."

24. Count Alexei A. Arakcheev (1769–1834), Russian soldier and statesman, was entrusted by the emperor Paul I (1754–1801) with the reform of the army, a task he carried out with notoriously ruthless discipline.

25. A reference to the Gospels: "And whosoever shall offend one of these little ones that believe in me, it is better for him that a millstone were hanged about his neck, and he were cast into the sea" (Mark 9:42; see also Matthew 18:6).

26. The litanies of the Orthodox liturgy include a petition "for a good defense before the dread Judgment Seat of Christ" at the Last Judgment.

27. Rudin, a restless, ineffectual idealist of the 1840s, is the hero of the novel of the same name (1856) by Ivan Turgenev (see note 3 above). He is killed on the barricades in Paris during the revolution of 1848.

28. Nikolai Leskov (1831–95), one of the greatest masters of Russian prose, published his "Legend of the Conscientious Danila" in 1888.

29. See the epistle of James 2:17: "Even so faith, if it hath not works, is dead, being alone," and Paul's epistle to the Galatians 2:16: "a man is not justified by the works of the law, but by the faith of Jesus Christ."

30. The Peter-and-Paul fortress, the oldest building in Petersburg, was a prison of formidable reputation, reserved mainly for political criminals.

31. The lines are from the poem "Remembrance" (1828).

32. See I Samuel 18:7: "Saul hath slain his thousands, and David his ten thousands."

THE STORY OF AN UNKNOWN MAN

1. The German title *Kammerjunker* ("gentleman of the bedchamber") was adopted by the Russian imperial court.

2. The Eliseev brothers founded a famous delicatessen on Nevsky Prospect in

Petersburg, which is still there and still
called Eliseevs'.

3. See note 5 to *The Duel*. Gogol is the
premier satirist (though much more than
a satirist) of Russian literature. M. E.
Saltykov (1826–89), who wrote under
the name of N. Shchedrin, was a radical
publicist most famous for his condensed
satirical history of Russia, *The History of
a Certain Town* (1869–70); the name of
the town is Glupov, i.e., "Stupidville."

4. Actual state councillor was second in the
table of ranks (see note 1 to *The Steppe*),
equivalent to the military rank of
general. The title conferred hereditary
nobility on its holder.

5. See note 5 to *The Duel*.

6. The Senate was not only a legislative
body but also the highest court of law in
imperial Russia.

7. Three young writers, Count Alexei K.
Tolstoy (1817–75) and his cousins Alexei
M. Zhemchuzhnikov (1821–1908) and
Vladimir M. Zhemchuzhnikov
(1830–84), invented the absurdly funny
writer Kozma Prutkov, and in his name
and style wrote verses, aphorisms ("fruits
of pondering"), and a project for the
introduction of unified thinking in
Russia.

8. A line from Pushkin's *Evgeny Onegin*,
Chapter 6, Stanza XXI, in which the
young poet Lensky ponders the future
(and Pushkin parodies bad romantic
poetry) before his fatal duel with
Onegin (see note 3 to *The Duel*).

9. The *Académie française* was founded in
1650 by Cardinal Richelieu for the
purpose of establishing a dictionary of
the French language. Its members,
chosen from among distinguished
literary figures, are known as immortals.

10. Diogenes of Synope was a Greek Cynic
philosopher of the fourth century B.C. It

is not clear what "perversity" is meant
here.

11. Marcus Cato the Elder (234–149 B.C.)
was a man of the strictest habits and diet,
but did indeed marry a young girl after
his wife's death. The story is told in
Plutarch's life of Cato.

12. A jumbled allusion to the Orthodox
marriage service, which includes in the
prayer for the married couple: "Grant
them of the fruit of their bodies, fair
children, concord of soul and of body;
exalt them like the cedars of Lebanon,
like a luxuriant vine."

13. Church Slavonic is the language of the
Russian and other Slavic Orthodox
Churches, derived from Old Bulgarian.

14. Margarete (Gretchen) is the young girl
who is seduced and abandoned by Faust
in the monumental two-part drama
Faust (1808, 1832), by the German poet
Johann Wolfgang von Goethe
(1749–1833).

15. See note 3 to *The Duel*.

16. Orlov is referring to Insarov, hero of
Turgenev's novel *On the Eve* (1860),
who goes to help liberate the Bulgarians
from Turkish rule but dies before he gets
there.

17. The German philosopher Eduard von
Hartmann (1842–1906) published his
major work, *The Philosophy of the
Unconscious (Philosophie des Unbewussten)*,
in 1869. It was widely read and introduced the notion of the unconscious
into intelligent conversation.

18. An adapted quotation from Act III,
Scene iii, of *Woe from Wit* (see note 3 to
The Duel), in which the smarmy young
wooer Molchalin says to Chatsky: "At
my age I should not dare my own
judgment to bear."

19. Camille Saint-Saëns (1835–1921) wrote
"The Swan" (*Le cygne*) for his *Carnival of
Animals*, of which it was the only part

published in his lifetime. Originally scored for the double bass, it has been adapted for cello, violin, flute, guitar, and piano solo. It was choreographed as "The Dying Swan" by Mikhail Fokine in 1905.

20. See Judges 16:3: "And Samson lay till midnight, and arose at midnight, and took the doors of the gate of the city, and the two posts, and went away with them, bar and all, and put them upon his shoulders, and carried them up to the top of an hill that is before Hebron."

21. See Genesis 1:26: "And God said, Let us make man in our image, after our likeness."

22. The episode occurs in part one, chapter 13, of *The Humiliated and the Injured* (1861) by Fyodor Dostoevsky (1821–81).

23. See Luke 23:39–43, where one of the two thieves crucified with Christ turns to Him and says: "Lord, remember me when thou comest into thy kingdom. And Jesus said unto him, Verily I say unto thee, Today shalt thou be with me in paradise."

24. *Le Père Goriot* (1835) is one of the major novels from the series *La comédie humaine*, by Honoré de Balzac (1799–1850). Zinaida Fyodorovna quotes the words of the novel's hero, the penniless young Rastignac, at the very end of the novel.

25. Antonio Canova (1757–1822) was the greatest Italian neoclassical sculptor.

26. Marino Faliero (1274–1355), from an illustrious Venetian family that supplied the city with several doges, was himself made doge in 1354. Caught up in a plot to assassinate the nobles and establish himself as dictator, he was tried by the Council of Ten and decapitated. He is the only one of the seventy-six doges of Venice whose portrait has been removed from the wall of the Sala del Maggior

Consiglio in the ducal palace on Saint Mark's Square.

27. See note 3 to *The Duel*.

28. A line from a popular song, probably about the battle of Poltava in 1709 (see note 23 to *The Steppe*).

29. Orlov paraphrases two lines from Act I, Scene ix, of *Woe from Wit*: "What a chore, O Creator, to be the father of a grown-up daughter!"

THREE YEARS

1. See note 13 to *The Duel*.

2. See note 22 to *The Steppe*.

3. *Anton the Wretch* (1846) is a short novel by D. V. Grigorovich (1822–99) depicting peasant life in the darkest colors.

4. The valet Matvei consoles Stiva Oblonsky with this phrase at the very beginning of Tolstoy's *Anna Karenina* (1877).

5. See note 18 to *The Steppe*.

6. *The Bells of Corneville* (also known in English as *The Chimes of Normandy*) is a comic operetta by the French composer Robert Planquette (1848–1903), first performed in Paris at the Théâtre des Folies Dramatiques in April 1877 and in New York at the Fifth Avenue Theater in October of the same year.

7. The imam Shamil (1796–1871) was the leader of a jihad against the Russians among the mountaineers of Dagestan and Chechnya that lasted for twenty-five years.

8. See note 3 to *The Story of an Unknown Man*. Porphyry Golovlyov, known as "Iudushka" or "Little Judas," the second son in Shchedrin's only novel, *The Golovlyov Family* (1876), is an unctuous hypocrite and moral torturer.

9. A kamilavka is a stiff upright hat awarded to Russian Orthodox priests and archpriests as a token of merit.

10. An akathist (from the Greek *akathizo*, "standing up") is a special canticle sung in honor of Christ, the Mother of God, or one of the saints.

11. The prayer "Many Years," asking for a peaceful life, health, salvation, prosperity in all things, and many years, is sung for specific persons on such occasions as baptism, marriage, birthdays, and so on.

12. See I Samuel 16:4–5.

13. Anton Rubinstein (1829–94) was a Russian pianist, composer, and conductor and cofounder of the Petersburg Conservatory.

14. Guerrier courses were higher courses in the humanities for women, first offered through Moscow University in 1872; they were later expanded into a three-year university program.

15. Jacob Becker built fine pianos in Petersburg, starting in 1841.

16. The Iverskaya Chapel, at the Voskresensky Gate on Red Square in Moscow, housed a copy—made in 1648 at the request of the tsar Alexei Mikhailovich (1629–76)—of a wonder-working icon known as the Iverskaya Mother of God, thought to have been painted in Byzantium in the eighth century and kept in the Iveron ("Iberian") Monastery on Mount Athos. One of the holiest sites in Moscow, the chapel was demolished in Soviet times and replaced by a statue of a worker, but was rebuilt in 1999.

17. *The Maid of Orleans (Die Jungfrau von Orleans)* is a romantic tragedy about Joan of Arc, written in 1801 by the German poet and playwright Friedrich Schiller (1759–1805). Marya N. Ermolova (1853–1928) was one of the most famous Russian actresses of her time.

18. See Genesis 3:19, God's punishment of Adam: "In the sweat of thy face shalt thou eat bread, till thou return unto the ground."

19. Ivan Shishkin (1832–98) was a Russian painter who belonged to the group known as Peredvizhniki ("Itinerants") because they jointly organized itinerant exhibitions of their work. He was chiefly a painter of forest scenes.

20. The Orthodox feast of the Elevation of the Cross is celebrated on September 14.

21. Yaroslav (980–1054), grand prince of Kiev, was the son of Vladimir I (see note 7 to *The Duel*). Vladimir II Monomakh (1053–1125), grand prince of Kiev, was the grandson of Yaroslav.

22. Pimen is the monk-chronicler in Pushkin's tragedy *Boris Godunov* (1831). Pimen's monologue in the scene "Night: A Cell in the Chudovo Monastery, 1603" is one of the most famous passages from the play.

23. The Kumans, called Polovtsi in Russia, were a nomadic East Turkic people who invaded southern Russia in the eleventh century and fought with the Kievan princes. They were eventually defeated by the eastern Slavs and were crushed definitively by the invading Mongols in 1245.

24. A memorial service *(panikhida)* for a dead person is traditionally served on the ninth, twentieth, and fortieth days following the death.

25. Dulcinea is Don Quixote's name for the peasant girl whom he idealizes as his chivalric lady love in Cervantes's novel.

26. Rassudina crudely rephrases a remark made by Chatsky in Act III, Scene iii, of Griboedov's *Woe from Wit* (see note 3 to *The Duel*).

27. A reference to the poem "The Dream" (1841) by Mikhail Lermontov (see note 3 to *The Duel*), about a soldier who dies

in the battle of Dargo, in which the imam Shamil delivered a crushing defeat to the Russian forces under General Vorontsov (see note 7 above).

28. See note 4 to *The Story of an Unknown Man*.

29. Grigory Lukyanovich Skuratov-Belsky (?–1573), known as Malyuta Skuratov, was the right-hand man of the tsar Ivan the Terrible (1530–84), who made him head of the Oprichnina, a special force opposed to the nobility, which terrorized Russia, burning, pillaging, and murdering many people.

30. That is, the Chicago World's Fair of 1893, known officially as the World's Columbian Exposition.

MY LIFE

1. Borodino was the scene of the first pitched battle between the Russians under General Kutuzov and the French under Napoleon, fought on September 7, 1812. It ended in a draw, with heavy casualties on both sides.

2. Marshal of the nobility was the highest elective office among the Russian nobility before the reforms of the 1860s.

3. Collegiate assessor was eighth of the fourteen civil ranks in Russia (see note 1 to *The Steppe*), equivalent to the military rank of major.

4. There were seven classes in the Russian gymnasium, or high school, the seventh being the last.

5. In the Book of Daniel, I:6–7, the names of Daniel's three companions— Hananiah, Mishael, and Azariah— are changed by the prince of King Nebuchadnessar's eunuchs to Shadrach, Meshach, and Abednego. Mishael (Misail in Slavonic) is a name often

adopted by Orthodox monks, but highly unusual and pretentious as a given name (Cleopatra is only slightly less so).

6. In Russian, a duma is a representative body, in this case a municipal assembly.

7. That is, the two-week fast preceding the feast of Saints Peter and Paul on June 29.

8. At the end of Gogol's comedy *Revizor* ("The Inspector General"), which opened in April 1836, the governor in his final monologue looks out at the audience and says he sees "pig snouts" instead of human faces.

9. Batu Khan (c. 1205–55), grandson of Genghis Khan, invaded southern Russia and by 1240 was in control of the Kievan principality. His territory, known as the Kipchak khanate and in Russia as the Golden Horde, had its seat in Saray on the lower Volga.

10. See note 17 to *The Steppe*.

11. See Luke 16:9, Christ's reproach to the Pharisees: "And I say unto you, Make to yourselves friends of the mammon of unrighteousness; that, when ye fail, they may receive you into everlasting habitations."

12. The deceased peasant (or "dead soul") Pyotr Saveliev Disrespect-Trough is mentioned in Volume One, Chapter 7, of Gogol's novel-poem *Dead Souls* (1842).

13. In imperial Russia, seminaries were often the only schools open to the children of poorer tradesmen and peasants, who would attend them without necessarily preparing for a clerical career. Seminaries acquired a reputation for being coarse, rowdy, and half educated. Many nineteenth- and twentieth-century Russian revolutionaries were former seminarians, among them Joseph Stalin.

14. That is, Theophany (see note 20 to *The Steppe*).

15. The decoration of the Order of Saint Vladimir (see note 7 to *The Duel*), worn on a ribbon around the neck.

16. Saint Thomas's Sunday is the first Sunday after Easter. Marriages were not performed during the fifty days preceding Easter, comprising the forty days of Lent and Holy Week; thus, they were married as soon as possible after Easter.

17. See note 11 to *The Steppe*.

18. The Pechenegs were Turkic nomads who inhabited the lower Volga region in the eighth and ninth centuries. Driven west by the Kumans, they settled in the southern Ukraine, where they harassed the Kievan principality. In 1061 they even besieged Constantinople, where they were virtually annihilated by the emperor Alexis I.

19. Bast, the inner bark of the linden, is a fiber used by Russian peasants to make shoes, mats, and so on.

20. A kulak is a rich and, by implication, tight-fisted peasant (the word "kulak" means "fist").

21. The sect of the flagellants ("khlysty") emerged among Russian peasants in the seventeenth century. Its adherents practiced self-flagellation as a means of purification from sin. Both the sect and the practice were condemned by the Church.

22. Among the Russian intelligentsia, the 1840s were the period of liberal idealism, the 1860s the period of radical nihilism.

23. The year that the Varangian chief Rurik (d. 879), founder of the first dynasty of Russian tsars, settled in Novgorod.

24. It was customary to hold a prayer service in any new building (or old building with new inhabitants) and bless the rooms with the sprinkling of holy water.

25. The romance "Night," by Pyotr Ilyich Tchaikovsky (1840–93), to words by the poet Yakov Polonsky (1819–98).

26. The mud stove of Russian peasant cottages was (and is) an elaborate construction that includes a shelf for sleeping. Old people commonly slept on the stove, it being the warmest place in the house.

27. See note 30 to *Three Years*.

28. Alexander Ostrovsky (1823–96) was the most prolific Russian playwright of his time, author of dramatic chronicles, the poetic folk play *Snegurochka*, and numerous realistic/satirical dramas set among the merchant class.

ABOUT THE TRANSLATORS

RICHARD PEVEAR has published translations of Alain, Yves Bonnefoy, Alberto Savinio, Pavel Florensky, and Henri Volohonsky, as well as two books of poetry. He has received fellowships or grants for translation from the National Endowment for the Arts, the Ingram Merrill Foundation, the Guggenheim Foundation, the National Endowment for the Humanities, and the French Ministry of Culture.

LARISSA VOLOKHONSKY was born in Leningrad. She has translated works by the prominent Orthodox theologians Alexander Schmemann and John Meyendorff into Russian.

Together, Pevear and Volokhonsky have translated *Dead Souls* and *The Collected Tales* by Nikolai Gogol, and *The Brothers Karamazov*, *Crime and Punishment*, *Notes from Underground*, *Demons*, *The Idiot*, and *The Adolescent* by Fyodor Dostoevsky. They have been twice awarded the PEN Book-of-the-Month Club Translation Prize, for their version of *The Brothers Karamazov* and more recently for *Anna Karenina*. They are married and live in France.

GIUSEPPE TOMASI DI
LAMPEDUSA
The Leopard

WILLIAM LANGLAND
Piers Plowman
with (anon.) Sir Gawain and the
Green Knight, Pearl, Sir Orfeo
(UK only)

D. H. LAWRENCE
Collected Stories
The Rainbow
Sons and Lovers
Women in Love

MIKHAIL LERMONTOV
A Hero of Our Time

PRIMO LEVI
If This is a Man and The Truce
(UK only)
The Periodic Table

THE MABINOGION

NICCOLÒ MACHIAVELLI
The Prince

NAGUIB MAHFOUZ
The Cairo Trilogy

THOMAS MANN
Buddenbrooks
Collected Stories (UK only)
Death in Venice and Other Stories
(US only)
Doctor Faustus
Joseph and His Brothers
The Magic Mountain

KATHERINE MANSFIELD
The Garden Party and Other
Stories

MARCUS AURELIUS
Meditations

GABRIEL GARCÍA MÁRQUEZ
The General in His Labyrinth
Love in the Time of Cholera
One Hundred Years of Solitude

ANDREW MARVELL
The Complete Poems

W. SOMERSET MAUGHAM
Collected Stories

CORMAC McCARTHY
The Border Trilogy (US only)

HERMAN MELVILLE
The Complete Shorter Fiction
Moby-Dick

JOHN STUART MILL
On Liberty and Utilitarianism

JOHN MILTON
The Complete English Poems

YUKIO MISHIMA
The Temple of the
Golden Pavilion

MARY WORTLEY MONTAGU
Letters

MICHEL DE MONTAIGNE
The Complete Works

THOMAS MORE
Utopia

TONI MORRISON
Song of Solomon

MURASAKI SHIKIBU
The Tale of Genji

VLADIMIR NABOKOV
Lolita
Pale Fire
Pnin
Speak, Memory

V. S. NAIPAUL
A House for Mr Biswas

R. K. NARAYAN
Swami and Friends
The Bachelor of Arts
The Dark Room
The English Teacher
(in 1 vol.)
Mr Sampath – The Printer of
Malgudi
The Financial Expert
Waiting for the Mahatma
(in 1 vol.)

THE NEW TESTAMENT
(King James Version)

THE OLD TESTAMENT
(King James Version)

This book is set in BEMBO which was cut
by the punch-cutter Francesco Griffo
for the Venetian printer-publisher
Aldus Manutius in early 1495
and first used in a pamphlet
by a young scholar
named Pietro
Bembo.